# THE HOUSE OF THE SEVEN GABLES

### AN AUTHORITATIVE TEXT
### BACKGROUNDS AND SOURCES
### ESSAYS IN CRITICISM

A NORTON CRITICAL EDITION

NATHANIEL HAWTHORNE

# THE HOUSE OF THE SEVEN GABLES

AN AUTHORITATIVE TEXT
BACKGROUNDS AND SOURCES
ESSAYS IN CRITICISM

Edited by
SEYMOUR L. GROSS
THE UNIVERSITY OF DETROIT

W · W · NORTON & COMPANY
New York · London

Library of Congress Catalog Card No. 67-11080

CENTER FOR EDITIONS OF
AMERICAN AUTHORS

*AN APPROVED TEXT*

MODERN LANGUAGE
ASSOCIATION OF AMERICA

®

FOR
MY DAUGHTER

Thelma Lee Gross

W. W. Norton & Company, Inc., 500 Fifth Avenue, New York, N.Y. 10110

# Contents

# Introduction

About six months after the publication of *The Scarlet Letter* on March 16, 1850, Hawthorne began writing *The House of the Seven Gables*. On January 27, 1851, it was done, and Hawthorne said he preferred it to the earlier romance. Neither the general reading public nor the literary critics, it has turned out, have agreed with him. *The Scarlet Letter* has, almost from the beginning, outsold *Gables*, and has evoked a massive number of critical essays that, it is safe to say, *Gables* will never approach. But what is curious about Hawthorne's averred preference is not so much that it runs counter to the usual response to the two books—after all, authors customarily consider their most recent work their best—but the terms in which he asserted the preference. To one friend he confided that *Gables* was "a more natural and healthy product of my mind"; to another that it was "more characteristic of my mind, and more proper and natural for me to write, than 'The Scarlet Letter.' " The terms here, it should be noted, are not all of the same order: "characteristic" and "natural" imply a view of what Hawthorne thought the true bent of his talent was; "proper" and "healthy" indicate what he thought his talent ought to be. These are two quite different judgments and so pose two quite different questions.

Whether Hawthorne was correct in thinking that the happy-ending hopefulness of *Gables* was a more natural and characteristic reflection of his imagination than the tragic hardness of *The Scarlet Letter* is an open question to which we will turn in a moment. But that he *wanted* to think so is clear. More than most of the writers of his time, Hawthorne had a firm hold on life's negative capabilities, but he was no romantic pessimist who takes a kind of perverse pleasure in exposing the skull beneath the skin. Unlike Poe, for example, he seems to have been troubled periodically by the propriety and healthiness of disclosing to the public the results of his dark imaginings. Because he felt a case could be made for the morally hopeful in literature, he could never wholly dismiss as irrelevant the fact that the average reader, as a famous publisher of the time put it, preferred to "ascend to the sunny climes with Nathaniel Parker Willis than descend to the charnel house with Nathaniel Hawthorne." Hawthorne seems to have become increasingly persuaded that "the charnel house" was a moral dead-end, especially after his marriage to Sophia Peabody, whose sunny ways, he felt, had freed him from the "dungeon" of his brooding heart. When Hawthorne read Sophia *The Scarlet Letter*, she took to her bed with a psychosomatic headache; but when he read her *Gables*, it was, she said, "Joy unspeakable!" Here then, close to home, was proof that *Gables* was more "healthy" and "proper" than *The Scarlet Letter*, which even Hawthorne's favorite critic, E. P. Whipple, described as "tragic even to ghastliness."

But is *The House of the Seven Gables* really more *characteristic* of Hawthorne's genius than his tales of "sin and sorrow?" For those whose knowledge of his work consists primarily of these two novels and the half-dozen or so of his most frequently reprinted stories, Hawthorne's estimate of himself must verge on the eccentric. Nevertheless, *Gables* is not all that much of a sport. Among the hundred-odd short stories and sketches he wrote, there are a substantial number of "shadowless" pieces which anticipate *Gables* in the sense that, say, "Young Goodman Brown" or "The Minister's Black Veil" anticipates *The Scarlet Letter*. Even Melville, who was hardly disposed to, noted the "humor and love" of many of the shorter works; but, being Melville, naturally emphasized the "blackness." And in recent years various Hawthorne critics and scholars have marshaled evidence for reversing, or at least modifying, the traditional image of Hawthorne as the dark geographer of the haunted mind. Edward Wagenknecht in his *Nathaniel Hawthorne* (1960) and Hubert Hoeltje in his *Inward Sky* (1962), for example, find that Hawthorne essentially "faced the light," that his most "prominent" quality was "a quiet, deeply joyful affirmation." *The House of the Seven Gables* obviously stands at the dead center of such a view.

If there are reasons for accepting Hawthorne's view of the natural bias of his mind, there are also reasons for not accepting it. Surely, great works of literature carry their own powerful authority, and it seems to be a fact that his greatest, or at least more frequently read and discussed, works—*The Scarlet Letter*, "My Kinsman, Major Molineux," "Young Goodman Brown," "Rappacini's Daughter," "Ethan Brand," "The Minister's Black Veil," "The Birthmark"—are all notably lacking in "sunshine," to use Hawthorne's term for moral cheerfulness. To say that these works are great but somehow not characteristic is critically self-annihilative, since such a statement assumes that imaginative creations are not organically related to the imagination that produced them. Moreover, when an author finds that he cannot honestly lighten a story, much as he may want to, as Hawthorne said of *The Scarlet Letter* ("[it] is positively a hell-fired story, into which I found it almost impossible to throw any cheering light"), we have a rather persuasive argument for accepting that work as characteristic of his mind. Indeed, even *The House of the Seven Gables,* which Hawthorne deliberately intended "to bring . . . to a prosperous close," almost wrote an ending different from the one it has: "It darkens damnably towards the close," he admitted to his publisher, "but I shall try hard to pour some setting sunshine over it." If it is true, then, that part of Hawthorne was drawn towards the light, it is also true that part of him was also drawn to peer unblinkingly into what he called "the midnight of the moral world."

There is perhaps no final answer to the question of which was the "real" Hawthorne, nor need there be. Certainly part of the fascination of *The House of the Seven Gables* lies in the way it serves as a theatre for the rival claims made upon Hawthorne of democratic expectancy and the conservative impulse, pragmatism and estheticism, a deterministic view of history and a belief in man's capacity to resist the pressures of his inheritance. The critical essays included in this volume address themselves to these and other problems—and emerge with various viewpoints. And this is as it should be; for an enduring work of literature endures not as an ironclad structure of absolute meanings, but as a dialogue between an artifact capable of stimulating and sustaining significant questions and an audience which will formulate these questions according to the language it has and the answers it thinks it needs to find.

The text of *The House of the Seven Gables* here reprinted is that of the Centenary Edition of the Works of Nathaniel Hawthorne produced at the Ohio State University Center for Textual Studies. It is "a critical unmodernized reconstruction"—a text as close to Hawthorne's own inscription as the surviving documents allow, subject to normal editorial procedures. A number of spellings in the text (e.g., *ancles, aukward, artizan*) will startle the modern reader; they are, however, Hawthorne's. In Backgrounds and Sources, the editor has brought together several relevant passages from Hawthorne's notebooks and letters, as well as two excerpts from historical works which Hawthorne knew, to serve as materials for a study of the background of the novel. (Where, however, the source or analogue was brief enough to be conveniently contained in a footnote, it has been placed at the bottom of the appropriate page.) One modern essay, on daguerreotypy and its relationship to the novel, has also been included in this section.

The three contemporary reviews of Hawthorne's novel which introduce the Reviews and Essays in Criticism section of this volume are meant to serve both as an indication of the response to *Gables* in Hawthorne's own time and as a contrast to the eleven critical essays, written in the last quarter century, which follow them. Henry James's piece (1879), which is interesting in its own right, can also be viewed as transitional in method. The editor has tried to include a fair sampling of the best thinking and writing that has been done on the novel, while still covering as wide a range of critical approaches as possible. Unfortunately, the exigencies of space necessitated the omission of several fine essays—those by Austin Warren, Marcus Cunliffe, Terrence Martin, and Maurice Beebe; these have all been listed in the Bibliography, which is a reasonably complete checklist of the significant criticism and scholarship done on the novel.

I want to express my gratitude to Professors John McGalliard, Francis Moran, and Marshall Smelser, who never got tired of my questions, graciously gave me the answers, or told me where to look. I wish that the late Professor Randall Stewart might know how deeply indebted I am to his magisterial edition of Hawthorne's *American Notebooks*. Finally, I am grateful to my twelve-year-old daughter for being young enough to think that proofreading was fun, and to whom, in consequence, I have affectionately dedicated this book.

SEYMOUR L. GROSS

The Text of
# The House of the
# Seven Gables

# CONTENTS

The text of *The House of the Seven Gables* is that of the Centenary Edition of the Works of Nathaniel Hawthorne, a publication of the Ohio State University Center for Textual Studies and the Ohio State University Press.

# PREFACE

WHEN a writer calls his work a Romance, it need hardly be observed that he wishes to claim a certain latitude, both as to its fashion and material, which he would not have felt himself entitled to assume, had he professed to be writing a Novel. The latter form of composition is presumed to aim at a very minute fidelity, not merely to the possible, but to the probable and ordinary course of man's experience. The former—while, as a work of art, it must rigidly subject itself to laws, and while it sins unpardonably, so far as it may swerve aside from the truth of the human heart—has fairly a right to present that truth under circumstances, to a great extent, of the writer's own choosing or creation. If he think fit, also, he may so manage his atmospherical medium as to bring out or mellow the lights and deepen and enrich the shadows of the picture. He will be wise, no doubt, to make a very moderate use of the privileges here stated, and, especially, to mingle the Marvellous rather as a slight, delicate, and evanescent flavor, than as any portion of the actual substance of the dish offered to the Public. He can hardly be said, however, to commit a literary crime, even if he disregard this caution.

In the present work, the Author has proposed to himself (but with what success, fortunately, it is not for him to judge) to keep undeviatingly within his immunities. The point of view in which this Tale comes under the Romantic definition, lies in the attempt to connect a by-gone time with the very Present that is flitting away from us. It is a Legend, prolonging itself, from an epoch now gray in the distance, down into our own broad daylight, and bringing along with it some of its legendary mist, which the Reader, according to his pleasure, may either disregard, or allow it to float almost imperceptibly about the characters and events, for the sake of a picturesque effect. The narrative, it may be, is woven of so humble a texture as to require this advantage, and, at the same time, to render it the more difficult of attainment.

Many writers lay very great stress upon some definite moral purpose, at which they profess to aim their works. Not to be deficient, in this particular, the Author has provided himself with a moral;—the truth, namely, that the wrong-doing of one generation lives into the successive ones, and, divesting itself of every temporary advantage, becomes a pure and uncontrollable mischief;—and he would feel it a singular gratification, if this Romance might effectually convince mankind (or, indeed, any one man) of the folly of tumbling down an avalanche of ill-gotten gold, or real estate, on the heads of an unfortunate posterity, thereby to maim and crush them, until the accumulated mass shall be scattered abroad in its original atoms.[1] In good faith, however, he is not sufficiently imaginative to flatter himself with the slightest hope of this kind. When romances do really teach anything, or produce any effective operation, it is usually through a far more subtile process than the ostensible one. The Author has considered it hardly worth his while, therefore, relentlessly to impale the story with its moral, as with an iron rod—or rather, as by sticking a pin through a butterfly—thus at once depriving it of life, and causing it to stiffen in an ungainly and unnatural attitude. A high truth, indeed, fairly, finely, and skilfully wrought out, brightening at every step, and crowning the

1. All his adult life Hawthorne was absorbed by this theme. For several actual instances of the crushing power of real estate on posterity, as recorded in his journals, see "Passages from *The American Notebooks*," p. 323.

final developement of a work of fiction, may add an artistic glory, but is never any truer, and seldom any more evident, at the last page than at the first.

The Reader may perhaps choose to assign an actual locality to the imaginary events of this narrative. If permitted by the historical connection, (which, though slight, was essential to his plan,) the Author would very willingly have avoided anything of this nature. Not to speak of other objections, it exposes the Romance to an inflexible and exceedingly dangerous species of criticism, by bringing his fancy-pictures almost into positive contact with the realities of the moment. It has been no part of his object, however, to describe local manners, nor in any way to meddle with the characteristics of a community for whom he cherishes a proper respect and a natural regard. He trusts not to be considered as unpardonably offending, by laying out a street that infringes upon nobody's private rights, and appropriating a lot of land which had no visible owner, and building a house, of materials long in use for constructing castles in the air. The personages of the Tale—though they give themselves out to be of ancient stability and considerable prominence—are really of the Author's own making, or, at all events, of his own mixing;[2] their virtues can shed no lustre, nor their defects redound, in the remotest degree, to the discredit of the venerable town of which they profess to be inhabitants. He would be glad, therefore, if—especially in the quarter to which he alludes—the book may be read strictly as a Romance, having a great deal more to do with the clouds overhead, than with any portion of the actual soil of the County of Essex.

Lenox, January 27, 1851.

---

2. There was, however, an historical Judge Pyncheon who had lived in Salem. Several of Pyncheon's descendants ("jackasses," Hawthorne called them) complained that Hawthorne had subjected the family to "derision and contempt." (See Holmes's essay listed in the Bibliography.)

# THE HOUSE OF THE
# SEVEN GABLES

## I

## THE OLD PYNCHEON FAMILY

HALF-WAY down a by-street of one of our New England towns, stands a rusty wooden house, with seven acutely peaked gables facing towards various points of the compass, and a huge, clustered chimney in the midst.[1] The street is Pyncheon-street; the house is the old Pyncheon-house; and an elm-tree of wide circumference, rooted before the door, is familiar to every town-born child by the title of the Pyncheon-elm. On my occasional visits to the town aforesaid, I seldom fail to turn down Pyncheon-street, for the sake of passing through the shadow of these two antiquities; the great elm-tree, and the weather-beaten edifice.

The aspect of the venerable mansion has always affected me like a human countenance, bearing the traces not merely of outward storm and sunshine, but expressive also of the long lapse of mortal life, and accompanying vicissitudes, that have passed within. Were these to be worthily recounted, they would form a narrative of no small interest and instruction, and possessing, moreover, a certain remarkable unity, which might almost seem the result of artistic arrangement. But the story would include a chain of events, extending over the better part of two centuries, and, written out with reason-

1. Several Salem houses have competed for the honor of being the house in the novel. One, the house on Turner Street, was owned by Hawthorne's cousin, Susan Ingersoll. Upon hearing that this house had once had seven gables, Hawthorne reputedly murmured, "House of the Seven Gables—that

able amplitude, would fill a bigger folio volume, or a longer series of duodecimos,[2] than could prudently be appropriated to the annals of all New England, during a similar period. It consequently becomes imperative to make short work with most of the traditionary lore of which the old Pyncheon-house, otherwise known as the House of the Seven Gables, has been the theme. With a brief sketch, therefore, of the circumstances amid which the foundation of the house was laid, and a rapid glimpse at its quaint exterior, as it grew black in the prevalent east-wind—pointing, too, here and there, at some spot of more verdant mossiness on its roof and walls—we shall commence the real action of our tale at an epoch not very remote from the present day. Still, there will be a connection with the long past—a reference to forgotten events and personages, and to manners, feelings, and opinions, almost or wholly obsolete—which, if adequately translated to the reader, would serve to illustrate how much of old material goes to make up the freshest novelty of human life. Hence, too, might be drawn a weighty lesson from the little regarded truth, that the act of the passing generation is the germ which may and must produce good or evil fruit, in a far distant time; that, together with the seed of the merely temporary crop, which mortals term expediency, they inevitably sow the acorns of a more enduring growth, which may darkly overshadow their posterity.

The House of the Seven Gables, antique as it now looks, was not the first habitation erected by civilized man, on precisely the same spot of ground. Pyncheon-street formerly bore the humbler appellation of Maule's Lane, from the name of the original occupant of the soil, before whose cottage-door it was a cow-path. A natural spring of soft and pleasant water—a rare treasure on the sea-girt peninsula, where the Puritan settlement was made—had early induced Matthew Maule to build a hut, shaggy with thatch, at this point, although somewhat too remote from what was then

sounds well."
2. A folio is a book printed on a sheet folded into two leaves—loosely applied to books over fifteen inches high; a duodecimo is a book printed on a sheet folded into twelve leaves—loosely applied to books six to eight inches high.

the centre of the village. In the growth of the town, however, after some thirty or forty years, the site covered by this rude hovel had become exceedingly desirable in the eyes of a prominent and powerful personage, who asserted plausible claims to the proprietorship of this, and a large adjacent tract of land, on the strength of a grant from the legislature. Colonel Pyncheon, the claimant, as we gather from whatever traits of him are preserved, was characterized by an iron energy of purpose. Matthew Maule, on the other hand, though an obscure man, was stubborn in the defence of what he considered his right; and, for several years, he succeeded in protecting the acre or two of earth which, with his own toil, he had hewn out of the primeval forest, to be his garden-ground and homestead. No written record of this dispute is known to be in existence. Our acquaintance with the whole subject is derived chiefly from tradition. It would be bold, therefore, and possibly unjust, to venture a decisive opinion as to its merits; although it appears to have been at least a matter of doubt, whether Colonel Pyncheon's claim were not unduly stretched, in order to make it cover the small metes and bounds of Matthew Maule. What greatly strengthens such a suspicion is the fact, that this controversy between two ill-matched antagonists—at a period, moreover, laud it as we may, when personal influence had far more weight than now —remained for years undecided, and came to a close only with the death of the party occupying the disputed soil. The mode of his death, too, affects the mind differently, in our day, from what it did a century and a half ago. It was a death that blasted with strange horror the humble name of the dweller in the cottage, and made it seem almost a religious act to drive the plough over the little area of his habitation, and obliterate his place and memory from among men.

Old Matthew Maule, in a word, was executed for the crime of witchcraft.[3] He was one of the martyrs to that terrible

3. Hawthorne's Maule is based on an actual person, Thomas Maule (1645–1724), a tough Quaker who was persecuted not for witchcraft but for his religion. His *Truth Held Forth and Maintained* (1695) indicted the authorities' conduct during the Salem witchcraft panic in 1692, for which he was

delusion which should teach us, among its other morals, that the influential classes, and those who take upon themselves to be leaders of the people, are fully liable to all the passionate error that has ever characterized the maddest mob. Clergymen, judges, statesmen—the wisest, calmest, holiest persons of their day—stood in the inner circle roundabout the gallows, loudest to applaud the work of blood, latest to confess themselves miserably deceived.[4] If any one part of their proceedings can be said to deserve less blame than another, it was the singular indiscrimination with which they persecuted, not merely the poor and aged, as in former judicial massacres, but people of all ranks; their own equals, brethren, and wives. Amid the disorder of such various ruin, it is not strange that a man of inconsiderable note, like Maule, should have trodden the martyr's path to the hill of execution, almost unremarked in the throng of his fellow-sufferers. But, in after days, when the frenzy of that hideous epoch had subsided, it was remembered how loudly Colonel Pyncheon had joined in the general cry, to purge the land from witchcraft; nor did it fail to be whispered, that there was an invidious acrimony in the zeal with which he had sought the condemnation of Matthew Maule. It was well known, that the victim had recognized the bitterness of personal enmity in his persecutor's conduct towards him, and that he declared himself hunted to death for his spoil. At the moment of execution—with the halter about his neck, and while Colonel Pyncheon sat on horseback, grimly gazing at the scene—Maule had addressed him from the scaffold, and uttered a prophecy, of which history, as well as fireside tradition, has preserved the very words.—"God," said the dying man, pointing his finger with a ghastly look at the undismayed countenance of his enemy, "God will give him blood to drink!"[5]

After the reputed wizard's death, his humble homestead had fallen an easy spoil into Colonel Pyncheon's grasp. When it was understood, however, that the Colonel intended to

imprisoned.
4. The Salem witchcraft panic of 1692 in which 20 people were executed and about 400 accused. In "Alice Doane's Appeal," Hawthorne described the occurrence as "the most execrable scene that our history blushes to record."

erect a family-mansion—spacious, ponderously framed of
oaken timber, and calculated to endure for many generations
of his posterity—over the spot first covered by the log-built
hut of Matthew Maule, there was much shaking of the head
among the village-gossips. Without absolutely expressing a
doubt whether the stalwart Puritan had acted as a man of
conscience and integrity, throughout the proceedings which
have been sketched, they nevertheless hinted that he was
about to build his house over an unquiet grave. His home
would include the home of the dead and buried wizard, and
would thus afford the ghost of the latter a kind of privilege
to haunt its new apartments, and the chambers into which
future bridegrooms were to lead their brides, and where
children of the Pyncheon blood were to be born. The terror
and ugliness of Maule's crime, and the wretchedness of his
punishment, would darken the freshly plastered walls, and
infect them early with the scent of an old and melancholy
house. Why, then—while so much of the soil around him
was bestrewn with the virgin forest-leaves—why should Colonel Pyncheon prefer a site that had already been accurst?

But the Puritan soldier and magistrate was not a man to
be turned aside from his well-considered scheme, either by
dread of the wizard's ghost, or by flimsy sentimentalities of
any kind, however specious. Had he been told of a bad
air, it might have moved him somewhat; but he was ready
to encounter an evil spirit, on his own ground. Endowed
with common-sense, as massive and hard as blocks of granite,
fastened together by stern rigidity of purpose, as with iron
clamps, he followed out his original design, probably without
so much as imagining an objection to it. On the score of
delicacy, or any scrupulousness which a finer sensibility might
have taught him, the Colonel, like most of his breed and generation, was impenetrable. He therefore dug his cellar, and
laid the deep foundations of his mansion, on the square of
earth whence Matthew Maule, forty years before, had first

His ancestor, John Hathorne, was one of the seven judges at the trials.
5. This malediction was actually delivered by an accused witch to the
Reverend Nicholas Noyes, a judge at the witchcraft trials. See "Thomas
Hutchinson," p. 328.

swept away the fallen leaves. It was a curious, and, as some people thought, an ominous fact, that, very soon after the workmen began their operations, the spring of water, above-mentioned, entirely lost the deliciousness of its pristine quality. Whether its sources were disturbed by the depth of the new cellar, or whatever subtler cause might lurk at the bottom, it is certain that the water of Maule's Well, as it continued to be called, grew hard and brackish. Even such we find it now; and any old woman of the neighborhood will certify, that it is productive of intestinal mischief to those who quench their thirst there.

The reader may deem it singular, that the head-carpenter of the new edifice was no other than the son of the very man, from whose dead gripe the property of the soil had been wrested. Not improbably, he was the best workman of his time; or, perhaps, the Colonel thought it expedient, or was impelled by some better feeling, thus openly to cast aside all animosity against the race of his fallen antagonist. Nor was it out of keeping with the general coarseness and matter-of-fact character of the age, that the son should be willing to earn an honest penny—or rather, a weighty amount of sterling pounds—from the purse of his father's deadly enemy. At all events, Thomas Maule became the architect of the House of the Seven Gables, and performed his duty so faithfully, that the timber frame-work, fastened by his hands, still holds together.[6]

Thus the great house was built. Familiar as it stands in the writer's recollection—for it has been an object of curiosity with him from boyhood, both as a specimen of the best and stateliest architecture of a long-past epoch, and as the scene of events more full of human interest, perhaps, than those of a gray, feudal castle—familiar as it stands, in its rusty old-age, it is therefore only the more difficult to imagine the bright novelty with which it first caught the sunshine. The impression of its actual state, at this distance of a hundred

6. The historical Thomas Maule was an excellent "architect"; he personally designed and had built the first Quaker church in Salem in 1688.

and sixty years, darkens inevitably through the picture which we would fain give of its appearance, on the morning when the Puritan magnate bade all the town to be his guests. A ceremony of consecration, festive, as well as religious, was now to be performed. A prayer and discourse from the Reverend Mr. Higginson,[7] and the outpouring of a psalm from the general throat of the community, was to be made acceptable to the grosser sense by ale, cider, wine, and brandy, in copious effusion, and, as some authorities aver, by an ox roasted whole, or, at least, by the weight and substance of an ox, in more manageable joints and sirloins. The carcass of a deer, shot within twenty miles, had supplied material for the vast circumference of a pasty. A cod-fish of sixty pounds, caught in the bay, had been dissolved into the rich liquid of a chowder. The chimney of the new house, in short, belching forth its kitchen-smoke, impregnated the whole air with the scent of meats, fowls, and fishes, spicily concocted with odoriferous herbs, and onions in abundance. The mere smell of such festivity, making its way to everybody's nostrils, was at once an invitation and an appetite.

Maule's Lane—or Pyncheon-street, as it were now more decorous to call it—was thronged, at the appointed hour, as with a congregation on its way to church. All, as they approached, looked upward at the imposing edifice, which was henceforth to assume its rank among the habitations of mankind. There it rose, a little withdrawn from the line of the street, but in pride, not modesty. Its whole visible exterior was ornamented with quaint figures, conceived in the grotesqueness of a Gothic fancy, and drawn or stamped in the glittering plaster, composed of lime, pebbles, and bits of glass, with which the wood-work of the walls was overspread. On every side, the seven gables pointed sharply towards the sky, and presented the aspect of a whole sisterhood of edifices, breathing through the spiracles of one great chimney. The many lattices, with their small, diamond-shaped panes, ad-

---

7. John Higginson (1616–1708), pastor of the First Church of Salem, was noted for his violent anti-Quakerism. The historical Maule was once given "Ten stripes well laid on" for saying that Higginson "preached lies and that his doctrine was of the devil."

mitted the sunlight into hall and chamber; while, nevertheless, the second story, projecting far over the base, and itself retiring beneath the third, threw a shadow and thoughtful gloom into the lower rooms. Carved globes of wood were affixed under the jutting stories. Little, spiral rods of iron beautified each of the seven peaks. On the triangular portion of the gable that fronted next the street, was a dial, put up that very morning, and on which the sun was still marking the passage of the first bright hour in a history, that was not destined to be all so bright. All around were scattered shavings, chips, shingles, and broken halves of bricks; these—together with the lately turned earth, on which the grass had not begun to grow—contributed to the impression of strangeness and novelty, proper to a house that had yet its place to make among men's daily interests.

The principal entrance, which had almost the breadth of a church-door, was in the angle between the two front gables, and was covered by an open porch, with benches beneath its shelter. Under this arched door-way, scraping their feet on the unworn threshold, now trod the clergymen, the elders, the magistrates, the deacons, and whatever of aristocracy there was in town or county. Thither, too, thronged the plebeian classes, as freely as their betters, and in larger number. Just within the entrance, however, stood two serving-men, pointing some of the guests to the neighborhood of the kitchen, and ushering others into the statelier rooms; hospitable alike to all, but still with a scrutinizing regard to the high or low degree of each. Velvet garments, sombre, but rich, stiffly plaited ruffs and bands, embroidered gloves, venerable beards, the mien and countenance of authority, made it easy to distinguish the gentleman of worship, at that period, from the tradesman, with his plodding air, or the laborer in his leathern jerkin, stealing awe-stricken into the house which he had perhaps helped to build.

One inauspicious circumstance there was, which awakened

a hardly concealed displeasure in the breasts of a few of the more punctilious visitors. The founder of this stately mansion —a gentleman noted for the square and ponderous courtesy of his demeanor—ought surely to have stood in his own hall, and to have offered the first welcome to so many eminent personages as here presented themselves, in honor of his solemn festival. He was as yet invisible; the most favored of the guests had not beheld him. This sluggishness on Colonel Pyncheon's part became still more unaccountable, when the second dignitary of the province made his appearance, and found no more ceremonious a reception. The Lieutenant Governor, although his visit was one of the anticipated glories of the day, had alighted from his horse, and assisted his lady from her side-saddle, and crossed the Colonel's threshold, without other greeting than that of the principal domestic.

This person—a gray-headed man of quiet and most respectful deportment—found it necessary to explain that his master still remained in his study, or private apartment; on entering which, an hour before, he had expressed a wish on no account to be disturbed.

"Do not you see, fellow," said the high-sheriff of the county, taking the servant aside, "that this is no less a man than the Lieutenant Governor? Summon Colonel Pyncheon at once! I know that he received letters from England, this morning; and, in the perusal and consideration of them, an hour may have passed away, without his noticing it. But he will be ill-pleased, I judge, if you suffer him to neglect the courtesy due to one of our chief rulers, and who may be said to represent King William,[8] in the absence of the Governor himself. Call your master instantly!"

"Nay, please your worship," answered the man, in much perplexity, but with a backwardness that strikingly indicated the hard and severe character of Colonel Pyncheon's domestic rule, "my master's orders were exceedingly strict; and, as your worship knows, he permits of no discretion in the obedience

8. William III, king of England, 1689–1702.

of those who owe him service. Let who list open yonder door! I dare not, though the Governor's own voice should bid me do it!"

"Pooh, pooh, Master High Sheriff!" cried the Lieutenant Governor, who had overheard the foregoing discussion, and felt himself high enough in station to play a little with his dignity.—"I will take the matter into my own hands. It is time that the good Colonel came forth to greet his friends; else we shall be apt to suspect that he has taken a sip too much of his Canary wine, in his extreme deliberation which cask it were best to broach, in honor of the day! But since he is so much behindhand, I will give him a remembrancer myself!"

Accordingly—with such a tramp of his ponderous riding-boots as might of itself have been audible in the remotest of the seven gables—he advanced to the door, which the servant pointed out, and made its new panels re-echo with a loud, free knock. Then, looking round with a smile to the spectators, he awaited a response. As none came, however, he knocked again, but with the same unsatisfactory result as at first. And, now, being a trifle choleric in his temperament, the Lieutenant Governor uplifted the heavy-hilt of his sword, wherewith he so beat and banged upon the door, that, as some of the bystanders whispered, the racket might have disturbed the dead. Be that as it might, it seemed to produce no awakening effect on Colonel Pyncheon. When the sound subsided, the silence through the house was deep, dreary, and oppressive; notwithstanding that the tongues of many of the guests had already been loosened by a surreptitious cup or two of wine or spirits.

"Strange, forsooth!—very strange!" cried the Lieutenant Governor, whose smile was changed to a frown. "But, seeing that our host sets us the good example of forgetting ceremony, I shall likewise throw it aside, and make free to intrude on his privacy!"

He tried the door, which yielded to his hand, and was flung wide open by a sudden gust of wind that passed, as with a loud sigh, from the outermost portal through all the passages and apartments of the new house. It rustled the silken garments of the ladies, and waved the long curls of the gentlemen's wigs, and shook the window-hangings and the curtains of the bed-chambers; causing everywhere a singular stir, which yet was more like a hush. A shadow of awe and half-fearful anticipation—nobody knew wherefore, nor of what—had all at once fallen over the company.

They thronged, however, to the now open door, pressing the Lieutenant Governor, in the eagerness of their curiosity, into the room in advance of them. At the first glimpse, they beheld nothing extraordinary; a handsomely furnished room of moderate size, somewhat darkened by curtains; books arranged on shelves; a large map on the wall, and likewise a portrait of Colonel Pyncheon, beneath which sat the original Colonel himself, in an oaken elbow-chair, with a pen in his hand. Letters, parchments, and blank sheets of paper were on the table before him. He appeared to gaze at the curious crowd, in front of which stood the Lieutenant Governor; and there was a frown on his dark and massive countenance, as if sternly resentful of the boldness that had impelled them into his private retirement.

A little boy—the Colonel's grandchild, and the only human being that ever dared to be familiar with him—now made his way among the guests and ran towards the seated figure; then pausing half-way, he began to shriek with terror. The company—tremulous as the leaves of a tree, when all are shaking together—drew nearer, and perceived that there was an unnatural distortion in the fixedness of Colonel Pyncheon's stare; that there was blood on his ruff, and that his hoary beard was saturated with it. It was too late to give assistance. The iron-hearted Puritan—the relentless persecutor—the grasping and strong-willed man—was dead! Dead, in his new house! There is a tradition—only worth alluding to, as lending a tinge of superstitious awe to a scene, perhaps gloomy enough without it—that a voice spoke loudly among the guests, the tones of which were like those of old Matthew Maule, the executed wizard:—"God hath given him blood to drink!"

Thus early had that one guest—the only guest who is certain, at one time or another, to find his way into every human dwelling—thus early had Death stept across the threshold of the House of the Seven Gables!

Colonel Pyncheon's sudden and mysterious end made a vast deal of noise in its day. There were many rumors, some of which have vaguely drifted down to the present time, how that appearances indicated violence; that there were the marks of fingers on his throat, and the print of a bloody hand on his plaited ruff; and that his peaked beard was dishevelled, as if it had been fiercely clutched and pulled. It was averred, likewise, that the lattice-window, near the Colonel's chair, was open, and that, only a few minutes before the fatal occurrence, the figure of a man had been seen clambering over the garden-fence, in the rear of the house. But it were folly to lay any stress on stories of this kind, which are sure to spring up around such an event as that now related, and which, as in the present case, sometimes prolong themselves for ages afterwards, like the toadstools that indicate where the fallen and buried trunk of a tree has long since mouldered into the earth. For our own part, we allow them just as little credence as to that other fable of the skeleton hand, which the Lieutenant Governor was said to have seen at the Colonel's throat, but which vanished away, as he advanced farther into the room. Certain it is, however, that there was a great consultation and dispute of doctors over the dead body. One —John Swinnerton[9] by name—who appears to have been a man of eminence, upheld it, if we have rightly understood his terms of art, to be a case of apoplexy.[1] His professional

9. Although John Swinnerton, a well-known Salem physician, died in 1690, what may have prompted Hawthorne to use him anyhow, was the connection he had to Maule: Swinnerton's stepson married Maule's daughter in 1693.

brethren, each for himself, adopted various hypotheses, more or less plausible, but all dressed out in a perplexing mystery of phrase, which, if it do not show a bewilderment of mind in these erudite physicians, certainly causes it in the unlearned peruser of their opinions. The coroner's jury sat upon the corpse, and, like sensible men, returned an unassailable verdict of "Sudden Death!"

It is indeed difficult to imagine that there could have been a serious suspicion of murder, or the slightest grounds for implicating any particular individual as the perpetrator. The rank, wealth, and eminent character of the deceased, must have ensured the strictest scrutiny into every ambiguous circumstance. As none such is on record, it is safe to assume that none existed. Tradition—which sometimes brings down truth that history has let slip, but is oftener the wild babble of the time, such as was formerly spoken at the fireside, and now congeals in newspapers—tradition is responsible for all contrary averments. In Colonel Pyncheon's funeral sermon, which was printed and is still extant, the Reverend Mr. Higginson enumerates, among the many felicities of his distinguished parishioner's earthly career, the happy seasonableness of his death. His duties all performed,—the highest prosperity attained,—his race and future generations fixed on a stable basis, and with a stately roof to shelter them, for centuries to come,—what other upward step remained for this good man to take, save the final step from earth to the golden gate of Heaven! The pious clergyman surely would not have uttered words like these, had he in the least suspected that the Colonel had been thrust into the other world with the clutch of violence upon his throat.

The family of Colonel Pyncheon, at the epoch of his death, seemed destined to as fortunate a permanence as can anywise consist with the inherent instability of human affairs. It might fairly be anticipated that the progress of time would rather increase and ripen their prosperity, than wear away and de-

1. Apoplexy, or stroke (cerebral hemorrhage), is not a condition in which blood would flow from the mouth so copiously as to saturate a beard and stain a ruff. But in Hawthorne's day apoplexy was often the diagnosis for any sudden death, including pulmonary hemorrhage, in which blood is forced

stroy it. For, not only had his son and heir come into immediate enjoyment of a rich estate, but there was a claim,
through an Indian deed, confirmed by a subsequent grant
of the General Court, to a vast, and as yet unexplored and
unmeasured tract of eastern lands. These possessions—for as
such they might almost certainly be reckoned—comprised the
greater part of what is now known as Waldo County, in the
State of Maine, and were more extensive than many a dukedom, or even a reigning prince's territory, on European soil.[2]
When the pathless forest, that still covered this wild principality, should give place—as it inevitably must, though perhaps not till ages hence—to the golden fertility of human
culture, it would be the source of incalculable wealth to the
Pyncheon blood. Had the Colonel survived only a few weeks
longer, it is probable that his great political influence, and
powerful connections, at home and abroad, would have consummated all that was necessary to render the claim available.
But, in spite of good Mr. Higginson's congratulatory eloquence, this appeared to be the one thing which Colonel Pyncheon, provident and sagacious as he was, had allowed to go
at loose ends. So far as the prospective territory was concerned,
he unquestionably died too soon. His son lacked not merely
the father's eminent position, but the talent and force of
character to achieve it; he could therefore effect nothing by
dint of political interest; and the bare justice or legality of the
claim was not so apparent, after the Colonel's decease, as it
had been pronounced in his lifetime. Some connecting link
had slipt out of the evidence, and could not anywhere be
found.

Efforts, it is true, were made by the Pyncheons, not only
then, but, at various periods, for nearly a hundred years afterwards, to obtain what they stubbornly persisted in deeming
their right. But, in course of time, the territory was partly
re-granted to more favored individuals, and partly cleared
and occupied by actual settlers. These last, if they ever heard

up into the throat and mouth of the victim.
2. In a journal entry dated August 12, 1837, Hawthorne comments on General
Henry Knox's plan to establish a feudal-like estate on his thirty square miles
of territory in Waldo County, Maine. See "Passages from *The American*

of the Pyncheon title, would have laughed at the idea of any man's asserting a right—on the strength of mouldy parchments, signed with the faded autographs of governors and legislators, long dead and forgotten—to the lands which they or their fathers had wrested from the wild hand of Nature, by their own sturdy toil. This impalpable claim, therefore, resulted in nothing more solid than to cherish, from generation to generation, an absurd delusion of family importance, which all along characterized the Pyncheons. It caused the poorest member of the race to feel as if he inherited a kind of nobility, and might yet come into the possession of princely wealth to support it. In the better specimens of the breed, this peculiarity threw an ideal grace over the hard material of human life, without stealing away any truly valuable quality. In the baser sort, its effect was to increase the liability to sluggishness and dependence, and induce the victim of a shadowy hope to remit all self-effort, while awaiting the realization of his dreams. Years and years after their claim had passed out of the public memory, the Pyncheons were accustomed to consult the Colonel's ancient map, which had been projected while Waldo County was still an unbroken wilderness. Where the old land-surveyor had put down woods, lakes, and rivers, they marked out the cleared spaces, and dotted the villages and towns, and calculated the progressively increasing value of the territory, as if there were yet a prospect of its ultimately forming a princedom for themselves.[3]

In almost every generation, nevertheless, there happened to be some one descendant of the family, gifted with a portion of the hard, keen sense, and practical energy, that had so remarkably distinguished the original founder. His character, indeed, might be traced all the way down, as distinctly as if the Colonel himself, a little diluted, had been gifted with a sort of intermittent immortality on earth. At two or three epochs, when the fortunes of the family were low, this representative of hereditary qualities had made his appearance,

Notebooks," p. 323.
3. This lost claim has a biographical parallel in Hawthorne's family, on his mother's side, which hoped to resurrect the dwindling family fortune through the recovery of a title to thousands of acres in Maine deeded to an ancestor

and caused the traditionary gossips of the town to whisper among themselves:—"Here is the old Pyncheon come again! Now the Seven Gables will be new-shingled!" From father to son, they clung to the ancestral house, with singular tenacity of home-attachment. For various reasons, however, and from impressions often too vaguely founded to be put on paper, the writer cherishes the belief that many, if not most, of the successive proprietors of this estate, were troubled with doubts as to their moral right to hold it. Of their legal tenure, there could be no question; but old Matthew Maule, it is to be feared, trode downward from his own age to a far later one, planting a heavy footstep, all the way, on the conscience of a Pyncheon. If so, we are left to dispose of the awful query, whether each inheritor of the property—conscious of wrong, and failing to rectify it—did not commit anew the great guilt of his ancestor, and incur all its original responsibilities. And supposing such to be the case, would it not be a far truer mode of expression to say, of the Pyncheon family, that they inherited a great misfortune, than the reverse?[4]

We have already hinted, that it is not our purpose to trace down the history of the Pyncheon family, in its unbroken connection with the House of the Seven Gables; nor to show, as in a magic picture, how the rustiness and infirmity of age gathered over the venerable house itself. As regards its interior life, a large, dim looking-glass used to hang in one of the rooms, and was fabled to contain within its depths all the shapes that had ever been reflected there; the old Colonel himself, and his many descendants, some in the garb of antique babyhood, and others in the bloom of feminine beauty, or manly prime, or saddened with the wrinkles of frosty age. Had we the secret of that mirror, we would gladly sit down before it, and transfer its revelations to our page. But there was a story, for which it is difficult to conceive any foundation, that the posterity of Matthew Maule had some connection with the mystery of the looking-glass, and that—by

in the seventeenth century by an Indian.
4. "To inherit a great fortune. To inherit a great misfortune." (*American Notebooks*, entry made between October 27 and December 4, 1849.)

what appears to have been a sort of mesmeric process—they could make its inner region all alive with the departed Pyncheons; not as they had shown themselves to the world, nor in their better and happier hours, but as doing over again some deed of sin, or in the crisis of life's bitterest sorrow. The popular imagination, indeed, long kept itself busy with the affair of the old Puritan Pyncheon and the wizard Maule; the curse, which the latter flung from his scaffold, was remembered, with the very important addition, that it had become a part of the Pyncheon inheritance. If one of the family did but gurgle in his throat, a bystander would be likely enough to whisper, between jest and earnest—"He has Maule's blood to drink!"—The sudden death of a Pyncheon, about a hundred years ago, with circumstances very similar to what have been related of the Colonel's exit, was held as giving additional probability to the received opinion on this topic. It was considered, moreover, an ugly and ominous circumstance, that Colonel Pyncheon's picture—in obedience, it was said, to a provision of his will—remained affixed to the wall of the room in which he died. Those stern, immitigable features seemed to symbolize an evil influence, and so darkly to mingle the shadow of their presence with the sunshine of the passing hour, that no good thoughts or purposes could ever spring up and blossom there. To the thoughtful mind, there will be no tinge of superstition in what we figuratively express, by affirming that the ghost of a dead progenitor—perhaps as a portion of his own punishment—is often doomed to become the Evil Genius of his family.

The Pyncheons, in brief, lived along, for the better part of two centuries, with perhaps less of outward vicissitude than has attended most other New England families, during the same period of time. Possessing very distinctive traits of their own, they nevertheless took the general characteristics of the little community in which they dwelt; a town noted for its frugal, discreet, well-ordered, and home-loving inhabitants, as well as for the somewhat confined scope of its sympathies; but in which, be it said, there are odder individuals, and, now and then, stranger occurrences, than one meets with almost anywhere else. During the revolution, the Pyncheon of that epoch, adopting the royal side, became a refugee, but repented, and made his re-appearance, just at the point of time to preserve the House of the Seven Gables from confiscation.[5] For the last seventy years, the most noted event in the Pyncheon annals had been likewise the heaviest calamity that ever befell the race; no less than the violent death—for so it was adjudged—of one member of the family, by the criminal act of another. Certain circumstances, attending this fatal occurrence, had brought the deed irresistibly home to a nephew of the deceased Pyncheon. The young man was tried and convicted of the crime; but either the circumstantial nature of the evidence, and possibly some lurking doubt in the breast of the Executive, or, lastly—an argument of greater weight in a republic, than it could have been under a monarchy—the high respectability and political influence of the criminal's connections, had availed to mitigate his doom from death to perpetual imprisonment. This sad affair had chanced about thirty years before the action of our story commences. Latterly, there were rumors (which few believed, and only one or two felt greatly interested in) that this long-buried man was likely, for some reason or other, to be summoned forth from his living tomb.

It is essential to say a few words respecting the victim of this now almost forgotten murder. He was an old bachelor, and possessed of great wealth, in addition to the house and real estate which constituted what remained of the ancient Pyncheon property. Being of an eccentric and melancholy turn of mind, and greatly given to rummaging old records and hearkening to old traditions, he had brought himself, it is averred, to the conclusion, that Matthew Maule, the wizard, had been foully wronged out of his homestead, if not out

---

5. "Notorious Conspirators," that is, Loyalists who gave active civil or military aid to the British during the Revolution, often had their property confiscated and put up for public auction.

of his life. Such being the case, and he, the old bachelor, in possession of the ill-gotten spoil—with the black stain of blood sunken deep into it, and still to be scented by conscientious nostrils—the question occurred, whether it were not imperative upon him, even at this late hour, to make restitution to Maule's posterity. To a man living so much in the past, and so little in the present, as the secluded and antiquarian old bachelor, a century and a half seemed not so vast a period as to obviate the propriety of substituting right for wrong. It was the belief of those who knew him best, that he would positively have taken the very singular step of giving up the House of the Seven Gables to the representative of Matthew Maule, but for the unspeakable tumult which a suspicion of the old gentleman's project awakened among his Pyncheon relatives. Their exertions had the effect of suspending his purpose; but it was feared that he would perform, after death, by the operation of his last will, what he had so hardly been prevented from doing, in his proper lifetime. But there is no one thing which men so rarely do, whatever the provocation or inducement, as to bequeath patrimonial property away from their own blood. They may love other individuals far better than their relatives; they may even cherish dislike, or positive hatred, to the latter; but yet, in view of death, the strong prejudice of propinquity revives, and impels the testator to send down his estate in the line marked out by custom, so immemorial, that it looks like nature. In all the Pyncheons, this feeling had the energy of disease. It was too powerful for the conscientious scruples of the old bachelor; at whose death, accordingly, the mansion-house, together with most of his other riches, passed into the possession of his next legal representative.[6]

This was a nephew; the cousin of the miserable young man who had been convicted of the uncle's murder. The new heir, up to the period of his accession, was reckoned rather a dissipated youth, but had at once reformed, and made himself an

6. George Parsons Lathrop, Hawthorne's son-in-law, was the first to conjecture that the murder in the novel was connected in Hawthorne's mind with the murder of Captain Joseph White in Salem on April 6, 1830. (See "Joseph B. Felt," p. 329.)

exceedingly respectable member of society. In fact, he showed more of the Pyncheon quality, and had won higher eminence in the world, than any of his race since the time of the original Puritan. Applying himself, in earlier manhood, to the study of the law, and having a natural tendency towards office, he had attained, many years ago, to a judicial situation in some inferior court, which gave him, for life, the very desirable and imposing title of Judge. Later, he had engaged in politics, and served a part of two terms in Congress, besides making a considerable figure in both branches of the state legislature. Judge Pyncheon was unquestionably an honor to his race. He had built himself a country-seat, within a few miles of his native town, and there spent such portions of his time as could be spared from public service, in the display of every grace and virtue—as a newspaper phrased it, on the eve of an election—befitting the christian, the good citizen, the horticulturist, and the gentleman![7]

There were few of the Pyncheons left, to sun themselves in the glow of the Judge's prosperity. In respect to natural increase, the breed had not thriven; it appeared rather to be dying out. The only members of the family, known to be extant, were, first, the Judge himself, and a single surviving son, who was now travelling in Europe; next, the thirty-years' prisoner, already alluded to, and a sister of the latter, who occupied, in an extremely retired manner, the House of the Seven Gables, in which she had a life-estate by the will of the old bachelor. She was understood to be wretchedly poor, and seemed to make it her choice to remain so; inasmuch as her affluent cousin, the Judge, had repeatedly offered her all the comforts of life, either in the old mansion or his own modern residence. The last and youngest Pyncheon was a little country-girl of seventeen, the daughter of another of the Judge's cousins, who had married a young woman of no family or property, and died early, and in poor circumstances. His widow had recently taken another husband.

7. In creating Judge Pyncheon, Hawthorne had Rev. Charles W. Upham mainly in mind. Upham, a Salem Whig, was chiefly responsible for having Hawthorne, a Democrat, removed from his position in the Salem Custom House when the national administration changed. According to Mrs. Haw-

As for Matthew Maule's posterity, it was supposed now to be extinct. For a very long period after the witchcraft delusion, however, the Maules had continued to inhabit the town, where their progenitor had suffered so unjust a death. To all appearance, they were a quiet, honest, well-meaning race of people, cherishing no malice against individuals or the public, for the wrong which had been done them; or if, at their own fireside, they transmitted, from father to child, any hostile recollection of the wizard's fate, and their lost patrimony, it was never acted upon, nor openly expressed. Nor would it have been singular, had they ceased to remember that the House of the Seven Gables was resting its heavy frame-work on a foundation that was rightfully their own. There is something so massive, stable, and almost irresistibly imposing, in the exterior presentment of established rank and great possessions, that their very existence seems to give them a right to exist; at least, so excellent a counterfeit of right, that few poor and humble men have moral force enough to question it, even in their secret minds. Such is the case now, after so many ancient prejudices have been overthrown; and it was far more so in ante revolutionary days, when the aristocracy could venture to be proud, and the low were content to be abased. Thus the Maules, at all events, kept their resentments within their own breasts. They were generally poverty-stricken; always plebeian and obscure; working with unsuccessful diligence at handicrafts; laboring on the wharves, or following the sea, as sailors before the mast; living here and there about the town, in hired tenements, and coming finally to the alms house, as the natural home of their old age. At last, after creeping, as it were, for such a length of time, along the utmost verge of the opaque puddle of obscurity, they had taken that downright plunge, which, sooner or later, is the destiny of all families, whether princely or plebeian. For thirty years past, neither town-record, nor grave-stone, nor the directory, nor the knowledge or memory of man, bore

_____

thorne, her husband thought Upham "the most satisfactory villain that ever was, for at every point he is consummate." Like Judge Pyncheon, Upham had served one term in each branch of the state legislature, was (in Hawany trace of Matthew Maule's descendants. His blood might possibly exist elsewhere; here, where its lowly current could be traced so far back, it had ceased to keep an onward course.

So long as any of the race were to be found, they had been marked out from other men—not strikingly, nor as with a sharp line, but with an effect that was felt, rather than spoken of—by an hereditary character of reserve. Their companions, or those who endeavored to become such, grew conscious of a circle roundabout the Maules, within the sanctity or the spell of which—in spite of an exterior of sufficient frankness and good-fellowship—it was impossible for any man to step. It was this indefinable peculiarity, perhaps, that, by insulating them from human aid, kept them always so unfortunate in life. It certainly operated to prolong, in their case, and to confirm to them, as their only inheritance, those feelings of repugnance and superstitious terror with which the people of the town, even after awakening from their frenzy, continued to regard the memory of the reputed witches. The mantle, or rather, the ragged cloak of old Matthew Maule, had fallen upon his children. They were half-believed to inherit mysterious attributes; the family eye was said to possess strange power. Among other good-for-nothing properties and privileges, one was especially assigned them, of exercising an influence over people's dreams. The Pyncheons, if all stories were true, haughtily as they bore themselves in the noonday streets of their native town, were no better than bond-servants to these plebeian Maules, on entering the topsyturvy commonwealth of sleep. Modern psychology, it may be, will endeavor to reduce these alleged necromancies within a system, instead of rejecting them as altogether fabulous.

A descriptive paragraph or two, treating of the seven-gabled mansion in its more recent aspect, will bring this preliminary chapter to a close. The street, in which it upreared its venerable peaks, has long ceased to be a fashionable quarter of the town; so that, though the old edifice was surrounded by habi-

---

thorne's view) a hypocrite, and had a forebear who was a Loyalist during the American Revolution.

tations of modern date, they were mostly small, built entirely of wood, and typical of the most plodding uniformity of common life. Doubtless, however, the whole story of human existence may be latent in each of them, but with no picturesqueness, externally, that can attract the imagination or sympathy to seek it there. But as for the old structure of our story, its white-oak frame, and its boards, shingles, and crumbling plaster, and even the huge, clustered chimney in the midst, seemed to constitute only the least and meanest part of its reality. So much of mankind's varied experience had passed there—so much had been suffered, and something, too, enjoyed—that the very timbers were oozy, as with the moisture of a heart. It was itself like a great human heart, with a life of its own, and full of rich and sombre reminiscences.

The deep projection of the second story gave the house such a meditative look, that you could not pass it without the idea that it had secrets to keep, and an eventful history to moralize upon. In front, just on the edge of the unpaved sidewalk, grew the Pyncheon-elm, which, in reference to such trees as one usually meets with, might well be termed gigantic. It had been planted by a great-grandson of the first Pyncheon, and, though now fourscore years of age, or perhaps nearer a hundred, was still in its strong and broad maturity, throwing its shadow from side to side of the street, overtopping the seven gables, and sweeping the whole black roof with its pendent foliage. It gave beauty to the old edifice, and seemed to make it a part of nature. The street having been widened, about forty years ago, the front gable was now precisely on a line with it. On either side extended a ruinous wooden fence, of open lattice-work, through which could be seen a grassy yard, and, especially in the angles of the building, an enormous fertility of burdocks, with leaves, it is hardly an exaggeration to say, two or three feet long. Behind the house, there appeared to be a garden, which undoubtedly had once been extensive, but was now infringed upon by other enclosures, or shut in by habitations and outbuildings that stood on another street. It would be an omission, trifling, indeed, but unpardonable, were we to forget the green moss that had long since gathered over the projections of the windows, and on the slopes of the roof; nor must we fail to direct the reader's eye to a crop, not of weeds, but flower-shrubs, which were growing aloft in the air not a great way from the chimney, in the nook between two of the gables. They were called Alice's Posies. The tradition was, that a certain Alice Pyncheon had flung up the seeds, in sport, and that the dust of the street and the decay of the roof gradually formed a kind of soil for them, out of which they grew, when Alice had long been in her grave. However the flowers might have come there, it was both sad and sweet to observe how Nature adopted to herself this desolate, decaying, gusty, rusty, old house of the Pyncheon family; and how the ever-returning Summer did her best to gladden it with tender beauty, and grew melancholy in the effort.

There is one other feature, very essential to be noticed, but which, we greatly fear, may damage any picturesque and romantic impression, which we have been willing to throw over our sketch of this respectable edifice. In the front gable, under the impending brow of the second story, and contiguous to the street, was a shop-door, divided horizontally in the midst, and with a window for its upper segment, such as is often seen in dwellings of a somewhat ancient date. This same shop-door had been a subject of no slight mortification to the present occupant of the august Pyncheon-house, as well as to some of her predecessors. The matter is disagreeably delicate to handle; but, since the reader must needs be let into the secret, he will please to understand, that, about a century ago, the head of the Pyncheons found himself involved in serious financial difficulties. The fellow (gentleman as he styled himself) can hardly have been other than a spurious interloper; for, instead of seeking office from the King or the royal Governor, or urging his hereditary claim to eastern lands, he bethought himself of no better avenue to wealth, than by cutting a shop-door through the side of his ancestral residence. It was the custom of the time, indeed, for merchants to store their goods, and transact business, in their own dwellings. But there was something pitifully small in this old Pyncheon's mode of setting about his commercial operations; it was whispered, that, with his own hands, all be-ruffled as they were, he used to give change for a shilling, and would turn a half-penny twice over, to make sure that it was a good one. Beyond all question, he had the blood of a petty huckster in his veins, through whatever channel it may have found its way there.

Immediately on his death, the shop-door had been locked, bolted, and barred, and, down to the period of our story, had probably never once been opened. The old counter, shelves, and other fixtures of the little shop, remained just as he had left them. It used to be affirmed, that the dead shopkeeper, in a white wig, a faded velvet coat, an apron at his waist, and his ruffles carefully turned back from his wrists, might be seen through the chinks of the shutters, any night of the year, ransacking his till, or poring over the dingy pages of his day-book. From the look of unutterable woe upon his face, it appeared to be his doom to spend eternity in a vain effort to make his accounts balance.

And now—in a very humble way, as will be seen—we proceed to open our narrative.

# II

# THE LITTLE SHOP-WINDOW

I T STILL lacked half-an-hour of sunrise, when Miss Hepzibah Pyncheon—we will not say awoke; it being doubtful whether the poor lady had so much as closed her eyes,
during the brief night of mid-summer—but, at all events, arose
from her solitary pillow, and began what it would be mockery to term the adornment of her person. Far from us be the
indecorum of assisting, even in imagination, at a maiden
lady's toilet! Our story must therefore await Miss Hepzibah at
the threshold of her chamber; only presuming, meanwhile, to
note some of the heavy sighs that labored from her bosom,
with little restraint as to their lugubrious depth and volume
of sound, inasmuch as they could be audible to nobody, save
a disembodied listener like ourself. The old maid was alone
in the old house. Alone, except for a certain respectable and
orderly young man, an artist in the daguerreotype line, who,
for about three months back, had been a lodger in a remote
gable—quite a house by itself, indeed—with locks, bolts, and
oaken bars, on all the intervening doors. Inaudible, consequently, were poor Miss Hepzibah's gusty sighs. Inaudible,
the creaking joints of her stiffened knees, as she knelt down
by the bedside. And inaudible, too, by mortal ear, but heard
with all-comprehending love and pity, in the farthest Heaven,
that almost agony of prayer—now whispered, now a groan,

now a struggling silence—wherewith she besought the Divine
assistance through the day! Evidently, this is to be a day of
more than ordinary trial to Miss Hepzibah, who, for above
a quarter of a century gone-by, has dwelt in strict seclusion;
taking no part in the business of life, and just as little in its
intercourse and pleasures. Not with such fervor prays the
torpid recluse, looking forward to the cold, sunless, stagnant
calm of a day that is to be like innumerable yesterdays!

The maiden lady's[1] devotions are concluded. Will she now
issue forth over the threshold of our story? Not yet, by many
moments. First, every drawer in the tall, old-fashioned bureau
is to be opened, with difficulty, and with a succession of spas-
modic jerks; then, all must close again, with the same fidgety
reluctance. There is a rustling of stiff silks; a tread of backward and forward footsteps, to-and-fro, across the chamber.
We suspect Miss Hepzibah, moreover, of taking a step upward into a chair, in order to give heedful regard to her
appearance, on all sides, and at full length, in the oval, dingy-
framed toilet-glass, that hangs above her table. Truly! Well,
indeed! Who would have thought it! Is all this precious time
to be lavished on the matutinal repair and beautifying of an
elderly person, who never goes abroad—whom nobody ever
visits—and from whom, when she shall have done her utmost,
it were the best charity to turn one's eyes another way!

Now, she is almost ready. Let us pardon her one other
pause; for it is given to the sole sentiment, or we might better
say—heightened and rendered intense, as it has been, by
sorrow and seclusion—to the strong passion of her life. We
heard the turning of a key in a small lock; she has opened a
secret drawer of an escritoir, and is probably looking at a certain miniature, done in Malbone's most perfect style, and representing a face worthy of no less delicate a pencil.[2] It was
once our good fortune to see this picture. It is the likeness

1. In the manuscript Hawthorne had originally almost always referred to
Hepzibah as "the Old Maid." In the course of writing the novel, however,
Hawthorne became more sympathetic towards her; and so he went back
and substituted either her name or some kinder term.
2. Edward Greene Malbone (1777-1807), who did exquisite small-scale portraits on ivory, is considered the finest American miniaturist.

of a young man, in a silken dressing-gown of an old fashion, the soft richness of which is well adapted to the countenance of reverie, with its full, tender lips, and beautiful eyes, that seem to indicate not so much capacity of thought, as gentle and voluptuous emotion. Of the possessor of such features we should have a right to ask nothing, except that he would take the rude world easily, and make himself happy in it. Can it have been an early lover of Miss Hepzibah? No; she never had a lover—poor thing, how could she?—nor ever knew, by her own experience, what love technically means. And yet, her undying faith and trust, her fresh remembrance, and continual devotedness towards the original of that miniature, have been the only substance for her heart to feed upon.

She seems to have put aside the miniature, and is standing again before the toilet-glass. There are tears to be wiped off. A few more footsteps to-and-fro; and here, at last—with another pitiful sigh, like a gust of chill, damp wind out of a long-closed vault, the door of which has accidentally been set ajar—here comes Miss Hepzibah Pyncheon! Forth she steps into the dusky, time-darkened passage; a tall figure, clad in black silk, with a long and shrunken waist, feeling her way towards the stairs like a near-sighted person, as in truth she is.

The sun, meanwhile, if not already above the horizon, was ascending nearer and nearer to its verge. A few clouds, floating high upward, caught some of the earliest light, and threw down its golden gleam on the windows of all the houses in the street; not forgetting the House of the Seven Gables, which—many such sunrises as it had witnessed—looked cheerfully at the present one. The reflected radiance served to show, pretty distinctly, the aspect and arrangement of the room which Hepzibah entered, after descending the stairs. It was a low-studded-room, with a beam across the ceiling, panelled with dark wood, and having a large chimney-piece, set round with pictured tiles, but now closed by an iron fireboard, through which ran the funnel of a modern stove. There was a carpet on the floor, originally of rich texture, but so worn and faded, in these latter years, that its once brilliant figure had quite vanished into one indistinguishable hue. In the way of furniture, there were two tables; one, constructed with perplexing intricacy, and exhibiting as many feet as a centipede; the other, most delicately wrought, with four long and slender legs, so apparently frail, that it was almost incredible what a length of time the ancient tea-table had stood upon them. Half-a-dozen chairs stood about the room, straight and stiff, and so ingeniously contrived for the discomfort of the human person, that they were irksome even to sight, and conveyed the ugliest possible idea of the state of society to which they could have been adapted. One exception there was, however, in a very antique elbow-chair, with a high back, carved elaborately in oak, and a roomy depth within its arms, that made up, by its spacious comprehensiveness, for the lack of any of those artistic curves which abound in a modern chair.

As for ornamental articles of furniture, we recollect but two, if such they may be called. One was a map of the Pyncheon territory at the eastward, not engraved, but the handiwork of some skilful old draftsman, and grotesquely illuminated with pictures of Indians and wild beasts, among which was seen a lion; the natural history of the region being as little known as its geography, which was put down most fantastically awry. The other adornment was the portrait of old Colonel Pyncheon, at two thirds length, representing the stern features of a Puritanic-looking personage, in a scull-cap, with a laced band and a grizzly beard; holding a Bible with one hand, and in the other uplifting an iron sword-hilt. The latter object, being more successfully depicted by the artist, stood out in far greater prominence than the sacred volume.[3] Face to face with this picture, on entering the apartment, Miss Hepzibah Pyncheon came to a pause; regarding it with a singular scowl—a strange contortion of the brow—which, by people who did not know her, would probably have been interpreted as an expression of bitter anger and ill-will. But

3. Compare the "portrait" of William Hathorne in "The Custom-House": "The figure of that first ancestor *** haunts me. *** I seem to have a stronger claim to a residence here [in Salem] on account of this grave, bearded, sable-cloaked, and steeple-crowned progenitor,—who came so early,

it was no such thing. She, in fact, felt a reverence for the pictured visage, of which only a far-descended and time-stricken virgin could be susceptible; and this forbidding scowl was the innocent result of her near-sightedness, and an effort so to concentrate her powers of vision, as to substitute a firm outline of the object, instead of a vague one.

We must linger, a moment, on this unfortunate expression of poor Hepzibah's brow. Her scowl—as the world, or such part of it as sometimes caught a transitory glimpse of her at the window, wickedly persisted in calling it—her scowl had done Miss Hepzibah a very ill-office, in establishing her character as an ill-tempered old maid; nor does it appear improbable, that, by often gazing at herself in a dim looking-glass, and perpetually encountering her own frown within its ghostly sphere, she had been led to interpret the expression almost as unjustly as the world did.— "How miserably cross I look!"—she must often have whispered to herself;—and ultimately have fancied herself so, by a sense of inevitable doom. But her heart never frowned. It was naturally tender, sensitive, and full of little tremors and palpitations; all of which weaknesses it retained, while her visage was growing so perversely stern, and even fierce. Nor had Hepzibah ever any hardihood, except what came from the very warmest nook in her affections.

All this time, however, we are loitering faint-heartedly on the threshold of our story. In very truth, we have an invincible reluctance to disclose what Miss Hepzibah Pyncheon was about to do.

It has already been observed, that, in the basement story of the gable fronting on the street, an unworthy ancestor, nearly a century ago, had fitted up a shop. Ever since the old gentleman retired from trade, and fell asleep under his coffin-lid, not only the shop-door, but the inner arrangements, had been suffered to remain unchanged; while the dust of ages gathered inch-deep over the shelves and counter, and

with his Bible and his sword."

partly filled an old pair of scales, as if it were of value enough to be weighed.—It treasured itself up, too, in the half-open till, where there still lingered a base sixpence, worth neither more nor less than the hereditary pride which had here been put to shame. Such had been the state and condition of the little shop, in old Hepzibah's childhood, when she and her brother used to play at hide-and-seek in its forsaken precincts. So it had remained, until within a few days past.

But now, though the shop-window was still closely curtained from the public gaze, a remarkable change had taken place in its interior. The rich and heavy festoons of cobweb, which it had cost a long ancestral succession of spiders their life's labor to spin and weave, had been carefully brushed away from the ceiling. The counter, shelves, and floor had all been scoured, and the latter was overstrewn with fresh blue sand. The brown scales, too, had evidently undergone rigid discipline, in an unavailing effort to rub off the rust, which, alas! had eaten through and through their substance. Neither was the little old shop any longer empty of merchantable goods. A curious eye, privileged to take an account of stock and investigate behind the counter, would have discovered a barrel—yea, two or three barrels and half-ditto—[4] one containing flour, another apples, and a third, perhaps, Indian meal.[5] There was likewise a square box of pine-wood, full of soap in bars; also, another of the same size, in which were tallow-candles, ten to the pound. A small stock of brown sugar, some white beans and split peas, and a few other commodities of low price, and such as are constantly in demand, made up the bulkier portion of the merchandize. It might have been taken for a ghostly or phantasmagoric reflection of the old shopkeeper Pyncheon's shabbily provided shelves; save that some of the articles were of a description and outward form, which could hardly have been known in his day. For instance, there was a glass pickle-jar, filled with fragments of Gibraltar-rock; not, indeed, splinters of the veritable

4. Ledger style for half a barrel; an amusing reminder of Hawthorne's Custom House days.
5. Cornmeal.

stone foundation of the famous fortress, but bits of delectable candy, neatly done up in white paper. Jim Crow, moreover, was seen executing his world-renowned dance, in ginger-bread. A party of leaden dragoons were galloping along one of the shelves, in equipments and uniform of modern cut; and there were some sugar figures, with no strong resemblance to the humanity of any epoch, but less unsatisfactorily representing our own fashions, than those of a hundred years ago. Another phenomenon, still more strikingly modern, was a package of lucifer-matches, which, in old times, would have been thought actually to borrow their instantaneous flame from the nether fires of Tophet.[6]

In short, to bring the matter at once to a point, it was incontrovertibly evident that somebody had taken the shop and fixtures of the long retired and forgotten Mr. Pyncheon, and was about to renew the enterprise of that departed worthy, with a different set of customers. Who could this bold adventurer be? And, of all places in the world, why had he chosen the House of the Seven Gables as the scene of his commercial speculations?

We return to the elderly maiden. She at length withdrew her eyes from the dark countenance of the Colonel's portrait, heaved a sigh—indeed, her breast was a very cave of Æolus,[7] that morning—and stept across the room on tiptoe, as is the customary gait of elderly women. Passing through an intervening passage, she opened a door that communicated with the shop, just now so elaborately described. Owing to the projection of the upper story—and, still more, to the thick shadow of the Pyncheon-elm, which stood almost directly in front of the gable—the twilight, here, was still as much akin to night as morning. Another heavy sigh from Miss Hepzibah! After a moment's pause on the threshold, peering towards the window with her near-sighted scowl, as if frowning down some bitter enemy, she suddenly projected herself into the

6. Hell.
7. God of the winds.

shop. The haste, and, as it were, the galvanic impulse of the movement, were really quite startling.

Nervously—in a sort of frenzy, we might almost say—she began to busy herself in arranging some children's playthings and other little wares, on the shelves and at the shop-window. In the aspect of this dark-arrayed, pale-faced, ladylike, old figure, there was a deeply tragic character that contrasted irreconcilably with the ludicrous pettiness of her employment. It seemed a queer anomaly, that so gaunt and dismal a personage should take a toy in hand;—a miracle, that the toy did not vanish in her grasp;—a miserably absurd idea, that she should go on perplexing her stiff and sombre intellect with the question how to tempt little boys into her premises! Yet such is undoubtedly her object! Now, she places a gingerbread elephant against the window, but with so tremulous a touch that it tumbles upon the floor, with the dismemberment of three legs and its trunk; it has ceased to be an elephant, and has become a few bits of musty gingerbread. There, again, she has upset a tumbler of marbles, all of which roll different ways, and each individual marble, devil-directed, into the most difficult obscurity that it can find. Heaven help our poor old Hepzibah, and forgive us for taking a ludicrous view of her position! As her rigid and rusty frame goes down upon its hands and knees, in quest of the absconding marbles, we positively feel so much the more inclined to shed tears of sympathy, from the very fact that we must needs turn aside and laugh at her! For here—and if we fail to impress it suitably upon the reader, it is our own fault, not that of the theme—here is one of the truest points of melancholy interest that occur in ordinary life. It was the final term of what called itself old gentility. A lady—who had fed herself from childhood with the shadowy food of aristocratic reminiscences, and whose religion it was, that a lady's hand soils itself irremediably by doing aught for bread—this born lady, after sixty years of narrowing means, is fain to step down from her pedestal of imaginary rank. Poverty, treading closely at her heels for a lifetime, has come up with her at last. She must earn her own food, or starve! And we have stolen upon Miss Hepzibah Pyncheon, too irreverently, at the instant of time when the patrician lady is to be transformed into the plebeian woman.

In this republican country, amid the fluctuating waves of our social life, somebody is always at the drowning-point. The tragedy is enacted with as continual a repetition as that of a popular drama on a holiday, and, nevertheless, is felt as deeply, perhaps, as when an hereditary noble sinks below his order. More deeply; since, with us, rank is the grosser substance of wealth and a splendid establishment, and has no spiritual existence after the death of these, but dies hopelessly along with them. And, therefore, since we have been unfortunate enough to introduce our heroine at so inauspicious a juncture, we would entreat for a mood of due solemnity in the spectators of her fate. Let us behold, in poor Hepzibah, the immemorial lady—two hundred years old, on this side of the water, and thrice as many, on the other—with her antique portraits, pedigrees, coats of arms, records, and traditions, and her claim, as joint heiress, to that princely territory at the eastward, no longer a wilderness, but a populous fertility—born, too, in Pyncheon-street, under the Pyncheon-elm, and in the Pyncheon-house, where she has spent all her days—reduced now, in that very house, to be the huckstercss of a cent shop!

This business of setting up a petty shop is almost the only resource of women, in circumstances at all similar to those of our unfortunate recluse. With her near-sightedness, and those tremulous fingers of hers, at once inflexible and delicate, she could not be a seamstress; although her sampler, of fifty years gone-by, exhibited some of the most recondite specimens of ornamental needlework. A school for little children had been often in her thoughts; and, at one time, she had begun a review of her early studies in the New England primer, with a view to prepare herself for the office of instructress. But the love of children had never been quickened in Hepzibah's heart, and was now torpid, if not extinct; she watched the little people of the neighborhood, from her chamber-window, and doubted whether she could tolerate a more intimate acquaintance with them. Besides, in our day, the very A. B. C. has become a science, greatly too abstruse to be any longer taught by pointing a pin from letter to letter. A modern child could teach old Hepzibah more than old Hepzibah could teach the child. So—with many a cold, deep heartquake at the idea of at last coming into sordid contact with the world, from which she had so long kept aloof, while every added day of seclusion had rolled another stone against the cavern-door of her hermitage—the poor thing bethought herself of the ancient shop-window, the rusty scales, and dusty till. She might have held back a little longer; but another circumstance, not yet hinted at, had somewhat hastened her decision. Her humble preparations, therefore, were duly made, and the enterprise was now to be commenced. Nor was she entitled to complain of any remarkable singularity in her fate; for, in the town of her nativity, we might point to several little shops of a similar description; some of them in houses as ancient as that of the seven gables; and one or two, it may be, where a decayed gentlewoman stands behind the counter, as grim an image of family-pride as Miss Hepzibah Pyncheon herself.

It was overpoweringly ridiculous—we must honestly confess it—the deportment of the maiden lady, while setting her shop in order for the public eye. She stole on tiptoe to the window, as cautiously as if she conceived some bloody-minded villain to be watching behind the elm-tree, with intent to take her life. Stretching out her long, lank arm, she put a paper of pearl-buttons, a jewsharp, or whatever the small article might be, in its destined place, and straightway vanished back into the dusk, as if the world need never hope for another glimpse of her. It might have been fancied, indeed, that she expected to minister to the wants of the community, unseen, like a disembodied divinity, or enchantress, holding forth her bargains to the reverential and awe-stricken purchaser, in an invisible hand. But Hepzibah had no such flattering dream. She was well aware that she must ultimately come forward, and stand revealed in her proper individuality; but, like other sensitive persons, she could not bear to be observed in the gradual process, and chose rather to flash forth on the world's astonished gaze, at once.

The inevitable moment was not much longer to be delayed. The sunshine might now be seen stealing down the front of the opposite house, from the windows of which came a reflected gleam, struggling through the boughs of the elm-tree, and enlightening the interior of the shop, more distinctly than heretofore. The town appeared to be waking-up. A baker's cart had already rattled through the street, chasing away the latest vestige of night's sanctity with the jingle-jangle of its dissonant bells. A milkman was distributing the contents of his cans from door to door; and the harsh peal of a fisherman's conch-shell was heard far off, around the corner. None of these tokens escaped Hepzibah's notice. The moment had arrived. To delay longer, would be only to lengthen out her misery. Nothing remained, except to take down the bar from the shop-door, leaving the entrance free—more than free—welcome, as if all were household friends—to every passer-by, whose eyes might be attracted by the commodities at the window. This last act Hepzibah now performed, letting the bar fall, with what smote upon her excited nerves as a most astounding clatter. Then—as if the only barrier betwixt herself and the world had been thrown down, and a flood of evil consequences would come tumbling through the gap—she fled into the inner parlor, threw herself into the ancestral elbow-chair, and wept.

Our miserable old Hepzibah! It is a heavy annoyance to

a writer, who endeavors to represent nature, its various attitudes and circumstances, in a reasonably correct outline and true coloring, that so much of the mean and ludicrous should be hopelessly mixed up with the purest pathos which life anywhere supplies to him. What tragic dignity, for example, can be wrought into a scene like this! How can we elevate our history of retribution for the sin of long ago, when, as one of our most prominent figures, we are compelled to introduce —not a young and lovely woman, nor even the stately remains of beauty, storm-shattered by affliction—but a gaunt, sallow, rusty-jointed maiden, in a long-waisted silk-gown, and with the strange horror of a turban on her head! Her visage is not even ugly. It is redeemed from insignificance only by the contraction of her eyebrows into a near-sighted scowl. And, finally, her great life-trial seems to be, that, after sixty years of idleness, she finds it convenient to earn comfortable bread by setting up a shop, in a small way. Nevertheless, if we look through all the heroic fortunes of mankind, we shall find this same entanglement of something mean and trivial with whatever is noblest in joy or sorrow. Life is made up of marble and mud. And, without all the deeper trust in a comprehensive sympathy above us, we might hence be led to suspect the insult of a sneer, as well as an immitigable frown, on the iron countenance of fate. What is called poetic insight is the gift of discerning, in this sphere of strangely mingled elements, the beauty and the majesty which are compelled to assume a garb so sordid.

# III

# THE FIRST CUSTOMER

MISS Hepzibah Pyncheon sat in the oaken elbow-chair, with her hands over her face, giving way to that heavy downsinking of the heart which most persons have experienced, when the image of Hope itself seems ponderously moulded of lead, on the eve of an enterprise, at once doubtful and momentous. She was suddenly startled by the tinkling alarum—high, sharp, and irregular—of a little bell. The maiden lady arose upon her feet, as pale as a ghost at cock-crow; for she was an enslaved spirit, and this the talisman to which she owed obedience.[1] This little bell—to speak in plainer terms—being fastened over the shop-door, was so contrived as to vibrate by means of a steel-spring, and thus convey notice to the inner regions of the house, when any customer should cross the threshold. Its ugly and spiteful little din, (heard now for the first time, perhaps, since Hepzibah's periwigged predecessor had retired from trade,) at once set every nerve of her body in responsive and tumultuous vibration. The crisis was upon her! Her first customer was at the door!

Without giving herself time for a second thought, she rushed into the shop, pale, wild, desperate in gesture and expression, scowling portentously, and looking far better qualified to do fierce battle with a housebreaker than to stand

---

1. The legend of a ghost's blanching at cock-crow goes back to the Middle Ages. Cf. the first appearance of the ghost in *Hamlet* (I, i, 147–49): "It was about to speak when the cock crew./And then it started like a guilty thing/ Upon a fearful summons."

smiling behind the counter, bartering small wares for a copper recompense. Any ordinary customer, indeed, would have turned his back, and fled. And yet there was nothing fierce in Hepzibah's poor old heart; nor had she, at the moment, a single bitter thought against the world at large, or one individual man or woman. She wished them all well, but wished, too, that she herself were done with them, and in her quiet grave.

The applicant, by this time, stood within the door-way. Coming freshly, as he did, out of the morning light, he appeared to have brought some of its cheery influences into the shop along with him. It was a slender young man, not more than one or two and twenty years old, with rather a grave and thoughtful expression, for his years, but likewise a springy alacrity and vigor. These qualities were not only perceptible, physically, in his make and motions, but made themselves felt, almost immediately, in his character. A brown beard, not too silken in its texture, fringed his chin, but as yet without completely hiding it; he wore a short moustache, too; and his dark, high-featured countenance looked all the better for these natural ornaments. As for his dress, it was of the simplest kind; a summer sack of cheap and ordinary material, thin checkered pantaloons, and a straw hat, by no means of the finest braid. Oak-hall might have supplied his entire equipment.[2] He was chiefly marked as a gentleman—if such, indeed, he made any claim to be—by the rather remarkable whiteness and nicety of his clean linen.

He met the scowl of old Hepzibah without apparent alarm, as having heretofore encountered it, and found it harmless.

"So, my dear Miss Pyncheon," said the Daguerreotypist—[3] for it was that sole other occupant of the seven-gabled mansion—"I am glad to see that you have not shrunk from your good purpose. I merely look in, to offer my best wishes, and to ask if I can assist you any further in your preparations?"

People in difficulty and distress, or in any manner at odds

2. Oak Hall was a department store in Boston which sold men's ready-to-wear clothing cheaply.
3. For a discussion of daguerreotypy and its relationship to the novel, see

with the world, can endure a vast amount of harsh treatment, and perhaps be only the stronger for it; whereas, they give way at once before the simplest expression of what they perceive to be genuine sympathy. So it proved with poor Hepzibah; for when she saw the young man's smile—looking so much the brighter on a thoughtful face—and heard his kindly tone, she broke first into an hysteric giggle, and then began to sob.

"Ah, Mr. Holgrave," cried she, as soon as she could speak, "I never can go through with it! Never, never, never! I wish I were dead, and in the old family-tomb, with all my forefathers! With my father, and my mother, and my sister! Yes; —and with my brother, who had far better find me there than here! The world is too chill and hard—and I am too old, and too feeble, and too hopeless!"

"Oh, believe me, Miss Hepzibah," said the young man quietly, "these feelings will not trouble you any longer, after you are once fairly in the midst of your enterprise. They are unavoidable at this moment, standing, as you do, on the outer verge of your long seclusion, and peopling the world with ugly shapes, which you will soon find to be as unreal as the giants and ogres of a child's story-book. I find nothing so singular in life, as that everything appears to lose its substance, the instant one actually grapples with it. So it will be with what you think so terrible."

"But I am a woman!" said Hepzibah piteously. "I was going to say, a lady,—but I consider that as past."

"Well; no matter if it be past!" answered the artist, a strange gleam of half-hidden sarcasm flashing through the kindliness of his manner. "Let it go! You are the better without it. I speak frankly, my dear Miss Pyncheon:—for are we not friends? I look upon this as one of the fortunate days of your life. It ends an epoch, and begins one. Hitherto, the life-blood has been gradually chilling in your veins, as you sat aloof, within your circle of gentility, while the rest of the

Alfred H. Marks, "Hawthorne's Daguerreotypist: Scientist, Artist, Reformer," p. 330.

world was fighting out its battle with one kind of necessity or another. Henceforth, you will at least have the sense of healthy and natural effort for a purpose, and of lending your strength—be it great or small—to the united struggle of mankind. This is success—all the success that anybody meets with!"

"It is natural enough, Mr. Holgrave, that you should have ideas like these," rejoined Hepzibah, drawing up her gaunt figure with slightly offended dignity.—"You are a man—a young man—and brought up, I suppose, as almost everybody is, now-a-days, with a view to seeking your fortune. But I was born a lady, and have always lived one—no matter in what narrowness of means, always a lady!"

"But I was not born a gentleman; neither have I lived like one," said Holgrave, slightly smiling; "so, my dear Madam, you will hardly expect me to sympathize with sensibilities of this kind; though—unless I deceive myself—I have some imperfect comprehension of them. These names of gentleman and lady had a meaning, in the past history of the world, and conferred privileges, desirable, or otherwise, on those entitled to bear them. In the present—and still more in the future condition of society—they imply, not privilege, but restriction."

"These are new notions," said the old gentlewoman, shaking her head. "I shall never understand them; neither do I wish it."

"We will cease to speak of them, then," replied the artist, with a friendlier smile than his last one; "and I will leave you to feel whether it is not better to be a true woman, than a lady. Do you really think, Miss Hepzibah, that any lady of your family has ever done a more heroic thing, since this house was built, than you are performing in it to-day? Never; —and if the Pyncheons had always acted so nobly, I doubt whether the old wizard Maule's anathema, of which you told me once, would have had much weight with Providence against them."

"Ah!—no, no!" said Hepzibah, not displeased at this allusion to the sombre dignity of an inherited curse. "If old Maule's ghost, or a descendant of his, could see me behind the counter to-day, he would call it the fulfilment of his worst wishes. But I thank you for your kindness, Mr. Holgrave, and will do my utmost to be a good shopkeeper!"

"Pray do," said Holgrave, "and let me have the pleasure of being your first customer. I am about taking a walk to the sea-shore, before going to my rooms, where I misuse Heaven's blessed sunshine by tracing out human features, through its agency. A few of those biscuits, dipt in sea-water, will be just what I need for breakfast. What is the price of half-a-dozen?"

"Let me be a lady a moment longer," replied Hepzibah, with a manner of antique stateliness, to which a melancholy smile lent a kind of grace. She put the biscuits into his hand, but rejected the compensation.—"A Pyncheon must not, at all events, under her forefathers' roof, receive money for a morsel of bread, from her only friend!"

Holgrave took his departure, leaving her, for the moment, with spirits not quite so much depressed. Soon, however, they had subsided nearly to their former dead-level. With a beating heart, she listened to the footsteps of early passengers, which now began to be frequent along the street. Once or twice, they seemed to linger; these strangers, or neighbors, as the case might be, were looking at the display of toys and petty commodities in Hepzibah's shop-window. She was doubly tortured;—in part, with a sense of overwhelming shame, that strange and unloving eyes should have the privilege of gazing;—and, partly, because the idea occurred to her, with ridiculous importunity, that the window was not arranged so skilfully, nor nearly to so much advantage, as it might have been. It seemed as if the whole fortune or failure of her shop might depend on the display of a different set of articles, or substituting a fairer apple for one which appeared to be specked. So she made the change, and straightway fancied that everything was spoiled by it; not recognizing that it was the nervousness of the juncture, and her own native squeamishness, as an old maid, that wrought all the seeming mischief.

Anon, there was an encounter, just at the door-step, betwixt two laboring men, as their rough voices denoted them to be. After some slight talk about their own affairs, one of them chanced to notice the shop-window, and directed the other's attention to it.

"See here!" cried he. "What do you think of this? Trade seems to be looking up, in Pyncheon-street!"

"Well, well, this is a sight, to be sure!" exclaimed the other. "In the old Pyncheon-house, and underneath the Pyncheon-elm! Who would have thought it! Old Maid Pyncheon is setting up a cent-shop!"

"Will she make it go, think you, Dixey?" said his friend. "I don't call it a very good stand. There's another shop, just round the corner."

"Make it go!" cried Dixey, with a most contemptuous expression, as if the very idea were impossible to be conceived. "Not a bit of it! Why, her face—I've seen it; for I dug her garden for her, one year—her face is enough to frighten the Old Nick himself, if he had ever so great a mind to trade with her. People can't stand it, I tell you! She scowls dreadfully, reason or none, out of pure ugliness of temper!"

"Well; that's not so much matter," remarked the other man. "These sour-tempered folks are mostly handy at business, and know pretty well what they are about. But, as you say, I don't think she'll do much. This business of keeping cent-shops is overdone, like all other kinds of trade, handicraft, and bodily labor. I know it, to my cost! My wife kept a cent-shop, three months, and lost five dollars on her outlay!"

"Poor business!" responded Dixey, in a tone as if he were shaking his head.—"Poor business!"

For some reason or other, not very easy to analyze, there had hardly been so bitter a pang in all her previous misery about the matter, as what thrilled Hepzibah's heart, on over-hearing the above conversation. The testimony in regard to her scowl was frightfully important; it seemed to hold up her image, wholly relieved from the false light of her self-partialities, and so hideous that she dared not look at it. She was absurdly hurt, moreover, by the slight and idle effect that her setting-up shop—an event of such breathless interest to herself—appeared to have upon the public, of which these two men were the nearest representatives. A glance; a passing word or two; a coarse laugh;—and she was doubtless forgotten, before they turned the corner! They cared nothing for her dignity, and just as little for her degradation. Then, also, the augury of ill-success, uttered from the sure wisdom of experience, fell upon her half-dead hope, like a clod into a grave. The man's wife had already tried the same experiment, and failed! How could the born lady—the recluse of half-a-lifetime, utterly unpractised in the world, at sixty years of age—how could she ever dream of succeeding, when the hard, vulgar, keen, busy, hackneyed New England woman had lost five dollars on her little outlay? Success presented itself as an impossibility, and the hope of it as a wild hallu-cination.

Some malevolent spirit, doing his utmost to drive Hepzibah mad, unrolled before her imagination a kind of panorama, representing the great thoroughfare of a city, all astir with customers. So many and so magnificent shops as there were! Groceries, toy-shops, dry-goods stores, with their immense panes of plate-glass, their gorgeous fixtures, their vast and complete assortments of merchandize, in which fortunes had been invested; and those noble mirrors at the farther end of each establishment, doubling all this wealth by a brightly burnished vista of unrealities! On one side of the street, this splendid bazaar, with a multitude of perfumed and glossy salesmen, smirking, smiling, bowing, and measuring out the goods! On the other, the dusky old House of the Seven Gables, with the antiquated shop-window under its projecting story, and Hepzibah herself in a gown of rusty black silk, behind the counter, scowling at the world as it went by! This mighty contrast thrust itself forward as a fair expression of the odds against which she was to begin her struggle for a subsistence. Success? Preposterous! She would never think of it again! The house might just as well be buried in an eternal fog, while all other houses had the sunshine on them; for not a foot would ever cross the threshold, nor a hand so much as try the door!

But, at this instant, the shop-bell, right over her head, tinkled as if it were bewitched. The old gentlewoman's heart seemed to be attached to the same steel-spring; for it went through a series of sharp jerks, in unison with the sound. The door was thrust open, although no human form was perceptible on the other side of the half-window. Hepzibah, nevertheless, stood at a gaze, with her hands clasped, looking very much as if she had summoned up an evil spirit, and were afraid, yet resolved, to hazard the encounter.

"Heaven help me!" she groaned mentally. "Now is my hour of need!"

The door, which moved with difficulty on its creaking and rusty hinges, being forced quite open, a square and sturdy little urchin became apparent, with cheeks as red as an apple. He was clad rather shabbily, (but, as it seemed, more owing to his mother's carelessness than his father's poverty,) in a blue apron, very wide and short trowsers, shoes somewhat out at the toes, and a chip-hat,[4] with the frizzles of his curly hair sticking through its crevices. A book and a small slate, under his arm, indicated that he was on his way to school. He stared at Hepzibah, a moment, as an elder customer than himself

4. A hat made of thin strips of wood or woody fiber.

would have been likely enough to do; not knowing what to make of the tragic attitude and queer scowl, wherewith she regarded him.

"Well, child!" said she, taking heart at sight of a personage so little formidable.—"Well, my child, what did you wish for?"

"That Jim Crow there, in the window!" answered the urchin, holding out a cent, and pointing to the gingerbread figure that had attracted his notice, as he loitered along to school.—"The one that has not a broken foot!"

So Hepzibah put forth her lank arm, and taking the effigy from the shop-window, delivered it to her first customer.

"No matter for the money!" said she, giving him a little push towards the door—for her old gentility was contumaciously squeamish at sight of the copper-coin; and, besides, it seemed such pitiful meanness to take the child's pocket-money, in exchange for a bit of stale gingerbread.—"No matter for the cent! You are welcome to Jim Crow!"

The child—staring with round eyes at this instance of liberality, wholly unprecedented in his large experience of cent-shops—took the man of gingerbread, and quitted the premises. No sooner had he reached the sidewalk (little cannibal that he was!) than Jim Crow's head was in his mouth. As he had not been careful to shut the door, Hepzibah was at the pains of closing it after him, with a pettish ejaculation or two about the troublesomeness of young people, and particularly of small boys. She had just placed another representative of the renowned Jim Crow at the window, when again the shop-bell tinkled clamorously; and again the door being thrust open, with its characteristic jerk and jar, disclosed the same sturdy little urchin who, precisely two minutes ago, had made his exit. The crumbs and discoloration of the cannibal-feast, as yet hardly consummated, were exceedingly visible about his mouth!

"What is it now, child?" asked the maiden lady, rather impatiently.—"Did you come back to shut the door?"

"No!" answered the urchin, pointing to the figure that had just been put up.—"I want that other Jim Crow!"

"Well, here it is for you," said Hepzibah, reaching it down; but, recognizing that this pertinacious customer would not quit her on any other terms, so long as she had a gingerbread figure in her shop, she partly drew back her extended hand— "Where is the cent?"

The little boy had the cent ready, but, like a true-born Yankee, would have preferred the better bargain to the worse. Looking somewhat chagrined, he put the coin into Hepzibah's hand, and departed, sending the second Jim Crow in quest of the former one. The new shopkeeper dropt the first solid result of her commercial enterprise into the till. It was done! The sordid stain of that copper-coin could never be washed away from her palm. The little schoolboy, aided by the impish figure of the negro dancer, had wrought an irreparable ruin. The structure of ancient aristocracy had been demolished by him, even as if his childish gripe had torn down the seven-gabled mansion! Now let Hepzibah turn the old Pyncheon portraits with their faces to the wall, and take the map of her eastern-territory to kindle the kitchen-fire, and blow up the flame with the empty breath of her ancestral traditions! What had she to do with ancestry? Nothing;—no more than with posterity! No lady, now, but simply Hepzibah Pyncheon, a forlorn old maid, and keeper of a cent-shop!

Nevertheless—even while she paraded these ideas somewhat ostentatiously through her mind—it is altogether surprising what a calmness had come over her. The anxiety and misgivings which had tormented her, whether asleep or in melancholy day-dreams, ever since her project began to take an aspect of solidity, had now vanished quite away. She felt the novelty of her position, indeed, but no longer with disturbance or affright. Now and then, there came a thrill of almost youthful enjoyment. It was the invigorating breath of a fresh outward atmosphere, after the long torpor and monotonous seclusion of her life. So wholesome is effort!

So miraculous the strength that we do not know of! The healthiest glow, that Hepzibah had known for years, had come now, in the dreaded crisis, when, for the first time, she had put forth her hand to help herself. That little circlet of the schoolboy's copper-coin—dim and lustreless though it was, with the small services which it had been doing, here and there about the world—had proved a talisman, fragrant with good, and deserving to be set in gold and worn next her heart. It was as potent, and perhaps endowed with the same kind of efficacy, as a galvanic ring![5] Hepzibah, at all events, was indebted to its subtile operation, both in body and spirit; so much the more, as it inspired her with energy to get some breakfast, at which—still the better to keep up her courage—she allowed herself an extra spoonful in her infusion of black tea.

Her introductory day of shopkeeping did not run on, however, without many and serious interruptions of this mood of cheerful vigor. As a general rule, Providence seldom vouchsafes to mortals any more than just that degree of encouragement, which suffices to keep them at a reasonably full exertion of their powers. In the case of our old gentlewoman, after the excitement of new effort had subsided, the despondency of her whole life threatened, ever and anon, to return. It was like the heavy mass of clouds, which we may often see obscuring the sky, and making a gray twilight everywhere, until, towards nightfall, it yields temporarily to a glimpse of sunshine. But, always, the envious cloud strives to gather again across the streak of celestial azure.

Customers came in, as the forenoon advanced, but rather slowly; in some cases, too, it must be owned, with little satisfaction either to themselves or Miss Hepzibah; nor on the whole, with an aggregate of very rich emolument to the till. A little girl, sent by her mother to match a skein of cotton-thread, of a peculiar hue, took one that the near-sighted old lady pronounced extremely like, but soon came running back,

5. A ring made of different metals; the chemical effect of one on the other was supposed to set up an electrical current that had a beneficial effect on the wearer.

with a blunt and cross message, that it would not do, and, besides, was very rotten! Then there was a pale, care-wrinkled woman, not old, but haggard, and already with streaks of gray among her hair, like silver ribbons; one of those women, naturally delicate, whom you at once recognize as worn to death by a brute—probably, a drunken brute—of a husband, and at least nine children. She wanted a few pounds of flour, and offered the money, which the decayed gentlewoman silently rejected, and gave the poor soul better measure than if she had taken it. Shortly afterwards, a man in a blue cotton-frock, much soiled, came in and bought a pipe; filling the whole shop, meanwhile, with the hot odor of strong drink, not only exhaled in the torrid atmosphere of his breath, but oozing out of his entire system, like an inflammable gas. It was impressed on Hepzibah's mind, that this was the husband of the care-wrinkled woman. He asked for a paper of tobacco; and, as she had neglected to provide herself with the article, her brutal customer dashed down his newly-bought pipe, and left the shop, muttering some unintelligible words, which had the tone and bitterness of a curse. Hereupon, Hepzibah threw up her eyes, unintentionally scowling in the face of Providence!

No less than five persons, during the forenoon, inquired for ginger-beer, or root-beer, or any drink of a similar brewage, and, obtaining nothing of the kind, went off in an exceedingly bad humor. Three of them left the door open; and the other two pulled it so spitefully, in going out, that the little bell played the very deuce with Hepzibah's nerves. A round, bustling, fire-ruddy housewife, of the neighborhood, burst breathless into the shop, fiercely demanding yeast; and when the poor gentlewoman, with her cold shyness of manner, gave her hot customer to understand that she did not keep the article, this very capable housewife took upon herself to administer a regular rebuke.

"A cent-shop, and no yeast!" quoth she. "That will never

do! Who ever heard of such a thing? Your loaf will never rise, no more than mine will to-day. You had better shut up shop at once!"

"Well," said Hepzibah, heaving a deep sigh, "perhaps I had!"

Several times, moreover, besides the above instance, her ladylike sensibilities were seriously infringed upon by the familiar, if not rude tone with which people addressed her. They evidently considered themselves not merely her equals, but her patrons and superiors. Now, Hepzibah had unconsciously flattered herself with the idea, that there would be a gleam or halo of some kind or other, about her person, which would ensure an obeisance to her sterling gentility, or, at least, a tacit recognition of it. On the other hand, nothing tortured her more intolerably than when this recognition was too prominently expressed. To one or two rather officious offers of sympathy, her responses were little short of acrimonious; and, we regret to say, Hepzibah was thrown into a positively unchristian state of mind by the suspicion that one of her customers was drawn to the shop, not by any real need of the article which she pretended to seek, but by a wicked wish to stare at her. The vulgar creature was determined to see for herself what sort of a figure a mildewed piece of aristocracy—after wasting all the bloom and much of the decline of her life, apart from the world—would cut behind a counter. In this particular case—however mechanical and innocuous it might be, at other times—Hepzibah's contortion of brow served her in good stead.

"I never was so frightened in my life!" said the curious customer in describing the incident to one of her acquaintances. "She's a real old vixen, take my word of it. She says little, to be sure;—but if you could only see the mischief in her eye!"

On the whole, therefore, her new experience led our decayed gentlewoman to very disagreeable conclusions as to the temper and manners of what she termed the lower classes, whom, heretofore, she had looked down upon with a gentle and pitying complacence, as herself occupying a sphere of unquestionable superiority. But, unfortunately, she had likewise to struggle against a bitter emotion, of a directly opposite kind; a sentiment of virulence, we mean, towards the idle aristocracy to which it had so recently been her pride to belong. When a lady, in a delicate and costly summer garb, with a floating veil and gracefully swaying gown, and, altogether, an ethereal lightness that made you look at her beautifully slippered feet, to see whether she trod on the dust or floated in the air—when such a vision happened to pass through this retired street, leaving it tenderly and delusively fragrant with her passage, as if a boquet of tea-roses had been borne along—then, again, it is to be feared, old Hepzibah's scowl could no longer vindicate itself entirely on the plea of near-sightedness.

"For what end," thought she, giving vent to that feeling of hostility, which is the only real abasement of the poor, in presence of the rich, "for what good end, in the wisdom of Providence, does that woman live! Must the whole world toil, that the palms of her hands may be kept white and delicate?"

Then, ashamed and penitent, she hid her face.

"May God forgive me!" said she.

Doubtless, God did forgive her. But, taking the inward and outward history of the first half-day into consideration, Hepzibah began to fear that the shop would prove her ruin, in a moral and religious point of view, without contributing very essentially towards even her temporal welfare.

# IV

# A DAY BEHIND THE COUNTER

TOWARDS noon, Hepzibah saw an elderly gentleman, large and portly, and of remarkably dignified demeanor, passing slowly along, on the opposite side of the white and dusty street. On coming within the shadow of the Pyncheon-elm, he stopt, and (taking off his hat, meanwhile, to wipe the perspiration from his brow) seemed to scrutinize, with especial interest, the dilapidated and rusty-visaged House of the Seven Gables. He himself, in a very different style, was as well worth looking at as the house. No better model need be sought, nor could have been found, of a very high order of respectability, which by some indescribable magic, not merely expressed itself in his looks and gestures, but even governed the fashion of his garments, and rendered them all proper and essential to the man. Without appearing to differ, in any tangible way, from other people's clothes, there was yet a wide and rich gravity about them, that must have been a characteristic of the wearer, since it could not be defined as pertaining either to the cut or material. His gold-headed cane, too—a serviceable staff, of dark, polished wood—had similar traits, and, had it chosen to take a walk by itself, would have been recognized anywhere as a tolerably adequate representative of its master. This character—which showed itself so strikingly in everything about him, and the effect of which we seek to convey to the reader—went no deeper than his station, habits of life, and external circumstances. One perceived him to be a personage of mark, influence, and authority; and, especially, you could feel just as certain that he was opulent, as if he had exhibited his bank account—or as if you had seen him touching the twigs of the Pyncheon-elm, and, Midas-like, transmuting them to gold.

In his youth, he had probably been considered a handsome man; at his present age, his brow was too heavy, his temples too bare, his remaining hair too gray, his eye too cold, his lips too closely compressed, to bear any relation to mere personal beauty. He would have made a good and massive portrait; better now, perhaps, than at any previous period of his life, although his look might grow positively harsh, in the process of being fixed upon the canvass. The artist would have found it desirable to study his face, and prove its capacity for varied expression; to darken it with a frown—to kindle it up with a smile.

While the elderly gentleman stood looking at the Pyncheon-house, both the frown and the smile passed successively over his countenance. His eye rested on the shop window, and putting up a pair of gold-bowed spectacles, which he held in his hand, he minutely surveyed Hepzibah's little arrangement of toys and commodities. At first, it seemed not to please him—nay, to cause him exceeding displeasure—and yet, the very next moment, he smiled. While the latter expression was yet on his lips, he caught a glimpse of Hepzibah, who had involuntarily bent forward to the window; and then the smile changed from acrid and disagreeable, to the sunniest complaisancy and benevolence. He bowed, with a happy mixture of dignity and courteous kindliness, and pursued his way.

"There he is!" said Hepzibah to herself, gulping down a very bitter emotion, and, since she could not rid herself of it, trying to drive it back into her heart.—"What does he think of it, I wonder? Does it please him? Ah!—he is looking back!"

The gentleman had paused in the street, and turned himself half about, still with his eyes fixed on the shop-window. In fact, he wheeled wholly round, and commenced a step or two, as if designing to enter the shop; but, as it chanced, his purpose was anticipated by Hepzibah's first customer, the little cannibal of Jim Crow, who, staring up at the window, was irresistibly attracted by an elephant of gingerbread. What a grand appetite had this small urchin!—two Jim Crows, immediately after breakfast!—and now an elephant, as a preliminary whet before dinner! By the time this latter purchase was completed, the elderly gentleman had resumed his way, and turned the street-corner.

"Take it as you like, Cousin Jaffrey!" muttered the maiden lady, as she drew back after cautiously thrusting out her head, and looking up and down the street. "Take it as you like! You have seen my little shop-window! Well!—what have you to say?—is not the Pyncheon-house my own, while I'm alive?"

After this incident, Hepzibah retreated to the back parlor, where she at first caught up a half-finished stocking, and began knitting at it with nervous and irregular jerks; but quickly finding herself at odds with the stitches, she threw it aside, and walked hurriedly about the room. At length, she paused before the portrait of the stern old Puritan, her ancestor, and the founder of the house. In one sense, this picture had almost faded into the canvass, and hidden itself behind the duskiness of age; in another, she could not but fancy that it had been growing more prominent, and strikingly expressive, ever since her earliest familiarity with it, as a child. For, while the physical outline and substance were darkening away from the beholder's eye, the bold, hard, and, at the same time, indirect character of the man seemed to be brought out in a kind of spiritual relief. Such an effect may occasionally be observed in pictures of antique date.

They acquire a look which an artist (if he have anything like the complaisancy of artists, now-a-days) would never dream of presenting to a patron as his own characteristic expression, but which, nevertheless, we at once recognize as reflecting the unlovely truth of a human soul. In such cases, the painter's deep conception of his subject's inward traits has wrought itself into the essence of the picture, and is seen, after the superficial coloring has been rubbed off by time.

While gazing at the portrait, Hepzibah trembled under its eye. Her hereditary reverence made her afraid to judge the character of the original so harshly, as a perception of the truth compelled her to do. But still she gazed, because the face of the picture enabled her—at least, she fancied so—to read more accurately, and to a greater depth, the face which she had just seen in the street.

"This is the very man!" murmured she to herself. "Let Jaffrey Pyncheon smile as he will, there is that look beneath! Put on him a scull cap, and a band, and a black cloak, and a Bible in one hand and a sword in the other—then let Jaffrey smile as he might—nobody would doubt that it was the old Pyncheon come again! He has proved himself the very man to build up a new house! Perhaps, too, to draw down a new curse!"

Thus did Hepzibah bewilder herself with these fantasies of the old time. She had dwelt too much alone—too long in the Pyncheon-house—until her very brain was impregnated with the dry-rot of its timbers. She needed a walk along the noonday street, to keep her sane.

By the spell of contrast, another portrait rose up before her, painted with more daring flattery than any artist would have ventured upon, but yet so delicately touched that the likeness remained perfect. Malbone's miniature, though from the same original, was far inferior to Hepzibah's air-drawn picture, at which affection and sorrowful remembrance wrought together. Soft, mildly and cheerfully contemplative, with full, red lips, just on the verge of a smile, which the eyes seemed to herald by a gentle kindling-up of their orbs! Feminine traits, moulded inseparably with those of the other sex! The miniature, likewise, had this last peculiarity; so that you inevitably thought of the original as resembling his mother; and she, a lovely and loveable woman, with perhaps some beautiful infirmity of character, that made it all the pleasanter to know, and easier to love her.

"Yes," thought Hepzibah, with grief of which it was only the more tolerable portion that welled up from her heart to her eyelids, "they persecuted his mother in him! He never was a Pyncheon!"

But here the shop-bell rang; it was like a sound from a remote distance—so far had Hepzibah descended into the sepulchral depths of her reminiscences. On entering the shop, she found an old man there, a humble resident of Pyncheon-street, and whom, for a great many years past, she had suffered to be a kind of familiar of the house. He was an immemorial personage, who seemed always to have had a white head and wrinkles, and never to have possessed but a single tooth, and that a half-decayed one, in the front of the upper jaw. Well advanced as Hepzibah was, she could not remember when Uncle Venner, as the neighborhood called him, had not gone up and down the street, stooping a little and drawing his feet heavily over the gravel or pavement. But still there was something tough and vigorous about him, that not only kept him in daily breath, but enabled him to fill a place which would else have been vacant, in the apparently crowded world. To go of errands, with his slow and shuffling gait, which made you doubt how he ever was to arrive anywhere; to saw a small household's foot or two of firewood, or knock to pieces an old barrel, or split up a pine board, for kindling-stuff; in summer, to dig the few yards of garden-ground, appertaining to a low-rented tenement, and share the produce of his labor at the halves; in winter, to

shovel away the snow from the sidewalk, or open paths to
the wood-shed, or along the clothes-line;—such were some of
the essential offices which Uncle Venner performed among
at least a score of families. Within that circle, he claimed the
same sort of privilege, and probably felt as much warmth of
interest, as a clergyman does in the range of his parishioners.
Not that he laid claim to the tithe pig;[1] but, as an analogous
mode of reverence, he went his rounds, every morning, to
gather up the crumbs of the table and overflowings of the
dinner-pot, as food for a pig of his own.

In his younger days—for, after all, there was a dim tradition
that he had been, not young, but younger—Uncle Venner
was commonly regarded as rather deficient, than otherwise,
in his wits. In truth, he had virtually pleaded guilty to the
charge, by scarcely aiming at such success as other men seek,
and by taking only that humble and modest part in the intercourse of life, which belongs to the alleged deficiency. But,
now, in his extreme old age—whether it were, that his long
and hard experience had actually brightened him, or that
his decaying judgement rendered him less capable of fairly
measuring himself—the venerable man made pretensions to
no little wisdom, and really enjoyed the credit of it. There
was likewise, at times, a vein of something like poetry in
him; it was the moss or wall-flower of his mind in its small
dilapidation, and gave a charm to what might have been vulgar and common-place, in his earlier and middle life. Hepzibah had a regard for him, because his name was ancient in
the town, and had formerly been respectable. It was a still
better reason for awarding him a species of familiar reverence,
that Uncle Venner was himself the most ancient existence,
whether of man or thing, in Pyncheon-street; except the
House of the Seven Gables, and perhaps the elm that overshadowed it.

This patriarch now presented himself before Hepzibah,
clad in an old blue coat, which had a fashionable air, and

1. A pig given to the church in payment of a parishioner's share of the support of the church.

must have accrued to him from the cast-off wardrobe of some dashing clerk. As for his trowsers, they were of tow-cloth,[2] very short in the legs, and bagging down strangely in the rear, but yet having a suitableness to his figure, which his other garment entirely lacked. His hat had relation to no other part of his dress, and but very little to the head that wore it. Thus Uncle Venner was a miscellaneous old gentleman, partly himself, but, in good measure, somebody else; patched together, too, of different epochs; an epitome of times and fashions.

"So, you have really begun trade," said he—"really begun trade! Well, I'm glad to see it. Young people should never live idle in the world, nor old ones neither, unless when the rheumatize gets hold of them. It has given me warning already; and in two or three years longer, I shall think of putting aside business, and retiring to my farm. That's yonder— the great brick house, you know—the work-house, most folks call it; but I mean to do my work first, and go there to be idle and enjoy myself. And I'm glad to see you beginning to do your work, Miss Hepzibah!"

"Thank you, Uncle Venner," said Hepzibah smiling; for she always felt kindly towards the simple and talkative old man. Had he been an old woman, she might probably have repelled the freedom which she now took in good part.—"It is time for me to begin work, indeed! Or, to speak the truth, I have but just begun, when I ought to be giving it up."

"Oh, never say that, Miss Hepzibah," answered the old man. "You are a young woman yet. Why, I hardly thought myself younger than I am now—it seems so little while ago— since I used to see you playing about the door of the old house, quite a small child! Oftener, though, you used to be sitting at the threshold and looking gravely into the street; for you had always a grave kind of way with you—a grown-up air, when you were only the height of my knee. It seems as if I saw you now; and your grandfather, with his red cloak,

2. A cheap, usually homespun, linen material.

and his white wig, and his cocked hat, and his cane, coming out of the house, and stepping so grandly up the street! Those old gentlemen, that grew up before the revolution, used to put on grand airs. In my young days, the great man of the town was commonly called King, and his wife—not Queen, to be sure—but Lady. Now-a-days, a man would not dare to be called King; and if he feels himself a little above common folks, he only stoops so much the lower to them. I met your cousin, the Judge, ten minutes ago; and, in my old tow-cloth trowsers, as you see, the Judge raised his hat to me, I do believe! At any rate, the Judge bowed and smiled!"

"Yes," said Hepzibah, with something bitter stealing unawares into her tone; "my Cousin Jaffrey is thought to have a very pleasant smile!"

"And so he has!" replied Uncle Venner. "And that's rather remarkable, in a Pyncheon; for—begging your pardon, Miss Hepzibah—they never had the name of being an easy and agreeable set of folks. There was no getting close to them. But, now, Miss Hepzibah, if an old man may be bold to ask, why don't Judge Pyncheon, with his great means, step forward, and tell his cousin to shut up her little shop at once? It's for your credit to be doing something; but it's not for the Judge's credit to let you!"

"We won't talk of this, if you please, Uncle Venner," said Hepzibah coldly. "I ought to say, however, that, if I choose to earn bread for myself, it is not Judge Pyncheon's fault. Neither will he deserve the blame," added she more kindly, remembering Uncle Venner's privileges of age and humble familiarity, "if I should, by-and-by, find it convenient to retire with you to your farm."

"And it's no bad place neither, that farm of mine!" cried the old man cheerily, as if there were something positively delightful in the prospect.—"No bad place is the great brick farm-house, especially for them that will find a good many old cronies there, as will be my case. I quite long to be among them, sometimes, of the winter evenings; for it is but dull business for a lonesome elderly man, like me, to be nodding, by the hour together, with no company but his air-tight stove. Summer or winter, there's a great deal to be said in favor of my farm! And, take it in the autumn, what can be pleasanter than to spend a whole day, on the sunny side of a barn or a wood-pile, chatting with somebody as old as one's self; or perhaps idling away the time with a natural-born simpleton, who knows how to be idle, because even our busy Yankees have never found out how to put him to any use? Upon my word, Miss Hepzibah, I doubt whether I've ever been so comfortable as I mean to be at my farm, which most folks call the work-house. But you—you're a young woman yet—you never need go there! Something still better will turn up for you. I'm sure of it!"

Hepzibah fancied that there was something peculiar in her venerable friend's look and tone; insomuch that she gazed into his face with considerable earnestness, endeavoring to discover what secret meaning, if any, might be lurking there. Individuals, whose affairs have reached an utterly desperate crisis, almost invariably keep themselves alive with hopes, so much the more airily magnificent, as they have the less of solid matter within their grasp, whereof to mould any judicious and moderate expectation of good. Thus, all the while Hepzibah was projecting the scheme of her little shop, she had cherished an unacknowledged idea that some harlequin-trick of fortune would intervene, in her favor. For example, an uncle who had sailed for India, fifty years before, and never been heard of since—might yet return, and adopt her to be the comfort of his very extreme and decrepit age, and adorn her with pearls, diamonds, and oriental shawls and turbans, and make her the ultimate heiress of his unreckonable riches. Or the member of parliament, now at the head of the English branch of the family—with which the elder

stock, on this side of the Atlantic, had held little or no intercourse for the last two centuries—this eminent gentleman
might invite Hepzibah to quit the ruinous House of the Seven
Gables, and come over to dwell with her kindred, at Pyncheon
Hall. But, for reasons the most imperative, she could not yield
to his request. It was more probable, therefore, that the descendants of a Pyncheon who had emigrated to Virginia, in
some past generation, and become a great planter there—
hearing of Hepzibah's destitution, and impelled by the splendid generosity of character, with which their Virginian mixture must have enriched the New England blood—would send
her a remittance of a thousand dollars, with a hint of repeating the favor, annually. Or—and, surely, anything so undeniably just could not be beyond the limits of reasonable
anticipation—the great claim to the heritage of Waldo County
might finally be decided in favor of the Pyncheons; so that,
instead of keeping a cent-shop, Hepzibah would build a
palace, and look down from its highest tower on hill, dale,
forest, field, and town, as her own share of the ancestral
territory!

These were some of the fantasies which she had long
dreamed about; and, aided by these, Uncle Venner's casual
attempt at encouragement kindled a strange festal glory in
the poor, bare, melancholy chambers of her brain, as if that
inner world were suddenly lighted up with gas. But either
he knew nothing of her castles in the air—as how should he?
—or else her earnest scowl disturbed his recollection, as it
might a more courageous man's. Instead of pursuing any
weightier topic, Uncle Venner was pleased to favor Hepzibah
with some sage counsel in her shop-keeping capacity.

"Give no credit!"—these were some of his golden maxims—
"Never take paper-money! Look well to your change! Ring
the silver on the four-pound weight! Shove back all English
half-pence and base copper-tokens, such as are very plenty

about town! At your leisure hours, knit children's woollen socks and mittens! Brew your own yeast, and make your own ginger-beer!"

And while Hepzibah was doing her utmost to digest the hard little pellets of his already uttered wisdom, he gave vent to his final, and what he declared to be his all-important advice, as follows:—

"Put on a bright face for your customers, and smile pleasantly as you hand them what they ask for! A stale article, if you dip it in a good, warm, sunny smile, will go off better than a fresh one that you've scowled upon!"

To this last apothegm, poor Hepzibah responded with a sigh, so deep and heavy that it almost rustled Uncle Venner quite away, like a withered leaf, as he was, before an autumnal gale. Recovering himself, however, he bent forward, and, with a good deal of feeling in his ancient visage, beckoned her nearer to him.

"When do you expect him home?" whispered he.

"Whom do you mean?" asked Hepzibah, turning pale.

"Ah!—You don't love to talk about it," said Uncle Venner. "Well, well, we'll say no more, though there's word of it, all over town. I remember him, Miss Hepzibah, before he could run alone!"

During the remainder of the day, poor Hepzibah acquitted herself even less creditably, as a shopkeeper, than in her earlier efforts. She appeared to be walking in a dream; or, more truly, the vivid life and reality, assumed by her emotions, made all outward occurrences unsubstantial, like the teasing phantasms of a half-conscious slumber. She still responded, mechanically, to the frequent summons of the shop-bell, and, at the demand of her customers, went prying with vague eyes about the shop; proffering them one article after another, and thrusting aside—perversely, as most of them supposed—the identical thing they asked for. There is sad confusion, indeed, when the spirit thus flits away into the past, or into the more awful future, or, in any manner, steps across the spaceless boundary betwixt its own region and the actual world; where the body remains to guide itself, as best it may, with little more than the mechanism of animal life. It is like death, without death's quiet privilege; its freedom from mortal care. Worst of all, when the actual duties are comprised in such petty details as now vexed the brooding soul of the old gentle-woman. As the animosity of fate would have it, there was a great influx of custom, in the course of the afternoon. Hepzi-bah blundered to-and-fro about her small place of business, committing the most unheard of errors; now stringing up twelve, and now seven tallow-candles, instead of ten to the pound; selling ginger for Scotch snuff, pins for needles, and needles for pins; misreckoning her change, sometimes to the public detriment, and much oftener to her own; and thus she went on, doing her utmost to bring chaos back again, until, at the close of the day's labor, to her inexplicable astonishment, she found the money-drawer almost destitute of coin. After all her painful traffic, the whole proceeds were perhaps half-a-dozen coppers, and a questionable ninepence, which ulti-mately proved to be copper likewise.

At this price, or at whatever price, she rejoiced that the day had reached its end. Never before had she had such a sense of the intolerable length of time that creeps between dawn and sunset, and of the miserable irksomeness of having aught to do, and of the better wisdom that it would be, to lie down at once, in sullen resignation, and let life, and its toils and vexations, trample over one's prostrate body, as they may! Hepzibah's final operation was with the little devourer of Jim Crow and the elephant, who now proposed to eat a camel. In her bewilderment, she offered him first a wooden dragoon, and next a handfull of marbles; neither of which being adapted to his else omnivorous appetite, she hastily held out her whole remaining stock of natural history, in ginger-bread, and huddled the small customer out of the shop. She then muffled the bell in an unfinished stocking, and put up the oaken bar across the door.

During the latter process, an omnibus came to a standstill under the branches of the elm-tree. Hepzibah's heart was in her mouth. Remote and dusky, and with no sunshine on all the intervening space, was that region of the Past, whence her only guest might be expected to arrive! Was she to meet him now?

Somebody, at all events, was passing from the farthest interior of the omnibus, towards its entrance. A gentleman alighted; but it was only to offer his hand to a young girl, whose slender figure, nowise needing such assistance, now lightly descended the steps, and made an airy little jump from the final one to the sidewalk. She rewarded her cavalier with a smile, the cheery glow of which was seen reflected on his own face, as he re-entered the vehicle. The girl then turned towards the House of the Seven Gables; to the door of which, meanwhile—not the shop-door, but the antique-portal—the omnibus-man had carried a light trunk and a bandbox. First giving a sharp rap of the old iron knocker, he left his passenger and her luggage at the door-step, and departed.

"Who can it be?" thought Hepzibah, who had been screwing her visual organs into the acutest focus of which they were capable. "The girl must have mistaken the house!"

She stole softly into the hall, and, herself invisible, gazed through the dusty side-lights of the portal at the young, blooming, and very cheerful face, which presented itself for admittance into the gloomy old mansion. It was a face to which almost any door would have opened of its own accord.

The young girl, so fresh, so unconventional, and yet so orderly and obedient to common rules, as you at once recognized her to be, was widely in contrast, at that moment, with everything about her. The sordid and ugly luxuriance of gigantic weeds, that grew in the angle of the house, and the heavy projection that overshadowed her, and the time-worn frame-work of the door;—none of these things belonged to her sphere. But—even as a ray of sunshine, fall into what dismal place it may, instantaneously creates for itself a propriety in being there—so did it seem altogether fit that the girl should be standing at the threshold. It was no less evidently proper, that the door should swing open to admit her. The maiden lady herself, sternly inhospitable in her first purposes, soon began to feel that the bolt ought to be shoved back, and the rusty key be turned in the reluctant lock.

"Can it be Phoebe?" questioned she within herself. "It must be little Phoebe; for it can be nobody else—and there is a look of her father about her, too! But what does she want here? And how like a country-cousin, to come down upon a poor body in this way, without so much as a day's notice, or asking whether she would be welcome! Well; she must have a night's lodging, I suppose; and tomorrow the child shall go back to her mother."

Phoebe, it must be understood, was that one little offshoot of the Pyncheon race to whom we have already referred, as a native of a rural part of New England, where the old fashions and feelings of relationship are still partially kept up. In her own circle, it was regarded as by no means improper for kinsfolk to visit one another, without invitation, or preliminary and ceremonious warning. Yet, in consideration of Miss Hepzibah's recluse way of life, a letter had actually been written and despatched, conveying information of Phoebe's projected visit. This epistle, for three or four days past, had been in the pocket of the penny-postman, who, happening to have no other business in Pyncheon-street, had not yet made it convenient to call at the House of the Seven Gables.

"No!—she can stay only one night," said Hepzibah, unbolting the door. "If Clifford were to find her here, it might disturb him!"

# V

## MAY AND NOVEMBER

PHOEBE PYNCHEON slept, on the night of her arrival, in a chamber that looked down on the garden of the old house. It fronted towards the east, so that, at a very seasonable hour, a glow of crimson light came flooding through the window, and bathed the dingy ceiling and paper-hangings in its own hue. There were curtains to Phoebe's bed; a dark, antique canopy and ponderous festoons, of a stuff which had been rich, and even magnificent, in its time; but which now brooded over the girl like a cloud, making a night in that one corner, while elsewhere it was beginning to be day. The morning-light, however, soon stole into the aperture at the foot of the bed, betwixt those faded curtains. Finding the new guest there—with a bloom on her cheeks, like the morning's own, and a gentle stir of departing slumber in her limbs, as when an early breeze moves the foliage—the Dawn kissed her brow. It was the caress which a dewy maiden—such as the Dawn is, immortally—gives to her sleeping sister, partly from the impulse of irresistible fondness, and partly as a pretty hint, that it is time now to unclose her eyes.

At the touch of those lips of light, Phoebe quietly awoke, and, for a moment, did not recognize where she was, nor how those heavy curtains chanced to be festooned around

her. Nothing, indeed, was absolutely plain to her, except
that it was now early morning, and that, whatever might
happen next, it was proper, first of all, to get up and say her
prayers. She was the more inclined to devotion, from the
grim aspect of the chamber and its furniture, especially the
tall, stiff chairs; one of which stood close by her bedside,
and looked as if some old-fashioned personage had been sitting there, all night, and had vanished only just in season to
escape discovery.

When Phoebe was quite dressed, she peeped out of the
window, and saw a rose-bush in the garden. Being a very
tall one, and of luxurious growth, it had been propt up
against the side of the house, and was literally covered with
a rare and very beautiful species of white rose. A large portion
of them, as the girl afterwards discovered, had blight or mildew at their hearts; but, viewed at a fair distance, the whole
rose-bush looked as if it had been brought from Eden, that
very summer, together with the mould in which it grew. The
truth was, nevertheless, that it had been planted by Alice
Pyncheon—she was Phoebe's great-great-grand-aunt—in soil
which, reckoning only its cultivation as a garden-plat, was
now unctuous with nearly two hundred years of vegetable
decay. Growing as they did, however, out of the old earth,
the flowers still sent a fresh and sweet incense up to their
Creator; nor could it have been the less pure and acceptable,
because Phoebe's young breath mingled with it, as the fragrance floated past the window. Hastening down the creaking and carpetless staircase, she found her way into the
garden, gathered some of the most perfect of the roses, and
brought them to her chamber.

Little Phoebe was one of those persons who possess, as
their exclusive patrimony, the gift of practical arrangement.
It is a kind of natural magic, that enables these favored ones
to bring out the hidden capabilities of things around them;
and particularly to give a look of comfort and habitableness

to any place which, for however brief a period, may happen to be their home.[1] A wild hut of underbrush, tossed together by wayfarers through the primitive forest, would acquire the home-aspect by one night's lodging of such a woman, and would retain it, long after her quiet figure had disappeared into the surrounding shade. No less a portion of such homely witchcraft was requisite, to reclaim, as it were, Phoebe's waste, cheerless, and dusky chamber, which had been untenanted so long—except by spiders, and mice, and rats, and ghosts—that it was all overgrown with the desolation, which watches to obliterate every trace of man's happier hours. What was precisely Phoebe's process, we find it impossible to say. She appeared to have no preliminary design, but gave a touch here, and another there; brought some articles of furniture to light, and dragged others into the shadow; looped up or let down a window-curtain; and, in the course of halfan-hour, had fully succeeded in throwing a kindly and hospitable smile over the apartment. No longer ago than the night before, it had resembled nothing so much as the old maid's heart; for there was neither sunshine nor household-fire in one nor the other, and, save for ghosts, and ghostly reminiscences, not a guest, for many years gone-by, had entered the heart or the chamber.

There was still another peculiarity of this inscrutable charm. The bed-chamber, no doubt, was a chamber of very great and varied experience, as a scene of human life; the joy of bridal nights had throbbed itself away here; new immortals had first drawn earthly breath here; and here old people had died. But—whether it were the white roses, or whatever the subtile influence might be—a person of delicate instinct would have known, at once, that it was now a maiden's bed-chamber, and had been purified of all former evil and sorrow by her sweet breath and happy thoughts. Her dreams of the past night, being such cheerful ones, had exorcised the gloom, and now haunted the chamber in its stead.

1. Sophia Hawthorne also had, in her husband's eyes, just this "natural magic" with things. Undoubtedly Phoebe (one of Hawthorne's pet names for his wife) owes much to Sophia, who herself noted the resemblance. Like Phoebe, Sophia was diminutive in body, incorrigibly optimistic, excellent with

After arranging matters to her satisfaction, Phoebe emerged from her chamber, with a purpose to descend again into the garden. Besides the rose-bush, she had observed several other species of flowers, growing there in a wilderness of neglect, and obstructing one another's developement (as is often the parallel case in human society) by their uneducated entanglement and confusion. At the head of the stairs, however, she met Hepzibah, who, it being still early, invited her into a room which she would probably have called her boudoir, had her education embraced any such French phrase. It was strewn about with a few old books, and a work-basket, and a dusty writing-desk, and had, on one side, a large, black article of furniture, of very strange appearance, which the old gentlewoman told Phoebe was a harpsichord. It looked more like a coffin than anything else; and, indeed—not having been played upon, or opened, for years—there must have been a vast deal of dead music in it, stifled for want of air. Human finger was hardly known to have touched its chords, since the days of Alice Pyncheon, who had learned the sweet accomplishment of melody, in Europe.

Hepzibah bade her young guest sit down, and, herself taking a chair near by, looked as earnestly at Phoebe's trim little figure as if she expected to see right into its springs and motive secrets.

"Cousin Phoebe," said she, at last, "I really can't see my way clear to keep you with me."

These words, however, had not the inhospitable bluntness with which they may strike the reader; for the two relatives, in a talk before bedtime, had arrived at a certain degree of mutual understanding. Hepzibah knew enough to enable her to appreciate the circumstances (resulting from the second marriage of the girl's mother) which made it desirable for Phoebe to establish herself in another home. Nor did she misinterpret Phoebe's character, and the genial activity pervading it—one of the most valuable traits of the true New

---

flowers, a genius in household management, and, in Hawthorne's view of the effect his marriage had on him, magically capable of drawing a life from the shadows into the sunshine.

England woman—which had impelled her forth, as might be said, to seek her fortune, but with a self-respecting purpose to confer as much benefit as she could anywise receive. As one of her nearest kindred, she had naturally betaken herself to Hepzibah, with no idea of forcing herself on her cousin's protection, but only for a visit of a week or two, which might be indefinitely extended, should it prove for the happiness of both.

To Hepzibah's blunt observation, therefore, Phoebe replied as frankly, and more cheerfully.

"Dear Cousin, I cannot tell how it will be," said she. "But I really think we may suit one another, much better than you suppose."

"You are a nice girl—I see it plainly," continued Hepzibah; "and it is not any question, as to that point, which makes me hesitate. But, Phoebe, this house of mine is but a melancholy place for a young person to be in. It lets in the wind and rain —and the snow, too, in the garret and upper chambers, in winter-time—but it never lets in the sunshine! And as for myself, you see what I am;—a dismal and lonesome old woman (for I begin to call myself old, Phoebe) whose temper, I am afraid, is none of the best, and whose spirits are as bad as can be! I cannot make your life pleasant, Cousin Phoebe; neither can I so much as give you bread to eat."

"You will find me a cheerful little body," answered Phoebe smiling, and yet with a kind of gentle dignity; "and I mean to earn my bread. You know, I have not been brought up a Pyncheon. A girl learns many things in a New England village."

"Ah, Phoebe," said Hepzibah sighing, "your knowledge would do but little for you here! And then it is a wretched thought, that you should fling away your young days in a place like this. Those cheeks would not be so rosy, after a month or two. Look at my face!"—and, indeed, the contrast was very striking—"you see how pale I am! It is my idea that the dust and continual decay of these old houses are unwholesome for the lungs."

"There is the garden—the flowers to be taken care of," observed Phoebe. "I should keep myself healthy with exercise in the open air."

"And, after all, child," exclaimed Hepzibah, suddenly rising, as if to dismiss the subject, "it is not for me to say who shall be a guest, or inhabitant of the old Pyncheon-house! Its master is coming!"

"Do you mean Judge Pyncheon?" asked Phoebe in surprise.

"Judge Pyncheon!" answered her cousin angrily. "He will hardly cross the threshold, while I live. No, no! But, Phoebe, you shall see the face of him I speak of!"

She went in quest of the miniature already described, and returned with it in her hand. Giving it to Phoebe, she watched her features narrowly, and with a certain jealousy as to the mode in which the girl would show herself affected by the picture.

"How do you like the face?" asked Hepzibah.

"It is handsome!—it is very beautiful!" said Phoebe admiringly. "It is as sweet a face as a man's can be, or ought to be. It has something of a child's expression—and yet not childish —only, one feels so very kindly towards him! He ought never to suffer anything. One would bear much, for the sake of sparing him toil or sorrow. Who is it, Cousin Hepzibah?"

"Did you never hear," whispered her cousin, bending towards her, "of Clifford Pyncheon?"

"Never! I thought there were no Pyncheons left, except yourself and our Cousin Jaffrey," answered Phoebe. "And, yet, I seem to have heard the name of Clifford Pyncheon. Yes!—from my father, or my mother—but has he not been a long while dead?"

"Well, well, child, perhaps he has!" said Hepzibah, with a sad, hollow laugh. "But, in old houses like this, you know, dead people are very apt to come back again! We shall see! And, Cousin Phoebe—since, after all that I have said, your courage does not fail you—we will not part so soon. You are welcome, my child, for the present, to such a home as your kinswoman can offer you."

With this measured, but not exactly cold assurance of a hospitable purpose, Hepzibah kissed her cheek.

They now went below stairs, where Phoebe—not so much assuming the office as attracting it to herself, by the magnetism of innate fitness—took the most active part in preparing breakfast. The mistress of the house, meanwhile, as is usual with persons of her stiff and unmalleable cast, stood mostly aside; willing to lend her aid, yet conscious that her natural inaptitude would be likely to impede the business in hand. Phoebe, and the fire that boiled the teakettle, were equally bright, cheerful, and efficient, in their respective offices. Hepzibah gazed forth from her habitual sluggishness, the necessary result of long solitude, as from another sphere. She could not help being interested, however, and even amused, at the readiness with which her new inmate adapted herself to the circumstances, and brought the house, moreover, and all its rusty old appliances, into a suitableness for her purposes. Whatever she did, too, was done without conscious effort, and with frequent outbreaks of song which were exceedingly pleasant to the ear. This natural tunefulness made Phoebe seem like a bird in a shadowy tree; or conveyed the idea that the stream of life warbled through her heart, as a brook sometimes warbles through a pleasant little dell. It betokened the cheeriness of an active temperament, finding joy in its activity, and therefore rendering it beautiful; it was a New England trait—the stern old stuff of Puritanism, with a gold thread in the web.

Hepzibah brought out some old silver spoons, with the family crest upon them, and a China tea-set, painted over with grotesque figures of man, bird, and beast, in as grotesque a landscape. These pictured people were odd humorists, in a world of their own; a world of vivid brilliancy, so far as color went, and still unfaded, although the tea-pot and small cups were as ancient as the custom itself of tea-drinking.

"Your great, great, great, great grandmother had these cups, when she was married," said Hepzibah to Phoebe. "She was a Davenport, of a good family.[2] They were almost the first tea-cups ever seen in the colony; and if one of them were to be broken, my heart would break with it. But it is nonsense to speak so, about a brittle tea-cup, when I remember what my heart has gone through without breaking!"

The cups—not having been used, perhaps, since Hepzibah's youth—had contracted no small burthen of dust, which Phoebe washed away with so much care and delicacy, as to satisfy even the proprietor of this invaluable China.

"What a nice little housewife you are!" exclaimed the latter smiling, and, at the same time, frowning so prodigiously that the smile was sunshine under a thunder-cloud.—"Do you do other things as well? Are you as good at your book as you are at washing tea-cups?"

"Not quite, I am afraid," said Phoebe, laughing at the form of Hepzibah's question.—"But I was schoolmistress for the little children, in our district, last summer, and might have been so still."

"Ah; 'tis all very well!" observed the maiden lady, drawing herself up.—"But these things must have come to you with your mother's blood. I never knew a Pyncheon that had any turn for them!"

It is very queer, but not the less true, that people are generally quite as vain, or even more so, of their deficiencies, than of their available gifts; as was Hepzibah of this native inapplicability, so to speak, of the Pyncheons to any useful purpose. She regarded it as an hereditary trait; and so, per-

2. This would be a descendant of Rev. John Davenport, who came to America in 1637. Hepzibah's "of a good family" is perhaps meant to distinguish this Davenport from Richard Davenport, an indentured servant who came to Salem in 1628.

haps, it was, but, unfortunately, a morbid one, such as is often generated in families that remain long above the surface of society.

Before they left the breakfast-table, the shop-bell rang sharply; and Hepzibah set down the remnant of her final cup of tea, with a look of sallow despair that was truly piteous to behold. In cases of distasteful occupation, the second day is generally worse than the first; we return to the rack, with all the soreness of the preceding torture in our limbs. At all events, Hepzibah had fully satisfied herself of the impossibility of ever becoming wonted to this peevishly obstreperous little bell. Ring as often as it might, the sound always smote upon her nervous system rudely and suddenly. And especially now, while, with her crested tea-spoons and antique China, she was flattering herself with ideas of gentility, she felt an unspeakable disinclination to confront a customer.

"Do not trouble yourself, dear Cousin!" cried Phoebe, starting lightly up. "I am shopkeeper to-day."

"You, child!" exclaimed Hepzibah. "What can a little country-girl know of such matters?"

"Oh, I have done all the shopping for the family, at our village-store," said Phoebe. "And I have had a table at a fancy-fair, and made better sales than anybody. These things are not to be learnt; they depend upon a knack that comes, I suppose," added she smiling, "with one's mother's blood. You shall see that I am as nice a little saleswoman, as I am a housewife!"

The old gentlewoman stole behind Phoebe, and peeped from the passage-way into the shop, to note how she would manage her undertaking. It was a case of some intricacy. A very ancient woman, in a white, short gown, and a green petticoat, with a string of gold beads about her neck, and what looked like a night-cap on her head, had brought a quantity of yarn to barter for the commodities of the shop. She was probably the very last person in town, who still kept the time-honored spinning-wheel in constant revolution. It was worth while to hear the croaking and hollow tones of the old lady and the pleasant voice of Phoebe, mingling in one twisted thread of talk; and still better, to contrast their figures —so light and bloomy—so decrepit and dusky—with only the counter betwixt them, in one sense, but more than threescore years, in another. As for the bargain, it was wrinkled slyness and craft, pitted against native truth and sagacity.

"Was not that well done?" asked Phoebe laughing, when the customer was gone.

"Nicely done, indeed, child!" answered Hepzibah. "I could not have gone through with it nearly so well. As you say, it must be a knack that belongs to you on the mother's side."

It is a very genuine admiration, that with which persons, too shy, or too aukward, to take a due part in the bustling world, regard the real actors in life's stirring scenes;—so genuine, in fact, that the former are usually fain to make it palatable to their self-love, by assuming that these active and forcible qualities are incompatible with others, which they choose to deem higher and more important. Thus, Hepzibah was well content to acknowledge Phoebe's vastly superior gifts as a shopkeeper; she listened, with compliant ear, to her suggestion of various methods whereby the influx of trade might be increased, and rendered profitable, without a hazardous outlay of capital. She consented that the village-maiden should manufacture yeast, both liquid and in cakes; and should brew a certain kind of beer, nectareous to the palate, and of rare stomachic virtues; and, moreover, should bake and exhibit for sale some little spice-cakes, which whosoever tasted, would longingly desire to taste again. All such proofs of a ready mind, and skilful handiwork, were highly acceptable to the aristocratic hucksteress, so long as she could murmur to herself, with a grim smile, and a half-natural sigh, and a sentiment of mixed wonder, pity, and growing affection:—

"What a nice little body she is! If she could only be a lady, too!—but that's impossible! Phoebe is no Pyncheon. She takes everything from her mother!"

As to Phoebe's not being a lady, or whether she were a lady or no, it was a point perhaps difficult to decide, but which could hardly have come up for judgement at all, in any fair and healthy mind. Out of New England, it would be impossible to meet with a person, combining so many ladylike attributes with so many others, that form no necessary, if compatible, part of the character. She shocked no canon of taste; she was admirably in keeping with herself, and never jarred against surrounding circumstances. Her figure, to be sure—so small as to be almost childlike, and so elastic that motion seemed as easy, or easier to it than rest— would hardly have suited one's idea of a countess. Neither did her face—with the brown ringlets on either side, and the slightly piquant nose, and the wholesome bloom, and the clear shade of tan, and the half-a-dozen freckles, friendly remembrancers of the April sun and breeze—precisely give us a right to call her beautiful. But there was both lustre and depth, in her eyes. She was very pretty; as graceful as a bird, and graceful much in the same way; as pleasant, about the house, as a gleam of sunshine falling on the floor through a shadow of twinkling leaves, or as a ray of firelight that dances on the wall, while evening is drawing nigh. Instead of discussing her claim to rank among ladies, it would be preferable to regard Phoebe as the example of feminine grace and availability combined, in a state of society, if there were any such, where ladies did not exist. There, it should be woman's office to move in the midst of practical affairs, and to gild them all— the very homeliest, were it even the scouring of pots and kettles—with an atmosphere of loveliness and joy.

Such was the sphere of Phoebe. To find the born and educated lady, on the other hand, we need look no farther than Hepzibah, our forlorn old maid, in her rustling and rusty silks, with her deeply cherished and ridiculous consciousness of long descent, her shadowy claims to princely

territory; and, in the way of accomplishment, her recollections, it may be, of having formerly thrummed on a harpsichord, and walked a minuet, and worked an antique tapestry-
stitch on her sampler. It was a fair parallel between new
Plebeianism and old Gentility!

It really seemed as if the battered visage of the House of
the Seven Gables, black and heavy-browed as it still certainly
looked, must have shown a kind of cheerfulness glimmering
through its dusky windows, as Phoebe passed to-and-fro in
the interior. Otherwise, it is impossible to explain how the
people of the neighborhood so soon became aware of the
girl's presence. There was a great run of custom, setting
steadily in from about ten o'clock until towards noon—relax-
ing, somewhat, at dinner-time—but re-commencing in the
afternoon, and finally dying-away, a half-an-hour or so before
the long day's sunset. One of the staunchest patrons was
little Ned Higgins, the devourer of Jim Crow and the elephant, who, to-day, had signalized his omnivorous prowess
by swallowing two dromedaries and a locomotive. Phoebe
laughed, as she summed up her aggregate of sales, upon the
slate; while Hepzibah, first drawing on a pair of silk gloves,
reckoned over the sordid accumulation of copper-coin, not
without silver intermixed, that had jingled into the till.

"We must renew our stock, Cousin Hepzibah!" cried the
little saleswoman. "The gingerbread figures are all gone,
and so are those Dutch wooden milk-maids, and most of our
other playthings. There has been constant inquiry for cheap
raisins, and a great cry for whistles, and trumpets, and
jewsharps, and at least a dozen little boys have asked for
molasses-candy. And we must contrive to get a peck of russet-
apples, late in the season as it is. But, dear Cousin, what an
enormous heap of copper! Positively a copper-mountain!"

"Well done! Well done! Well done!" quoth Uncle Venner, who had taken occasion to shuffle in and out of the shop,

several times in the course of the day. "Here's a girl that will never end her days at my farm! Bless my eyes, what a brisk little soul!"

"Yes!—Phoebe is a nice girl," said Hepzibah, with a scowl of austere approbation. "But, Uncle Venner, you have known the family a great many years. Can you tell me whether there ever was a Pyncheon whom she takes after?"

"I don't believe there ever was," answered the venerable man. "At any rate, it never was my luck to see her like among them, nor—for that matter—anywhere else. I've seen a great deal of the world, not only in people's kitchens and back-yards, but at the street-corners, and on the wharves, and in other places where my business calls me; and I'm free to say, Miss Hepzibah, that I never knew a human creature do her work so much like one of God's angels, as this child Phoebe does!"

Uncle Venner's eulogium, if it appear rather too high-strained for the person and occasion, had nevertheless a sense in which it was both subtle and true. There was a spiritual quality in Phoebe's activity. The life of the long and busy day —spent in occupations that might so easily have taken a squalid and ugly aspect—had been made pleasant, and even lovely, by the spontaneous grace with which these homely duties seemed to bloom out of her character; so that labor, while she dealt with it, had the easy and flexible charm of play. Angels do not toil, but let their good works grow out of them; and so did Phoebe.

The two relatives—the young maid and the old one—found time, before nightfall, in the intervals of trade, to make rapid advances towards affection and confidence. A recluse, like Hepzibah, usually displays remarkable frankness, and at least temporary affability, on being absolutely cornered, and brought to the point of personal intercourse;—like the angel whom Jacob wrestled with, she is ready to bless you, when once overcome.[3]

The old gentlewoman took a dreary and proud satisfaction,

3. In Genesis xxxii: 24–29, Jacob (Israel) wrestles an angel all night until the angel blesses him.

in leading Phœbe from room to room of the house, and re-
counting the traditions with which, as we may say, the walls
were lugubriously frescoed. She showed the indentations,
made by the Lieutenant Governor's sword-hilt, in the door-
panels of the apartment where old Colonel Pyncheon, a dead
host, had received his affrighted visitors with an awful frown.
The dusky terror of that frown, Hepzibah observed, was
thought to be lingering ever since in the passage-way. She
bade Phœbe step into one of the tall chairs, and inspect the
ancient map of the Pyncheon territory, at the eastward. In a
tract of land, on which she laid her finger, there existed a
silver-mine, the locality of which was precisely pointed out in
some memoranda of Colonel Pyncheon himself, but only to
be made known when the family-claim should be recognized
by government. Thus, it was for the interest of all New England that the Pyncheons should have justice done them. She
told, too, how that there was undoubtedly an immense treasure of English guineas, hidden somewhere about the house,
or in the cellar, or possibly in the garden.

"If you should happen to find it, Phœbe," said Hepzibah,
glancing aside at her, with a grim, yet kindly smile, "we will
tie up the shop-bell for good and all!"

"Yes, dear Cousin," answered Phœbe; "but, in the meantime, I hear somebody ringing it!"

When the customer was gone, Hepzibah talked rather
vaguely, and at great length, about a certain Alice Pyncheon,
who had been exceedingly beautiful and accomplished, in her
lifetime, a hundred years ago. The fragrance of her rich and
delightful character still lingered about the place where she
had lived, as a dried rosebud scents the drawer where it has
withered and perished. This lovely Alice had met with some
great and mysterious calamity, and had grown thin and white,
and gradually faded out of the world. But, even now, she was
supposed to haunt the House of the Seven Gables, and, a great
many times, especially when one of the Pynchcons was to
die, she had been heard playing sadly and beautifully on the

harpsichord. One of these tunes, just as it sounded from her spiritual touch, had been written down by an amateur of music; it was so exquisitely mournful that nobody, to this day, could bear to hear it played, unless when a great sorrow had made them know the still profounder sweetness of it.

"Was it the same harpsichord that you showed me?" inquired Phoebe.

"The very same," said Hepzibah. "It was Alice Pyncheon's harpsichord. When I was learning music, my father would never let me open it. So, as I could only play on my teacher's instrument, I have forgotten all my music, long ago."

Leaving these antique themes, the old lady began to talk about the Daguerreotypist, whom, as he seemed to be a well-meaning and orderly young man, and in narrow circumstances, she had permitted to take up his residence in one of the seven gables. But, on seeing more of Mr. Holgrave, she hardly knew what to make of him. He had the strangest companions imaginable;—men with long beards, and dressed in linen blouses, and other such new-fangled and ill-fitting garments;—reformers, temperance-lecturers, and all manner of cross-looking philanthropists;—community-men and come-outers, as Hepzibah believed, who acknowledged no law and ate no solid food, but lived on the scent of other people's cookery, and turned up their noses at the fare. As for the Daguerreotypist, she had read a paragraph in a penny-paper, the other day, accusing him of making a speech, full of wild and disorganizing matter, at a meeting of his banditti-like associates. For her own part, she had reason to believe that he practised animal-magnetism,[4] and, if such things were in fashion now-a-days, should be apt to suspect him of studying the Black Art, up there in his lonesome chamber.

"But, dear Cousin," said Phoebe, "if the young man is so dangerous, why do you let him stay? If he does nothing worse, he may set the house on fire!"

"Why, sometimes," answered Hepzibah, "I have seriously

4. The nineteenth-century term used to describe a mesmerist's (or hypnotist's) power over the will and nervous system of a subject.

made it a question, whether I ought not to send him away. But, with all his oddities, he is a quiet kind of a person, and has such a way of taking hold of one's mind, that, without exactly liking him, (for I don't know enough of the young man,) I should be sorry to lose sight of him entirely. A woman clings to slight acquaintances, when she lives so much alone as I do."

"But if Mr. Holgrave is a lawless person!" remonstrated Phoebe, a part of whose essence it was, to keep within the limits of law.

"Oh," said Hepzibah carelessly—for, formal as she was, still, in her life's experience, she had gnashed her teeth against human law—"I suppose he has a law of his own!"

## VI

## MAULE'S WELL

AFTER an early tea, the little country-girl strayed into the garden. The enclosure had formerly been very extensive, but was now contracted within small compass, and hemmed about, partly by high wooden fences, and partly by the outbuildings of houses that stood on another street. In its centre was a grass-plat, surrounding a ruinous little structure, which showed just enough of its original design to indicate that it had once been a summer-house. A hop-vine, springing from last year's root, was beginning to clamber over it, but would be long in covering the roof with its green mantle. Three of the seven gables either fronted, or looked sideways, with a dark solemnity of aspect, down into the garden.

The black, rich soil had fed itself with the decay of a long period of time; such as fallen leaves, the petals of flowers, and the stalks and seed-vessels of vagrant and lawless plants, more useful after their death, than ever while flaunting in the sun. The evil of these departed years would naturally have sprung up again, in such rank weeds (symbolic of the transmitted vices of society) as are always prone to root themselves about human dwellings. Phoebe saw, however, that their growth must have been checked by a degree of careful labor, bestowed daily and systematically on the garden. The

white double-rosebush had evidently been propt up anew
against the house, since the commencement of the season;
and a pear-tree and three damson-trees, which, except a row
of currant-bushes, constituted the only varieties of fruit, bore
marks of the recent amputation of several superfluous or
defective limbs. There were also a few species of antique and
hereditary flowers, in no very flourishing condition, but scrupulously weeded; as if some person, either out of love or
curiosity, had been anxious to bring them to such perfection
as they were capable of attaining. The remainder of the garden presented a well-selected assortment of esculent vegetables, in a praiseworthy state of advancement. Summer-
squashes, almost in their golden-blossom; cucumbers, now
evincing a tendency to spread away from the main-stock, and
ramble far and wide; two or three rows of string-beans, and
as many more, that were about to festoon themselves on poles;
tomatoes, occupying a site so sheltered and sunny, that the
plants were already gigantic, and promised an early and abundant harvest.

Phoebe wondered whose care and toil it could have been,
that had planted these vegetables, and kept the soil so clean
and orderly. Not, surely, her Cousin Hepzibah's, who had
no taste nor spirits for the ladylike employment of cultivating
flowers, and—with her recluse habits, and tendency to shelter
herself within the dismal shadow of the house—would hardly
have come forth, under the speck of open sky, to weed and
hoe, among the fraternity of beans and squashes.

It being her first day of complete estrangement from rural
objects, Phoebe found an unexpected charm in this little nook
of grass, and foliage, and aristocratic flowers, and plebeian
vegetables. The eye of Heaven seemed to look down into it,
pleasantly, and with a peculiar smile; as if glad to perceive
that Nature, elsewhere overwhelmed, and driven out of the
dusty town, had here been able to retain a breathing-place.
The spot acquired a somewhat wilder grace, and yet a very

gentle one, from the fact that a pair of robins had built their nest in the pear-tree, and were making themselves exceedingly busy and happy, in the dark intricacy of its boughs. Bees, too—strange to say—had thought it worth their while to come hither, possibly from the range of hives beside some farmhouse, miles away. How many aerial voyages might they have made, in quest of honey, or honey-laden, betwixt dawn and sunset! Yet, late as it now was, there still arose a pleasant hum out of one or two of the squash-blossoms, in the depths of which these bees were plying their golden labor. There was one other object in the garden, which Nature might fairly claim as her inalienable property, in spite of whatever man could do to render it his own. This was a fountain, set round with a rim of old, mossy stones, and paved, in its bed, with what appeared to be a sort of mosaic-work of variously colored pebbles. The play and slight agitation of the water, in its upward gush, wrought magically with these variegated pebbles, and made a continually shifting apparition of quaint figures, vanishing too suddenly to be definable. Thence, welling over the rim of moss-grown stones, the water stole away under the fence, through what we regret to call a gutter, rather than a channel.

Nor must we forget to mention a hen-coop, of very reverend antiquity, that stood in the farther corner of the garden, not a great way from the fountain. It now contained only Chanticleer,[1] his two wives, and a solitary chicken. All of them were pure specimens of a breed which had been transmitted down as an heirloom in the Pyncheon family, and were said, while in their prime, to have attained almost the size of turkeys, and, on the score of delicate flesh, to be fit for a prince's table. In proof of the authenticity of this legendary renown, Hepzibah could have exhibited the shell of a great egg, which an ostrich need hardly have been ashamed of. Be that as it might, the hens were now scarcely larger than pigeons, and had a queer, rusty, withered aspect, and a

1. Chanticleer is a generic name for a rooster, derived from the name of the cock in medieval beast epics, and made most famous by Chaucer in his Nun's Priest's Tale.

gouty kind of movement, and a sleepy and melancholy tone throughout all the variations of their clucking and cackling. It was evident that the race had degenerated, like many a noble race besides, in consequence of too strict a watchfulness to keep it pure. These feathered people had existed too long, in their distinct variety; a fact of which the present representatives, judging by their lugubrious deportment, seemed to be aware. They kept themselves alive, unquestionably, and laid now and then an egg, and hatched a chicken, not for any pleasure of their own, but that the world might not absolutely lose what had once been so admirable a breed of fowls. The distinguishing mark of the hens was a crest, of lamentably scanty growth, in these latter days, but so oddly and wickedly analogous to Hepzibah's turban, that Phoebe—to the poignant distress of her conscience, but inevitably—was led to fancy a general resemblance betwixt these forlorn bipeds and her respectable relative.

The girl ran into the house to get some crumbs of bread, cold potatoes, and other such scraps as were suitable to the accommodating appetite of fowls. Returning, she gave a peculiar call, which they seemed to recognize. The chicken crept through the pales of the coop, and ran with some show of liveliness to her feet; while Chanticleer and the ladies of his household regarded her with queer, sidelong glances, and then croaked one to another, as if communicating their sage opinions of her character. So wise as well as antique was their aspect, as to give color to the idea, not merely that they were the descendants of a time-honored race, but that they had existed, in their individual capacity, ever since the House of the Seven Gables was founded, and were somehow mixed up with its destiny. They were a species of tutelary sprite, or Banshee;[2] although winged and feathered differently from most other guardian-angels.

"Here, you odd little chicken!" cried Phoebe. "Here are some nice crumbs for you!"

2. In Irish and Scottish folklore, a supernatural creature who is supposed to wail beneath the window of someone about to die.

The chicken, hereupon, though almost as venerable in appearance as its mother—possessing, indeed, the whole antiquity of its progenitors, in miniature—mustered vivacity enough to flutter upward and alight on Phoebe's shoulder.

"That little fowl pays you a high compliment!" said a voice behind Phoebe.

Turning quickly, she was surprised at sight of a young man, who had found access into the garden by a door, opening out of another gable than that whence she had emerged. He held a hoe in his hand, and, while Phoebe was gone in quest of the crumbs, had begun to busy himself with drawing up fresh earth about the roots of the tomatoes.

"The chicken really treats you like an old acquaintance," continued he, in a quiet way, while a smile made his face pleasanter than Phoebe at first fancied it.—"Those venerable personages in the coop, too, seem very affably disposed. You are lucky to be in their good graces so soon! They have known me much longer, but never honor me with any familiarity, though hardly a day passes without my bringing them food. Miss Hepzibah, I suppose, will interweave the fact with her other traditions, and set it down that the fowls know you to be a Pyncheon!"

"The secret is," said Phoebe smiling, "that I have learned how to talk with hens and chickens."

"Ah; but these hens," answered the young man, "these hens of aristocratic lineage would scorn to understand the vulgar language of a barn-door fowl. I prefer to think—and so would Miss Hepzibah—that they recognize the family tone. For you are a Pyncheon?"

"My name is Phoebe Pyncheon," said the girl, with a manner of some reserve; for she was aware that her new acquaintance could be no other than the Daguerreotypist, of whose lawless propensities the old maid had given her a disagreeable idea. "I did not know that my Cousin Hepzibah's garden was under another person's care."

"Yes," said Holgrave, "I dig, and hoe, and weed, in this black old earth, for the sake of refreshing myself with what little nature and simplicity may be left in it, after men have so long sown and reaped here. I turn up the earth by way of pastime. My sober occupation, so far as I have any, is with a lighter material. In short, I make pictures out of sunshine; and, not to be too much dazzled with my own trade, I have prevailed with Miss Hepzibah to let me lodge in one of these dusky gables. It is like a bandage over one's eyes, to come into it. But would you like to see a specimen of my productions?"

"A daguerreotype likeness, do you mean?" asked Phoebe, with less reserve; for, in spite of prejudice, her own youthfulness sprang forward to meet his. "I don't much like pictures of that sort—they are so hard and stern; besides dodging away from the eye, and trying to escape altogether. They are conscious of looking very unamiable, I suppose, and therefore hate to be seen."

"If you would permit me," said the artist, looking at Phoebe, "I should like to try whether the daguerreotype can bring out disagreeable traits on a perfectly amiable face. But there certainly is truth in what you have said. Most of my likenesses do look unamiable; but the very sufficient reason, I fancy, is, because the originals are so. There is a wonderful insight in heaven's broad and simple sunshine. While we give it credit only for depicting the merest surface, it actually brings out the secret character with a truth that no painter would ever venture upon, even could he detect it. There is at least no flattery in my humble line of art. Now, here is a likeness which I have taken, over and over again, and still with no better result. Yet the original wears, to common eyes, a very different expression. It would gratify me to have your judgement on this character."

He exhibited a daguerreotype miniature, in a morocco case. Phoebe merely glanced at it, and gave it back.

"I know the face," she replied; "for its stern eye has been following me about, all day. It is my Puritan ancestor, who hangs yonder in the parlor. To be sure, you have found some way of copying the portrait without its black velvet cap and gray beard, and have given him a modern coat and satin cravat, instead of his cloak and band. I don't think him improved by your alterations."

"You would have seen other differences, had you looked a little longer," said Holgrave, laughing, yet apparently much struck.—"I can assure you that this is a modern face, and one which you will very probably meet. Now, the remarkable point is, that the original wears, to the world's eye—and, for aught I know, to his most intimate friends—an exceedingly pleasant countenance, indicative of benevolence, openness of heart, sunny good humor, and other praiseworthy qualities of that cast. The sun, as you see, tells quite another story, and will not be coaxed out of it, after half-a-dozen patient attempts on my part. Here we have the man, sly, subtle, hard, imperious, and, withal, cold as ice. Look at that eye! Would you like to be at its mercy? At that mouth! Could it ever smile? And yet, if you could only see the benign smile of the original! It is so much the more unfortunate, as he is a public character of some eminence, and the likeness was intended to be engraved."

"Well; I don't wish to see it any more," observed Phoebe, turning away her eyes. "It is certainly very like the old portrait. But my Cousin Hepzibah has another picture; a miniature. If the original is still in the world, I think he might defy the sun to make him look stern and hard."

"You have seen that picture, then?" exclaimed the artist, with an expression of much interest.—"I never did, but have a great curiosity to do so. And you judge favorably of the face?"

"There never was a sweeter one," said Phoebe. "It is almost too soft and gentle for a man's."

"Is there nothing wild in the eye?" continued Holgrave,

so earnestly that it embarrassed Phoebe, as did also the quiet
freedom with which he presumed on their so recent acquaintance. "Is there nothing dark or sinister, anywhere? Could
you not conceive the original to have been guilty of a great
crime?"

"It is nonsense," said Phoebe, a little impatiently, "for us
to talk about a picture which you have never seen. You mistake it for some other. A crime, indeed! Since you are a
friend of my Cousin Hepzibah's, you should ask her to show
you the picture."

"It will suit my purpose still better, to see the original,"
replied the Daguerreotypist coolly. "As to his character, we
need not discuss its points—they have already been settled
by a competent tribunal, or one which called itself competent.—But, stay! Do not go yet, if you please! I have a proposition to make you."

Phoebe was on the point of retreating, but turned back,
with some hesitation; for she did not exactly comprehend his
manner, although, on better observation, its feature seemed
rather to be lack of ceremony, than any approach to offensive
rudeness. There was an odd kind of authority, too, in what
he now proceeded to say; rather as if the garden were his
own, than a place to which he was admitted merely by
Hepzibah's courtesy.

"If agreeable to you," he observed, "it would give me
pleasure to turn over these flowers, and those ancient and
respectable fowls, to your care. Coming fresh from country-
air and occupations, you will soon feel the need of some
such out-of-door employment. My own sphere does not so
much lie among flowers. You can trim and tend them, therefore, as you please; and I will ask only the least trifle of a
blossom, now and then, in exchange for all the good, honest
kitchen-vegetables with which I propose to enrich Miss Hepzibah's table. So, we will be fellow-laborers, somewhat on the
community-system."

Silently, and rather surprised at her own compliance,

Phoebe accordingly betook herself to weeding a flower-bed, but busied herself still more with cogitations respecting this young man, with whom she so unexpectedly found herself on terms approaching to familiarity. She did not altogether like him. His character perplexed the little country-girl, as it might a more practised observer; for, while the tone of his conversation had generally been playful, the impression left on her mind was that of gravity, and, except as his youth modified it, almost sternness. She rebelled, as it were, against a certain magnetic element in the artist's nature, which he exercised towards her, possibly without being conscious of it.

After a little while, the twilight, deepened by the shadows of the fruit-trees and the surrounding buildings, threw an obscurity over the garden.

"There," said Holgrave; "it is time to give over work! That last stroke of the hoe has cut off a bean-stalk. Good night, Miss Phoebe Pyncheon! Any bright day, if you will put one of those rosebuds in your hair, and come to my rooms in Central-street, I will seize the purest ray of sunshine, and make a picture of the flower and its wearer."

He retired towards his own solitary gable, but turned his head, on reaching the door, and called to Phoebe, with a tone which certainly had laughter in it, yet which seemed to be more than half in earnest.

"Be careful not to drink at Maule's Well!" said he. "Neither drink nor bathe your face in it!"

"Maule's Well!" answered Phoebe. "Is that it, with the rim of mossy stones? I have no thought of drinking there—but why not?"

"Oh," rejoined the Daguerreotypist, "because, like an old lady's cup of tea, it is water bewitched!"

He vanished; and Phoebe, lingering a moment, saw a glimmering light, and then the steady beam of a lamp, in a chamber of the gable. On returning into Hepzibah's depart-

ment of the house, she found the low-studded parlor so dim
and dusky, that her eyes could not penetrate the interior.
She was indistinctly aware, however, that the gaunt figure of
the old gentlewoman was sitting in one of the straight-backed
chairs, a little withdrawn from the window, the faint gleam
of which showed the blanched paleness of her cheek, turned
sideway towards a corner.

"Shall I light a lamp, Cousin Hepzibah?" she asked.

"Do, if you please, my dear child," answered Hepzibah.
"But put it on the table in the corner of the passage. My
eyes are weak; and I can seldom bear the lamplight on them."

What an instrument is the human voice! How wonderfully
responsive to every emotion of the human soul! In Hepzibah's
tone, at that moment, there was a certain rich depth and
moisture, as if the words, common-place as they were, had
been steeped in the warmth of her heart. Again, while lighting the lamp in the kitchen, Phoebe fancied that her cousin
spoke to her.

"In a moment, Cousin!" answered the girl. "These matches
just glimmer, and go out."

But, instead of a response from Hepzibah, she seemed to
hear the murmur of an unknown voice. It was strangely
indistinct, however, and less like articulate words than an
unshaped sound, such as would be the utterance of feeling
and sympathy, rather than of the intellect. So vague was
it, that its impression or echo, in Phoebe's mind, was that of
unreality. She concluded that she must have mistaken some
other sound for that of the human voice; or else that it was
altogether in her fancy.

She set the lighted lamp in the passage, and again entered
the parlor. Hepzibah's form, though its sable outline mingled
with the dusk, was now less imperfectly visible. In the remoter
parts of the room, however, its walls being so ill adapted to
reflect light, there was nearly the same obscurity as before.

"Cousin," said Phoebe, "did you speak to me just now?"
"No, child!" replied Hepzibah.

Fewer words than before, but with the same mysterious music in them! Mellow, melancholy, yet not mournful, the tone seemed to gush up out of the deep well of Hepzibah's heart, all steeped in its profoundest emotion. There was a tremor in it, too, that—as all strong feeling is electric—partly communicated itself to Phoebe. The girl sat silently for a moment. But soon, her senses being very acute, she became conscious of an irregular respiration in an obscure corner of the room. Her physical organization, moreover, being at once delicate and healthy, gave her a perception, operating with almost the effect of a spiritual medium, that somebody was near at hand.

"My dear Cousin," asked she, overcoming an indefinable reluctance, "is there not some one in the room with us?"

"Phoebe, my dear little girl," said Hepzibah, after a moment's pause, "you were up betimes, and have been busy all day. Pray go to bed; for I am sure you must need rest. I will sit in the parlor, awhile, and collect my thoughts. It has been my custom for more years, child, than you have lived!"

While thus dismissing her, the maiden lady stept forward, kissed Phoebe, and pressed her to her heart, which beat against the girl's bosom with a strong, high, and tumultuous swell. How came there to be so much love in this desolate old heart, that it could afford to well over thus abundantly!

"Good night, Cousin," said Phoebe, strangely affected by Hepzibah's manner. "If you begin to love me, I am glad!"

She retired to her chamber, but did not soon fall asleep, nor then very profoundly. At some uncertain period in the depths of night, and, as it were, through the thin veil of a dream, she was conscious of a footstep mounting the stairs, heavily, but not with force and decision. The voice of Hepzibah, with a hush through it, was going up along with the footsteps; and, again, responsive to her cousin's voice, Phoebe heard that strange, vague murmur, which might be likened to an indistinct shadow of human utterance.

## VII

# THE GUEST

W HEN Phoebe awoke—which she did with the early twittering of the conjugal couple of robins, in the pear-tree—she heard movements below stairs, and hastening down, found Hepzibah already in the kitchen. She stood by a window, holding a book in close contiguity to her nose; as if with the hope of gaining an olfactory acquaintance with its contents, since her imperfect vision made it not very easy to read them. If any volume could have manifested its essential wisdom, in the mode suggested, it would certainly have been the one now in Hepzibah's hand; and the kitchen, in such an event, would forthwith have steamed with the fragrance of venison, turkeys, capons, larded partridges, puddings, cakes, and Christmas pies, in all manner of elaborate mixture and concoction. It was a Cookery Book, full of innumerable old fashions of English dishes, and illustrated with engravings, which represented the arrangements of the table, at such banquets as it might have befitted a nobleman to give, in the great hall of his castle. And, amid these rich and potent devices of the culinary art, (not one of which, probably, had been tested, within the memory of any man's grandfather,) poor Hepzibah was seeking for some nimble little tidbit, which, with what skill she had, and such materials as were at hand, she might toss up for breakfast!

Soon, with a deep sigh, she put aside the savory volume, and inquired of Phoebe whether old Speckle, as she called one of the hens, had laid an egg, the preceding day. Phoebe ran to see, but returned without the expected treasure in her hand. At that instant, however, the blast of a fishdealer's conch was heard, announcing his approach along the street. With energetic raps at the shop-window, Hepzibah summoned the man in, and made purchase of what he warranted as the finest mackerel in his cart, and as fat a one as ever he felt with his finger, so early in the season. Requesting Phoebe to roast some coffee—which she casually observed was the real Mocha,[1] and so long kept that each of the small berries ought to be worth its weight in gold—the maiden lady heaped fuel into the vast receptacle of the ancient fireplace, in such quantity as soon to drive the lingering dusk out of the kitchen. The country-girl, willing to give her utmost assistance, proposed to make an Indian cake,[2] after her mother's peculiar method, of easy manufacture, and which she could vouch for as possessing a richness, and, if rightly prepared, a delicacy, unequalled by any other mode of breakfast-cake. Hepzibah gladly assenting, the kitchen was soon the scene of savory preparation. Perchance, amid their proper element of smoke, which eddied forth from the ill-constructed chimney, the ghosts of departed cook-maids looked wonderingly on, or peeped down the great breadth of the flue, despising the simplicity of the projected meal, yet ineffectually pining to thrust their shadowy hands into each inchoate dish. The half-starved rats, at any rate, stole visibly out of their hiding-places, and sat on their hind-legs, snuffing the fumy atmosphere, and wistfully awaiting an opportunity to nibble.

Hepzibah had no natural turn for cookery, and, to say the truth, had fairly incurred her present meagerness by often choosing to go without her dinner, rather than be attendant on the rotation of the spit or ebullition of the pot. Her zeal over the fire, therefore, was quite an heroic test of sentiment.

1. A fine quality coffee originally produced in Mocha, Yemen Province, Arabia.
2. Cornbread.

It was touching, and positively worthy of tears, (if Phoebe, the only spectator, except the rats and ghosts aforesaid, had not been better employed than in shedding them,) to see her rake out a bed of fresh and glowing coals, and proceed to broil the mackerel. Her usually pale cheeks were all a-blaze with heat and hurry. She watched the fish with as much tender care, and minuteness of attention, as if—we know not how to express it otherwise—as if her own heart were on the gridiron, and her immortal happiness were involved in its being done precisely to a turn!

Life, within doors, has few pleasanter prospects than a neatly arranged and well-provisioned breakfast-table. We come to it freshly, in the dewy youth of the day, and when our spiritual and sensual elements are in better accord than at a later period; so that the material delights of the morning meal are capable of being fully enjoyed, without any very grievous reproaches, whether gastric or conscientious, for yielding even a trifle overmuch to the animal department of our nature. The thoughts, too, that run around the ring of familiar guests, have a piquancy and mirthfulness, and oftentimes a vivid truth, which more rarely find their way into the elaborate intercourse of dinner. Hepzibah's small and ancient table, supported on its slender and graceful legs, and covered with a cloth of the richest damask, looked worthy to be the scene and centre of one of the cheerfullest of parties. The vapor of the broiled fish arose like incense from the shrine of a barbarian idol; while the fragrance of the Mocha might have gratified the nostrils of a tutelary Lar,[3] or whatever power has scope over a modern breakfast-table. Phoebe's Indian cakes were the sweetest offering of all—in their hue, befitting the rustic altars of the innocent and golden age— or, so brightly yellow were they, resembling some of the bread which was changed to glistening gold, when Midas tried to eat it. The butter must not be forgotten—butter which Phoebe herself had churned, in her own rural home,

3. A household deity in Roman and Etruscan mythology.

and brought it to her cousin as a propitiatory gift—smelling of clover-blossoms, and diffusing the charm of pastoral scenery through the dark-panelled parlor. All this, with the quaint gorgeousness of the old China cups and saucers, and the crested spoons, and a silver cream-jug (Hepzibah's only other article of plate, and shaped like the rudest porringer) set out a board, at which the stateliest of old Colonel Pyncheon's guests need not have scorned to take his place. But the Puritan's face scowled down out of the picture, as if nothing on the table pleased his appetite.

By way of contributing what grace she could, Phoebe gathered some roses and a few other flowers, possessing either scent or beauty, and arranged them in a glass pitcher, which, having long ago lost its handle, was so much the fitter for a flower-vase. The early sunshine—as fresh as that which peeped into Eve's bower, while she and Adam sat at breakfast there—came twinkling through the branches of the pear-tree, and fell quite across the table. All was now ready. There were chairs and plates for three. A chair and plate for Hepzibah—the same for Phoebe:—but what other guest did her cousin look for?

Throughout this preparation, there had been a constant tremor in Hepzibah's frame; an agitation so powerful, that Phoebe could see the quivering of her gaunt shadow, as thrown by the firelight on the kitchen-wall, or by the sunshine on the parlor-floor. Its manifestations were so various, and agreed so little with one another, that the girl knew not what to make of it. Sometimes, it seemed an ecstacy of delight and happiness. At such moments, Hepzibah would fling out her arms, and enfold Phoebe in them, and kiss her cheek, as tenderly as ever her mother had; she appeared to do so by an inevitable impulse, and as if her bosom were oppressed with tenderness, of which she must needs pour out a little, in order to gain breathing-room. The next moment, without any visible cause for the change, her unwonted joy shrank back, appalled, as it were, and clothed itself in mourning; or it ran and hid itself, so to speak, in the dungeon of her heart, where it had long lain chained; while a cold, spectral sorrow took the place of the imprisoned joy, that was afraid to be enfranchised—a sorrow as black as that was bright. She often broke into a little, nervous, hysteric laugh, more touching than any tears could be; and forthwith, as if to try which was the most touching, a gust of tears would follow; or perhaps the laughter and tears came both at once, and surrounded our poor Hepzibah, in a moral sense, with a kind of pale, dim rainbow. Towards Phoebe, as we have said, she was affectionate—far tenderer than ever before, in their brief acquaintance, except for that one kiss, on the preceding night —yet with a continually recurring pettishness and irritability. She would speak sharply to her; then, throwing aside all the starched reserve of her ordinary manner, ask pardon, and, the next instant, renew the just forgiven injury.

At last, when their mutual labor was all finished, she took Phoebe's hand in her own trembling one.

"Bear with me, my dear child," she cried, "for truly my heart is full to the brim! Bear with me; for I love you, Phoebe, though I speak so roughly! Think nothing of it, dearest child! By-and-by, I shall be kind, and only kind!"

"My dearest Cousin, cannot you tell me what has happened?" asked Phoebe, with a sunny and tearful sympathy. "What is it that moves you so?"

"Hush! hush! He is coming!" whispered Hepzibah, hastily wiping her eyes. "Let him see you first, Phoebe; for you are young and rosy, and cannot help letting a smile break out, whether or no. He always liked bright faces! And mine is old, now, and the tears are hardly dry on it. He never could abide tears. There; draw the curtain a little, so that the shadow may fall across his side of the table! But let there be a good deal of sunshine, too; for he never was fond of gloom, as some people are. He has had but little sunshine in his life

—poor Clifford—and, Oh, what a black shadow! Poor, poor, Clifford!"

Thus murmuring, in an undertone, as if speaking rather to her own heart than to Phoebe, the old gentlewoman stept on tiptoe about the room, making such arrangements as suggested themselves at the crisis.

Meanwhile, there was a step in the passage-way, above-stairs. Phoebe recognized it as the same which had passed upward, as through her dream, in the night-time. The approaching guest, whoever it might be, appeared to pause at the head of the staircase; he paused, twice or thrice, in the descent; he paused again at the foot. Each time, the delay seemed to be without purpose, but rather from a forgetfulness of the purpose which had set him in motion, or as if the person's feet came involuntarily to a standstill, because the motive power was too feeble to sustain his progress. Finally, he made a long pause at the threshold of the parlor. He took hold of the knob of the door; then loosened his grasp, without opening it. Hepzibah, her hands convulsively clasped, stood gazing at the entrance.

"Dear Cousin Hepzibah, pray don't look so!" said Phoebe, trembling; for her cousin's emotion, and this mysteriously reluctant step, made her feel as if a ghost were coming into the room.—"You really frighten me! Is something awful going to happen?"

"Hush!" whispered Hepzibah. "Be cheerful! Whatever may happen, be nothing but cheerful!"

The final pause at the threshold proved so long, that Hepzibah, unable to endure the suspense, rushed forward, threw open the door, and led in the stranger by the hand. At the first glance, Phoebe saw an elderly personage, in an old-fashioned dressing-gown of faded damask, and wearing his gray, or almost white hair, of an unusual length. It quite overshadowed his forehead, except when he thrust it back, and stared vaguely about the room. After a very brief inspection of his face, it was easy to conceive that his footstep must necessarily be such an one as that which—slowly, and with as indefinite an aim as a child's first journey across a floor—had just brought him hitherward. Yet there were no tokens that his physical strength might not have sufficed for a free and determined gait. It was the spirit of the man, that could not walk. The expression of his countenance—while, notwithstanding, it had the light of reason in it—seemed to waver, and glimmer, and nearly to die away, and feebly to recover itself again. It was like a flame which we see twinkling among half-extinguished embers; we gaze at it, more intently than if it were a positive blaze, gushing vividly upward—more intently, but with a certain impatience, as if it ought either to kindle itself into satisfactory splendor, or be at once extinguished.

For an instant after entering the room, the guest stood still, retaining Hepzibah's hand, instinctively, as a child does that of the grown person who guides it. He saw Phoebe, however, and caught an illumination from her youthful and pleasant aspect, which, indeed, threw a cheerfulness about the parlor, like the circle of reflected brilliancy around the glass vase of flowers that was standing in the sunshine. He made a salutation, or, to speak nearer the truth, an ill-defined, abortive attempt at courtesy. Imperfect as it was, however, it conveyed an idea, or, at least, gave a hint, of indescribable grace, such as no practised art of external manners could have attained. It was too slight to seize upon, at the instant, yet, as recollected afterwards, seemed to transfigure the whole man.

"Dear Clifford," said Hepzibah, in the tone with which one soothes a wayward infant, "this is our Cousin Phoebe— little Phoebe Pyncheon—Arthur's only child, you know! She has come from the country to stay with us awhile; for our old house has grown to be very lonely now."

"Phoebe? — Phoebe Pyncheon! — Phoebe?" repeated the

guest, with a strange, sluggish, ill-defined utterance.—"Arthur's child! Ah, I forget! No matter! She is very welcome!"

"Come, dear Clifford, take this chair," said Hepzibah, leading him to his place.—"Pray, Phoebe, lower the curtain a very little more. Now let us begin breakfast!"

The guest seated himself in the place assigned him, and looked strangely around. He was evidently trying to grapple with the present scene, and bring it home to his mind with a more satisfactory distinctness. He desired to be certain, at least, that he was here, in the low-studded, cross-beamed, oaken-panelled parlor, and not in some other spot, which had stereotyped itself into his senses. But the effort was too great to be sustained with more than a fragmentary success. Continually, as we may express it, he faded away out of his place; or, in other words, his mind and consciousness took their departure, leaving his wasted, gray, and melancholy figure—a substantial emptiness, a material ghost—to occupy his seat at table. Again, after a blank moment, there would be a flickering taper-gleam in his eyeballs. It betokened that his spiritual part had returned, and was doing its best to kindle the heart's household-fire, and light up intellectual lamps in the dark and ruinous mansion, where it was doomed to be a forlorn inhabitant.

At one of these moments of less torpid, yet still imperfect animation, Phoebe became convinced of what she had at first rejected as too extravagant and startling an idea. She saw that the person before her must have been the original of the beautiful miniature in her Cousin Hepzibah's possession. Indeed, with a feminine eye for costume, she had at once identified the damask dressing-gown, which enveloped him, as the same in figure, material, and fashion, with that so elaborately represented in the picture. This old, faded garment, with all its pristine brilliancy extinct, seemed, in some indescribable way, to translate the wearer's untold misfortune, and make it perceptible to the beholder's eye. It was the better to be discerned, by this exterior type, how worn and old were the soul's more immediate garments; that form and countenance, the beauty and grace of which had almost transcended the skill of the most exquisite of artists. It could the more adequately be known, that the soul of the man must have suffered some miserable wrong from its earthly experience. There he seemed to sit, with a dim veil of decay and ruin betwixt him and the world, but through which, at flitting intervals, might be caught the same expression, so refined, so softly imaginative, which Malbone—venturing a happy touch, with suspended breath—had imparted to the miniature! There had been something so innately characteristic in this look, that all the dusky years, and the burthen of unfit calamity which had fallen upon him, did not suffice utterly to destroy it.

Hepzibah had now poured out a cup of deliciously fragrant coffee, and presented it to her guest. As his eyes met hers, he seemed bewildered and disquieted.

"Is this you, Hepzibah?" he murmured sadly; then, more apart, and perhaps unconscious that he was overheard.—"How changed! How changed! And is she angry with me? Why does she bend her brow so!"

Poor Hepzibah! It was that wretched scowl, which time, and her near-sightedness, and the fret of inward discomfort, had rendered so habitual, that any vehemence of mood invariably evoked it. But, at the indistinct murmur of his words, her whole face grew tender, and even lovely, with sorrowful affection; the harshness of her features disappeared, as it were, behind the warm and misty glow.

"Angry!" she repeated. "Angry with you, Clifford!"

Her tone, as she uttered this exclamation, had a plaintive and really exquisite melody thrilling through it, yet without subduing a certain something which an obtuse auditor might still have mistaken for asperity. It was as if some transcendent musician should draw a soul-thrilling sweetness out of a cracked instrument, which makes its physical imperfection heard in the midst of ethereal harmony. So deep was the sensibility that found an organ in Hepzibah's voice!

"There is nothing but love here, Clifford," she added—"nothing but love! You are at home!"

The guest responded to her tone by a smile, which did not half light up his face. Feeble as it was, however, and gone in a moment, it had a charm of wonderful beauty. It was followed by a coarser expression; or one that had the effect of coarseness on the fine mould and outline of his countenance, because there was nothing intellectual to temper it. It was a look of appetite. He ate food with what might almost be termed voracity, and seemed to forget himself, Hepzibah, the young girl, and everything else around him, in the sensual enjoyment which the bountifully spread table afforded. In his natural system, though high-wrought and delicately refined, a sensibility to the delights of the palate was probably inherent. It would have been kept in check, however, and even converted into an accomplishment, and one of the thousand modes of intellectual culture, had his more ethereal characteristics retained their vigor. But, as it existed now, the effect was painful, and made Phoebe droop her eyes.

In a little while, the guest became sensible of the fragrance of the yet untasted coffee. He quaffed it eagerly. The subtle essence acted on him like a charmed draught, and caused the opaque substance of his animal being to grow transparent, or, at least, translucent; so that a spiritual gleam was transmitted through it, with a clearer lustre than hitherto.

"More, more!" he cried, with nervous haste in his utterance, as if anxious to retain his grasp of what sought to escape him. —"This is what I need! Give me more!"

Under this delicate and powerful influence, he sat more erect, and looked out from his eyes with a glance that took note of what it rested on. It was not so much, that his expression grew more intellectual; this, though it had its share, was not the most peculiar effect. Neither was what we call the moral nature so forcibly awakened, as to present itself in remarkable prominence. But a certain fine temper of being was now—not brought out in full relief, but changeably and imperfectly betrayed—of which it was the function to deal with all beautiful and enjoyable things. In a character where it should exist as the chief attribute, it would bestow on its possessor an exquisite taste, and an enviable susceptibility of happiness. Beauty would be his life; his aspirations would all tend towards it; and, allowing his frame and physical organs to be in consonance, his own developements would likewise be beautiful. Such a man should have nothing to do with sorrow; nothing with strife; nothing with the martyrdom which, in an infinite variety of shapes, awaits those who have the heart, and will, and conscience, to fight a battle with the world. To these heroic tempers, such martyrdom is the richest meed in the world's gift. To the individual before us, it could only be a grief, intense in due proportion with the severity of the infliction. He had no right to be a martyr; and, beholding him so fit to be happy, and so feeble for all other purposes, a generous, strong, and noble spirit would, methinks, have been ready to sacrifice what little enjoyment it might have planned for itself—it would have flung down the hopes, so paltry in its regard—if thereby the wintry blasts of our rude sphere might come tempered to such a man.

Not to speak it harshly or scornfully, it seemed Clifford's nature to be a Sybarite.[4] It was perceptible, even there, in the dark, old parlor, in the inevitable polarity with which his eyes were attracted towards the quivering play of sunbeams through the shadowy foliage. It was seen in his appreciating notice of the vase of flowers, the scent of which he inhaled with a zest, almost peculiar to a physical organization so refined that spiritual ingredients are moulded in with it. It was betrayed in the unconscious smile with which he regarded Phoebe, whose fresh and maidenly figure was both sunshine

---

4. A generic name for an effeminate sensualist, derived from Sybaris, an ancient Greek city in southern Italy noted for its devotion to sensual pleasure.

and flowers, their essence, in a prettier and more agreeable mode of manifestation. Not less evident was this love and necessity for the Beautiful, in the instinctive caution with which, even so soon, his eyes turned away from his hostess, and wandered to any quarter, rather than come back. It was Hepzibah's misfortune; not Clifford's fault. How could he—so yellow as she was, so wrinkled, so sad of mien, with that odd uncouthness of a turban on her head, and that most perverse of scowls contorting her brow—how could he love to gaze at her! But, did he owe her no affection for so much as she had silently given? He owed her nothing. A nature like Clifford's can contract no debts of that kind. It is—we say it without censure, nor in diminution of the claim which it indefeasibly possesses on beings of another mould—it is always selfish in its essence; and we must give it leave to be so, and heap up our heroic and disinterested love upon it, so much the more, without a recompense. Poor Hepzibah knew this truth, or, at least, acted on the instinct of it. So long estranged from what was lovely, as Clifford had been, she rejoiced—rejoiced, though with a present sigh, and a secret purpose to shed tears in her own chamber—that he had brighter objects now before his eyes, than her aged and uncomely features. They never possessed a charm; and if they had, the canker of her grief for him would long since have destroyed it.

The guest leaned back in his chair. Mingled in his countenance with a dreamy delight, there was a troubled look of effort and unrest. He was seeking to make himself more fully sensible of the scene around him; or perhaps, dreading it to be a dream, or a play of imagination, was vexing the fair moment with a struggle for some added brilliancy and more durable illusion.

"How pleasant!—How delightful!" he murmured, but not as if addressing any one. "Will it last? How balmy the atmosphere, through that open window! An open window! How beautiful that play of sunshine! Those flowers, how very fragrant! That young girl's face, how cheerful, how blooming; a flower with the dew on it, and sunbeams in the dewdrops! Ah; this must be all a dream! A dream! A dream! But it has quite hidden the four stone-walls!"

Then his face darkened, as if the shadow of a cavern or a dungeon had come over it; there was no more light in its expression than might have come through the iron grates of a prison-window—still lessening, too, as if he were sinking farther into the depths. Phoebe (being of that quickness and activity of temperament that she seldom long refrained from taking a part, and generally a good one, in what was going forward) now felt herself moved to address the stranger.

"Here is a new kind of rose, which I found, this morning, in the garden," said she, choosing a small crimson one from among the flowers in the vase. "There will be but five or six on the bush, this season. This is the most perfect of them all; not a speck of blight or mildew in it. And how sweet it is!—sweet like no other rose! One can never forget that scent!"

"Ah!—let me see!—let me hold it!" cried the guest, eagerly seizing the flower, which, by the spell peculiar to remembered odors, brought innumerable associations along with the fragrance that it exhaled.—"Thank you! This has done me good. I remember how I used to prize this flower—long ago, I suppose, very long ago!—or was it only yesterday? It makes me feel young again! Am I young? Either this remembrance is singularly distinct, or this consciousness strangely dim! But how kind of the fair young girl! Thank you! Thank you!"

The favorable excitement, derived from this little crimson rose, afforded Clifford the brightest moment which he enjoyed at the breakfast-table. It might have lasted longer, but that his eyes happened, soon afterwards, to rest on the face of the old Puritan, who, out of his dingy frame and lustreless canvass, was looking down on the scene like a ghost, and a most ill-tempered and ungenial one. The guest made an impatient gesture of the hand, and addressed Hepzibah with what might easily be recognized as the licensed irritability of a petted member of the family.

"Hepzibah!—Hepzibah!" cried he, with no little force and distinctness. "Why do you keep that odious picture on the wall? Yes, yes!—that is precisely your taste! I have told you, a thousand times, that it was the evil genius of the house!—my evil genius particularly! Take it down at once!"

"Dear Clifford," said Hepzibah sadly, "you know it cannot be!"

"Then, at all events," continued he, still speaking with some energy, "pray cover it with a crimson curtain, broad enough to hang in folds, and with a golden border and tassels! I cannot bear it! It must not stare me in the face!"

"Yes, dear Clifford, the picture shall be covered," said Hepzibah soothingly. "There is a crimson curtain in a trunk above-stairs—a little faded and moth-eaten, I'm afraid—but Phoebe and I will do wonders with it."

"This very day, remember!" said he; and then added, in a low, self-communing voice,—"Why should we live in this dismal house at all? Why not go to the south of France?—to Italy?—Paris, Naples, Venice, Rome? Hepzibah will say, we have not the means. A droll idea, that!"

He smiled to himself, and threw a glance of fine, sarcastic meaning towards Hepzibah.

But the several moods of feeling, faintly as they were marked, through which he had passed, occurring in so brief an interval of time, had evidently wearied the stranger. He was probably accustomed to a sad monotony of life, not so much flowing in a stream, however sluggish, as stagnating in a pool around his feet. A slumberous veil diffused itself over his countenance, and had an effect, morally speaking, on its naturally delicate and elegant outline, like that which a brooding mist, with no sunshine in it, throws over the features of a landscape. He appeared to become grosser; almost cloddish. If aught of interest or beauty—even ruined beauty—had heretofore been visible in this man, the beholder might now begin to doubt it, and to accuse his own imagination of deluding him with whatever grace had flickered over that visage, and whatever exquisite lustre had gleamed in those filmy eyes.

Before he had quite sunken away, however, the sharp and peevish tinkle of the shop-bell made itself audible. Striking most disagreeably on Clifford's auditory organs and the characteristic sensibility of his nerves, it caused him to start upright out of his chair.

"Good Heavens, Hepzibah, what horrible disturbance have we now in the house?" cried he, wreaking his resentful impatience—as a matter of course, and a custom of old—on the one person in the world that loved him. "I have never heard such a hateful clamor! Why do you permit it? In the name of all dissonance, what can it be?"

It was very remarkable into what prominent relief—even as if a dim picture should leap suddenly from its canvass—Clifford's character was thrown by this apparently trifling annoyance. The secret was, that an individual of his temper can always be pricked more acutely through his sense of the beautiful and harmonious, than through his heart. It is even possible—for similar cases have often happened—that if Clifford, in his foregoing life, had enjoyed the means of cultivating his taste to its utmost perfectibility, that subtle attribute might, before this period, have completely eaten out or filed away his affections. Shall we venture to pronounce, therefore, that his long and black calamity may not have had a redeeming drop of mercy, at the bottom?

"Dear Clifford, I wish I could keep the sound from your ears," said Hepzibah patiently, but reddening with a painful suffusion of shame. "It is very disagreeable even to me. But, do you know, Clifford, I have something to tell you? This ugly noise—pray run, Phoebe, and see who is there!—this naughty little tinkle is nothing but our shop-bell!"

"Shop-bell!" repeated Clifford, with a bewildered stare.

"Yes; our shop-bell!" said Hepzibah; a certain natural dignity, mingled with deep emotion, now asserting itself in her manner. "For you must know, dearest Clifford, that we are very poor. And there was no resource, but either to accept assistance from a hand that I would push aside, (and so would you!) were it to offer bread when we were dying for it—no help, save from him, or else to earn our subsistence with my own hands! Alone, I might have been content to starve. But you were to be given back to me! Do you think, then, dear Clifford," added she, with a wretched smile, "that I have brought an irretrievable disgrace on the old house, by opening a little shop in the front gable? Our great, great-grandfather did the same, when there was far less need! Are you ashamed of me?"

"Shame! Disgrace! Do you speak these words to me, Hepzibah?" said Clifford, not angrily, however; for when a man's spirit has been thoroughly crushed, he may be peevish at small offences, but never resentful of great ones. So he spoke with only a grieved emotion.—"It was not kind to say so, Hepzibah! What shame can befall me now?"

And then the unnerved man—he that had been born for enjoyment, but had met a doom so very wretched—burst into a woman's passion of tears. It was but of brief continuance, however; soon leaving him in a quiescent, and, to judge by his countenance, not an uncomfortable state. From this mood, too, he partially rallied, for an instant, and looked at Hepzibah with a smile, the keen, half-derisory purport of which was a puzzle to her.

"Are we so very poor, Hepzibah?" said he.

Finally, his chair being deep and softly cushioned, Clifford fell asleep. Hearing the more regular rise and fall of his breath—(which, however, even then, instead of being strong and full, had a feeble kind of tremor, corresponding with the lack of vigor in his character)—hearing these tokens of settled slumber, Hepzibah seized the opportunity to peruse his face, more attentively than she had yet dared to do. Her heart melted away in tears; her profoundest spirit sent forth a moaning voice, low, gentle, but inexpressibly sad. In this depth of grief and pity, she felt that there was no irreverence in gazing at his altered, aged, faded, ruined face. But, no sooner was she a little relieved, than her conscience smote her for gazing curiously at him, now that he was so changed; and, turning hastily away, Hepzibah let down the curtain over the sunny window, and left Clifford to slumber there.

# VIII

# THE PYNCHEON OF TO-DAY

PHOEBE, on entering the shop, beheld there the already familiar face of the little devourer—if we can reckon his mighty deeds aright—of Jim Crow, the elephant, the camel, the dromedaries, and the locomotive. Having expended his private fortune, on the two preceding days, in the purchase of the above unheard-of luxuries, the young gentleman's present errand was on the part of his mother, in quest of three eggs and half-a-pound of raisins. These articles Phoebe accordingly supplied, and—as a mark of gratitude for his previous patronage, and a slight, superadded morsel, after breakfast—put likewise into his hand a whale! The great fish —reversing his experience with the prophet of Nineveh[1]—immediately began his progress down the same red pathway of fate, whither so varied a caravan had preceded him. This remarkable urchin, in truth, was the very emblem of old Father Time, both in respect of his all-devouring appetite for men and things, and because he, as well as Time, after engulfing thus much of creation, looked almost as youthful as if he had been just that moment made.

After partly closing the door, the child turned back, and mumbled something to Phoebe which, as the whale was but half-disposed of, she could not perfectly understand.

"What did you say, my little fellow?" asked she.

1. Jonah, on being commanded by the Lord to go to Nineveh to preach, tried to escape to Tarshish, but his shipmates threw him overboard and he was swallowed by a whale (1 Jonah, 1–17).

"Mother wants to know," repeated Ned Higgins, more distinctly, "how Old Maid Pyncheon's brother does? Folks say he has got home!"

"My Cousin Hepzibah's brother!" exclaimed Phoebe, surprised at this sudden explanation of the relationship between Hepzibah and her guest.—"Her brother! And where can he have been!"

The little boy only put his thumb to his broad snub-nose, with that look of shrewdness which a child, spending much of his time in the street, so soon learns to throw over his features, however unintelligent in themselves. Then, as Phoebe continued to gaze at him without answering his mother's message, he took his departure.

As the child went down the steps, a gentleman ascended them, and made his entrance into the shop. It was the portly, and, had it possessed the advantage of a little more height, would have been the stately figure of a man considerably in the decline of life, dressed in a black suit of some thin stuff, resembling broadcloth as closely as possible. A gold-headed cane of rare, oriental wood, added materially to the high respectability of his aspect; as did also a white neckcloth of the utmost snowy purity, and the conscientious polish of his boots. His dark, square countenance, with its almost shaggy depth of eyebrows, was naturally impressive, and would perhaps have been rather stern, had not the gentleman considerately taken upon himself to mitigate the harsh effect by a look of exceeding good-humor and benevolence. Owing, however, to a somewhat massive accumulation of animal substance about the lower region of his face, the look was perhaps unctuous, rather than spiritual, and had, so to speak, a kind of fleshly effulgence, not altogether so satisfactory as he doubtless intended it to be. A susceptible observer, at any rate, might have regarded it as affording very little evidence of the genuine benignity of soul, whereof it purported to be the outward reflection. And if the observer chanced to be ill-natured, as well as acute and susceptible, he would probably suspect, that the smile on the gentleman's face was a good deal akin to the shine on his boots, and that each must have cost him and his boot-black, respectively, a good deal of hard labor to bring out and preserve them.

As the stranger entered the little shop—where the projection of the second story and the thick foliage of the elm-tree, as well as the commodities at the window, created a sort of gray medium—his smile grew as intense as if he had set his heart on counteracting the whole gloom of the atmosphere (besides any moral gloom pertaining to Hepzibah and her inmates) by the unassisted light of his countenance. On perceiving a young rosebud of a girl, instead of the gaunt presence of the old maid, a look of surprise was manifest. He at first knit his brows; then smiled with more unctuous benignity than ever.

"Ah, I see how it is!" said he, in a deep voice—a voice which, had it come from the throat of an uncultivated man, would have been gruff, but, by dint of careful training, was now sufficiently agreeable—"I was not aware that Miss Hepzibah Pyncheon had commenced business under such favorable auspices. You are her assistant, I suppose?"

"I certainly am," answered Phoebe, and added, with a little air of ladylike assumption—(for, civil as the gentleman was, he evidently took her to be a young person serving for wages)—"I am a cousin of Miss Hepzibah, on a visit to her."

"Her cousin?—and from the country? Pray pardon me, then," said the gentleman, bowing and smiling as Phoebe never had been bowed to nor smiled on before.—"In that case, we must be better acquainted; for, unless I am sadly mistaken, you are my own little kinswoman likewise! Let me see—Mary? —Dolly?—Phoebe?—yes, Phoebe is the name! Is it possible that you are Phoebe Pyncheon, only child of my dear cousin and classmate, Arthur? Ah, I see your father now, about your mouth! Yes; yes; we must be better acquainted! I am your kinsman, my dear. Surely you must have heard of Judge Pyncheon?"

As Phoebe courtesied in reply, the Judge bent forward, with the pardonable and even praiseworthy purpose—considering the nearness of blood and the difference of age—of bestowing on his young relative a kiss of acknowledged kindred and natural affection. Unfortunately, (without design, or only with such instinctive design as gives no account of itself to the intellect,) Phoebe, just at the critical moment, drew back; so that her highly respectable kinsman, with his body bent over the counter, and his lips protruded, was betrayed into the rather absurd predicament of kissing the empty air. It was a modern parallel to the case of Ixion embracing a cloud,[2] and was so much the more ridiculous, as the Judge prided himself on eschewing all airy matter, and never mistaking a shadow for a substance. The truth was—and it is Phoebe's only excuse—that, although Judge Pyncheon's glowing benignity might not be absolutely unpleasant to the feminine beholder, with the width of a street or even an ordinary sized room interposed between, yet it became quite too intense, when this dark, full-fed physiognomy (so roughly bearded, too, that no razor could ever make it smooth) sought to bring itself into actual contact with the object of its regards. The man, the sex, somehow or other, was entirely too prominent in the Judge's demonstrations of that sort. Phoebe's eyes sank, and, without knowing why, she felt herself blushing deeply under his look. Yet she had been kissed before, and without any particular squeamishness, by perhaps half-a-dozen different cousins, younger, as well as older, than this dark-browed, grisly bearded, white neckclothed, and unctuously benevolent Judge! Then why not by him?

On raising her eyes, Phoebe was startled by the change in Judge Pyncheon's face. It was quite as striking, allowing for the difference of scale, as that betwixt a landscape under a broad sunshine, and just before a thunder-storm; not that

2. Zeus punished Ixion for attempting to seduce Hera by deceiving him with a cloud image of her (on which he begat the Centaurs) before attaching him to a revolving wheel.

it had the passionate intensity of the latter aspect, but was cold, hard, immitigable, like a day-long brooding cloud.

"Dear me, what is to be done now?" thought the country-girl to herself.—"He looks as if there were nothing softer in him than a rock, nor milder than the east-wind! I meant no harm! Since he is really my cousin, I would have let him kiss me, if I could!"

Then, all at once, it struck Phoebe, that this very Judge Pyncheon was the original of the miniature, which the Daguerreotypist had shown her in the garden, and that the hard, stern, relentless look, now on his face, was the same that the sun had so inflexibly persisted in bringing out. Was it, therefore, no momentary mood, but, however skilfully concealed, the settled temper of his life? And not merely so, but was it hereditary in him, and transmitted down as a precious heir-loom from that bearded ancestor, in whose picture both the expression, and, to a singular degree, the features of the modern Judge, were shown as by a kind of prophecy? A deeper philosopher than Phoebe might have found something very terrible in this idea. It implied that the weaknesses and defects, the bad passions, the mean tendencies, and the moral diseases which lead to crime, are handed down from one generation to another, by a far surer process of transmission than human law has been able to establish, in respect to the riches and honors which it seeks to entail upon posterity.

But, as it happened, scarcely had Phoebe's eyes rested again on the Judge's countenance, than all its ugly sternness vanished; and she found herself quite overpowered by the sultry, dog-day heat, as it were, of benevolence, which this excellent man diffused out of his great heart into the surrounding atmosphere;—very much like a serpent, which, as a preliminary to fascination, is said to fill the air with his peculiar odor.

"I like that, Cousin Phoebe!" cried he, with an emphatic nod of approbation.—"I like it much, my little cousin! You are a good child, and know how to take care of yourself. A young girl—especially if she be a very pretty one—can never be too chary of her lips."

"Indeed, Sir," said Phoebe, trying to laugh the matter off, "I did not mean to be unkind."

Nevertheless, whether or no it were entirely owing to the inauspicious commencement of their acquaintance, she still acted under a certain reserve, which was by no means customary to her frank and genial nature. The fantasy would not quit her, that the original Puritan, of whom she had heard so many sombre traditions—the progenitor of the whole race of New England Pyncheons, the founder of the House of the Seven Gables, and who had died so strangely in it—had now stept into the shop. In these days of off-hand equipment, the matter was easily enough arranged. On his arrival from the other world, he had merely found it necessary to spend a quarter-of-an-hour at a barber's, who had trimmed down the Puritan's full beard into a pair of grizzled whiskers; then, patronizing a ready-made clothing establishment, he had exchanged his velvet doublet and sable cloak, with the richly worked band under his chin, for a white collar and cravat, coat, vest, and pantaloons; and, lastly, putting aside his steel-hilted broadsword to take up a gold-headed cane, the Colonel Pyncheon, of two centuries ago, steps forward as the Judge, of the passing moment!

Of course, Phoebe was far too sensible a girl to entertain this idea in any other way than as matter for a smile. Possibly, also, could the two personages have stood together before her eye, many points of difference would have been perceptible, and perhaps only a general resemblance. The long lapse of intervening years, in a climate so unlike that which had fostered the ancestral Englishman, must inevitably have wrought important changes in the physical system of his descendant. The Judge's volume of muscle could hardly be the same as the Colonel's; there was undoubtedly less beef in him. Though looked upon as a weighty man among his contemporaries, in respect of animal substance; and as favored with a remarkable degree of fundamental developement, well adapting him for the judicial bench, we conceive that the modern Judge Pyncheon, if weighed in the same balance with his ancestor, would have required at least an old-fashioned fifty-six,[3] to keep the scale in equilibrio. Then the Judge's face had lost the ruddy English hue, that showed its warmth through all the duskiness of the Colonel's weather-beaten cheek, and had taken a sallow shade, the established complexion of his countrymen. If we mistake not, moreover, a certain quality of nervousness had become more or less manifest, even in so solid a specimen of Puritan descent, as the gentleman now under discussion. As one of its effects, it bestowed on his countenance a quicker mobility than the old Englishman's had possessed, and keener vivacity, but at the expense of a sturdier something, on which these acute endowments seemed to act like dissolving acids. This process, for aught we know, may belong to the great system of human progress, which, with every ascending footstep, as it diminishes the necessity for animal force, may be destined gradually to spiritualize us by refining away our grosser attributes of body. If so, Judge Pyncheon could endure a century or two more of such refinement, as well as most other men.

The similarity, intellectual and moral, between the Judge and his ancestor, appears to have been at least as strong as the resemblance of mien and feature would afford reason to anticipate. In old Colonel Pyncheon's funeral discourse, the clergyman absolutely canonized his deceased parishioner, and opening, as it were, a vista through the roof of the church, and thence through the firmament above, showed him seated, harp in hand, among the crowned choristers of the spiritual world. On his tombstone, too, the record is highly eulogistic; nor does history, so far as he holds a place upon its page, assail the consistency and uprightness of his

3. A colloquial way of referring to the Winchester Bushel of 2,150.42 cubic inches, which became the standard of dry measure in U.S. Custom Houses in 1832. It was called a "fifty-six" because a bushel of wheat was supposed to weigh fifty-six pounds.

character. So also, as regards the Judge Pyncheon of to-day, neither clergyman, nor legal critic, nor inscriber of tomb-stones, nor historian of general or local politics, would venture a word against this eminent person's sincerity as a christian, or respectability as a man, or integrity as a judge, or courage and faithfulness as the often-tried representative of his political party. But, besides these cold, formal, and empty words of the chisel that inscribes, the voice that speaks, and the pen that writes for the public eye and for distant time—and which inevitably lose much of their truth and freedom by the fatal consciousness of so doing—there were traditions about the ancestor, and private diurnal gossip about the Judge, remark-ably accordant in their testimony. It is often instructive to take the woman's, the private and domestic view, of a public man; nor can anything be more curious than the vast dis-crepancy between portraits intended for engraving, and the pencil-sketches that pass from hand to hand, behind the original's back.

For example, tradition affirmed that the Puritan had been greedy of wealth; the Judge, too, with all the show of liberal expenditure, was said to be as close-fisted as if his gripe were of iron. The ancestor had clothed himself in a grim assump-tion of kindliness, a rough heartiness of word and manner, which most people took to be the genuine warmth of nature, making its way through the thick and inflexible hide of a manly character. His descendant, in compliance with the requirements of a nicer age, had etherealized this rude benev-olence into that broad benignity of smile, wherewith he shone like a noonday sun along the streets, or glowed like a house-hold fire, in the drawing-rooms of his private acquaintance. The Puritan—if not belied by some singular stories, mur-mured, even at this day, under the narrator's breath—had fallen into certain transgressions to which men of his great animal developement, whatever their faith or principles, must continue liable, until they put off impurity, along with the

gross earthly substance that involves it. We must not stain
our page with any contemporary scandal, to a similar purport,
that may have been whispered against the Judge. The Puritan, again, an autocrat in his own household, had worn out
three wives, and, merely by the remorseless weight and hardness of his character in the conjugal relation, had sent them,
one after another, broken hearted, to their graves. Here, the
parallel, in some sort, fails. The Judge had wedded but a
single wife, and lost her in the third or fourth year of their
marriage. There was a fable, however—for such we choose to
consider it, though, not impossibly, typical of Judge Pyncheon's marital deportment—that the lady got her death-blow
in the honey-moon, and never smiled again, because her husband compelled her to serve him with coffee, every morning,
at his bedside, in token of fealty to her liege-lord and master.

But it is too fruitful a subject, this of hereditary resem-
blances,—the frequent recurrence of which, in a direct line,
is truly unaccountable, when we consider how large an accumulation of ancestry lies behind every man, at the distance
of one or two centuries. We shall only add, therefore, that
the Puritan—so, at least, says chimney-corner tradition, which
often preserves traits of character with marvellous fidelity—
was bold, imperious, relentless, crafty; laying his purposes
deep, and following them out with an inveteracy of pursuit
that knew neither rest nor conscience; trampling on the
weak, and, when essential to his ends, doing his utmost to
beat down the strong. Whether the Judge in any degree
resembled him, the farther progress of our narrative may
show.

Scarcely any of the items in the above-drawn parallel occurred to Phoebe, whose country-birth and residence, in truth,
had left her pitifully ignorant of most of the family traditions,
which lingered, like cobwebs and incrustations of smoke,
about the rooms and chimney-corners of the House of the
Seven Gables. Yet there was a circumstance, very trifling in

itself, which impressed her with an odd degree of horror. She had heard of the anathema flung by Maule, the executed wizard, against Colonel Pyncheon and his posterity—that God would give them blood to drink—and likewise of the popular notion, that this miraculous blood might now and then be heard gurgling in their throats. The latter scandal (as became a person of sense, and, more especially, a member of the Pyncheon family) Phoebe had set down for the absurdity which it unquestionably was. But ancient superstitions, after being steeped in human hearts, and embodied in human breath, and passing from lip to ear in manifold repetition, through a series of generations, become imbued with an effect of homely truth. The smoke of the domestic hearth has scented them, through and through. By long transmission among household facts, they grow to look like them, and have such a familiar way of making themselves at home, that their influence is usually greater than we suspect. Thus it happened, that when Phoebe heard a certain noise in Judge Pyncheon's throat—rather habitual with him, not altogether voluntary, yet indicative of nothing, unless it were a slight bronchial complaint, or, as some people hinted, an apoplectic symptom—when the girl heard this queer and aukward ingurgitation, (which the writer never did hear, and therefore cannot describe,) she, very foolishly, started, and clasped her hands.

Of course, it was exceedingly ridiculous in Phoebe to be discomposed by such a trifle, and still more unpardonable to show her discomposure to the individual most concerned in it. But the incident chimed in so oddly with her previous fancies about the Colonel and the Judge, that, for the moment, it seemed quite to mingle their identity.

"What is the matter with you, young woman?" said Judge Pyncheon, giving her one of his harsh looks. "Are you afraid of anything?"

"Oh, nothing, Sir, nothing in the world!" answered Phoebe, with a little laugh of vexation at herself.—"But perhaps you wish to speak with my Cousin Hepzibah. Shall I call her?"

"Stay a moment, if you please!" said the Judge, again beaming sunshine out of his face.—"You seem to be a little nervous, this morning. The town air, Cousin Phoebe, does not agree with your good, wholesome country-habits. Or, has anything happened to disturb you?—anything remarkable in Cousin Hepzibah's family? An arrival, eh? I thought so! No wonder you are out of sorts, my little cousin. To be an inmate with such a guest may well startle an innocent young girl!"

"You quite puzzle me, Sir," replied Phoebe, gazing inquiringly at the Judge. "There is no frightful guest in the house, but only a poor, gentle, childlike man, whom I believe to be Cousin Hepzibah's brother. I am afraid (but you, Sir, will know better than I) that he is not quite in his sound senses; but so mild and quiet, he seems to be, that a mother might trust her baby with him; and I think he would play with the baby as if he were only a few years older than itself. He startle me! Oh, no indeed!"

"I rejoice to hear so favorable and so ingenuous an account of my Cousin Clifford," said the benevolent Judge. "Many years ago, when we were boys and young men together, I had a great affection for him, and still feel a tender interest in all his concerns. You say, Cousin Phoebe, he appears to be weak-minded. Heaven grant him at least enough of intellect to repent of his past sins!"

"Nobody, I fancy," observed Phoebe, "can have fewer to repent of."

"And is it possible, my dear," rejoined the Judge, with a commiserating look, "that you have never heard of Clifford Pyncheon?—that you know nothing of his history? Well; it is all right; and your mother has shown a very proper regard for the good name of the family with which she connected herself. Believe the best you can of this unfortunate person, and hope the best! It is a rule which christians should always follow, in their judgements of one another; and especially is it right and wise among near relatives, whose characters have necessarily a degree of mutual dependence. But is Clifford in the parlor? I will just step in and see!"

"Perhaps, Sir, I had better call my Cousin Hepzibah," said Phoebe; hardly knowing, however, whether she ought to obstruct the entrance of so affectionate a kinsman, into the private regions of the house.—"Her brother seemed to be just falling asleep, after breakfast; and I am sure she would not like him to be disturbed. Pray, Sir, let me give her notice!"

But the Judge showed a singular determination to enter unannounced; and as Phoebe, with the vivacity of a person whose movements unconsciously answer to her thoughts, had stept towards the door, he used little or no ceremony in putting her aside.

"No, no, Miss Phoebe!" said Judge Pyncheon, in a voice as deep as a thunder-growl, and with a frown as black as the cloud whence it issues. "Stay you here! I know the house, and know my Cousin Hepzibah, and know her brother Clifford likewise!—nor need my little country-cousin put herself to the trouble of announcing me!"—in these latter words, by-the-by, there were symptoms of a change from his sudden harshness into his previous benignity of manner—"I am at home here, Phoebe, you must recollect, and you are the stranger. I will just step in, therefore, and see for myself how Clifford is, and assure him and Hepzibah of my kindly feelings and best wishes. It is right, at this juncture, that they should both hear from my own lips how much I desire to serve them. Ha! Here is Hepzibah herself!"

Such was the case. The vibrations of the Judge's voice had reached the old gentlewoman in the parlor, where she sat, with face averted, waiting on her brother's slumber. She now issued forth, as would appear, to defend the entrance, looking, we must needs say, amazingly like the dragon which, in fairy tales, is wont to be the guardian over an enchanted beauty. The habitual scowl of her brow was, undeniably, too fierce, at this moment, to pass itself off on the innocent score of near-sightedness; and it was bent on Judge Pyncheon in a way that seemed to confound, if not alarm him—so inadequately had he estimated the moral force of a deeply grounded antipathy. She made a repelling gesture with her hand, and stood, a perfect picture of Prohibition, at full length, in the dark frame of the door-way. But we must betray Hepzibah's secret, and confess, that the native timorousness of her character even now developed itself, in a quick tremor, which, to her own perception, set each of her joints at variance with its fellow.

Possibly, the Judge was aware how little true hardihood lay behind Hepzibah's formidable front. At any rate, being a gentleman of sturdy nerves, he soon recovered himself, and failed not to approach his cousin with outstretched hand; adopting the sensible precaution, however, to cover his advance with a smile, so broad and sultry, that, had it been only half as warm as it looked, a trellis of grapes might at once have turned purple under its summer-like exposure. It may have been his purpose, indeed, to melt poor Hepzibah, on the spot, as if she were a figure of yellow wax.

"Hepzibah, my beloved Cousin, I am rejoiced!" exclaimed the Judge, most emphatically. "Now, at length, you have something to live for. Yes; and all of us, let me say, your friends and kindred, have more to live for than we had yesterday. I have lost no time in hastening to offer any assistance in my power towards making Clifford comfortable. He belongs to us all. I know how much he requires—how much he used to require—with his delicate taste, and his love of the beautiful. Anything in my house—pictures, books, wine, luxuries of the table—he may command them all! It would afford me a most heartfelt gratification to see him! Shall I step in, this moment?"

"No," replied Hepzibah, her voice quivering too painfully to allow of many words. "He cannot see visitors!"

"A visitor, my dear Cousin?—do you call me so?" cried

the Judge, whose sensibility, it seems, was hurt by the coldness of the phrase. "Nay, then, let me be Clifford's host, and your own likewise. Come at once to my house! The country-air, and all the conveniences—I may say, luxuries— that I have gathered about me, will do wonders for him. And you and I, dear Hepzibah, will consult together, and watch together, and labor together, to make our dear Clifford happy. Come! Why should we make more words about what is both a duty and a pleasure, on my part? Come to me at once!"

On hearing these so hospitable offers, and such generous recognition of the claims of kindred, Phoebe felt very much in the mood of running up to Judge Pyncheon, and giving him, of her own accord, the kiss from which she had so recently shrunk away. It was quite otherwise with Hepzibah; the Judge's smile seemed to operate on her acerbity of heart like sunshine upon vinegar, making it ten times sourer than ever.

"Clifford," said she—still too agitated to utter more than an abrupt sentence—"Clifford has a home here!"

"May Heaven forgive you, Hepzibah," said Judge Pyncheon—reverently lifting his eyes towards that high court of equity to which he appealed—"if you suffer any ancient prejudice or animosity to weigh with you, in this matter! I stand here, with an open heart, willing and anxious to receive yourself and Clifford into it. Do not refuse my good offices—my earnest propositions for your welfare! They are such, in all respects, as it behoves your nearest kinsman to make. It will be a heavy responsibility, Cousin, if you confine your brother to this dismal house and stifled air, when the delightful freedom of my country-seat is at his command."

"It would never suit Clifford," said Hepzibah, as briefly as before.

"Woman," broke forth the Judge, giving way to his resent-

ment, "what is the meaning of all this? Have you other
resources? Nay; I suspected as much! Take care, Hepzibah,
take care! Clifford is on the brink of as black a ruin as ever
befell him yet! But why do I talk with you, woman as you
are! Make way! I must see Clifford!"

Hepzibah spread out her gaunt figure across the door, and
seemed really to increase in bulk; looking the more terrible,
also, because there was so much terror and agitation in her
heart. But Judge Pyncheon's evident purpose of forcing a
passage was interrupted by a voice from the inner room; a
weak, tremulous, wailing voice, indicating helpless alarm,
with no more energy for self-defence than belongs to a frightened infant.

"Hepzibah, Hepzibah," cried the voice, "go down on your
knees to him! Kiss his feet! Entreat him not to come in!
Oh, let him have mercy on me! Mercy!—mercy!"

For the instant, it appeared doubtful whether it were not
the Judge's resolute purpose to set Hepzibah aside, and step
across the threshold into the parlor, whence issued that
broken and miserable murmur of entreaty. It was not pity
that restrained him; for, at the first sound of the enfeebled
voice, a red fire kindled in his eyes; and he made a quick
pace forward, with something inexpressibly fierce and grim,
darkening forth, as it were, out of the whole man. To know
Judge Pyncheon, was to see him at that moment. After such
a revelation, let him smile with what sultriness he would, he
could much sooner turn grapes purple, or pumpkins yellow,
than melt the iron-branded impression out of the beholder's
memory. And it rendered his aspect not the less, but more
frightful, that it seemed not to express wrath or hatred, but
a certain hot fellness of purpose, which annihilated everything but itself.

Yet, after all, are we not slandering an excellent and amiable man? Look at the Judge now! He is apparently conscious

of having erred, in too energetically pressing his deeds of loving-kindness on persons unable to appreciate them. He will await their better mood, and hold himself as ready to assist them, then, as at this moment. As he draws back from the door, an all-comprehensive benignity blazes from his visage, indicating that he gathers Hepzibah, little Phoebe, and the invisible Clifford, all three, together with the whole world besides, into his immense heart, and gives them a warm bath in its flood of affection.

"You do me great wrong, dear Cousin Hepzibah," said he, first kindly offering her his hand, and then drawing on his glove preparatory to departure. "Very great wrong! But I forgive it, and will study to make you think better of me. Of course, our poor Clifford being in so unhappy a state of mind, I cannot think of urging an interview at present. But I shall watch over his welfare, as if he were my own beloved brother; nor do I at all despair, my dear Cousin, of constraining both him and you to acknowledge your injustice. When that shall happen, I desire no other revenge than your acceptance of the best offices in my power to do you."

With a bow to Hepzibah, and a degree of paternal benevolence in his parting nod to Phoebe, the Judge left the shop, and went smiling along the street. As is customary with the rich, when they aim at the honors of a republic, he apologized, as it were, to the people, for his wealth, prosperity, and elevated station, by a free and hearty manner towards those who knew him; putting off the more of his dignity, in due proportion with the humbleness of the man whom he saluted; and thereby proving a haughty consciousness of his advantages, as irrefragably as if he had marched forth, preceded by a troop of lackeys to clear the way. On this particular forenoon, so excessive was the warmth of Judge Pyncheon's kindly aspect, that (such, at least, was the rumor about town) an extra passage of the water-carts was found essential, in order to lay the dust occasioned by so much extra sunshine!

No sooner had he disappeared, than Hepzibah grew deadly white, and staggering towards Phoebe, let her head fall on the young girl's shoulder.

"Oh, Phoebe," murmured she, "that man has been the horror of my life! Shall I never, never have the courage—will my voice never cease from trembling long enough—to let me tell him what he is!"

"Is he so very wicked?" asked Phoebe. "Yet his offers were surely kind!"

"Do not speak of them—he has a heart of iron!" rejoined Hepzibah.—"Go now, and talk to Clifford! Amuse, and keep him quiet! It would disturb him wretchedly, to see me so agitated as I am. There, go, dear child, and I will try to look after the shop!"

Phoebe went, accordingly, but perplexed herself, meanwhile, with queries as to the purport of the scene which she had just witnessed, and also whether judges, clergymen, and other characters of that eminent stamp and respectability, could really, in any single instance, be otherwise than just and upright men. A doubt of this nature has a most disturbing influence, and, if shown to be a fact, comes with fearful and startling effect, on minds of the trim, orderly, and limit-loving class, in which we find our little country-girl. Dispositions more boldly speculative may derive a stern enjoyment from the discovery, since there must be evil in the world, that a high man is as likely to grasp his share of it, as a low one. A wider scope of view, and a deeper insight, may see rank, dignity, and station, all proved illusory, so far as regards their claim to human reverence, and yet not feel as if the universe were thereby tumbled headlong into chaos. But Phoebe, in order to keep the universe in its old place, was fain to smother, in some degree, her own intuitions as to Judge Pyncheon's character. And as for her cousin's testimony in disparagement of it, she concluded that Hepzibah's judgement was embittered by one of those family feuds, which render hatred the more deadly, by the dead and corrupted love that they intermingle with its native poison.

## IX

## CLIFFORD AND PHOEBE

TRULY was there something high, generous, and noble, in the native composition of our poor old Hepzibah! Or else—and it was quite as probably the case—she had been enriched by poverty, developed by sorrow, elevated by the strong and solitary affection of her life, and thus endowed with heroism, which never could have characterized her in what are called happier circumstances. Through dreary years, Hepzibah had looked forward—for the most part, despairingly, never with any confidence of hope, but always with the feeling that it was her brightest possibility—to the very position in which she now found herself. In her own behalf, she had asked nothing of Providence, but the opportunity of devoting herself to this brother whom she had so loved—so admired for what he was, or might have been—and to whom she had kept her faith, alone of all the world, wholly, unfaulteringly, at every instant, and throughout life. And here, in his late decline, the lost one had come back out of his long and strange misfortune, and was thrown on her sympathy, as it seemed, not merely for the bread of his physical existence, but for everything that should keep him morally alive. She had responded to the call! She had come forward—our poor, gaunt Hepzibah, in her rusty silks, with her rigid joints, and the sad perversity of her scowl—ready to do her utmost, and with affection enough, if that were all, to do a hundred times as much!—There could be few more tearful sights—and Heaven forgive us, if a smile insist on mingling with our conception of it!—few sights with truer pathos in them, than Hepzibah presented, on that first afternoon.

How patiently did she endeavor to wrap Clifford up in her great, warm love, and make it all the world to him, so that he should retain no torturing sense of the coldness and dreariness, without! Her little efforts to amuse him! How pitiful, yet magnanimous, they were!

Remembering his early love of poetry and fiction, she un-locked a bookcase, and took down several books that had been excellent reading, in their day. There was a volume of Pope, with the Rape of the Lock in it, and another of the Tatler, and an odd one of Dryden's Miscellanies,[1] all with tarnished gilding on their covers, and thoughts of tarnished brilliancy, inside. They had no success with Clifford. These, and all such writers of society, whose new works glow like the rich texture of a just-woven carpet, must be content to relinquish their charm, for every reader, after an age or two, and could hardly be supposed to retain any portion of it for a mind, that had utterly lost its estimate of modes and manners. Hep-zibah then took up Rasselas,[2] and began to read of the Happy Valley, with a vague idea that some secret of a contented life had there been elaborated, which might at least serve Clifford and herself for this one day. But the Happy Valley had a cloud over it. Hepzibah troubled her auditor, moreover, by innumerable sins of emphasis, which he seemed to detect without any reference to the meaning; nor, in fact, did he appear to take much note of the sense of what she read, but evidently felt the tedium of the lecture without harvesting its profit. His sister's voice, too, naturally harsh, had, in the course of her sorrowful lifetime, contracted a kind of croak, which, when it once gets into the human throat, is as ineradi-cable as sin. In both sexes, occasionally, this life-long croak,

1. Alexander Pope's *The Rape of the Lock* (1714) is a mock-heroic epic satirizing the absurd frivolities of a polite age; *The Tatler* (1709–1711) is a series of periodical essays written by Richard Steele and Joseph Addison, satirizing the vanity and affectations of its time. John Dryden's miscellanies

accompanying each word of joy or sorrow, is one of the symptoms of a settled melancholy; and wherever it occurs, the whole history of misfortune is conveyed in its slightest accent. The effect is as if the voice had been dyed black; or—if we must use a more moderate simile—this miserable croak, running through all the variations of the voice, is like a black silken thread, on which the crystal beads of speech are strung, and whence they take their hue. Such voices have put on mourning for dead hopes; and they ought to die and be buried along with them!

Discerning that Clifford was not gladdened by her efforts, Hepzibah searched about the house for the means of more exhilarating pastime. At one time, her eyes chanced to rest on Alice Pyncheon's harpsichord. It was a moment of great peril; for—despite the traditionary awe that had gathered over this instrument of music, and the dirges which spiritual fingers were said to play on it—the devoted sister had solemn thoughts of thrumming on its chords for Clifford's benefit, and accompanying the performance with her voice. Poor Clifford! Poor Hepzibah! Poor harpsichord! All three would have been miserable together. By some good agency—possibly, by the unrecognized interposition of the long-buried Alice, herself—the threatening calamity was averted.

But the worst of all—the hardest stroke of fate for Hepzibah to endure, and perhaps for Clifford too—was his invincible distaste for her appearance. Her features, never the most agreeable, and now harsh with age and grief, and resentment against the world for his sake; her dress, and especially her turban; the queer and quaint manners, which had unconsciously grown upon her in solitude;—such being the poor gentlewoman's outward characteristics, it is no great marvel, although the mournfullest of pities, that the instinctive lover of the Beautiful was fain to turn away his eyes! There was no help for it. It would be the latest impulse to die within him. In his last extremity, the expiring breath

began to appear in 1684.
2. Samuel Johnson's *History of Rasselas, Prince of Abissinia* (1759) is the story of a young man who escapes from a mythical "Happy Valley" into the real world, where happiness, he learns, is never to be found.

stealing faintly through Clifford's lips, he would doubtless press Hepzibah's hand, in fervent recognition of all her lavished love, and close his eyes—but not so much to die, as to be constrained to look no longer on her face! Poor Hepzibah! She took counsel with herself what might be done, and thought of putting ribbons on her turban, but, by the instant rush of several guardian angels, was withheld from an experiment, that could hardly have proved less than fatal to the beloved object of her anxiety.[3]

To be brief, besides Hepzibah's disadvantages of person, there was an uncouthness pervading all her deeds; a clumsy something, that could but ill adapt itself for use, and not at all for ornament. She was a grief to Clifford, and she knew it. In this extremity, the antiquated virgin turned to Phoebe. No grovelling jealousy was in her heart. Had it pleased Heaven to crown the heroic fidelity of her life by making her personally the medium of Clifford's happiness, it would have rewarded her for all the past, by a joy with no bright tints, indeed, but deep and true, and worth a thousand gayer ecstacies. This could not be. She therefore turned to Phoebe, and resigned the task into the young girl's hands. The latter took it up, cheerfully, as she did everything, but with no sense of a mission to perform, and succeeding all the better for that same simplicity.

By the involuntary effect of a genial temperament, Phoebe soon grew to be absolutely essential to the daily comfort, if not the daily life, of her two forlorn companions. The grime and sordidness of the House of the Seven Gables seemed to have vanished, since her appearance there; the gnawing tooth of the dry-rot was stayed, among the old timbers of its skeleton-frame; the dust had ceased to settle down so densely from the antique ceilings, upon the floors and furniture of the rooms below;—or, at any rate, there was a little housewife, as light-footed as the breeze that sweeps a garden-walk, gliding hither and thither, to brush it all away. The shadows

3. An allusion, comic in its inappropriateness, to the sylphs who preside over the toilet of the elegant lady of society, Belinda, in *The Rape of the Lock* (I, 145-6): "The busy Sylphs surround their darling care,/These set the head, and those divide the hair *** "

of gloomy events, that haunted the else lonely and desolate apartments; the heavy, breathless scent which Death had
left in more than one of the bed-chambers, ever since his
visits of long ago;—these were less powerful than the purify-
ing influence, scattered throughout the atmosphere of the
household by the presence of one, youthful, fresh, and thoroughly wholesome heart. There was no morbidness in
Phoebe; if there had been, the old Pyncheon-house was the
very locality to ripen it into incurable disease. But, now, her
spirit resembled, in its potency, a minute quantity of attar of
rose in one of Hepzibah's huge, iron-bound trunks, diffusing
its fragrance through the various articles of linen and wrought-
lace, kerchiefs, caps, stockings, folded dresses, gloves, and
whatever else was treasured there. As every article in the
great trunk was the sweeter for the rose-scent, so did all the
thoughts and emotions of Hepzibah and Clifford, sombre as
they might seem, acquire a subtle attribute of happiness from
Phoebe's intermixture with them. Her activity of body, intellect, and heart, impelled her continually to perform the ordinary little toils that offered themselves around her, and to
think the thought, proper for the moment, and to sympathize
—now with the twittering gaiety of the robins in the pear-
tree—and now, to such depth as she could, with Hepzibah's
dark anxiety, or the vague moan of her brother. This facile
adaptation was at once the symptom of perfect health, and
its best preservative.

A nature like Phoebe's has invariably its due influence,
but is seldom regarded with due honor. Its spiritual force,
however, may be partially estimated by the fact of her having
found a place for herself, amid circumstances so stern, as
those which surrounded the mistress of the house; and also
by the effect which she produced on a character of so much
more mass than her own. For the gaunt, bony frame and
limbs of Hepzibah, as compared with the tiny lightsomeness
of Phoebe's figure, were perhaps in some fit proportion with

the moral weight and substance, respectively, of the woman and the girl.

To the guest—to Hepzibah's brother—or Cousin Clifford, as Phoebe now began to call him—she was especially necessary. Not that he could ever be said to converse with her, or often manifest, in any other very definite mode, his sense of a charm in her society. But, if she were a long while absent, he became pettish and nervously restless, pacing the room to-and-fro, with the uncertainty that characterized all his movements; or else would sit broodingly in his great chair, resting his head on his hands, and evincing life only by an electric sparkle of ill-humor, whenever Hepzibah endeavored to arouse him. Phoebe's presence, and the contiguity of her fresh life to his blighted one, was usually all that he required. Indeed, such was the native gush and play of her spirit, that she was seldom perfectly quiet and undemonstrative, any more than a fountain ever ceases to dimple and warble with its flow. She possessed the gift of song, and that too so naturally, that you would as little think of inquiring whence she had caught it, or what master had taught her, as of asking the same questions about a bird, in whose small strain of music we recognize the voice of the Creator, as distinctly as in the loudest accents of His thunder. So long as Phoebe sang, she might stray at her own will about the house. Clifford was content, whether the sweet, airy homeliness of her tones came down from the upper chambers, or along the passage-way from the shop, or was sprinkled through the foliage of the pear-tree, inward from the garden, with the twinkling sunbeams. He would sit quietly, with a gentle pleasure gleaming over his face, brighter now, and now a little dimmer, as the song happened to float near him, or was more remotely heard. It pleased him best, however, when she sat on a low footstool at his knee.

It is perhaps remarkable, considering her temperament, that Phoebe oftener chose a strain of pathos than of gaiety.

But the young and happy are not ill-pleased to temper their life with a transparent shadow. The deepest pathos of Phoebe's voice and song, moreover, came sifted through the golden texture of a cheery spirit, and was somehow so interfused with the quality thence acquired, that one's heart felt all the lighter for having wept at it. Broad mirth, in the sacred presence of dark misfortune, would have jarred harshly and irreverently with the solemn symphony, that rolled its undertone through Hepzibah's and her brother's life. Therefore it was well that Phoebe so often chose sad themes, and not amiss that they ceased to be so sad, while she was singing them.

Becoming habituated to her companionship, Clifford readily showed how capable of imbibing pleasant tints, and gleams of cheerful light from all quarters, his nature must originally have been. He grew youthful, while she sat by him. A beauty—not precisely real, even in its utmost manifestation, and which a painter would have watched long to seize, and fix upon his canvass, and, after all, in vain—beauty, nevertheless, that was not a mere dream, would sometimes play upon and illuminate his face. It did more than to illuminate; it transfigured him with an expression that could only be interpreted as the glow of an exquisite and happy spirit. That gray hair, and those furrows—with their record of infinite sorrow, so deeply written across his brow, and so compressed, as with a futile effort to crowd in all the tale, that the whole inscription was made illegible—these, for the moment, vanished. An eye, at once tender and acute, might have beheld in the man some shadow of what he was meant to be. Anon, as age came stealing, like a sad twilight, back over his figure, you would have felt tempted to hold an argument with Destiny, and affirm, that either this being should not have been made mortal, or mortal existence should have been tempered to his qualities. There seemed no necessity for his having drawn breath, at all;—the world never wanted him;—but, as he had breathed, it ought always to have been the balmicst of summer air. The same perplexity will invariably haunt us with regard to natures, that tend to feed exclusively upon the Beautiful, let their earthly fate be as lenient as it may.

Phoebe, it is probable, had but a very imperfect comprehension of the character, over which she had thrown so beneficent a spell. Nor was it necessary. The fire upon the hearth can gladden a whole semi-circle of faces roundabout it, but need not know the individuality of one among them all. Indeed, there was something too fine and delicate in Clifford's traits, to be perfectly appreciated by one whose sphere lay so much in the Actual as Phoebe's did. For Clifford, however, the reality, and simplicity, and thorough homeliness of the girl's nature, were as powerful a charm as any that she possessed. Beauty, it is true, and beauty almost perfect in its own style, was indispensable. Had Phoebe been coarse in feature, shaped clumsily, of a harsh voice, and uncouthly mannered, she might have been rich with all good gifts, beneath this unfortunate exterior; and still, so long as she wore the guise of woman, she would have shocked Clifford and depressed him by her lack of beauty. But nothing more beautiful—nothing prettier, at least—was ever made, than Phoebe. And, therefore, to this man—whose whole poor and impalpable enjoyment of existence, heretofore, and until both his heart and fancy died within him, had been a dream —whose images of women had more and more lost their warmth and substance, and been frozen, like the pictures of secluded artists, into the chillest ideality—to him, this little figure of the cheeriest household-life was just what he required, to bring him back into the breathing world. Persons who have wandered, or been expelled, out of the common track of things, even were it for a better system, desire nothing so much as to be led back. They shiver in their loneliness, be it on a mountain-top or in a dungeon. Now, Phoebe's presence made a home about her—that very sphere which the outcast, the prisoner, the potentate, the wretch beneath mankind, the wretch aside from it, or the wretch above it, instinctively pines after—a home! She was real! Holding her hand, you felt something; a tender something; a substance, and a warm one; and so long as you should feel its grasp, soft as it was, you might be certain that your place was good in the whole sympathetic chain of human nature. The world was no longer a delusion.

By looking a little farther in this direction, we might suggest an explanation of an often suggested mystery. Why are poets so apt to choose their mates, not for any similarity of poetic endowment, but for qualities which might make the happiness of the rudest handicraftsman, as well as that of the ideal craftsman of the spirit? Because, probably, at his highest elevation, the poet needs no human intercourse; but he finds it dreary to descend, and be a stranger.

There was something very beautiful in the relation that grew up between this pair; so closely and constantly linked together, yet with such a waste of gloomy and mysterious years from his birth-day to hers. On Clifford's part, it was the feeling of a man naturally endowed with the liveliest sensibility to feminine influence, but who had never quaffed the cup of passionate love, and knew that it was now too late. He knew it, with the instinctive delicacy that had survived his intellectual decay. Thus, his sentiment for Phoebe, without being paternal, was not less chaste than if she had been his daughter. He was a man, it is true, and recognized her as a woman. She was his only representative of womankind. He took unfailing note of every charm that appertained to her sex, and saw the ripeness of her lips, and the virginal developement of her bosom. All her little, womanly ways, budding out of her like blossoms on a young fruit-tree, had their effect on him, and sometimes caused his very heart to tingle with the keenest thrills of pleasure. At such moments—

for the effect was seldom more than momentary—the half-torpid man would be full of harmonious life, just as a long-silent harp is full of sound, when the musician's fingers sweep across it. But, after all, it seemed rather a perception, or a sympathy, than a sentiment belonging to himself as an individual. He read Phoebe, as he would a sweet and simple story; he listened to her, as if she were a verse of household poetry, which God, in requital of his bleak and dismal lot, had permitted some angel, that most pitied him, to warble through the house. She was not an actual fact for him, but the interpretation of all that he had lacked on earth, brought warmly home to his conception; so that this mere symbol or lifelike picture had almost the comfort of reality.

But we strive in vain to put the idea into words. No adequate expression of the beauty and profound pathos, with which it impresses us, is attainable. This being, made only for happiness, and heretofore so miserably failing to be happy —his tendencies so hideously thwarted, that, some unknown time ago, the delicate springs of his character, never morally or intellectually strong, had given way, and he was now imbecile—this poor, forlorn voyager from the Islands of the Blest,[4] in a frail bark, on a tempestuous sea, had been flung, by the last mountain-wave of his shipwreck, into a quiet harbor. There, as he lay more than half-lifeless on the strand, the fragrance of an earthly rosebud had come to his nostrils, and, as odors will, had summoned up reminiscences or visions of all the living and breathing beauty, amid which he should have had his home. With his native susceptibility of happy influences, he inhales the slight, ethereal rapture into his soul, and expires!

And how did Phoebe regard Clifford? The girl's was not one of those natures which are most attracted by what is strange and exceptional in human character. The path, which would best have suited her, was the well-worn track of ordinary life; the companions, in whom she would most have

4. The Islands of the Blest, or Elysium, first mentioned by Homer and Hesoid, was a mythical place at the end of the earth where those who had died, but were exempted from death, were translated by the gods; therefore, as Hawthorne uses it, a state which is neither life nor death.

delighted, were such as one encounters at every turn. The mystery which enveloped Clifford, so far as it affected her at all, was an annoyance, rather than the piquant charm which many women might have found in it. Still, her native kindliness was brought strongly into play, not by what was darkly picturesque in his situation, nor so much even by the finer grace of his character, as by the simple appeal of a heart so forlorn as his, to one so full of genuine sympathy as hers. She gave him an affectionate regard, because he needed so much love, and seemed to have received so little. With a ready tact, the result of ever-active and wholesome sensibility, she discerned what was good for him, and did it. Whatever was morbid in his mind and experience, she ignored, and thereby kept their intercourse healthy by the incautious, but, as it were, heaven-directed freedom of her whole conduct. The sick in mind, and perhaps in body, are rendered more darkly and hopelessly so, by the manifold reflection of their disease, mirrored back from all quarters, in the deportment of those about them; they are compelled to inhale the poison of their own breath, in infinite repetition. But Phoebe afforded her poor patient a supply of purer air. She impregnated it, too, not with a wild-flower scent—for wildness was no trait of hers—but with the perfume of garden-roses, pinks, and other blossoms of much sweetness, which nature and man have consented together in making grow, from summer to summer, and from century to century. Such a flower was Phoebe, in her relation with Clifford, and such the delight that he inhaled from her.

Yet, it must be said, her petals sometimes drooped a little, in consequence of the heavy atmosphere about her. She grew more thoughtful than heretofore. Looking aside at Clifford's face, and seeing the dim, unsatisfactory elegance, and the intellect almost quenched, she would try to inquire what had been his life. Was he always thus? Had this veil been over him from his birth?—this veil, under which far more of his spirit was hidden than revealed, and through which he so imperfectly discerned the actual world—or was its gray texture woven of some dark calamity? Phoebe loved no riddles, and would have been glad to escape the perplexity of this one. Nevertheless, there was so far a good result of her meditations on Clifford's character, that, when her involuntary conjectures, together with the tendency of every strange circumstance to tell its own story, had gradually taught her the fact, it had no terrible effect upon her. Let the world have done him what vast wrong it might, she knew Cousin Clifford too well—or fancied so—ever to shudder at the touch of his thin, delicate fingers.

Within a few days after the appearance of this remarkable inmate, the routine of life had established itself with a good deal of uniformity in the old house of our narrative. In the morning, very shortly after breakfast, it was Clifford's custom to fall asleep in his chair; nor, unless accidentally disturbed, would he emerge from a dense cloud of slumber, or the thinner mists that flitted to-and-fro, until well towards noonday. These hours of drowsyhead were the season of the old gentlewoman's attendance on her brother, while Phoebe took charge of the shop; an arrangement which the public speedily understood, and evinced their decided preference of the younger shopwoman by the multiplicity of their calls, during her administration of affairs. Dinner over, Hepzibah took her knitting-work—a long stocking of gray yarn, for her brother's winter-wear—and with a sigh, and a scowl of affectionate farewell to Clifford, and a gesture enjoining watchfulness on Phoebe, went to take her seat behind the counter. It was now the young girl's turn to be the nurse, the guardian, the playmate—or whatever is the fitter phrase—of the gray haired man.

## X

# THE PYNCHEON-GARDEN

CLIFFORD, except for Phoebe's more active instigation, would ordinarily have yielded to the torpor which had crept through all his modes of being, and which sluggishly counselled him to sit in his morning chair, till eventide. But the girl seldom failed to propose a removal to the garden, where Uncle Venner and the Daguerreotypist had made such repairs on the roof of the ruinous arbor, or summer-house, that it was now a sufficient shelter from sunshine and casual showers. The hop-vine, too, had begun to grow luxuriantly over the sides of the little edifice, and made an interior of verdant seclusion, with innumerable peeps and glimpses into the wider solitude of the garden.

Here, sometimes, in this green play-place of flickering light, Phoebe read to Clifford. Her acquaintance, the artist, who appeared to have a literary turn, had supplied her with works of fiction, in pamphlet-form, and a few volumes of poetry, in altogether a different style and taste from those which Hepzibah selected for his amusement. Small thanks were due to the books, however, if the girl's readings were in any degree more successful than her elderly cousin's. Phoebe's voice had always a pretty music in it, and could either enliven Clifford, by its sparkle and gaiety of tone, or soothe him by a continued flow of pebbly and brook-like cadences. But the fictions—in which the country-girl, unused to works of that nature, often became deeply absorbed—interested her strange auditor very little, or not at all. Pictures of life, scenes of passion or sentiment, wit, humor, and pathos, were all thrown away, or worse than thrown away, on Clifford; either because he lacked an experience by which to test their truth, or because his own griefs were a touch-stone of reality that few feigned emotions could withstand. When Phoebe broke into a peal of merry laughter at what she read, he would now and then laugh for sympathy, but oftener respond with a troubled, questioning look. If a tear—a maiden's sunshiny tear, over imaginary woe—dropt upon some melancholy page, Clifford either took it as a token of actual calamity, or else grew peevish, and angrily motioned her to close the volume. And wisely, too! Is not the world sad enough, in genuine earnest, without making a pastime of mock-sorrows?

With poetry, it was rather better. He delighted in the swell and subsidence of the rhythm, and the happily recurring rhyme. Nor was Clifford incapable of feeling the sentiment of poetry—not perhaps where it was highest or deepest—but where it was most flitting and ethereal. It was impossible to foretell in what exquisite verse the awakening spell might lurk; but, on raising her eyes from the page to Clifford's face, Phoebe would be made aware, by the light breaking through it, that a more delicate intelligence than her own had caught a lambent flame from what she read. One glow of this kind, however, was often the precursor of gloom, for many hours afterward, because, when the glow left him, he seemed conscious of a missing sense and power, and groped about for them, as if a blind man should go seeking his lost eyesight.

It pleased him more, and was better for his inward welfare, that Phoebe should talk, and make passing occurrences vivid to his mind by her accompanying description and remarks. The life of the garden offered topics enough for such discourse as suited Clifford best. He never failed to inquire what flowers had bloomed, since yesterday. His feeling for flowers was very exquisite, and seemed not so much a taste, as an emotion; he was fond of sitting with one in his hand, intently observing it, and looking from its petals into Phoebe's face, as if the garden-flower were the sister of the household-maiden. Not merely was there a delight in the flower's perfume, or pleasure in its beautiful form, and the delicacy or brightness of its hue; but Clifford's enjoyment was accompanied with a perception of life, character, and individuality, that made him love these blossoms of the garden, as if they were endowed with sentiment and intelligence. This affection and sympathy for flowers is almost exclusively a woman's trait. Men, if endowed with it by nature, soon lose, forget, and learn to despise it, in their contact with coarser things than flowers. Clifford, too, had long forgotten it, but found it again, now, as he slowly revived from the chill torpor of his life.[1]

It is wonderful how many pleasant incidents continually came to pass in that secluded garden-spot, when once Phoebe had set herself to look for them. She had seen or heard a bee there, on the first day of her acquaintance with the place. And often—almost continually, indeed—since then, the bees kept coming thither, Heaven knows why, or by what pertinacious desire for far-fetched sweets; when, no doubt, there were broad clover-fields, and all kinds of garden-growth, much nearer home than this. Thither the bees came, however, and plunged into the squash-blossoms, as if there were no other squash vines within a long day's flight, or as if the soil of Hepzibah's garden gave its productions just the very quality which these laborious little wizards wanted, in order to impart the Hymettus[2] odor to their whole hive of New England honey. When Clifford heard their sunny, buzzing murmur, in the heart of the great, yellow blossoms, he looked about him with a joyful sense of warmth, and blue sky, and green

1. "My wife *** has, in perfection, the love and taste for flowers, without which a woman is a monster—and which it would be well for men to possess if they can." (*American Notebooks*, entry dated August 6, 1842.)
2. A mountain in east-central Greece noted for its honey.

grass, and of God's free air in the whole height from earth to heaven. After all, there need be no question why the bees came to that one green nook, in the dusty town. God sent them thither to gladden our poor Clifford! They brought the rich summer with them, in requital of a little honey.

When the bean-vines began to flower on the poles, there was one particular variety which bore a vivid scarlet blossom. The Daguerreotypist had found these beans in a garret, over one of the seven gables, treasured up in an old chest of drawers by some horticultural Pyncheon of days gone-by, who doubtless meant to sow them, the next summer, but was himself first sown in Death's garden-ground. By way of testing whether there was still a living germ in such ancient seeds, Holgrave had planted some of them; and the result of his experiment was a splendid row of bean-vines, clambering early to the full height of the poles, and arraying them, from top to bottom, in a spiral profusion of red blossoms. And, ever since the unfolding of the first bud, a multitude of humming-birds had been attracted thither. At times, it seemed as if, for every one of the hundred blossoms, there was one of these tiniest fowls of the air, a thumb's bigness of burnished plumage, hovering and vibrating about the bean-poles. It was with indescribable interest, and even more than childish delight, that Clifford watched the humming-birds. He used to thrust his head softly out of the arbor, to see them the better; all the while, too, motioning Phoebe to be quiet, and snatching glimpses of the smile upon her face, so as to heap his enjoyment up the higher with her sympathy. He had not merely grown young; he was a child again.

Hepzibah, whenever she happened to witness one of these fits of miniature enthusiasm, would shake her head, with a strange mingling of the mother and sister, and of pleasure and sadness, in her aspect. She said that it had always been thus with Clifford, when the humming-birds came—always, from his babyhood—and that his delight in them had been one of the earliest tokens by which he showed his love for beautiful things. And it was a wonderful coincidence, the good lady thought, that the artist should have planted these scarlet-flowering beans—which the humming-birds sought, far and wide, and which had not grown in the Pyncheon-garden before, for forty years—on the very summer of Clifford's return.

Then would the tears stand in poor Hepzibah's eyes, or overflow them with a too abundant gush, so that she was fain to betake herself into some corner, lest Clifford should espy her agitation. Indeed, all the enjoyments of this period were provocative of tears. Coming so late as it did, it was a kind of Indian summer, with a mist in its balmiest sunshine, and decay and death in its gaudiest delight. The more Clifford seemed to taste the happiness of a child, the sadder was the difference to be recognized. With a mysterious and terrible Past, which had annihilated his memory, and a blank Future before him, he had only this visionary and impalpable Now, which, if you once look closely at it, is nothing. He himself, as was perceptible by many symptoms, lay darkly behind his pleasure, and knew it to be a baby-play, which he was to toy and trifle with, instead of thoroughly believing. Clifford saw, it may be, in the mirror of his deeper consciousness, that he was an example and representative of that great chaos of people, whom an inexplicable Providence is continually putting at cross-purposes with the world; breaking what seems its own promise in their nature; withholding their proper food, and setting poison before them for a banquet; and thus—when it might so easily, as one would think, have been adjusted otherwise—making their existence a strangeness, a solitude, and torment. All his life long, he had been learning how to be wretched, as one learns a foreign tongue;[3] and now, with the lesson thoroughly at heart, he could with difficulty comprehend his little, airy happiness. Frequently, there was a dim shadow of doubt in his eyes.—"Take my

3. This curious comparison can be ascribed to Hawthorne's great difficulty in learning German. In his *American Notebooks* in an entry dated April 25, 1843, he mentions being "on the point of choking with a huge German word."

hand, Phoebe," he would say, "and pinch it hard with your little fingers! Give me a rose, that I may press its thorns, and prove myself awake, by the sharp touch of pain!"— Evidently, he desired this prick of a trifling anguish, in order to assure himself, by that quality which he best knew to be real, that the garden, and the seven weather-beaten gables, and Hepzibah's scowl and Phoebe's smile, were real, like-wise. Without this signet in his flesh, he could have attrib-uted no more substance to them, than to the empty confusion of imaginary scenes with which he had fed his spirit, until even that poor sustenance was exhausted.

The author needs great faith in his reader's sympathy; else he must hesitate to give details so minute, and incidents apparently so trifling, as are essential to make up the idea of this garden-life. It was the Eden of a thunder-smitten Adam, who had fled for refuge thither out of the same dreary and perilous wilderness, into which the original Adam was expelled.

One of the available means of amusement, of which Phoebe made the most, in Clifford's behalf, was that feath-ered society, the hens, a breed of whom, as we have already said, was an immemorial heirloom in the Pyncheon family. In compliance with a whim of Clifford, as it troubled him to see them in confinement, they had been set at liberty, and now roamed at will about the garden; doing some little mischief, but hindered from escape by buildings, on three sides, and the difficult peaks of a wooden fence, on the other. They spent much of their abundant leisure on the margin of Maule's Well, which was haunted by a kind of snail, evi-dently a tidbit to their palates; and the brackish water itself, however nauseous to the rest of the world, was so greatly esteemed by these fowls, that they might be seen tasting, turning up their heads, and smacking their bills, with pre-cisely the air of wine-bibbers round a probationary cask. Their generally quiet, yet often brisk, and constantly diversified talk, one to another, or sometimes in soliloquy—as they scratched worms out of the rich, black soil, or pecked at such plants as suited their taste—had such a domestic tone, that it was almost a wonder why you could not establish a regular interchange of ideas about household matters, human and gallinaceous. All hens are well-worth studying, for the piquancy and rich variety of their manners; but by no possibility can there have been other fowls, of such odd appearance and deportment as these ancestral ones. They probably embodied the traditionary peculiarities of their whole line of progenitors, derived through an unbroken succession of eggs; or else this individual Chanticleer and his two wives had grown to be humorists, and a little crack-brained withal, on account of their solitary way of life, and out of sympathy for Hepzibah, their lady-patroness.

Queerly indeed they looked! Chanticleer himself, though stalking on two stilt-like legs, with the dignity of interminable descent in all his gestures, was hardly bigger than an ordinary partridge; his two wives were about the size of quails; and as for the one chicken, it looked small enough to be still in the egg, and, at the same time, sufficiently old, withered, wizened, and experienced, to have been the founder of the antiquated race. Instead of being the youngest of the family, it rather seemed to have aggregated into itself the ages, not only of these living specimens of the breed, but of all its forefathers and fore-mothers, whose united excellencies and oddities were squeezed into its little body. Its mother evidently regarded it as the one chicken of the world, and as necessary, in fact, to the world's continuance, or, at any rate, to the equilibrium of the present system of affairs, whether in church or state. No lesser sense of the infant fowl's importance could have justified, even in a mother's eyes, the perseverance with which she watched over its safety, ruffling her small person to twice its proper size, and flying in everybody's face that so much as looked towards her hopeful

progeny. No lower estimate could have vindicated the indefatigable zeal with which she scratched, and her unscrupulousness in digging up the choicest flower or vegetable, for
the sake of the fat earth-worm at its root. Her nervous cluck,
when the chicken happened to be hidden in the long grass
or under the squash-leaves; her gentle croak of satisfaction,
while sure of it beneath her wing; her note of ill-concealed
fear and obstreperous defiance, when she saw her arch-enemy,
a neighbor's cat, on the top of the high fence;—one or other
of these sounds was to be heard at almost every moment of
the day. By degrees, the observer came to feel nearly as much
interest in this chicken of illustrious race, as the mother-
hen did.

Phoebe, after getting well acquainted with the old hen,
was sometimes permitted to take the chicken in her hand,
which was quite capable of grasping its cubic inch or two
of body. While she curiously examined its hereditary marks—
the peculiar speckle of its plumage, the funny tuft on its
head, and a knob on each of its legs—the little biped, as she
insisted, kept giving her a sagacious wink. The Daguerreotypist once whispered her, that these marks betokened the
oddities of the Pyncheon family, and that the chicken itself
was a symbol of the life of the old house; embodying its interpretation, likewise, although an unintelligible one, as such
clues generally are. It was a feathered riddle; a mystery
hatched out of an egg, and just as mysterious as if the egg
had been addle!

The second of Chanticleer's two wives, ever since Phoebe's
arrival, had been in a state of heavy despondency, caused,
as it afterwards appeared, by her inability to lay an egg. One
day, however, by her self-important gait, the sideway turn
of her head, and the cock of her eye, as she pried into one
and another nook of the garden—croaking to herself, all the
while, with inexpressible complacency—it was made evident
that this identical hen, much as mankind undervalued her,

carried something about her person, the worth of which was not to be estimated either in gold or precious stones.[4] Shortly after, there was a prodigious cackling and gratulation of Chanticleer and all his family, including the wizened chicken, who appeared to understand the matter, quite as well as did his sire, his mother, or his aunt. That afternoon, Phoebe found a diminutive egg—not in the regular nest—it was far too precious to be trusted there—but cunningly hidden under the currant-bushes, on some dry stalks of last year's grass. Hepzibah, on learning the fact, took possession of the egg and appropriated it to Clifford's breakfast, on account of a certain delicacy of flavor, for which, as she affirmed, these eggs had always been famous. Thus unscrupulously did the old gentlewoman sacrifice the continuance, perhaps, of an ancient feathered race, with no better end than to supply her brother with a dainty that hardly filled the bowl of a teaspoon! It must have been in reference to this outrage, that Chanticleer, the next day, accompanied by the bereaved mother of the egg, took his post in front of Phoebe and Clifford, and delivered himself of a harangue that might have proved as long as his own pedigree, but for a fit of merriment on Phoebe's part. Hereupon, the offended fowl stalked away on his long stilts, and utterly withdrew his notice from Phoebe and the rest of human nature; until she made her peace with an offering of spice-cake, which, next to snails, was the delicacy most in favor with his aristocratic taste.

We linger too long, no doubt, beside this paltry rivulet of life that flowed through the garden of the Pyncheon-house. But we deem it pardonable to record these mean incidents, and poor delights, because they proved so greatly to Clifford's benefit. They had the earth-smell in them, and contributed to give him health and substance. Some of his occupations wrought less desirably upon him. He had a singular propensity, for example, to hang over Maule's Well, and look at the constantly shifting phantasmagoria of figures,

4. "The queer gestures and sounds of a hen, looking about for a place to deposit her egg; her self-important gait; the side-way turn of her head, and cock of her eye, as she prys [sic] into one and another nook, croaking all the while—evidently with the idea that the egg in question is the most important

produced by the agitation of the water over the mosaic-work of colored pebbles, at the bottom. He said that faces looked upward to him there—beautiful faces, arrayed in be-witching smiles—each momentary face so fair and rosy, and every smile so sunny, that he felt wronged at its departure, until the same flitting witchcraft made a new one. But some-times he would suddenly cry out—"The dark face gazes at me!"—and be miserable, the whole day afterwards. Phoebe, when she hung over the fountain by Clifford's side, could see nothing of all this—neither the beauty nor the ugliness—but only the colored pebbles, looking as if the gush of the water shook and disarranged them. And the dark face, that so troubled Clifford, was no more than the shadow, thrown from a branch of one of the damson-trees, and breaking the inner light of Maule's Well. The truth was, however, that his fancy—reviving faster than his will and judgement, and always stronger than they—created shapes of loveliness that were symbolic of his native character, and now and then a stern and dreadful shape, that typified his fate.

On Sundays, after Phoebe had been at church—for the girl had a church-going conscience, and would hardly have been at ease, had she missed either prayer, singing, sermon, or benediction—after church-time, therefore, there was ordi-narily a sober little festival in the garden. In addition to Clifford, Hepzibah, and Phoebe, two guests made up the company. One was the artist, Holgrave, who, in spite of his consociation with reformers, and his other queer and ques-tionable traits, continued to hold an elevated place in Hep-zibah's regard. The other, we are almost ashamed to say, was the venerable Uncle Venner, in a clean shirt, and a broad-cloth coat, more respectable than his ordinary wear; inasmuch as it was neatly patched on each elbow, and might be called an entire garment, except for a slight inequality in the length of its skirts. Clifford, on several occasions, had seemed to enjoy the old man's intercourse, for the sake of his mellow,

thing that has been brought to pass since the world began. A speckled black and white and tufted hen of ours does it to most ludicrous perfection; and there is something laughably womanish in it too." (*American Notebooks*, en-try dated July 14, 1850.)

cheerful vein, which was like the sweet flavor of a frost-bitten apple, such as one picks up under the tree, in December. A man, at the very lowest point of the social scale, was easier and more agreeable for the fallen gentleman to encounter, than a person at any of the intermediate degrees; and, moreover, as Clifford's young manhood had been lost, he was fond of feeling himself comparatively youthful, now, in apposition with the patriarchal age of Uncle Venner. In fact, it was sometimes observable, that Clifford half wilfully hid from himself the consciousness of being stricken in years, and cherished visions of an earthly future still before him; visions, however, too indistinctly drawn to be followed by disappointment—though, doubtless, by depression—when any casual incident or recollection made him sensible of the withered leaf.

So this oddly composed little social party used to assemble under the ruinous arbor. Hepzibah—stately as ever, at heart, and yielding not an inch of her old gentility, but resting upon it so much the more, as justifying a princesslike condescension —exhibited a not ungraceful hospitality. She talked kindly to the vagrant artist, and took sage counsel, lady as she was, with the wood-sawyer, the messenger of everybody's petty errands, the patched philosopher. And Uncle Venner, who had studied the world at street-corners, and at other posts equally well adapted for just observation, was as ready to give out his wisdom as a town-pump to give water.

"Miss Hepzibah, Ma'am," said he once, after they had all been cheerful together, "I really enjoy these quiet little meetings, of a Sabbath afternoon. They are very much like what I expect to have, after I retire to my farm!"

"Uncle Venner," observed Clifford, in a drowsy, inward tone, "is always talking about his farm. But I have a better scheme for him, by-and-by. We shall see!"

"Ah, Mr. Clifford Pyncheon," said the man of patches, "you may scheme for me as much as you please; but I'm not going to give up this one scheme of my own, even if I never bring it really to pass. It does seem to me that men make a wonderful mistake in trying to heap up property upon property. If I had done so, I should feel as if Providence was not bound to take care of me; and, at all events, the city wouldn't be! I'm one of those people who think that Infinity is big enough for us all—and Eternity long enough!"

"Why, so they are, Uncle Venner," remarked Phoebe after a pause; for she had been trying to fathom the profundity and appositeness of this concluding apothegm. "But, for this short life of ours, one would like a house and a moderate garden-spot of one's own."

"It appears to me," said the Daguerreotypist smiling, "that Uncle Venner has the principles of Fourier at the bottom of his wisdom; only they have not quite so much distinctness, in his mind, as in that of the systematizing Frenchman." [5]

"Come, Phoebe," said Hepzibah, "it is time to bring the currants."

And then, while the yellow richness of the declining sunshine still fell into the open space of the garden, Phoebe brought out a loaf of bread, and a China bowl of currants, freshly gathered from the bushes, and crushed with sugar. These, with water—but not from the fountain of ill-omen, close at hand—constituted all the entertainment. Meanwhile, Holgrave took some pains to establish an intercourse with Clifford; actuated, it might seem, entirely by an impulse of kindliness, in order that the present hour might be cheerfuller than most which the poor recluse had spent, or was destined yet to spend. Nevertheless, in the artist's deep, thoughtful, all-observant eyes, there was now-and-then an expression, not sinister, but questionable; as if he had some other interest in the scene than a stranger, a youthful and unconnected adventurer, might be supposed to have. With great mobility of outward mood, however, he applied himself to the task of enlivening the party, and with so much success, that even

5. Charles Fourier (1772–1837) was a French socialist writer. His projected Utopian reorganization of society along communistic principles was based on the harmonious interrelationship among all parts of the universe, animate and inanimate, spiritual and material. Fourier planned on social units of about

dark-hued Hepzibah threw off one tint of melancholy, and made what shift she could with the remaining portion. Phoebe said to herself—"How pleasant he can be!" As for Uncle Venner, as a mark of friendship and approbation, he readily consented to afford the young man his countenance in the way of his profession—not metaphorically, be it understood—but literally, by allowing a daguerreotype of his face, so familiar to the town, to be exhibited at the entrance of Holgrave's studio.

Clifford, as the company partook of their little banquet, grew to be the gayest of them all. Either it was one of those up-quivering flashes of the spirit, to which minds in an abnormal state are liable; or else the artist had subtly touched some chord that made musical vibration. Indeed, what with the pleasant summer-evening, and the sympathy of this little circle of not unkindly souls, it was perhaps natural that a character so susceptible as Clifford's should become animated, and show itself readily responsive to what was said around him. But he gave out his own thoughts, likewise, with an airy and fanciful glow; so that they glistened, as it were, through the arbor, and made their escape among the interstices of the foliage. He had been as cheerful, no doubt, while alone with Phoebe, but never with such tokens of acute, although partial intelligence.

But, as the sunlight left the peaks of the seven gables, so did the excitement fade out of Clifford's eyes. He gazed vaguely and mournfully about him, as if he missed something precious, and missed it the more drearily for not knowing precisely what it was.

"I want my happiness!" at last he murmured hoarsely and indistinctly, hardly shaping out the words. "Many, many years have I waited for it! It is late! It is late! I want my happiness!"

Alas, poor Clifford! You are old, and worn with troubles that ought never to have befallen you. You are partly crazy,

---

1,600 persons who would divide labor according to natural predilections. Hawthorne read Fourier in 1845 and, according to his wife, "was thoroughly disgusted." Sherbo (see BIBLIOGRAPHY) argues that Holgrave owes something to Albert Brisbane, America's leading Fourierist.

and partly imbecile; a ruin, a failure, as almost everybody is—though some in less degree, or less perceptibly, than their fellows. Fate has no happiness in store for you; unless your quiet home in the old family residence, with the faithful Hepzibah, and your long summer-afternoons with Phoebe, and these Sabbath festivals with Uncle Venner and the Daguerreotypist, deserve to be called happiness! Why not? If not the thing itself, it is marvellously like it, and the more so for that ethereal and intangible quality, which causes it all to vanish, at too close an introspection. Take it, therefore, while you may. Murmur not—question not—but make the most of it!

## XI

# THE ARCHED WINDOW

FROM the inertness, or what we may term the vegetative character of his ordinary mood, Clifford would perhaps have been content to spend one day after another, interminably—or, at least throughout the summer-time—in just the kind of life described in the preceding pages. Fancying, however, that it might be for his benefit occasionally to diversify the scene, Phoebe sometimes suggested that he should look out upon the life of the street. For this purpose, they used to mount the staircase together, to the second story of the house, where, at the termination of a wide entry, there was an arched window of uncommonly large dimensions, shaded by a pair of curtains. It opened above the porch, where there had formerly been a balcony, the balustrade of which had long since gone to decay, and been removed. At this arched window, throwing it open, but keeping himself in comparative obscurity by means of the curtain, Clifford had an opportunity of witnessing such a portion of the great world's movement, as might be supposed to roll through one of the retired streets of a not very populous city. But he and Phoebe made a sight as well worth seeing as any that the city could exhibit. The pale, gray, childish, aged, melancholy, yet often simply cheerful, and sometimes delicately intelligent, aspect of Clifford, peering from behind the faded crim-

son of the curtain—watching the monotony of every-day occurrences with a kind of inconsequential interest and earnestness—and, at every petty throb of his sensibility, turning for
sympathy to the eyes of the bright young girl!

If once he were fairly seated at the window, even Pyncheon-street would hardly be so dull and lonely but that,
somewhere or other along its extent, Clifford might discover
matter to occupy his eye, and titillate, if not engross, his observation. Things, familiar to the youngest child that had
begun its outlook at existence, seemed strange to him. A
cab; an omnibus, with its populous interior, dropping here-and-
there a passenger, and picking up another, and thus typifying
that vast rolling vehicle, the world, the end of whose journey
is everywhere, and nowhere;—these objects he followed
eagerly with his eyes, but forgot them, before the dust, raised
by the horses and wheels, had settled along their track. As
regarded novelties, (among which, cabs and omnibusses were
to be reckoned,) his mind appeared to have lost its proper
gripe and retentiveness. Twice or thrice, for example, during
the sunny hours of the day, a water-cart went along by the
Pyncheon-house, leaving a broad wake of moistened earth,
instead of the white dust that had risen at a lady's lightest
footfall; it was like a summer-shower, which the city-authori-
ties had caught and tamed, and compelled it into the com-
monest routine of their convenience. With the water-cart
Clifford could never grow familiar; it always affected him
with just the same surprise as at first. His mind took an apparently sharp impression from it, but lost the recollection of
this perambulatory shower, before its next re-appearance, as
completely as did the street itself, along which the heat so
quickly strewed white dust again. It was the same with the
railroad. Clifford could hear the obstreperous howl of the
steam-devil, and, by leaning a little way from the arched
window, could catch a glimpse of the trains of cars, flashing
a brief transit across the extremity of the street. The idea of

terrible energy, thus forced upon him, was new at every recurrence, and seemed to affect him as disagreeably, and with almost as much surprise, the hundredth time as the first.

Nothing gives a sadder sense of decay, than this loss or suspension of the power to deal with unaccustomed things and to keep up with the swiftness of the passing moment. It can merely be a suspended animation; for, were the power actually to perish, there would be little use of immortality. We are less than ghosts, for the time being, whenever this calamity befalls us.

Clifford was indeed the most inveterate of conservatives. All the antique fashions of the street were dear to him; even such as were characterized by a rudeness that would naturally have annoyed his fastidious senses. He loved the old rumbling and jolting carts, the former track of which he still found in his long-buried remembrance, as the observer of to-day finds the wheel-tracks of ancient vehicles, in Herculaneum.[1] The butcher's cart, with its snowy canopy, was an acceptable object; so was the fish-cart, heralded by its horn; so, likewise, was the countryman's cart of vegetables, plodding from door to door, with long pauses of the patient horse, while his owner drove a trade in turnips, carrots, summer-squashes, string-beans, green peas, and new potatoes, with half the housewives of the neighborhood. The baker's cart, with the harsh music of its bells, had a pleasant effect on Clifford, because, as few things else did, it jingled the very dissonance of yore. One afternoon, a scissor-grinder chanced to set his wheel a-going, under the Pyncheon-elm, and just in front of the arched window. Children came running with their mothers' scissors, or the carving-knife, or the paternal razor, or anything else that lacked an edge, (except, indeed, poor Clifford's wits,) that the grinder might apply the article to his magic wheel, and give it back as good as new. Round went the busily revolving machinery, kept in motion by the scissor-grinder's foot, and wore away the hard steel against the hard

1. The most prominent city, after Pompeii, destroyed by the eruption of Vesuvius in 79 A.D.

stone, whence issued an intense and spiteful prolongation of a hiss, as fierce as those emitted by Satan and his compeers in Pandemonium,[2] though squeezed into smaller compass. It was an ugly, little, venomous serpent of a noise, as ever did petty violence to human ears. But Clifford listened with rapturous delight. The sound, however disagreeable, had very brisk life in it, and, together with the circle of curious children, watching the revolutions of the wheel, appeared to give him a more vivid sense of active, bustling, and sunshiny existence, than he had attained in almost any other way. Nevertheless, its charm lay chiefly in the past; for the scissor-grinder's wheel had hissed in his childish ears.

He sometimes made doleful complaint, that there were no stage-coaches, now-a-days. And he asked, in an injured tone, what had become of all those old square-top chaises, with wings sticking out on either side, that used to be drawn by a plough-horse, and driven by a farmer's wife and daughter, peddling whortle-berries and black-berries about the town. Their disappearance made him doubt, he said, whether the berries had not left off growing in the broad pastures, and along the shady country-lanes.

✳    But anything that appealed to the sense of beauty, in however humble a way, did not require to be recommended by these old associations. This was observable, when one of those Italian boys (who are rather a modern feature of our streets) came along, with his barrel-organ, and stopt under the wide and cool shadows of the elm. With his quick professional eye, he took note of the two faces watching him from the arched window, and, opening his instrument, began to scatter its melodies abroad. He had a monkey on his shoulder, dressed in a highland plaid; and, to complete the sum of splendid attractions wherewith he presented himself to the public, there was a company of little figures, whose sphere and habitation was in the mahogany case of his organ, and whose principle of life was the music, which the Italian

2. The capital of Satan and his peers in John Milton's *Paradise Lost*. Hawthorne is thinking of the meeting of the fallen angels in Pandemonium when "dreadful was the din/of hissing through the Hall" (X.521–22).

made it his business to grind out. In all their variety of occupation—the cobbler, the blacksmith, the soldier, the lady with
her fan, the toper with his bottle, the milk-maid sitting by
her cow—this fortunate little society might truly be said to
enjoy a harmonious existence, and to make life literally a
dance. The Italian turned a crank; and, behold! every one
of these small individuals started into the most curious vivacity. The cobbler wrought upon a shoe; the blacksmith
hammered his iron; the soldier waved his glittering blade;
the lady raised a tiny breeze with her fan; the jolly toper
swigged lustily at his bottle; a scholar opened his book, with
eager thirst for knowledge, and turned his head to-and-fro
along the page; the milk-maid energetically drained her cow;
and a miser counted gold into his strong-box;—all at the same
turning of a crank. Yes; and moved by the self-same impulse,
a lover saluted his mistress on her lips! Possibly, some cynic,
at once merry and bitter, had desired to signify, in this pantomimic scene, that we mortals, whatever our business or
amusement—however serious, however trifling—all dance to
one identical tune, and, in spite of our ridiculous activity,
bring nothing finally to pass. For the most remarkable aspect
of the affair was, that, at the cessation of the music, everybody was petrified at once, from the most extravagant life
into a dead torpor. Neither was the cobbler's shoe finished,
nor the blacksmith's iron shaped out; nor was there a drop
less of brandy in the toper's bottle, nor a drop more of milk
in the milk-maid's pail, nor one additional coin in the miser's
strong-box; nor was the scholar a page deeper in his book.
All were precisely in the same condition as before they made
themselves so ridiculous by their haste to toil, to enjoy, to
accumulate gold, and to become wise. Saddest of all, moreover, the lover was none the happier for the maiden's granted
kiss! But, rather than swallow this last too acrid ingredient,
we reject the whole moral of the show.

The monkey, meanwhile, with a thick tail curling out into

preposterous prolixity from beneath his tartans, took his station at the Italian's feet. He turned a wrinkled and abominable little visage to every passer-by, and to the circle of children that soon gathered round, and to Hepzibah's shop-door, and upward to the arched window, whence Phoebe and Clifford were looking down. Every moment, also, he took off his highland bonnet, and performed a bow and scrape. Sometimes, moreover, he made personal application to individuals, holding out his small black palm, and otherwise plainly signifying his excessive desire for whatever filthy lucre might happen to be in anybody's pocket. The mean and low, yet strangely man-like expression of his wilted countenance; the prying and crafty glance, that showed him ready to gripe at every miserable advantage; his enormous tail, (too enormous to be decently concealed under his gabardine,) and the deviltry of nature which it betokened;—take this monkey just as he was, in short, and you could desire no better image of the Mammon[3] of copper-coin, symbolizing the grossest form of the love of money. Neither was there any possibility of satisfying the covetous little devil. Phoebe threw down a whole handfull of cents, which he picked up with joyless eagerness, handed them over to the Italian for safe-keeping, and immediately re-commenced a series of pantomimic petitions for more.

Doubtless, more than one New-Englander—or let him be of what country he might, it is as likely to be the case—passed by, and threw a look at the monkey, and went on, without imagining how nearly his own moral condition was here exemplified. Clifford, however, was a being of another order. He had taken childish delight in the music, and smiled, too, at the figures which it set in motion. But, after looking awhile at the long-tailed imp, he was so shocked by his horrible ugliness, spiritual as well as physical, that he actually began to shed tears; a weakness which men of merely delicate endowments—and destitute of the fiercer, deeper, and more tragic power of laughter—can hardly avoid, when the worst

3. The personification of material covetousness, who, as a character in *Paradise Lost,* is designated as the least of the fallen angels; for even in Heaven, Mammon admired more "The riches of Heaven's pavement, trodden gold,/ Than aught divine *** " (I.679–83).

and meanest aspect of life happens to be presented to them.[4]

Pyncheon-street was sometimes enlivened by spectacles of more imposing pretensions than the above, and which brought the multitude along with them. With a shivering repugnance at the idea of personal contact with the world, a powerful impulse still seized on Clifford, whenever the rush and roar of the human tide grew strongly audible to him. This was made evident, one day, when a political procession, with hundreds of flaunting banners, and drums, fifes, clarions, and cymbals, reverberating between the rows of buildings, marched all through town, and trailed its length of trampling footsteps, and most infrequent uproar, past the ordinarily quiet House of the Seven Gables. As a mere object of sight, nothing is more deficient in picturesque features than a procession, seen in its passage through narrow streets. The spectator feels it to be fool's play, when he can distinguish the tedious common-place of each man's visage, with the perspiration and weary self-importance on it, and the very cut of his pantaloons, and the stiffness or laxity of his shirt-collar, and the dust on the back of his black coat. In order to become majestic, it should be viewed from some vantage-point, as it rolls its slow and long array through the centre of a wide plain, or the stateliest public square of a city; for then, by its remoteness, it melts all the petty personalities, of which it is made up, into one broad mass of existence—one great life —one collected body of mankind, with a vast, homogeneous spirit animating it. But, on the other hand, if an impressible person, standing alone over the brink of one of these processions, should behold it, not in its atoms, but in its aggregate— as a mighty river of life, massive in its tide, and black with mystery, and, out of its depths, calling to the kindred depth within him—then the contiguity would add to the effect. It might so fascinate him, that he would hardly be restrained from plunging into the surging stream of human sympathies.

So it proved with Clifford. He shuddered; he grew pale,

4. This passage describing the organ-grinder's monkey and Clifford's response to it is based on an actual occurrence recorded in Hawthorne's notebook. See "Passages from *The American Notebooks*," p. 326.

he threw an appealing look at Hepzibah and Phoebe, who were with him at the window. They comprehended nothing of his emotions, and supposed him merely disturbed by the unaccustomed tumult. At last, with tremulous limbs, he started up, set his foot on the window-sill, and, in an instant more, would have been in the unguarded balcony. As it was, the whole procession might have seen him, a wild, haggard figure, his gray locks floating in the wind that waved their banners; a lonely being, estranged from his race, but now feeling himself man again, by virtue of the irrepressible instinct that possessed him. Had Clifford attained the balcony, he would probably have leaped into the street; but whether impelled by the species of terror, that sometimes urges its victim over the very precipice which he shrinks from, or by a natural magnetism, tending towards the great centre of humanity—it were not easy to decide. Both impulses might have wrought on him at once.

But his companions, affrighted by his gesture—which was that of a man hurried away, in spite of himself—seized Clifford's garment and held him back. Hepzibah shrieked. Phoebe, to whom all extravagance was a horror, burst into sobs and tears.

"Clifford, Clifford, are you crazy?" cried his sister.

"I hardly know, Hepzibah!" said Clifford, drawing a' long breath. "Fear nothing—it is over now—but had I taken that plunge, and survived it, methinks it would have made me another man!"

Possibly, in some sense, Clifford may have been right. He needed a shock; or perhaps he required to take a deep, deep plunge into the ocean of human life, and to sink down and be covered by its profoundness, and then to emerge, sobered, invigorated, restored to the world and to himself. Perhaps, again, he required nothing less than the great final remedy— death!

A similar yearning to renew the broken links of brotherhood with his kind sometimes showed itself in a milder form; and once it was made beautiful by the religion that lay even deeper than itself. In the incident now to be sketched, there was a touching recognition, on Clifford's part, of God's care and love towards him—towards this poor, forsaken man, who, if any mortal could, might have been pardoned for regarding himself as thrown aside, forgotten, and left to be the sport of some fiend, whose playfulness was an ecstacy of mischief.

It was the Sabbath morning; one of those bright, calm Sabbaths, with its own hallowed atmosphere, when Heaven seems to diffuse itself over the earth's face in a solemn smile, no less sweet than solemn. On such a Sabbath morn, were we pure enough to be its medium, we should be conscious of the earth's natural worship ascending through our frames, on whatever spot of ground we stood. The church-bells, with various tones, but all in harmony, were calling out, and responding to one another—"It is the Sabbath!—The Sabbath!—Yea; the Sabbath!"—and over the whole city, the bells scattered the blessed sounds, now slowly, now with livelier joy, now one bell alone, now all the bells together, crying earnestly —"It is the Sabbath!"—and flinging their accents afar off, to melt into the air, and pervade it with the holy word. The air, with God's sweetest and tenderest sunshine in it, was meet for mankind to breathe into their hearts, and send it forth again as the utterance of prayer.

Clifford sat at the window, with Hepzibah, watching the neighbors as they stept into the street. All of them, however unspiritual on other days, were transfigured by the Sabbath influence; so that their very garments—whether it were an old man's decent coat, well-brushed for the thousandth time, or a little boy's first sack and trowsers, finished yesterday by his mother's needle—had somewhat of the quality of ascension-robes. Forth, likewise, from the portal of the old house, stept Phoebe, putting up her small, green sunshade, and throwing upward a glance and smile of parting kindness to the faces at the arched window. In her aspect, there was a familiar gladness, and a holiness that you could play with, and yet reverence it as much as ever. She was like a prayer, offered up in the homeliest beauty of one's mother-tongue. Fresh was Phoebe, moreover, and airy and sweet in her apparel; as if nothing that she wore—neither her gown, nor her small straw bonnet, nor her little kerchief, any more than her snowy stockings—had ever been put on, before; or, if worn, were all the fresher for it, and with a fragrance as if they had lain among the rosebuds.

The girl waved her hand to Hepzibah and Clifford, and went up the street; a Religion in herself, warm, simple, true, with a substance that could walk on earth, and a spirit that was capable of Heaven.

"Hepzibah," asked Clifford, after watching Phoebe to the corner, "do you never go to church?"

"No, Clifford," she replied—"not these many, many years!"

"Were I to be there," he rejoined, "it seems to me that I could pray once more, when so many human souls were praying all around me!"

She looked into Clifford's face, and beheld there a soft, natural effusion; for his heart gushed out, as it were, and ran over at his eyes, in delightful reverence for God, and kindly affection for his human brethren. The emotion communicated itself to Hepzibah. She yearned to take him by the hand, and go and kneel down, they two together—both so long separate from the world, and, as she now recognized, scarcely friends with Him above—to kneel down among the people, and be reconciled to God and man at once.

"Dear brother," said she, earnestly, "let us go! We belong nowhere. We have not a foot of space, in any church, to kneel upon; but let us go to some place of worship, even if we stand in the broad aisle. Poor and forsaken as we are, some pew-door will be opened to us!"

So Hepzibah and her brother made themselves ready—as

ready as they could, in the best of their old-fashioned garments, which had hung on pegs, or been laid away in trunks,
so long that the dampness and mouldy smell of the past was
on them—made themselves ready, in their faded bettermost,
to go to church. They descended the staircase together, gaunt,
sallow Hepzibah, and pale, emaciated, age-stricken Clifford!
They pulled open the front-door, and stept across the threshold, and felt, both of them, as if they were standing in the
presence of the whole world, and with mankind's great and
terrible eye on them alone. The eye of their Father seemed
to be withdrawn, and gave them no encouragement. The
warm, sunny air of the street made them shiver. Their hearts
quaked within them, at the idea of taking one step further.

"It cannot be, Hepzibah!—it is too late," said Clifford with
deep sadness.—"We are ghosts! We have no right among
human beings—no right anywhere, but in this old house,
which has a curse on it, and which therefore we are doomed
to haunt. And, besides," he continued, with a fastidious
sensibility, inalienably characteristic of the man, "it would
not be fit nor beautiful, to go! It is an ugly thought, that I
should be frightful to my fellow-beings, and that children
would cling to their mothers' gowns, at sight of me!"

They shrank back into the dusky passage-way, and closed
the door. But, going up the staircase again, they found the
whole interior of the house tenfold more dismal, and the air
closer and heavier, for the glimpse and breath of freedom
which they had just snatched. They could not flee; their jailor
had but left the door ajar, in mockery, and stood behind it,
to watch them stealing out. At the threshold, they felt his
pitiless gripe upon them. For, what other dungeon is so dark
as one's own heart! What jailor so inexorable as one's self!

But it would be no fair picture of Clifford's state of mind,
were we to represent him as continually or prevailingly
wretched. On the contrary, there was no other man in the
city, we are bold to affirm, of so much as half his years, who

enjoyed so many lightsome and griefless moments, as himself.
He had no burthen of care upon him; there were none of
those questions and contingencies with the future to be
settled, which wear away all other lives, and render them
not worth having by the very process of providing for their
support. In this respect, he was a child; a child for the whole
term of his existence, be it long or short. Indeed, his life
seemed to be standing still at a period little in advance of
childhood, and to cluster all its reminiscences about that
epoch; just as, after the torpor of a heavy blow, the sufferer's
reviving consciousness goes back to a moment considerably
behind the accident that stupefied him. He sometimes told
Phoebe and Hepzibah his dreams, in which he invariably
played the part of a child, or a very young man. So vivid were
they, in his relation of them, that he once held a dispute
with his sister as to the particular figure or print of a chintz
morning-dress, which he had seen their mother wear, in the
dream of the preceding night. Hepzibah, piquing herself on
a woman's accuracy in such matters, held it to be slightly different from what Clifford described; but, producing the very
gown from an old trunk, it proved to be identical with his
remembrance of it. Had Clifford, every time that he emerged
out of dreams so lifelike, undergone the torture of transformation from a boy into an old and broken man, the daily
recurrence of the shock would have been too much to bear.
It would have caused an acute agony to thrill, from the morning twilight, all the day through, until bedtime, and even
then would have mingled a dull, inscrutable pain, and pallid
hue of misfortune, with the visionary bloom and adolescence
of his slumber. But the nightly moonshine interwove itself
with the morning mist, and enveloped him as in a robe, which
he hugged about his person, and seldom let realities pierce
through; he was not often quite awake, but slept open-eyed,
and perhaps fancied himself most dreaming, then.

Thus, lingering always so near his childhood, he had sympathies with children, and kept his heart the fresher thereby, like a reservoir into which rivulets come pouring, not far from the fountain-head. Though prevented, by a subtle sense of propriety, from desiring to associate with them, he loved few things better than to look out of the arched window, and see a little girl, driving her hoop along the sidewalk, or schoolboys at a game of ball. Their voices, also, were very pleasant to him, heard at a distance, all swarming and intermingling to-gether, as flies do in a sunny room.

Clifford would doubtless have been glad to share their sports. One afternoon, he was seized with an irresistible desire to blow soap-bubbles; an amusement, as Hepzibah told Phoebe apart, that had been a favorite one with her brother, when they were both children. Behold him, therefore, at the arched window, with an earthen pipe in his mouth! Behold him, with his gray hair, and a wan, unreal smile over his countenance, where still hovered a beautiful grace, which his worst enemy must have acknowledged to be spiritual and im-mortal, since it had survived so long! Behold him, scattering airy spheres abroad, from the window into the street! Little, impalpable worlds, were those soap-bubbles, with the big world depicted, in hues bright as imagination, on the nothing of their surface. It was curious to see how the passers-by re-garded these brilliant fantasies, as they came floating down, and made the dull atmosphere imaginative, about them. Some stopt to gaze, and perhaps carried a pleasant recollection of the bubbles, onward, as far as the street-corner; some looked angrily upward, as if poor Clifford wronged them, by setting an image of beauty afloat so near their dusty pathway. A great many put out their fingers, or their walking-sticks, to touch withal, and were perversely gratified, no doubt, when the bubble, with all its pictured earth and sky scene, vanished as if it had never been.

At length, just as an elderly gentleman of very dignified presence happened to be passing, a large bubble sailed majes-

tically down, and burst right against his nose! He looked up
—at first with a stern, keen glance, which penetrated at once
into the obscurity behind the arched window—then with a
smile, which might be conceived as diffusing a dog-day sultriness for the space of several yards about him.

"Aha, Cousin Clifford!" cried Judge Pyncheon. "What!
Still blowing soap-bubbles!"

The tone seemed as if meant to be kind and soothing, but
yet had a bitterness of sarcasm in it. As for Clifford, an absolute palsy of fear came over him. Apart from any definite
cause of dread, which his past experience might have given
him, he felt that native and original horror of the excellent
Judge, which is proper to a weak, delicate, and apprehensive
character, in the presence of massive strength. Strength is incomprehensible by weakness, and therefore the more terrible.
There is no greater bugbear than a strong-willed relative, in
the circle of his own connections.

# XII

# THE DAGUERREOTYPIST

IT MUST not be supposed that the life of a personage, naturally so active as Phoebe, could be wholly confined within the precincts of the old Pyncheon-house. Clifford's demands upon her time were usually satisfied, in those long days, considerably earlier than sunset. Quiet as his daily existence seemed, it nevertheless drained all the resources by which he lived. It was not physical exercise that overwearied him; for—except that he sometimes wrought a little with a hoe, or paced the garden-walk, or, in rainy weather, traversed a large, unoccupied room—it was his tendency to remain only too quiescent, as regarded any toil of the limbs and muscles. But either there was a smouldering fire within him, that consumed his vital energy, or the monotony, that would have dragged itself with benumbing effect over a mind differently situated, was no monotony to Clifford. Possibly, he was in a state of second growth and recovery, and was constantly assimilating nutriment for his spirit and intellect from sights, sounds, and events, which passed as a perfect void to persons more practised with the world. As all is activity and vicissitude to the new mind of a child, so might it be, likewise, to a mind that had undergone a kind of new creation, after its long-suspended life.

Be the cause what it might, Clifford commonly retired to

rest, thoroughly exhausted, while the sunbeams were still melting through his window-curtains, or were thrown with late lustre on the chamber-wall. And while he thus slept early, as other children do, and dreamed of childhood, Phoebe was free to follow her own tastes for the remainder of the day and evening.

This was a freedom essential to the health even of a character so little susceptible of morbid influences as that of Phoebe. The old house, as we have already said, had both the dry-rot and the damp-rot in its walls; it was not good to breathe no other atmosphere than that. Hepzibah, though she had her valuable and redeeming traits, had grown to be a kind of lunatic, by imprisoning herself so long in one place, with no other company than a single series of ideas, and but one affection, and one bitter sense of wrong. Clifford, the reader may perhaps imagine, was too inert to operate morally on his fellow-creatures, however intimate and exclusive their relations with him. But the sympathy or magnetism among human beings is more subtle and universal, than we think; it exists, indeed, among different classes of organized life, and vibrates from one to another. A flower, for instance, as Phoebe herself observed, always began to droop sooner in Clifford's hand, or Hepzibah's, than in her own; and by the same law, converting her whole daily life into a flower-fragrance for these two sickly spirits, the blooming girl must inevitably droop and fade, much sooner than if worn on a younger and happier breast. Unless she had now and then indulged her brisk impulses, and breathed rural air in a suburban walk, or ocean-breezes along the shore—had occasionally obeyed the impulse of nature, in New England girls, by attending a metaphysical or philosophical lecture, or viewing a seven-mile panorama, or listening to a concert—had gone shopping about the city, ransacking entire depôts of splendid merchandize, and bringing home a ribbon—had enjoyed, likewise, a little time to read the Bible in her chamber, and had stolen a little more, to think of her mother and her native place—unless for such moral medicines as the above, we should soon have beheld our poor Phoebe grow thin, and put on a bleached, unwholesome aspect, and assume strange, shy ways, prophetic of old-maidenhood and a cheerless future.

Even as it was, a change grew visible; a change partly to be regretted, although whatever charm it infringed upon was repaired by another, perhaps more precious. She was not so constantly gay, but had her moods of thought, which Clifford, on the whole, liked better than her former phase of unmingled cheerfulness; because now she understood him better and more delicately, and sometimes even interpreted him to himself. Her eyes looked larger, and darker, and deeper; so deep, at some silent moments, that they seemed like Artesian wells, down, down, into the infinite. She was less girlish than when we first beheld her, alighting from the omnibus; less girlish, but more a woman!

The only youthful mind, with which Phoebe had an opportunity of frequent intercourse, was that of the Daguerreotypist. Inevitably, by the pressure of the seclusion about them, they had been brought into habits of some familiarity. Had they met under different circumstances, neither of these young persons would have been likely to bestow much thought upon the other; unless, indeed, their extreme dissimilarity should have proved a principle of mutual attraction. Both, it is true, were characters proper to New England life, and possessing a common ground, therefore, in their more external developements; but as unlike, in their respective interiors, as if their native climes had been at world-wide distance. During the early part of their acquaintance, Phoebe had held back rather more than was customary with her frank and simple manners, from Holgrave's not very marked advances. Nor was she yet satisfied that she knew him well, although they almost daily met and talked together in a kind, friendly, and what seemed to be a familiar way.

The artist, in a desultory manner, had imparted to Phoebe something of his history. Young as he was, and had his career terminated at the point already attained, there had been enough of incident to fill, very creditably, an autobiographic volume. A romance on the plan of Gil Blas,[1] adapted to American society and manners, would cease to be a romance. The experience of many individuals among us, who think it hardly worth the telling, would equal the vicissitudes of the Spaniard's earlier life; while their ultimate success, or the point whither they tend, may be incomparably higher than any that a novelist would imagine for his hero. Holgrave, as he told Phoebe, somewhat proudly, could not boast of his origin, unless as being exceedingly humble, nor of his education, except that it had been the scantiest possible, and obtained by a few winter-months' attendance at a district-school. Left early to his own guidance, he had begun to be self-dependent while yet a boy; and it was a condition aptly suited to his natural force of will. Though now but twenty-two years old, (lacking some months, which are years, in such a life,) he had already been, first, a country-schoolmaster; next, a salesman in a country-store; and, either at the same time or afterwards, the political-editor of a country-newspaper. He had subsequently travelled New England and the middle states as a pedler, in the employment of a Connecticut manufactory of Cologne water and other essences. In an episodical way, he had studied and practised dentistry, and with very flattering success, especially in many of the factory-towns along our inland-streams. As a supernumerary official, of some kind or other, aboard a packet-ship, he had visited Europe, and found means, before his return, to see Italy, and part of France and Germany. At a later period, he had spent some months in a community of Fourierists.[2] Still more recently, he had been a public lecturer on Mesmerism,[3] for which science (as he assured Phoebe, and, indeed, satisfactorily proved by putting Chanticleer, who happened to be

1. *Gil Blas* (1715) by Alain René Le Sage is a famous French picaresque romance (the adventures of a rogue-hero) which humorously exposes the social and moral foibles of Spain.
2. Hawthorne spent "some months" in 1841 at Brook Farm, a Fourierist-like

scratching, near by, to sleep) he had very remarkable endowments.

His present phase, as a Daguerreotypist, was of no more
importance in his own view, nor likely to be more permanent,
than any of the preceding ones. It had been taken up with
the careless alacrity of an adventurer, who had his bread to
earn; it would be thrown aside as carelessly, whenever he
should choose to earn his bread by some other equally digres-
sive means. But what was most remarkable, and perhaps
showed a more than common poise in the young man, was
the fact, that, amid all these personal vicissitudes, he had
never lost his identity. Homeless as he had been—continually
changing his whereabout, and therefore responsible neither
to public opinion nor to individuals—putting off one exterior,
and snatching up another, to be soon shifted for a third—he
had never violated the innermost man, but had carried his
conscience along with him. It was impossible to know Holgrave, without recognizing this to be the fact. Hepzibah had
seen it. Phoebe soon saw it, likewise, and gave him the sort
of confidence which such a certainty inspires. She was
startled, however, and sometimes repelled—not by any doubt
of his integrity to whatever law he acknowledged—but by a
sense that his law differed from her own. He made her un-
easy, and seemed to unsettle everything around her, by his
lack of reverence for what was fixed; unless, at a moment's
warning, it could establish its right to hold its ground.

Then, moreover, she scarcely thought him affectionate in
his nature. He was too calm and cool an observer. Phoebe
felt his eye, often; his heart, seldom or never. He took a certain kind of interest in Hepzibah and her brother, and Phoebe
herself; he studied them attentively, and allowed no slightest
circumstance of their individualities to escape him; he was
ready to do them whatever good he might;—but, after all, he
never exactly made common cause with them, nor gave any
reliable evidence that he loved them better, in proportion as

Utopian socialist community in West Roxbury, Massachusetts. See also n. 1,
p. 156.
3. Hypnotism, taking its name from F. A. Mesmer (1734–1815), an Austrian
physician who popularized the practice. For Hawthorne's attitude toward

he knew them more. In his relations with them, he seemed to be in quest of mental food; not heart-sustenance. Phoebe could not conceive what interested him so much in her friends and herself, intellectually, since he cared nothing for them, or comparatively so little, as objects of human affection.

Always, in his interviews with Phoebe, the artist made especial inquiry as to the welfare of Clifford, whom, except at the Sunday festival, he seldom saw.

"Does he still seem happy?" he asked, one day.

"As happy as a child," answered Phoebe, "but—like a child, too—very easily disturbed."

"How disturbed?" inquired Holgrave.—"By things without? —or by thoughts within?"

"I cannot see his thoughts!—How should I?" replied Phoebe, with simple piquancy.—"Very often, his humor changes without any reason that can be guessed at, just as a cloud comes over the sun. Latterly, since I have begun to know him better, I feel it to be not quite right to look closely into his moods. He has had such a great sorrow, that his heart is made all solemn and sacred by it. When he is cheerful—when the sun shines into his mind—then I venture to peep in, just as far as the light reaches, but no farther. It is holy ground where the shadow falls!"

"How prettily you express this sentiment!" said the artist. "I can understand the feeling, without possessing it. Had I your opportunities, no scruples would prevent me from fathoming Clifford to the full depth of my plummet-line!"

"How strange that you should wish it!" remarked Phoebe involuntarily. "What is Cousin Clifford to you?"

"Oh, nothing, of course, nothing!" answered Holgrave with a smile. "Only this is such an odd and incomprehensible world! The more I look at it, the more it puzzles me; and I begin to suspect that a man's bewilderment is the measure of his wisdom. Men and women, and children, too, are such strange creatures, that one never can be certain that he really

Mesmerism, see *"Love Letters of Nathaniel Hawthorne,"* p. 328.

knows them; nor ever guess what they have been, from what he sees them to be, now. Judge Pyncheon! Clifford! What a complex riddle—a complexity of complexities—do they present! It requires intuitive sympathy, like a young girl's, to solve it. A mere observer, like myself, (who never have any intuitions, and am, at best, only subtle and acute,) is pretty certain to go astray."

The artist now turned the conversation to themes less dark than that which they had touched upon. Phoebe and he were young together; nor had Holgrave, in his premature experience of life, wasted entirely that beautiful spirit of youth, which, gushing forth from one small heart and fancy, may diffuse itself over the universe, making it all as bright as on the first day of creation. Man's own youth is the world's youth; at least, he feels as if it were, and imagines that the earth's granite substance is something not yet hardened, and which he can mould into whatever shape he likes. So it was with Holgrave. He could talk sagely about the world's old age, but never actually believed in what he said; he was a young man still, and therefore looked upon the world—that gray-bearded and wrinkled profligate, decrepit, without being venerable—as a tender stripling, capable of being improved into all that it ought to be, but scarcely yet had shown the remotest promise of becoming. He had that sense, or inward prophecy—which a young man had better never have been born, than not to have, and a mature man had better die at once, than utterly to relinquish—that we are not doomed to creep on forever in the old, bad way, but that, this very now, there are the harbingers abroad of a golden era, to be accomplished in his own lifetime. It seemed to Holgrave—as doubtless it has seemed to the hopeful of every century, since the epoch of Adam's grandchildren—that in this age, more than ever before, the moss-grown and rotten Past is to be torn down, and lifeless institutions to be thrust out of the way, and their dead corpses buried, and everything to begin anew.

As to the main point—may we never live to doubt it!—as to the better centuries that are coming, the artist was surely right. His error lay, in supposing that this age, more than any past or future one, is destined to see the tattered garments of Antiquity exchanged for a new suit, instead of gradually renewing themselves by patchwork; in applying his own little life-span as the measure of an interminable achievement; and, more than all, in fancying that it mattered anything to the great end in view, whether he himself should contend for it or against it. Yet it was well for him to think so. This enthusiasm, infusing itself through the calmness of his character, and thus taking an aspect of settled thought and wisdom, would serve to keep his youth pure, and make his aspirations high. And when, with the years settling down more weightily upon him, his early faith should be modified by inevitable experience, it would be with no harsh and sudden revolution of his sentiments. He would still have faith in man's brightening destiny, and perhaps love him all the better, as he should recognize his helplessness in his own behalf; and the haughty faith, with which he began life, would be well bartered for a far humbler one, at its close, in discerning that man's best-directed effort accomplishes a kind of dream, while God is the sole worker of realities.

Holgrave had read very little, and that little, in passing through the thoroughfare of life, where the mystic language of his books was necessarily mixed up with the babble of the multitude; so that both one and the other were apt to lose any sense, that might have been properly their own. He considered himself a thinker, and was certainly of a thoughtful turn, but, with his own path to discover, had perhaps hardly yet reached the point where an educated man begins to think. The true value of his character lay in that deep consciousness of inward strength, which made all his past vicissitudes seem merely like a change of garments; in that enthusiasm, so quiet that he scarcely knew of its existence, but which gave a warmth to everything that he laid his hand on; in that personal ambition, hidden—from his own as well as other eyes—among his more generous impulses, but in which lurked a certain efficacy, that might solidify him from a theorist into the champion of some practicable cause. Altogether, in his culture and want of culture; in his crude, wild, and misty philosophy, and the practical experience that counteracted some of its tendencies; in his magnanimous zeal for man's welfare, and his recklessness of whatever the ages had established in man's behalf; in his faith, and in his infidelity; in what he had, and in what he lacked—the artist might fitly enough stand forth as the representative of many compeers in his native land.

His career it would be difficult to prefigure. There appeared to be qualities in Holgrave, such as, in a country where everything is free to the hand that can grasp it, could hardly fail to put some of the world's prizes within his reach. But these matters are delightfully uncertain. At almost every step in life, we meet with young men of just about Holgrave's age, for whom we anticipate wonderful things, but of whom, even after much and careful inquiry, we never happen to hear another word. The effervescence of youth and passion, and the fresh gloss of the intellect and imagination, endow them with a false brilliancy, which makes fools of themselves and other people. Like certain chintzes, calicoes, and ginghams, they show finely in their first newness, but cannot stand the sun and rain, and assume a very sober aspect after washing-day.

But our business is with Holgrave, as we find him on this particular afternoon, and in the arbor of the Pyncheon-garden. In that point of view, it was a pleasant sight to behold this young man, with so much faith in himself, and so fair an appearance of admirable powers—so little harmed, too, by the many tests that had tried his metal—it was pleasant to see him in his kindly intercourse with Phoebe. Her thought had scarcely done him justice, when it pronounced him cold; or if so, he had grown warmer, now. Without such purpose, on her part, and unconsciously on his, she made the House of the Seven Gables like a home to him, and the garden a familiar precinct. With the insight on which he prided himself, he fancied that he could look through Phoebe, and all around her, and could read her off like a page of a child's story-book. But these transparent natures are often deceptive in their depth; those pebbles at the bottom of the fountain are farther from us than we think. Thus the artist, whatever he might judge of Phoebe's capacity, was beguiled, by some silent charm of hers, to talk freely of what he dreamed of doing in the world. He poured himself out as to another self. Very possibly, he forgot Phoebe while he talked to her, and was moved only by the inevitable tendency of thought, when rendered sympathetic by enthusiasm and emotion, to flow into the first safe reservoir which it finds. But, had you peeped at them through the chinks of the garden-fence, the young man's earnestness and heightened color might have led you to suppose that he was making love to the young girl!

At length, something was said by Holgrave, that made it apposite for Phoebe to inquire what had first brought him acquainted with her Cousin Hepzibah, and why he now chose to lodge in the desolate old Pyncheon-house. Without directly answering her, he turned from the Future, which had heretofore been the theme of his discourse, and began to speak of the influences of the Past. One subject, indeed, is but the reverberation of the other.

"Shall we never, never get rid of this Past!" cried he, keeping up the earnest tone of his preceding conversation.—"It lies upon the Present like a giant's dead body! In fact, the case is just as if a young giant were compelled to waste all his strength in carrying about the corpse of the old giant, his grandfather, who died a long while ago, and only needs to be decently buried. Just think, a moment; and it will startle you to see what slaves we are to by-gone times—to Death, if we give the matter the right word!"

"But I do not see it," observed Phoebe.

"For example, then," continued Holgrave, "a Dead Man, if he happen to have made a will, disposes of wealth no longer his own; or, if he die intestate, it is distributed in accordance with the notions of men much longer dead than he. A Dead Man sits on all our judgement-seats; and living judges do but search out and repeat his decisions. We read in Dead Men's books! We laugh at Dead Men's jokes, and cry at Dead Men's pathos! We are sick of Dead Men's diseases, physical and moral, and die of the same remedies with which dead doctors killed their patients! We worship the living Deity, according to Dead Men's forms and creeds! Whatever we seek to do, of our own free motion, a Dead Man's icy hand obstructs us! Turn our eyes to what point we may, a Dead Man's white, immitigable face encounters them, and freezes our very heart! And we must be dead ourselves, before we can begin to have our proper influence on our own world, which will then be no longer our world, but the world of another generation, with which we shall have no shadow of a right to interfere. I ought to have said, too, that we live in Dead Men's houses; as, for instance, in this of the seven gables!"[4]

"And why not," said Phoebe, "so long as we can be comfortable in them?"

"But we shall live to see the day, I trust," went on the artist, "when no man shall build his house for posterity. Why should he? He might just as reasonably order a durable suit of clothes—leather, or gutta percha, or whatever else lasts longest—so that his great-grandchildren should have the benefit of them, and cut precisely the same figure in the world that he himself does.[5] If each generation were allowed and expected to build its own houses, that single change, comparatively unimportant in itself, would imply almost every

4. See "Passages from *The American Notebooks*," p. 326.
5. "Eben [Hawthorne] passed from the matters of birth, pedigree, and ancestral pride, to give vent to the most arrant democracy and locofocoism [socialistic ideas], that I have happened to hear; saying that nobody ought

reform which society is now suffering for. I doubt whether even our public edifices—our capitols, state-houses, court-houses, city-halls, and churches—ought to be built of such permanent materials as stone or brick. It were better that they should crumble to ruin, once in twenty years, or there-abouts, as a hint to the people to examine into and reform the institutions which they symbolize."

"How you hate everything old!" said Phoebe in dismay. —"It makes me dizzy to think of such a shifting world!"

"I certainly love nothing mouldy," answered Holgrave. "Now this old Pyncheon-house! Is it a wholesome place to live in, with its black shingles, and the green moss that shows how damp they are?—its dark, low-studded rooms?—its grime and sordidness, which are the crystallization on its walls of the human breath, that has been drawn and exhaled here, in discontent and anguish? The house ought to be purified with fire—purified till only its ashes remain!"

"Then why do you live in it?" asked Phoebe, a little piqued.

"Oh, I am pursuing my studies here; not in books, how-ever!" replied Holgrave. "The house, in my view, is expres-sive of that odious and abominable Past, with all its bad influences, against which I have just been declaiming. I dwell in it for awhile, that I may know the better how to hate it. By-the-by, did you ever hear the story of Maule, the wizard, and what happened between him and your immeas-urably great-grandfather?"

"Yes indeed!" said Phoebe. "I heard it long ago from my father, and two or three times from my Cousin Hepzibah, in the month that I have been here. She seems to think that all the calamities of the Pyncheons began from that quarrel with the wizard, as you call him. And you, Mr. Holgrave, look as if you thought so too! How singular, that you should believe what is so very absurd, when you reject many things that are a great deal worthier of credit!"

---

to possess wealth longer than his own life, and that then it should return to the people &c. It was queer." (*American Notebooks,* entry dated August 27, 1837.)

"I do believe it," said the artist seriously—"not as a superstition, however—but as proved by unquestionable facts, and
as exemplifying a theory. Now, see! Under those seven
gables, at which we now look up—and which old Colonel
Pyncheon meant to be the home of his descendants, in prosperity and happiness, down to an epoch far beyond the
present—under that roof, through a portion of three centuries,
there has been perpetual remorse of conscience, a constantly
defeated hope, strife amongst kindred, various misery, a
strange form of death, dark suspicion, unspeakable disgrace,—
all, or most of which calamity, I have the means of tracing to
the old Puritan's inordinate desire to plant and endow a family. To plant a family! This idea is at the bottom of most
of the wrong and mischief which men do. The truth is, that,
once in every half-century, at longest, a family should be
merged into the great, obscure mass of humanity, and forget
all about its ancestors. Human blood, in order to keep its
freshness, should run in hidden streams, as the water of an
aqueduct is conveyed in subterranean pipes. In the family-
existence of these Pyncheons, for instance—forgive me,
Phoebe; but I cannot think of you as one of them—in their
brief, New England pedigree, there has been time enough
to infect them all with one kind of lunacy or another!"

"You speak very unceremoniously of my kindred," said
Phoebe, debating with herself whether she ought to take
offence.

"I speak true thoughts to a true mind!" answered Holgrave,
with a vehemence which Phoebe had not before witnessed in
him. "The truth is as I say! Furthermore, the original perpetrator and father of this mischief appears to have perpetuated himself, and still walks the street—at least, his very
image, in mind and body—with the fairest prospect of transmitting to posterity as rich, and as wretched, an inheritance
as he has received! Do you remember the daguerreotype, and
its resemblance to the old portrait?"

"How strangely in earnest you are," exclaimed Phoebe, looking at him with surprise and perplexity, half-alarmed, and partly inclined to laugh. "You talk of the lunacy of the Pyncheons! Is it contagious?"

"I understand you!" said the artist, coloring and laughing. "I believe I am a little mad! This subject has taken hold of my mind with the strangest tenacity of clutch, since I have lodged in yonder old gable. As one method of throwing it off, I have put an incident of the Pyncheon family-history, with which I happen to be acquainted, into the form of a legend, and mean to publish it in a magazine."

"Do you write for the magazines?" inquired Phoebe.

"Is it possible you did not know it?" cried Holgrave.— "Well; such is literary fame! Yes, Miss Phoebe Pyncheon, among the multitude of my marvellous gifts, I have that of writing stories; and my name has figured, I can assure you, on the covers of Graham and Godey,[6] making as respectable an appearance, for aught I could see, as any of the canonized bead-roll[7] with which it was associated. In the humorous line, I am thought to have a very pretty way with me; and as for pathos, I am as provocative of tears as an onion! But shall I read you my story?"

"Yes; if it is not very long," said Phoebe—and added, laughingly—"nor very dull!"

As this latter point was one which the Daguerreotypist could not decide for himself, he forthwith produced his roll of manuscript, and, while the late sunbeams gilded the seven gables, began to read.

---

6. *Graham's Magazine* (1826–1858) and Godey's *Magazine and Lady's Book* (1830–1898) were among the most successful periodicals of the nineteenth century; Hawthorne himself published one story in each.
7. Originally a list of saints to be prayed to; here the illustrious contributors to the magazine.

## XIII

# ALICE PYNCHEON

THERE was a message brought, one day, from the worshipful Gervayse Pyncheon to young Matthew Maule, the carpenter, desiring his immediate presence at the House of the Seven Gables.

"And what does your master want with me?" said the carpenter to Mr. Pyncheon's black servant. "Does the house need any repair? Well it may, by this time; and no blame to my father who built it, neither! I was reading the old Colonel's tombstone, no longer ago than last Sabbath; and reckoning from that date, the house has stood seven-and-thirty years. No wonder if there should be a job to do on the roof!"

"Don't know what Massa wants!" answered Scipio. "The house is a berry good house, and old Colonel Pyncheon think so too, I reckon;—else why the old man haunt it so, and frighten a poor nigger, as he does?"

"Well, well, friend Scipio, let your master know that I'm coming," said the carpenter with a laugh. "For a fair, workmanlike job, he'll find me his man. And so the house is haunted, is it? It will take a tighter workman than I am, to keep the spirits out of the seven gables. Even if the Colonel would be quit," he added, muttering to himself, "my old grandfather, the wizard, will be pretty sure to stick to the Pyncheons, as long as their walls hold together!"

"What's that you mutter to yourself, Matthew Maule?" asked Scipio. "And what for do you look so black at me?"

"No matter, darkey!" said the carpenter. "Do you think nobody is to look black but yourself? Go tell your master I'm coming; and if you happen to see Mistress Alice, his daughter, give Matthew Maule's humble respects to her. She has brought a fair face from Italy—fair, and gentle, and proud— has that same Alice Pyncheon!"

"He talk of Mistress Alice!" cried Scipio, as he returned from his errand. "The low carpenter-man! He no business so much as to look at her a great way off!"

This young Matthew Maule, the carpenter, it must be observed, was a person little understood, and not very generally liked, in the town where he resided; not that anything could be alleged against his integrity, or his skill and diligence in the handicraft which he exercised. The aversion (as it might justly be called) with which many persons regarded him, was partly the result of his own character and deportment, and partly an inheritance.

He was the grandson of a former Matthew Maule; one of the early settlers of the town, and who had been a famous and terrible wizard, in his day. This old reprobate was one of the sufferers, when Cotton Mather,[1] and his brother ministers, and the learned judges, and other wise men, and Sir William Phips, the sagacious Governor,[2] made such laudable efforts to weaken the great Enemy of souls, by sending a multitude of his adherents up the rocky pathway of Gallows-Hill.[3] Since those days, no doubt, it had grown to be suspected, that, in consequence of an unfortunate overdoing of a work praiseworthy in itself, the proceedings against the witches had proved far less acceptable to the Beneficent Father, than to that very Arch-Enemy, whom they were intended to distress and utterly overwhelm. It is not the less certain, however, that awe and terror brooded over the memories of those who died for this horrible crime of witchcraft.

1. Cotton Mather (1663–1728), a powerful Puritan minister and prolific writer, defended the Salem witchcraft trials in his *Wonders of the Invisible World* (1692).
2. William Phips (1651–1695), the Royal Governor of Massachusetts, con-

Their graves, in the crevices of the rocks, were supposed to be incapable of retaining the occupants, who had been so hastily thrust into them. Old Matthew Maule, especially, was known to have as little hesitation or difficulty in rising out of his grave, as an ordinary man in getting out of bed, and was as often seen at midnight, as living people at noonday. This pestilent wizard (in whom his just punishment seemed to have wrought no manner of amends) had an inveterate habit of haunting a certain mansion, styled the House of the Seven Gables, against the owner of which he pretended to hold an unsettled claim for ground-rent. The ghost, it appears—with the pertinacity which was one of his distinguishing characteristics, while alive—insisted that he was the rightful proprietor of the site upon which the house stood. His terms were, that either the aforesaid ground-rent, from the day when the cellar began to be dug, should be paid down, or the mansion itself given up; else he, the ghostly creditor, would have his finger in all the affairs of the Pyncheons, and make everything go wrong with them, though it should be a thousand years after his death. It was a wild story, perhaps, but seemed not altogether so incredible, to those who could remember what an inflexibly obstinate old fellow this wizard Maule had been!

Now, the wizard's grandson, the young Matthew Maule of our story, was popularly supposed to have inherited some of his ancestor's questionable traits. It is wonderful how many absurdities were promulgated in reference to the young man. He was fabled, for example, to have a strange power of getting into people's dreams, and regulating matters there according to his own fancy, pretty much like the stage-manager of a theatre. There was a great deal of talk among the neighbors, particularly the petticoated ones, about what they called the witchcraft of Maule's eye. Some said, that he could look into people's minds; others, that, by the marvellous power of this eye, he could draw people into his own mind,

vened the witchcraft court; after his own wife was accused, he dismissed it on October 29, 1692.
3. The site of the witchcraft executions.

or send them, if he pleased, to do errands to his grandfather, in the spiritual world; others again, that it was what is termed an Evil Eye, and possessed the valuable faculty of blighting corn, and drying children into mummies with the heart-burn. But, after all, what worked most to the young carpenter's disadvantage was, first, the reserve and sternness of his natural disposition, and next, the fact of his not being a church-communicant, and the suspicion of his holding heretical tenets in matters of religion and polity.

After receiving Mr. Pyncheon's message, the carpenter merely tarried to finish a small job, which he happened to have in hand, and then took his way towards the House of the Seven Gables. This noted edifice, though its style might be getting a little out of fashion, was still as respectable a family residence as that of any gentleman in town. The present owner, Gervayse Pyncheon, was said to have contracted a dislike to the house, in consequence of a shock to his sensibility, in early childhood, from the sudden death of his grandfather. In the very act of running to climb Colonel Pyncheon's knee, the boy had discovered the old Puritan to be a corpse! On arriving at manhood, Mr. Pyncheon had visited England, where he married a lady of fortune, and had subsequently spent many years, partly in the mother-country, and partly in various cities, on the continent of Europe. During this period, the family-mansion had been consigned to the charge of a kinsman, who was allowed to make it his home, for the time being, in consideration of keeping the premises in thorough repair. So faithfully had this contract been fulfilled, that now, as the carpenter approached the house, his practised eye could detect nothing to criticize in its condition. The peaks of the seven gables rose up sharply; the shingled roof looked thoroughly water-tight; and the glittering plaster-work entirely covered the exterior walls, and sparkled in the October sun, as if it had been new only a week ago.

The house had that pleasant aspect of life, which is like the cheery expression of comfortable activity, in the human countenance. You could see at once that there was the stir of a large family within it. A huge load of oak-wood was passing through the gateway, towards the outbuildings in the rear; the fat cook, or probably it might be the housekeeper, stood at the side-door, bargaining for some turkeys and poultry, which a countryman had brought for sale. Now and then, a maid-servant, neatly dressed, and now the shining, sable face of a slave,[4] might be seen bustling across the windows, in the lower part of the house. At an open window of a room in the second story, hanging over some pots of beautiful and delicate flowers—exotics, but which had never known a more genial sunshine than that of the New England autumn—was the figure of a young lady, an exotic, like the flowers, and beautiful and delicate as they. Her presence imparted an indescribable grace and faint witchery to the whole edifice. In other respects, it was a substantial, jolly-looking mansion, and seemed fit to be the residence of a patriarch, who might establish his own head-quarters in the front gable, and assign one of the remainder to each of his six children; while the great chimney, in the centre, should symbolize the old fellow's hospitable heart, which kept them all warm, and made a great whole of the seven smaller ones.

There was a vertical sun-dial on the front gable; and as the carpenter passed beneath it, he looked up and noted the hour.

"Three o'clock!" said he to himself. "My father told me, that dial was put up only an hour before the old Colonel's death. How truly it has kept time, these seven-and-thirty years past! The shadow creeps and creeps, and is always looking over the shoulder of the sunshine!"

It might have befitted a craftsman, like Matthew Maule, on being sent for to a gentleman's house, to go to the backdoor, where servants and work-people were usually admitted;

4. Slavery was not abolished in Massachusetts until 1779.

or at least to the side-entrance, where the better class of tradesmen made application. But the carpenter had a great deal of pride and stiffness in his nature; and at this moment, moreover, his heart was bitter with the sense of hereditary wrong, because he considered the great Pyncheon-house to be standing on soil which should have been his own. On this very site, beside a spring of delicious water, his grandfather had felled the pine-trees and built a cottage, in which children had been born to him; and it was only from a dead man's stiffened fingers, that Colonel Pyncheon had wrested away the title-deeds. So young Maule went straight to the principal entrance, beneath a portal of carved oak, and gave such a peal of the iron knocker, that you would have imagined the stern old wizard himself to be standing at the threshold.

Black Scipio answered the summons in a prodigious hurry, but showed the whites of his eyes, in amazement, on beholding only the carpenter.

"Lord-a-mercy, what a great man he be, this carpenter fellow!" mumbled Scipio, down in his throat. "Anybody think he beat on the door with his biggest hammer!"

"Here I am!" said Maule sternly. "Show me the way to your master's parlor!"

As he stept into the house, a note of sweet and melancholy music trilled and vibrated along the passage-way, proceeding from one of the rooms above-stairs. It was the harpsichord which Alice Pyncheon had brought with her from beyond the sea. The fair Alice bestowed most of her maiden leisure between flowers and music, although the former were apt to droop, and the melodies were often sad. She was of foreign education, and could not take kindly to the New England modes of life, in which nothing beautiful had ever been developed.

As Mr. Pyncheon had been impatiently awaiting Maule's arrival, black Scipio, of course, lost no time in ushering the carpenter into his master's presence. The room, in which this

gentleman sat, was a parlor of moderate size, looking out
upon the garden of the house, and having its windows partly
shadowed by the foliage of fruit-trees. It was Mr. Pyncheon's
peculiar apartment, and was provided with furniture, in an
elegant and costly style, principally from Paris; the floor
(which was unusual, at that day) being covered with a carpet, so skilfully and richly wrought, that it seemed to glow
as with living flowers. In one corner stood a marble woman,
to whom her own beauty was the sole and sufficient garment.
Some pictures—that looked old, and had a mellow tinge,
diffused through all their artful splendor—hung on the walls.
Near the fire-place was a large and very beautiful cabinet of
ebony, inlaid with ivory; a piece of antique furniture, which
Mr. Pyncheon had bought in Venice, and which he used as
the treasure-place for medals, ancient coins, and whatever
small and valuable curiosities he had picked up, on his
travels. Through all this variety of decoration, however, the
room showed its original characteristics; its low stud, its
cross-beam, its chimney-piece, with the old-fashioned Dutch
tiles;[5] so that it was the emblem of a mind, industriously stored
with foreign ideas, and elaborated into artificial refinement,
but neither larger, nor, in its proper self, more elegant, than
before.

There were two objects that appeared rather out of place
in this very handsomely furnished room. One was a large
map, or surveyor's plan of a tract of land, which looked as
if it had been drawn a good many years ago, and was now
dingy with smoke, and soiled, here and there, with the touch
of fingers. The other was a portrait of a stern old man, in
a Puritan garb, painted roughly, but with a bold effect, and
a remarkably strong expression of character.

At a small table, before a fire of English sea-coal,[6] sat Mr.
Pyncheon, sipping coffee, which had grown to be a very
favorite beverage with him, in France. He was a middle-aged
and really handsome man, with a wig flowing down upon

5. Decorated blue-on-white tiles made in the Netherlands; they were popular
in prosperous Colonial American homes.
6. Mineral coal as distinguished from charcoal.

his shoulders; his coat was of blue velvet, with lace on the borders and at the button-holes; and the firelight glistened on the spacious breadth of his waistcoat, which was flowered all over with gold. On the entrance of Scipio, ushering in the carpenter, Mr. Pyncheon turned partly round, but resumed his former position, and proceeded deliberately to finish his cup of coffee, without immediate notice of the guest whom he had summoned to his presence. It was not that he intended any rudeness, or improper neglect—which, indeed, he would have blushed to be guilty of—but it never occurred to him that a person in Maule's station had a claim on his courtesy, or would trouble himself about it, one way or the other.

The carpenter, however, stept at once to the hearth, and turned himself about, so as to look Mr. Pyncheon in the face.

"You sent for me!" said he. "Be pleased to explain your business, that I may go back to my own affairs!"

"Ah! excuse me," said Mr. Pyncheon quietly.—"I did not mean to tax your time without a recompense. Your name, I think, is Maule—Thomas or Matthew Maule—a son or grandson of the builder of this house?"

"Matthew Maule," replied the carpenter—"son of him who built the house—grandson of the rightful proprietor of the soil!"

"I know the dispute to which you allude," observed Mr. Pyncheon, with undisturbed equanimity. "I am well aware, that my grandfather was compelled to resort to a suit at law, in order to establish his claim to the foundation-site of this edifice. We will not, if you please, renew the discussion. The matter was settled at the time, and by the competent authorities—equitably, it is to be presumed—and, at all events, irrevocably. Yet, singularly enough, there is an incidental reference to this very subject in what I am now about to say to you. And this same inveterate grudge—excuse me, I mean no offence—this irritability, which you have just shown, is not entirely aside from the matter."

"If you can find anything for your purpose, Mr. Pyncheon," said the carpenter, "in a man's natural resentment for the wrongs done to his blood, you are welcome to it!"

"I take you at your word, Goodman[7] Maule," said the owner of the seven gables, with a smile, "and will proceed to suggest a mode in which your hereditary resentments—justifiable, or otherwise—may have had a bearing on my affairs. You have heard, I suppose, that the Pyncheon family, ever since my grandfather's days, have been prosecuting a still unsettled claim to a very large extent of territory at the eastward?"

"Often," replied Maule—and it is said that a smile came over his face—"very often—from my father!"

"This claim," continued Mr. Pyncheon, after pausing a moment, as if to consider what the carpenter's smile might mean, "appeared to be on the very verge of a settlement and full allowance, at the period of my grandfather's decease. It was well known, to those in his confidence, that he anticipated neither difficulty nor delay. Now, Colonel Pyncheon, I need hardly say, was a practical man, well acquainted with public and private business, and not at all the person to cherish ill-founded hopes, or to attempt the following out of an impracticable scheme. It is obvious to conclude, therefore, that he had grounds—not apparent to his heirs—for his confident anticipation of success in the matter of this eastern claim. In a word, I believe—and my legal advisers coincide in the belief, which, moreover, is authorized, to a certain extent, by the family-traditions—that my grandfather was in possession of some deed, or other document, essential to this claim, but which has since disappeared."

"Very likely," said Matthew Maule—and again, it is said, there was a dark smile on his face—"but what can a poor carpenter have to do with the grand affairs of the Pyncheon family?"

"Perhaps nothing," returned Mr. Pyncheon—"possibly, much!"

7. Originally prefixed to the names of males below the rank of "Gentleman"; in the early days of the Colonies, it was applied to men who were neither members of a profession nor eminent in commerce or farming.

Here ensued a great many words between Matthew Maule and the proprietor of the seven gables, on the subject which the latter had thus broached. It seems (although Mr. Pyncheon had some hesitation in referring to stories, so exceedingly absurd in their aspect) that the popular belief pointed to some mysterious connection and dependence, existing between the family of the Maules, and these vast, unrealized possessions of the Pyncheons. It was an ordinary saying, that the old wizard, hanged though he was, had obtained the best end of the bargain, in his contest with Colonel Pyncheon; inasmuch as he had got possession of the great eastern claim, in exchange for an acre or two of garden-ground. A very aged woman, recently dead, had often used the metaphorical expression, in her fireside-talk, that miles and miles of the Pyncheon lands had been shovelled into Maule's grave; which, by-the-by, was but a very shallow nook, between two rocks, near the summit of Gallows-Hill. Again, when the lawyers were making inquiry for the missing document, it was a by-word, that it would never be found, unless in the wizard's skeleton-hand. So much weight had the shrewd lawyers assigned to these fables, that—(but Mr. Pyncheon did not see fit to inform the carpenter of the fact)—they had secretly caused the wizard's grave to be searched. Nothing was discovered, however, except that, unaccountably, the right hand of the skeleton was gone.

Now, what was unquestionably important, a portion of these popular rumors could be traced, though rather doubtfully and indistinctly, to chance words and obscure hints of the executed wizard's son, and the father of this present Matthew Maule. And here Mr. Pyncheon could bring an item of his own personal evidence into play. Though but a child, at the time, he either remembered or fancied, that Matthew's father had had some job to perform, on the day before, or possibly the very morning, of the Colonel's decease, in the private room where he and the carpenter were at this moment talking. Certain papers belonging to Colonel Pyncheon, as his grandson distinctly recollected, had been spread out on the table.

Matthew Maule understood the insinuated suspicion.

"My father," he said—but still there was that dark smile, making a riddle of his countenance—"my father was an honester man than the bloody old Colonel! Not to get his rights back again, would he have carried off one of those papers!"

"I shall not bandy words with you," observed the foreign-bred Mr. Pyncheon, with haughty composure. "Nor will it become me to resent any rudeness towards either my grandfather or myself. A gentleman, before seeking intercourse with a person of your station and habits, will first consider whether the urgency of the end may compensate for the disagreeableness of the means. It does so, in the present instance."

He then renewed the conversation, and made great pecuniary offers to the carpenter, in case the latter should give information leading to the discovery of the lost document, and the consequent success of the eastern claim. For a long time, Matthew Maule is said to have turned a cold ear to these propositions. At last, however, with a strange kind of laugh, he inquired whether Mr. Pyncheon would make over to him the old wizard's homestead-ground, together with the House of the Seven Gables, now standing on it, in requital of the documentary evidence, so urgently required.

The wild, chimney-corner legend (which, without copying all its extravagances, my narrative essentially follows) here gives an account of some very strange behavior on the part of Colonel Pyncheon's portrait. This picture, it must be understood, was supposed to be so intimately connected with the fate of the house, and so magically built into its walls, that, if once it should be removed, that very instant, the whole edifice would come thundering down, in a heap of dusty ruin. All through the foregoing conversation between Mr. Pyncheon and the carpenter, the portrait had been frowning, clenching its fist, and giving many such proofs of excessive discomposure, but without attracting the notice of either of the two colloquists. And finally, at Matthew Maule's audacious suggestion of a transfer of the seven-gabled structure, the ghostly portrait is averred to have lost all patience, and to have shown itself on the point of descending bodily from its frame. But such incredible incidents are merely to be mentioned aside.

"Give up this house!" exclaimed Mr. Pyncheon, in amazement at the proposal. "Were I to do so, my grandfather would not rest quiet in his grave!"

"He never has, if all stories are true," remarked the carpenter, composedly. "But that matter concerns his grandson, more than it does Matthew Maule. I have no other terms to propose."

Impossible as he at first thought it, to comply with Maule's conditions, still, on a second glance, Mr. Pyncheon was of opinion that they might at least be made matter of discussion. He himself had no personal attachment for the house, nor any pleasant associations connected with his childish residence in it. On the contrary, after seven-and-thirty years, the presence of his dead grandfather seemed still to pervade it, as on that morning when the affrighted boy had beheld him, with so ghastly an aspect, stiffening in his chair. His long abode in foreign parts, moreover, and familiarity with many of the castles and ancestral halls of England, and the marble palaces of Italy, had caused him to look contemptuously at the House of the Seven Gables, whether in point of splendor or convenience. It was a mansion exceedingly inadequate to the style of living, which it would be incumbent on Mr. Pyncheon to support, after realizing his territorial rights. His steward might deign to occupy it, but never, certainly, the great landed proprietor himself. In the event of success, indeed, it was his purpose to return to England; nor, to say the truth, would he recently have quitted that more congenial home, had not his own fortune, as well as his deceased wife's, begun to give symptoms of exhaustion. The eastern claim once fairly settled, and put upon the firm basis of actual possession, Mr. Pyncheon's property—to be measured by miles, not acres—would be worth an earldom, and would reasonably entitle him to solicit, or enable him to purchase, that elevated dignity from the British monarch. Lord Pyncheon!—or the Earl of Waldo!—how could such a magnate be expected to contract his grandeur within the pitiful compass of seven shingled gables?

In short, on an enlarged view of the business, the carpenter's terms appeared so ridiculously easy, that Mr. Pyncheon could scarcely forbear laughing in his face. He was quite ashamed, after the foregoing reflections, to propose any diminution of so moderate a recompense for the immense service to be rendered.

"I consent to your proposition, Maule!" cried he. "Put me in possession of the document, essential to establish my rights, and the House of the Seven Gables is your own!"

According to some versions of the story, a regular contract to the above effect was drawn up by a lawyer, and signed and sealed in the presence of witnesses. Others say, that Matthew Maule was contented with a private, written agreement, in which Mr. Pyncheon pledged his honor and integrity to the fulfilment of the terms concluded upon. The gentleman then ordered wine, which he and the carpenter drank together, in confirmation of their bargain. During the whole preceding discussion and subsequent formalities, the old Puritan's portrait seems to have persisted in its shadowy gestures of disapproval, but without effect; except that, as Mr. Pyncheon set down the emptied glass, he thought he beheld his grandfather frown.

"This Sherry is too potent a wine for me;—it has affected

my brain already," he observed, after a somewhat startled look at the picture.—"On returning to Europe, I shall confine myself to the more delicate vintages of Italy and France, the best of which will not bear transportation."

"My Lord Pyncheon may drink what wine he will, and wherever he pleases!" replied the carpenter, as if he had been privy to Mr. Pyncheon's ambitious projects. "But first, Sir, if you desire tidings of this lost document, I must crave the favor of a little talk with your fair daughter Alice!"

"You are mad, Maule!" exclaimed Mr. Pyncheon haughtily; and now, at last, there was anger mixed up with his pride.—"What can my daughter have to do with a business like this?"

Indeed, at this new demand on the carpenter's part, the proprietor of the seven gables was even more thunderstruck, than at the cool proposition to surrender his house. There was, at least, an assignable motive for the first stipulation; there appeared to be none whatever, for the last. Nevertheless, Matthew Maule sturdily insisted on the young lady being summoned, and even gave her father to understand, in a mysterious kind of explanation—which made the matter considerably darker than it looked before—that the only chance of acquiring the requisite knowledge was through the clear, crystal medium of a pure and virgin intelligence, like that of the fair Alice. Not to encumber our story with Mr. Pyncheon's scruples, whether of conscience, pride, or fatherly affection, he at length ordered his daughter to be called. He well knew that she was in her chamber, and engaged in no occupation that could not readily be laid aside; for, as it happened, ever since Alice's name had been spoken, both her father and the carpenter had heard the sad and sweet music of her harpsichord, and the airier melancholy of her accompanying voice.

So Alice Pyncheon was summoned, and appeared. A portrait of this young lady, painted by a Venetian artist and

left by her father in England, is said to have fallen into the
hands of the present Duke of Devonshire, and to be now
preserved at Chatsworth;[8] not on account of any associations
with the original, but for its value as a picture, and the high
character of beauty, in the countenance. If ever there was
a lady born, and set apart from the world's vulgar mass by
a certain gentle and cold stateliness, it was this very Alice
Pyncheon. Yet there was the womanly mixture in her;—
the tenderness, or, at least, the tender capabilities. For the
sake of that redeeming quality, a man of generous nature
would have forgiven all her pride, and have been content,
almost, to lie down in her path, and let Alice set her slender
foot upon his heart. All that he would have required, was
simply the acknowledgement that he was indeed a man, and
a fellow-being, moulded of the same elements as she.

As Alice came into the room, her eyes fell upon the carpenter, who was standing near its centre, clad in a green,
woollen jacket, a pair of loose breeches, open at the knees,
and with a long pocket for his rule, the end of which protruded; it was as proper a mark of the artizan's calling, as
Mr. Pyncheon's full-dress sword, of that gentleman's aristocratic pretensions. A glow of artistic approval brightened over
Alice Pyncheon's face; she was struck with admiration—
which she made no attempt to conceal—of the remarkable
comeliness, strength, and energy of Maule's figure. But that
admiring glance (which most other men, perhaps, would
have cherished as a sweet recollection, all through life) the
carpenter never forgave. It must have been the devil himself
that made Maule so subtile in his perception.

"Does the girl look at me as if I were a brute beast!"
thought he, setting his teeth. "She shall know whether I
have a human spirit; and the worse for her, if it prove
stronger than her own!"

"My father, you sent for me," said Alice, in her sweet
and harp-like voice. "But, if you have business with this

8. One of the most splendid private residences in England, famous for its
collection of paintings by Titian, Rubens, Raphael, and Claude, whom Hawthorne mentions a few paragraphs on (see the following footnote).

young man, pray let me go again. You know I do not love this room, in spite of that Claude,[9] with which you try to bring back sunny recollections."

"Stay a moment, young lady, if you please!" said Matthew Maule. "My business with your father is over. With yourself, it is now to begin!"

Alice looked towards her father, in surprise and inquiry.

"Yes, Alice," said Mr. Pyncheon, with some disturbance and confusion. "This young man—his name is Matthew Maule—professes, so far as I can understand him, to be able to discover, through your means, a certain paper or parchment, which was missing long before your birth. The importance of the document in question renders it advisable to neglect no possible, even if improbable, method of regaining it. You will therefore oblige me, my dear Alice, by answering this person's inquiries, and complying with his lawful and reasonable requests, so far as they may appear to have the aforesaid object in view. As I shall remain in the room, you need apprehend no rude nor unbecoming deportment, on the young man's part; and, at your slightest wish, of course, the investigation, or whatever we may call it, shall immediately be broken off."

"Mistress Alice Pyncheon," remarked Matthew Maule, with the utmost deference, but yet a half-hidden sarcasm in his look and tone, "will no doubt feel herself quite safe in her father's presence, and under his all-sufficient protection."

"I certainly shall entertain no manner of apprehension, with my father at hand," said Alice, with maidenly dignity. "Neither do I conceive that a lady, while true to herself, can have aught to fear from whomsoever, or in any circumstances!"

Poor Alice! By what unhappy impulse did she thus put herself at once on terms of defiance against a strength which she could not estimate?

"Then, Mistress Alice," said Matthew Maule, handing a

9. Claude of Lorraine (1600–1682), a celebrated French landscape artist who did most of his painting in Italy.

chair—gracefully enough, for a craftsman—"will it please you only to sit down, and do me the favor (though altogether beyond a poor carpenter's deserts) to fix your eyes on mine!"

Alice complied. She was very proud. Setting aside all advantages of rank, this fair girl deemed herself conscious of a power—combined of beauty, high, unsullied purity, and the preservative force of womanhood—that could make her sphere impenetrable, unless betrayed by treachery within. She instinctively knew, it may be, that some sinister or evil potency was now striving to pass her barriers; nor would she decline the contest. So Alice put woman's might against man's might; a match not often equal, on the part of woman.

Her father, meanwhile, had turned away, and seemed absorbed in the contemplation of a landscape by Claude, where a shadowy and sun-streaked vista penetrated so remotely into an ancient wood, that it would have been no wonder if his fancy had lost itself in the picture's bewildering depths. But, in truth, the picture was no more to him, at that moment, than the blank wall against which it hung. His mind was haunted with the many and strange tales which he had heard, attributing mysterious, if not supernatural endowments to these Maules, as well the grandson, here present, as his two immediate ancestors. Mr. Pyncheon's long residence abroad, and intercourse with men of wit and fashion—courtiers, worldlings, and free thinkers—had done much towards obliterating the grim, Puritan superstitions, which no man of New England birth, at that early period, could entirely escape. But, on the other hand, had not a whole community believed Maule's grandfather to be a wizard? Had not the crime been proved? Had not the wizard died for it? Had he not bequeathed a legacy of hatred against the Pyncheons to this only grandson, who, as it appeared, was now about to exercise a subtle influence over the daughter of his enemy's house? Might not this influence be the same that was called witchcraft?

Turning half around, he caught a glimpse of Maule's figure

in the looking-glass. At some paces from Alice, with his arms uplifted in the air, the carpenter made a gesture, as if directing downward a slow, ponderous, and invisible weight upon the maiden.

"Stay, Maule!" exclaimed Mr. Pyncheon, stepping forward. "I forbid your proceeding farther!"

"Pray, my dear father, do not interrupt the young man!" said Alice, without changing her position. "His efforts, I assure you, will prove very harmless."

Again, Mr. Pyncheon turned his eyes towards the Claude. It was then his daughter's will, in opposition to his own, that the experiment should be fully tried. Henceforth, therefore, he did but consent, not urge it. And was it not for her sake, far more than for his own, that he desired its success? That lost parchment once restored, the beautiful Alice Pyncheon, with the rich dowry which he could then bestow, might wed an English duke, or a German reigning-prince, instead of some New England clergyman or lawyer! At the thought, the ambitious father almost consented, in his heart, that, if the devil's power were needed to the accomplishment of this great object, Maule might evoke him! Alice's own purity would be her safe-guard.

With his mind full of imaginary magnificence, Mr. Pyncheon heard a half-uttered exclamation from his daughter. It was very faint and low; so indistinct, that there seemed but half a will to shape out the words, and too undefined a purport, to be intelligible. Yet it was a call for help!—his conscience never doubted it!—and, little more than a whisper to his ear, it was a dismal shriek, and long re-echoed so, in the region round his heart! But, this time, the father did not turn.

After a farther interval, Maule spoke.

"Behold your daughter!" said he.

Mr. Pyncheon came hastily forward. The carpenter was standing erect in front of Alice's chair, and pointing his finger towards the maiden with an expression of triumphant power, the limits of which could not be defined; as, indeed, its scope stretched vaguely towards the unseen and the infinite. Alice sat in an attitude of profound repose, with the long, brown lashes drooping over her eyes.

"There she is!" said the carpenter. "Speak to her!"

"Alice! My daughter!" exclaimed Mr. Pyncheon. "My own Alice!"

She did not stir.

"Louder!" said Maule smiling.

"Alice! Awake!" cried her father. "It troubles me to see you thus! Awake!"

He spoke loudly, with terror in his voice, and close to that delicate ear which had always been so sensitive to every discord. But the sound evidently reached her not. It is indescribable what a sense of remote, dim, unattainable distance, betwixt himself and Alice, was impressed on the father by this impossibility of reaching her with his voice.

"Best touch her!" said Matthew Maule. "Shake the girl, and roughly too! My hands are hardened with too much use of axe, saw, and plane; else I might help you!"

Mr. Pyncheon took her hand, and pressed it with the earnestness of startled emotion. He kissed her, with so great a heart-throb in the kiss, that he thought she must needs feel it. Then, in a gust of anger at her insensibility, he shook her maiden form, with a violence which, the next moment, it affrighted him to remember. He withdrew his encircling arms; and Alice — whose figure, though flexible, had been wholly impassive—relapsed into the same attitude as before these attempts to arouse her. Maule having shifted his position, her face was turned towards him, slightly, but with what seemed to be a reference of her very slumber to his guidance.

Then, it was a strange sight to behold, how the man of conventionalities shook the powder out of his periwig; how the reserved and stately gentleman forgot his dignity; how the gold-embroidered waistcoat flickered and glistened in the firelight, with the convulsion of rage, terror, and sorrow, in the human heart that was beating under it!

"Villain!" cried Mr. Pyncheon, shaking his clenched fist at Maule. "You and the fiend together have robbed me of my daughter! Give her back—spawn of the old wizard!—or you shall climb Gallows-Hill in your grandfather's footsteps!"

"Softly, Mr. Pyncheon!" said the carpenter with scornful composure.—"Softly, an' it please your worship; else you will spoil those rich lace-ruffles, at your wrists! Is it my crime, if you have sold your daughter for the mere hope of getting a sheet of yellow parchment into your clutch? There sits Mistress Alice, quietly asleep! Now let Matthew Maule try whether she be as proud, as the carpenter found her awhile since!"

He spoke; and Alice responded, with a soft, subdued, inward acquiescence, and a bending of her form towards him, like the flame of a torch, when it indicates a gentle draft of air. He beckoned with his hand; and, rising from her chair—blindly, but undoubtingly, as tending to her sure and inevitable centre—the proud Alice approached him. He waved her back; and, retreating, Alice sank again into her seat!

"She is mine!" said Matthew Maule. "Mine, by the right of the strongest spirit!"

In the further progress of the legend, there is a long, grotesque, and occasionally awe-striking account of the carpenter's incantations (if so they are to be called) with a view of discovering the lost document. It appears to have been his object to convert the mind of Alice into a kind of telescopic medium, through which Mr. Pyncheon and himself might obtain a glimpse into the spiritual world.[1] He succeeded, accordingly, in holding an imperfect sort of intercourse, at one remove, with the departed personages, in whose custody the so much valued secret had been carried beyond the precincts of earth. During her trance, Alice described three figures, as being present to her spiritualized perception. One

1. "Questions as to unsettled points of History, and Mysteries of Nature, to be asked of a mesmerized person." (*American Notebooks*, entry made between January 23 and June 1, 1842.)

was an aged, dignified, stern-looking gentleman, clad, as for a solemn festival, in grave and costly attire, but with a great blood-stain on his richly wrought band;—the second, an aged man, meanly dressed, with a dark and malign countenance, and a broken halter about his neck;—the third, a person not so advanced in life as the former two, but beyond the middle-age, wearing a coarse woollen tunic and leather-breeches, and with a carpenter's rule sticking out of his side-pocket. These three visionary characters possessed a mutual knowledge of the missing document. One of them, in truth—it was he with the blood-stain on his band—seemed, unless his gestures were misunderstood, to hold the parchment in his immediate keeping, but was prevented, by his two partners in the mystery, from disburthening himself of the trust. Finally, when he showed a purpose of shouting forth the secret, loudly enough to be heard from his own sphere into that of mortals, his companions struggled with him, and pressed their hands over his mouth; and forthwith—whether that he were choked by it, or that the secret itself was of a crimson hue—there was a fresh flow of blood upon his band. Upon this, the two meanly-dressed figures mocked and jeered at the much-abashed old dignitary, and pointed their fingers at the stain!

At this juncture, Maule turned to Mr. Pyncheon.

"It will never be allowed!" said he. "The custody of this secret, that would so enrich his heirs, makes part of your grandfather's retribution. He must choke with it, until it is no longer of any value. And keep you the House of the Seven Gables! It is too dear bought an inheritance, and too heavy, with the curse upon it, to be shifted yet awhile from the Colonel's posterity!"

Mr. Pyncheon tried to speak, but—what with fear and passion—could make only a gurgling murmur in his throat. The carpenter smiled.

"Aha, worshipful Sir! So, you have old Maule's blood to drink!" said he jeeringly.

"Fiend in man's shape, why dost thou keep dominion over my child?" cried Mr. Pyncheon, when his choked utterance could make way.—"Give me back my daughter! Then go thy ways; and may we never meet again!"

"Your daughter!" said Matthew Maule. "Why, she is fairly mine! Nevertheless, not to be too hard with fair Mistress Alice, I will leave her in your keeping; but I do not warrant you, that she shall never have occasion to remember Maule, the carpenter."

He waved his hands with an upward motion; and, after a few repetitions of similar gestures, the beautiful Alice Pyncheon awoke from her strange trance. She awoke, without the slightest recollection of her visionary experience; but as one losing herself in a momentary reverie, and returning to the consciousness of actual life, in almost as brief an interval as the down-sinking flame of the hearth should quiver again up the chimney. On recognizing Matthew Maule, she assumed an air of somewhat cold, but gentle dignity; the rather, as there was a certain peculiar smile on the carpenter's visage, that stirred the native pride of the fair Alice. So ended, for that time, the quest for the lost title-deed of the Pyncheon territory at the eastward; nor, though often subsequently renewed, has it ever yet befallen a Pyncheon to set his eye upon that parchment.

But alas, for the beautiful, the gentle, yet too haughty Alice! A power, that she little dreamed of, had laid its grasp upon her maiden soul. A will, most unlike her own, constrained her to do its grotesque and fantastic bidding. Her father, as it proved, had martyred his poor child to an inordinate desire for measuring his land by miles, instead of acres. And, therefore, while Alice Pyncheon lived, she was Maule's slave, in a bondage more humiliating, a thousand-fold, than that which binds its chain around the body. Seated by his humble fireside, Maule had but to wave his hand; and, wherever the proud lady chanced to be—whether in her chamber,

or entertaining her father's stately guests, or worshipping at
church—whatever her place or occupation, her spirit passed
from beneath her own control, and bowed itself to Maule.
"Alice, laugh!"—the carpenter, beside his hearth, would say;
or perhaps intensely will it, without a spoken word. And,
even were it prayer-time, or at a funeral, Alice must break into
wild laughter. "Alice, be sad!"—and, at the instant, down
would come her tears, quenching all the mirth of those
around her, like sudden rain upon a bonfire. "Alice, dance!"
—and dance she would, not in such court-like measures as she
had learned abroad, but some high-paced jig, or hop-skip
rigadoon, befitting the brisk lasses at a rustic merry-making.
It seemed to be Maule's impulse, not to ruin Alice, nor to
visit her with any black or gigantic mischief, which would
have crowned her sorrow with the grace of tragedy, but to
wreak a low, ungenerous scorn upon her. Thus all the dignity
of life was lost. She felt herself too much abased, and longed
to change natures with some worm!

One evening, at a bridal party—(but not her own; for, so
lost from self-control, she would have deemed it sin to marry)
—poor Alice was beckoned forth by her unseen despot, and
constrained, in her gossamer white dress and satin slippers, to
hasten along the street to the mean dwelling of a laboring-
man. There was laughter and good cheer, within; for Matthew Maule, that night, was to wed the laborer's daughter, and
had summoned proud Alice Pyncheon to wait upon his bride.
And so she did; and when the twain were one, Alice awoke
out of her enchanted sleep. Yet, no longer proud—humbly,
and with a smile, all steeped in sadness—she kissed Maule's
wife, and went her way. It was an inclement night; the south-
east wind drove the mingled snow and rain into her thinly
sheltered bosom; her satin slippers were wet through and
through, as she trod the muddy sidewalks. The next day, a
cold; soon, a settled cough; anon, a hectic cheek, a wasted
form, that sat beside the harpsichord, and filled the house

with music! Music, in which a strain of the heavenly choristers was echoed! Oh, joy! For Alice had borne her last humiliation! Oh, greater joy! For Alice was penitent of her one earthly sin, and proud no more!

The Pyncheons made a great funeral for Alice. The kith and kin were there, and the whole respectability of the town besides. But, last in the procession, came Matthew Maule, gnashing his teeth, as if he would have bitten his own heart in twain; the darkest and wofullest man that ever walked behind a corpse. He meant to humble Alice, not to kill her;— but he had taken a woman's delicate soul into his rude gripe, to play with;—and she was dead!

## XIV

## PHOEBE'S GOOD BYE

HOLGRAVE, plunging into his tale with the energy and absorption natural to a young author, had given a good deal of action to the parts capable of being developed and exemplified in that manner. He now observed that a certain remarkable drowsiness (wholly unlike that with which the reader possibly feels himself affected) had been flung over the senses of his auditress. It was the effect, unquestionably, of the mystic gesticulations, by which he had sought to bring bodily before Phoebe's perception the figure of the mesmerizing carpenter. With the lids drooping over her eyes—now lifted, for an instant, and drawn down again, as with leaden weights—she leaned slightly towards him, and seemed almost to regulate her breath by his. Holgrave gazed at her, as he rolled up his manuscript, and recognized an incipient stage of that curious psychological condition, which, as he had himself told Phoebe, he possessed more than an ordinary faculty of producing. A veil was beginning to be muffled about her, in which she could behold only him, and live only in his thoughts and emotions. His glance, as he fastened it on the young girl, grew involuntarily more concentrated; in his attitude, there was the consciousness of power, investing his hardly mature figure with a dignity that did not belong to its physical manifestation. It was evident, that, with but one wave of his hand and a corresponding effort of his will, he could complete his mastery over Phoebe's yet free and virgin spirit; he could establish an influence over this good, pure, and simple child, as dangerous, and perhaps as disastrous, as that which the carpenter of his legend had acquired and exercised over the ill-fated Alice.

To a disposition like Holgrave's, at once speculative and active, there is no temptation so great as the opportunity of acquiring empire over the human spirit; nor any idea more seductive to a young man, than to become the arbiter of a young girl's destiny. Let us, therefore—whatever his defects of nature and education, and in spite of his scorn for creeds and institutions—concede to the Daguerreotypist the rare and high quality of reverence for another's individuality. Let us allow him integrity, also, forever after to be confided in; since he forbade himself to twine that one link more, which might have rendered his spell over Phoebe indissoluble.

He made a slight gesture upward, with his hand.

"You really mortify me, my dear Miss Phoebe!" he exclaimed, smiling half sarcastically at her. "My poor story, it is but too evident, will never do for Godey or Graham! Only think of your falling asleep, at what I hoped the newspaper critics would pronounce a most brilliant, powerful, imaginative, pathetic, and original winding up! Well; the manuscript must serve to light lamps with;—if, indeed, being so imbued with my gentle dulness, it is any longer capable of flame!"

"Me asleep! How can you say so?" answered Phoebe, as unconscious of the crisis through which she had passed, as an infant of the precipice to the verge of which it has rolled. "No, no! I consider myself as having been very attentive; and though I don't remember the incidents quite distinctly, yet I have an impression of a vast deal of trouble and calamity —so, no doubt, the story will prove exceedingly attractive."

By this time, the sun had gone down, and was tinting the clouds towards the zenith with those bright hues, which are not seen there until some time after sunset, and when the horizon has quite lost its richer brilliancy. The moon, too, which had long been climbing overhead, and unobtrusively melting its disk into the azure—like an ambitious demagogue, who hides his aspiring purpose by assuming the prevalent hue of popular sentiment—now began to shine out, broad and oval, in its middle pathway. These silvery beams were already powerful enough to change the character of the lingering daylight. They softened and embellished the aspect of the old house; although the shadows fell deeper into the angles of its many gables, and lay brooding under the projecting story, and within the half-open door. With the lapse of every moment, the garden grew more picturesque; the fruit-trees, shrubbery, and flower-bushes had a dark obscurity among them. The common-place characteristics—which, at noontide, it seemed to have taken a century of sordid life to accumulate —were now transfigured by a charm of romance. A hundred mysterious years were whispering among the leaves, whenever the slight sea-breeze found its way thither, and stirred them. Through the foliage that roofed the little summer-house, the moonlight flickered to-and-fro, and fell, silvery white, on the dark floor, the table, and the circular bench, with a continual shift and play, according as the chinks and wayward crevices among the twigs admitted or shut out the glimmer.

So sweetly cool was the atmosphere, after all the feverish day, that the summer Eve might be fancied as sprinkling dews and liquid moonlight, with a dash of icy temper in them, out of a silver vase. Here and there, a few drops of this freshness were scattered on a human heart, and gave it youth again, and sympathy with the eternal youth of nature. The artist chanced to be one, on whom the reviving influence fell. It made him feel—what he sometimes almost forgot, thrust so early, as he had been, into the rude struggle of man with man—how youthful he still was.

"It seems to me," he observed, "that I never watched the

coming of so beautiful an eve, and never felt anything so very much like happiness as at this moment. After all, what a good world we live in! How good, and beautiful! How young it is, too, with nothing really rotten or age-worn in it! This old house, for example, which sometimes has positively oppressed my breath with its smell of decaying timber! And this garden, where the black mould always clings to my spade, as if I were a sexton, delving in a grave-yard! Could I keep the feeling that now possesses me, the garden would every day be virgin soil, with the earth's first freshness in the flavor of its beans and squashes; and the house!—it would be like a bower in Eden, blossoming with the earliest roses that God ever made. Moonlight, and the sentiment in man's heart, responsive to it, is the greatest of renovators and reformers. And all other reform and renovation, I suppose, will prove to be no better than moonshine!"

"I have been happier than I am now—at least, much gayer," said Phoebe thoughtfully. "Yet I am sensible of a great charm in this brightening moonlight; and I love to watch how the day, tired as it is, lags away reluctantly, and hates to be called yesterday, so soon. I never cared much about moonlight before. What is there, I wonder, so beautiful in it, to-night?"

"And you have never felt it before?" inquired the artist, looking earnestly at the girl, through the twilight.

"Never," answered Phoebe; "and life does not look the same, now that I have felt it so. It seems as if I had looked at everything, hitherto, in broad daylight, or else in the ruddy light of a cheerful fire, glimmering and dancing through a room. Ah, poor me!" she added, with a half-melancholy laugh. "I shall never be so merry as before I knew Cousin Hepzibah and poor Cousin Clifford. I have grown a great deal older, in this little time. Older, and, I hope, wiser, and —not exactly sadder—but, certainly, with not half so much lightness in my spirits! I have given them my sunshine, and have been glad to give it; but, of course, I cannot both give and keep it. They are welcome, notwithstanding!"

"You have lost nothing, Phoebe, worth keeping, nor which it was possible to keep," said Holgrave, after a pause. "Our first youth is of no value; for we are never conscious of it, until after it is gone. But sometimes—always, I suspect, unless one is exceedingly unfortunate—there comes a sense of second youth, gushing out of the heart's joy at being in love; or, possibly, it may come to crown some other grand festival in life, if any other such there be. This bemoaning of one's self (as you do now) over the first, careless, shallow gaiety of youth departed, and this profound happiness at youth regained—so much deeper and richer than that we lost—are essential to the soul's developement. In some cases, the two states come almost simultaneously, and mingle the sadness and the rapture in one mysterious emotion."

"I hardly think I understand you," said Phoebe.

"No wonder," replied Holgrave, smiling; "for I have told you a secret which I hardly began to know, before I found myself giving it utterance. Remember it, however; and when the truth becomes clear to you, then think of this moonlight scene!"

"It is entirely moonlight now; except only a little flush of faint crimson, upward from the west, between those buildings," remarked Phoebe. "I must go in. Cousin Hepzibah is not quick at figures, and will give herself a headache over the day's accounts, unless I help her."

But Holgrave detained her a little longer.

"Miss Hepzibah tells me," observed he, "that you return to the country, in a few days."

"Yes; but only for a little while," answered Phoebe; "for I look upon this as my present home. I go to make a few arrangements, and to take a more deliberate leave of my mother and friends. It is pleasant to live where one is much desired, and very useful; and I think I may have the satisfaction of feeling myself so, here."

"You surely may, and more than you imagine," said the artist. "Whatever health, comfort, and natural life, exists in the house, is embodied in your person. These blessings came along with you, and will vanish when you leave the threshold. Miss Hepzibah, by secluding herself from society, has lost all true relation with it, and is in fact dead; although she galvanizes herself into a semblance of life, and stands behind her counter, afflicting the world with a greatly-to-be-deprecated scowl. Your poor Cousin Clifford is another dead and long-buried person, on whom the Governor and Council have wrought a necromantic miracle. I should not wonder if he were to crumble away, some morning, after you are gone, and nothing be seen of him more, except a heap of dust. Miss Hepzibah, at any rate, will lose what little flexibility she has. They both exist by you!"

"I should be very sorry to think so," answered Phoebe, gravely. "But it is true that my small abilities were precisely what they needed; and I have a real interest in their welfare—an odd kind of motherly sentiment—which I wish you would not laugh at! And let me tell you frankly, Mr. Holgrave, I am sometimes puzzled to know whether you wish them well or ill."

"Undoubtedly," said the Daguerreotypist, "I do feel an interest in this antiquated, poverty-stricken, old maiden lady; and this degraded and shattered gentleman—this abortive lover of the Beautiful. A kindly interest too, helpless old children that they are! But you have no conception what a different kind of heart mine is from your own. It is not my impulse—as regards these two individuals—either to help or hinder; but to look on, to analyze, to explain matters to myself, and to comprehend the drama which, for almost two hundred years, has been dragging its slow length over the ground, where you and I now tread. If permitted to witness the close, I doubt not to derive a moral satisfaction from it, go matters how they may. There is a conviction within me, that the end draws nigh. But, though Providence sent you hither to help, and sends me only as a privileged and meet spectator, I pledge myself to lend these unfortunate beings whatever aid I can!"

"I wish you would speak more plainly," cried Phoebe, perplexed and displeased;—"and, above all, that you would feel more like a christian and a human being! How is it possible to see people in distress, without desiring, more than anything else, to help and comfort them? You talk as if this old house were a theatre; and you seem to look at Hepzibah's and Clifford's misfortunes, and those of generations before them, as a tragedy, such as I have seen acted in the hall of a country-hotel; only the present one appears to be played exclusively for your amusement! I do not like this. The play costs the performers too much—and the audience is too cold-hearted!"

"You are severe!" said Holgrave, compelled to recognize a degree of truth in this piquant sketch of his own mood.

"And then," continued Phoebe, "what can you mean by your conviction, which you tell me of, that the end is drawing near? Do you know of any new trouble hanging over my poor relatives? If so, tell me at once, and I will not leave them!"

"Forgive me, Phoebe!" said the Daguerreotypist, holding out his hand, to which the girl was constrained to yield her own. "I am somewhat of a mystic, it must be confessed. The tendency is in my blood, together with the faculty of mesmerism, which might have brought me to Gallows-Hill, in the good old times of witchcraft. Believe me, if I were really aware of any secret, the disclosure of which would benefit your friends—who are my own friends, likewise—you should learn it, before we part. But I have no such knowledge."

"You hold something back!" said Phoebe.

"Nothing—no secrets, but my own," answered Holgrave. "I can perceive, indeed, that Judge Pyncheon still keeps his eye on Clifford, in whose ruin he had so large a share. His motives and intentions, however, are a mystery to me. He is a determined and relentless man, with the genuine character of an inquisitor; and had he any object to gain by putting Clifford to the rack, I verily believe that he would wrench his joints from their sockets in order to accomplish it. But, so wealthy and eminent as he is — so powerful in his own strength, and in the support of society on all sides—what can Judge Pyncheon have to hope or fear from the imbecile, branded, half-torpid Clifford?"

"Yet," urged Phoebe, "you did speak as if misfortune were impending!"

"Oh, that was because I am morbid!" replied the artist. "My mind has a twist aside, like almost everybody's mind, except your own. Moreover, it is so strange to find myself an inmate of this old Pyncheon-house, and sitting in this old garden—(hark, how Maule's Well is murmuring!)—that, were it only for this one circumstance, I cannot help fancying that Destiny is arranging its fifth act for a catastrophe."

"There!" cried Phoebe with renewed vexation; for she was by nature as hostile to mystery, as the sunshine to a dark corner. "You puzzle me more than ever!"

"Then let us part friends!" said Holgrave, pressing her hand. "Or, if not friends, let us part before you entirely hate me. You, who love everybody else in the world!"

"Good bye, then," said Phoebe frankly. "I do not mean to be angry a great while, and should be sorry to have you think so. There has Cousin Hepzibah been standing in the shadow of the door-way, this quarter-of-an-hour past! She thinks I stay too long in the damp garden. So, good night, and good bye!"

On the second morning thereafter, Phoebe might have been seen, in her straw bonnet, with a shawl on one arm and a little carpet-bag on the other, bidding adieu to Hepzibah and Cousin Clifford. She was to take a seat in the next train of cars, which would transport her to within half-a-dozen miles of her country village.

The tears were in Phoebe's eyes; a smile, dewy with affectionate regret, was glimmering around her pleasant mouth. She wondered how it came to pass, that her life of a few weeks, here in this heavy-hearted old mansion, had taken such hold of her, and so melted into her associations, as now to seem a more important centre-point of remembrance than all which had gone before. How had Hepzibah—grim, silent, and irresponsive to her overflow of cordial sentiment—contrived to win so much love? And Clifford—in his abortive decay, with the mystery of fearful crime upon him, and the close prison-atmosphere yet lurking in his breath—how had he transformed himself into the simplest child, whom Phoebe felt bound to watch over, and be, as it were, the Providence of his unconsidered hours! Everything, at that instant of farewell, stood out prominently to her view. Look where she would, lay her hand on what she might, the object responded to her consciousness, as if a moist human heart were in it.

She peeped from the window into the garden, and felt herself more regretful at leaving this spot of black earth, vitiated with such an age-long growth of weeds, than joyful at the idea of again scenting her pine-forests and fresh clover-fields. She called Chanticleer, his two wives, and the venerable chicken, and threw them some crumbs of bread from the breakfast-table. These being hastily gobbled up, the chicken spread its wings, and alighted close by Phoebe on the window-sill, where it looked gravely into her face and vented its emotions in a croak. Phoebe bade it be a good old chicken, during her absence, and promised to bring it a little bag of buckwheat.

"Ah, Phoebe," remarked Hepzibah, "you do not smile so naturally as when you came to us! Then, the smile chose to shine out;—now, you choose it should. It is well that you are going back, for a little while, into your native air! There has been too much weight on your spirits. The house is too gloomy and lonesome; the shop is full of vexations; and as for me, I have no faculty of making things look brighter than they are. Dear Clifford has been your only comfort!"

"Come hither, Phoebe!" suddenly cried her Cousin Clifford, who had said very little, all the morning.—"Close!—closer!—and look me in the face!"

Phoebe put one of her small hands on each elbow of his chair, and leaned her face towards him, so that he might peruse it as carefully as he would. It is probable that the latent emotions of this parting hour had revived, in some degree, his bedimmed and enfeebled faculties. At any rate, Phoebe soon felt that, if not the profound insight of a seer, yet a more than feminine delicacy of appreciation was making her heart the subject of its regard. A moment before, she had known nothing which she would have sought to hide. Now, as if some secret were hinted to her own consciousness through the medium of another's perception, she was fain to let her eyelids droop beneath Clifford's gaze. A blush, too—the redder, because she strove hard to keep it down—ascended higher and higher, in a tide of fitful progress, until even her brow was all suffused with it.

"It is enough, Phoebe!" said Clifford, with a melancholy smile. "When I first saw you, you were the prettiest little maiden in the world; and now you have deepened into beauty! Girlhood has passed into womanhood; the bud is a bloom! Go, now! I feel lonelier than I did."

Phoebe took leave of the desolate couple, and passed through the shop, twinkling her eyelids to shake off a dewdrop; for—considering how brief her absence was to be, and therefore the folly of being cast down about it she would not so far acknowledge her tears as to dry them with her handkerchief. On the door-step, she met the little urchin, whose marvellous feats of gastronomy have been recorded in the earlier pages of our narrative. She took from the window some specimen or other of natural history—her eyes being too dim with moisture to inform her accurately whether it was a rabbit or a hippopotamus—put it into the child's hand, as a parting gift, and went her way. Old Uncle Venner was just coming out of his door, with a wood-horse and saw on his shoulder; and, trudging along the street, he scrupled not to keep company with Phoebe, so far as their paths lay together; nor, in spite of his patched coat and rusty beaver, and the curious fashion of his tow-cloth trowsers, could she find it in her heart to outwalk him.

"We shall miss you, next Sabbath afternoon," observed the street-philosopher. "It is unaccountable how little while it takes some folks to grow just as natural to a man as his own breath; and, begging your pardon, Miss Phoebe, (though there can be no offence in an old man's saying it,) that's just what you've grown, to me! My years have been a great many, and your life is but just beginning; and yet, you are somehow as familiar to me as if I had found you at my mother's door, and you had blossomed, like a running vine, all along my pathway since. Come back soon, or I shall be gone to my farm; for I begin to find these wood-sawing jobs a little too tough for my back-ache."

"Very soon, Uncle Venner," replied Phoebe.

"And let it be all the sooner, Phoebe, for the sake of those poor souls yonder," continued her companion. "They can never do without you, now—never, Phoebe, never!—no more than if one of God's angels had been living with them, and making their dismal house pleasant and comfortable. Don't it seem to you they'd be in a sad case, if, some pleasant summer morning like this, the angel should spread his wings, and fly to the place he came from? Well; just so they feel, now that you're going home by the railroad! They can't bear it, Miss Phoebe; so be sure to come back!"

"I am no angel, Uncle Venner," said Phoebe, smiling, as she offered him her hand at the street-corner. "But, I suppose, people never feel so much like angels as when they are doing what little good they may. So I shall certainly come back!"

Thus parted the old man and the rosy girl; and Phoebe took the wings of the morning, and was soon flitting almost as rapidly away, as if endowed with the aerial locomotion of the angels, to whom Uncle Venner had so graciously compared her.

## XV

# THE SCOWL AND SMILE

SEVERAL days passed over the seven gables, heavily and drearily enough. In fact (not to attribute the whole gloom of sky and earth to the one inauspicious circum-. stance of Phoebe's departure) an easterly storm had set in, and indefatigably applied itself to the task of making the black roof and walls of the old house look more cheerless than ever before. Yet was the outside not half so cheerless as the interior. Poor Clifford was cut off, at once, from all his scanty resources of enjoyment. Phoebe was not there; nor did the sunshine fall upon the floor. The garden, with its muddy walks and the chill, dripping foliage of its summer-house, was an image to be shuddered at. Nothing flourished in the cold, moist, pitiless atmosphere, drifting with the brackish scud of sea-breezes, except the moss along the joints of the shingle-roof, and the great bunch of weeds, that had lately been suffering from drought, in the angle between the two front gables.

As for Hepzibah, she seemed not merely possessed with the east-wind, but to be, in her very person, only another phase of this gray and sullen spell of weather; the East-Wind itself, grim and disconsolate, in a rusty black silk-gown, and with a turban of cloud-wreaths on its head! The custom of the shop fell off, because a story got abroad that she soured her small beer and other damageable commodities, by scowling on them. It is perhaps true, that the public had something reasonably to complain of in her deportment; but towards Clifford she was neither ill-tempered nor unkind, nor felt less warmth of heart than always, had it been possible to make it reach him. The inutility of her best efforts, however, palsied the poor old gentlewoman. She could do little else than sit silently in a corner of the room, where the wet pear-tree branches, sweeping across the small windows, created a noonday dusk, which Hepzibah unconsciously darkened with her wo-begone aspect. It was no fault of Hepzibah's. Everything—even the old chairs and tables, that had known what weather was, for three or four such lifetimes as her own—looked as damp and chill as if the present were their worst experience. The picture of the Puritan Colonel shivered on the wall. The house itself shivered, from every attic of its seven gables, down to the great kitchen-fireplace, which served all the better as an emblem of the mansion's heart, because, though built for warmth, it was now so comfortless and empty.

Hepzibah attempted to enliven matters by a fire in the parlor. But the storm-demon kept watch above, and, whenever a flame was kindled, drove the smoke back again, choking the chimney's sooty throat with its own breath. Nevertheless, during four days of this miserable storm, Clifford wrapt himself in an old cloak, and occupied his customary chair. On the morning of the fifth, when summoned to breakfast, he responded only by a broken-hearted murmur, expressive of a determination not to leave his bed. His sister made no attempt to change his purpose. In fact, entirely as she loved him, Hepzibah could hardly have borne any longer the wretched duty—so impracticable by her few and rigid faculties—of seeking pastime for a still sensitive, but ruined mind, critical, and fastidious, without force or volition. It was, at least, something short of positive despair, that, to-day, she might sit shivering alone, and not suffer continually a new grief, and unreasonable pang of remorse, at every fitful sigh of her fellow-sufferer.

But Clifford, it seemed, though he did not make his appearance below stairs, had, after all, bestirred himself in quest of amusement. In the course of the forenoon, Hepzibah heard a note of music, which (there being no other tuneful contrivance in the House of the Seven Gables) she knew must proceed from Alice Pyncheon's harpsichord. She was aware that Clifford, in his youth, had possessed a cultivated taste for music, and a considerable degree of skill in its practice. It was difficult, however, to conceive of his retaining an accomplishment to which daily exercise is so essential, in the measure indicated by the sweet, airy, and delicate, though most melancholy strain, that now stole upon her ear. Nor was it less marvellous, that the long silent instrument should be capable of so much melody. Hepzibah involuntarily thought of the ghostly harmonies, prelusive of death in the family, which were attributed to the legendary Alice. But it was, perhaps, proof of the agency of other than spiritual fingers, that, after a few touches, the chords seemed to snap asunder with their own vibrations, and the music ceased.

But a harsher sound succeeded to the mysterious notes; nor was the easterly day fated to pass without an event, sufficient in itself to poison, for Hepzibah and Clifford, the balmiest air that ever brought the humming-birds along with it. The final echoes of Alice Pyncheon's performance, (or Clifford's, if his we must consider it,) were driven away by no less vulgar a dissonance than the ringing of the shop-bell. A foot was heard scraping itself on the threshold, and thence somewhat ponderously stepping on the floor. Hepzibah delayed, a moment, while muffling herself in a faded shawl, which had been her defensive armor in a forty years' warfare against the east-wind. A characteristic sound, however—neither a cough nor a hem, but a kind of rumbling and reverberating spasm in somebody's capacious depth of chest—impelled her to hurry forward, with that aspect of fierce faint-heartedness, so common to women in cases of perilous emergency. Few of her sex, on such occasions, have ever looked so terrible as our poor scowling Hepzibah. But the visitor quietly closed the shop-door behind him, stood up his umbrella against the counter, and turned a visage of composed benignity, to meet the alarm and anger which his appearance had excited.

Hepzibah's presentiment had not deceived her. It was no other than Judge Pyncheon, who, after in vain trying the front-door, had now effected his entrance into the shop.

"How do you do, Cousin Hepzibah?—and how does this most inclement weather affect our poor Clifford?" began the Judge; and wonderful it seemed, indeed, that the easterly storm was not put to shame, or, at any rate, a little mollified, by the genial benevolence of his smile. "I could not rest without calling to ask, once more, whether I can in any manner promote his comfort, or your own!"

"You can do nothing," said Hepzibah, controlling her agitation as well as she could. "I devote myself to Clifford. He has every comfort which his situation admits of."

"But, allow me to suggest, dear Cousin," rejoined the Judge, "you err—in all affection and kindness, no doubt, and with the very best intentions—but you do err, nevertheless, in keeping your brother so secluded. Why insulate him thus from all sympathy and kindness? Clifford, alas! has had too much of solitude. Now let him try society—the society, that is to say, of kindred and old friends. Let me, for instance, but see Clifford; and I will answer for the good effect of the interview."

"You cannot see him," answered Hepzibah. "Clifford has kept his bed since yesterday."

"What! How! Is he ill?" exclaimed Judge Pyncheon, starting with what seemed to be angry alarm; for the very frown of the old Puritan darkened through the room as he spoke.

"Nay, then, I must and will see him! What if he should die?"

"He is in no danger of death," said Hepzibah—and added, with bitterness that she could repress no longer, "None;—unless he shall be persecuted to death, now, by the same man who long ago attempted it!"

"Cousin Hepzibah," said the Judge, with an impressive earnestness of manner, which grew even to tearful pathos as he proceeded, "is it possible that you do not perceive how unjust, how unkind, how unchristian, is this constant, this long-continued bitterness against me, for a part which I was constrained by duty and conscience, by the force of law, and at my own peril, to act? What did I do, in detriment to Clifford, which it was possible to leave undone? How could you, his sister—if, for your never-ending sorrow, as it has been for mine, you had known what I did—have shown greater tenderness? And do you think, Cousin, that it has cost me no pang? —that it has left no anguish in my bosom, from that day to this, amidst all the prosperity with which Heaven has blessed me?—or that I do not now rejoice, when it is deemed consistent with the dues of public justice and the welfare of society, that this dear kinsman, this early friend, this nature so delicately and beautifully constituted—so unfortunate, let us pronounce him, and forbear to say, so guilty—that our own Clifford, in fine, should be given back to life and its possibilities of enjoyment? Ah, you little know me, Cousin Hepzibah! You little know this heart! It now throbs at the thought of meeting him! There lives not the human being—(except yourself; and you not more than I)—who has shed so many tears for Clifford's calamity! You behold some of them now. There is none who would so delight to promote his happiness! Try me, Hepzibah!—try me, Cousin!—try the man whom you have treated as your enemy and Clifford's!—try Jaffrey Pyncheon, and you shall find him true, to the heart's core!"

"In the name of Heaven," cried Hepzibah, provoked only to intenser indignation by this outgush of the inestimable tenderness of a stern nature—"in God's name, whom you insult—and whose power I could almost question, since He hears you utter so many false words, without palsying your tongue—give over, I beseech you, this loathsome pretence of affection for your victim! You hate him! Say so, like a man! You cherish, at this moment, some black purpose against him, in your heart! Speak it out, at once!—or, if you hope so to promote it better, hide it, till you can triumph in its success. But never speak again of your love for my poor brother! I cannot bear it! It will drive me beyond a woman's decency! It will drive me mad! Forbear! Not another word! It will make me spurn at you!" [1]

For once, Hepzibah's wrath had given her courage. She had spoken. But, after all, was this unconquerable distrust of Judge Pyncheon's integrity—and this utter denial, apparently, of his claim to stand in the ring of human sympathies— were they founded in any just perception of his character, or merely the offspring of a woman's unreasoning prejudice, deduced from nothing?

The Judge, beyond all question, was a man of eminent respectability. The church acknowledged it; the state acknowledged it. It was denied by nobody. In all the very extensive sphere of those who knew him, whether in his public or private capacities, there was not an individual— except Hepzibah, and some lawless mystic like the Daguerreo- typist, and possibly a few political opponents—who would have dreamed of seriously disputing his claim to a high and honorable place in the world's regard. Nor, we must do him the further justice to say, did Judge Pyncheon himself, prob- ably, entertain many or very frequent doubts, that his envi- able reputation accorded with his deserts. His conscience, therefore—usually considered the surest witness to a man's integrity—his conscience, unless, it might be for the little space of five minutes in the twenty-four hours, or, now and then, some black day in the whole year's circle—his conscience

1. This awkward construction is the result of Hawthorne's having substituted "spurn" for "spit" in the manuscript and then forgetting to cross out the no longer appropriate "at."

bore an accordant testimony with the world's laudatory voice. And yet, strong as this evidence may seem to be, we should hesitate to peril our own conscience on the assertion, that the Judge and the consenting world were right, and that poor Hepzibah, with her solitary prejudice, was wrong. Hidden from mankind—forgotten by himself, or buried so deeply under a sculptured and ornamented pile of ostentatious deeds, that his daily life could take no note of it—there may have lurked some evil and unsightly thing. Nay; we could almost venture to say farther, that a daily guilt might have been acted by him, continually renewed, and reddening forth afresh, like the miraculous blood-stain of a murder, without his necessarily, and at every moment, being aware of it.

Men of strong minds, great force of character, and a hard texture of the sensibilities, are very capable of falling into mistakes of this kind. They are ordinarily men to whom forms are of paramount importance. Their field of action lies among the external phenomena of life. They possess vast ability in grasping, and arranging, and appropriating to themselves, the big, heavy, solid unrealities, such as gold, landed estate, offices of trust and emolument, and public honors. With these materials, and with deeds of goodly aspect, done in the public eye, an individual of this class builds up, as it were, a tall and stately edifice, which, in the view of other people, and ultimately in his own view, is no other than the man's character, or the man himself. Behold, therefore, a palace! Its splendid halls and suites of spacious apartments are floored with a mosaic-work of costly marbles; its windows, the whole height of each room, admit the sunshine through the most transparent of plate-glass; its high cornices are gilded, and its ceilings gorgeously painted; and a lofty dome—through which, from the central pavement, you may gaze up to the sky, as with no obstructing medium between— surmounts the whole. With what fairer and nobler emblem could any man desire to shadow forth his character? Ah; but in some low and obscure nook—some narrow closet on the ground floor, shut, locked, and bolted, and the key flung away—or beneath the marble pavement, in a stagnant water-puddle, with the richest pattern of mosaic-work above—may lie a corpse, half-decayed, and still decaying, and diffusing its death-scent all through the palace! The inhabitant will not be conscious of it; for it has long been his daily breath! Neither will the visitors; for they smell only the rich odors which the master sedulously scatters through the palace, and the incense which they bring, and delight to burn before him! Now and then, perchance, comes in a seer, before whose sadly gifted eye the whole structure melts into thin air, leaving only the hidden nook, the bolted closet, with the cobwebs festooned over its forgotten door, or the deadly hole under the pavement, and the decaying corpse within. Here, then, we are to seek the true emblem of the man's character, and of the deed that gives whatever reality it possesses, to his life. And, beneath the show of a marble palace, that pool of stagnant water, foul with many impurities, and perhaps tinged with blood—that secret abomination, above which, possibly, he may say his prayers, without remembering it—is this man's miserable soul!

To apply this train of remark somewhat more closely to Judge Pyncheon! We might say (without, in the least, imputing crime to a personage of his eminent respectability) that there was enough of splendid rubbish in his life to cover up and paralyze a more active and subtle conscience than the Judge was ever troubled with. The purity of his judicial character, while on the bench; the faithfulness of his public service in subsequent capacities; his devotedness to his party, and the rigid consistency with which he had adhered to its principles, or, at all events, kept pace with its organized movements; his remarkable zeal as president of a Bible society; his unimpeachable integrity as treasurer of a Widow's and Orphan's fund; his benefits to horticulture, by

producing two much-esteemed varieties of the pear, and to
agriculture, through the agency of the famous Pyncheon-
bull; the cleanliness of his moral deportment, for a great
many years past; the severity with which he had frowned
upon, and finally cast off, an expensive and dissipated son,
delaying forgiveness until within the final quarter of an hour
of the young man's life; his prayers at morning and eventide,
and graces at mealtime; his efforts in furtherance of the
temperance-cause; his confining himself, since the last attack
of the gout, to five diurnal glasses of old Sherry wine; the
snowy whiteness of his linen, the polish of his boots, the
handsomeness of his gold-headed cane, the square and roomy
fashion of his coat, and the fineness of its material, and, in
general, the studied propriety of his dress and equipment;
the scrupulousness with which he paid public notice, in the
street, by a bow, a lifting of the hat, a nod, or a motion of the
hand, to all and sundry his acquaintances, rich or poor; the
smile of broad benevolence wherewith he made it a point to
gladden the whole world;—what room could possibly be found
for darker traits, in a portrait made up of lineaments like
these! This proper face was what he beheld in the looking-
glass. This admirably arranged life was what he was conscious of, in the progress of every day. Then, might not he
claim to be its result and sum, and say to himself and the
community—"Behold Judge Pyncheon, there"?

And, allowing that, many, many years ago, in his early
and reckless youth, he had committed some one wrong act—
or that, even now, the inevitable force of circumstances
should occasionally make him do one questionable deed,
among a thousand praiseworthy, or, at least, blameless ones—
would you characterize the Judge by that one necessary deed,
and that half-forgotten act, and let it overshadow the fair
aspect of a lifetime! What is there so ponderous in evil, that
a thumb's bigness of it should outweigh the mass of things
not evil, which were heaped into the other scale! This scale

and balance system is a favorite one with people of Judge Pyncheon's brotherhood. A hard, cold man, thus unfortunately situated, seldom or never looking inward, and resolutely taking his idea of himself from what purports to be his image, as reflected in the mirror of public opinion, can scarcely arrive at true self-knowledge, except through loss of property and reputation. Sickness will not always help him to it; not always the death-hour!

But our affair, now, is with Judge Pyncheon, as he stood confronting the fierce outbreak of Hepzibah's wrath. Without premeditation, to her own surprise, and indeed terror, she had given vent, for once, to the inveteracy of her resentment, cherished against this kinsman, for thirty years.

Thus far, the Judge's countenance had expressed mild forbearance—grave and almost gentle deprecation of his cousin's unbecoming violence—free and christianlike forgiveness of the wrong inflicted by her words. But, when those words were irrevocably spoken, his look assumed sternness, the sense of power, and immitigable resolve; and this with so natural and imperceptible a change, that it seemed as if the iron man had stood there from the first, and the meek man not at all. The effect was as when the light vapory clouds, with their soft coloring, suddenly vanish from the stony brow of a precipitous mountain, and leave there the frown which you at once feel to be eternal. Hepzibah almost adopted the insane belief, that it was her old Puritan ancestor, and not the modern Judge, on whom she had just been wreaking the bitterness of her heart. Never did a man show stronger proof of the lineage attributed to him, than Judge Pyncheon, at this crisis, by his unmistakeable resemblance to the picture in the inner room.

"Cousin Hepzibah," said he, very calmly, "it is time to have done with this."

"With all my heart!" answered she. "Then why do you

persecute us any longer? Leave poor Clifford and me in peace. Neither of us desires anything better!"

"It is my purpose to see Clifford before I leave this house," continued the Judge. "Do not act like a madwoman, Hepzibah! I am his only friend, and an all-powerful one. Has it never occurred to you—are you so blind as not to have seen—that, without not merely my consent, but my efforts, my representations, the exertion of my whole influence, political, official, personal—Clifford would never have been what you call free? Did you think his release a triumph over me? Not so, my good Cousin; not so, by any means! The farthest possible from that! No; but it was the accomplishment of a purpose long entertained on my part. I set him free!"

"You!" answered Hepzibah. "I never will believe it! He owed his dungeon to you; his freedom, to God's providence!"

"I set him free!" re-affirmed Judge Pyncheon, with the calmest composure. "And I come hither now to decide whether he shall retain his freedom. It will depend upon himself. For this purpose, I must see him."

"Never!—it would drive him mad!" exclaimed Hepzibah, but with an irresoluteness, sufficiently perceptible to the keen eye of the Judge; for, without the slightest faith in his good intentions, she knew not whether there was most to dread in yielding, or resistance. "And why should you wish to see this wretched, broken man, who retains hardly a fraction of his intellect, and will hide even that from an eye which has no love in it?"

"He shall see love enough in mine, if that be all!" said the Judge, with well-grounded confidence in the benignity of his aspect. "But, Cousin Hepzibah, you confess a great deal, and very much to the purpose. Now, listen, and I will frankly explain my reasons for insisting on this interview. At the death, thirty years since, of our Uncle Jaffrey, it was found—I know not whether the circumstance ever attracted much of your attention, among the sadder interests that clustered round that event—but it was found that his visible estate, of every kind, fell far short of any estimate ever made of it. He was supposed to be immensely rich. Nobody doubted that he stood among the weightiest men of his day. It was one of his eccentricities, however—and not altogether a folly, neither—to conceal the amount of his property by making distant and foreign investments, perhaps under other names than his own, and by various means, familiar enough to capitalists, but unnecessary here to be specified. By Uncle Jaffrey's last will and testament, as you are aware, his entire property was bequeathed to me, with the single exception of a life-interest, to yourself, in this old family-mansion, and the strip of patrimonial estate, remaining attached to it."

"And do you seek to deprive us of that?" asked Hepzibah, unable to restrain her bitter contempt. "Is this your price for ceasing to persecute poor Clifford?"

"Certainly not, my dear Cousin!" answered the Judge, smiling benevolently. "On the contrary, as you must do me the justice to own, I have constantly expressed my readiness to double or treble your resources, whenever you should make up your mind to accept any kindness of that nature, at the hands of your kinsman. No, no! But here lies the gist of the matter. Of my Uncle's unquestionably great estate, as I have said, not the half—no, not one third, as I am fully convinced—was apparent after his death. Now, I have the best possible reasons for believing, that your brother Clifford can give me a clue to the recovery of the remainder!"

"Clifford?—Clifford know of any hidden wealth? Clifford have it in his power to make you rich?" cried the old gentlewoman, affected with a sense of something like ridicule, at the idea. "Impossible! You deceive yourself! It is really a thing to laugh at!"

"It is as certain as that I stand here!" said Judge Pyncheon, striking his gold-headed cane on the floor, and at the same time stamping his foot, as if to express his conviction the more forcibly by the whole emphasis of his substantial person.—"Clifford told me so himself!"

"No, no!" exclaimed Hepzibah incredulously. "You are dreaming, Cousin Jaffrey!"

"I do not belong to the dreaming class of men," said the Judge quietly. "Some months before my Uncle's death, Clifford boasted to me of the possession of the secret of incalculable wealth. His purpose was to taunt me, and excite my curiosity. I know it well. But, from a pretty distinct recollection of the particulars of our conversation, I am thoroughly convinced that there was truth in what he said. Clifford, at this moment, if he chooses—and choose he must—can inform me where to find the schedule, the documents, the evidences, in whatever shape they exist, of the vast amount of Uncle Jaffrey's missing property. He has the secret. His boast was no idle word. It had a directness, an emphasis, a particularity, that showed a backbone of solid meaning within the mystery of his expression."

"But what could have been Clifford's object," asked Hepzibah, "in concealing it so long?"

"It was one of the bad impulses of our fallen nature," replied the Judge, turning up his eyes. "He looked upon me as his enemy. He considered me as the cause of his overwhelming disgrace, his imminent peril of death, his irretrievable ruin. There was no great probability, therefore, of his volunteering information, out of his dungeon, that should elevate me still higher on the ladder of prosperity. But the moment has now come, when he must give up his secret."

"And what if he should refuse?" inquired Hepzibah. "Or—as I steadfastly believe—what if he has no knowledge of this wealth?"

"My dear Cousin," said Judge Pyncheon, with a quietude which he had the power of making more formidable than any violence, "since your brother's return, I have taken the precaution (a highly proper one in the near kinsman and natural guardian of an individual so situated) to have his deportment and habits constantly and carefully overlooked. Your neighbors have been eye-witnesses to whatever has passed in the garden. The butcher, the baker, the fish-monger, some of the customers of your shop, and many a prying old woman, have told me several of the secrets of your interior. A still larger circle—I myself among the rest—can testify to his extravagances, at the arched window. Thousands beheld him, a week or two ago, on the point of flinging himself thence into the street. From all this testimony, I am led to apprehend—reluctantly, and with deep grief—that Clifford's misfortunes have so affected his intellect, never very strong, that he cannot safely remain at large. The alternative, you must be aware—and its adoption will depend entirely on the decision which I am now about to make—the alternative is his confinement, probably for the remainder of his life, in a public asylum for persons in his unfortunate state of mind."

"You cannot mean it!" shrieked Hepzibah.

"Should my Cousin Clifford," continued Judge Pyncheon, wholly undisturbed, "from mere malice, and hatred of one whose interests ought naturally to be dear to him—a mode of passion that, as often as any other, indicates mental disease—should he refuse me the information, so important to myself, and which he assuredly possesses, I shall consider it the one needed jot of evidence, to satisfy my mind of his insanity. And, once sure of the course pointed out by conscience, you know me too well, Cousin Hepzibah, to entertain a doubt that I shall pursue it."

"Oh, Jaffrey—Cousin Jaffrey," cried Hepzibah, mournfully, not passionately—"it is you that are diseased in mind, not Clifford! You have forgotten that a woman was your mother! —that you have had sisters, brothers, children of your own!— or that there ever was affection between man and man, or pity from one man to another, in this miserable world! Else, how could you have dreamed of this? You are not young, Cousin Jaffrey—no, nor middle-aged—but already an old man.

The hair is white upon your head! How many years have you
to live? Are you not rich enough for that little time? Shall
you be hungry?—shall you lack clothes, or a roof to shelter
you, between this point and the grave? No; but, with the
half of what you now possess, you could revel in costly food
and wines, and build a house twice as splendid as you now
inhabit, and make a far greater show to the world—and yet
leave riches to your only son, to make him bless the hour of
your death! Then why should you do this cruel, cruel thing?
—so mad a thing, that I know not whether to call it wicked!
Alas, Cousin Jaffrey, this hard and grasping spirit has run
in our blood, these two hundred years! You are but doing
over again, in another shape, what your ancestor before you
did, and sending down to your posterity the curse inherited
from him!"

"Talk sense, Hepzibah, for Heaven's sake!" exclaimed the
Judge, with the impatience natural to a reasonable man, on
hearing anything so utterly absurd as the above, in a discussion about matters of business. "I have told you my determination. I am not apt to change. Clifford must give up his
secret, or take the consequences. And let him decide quickly;
for I have several affairs to attend to, this morning, and an
important dinner-engagement with some political friends."

"Clifford has no secret!" answered Hepzibah. "And God
will not let you do the thing you meditate!"

"We shall see!" said the unmoved Judge. "Meanwhile,
choose whether you will summon Clifford, and allow this
business to be amicably settled by an interview between two
kinsmen; or drive me to harsher measures, which I should
be most happy to feel myself justified in avoiding. The responsibility is altogether on your part."

"You are stronger than I," said Hepzibah, after a brief
consideration; "and you have no pity in your strength. Clifford is not now insane; but the interview, which you insist
upon, may go far to make him so. Nevertheless, knowing you

as I do, I believe it to be my best course to allow you to judge
for yourself as to the improbability of his possessing any
valuable secret. I will call Clifford. Be merciful in your
dealings with him!—be far more merciful than your heart
bids you be!—for God is looking at you, Jaffrey Pyncheon!"

The Judge followed his cousin from the shop, where the
foregoing conversation had passed, into the parlor, and flung
himself heavily into the great, ancestral chair. Many a
former Pyncheon had found repose in its capacious arms;—
rosy children, after their sports, young men, dreamy with
love, grown men, weary with cares, old men, burthened with
winters;—they had mused, and slumbered, and departed, to a
yet profounder sleep. It had been a long tradition, though a
doubtful one, that this was the very chair, seated in which,
the earliest of the Judge's New England forefathers—he
whose picture still hung upon the wall—had given a dead
man's silent and stern reception to the throng of distinguished
guests. From that hour of evil omen, until the present, it may
be—though we know not the secret of his heart—but it may
be, that no wearier and sadder man had ever sunk into the
chair, than this same Judge Pyncheon, whom we have just
beheld so immitigably hard and resolute. Surely, it must have
been at no slight cost, that he had thus fortified his soul with
iron! Such calmness is a mightier effort than the violence of
weaker men. And there was yet a heavy task for him to do!
Was it a little matter—a trifle, to be prepared for in a single
moment, and to be rested from, in another moment—that he
must now, after thirty years, encounter a kinsman risen from
a living tomb, and wrench a secret from him, or else consign
him to a living tomb again?

"Did you speak?" asked Hepzibah, looking in from the
threshold of the parlor; for she imagined that the Judge had
uttered some sound, which she was anxious to interpret as
a relenting impulse. "I thought you called me back!"

"No, no!" gruffly answered Judge Pyncheon, with a harsh

frown, while his brow grew almost a black purple, in the shadow of the room. "Why should I call you back? Time flies! Bid Clifford come to me!"

The Judge had taken his watch from his vest-pocket, and now held it in his hand, measuring the interval which was to ensue before the appearance of Clifford.

## XVI

## CLIFFORD'S CHAMBER

NEVER had the old house appeared so dismal to poor Hepzibah, as when she departed on that wretched errand. There was a strange aspect in it. As she trode along the foot-worn passages, and opened one crazy door after another, and ascended the creaking staircase, she gazed wistfully and fearfully around. It would have been no marvel, to her excited mind, if, behind or beside her, there had been the rustle of dead people's garments, or pale visages awaiting her on the landing place above. Her nerves were set all ajar by the scene of passion and terror, through which she had just struggled. Her colloquy with Judge Pyncheon, who so perfectly represented the person and attributes of the founder of the family, had called back the dreary past. It weighed upon her heart. Whatever she had heard from legendary aunts and grandmothers, concerning the good or evil fortunes of the Pyncheons—stories, which had heretofore been kept warm in her remembrance by the chimney-corner glow, that was associated with them—now recurred to her, sombre, ghastly, cold, like most passages of family history, when brooded over in melancholy mood. The whole seemed little else but a series of calamity, reproducing itself in successive generations, with one general hue, and varying in little save the outline. But Hepzibah now felt as if the Judge, and Clifford, and herself—they three together—were on the point of adding another incident to the annals of the house, with a bolder relief of wrong and sorrow, which would cause it to stand out from all the rest. Thus it is, that the grief of the passing moment takes upon itself an individuality, and a character of climax, which it is destined to lose, after awhile, and to fade into the dark gray tissue, common to the grave or glad events of many years ago. It is but for a moment, comparatively, that anything looks strange or startling;—a truth, that has the bitter and the sweet in it!

But Hepzibah could not rid herself of the sense of something unprecedented, at that instant passing, and soon to be accomplished. Her nerves were in a shake. Instinctively, she paused before the arched window, and looked out upon the street, in order to seize its permanent objects with her mental grasp, and thus to steady herself from the reel and vibration which affected her more immediate sphere. It brought her up, as we may say, with a kind of shock, when she beheld everything under the same appearance as the day before, and numberless preceding days, except for the difference between sunshine and sullen storm. Her eyes travelled along the street, from door-step to door-step, noting the wet sidewalks, with here and there a puddle in hollows that had been imperceptible, until filled with water. She screwed her dim optics to their acutest point in the hope of making out, with greater distinctness, a certain window, where she half saw, half guessed, that a tailor's seamstress was sitting at her work. Hepzibah flung herself upon that unknown woman's companionship, even thus far off. Then she was attracted by a chaise rapidly passing, and watched its moist and glistening top, and its splashing wheels, until it had turned the corner, and refused to carry any further her idly trifling, because appalled and overburthened mind. When the vehicle had disappeared, she allowed herself still another loitering moment; for the patched figure of good Uncle Venner was now visible, coming slowly from the head of the street downward, with a rheumatic limp, because the east-wind had got into his joints. Hepzibah wished that he would pass yet more slowly, and befriend her shivering solitude, a little longer. Anything that would take her out of the grievous present, and interpose human beings betwixt herself and what was nearest to her—whatever would defer, for an instant, the inevitable errand on which she was bound—all such impediments were welcome. Next to the lightest heart, the heaviest is apt to be most playful.

Hepzibah had little hardihood for her own proper pain, and far less for what she must inflict on Clifford. Of so slight a nature, and so shattered by his previous calamities, it could not well be short of utter ruin, to bring him face to face with the hard, relentless man, who had been his Evil Destiny through life. Even had there been no bitter recollections, nor any hostile interest now at stake between them, the mere natural repugnance of the more sensitive system to the massive, weighty, and unimpressible one, must in itself have been disastrous to the former. It would be like flinging a porcelain vase, with already a crack in it, against a granite column. Never before had Hepzibah so adequately estimated the powerful character of her Cousin Jaffrey;—powerful by intellect, energy of will, the long habit of acting among men, and, as she believed, by his unscrupulous pursuit of selfish ends through evil means. It did but increase the difficulty, that Judge Pyncheon was under a delusion as to the secret which he supposed Clifford to possess. Men of his strength of purpose, and customary sagacity, if they chance to adopt a mistaken opinion in practical matters, so wedge it and fasten it among things known to be true, that to wrench it out of their minds is hardly less difficult than pulling up an oak. Thus, as the Judge required an impossibility of Clifford, the latter, as he could not perform it, must needs perish. For what, in the grasp of a man like this, was to become of Clifford's soft, poetic nature, that never should have had a task more stubborn than to set a life of beautiful enjoyment to the flow and rhythm of musical cadences! Indeed, what had become of it, already? Broken! Blighted! All but annihilated! Soon to be wholly so!

For a moment, the thought crossed Hepzibah's mind, whether Clifford might not really have such knowledge of their deceased uncle's vanished estate, as the Judge imputed to him. She remembered some vague intimations, on her brother's part, which—if the supposition were not essentially preposterous—might have been so interpreted. There had been schemes of travel and residence abroad, day-dreams of brilliant life at home, and splendid castles in the air, which it would have required boundless wealth to build and realize. Had this wealth been in her power, how gladly would Hepzibah have bestowed it all upon her iron-hearted kinsman, to buy for Clifford the freedom and seclusion of the desolate old house! But she believed that her brother's schemes were as destitute of actual substance and purpose, as a child's pictures of its future life, while sitting in a little chair by its mother's knee. Clifford had none but shadowy gold at his command; and it was not the stuff to satisfy Judge Pyncheon!

Was there no help in their extremity? It seemed strange that there should be none, with a city roundabout her. It would be so easy to throw up the window and send forth a shriek, at the strange agony of which, everybody would come hastening to the rescue, well understanding it to be the cry of a human soul, at some dreadful crisis! But how wild, how almost laughable the fatality—and yet how continually it comes to pass, thought Hepzibah, in this dull delirium of a world—that whosoever, and with however kindly a purpose, should come to help, they would be sure to help the strongest side! Might and wrong combined, like iron magnetized, are endowed with irresistible attraction. There would be Judge Pyncheon; a person eminent in the public view, of high station and great wealth, a philanthropist, a member of Congress and of the church, and intimately associated with whatever else bestows good name; so imposing, in these advantageous lights, that Hepzibah herself could hardly help shrinking from her own conclusions as to his hollow integrity! The Judge, on one side! And who, on the other? The guilty Clifford! Once, a by-word! Now, an indistinctly remembered ignominy!

Nevertheless, in spite of this perception that the Judge would draw all human aid to his own behalf, Hepzibah was so unaccustomed to act for herself, that the least word of counsel would have swayed her to any mode of action. Little Phoebe Pyncheon would at once have lighted up the whole scene, if not by any available suggestion, yet simply by the warm vivacity of her character. The idea of the artist occurred to Hepzibah. Young and unknown, mere vagrant adventurer as he was, she had been conscious of a force in Holgrave, which might well adapt him to be the champion of a crisis. With this thought in her mind, she unbolted a door, cobwebbed and long disused, but which had served as a former medium of communication between her own part of the house, and the gable where the wandering Daguerreotypist had now established his temporary home. He was not there. A book, face downward on the table, a roll of manuscript, a half-written sheet, a newspaper, some tools of his present occupation, and several rejected daguerreotypes, conveyed an impression as if he were close at hand. But, at this period of the day, as Hepzibah might have anticipated, the artist was at his public rooms. With an impulse of idle curiosity, that flickered among her heavy thoughts, she looked at one of the daguerreotypes, and beheld Judge Pyncheon frowning at her! Fate stared her in the face. She turned back from her fruitless quest, with a heart-sinking sense of disappointment. In all her years of seclusion, she had never felt, as now, what it was to be alone. It seemed as if the house stood in a desert, or, by some spell, was made invisible to those who dwelt around, or passed beside it; so that any mode of misfortune, miserable accident, or crime, might happen in it, without the possibility of aid. In her grief and wounded pride, Hepzibah had spent her life in divesting herself of friends;—she had wilfully cast off the support which God has ordained His creatures to need from one another;— and it was now her punishment, that Clifford and herself would fall the easier victims to their kindred enemy.

Returning to the arched window, she lifted her eyes— scowling, poor, dim-sighted Hepzibah, in the face of Heaven! —and strove hard to send up a prayer through the dense, gray pavement of clouds. Those mists had gathered, as if to symbolize a great, brooding mass of human trouble, doubt, confusion, and chill indifference, between earth and the better regions. Her faith was too weak; the prayer too heavy to be thus uplifted. It fell back, a lump of lead, upon her heart. It smote her with the wretched conviction, that Providence intermeddled not in these petty wrongs of one individual to his fellow, nor had any balm for these little agonies of a solitary soul, but shed its justice, and its mercy, in a broad, sunlike sweep, over half the universe at once. Its vastness made it nothing. But Hepzibah did not see, that, just as there comes a warm sunbeam into every cottage-window, so comes a love-beam of God's care and pity, for every separate need.

At last, finding no other pretext for deferring the torture that she was to inflict on Clifford, her reluctance to which was the true cause of her loitering at the window, her search for the artist, and even her abortive prayer—dreading also to hear the stern voice of Judge Pyncheon from below stairs, chiding her delay—she crept slowly, a pale, grief-stricken figure, a dismal shape of woman, with almost torpid limbs, slowly to her brother's door, and knocked.

There was no reply!

And how should there have been! Her hand, tremulous

with the shrinking purpose which directed it, had smitten so feebly against the door that the sound could hardly have gone inward. She knocked again. Still, no response! Nor was it to be wondered at. She had struck with the entire force of her heart's vibration, communicating by some subtle magnetism her own terror to the summons. Clifford would turn his face to the pillow, and cover his head beneath the bed-clothes, like a startled child at midnight. She knocked a third time, three regular strokes, gentle, but perfectly distinct, and with meaning in them; for, modulate it with what cautious art we will, the hand cannot help playing some tune of what we feel, upon the senseless wood.

Clifford returned no answer.

"Clifford! Dear brother!" said Hepzibah. "Shall I come in?"

A silence!

Two or three times, and more, Hepzibah repeated his name, without result; till, thinking her brother's sleep unwontedly profound, she undid the door, and entering, found the chamber vacant. How could he have come forth, and when, without her knowledge? Was it possible that, in spite of the stormy day, and worn out with the irksomeness within doors, he had betaken himself to his customary haunt, in the garden, and was now shivering under the cheerless shelter of the summer-house? She hastily threw up a window, thrust forth her turbaned head and the half of her gaunt figure, and searched the whole garden through, as completely as her dim vision would allow. She could see the interior of the summer-house, and its circular seat, kept moist by the droppings of the roof. It had no occupant. Clifford was not thereabouts; unless, indeed, he had crept for concealment—(as, for a moment, Hepzibah fancied might be the case)—into a great, wet mass of tangled and broad-leaved shadow, where the squash-vines were clambering tumultuously upon an old wooden frame-work, set casually aslant against the fence. This could not be, however; he was not there; for, while Hepzibah was looking, a strange Grimalkin[1] stole forth from the very spot, and picked his way across the garden. Twice, he paused to snuff the air, and then anew directed his course towards the parlor-window. Whether it was only on account of the stealthy, prying manner common to the race, or that this cat seemed to have more than ordinary mischief in his thoughts, the old gentlewoman, in spite of her much perplexity, felt an impulse to drive the animal away, and accordingly flung down a window-stick. The cat stared up at her, like a detected thief or murderer, and, the next instant, took to flight. No other living creature was visible in the garden. Chanticleer and his family had either not left their roost, disheartened by the interminable rain, or had done the next wisest thing, by seasonably returning to it. Hepzibah closed the window.

But where was Clifford? Could it be, that, aware of the presence of his Evil Destiny, he had crept silently down the staircase, while the Judge and Hepzibah stood talking in the shop, and had softly undone the fastenings of the outer door, and made his escape into the street? With that thought, she seemed to behold his gray, wrinkled, yet childlike aspect, in the old fashioned garments which he wore about the house; a figure such as one sometimes imagines himself to be, with the world's eye upon him, in a troubled dream. This figure of her wretched brother would go wandering through the city, attracting all eyes, and everybody's wonder and repugnance, like a ghost, the more to be shuddered at because visible at noontide. To incur the ridicule of the younger crowd, that knew him not; the harsher scorn and indignation of a few old men, who might recall his once familiar features! To be the sport of boys, who, when old enough to run about the streets, have no more reverence for what is beautiful and holy, nor pity for what is sad—no more sense of sacred misery, sanctifying the human shape in which it embodies itself— than if Satan were the father of them all! Goaded by their taunts, their loud, shrill cries, and cruel laughter—insulted

1. Originally an old gray she-cat; the capitalization (in the manuscript it was originally in lower case) is unusual.

by the filth of the public ways, which they would fling upon him—or, as it might well be, distracted by the mere strangeness of his situation, though nobody should afflict him with so much as a thoughtless word—what wonder if Clifford were to break into some wild extravagance, which was certain to be interpreted as lunacy? Thus Judge Pyncheon's fiendish scheme would be ready accomplished to his hands!

Then Hepzibah reflected that the town was almost completely water-girdled. The wharves stretched out towards the centre of the harbor, and, in this inclement weather, were deserted by the ordinary throng of merchants, laborers, and sea-faring men; each wharf a solitude, with the vessels moored stem and stern, along its misty length. Should her brother's aimless footsteps stray thitherward, and he but bend, one moment, over the deep, black tide, would he not bethink himself that here was the sure refuge within his reach, and that, with a single step, or the slightest overbalance of his body, he might be forever beyond his kinsman's gripe? Oh, the temptation! To make of his ponderous sorrow a security! To sink, with its leaden weight upon him, and never rise again!

The horror of this last conception was too much for Hepzibah. Even Jaffrey Pyncheon must help her now! She hastened down the staircase, shrieking as she went.

"Clifford is gone!" she cried. "I cannot find my brother! Help, Jaffrey Pyncheon! Some harm will happen to him!"

She threw open the parlor-door. But, what with the shade of branches across the windows, and the smoke-blackened ceiling, and the dark oak-panelling of the walls, there was hardly so much daylight in the room that Hepzibah's imperfect sight could accurately distinguish the Judge's figure. She was certain, however, that she saw him sitting in the ancestral arm-chair, near the centre of the floor, with his face somewhat averted, and looking towards a window. So firm and quiet is the nervous system of such men as Judge Pyncheon, that he had perhaps stirred not more than once since her departure, but, in the hard composure of his temperament, retained the position into which accident had thrown him.

"I tell you, Jaffrey," cried Hepzibah impatiently, as she turned from the parlor-door to search other rooms, "my brother is not in his chamber! You must help me seek him!"

But Judge Pyncheon was not the man to let himself be startled from an easy-chair, with haste ill-befitting either the dignity of his character or his broad personal basis, by the alarm of an hysteric woman. Yet, considering his own interest in the matter, he might have bestirred himself with a little more alacrity!

"Do you hear me, Jaffrey Pyncheon?" screamed Hepzibah, as she again approached the parlor-door, after an ineffectual search elsewhere. "Clifford is gone!"

At this instant, on the threshold of the parlor, emerging from within, appeared Clifford himself! His face was preternaturally pale; so deadly white, indeed, that, through all the glimmering indistinctness of the passage-way, Hepzibah could discern his features, as if a light fell on them alone. Their vivid and wild expression seemed likewise sufficient to illuminate them; it was an expression of scorn and mockery, coinciding with the emotions indicated by his gesture. As Clifford stood on the threshold, partly turning back, he pointed his finger within the parlor, and shook it slowly, as though he would have summoned not Hepzibah alone, but the whole world, to gaze at some object inconceivably ridiculous. This action, so ill-timed and extravagant—accompanied, too, with a look that showed more like joy than any other kind of excitement—compelled Hepzibah to dread that her stern kinsman's ominous visit had driven her poor brother to absolute insanity. Nor could she otherwise account for the Judge's quiescent mood, than by supposing him craftily on the watch, while Clifford developed these symptoms of a distracted mind.

"Be quiet, Clifford!" whispered his sister, raising her hand to impress caution. "Oh, for Heaven's sake, be quiet!"

"Let him be quiet!—What can he do better?" answered Clifford, with a still wilder gesture, pointing into the room which he had just quitted. "As for us, Hepzibah, we can dance now!—we can sing, laugh, play, do what we will! The weight is gone, Hepzibah; it is gone off this weary old world; and we may be as light-hearted as little Phoebe herself!"

And, in accordance with his words, he began to laugh, still pointing his finger at the object, invisible to Hepzibah, within the parlor. She was seized with a sudden intuition of some horrible thing. She thrust herself past Clifford, and disappeared into the room, but almost immediately returned, with a cry choking in her throat. Gazing at her brother, with an affrighted glance of inquiry, she beheld him all in a tremor and a quake, from head to foot; while, amid these commoted elements of passion or alarm, still flickered his gusty mirth.

"My God, what is to become of us!" gasped Hepzibah.

"Come!" said Clifford, in a tone of brief decision, most unlike what was usual with him. "We stay here too long! Let us leave the old house to our Cousin Jaffrey! He will take good care of it!"

Hepzibah now noticed that Clifford had on a cloak—a garment of long ago—in which he had constantly muffled himself during these days of easterly storm. He beckoned with his hand, and intimated, so far as she could comprehend him, his purpose that they should go together from the house. There are chaotic, blind, or drunken moments, in the lives of persons who lack real force of character—moments of test, in which courage would most assert itself—but where these individuals, if left to themselves, stagger aimlessly along, or follow implicitly whatever guidance may befall them, even if it be a child's. No matter how preposterous or insane, a purpose is a god-send to them. Hepzibah had reached this point. Unaccustomed to action or responsibility—full of horror at what she had seen, and afraid to inquire, or almost to imagine, how it had come to pass—affrighted at the fatality which seemed to pursue her brother—stupefied by the dim, thick, stifling atmosphere of dread, which filled the house as with a death-smell, and obliterated all definiteness of thought —she yielded without a question, and on the instant, to the will which Clifford expressed. For herself, she was like a person in a dream, when the will always sleeps. Clifford, ordinarily so destitute of this faculty, had found it in the tension of the crisis.

"Why do you delay so?" cried he sharply. "Put on your cloak and hood, or whatever it pleases you to wear! No matter what;—you cannot look beautiful nor brilliant, my poor Hepzibah! Take your purse, with money in it, and come along!"

Hepzibah obeyed these instructions, as if nothing else were to be done or thought of. She began to wonder, it is true, why she did not wake up, and at what still more intolerable pitch of dizzy trouble her spirit would struggle out of the maze, and make her conscious that nothing of all this had actually happened. Of course, it was not real; no such black, easterly day as this had yet begun to be; Judge Pyncheon had not talked with her; Clifford had not laughed, pointed, beckoned her away with him; but she had merely been afflicted — as lonely sleepers often are—with a great deal of unreasonable misery in a morning dream!

"Now—now—I shall certainly awake!" thought Hepzibah, as she went to-and-fro, making her little preparations. "I can bear it no longer! I must wake up now!"

But it came not, that awakening moment! It came not, even when, just before they left the house, Clifford stole to the parlor-door, and made a parting obeisance to the sole occupant of the room.

"What an absurd figure the old fellow cuts now!" whispered he to Hepzibah. "Just when he fancied he had me completely under his thumb! Come, come; make haste; or he will start up like Giant Despair in pursuit of Christian and Hopeful, and catch us yet!"[2]

As they passed into the street, Clifford directed Hepzibah's attention to something on one of the posts of the front-door. It was merely the initials of his own name, which, with somewhat of his characteristic grace about the forms of the letters, he had cut there, when a boy. The brother and sister departed, and left Judge Pyncheon sitting in the old home of his forefathers, all by himself; so heavy and lumpish that we can liken him to nothing better than a defunct nightmare, which had perished in the midst of its wickedness, and left its flabby corpse on the breast of the tormented one, to be gotten rid of as it might!

2. An allusion to John Bunyan's *The Pilgrim's Progress* (1678), a Puritan allegory of the soul's search for salvation. In Part I Christian and Hopeful escape from Giant Despair's dungeon by means of Promise, a key which can "open any lock in Doubting Castle."

# XVII

# THE FLIGHT OF TWO OWLS

SUMMER as it was, the east-wind set poor Hepzibah's few remaining teeth chattering in her head, as she and Clifford faced it, on their way up Pyncheon-street, and towards the centre of the town. Not merely was it the shiver which this pitiless blast brought to her frame, (although her feet and hands, especially, had never seemed so death-a-cold as now,) but there was a moral sensation, mingling itself with the physical chill, and causing her to shake more in spirit than in body. The world's broad, bleak atmosphere was all so comfortless! Such, indeed, is the impression which it makes on every new adventurer, even if he plunge into it while the warmest tide of life is bubbling through his veins. What then must it have been to Hepzibah and Clifford—so time-stricken as they were, yet so like children in their inexperience—as they left the door-step, and passed from beneath the wide shelter of the Pyncheon-elm! They were wandering all abroad, on precisely such a pilgrimage as a child often meditates, to the world's end, with perhaps a sixpence and a biscuit in his pocket. In Hepzibah's mind, there was the wretched consciousness of being adrift. She had lost the faculty of self-guidance, but, in view of the difficulties around her, felt it hardly worth an effort to regain it, and was, moreover, incapable of making one.

As they proceeded on their strange expedition, she now and then cast a look sidelong at Clifford, and could not but observe that he was possessed and swayed by a powerful excitement. It was this, indeed, that gave him the control which he had at once, and so irresistibly, established over her movements. It not a little resembled the exhilaration of wine. Or it might more fancifully be compared to a joyous piece of music, played with wild vivacity, but upon a disordered instrument. As the cracked, jarring note might always be heard, and as it jarred loudest amid the loftiest exultation of the melody, so was there a continual quake through Clifford, causing him most to quiver while he wore a triumphant smile, and seemed almost under a necessity to skip in his gait.

They met few people abroad, even on passing from the retired neighborhood of the House of the Seven Gables into what was ordinarily the more thronged and busier portion of the town. Glistening sidewalks, with little pools of rain, here and there, along their unequal surface; umbrellas, displayed ostentatiously in the shop-windows, as if the life of trade had concentred itself in that one article; wet leaves of the horse-chestnut or elm-trees, torn off untimely by the blast, and scattered along the public-way; an unsightly accumulation of mud in the middle of the street, which perversely grew the more unclean for its long and laborious washing;—these were the more definable points of a very sombre picture. In the way of movement, and human life, there was the hasty rattle of a cab or coach, its driver protected by a water-proof cap over his head and shoulders; the forlorn figure of an old man, who seemed to have crept out of some subterranean sewer, and was stooping along the kennel, and poking the wet rubbish with a stick, in quest of rusty nails; a merchant or two, at the door of the post-office, together with an editor, and a miscellaneous politician, awaiting a dilatory mail; a few visages of retired sea-captains at the window of an Insurance Office,[1] looking out vacantly at the vacant street, blas-

1. The office of a marine insurance company (there were about a half-dozen in Salem in Hawthorne's day), where merchants and sea-captains assembled to transact business, read the newspapers, and hear the gossip of the day.

pheming at the weather, and fretting at the dearth as well of
public news as local gossip. What a treasure-trove to these
venerable quidnuncs, could they have guessed the secret
which Hepzibah and Clifford were carrying along with them!
But their two figures attracted hardly so much notice as that
of a young girl, who passed, at the same instant, and happened to raise her skirt a trifle too high above her ancles.
Had it been a sunny and cheerful day, they could hardly have
gone through the streets without making themselves obnox-
ious to remark. Now, probably, they were felt to be in keeping with the dismal and bitter weather, and therefore did not
stand out in strong relief, as if the sun were shining on them,
but melted into the gray gloom, and were forgotten as soon as
gone.

Poor Hepzibah! Could she have understood this fact, it
would have brought her some little comfort; for, to all her
other troubles—strange to say!—there was added the womanish
and old-maidenlike misery, arising from a sense of unseemli-
ness in her attire. Thus, she was fain to shrink deeper into
herself, as it were, as if in the hope of making people suppose
that here was only a cloak and hood, threadbare and wofully
faded, taking an airing in the midst of the storm, without any
wearer!

As they went on, the feeling of indistinctness and unreality
kept dimly hovering roundabout her, and so diffusing itself
into her system that one of her hands was hardly palpable to
the touch of the other. Any certainty would have been preferable to this. She whispered to herself, again and again—
'Am I awake?—Am I awake?'—and sometimes exposed her
face to the chill spatter of the wind, for the sake of its rude
assurance, that she was. Whether it were Clifford's purpose,
or only chance had led them thither, they now found themselves passing beneath the arched entrance of a large structure
of gray stone. Within, there was a spacious breadth, and an
airy height from floor to roof, now partially filled with smoke

and steam, which eddied voluminously upward, and formed a mimic cloud-region over their heads. A train of cars was just ready for a start; the locomotive was fretting and fuming, like a steed impatient for a headlong rush; and the bell rang out its hasty peal, so well expressing the brief summons which life vouchsafes to us, in its hurried career. Without question or delay—with the irresistible decision, if not rather to be called recklessness, which had so strangely taken possession of him, and through him of Hepzibah—Clifford impelled her towards the cars, and assisted her to enter. The signal was given; the engine puffed forth its short, quick breaths; the train began its movement; and, along with a hundred other passengers, these two unwonted travellers sped onward like the wind.

At last, therefore, and after so long estrangement from everything that the world acted or enjoyed, they had been drawn into the great current of human life, and were swept away with it, as by the suction of fate itself.

Still haunted with the idea that not one of the past incidents, inclusive of Judge Pyncheon's visit, could be real, the recluse of the seven gables murmured in her brother's ear:—

"Clifford! Clifford! Is not this a dream?"

"A dream, Hepzibah!" repeated he, almost laughing in her face. "On the contrary, I have never been awake before!"

Meanwhile, looking from the window, they could see the world racing past them. At one moment, they were rattling through a solitude;—the next, a village had grown up around them;—a few breaths more, and it had vanished, as if swallowed by an earthquake. The spires of meeting-houses seemed set adrift from their foundations; the broad based hills glided away. Everything was unfixed from its age-long rest, and moving at whirlwind speed in a direction opposite to their own.

Within the car, there was the usual interior life of the railroad, offering little to the observation of other passengers, but full of novelty for this pair of strangely enfranchised prisoners. It was novelty enough, indeed, that there were fifty human beings in close relation with them, under one long and narrow roof, and drawn onward by the same mighty influence that had taken their two selves into its grasp. It seemed marvellous how all these people could remain so quietly in their seats, while so much noisy strength was at work in their behalf. Some, with tickets in their hats, (long travellers these, before whom lay a hundred miles of railroad,) had plunged into the English scenery and adventures of pamphlet-novels, and were keeping company with dukes and earls. Others, whose briefer span forbade their devoting themselves to studies so abstruse, beguiled the little tedium of the way with penny-papers. A party of girls, and one young man, on opposite sides of the car, found huge amusement in a game of ball. They tossed it to-and-fro, with peals of laughter that might be measured by mile-lengths; for, faster than the nimble ball could fly, the merry players fled unconsciously along, leaving the trail of their mirth afar behind, and ending their game under another sky than had witnessed its commencement. Boys, with apples, cakes, candy, and rolls of variously tinctured lozenges—merchandize that reminded Hepzibah of her deserted shop—appeared at each momentary stopping-place, doing up their business in a hurry, or breaking it short off, lest the market should ravish them away with it. New people continually entered. Old acquaintances—for such they soon grew to be, in this rapid current of affairs—continually departed. Here and there, amid the rumble and the tumult, sat one asleep. Sleep; sport; business; graver or lighter study;—and the common and inevitable movement onward! It was life itself![2]

Clifford's naturally poignant sympathies were all aroused. He caught the color of what was passing about him, and threw it back more vividly than he received it, but mixed, nevertheless, with a lurid and portentous hue. Hepzibah, on the other hand, felt herself more apart from humankind than even in the seclusion which she had just quitted.

"You are not happy, Hepzibah!" said Clifford apart, in a

2. For the notebook entry (May 5, 1850) on which this paragraph is based, see "Passages from *The American Notebooks*," p. 327.

tone of reproach. "You are thinking of that dismal old house, and of Cousin Jaffrey"—here came the quake through him—"and of Cousin Jaffrey sitting there, all by himself! Take my advice—follow my example—and let such things slip aside. Here we are, in the world, Hepzibah!—in the midst of life!—in the throng of our fellow-beings! Let you and I be happy! As happy as that youth, and those pretty girls, at their game of ball!"

"Happy!" thought Hepzibah, bitterly conscious, at the word, of her dull and heavy heart, with the frozen pain in it. "Happy! He is mad already; and, if I could once feel myself broad awake, I should go mad too!"

If a fixed idea be madness, she was perhaps not remote from it. Fast and far as they had rattled and clattered along the iron track, they might just as well, as regarded Hepzibah's mental images, have been passing up and down Pyncheon-street. With miles and miles of varied scenery between, there was no scene for her, save the seven old gable-peaks, with their moss, and the tuft of weeds in one of the angles, and the shop-window, and a customer shaking the door, and compelling the little bell to jingle fiercely, but without disturbing Judge Pyncheon! This one old house was everywhere! It transported its great, lumbering bulk, with more than railroad speed, and set itself phlegmatically down on whatever spot she glanced at. The quality of Hepzibah's mind was too unmalleable to take new impressions so readily as Clifford's. He had a winged nature; she was rather of the vegetable kind, and could hardly be kept long alive, if drawn up by the roots. Thus it happened, that the relation heretofore existing between her brother and herself was changed. At home, she was his guardian; here, Clifford had become hers, and seemed to comprehend whatever belonged to their new position, with a singular rapidity of intelligence. He had been startled into manhood and intellectual vigor; or, at least, into a condition that resembled them, though it might be both diseased and transitory.

The conductor now applied for their tickets; and Clifford, who had made himself the purse-bearer, put a bank-note into his hand, as he had observed others do.

"For the lady and yourself?" asked the conductor. "And how far?"

"As far as that will carry us," said Clifford. "It is no great matter. We are riding for pleasure, merely!"

"You choose a strange day for it, Sir!" remarked a gimlet-eyed old gentleman, on the other side of the car, looking at Clifford and his companion as if curious to make them out.— "The best chance of pleasure in an easterly rain, I take it, is in a man's own house, with a nice little fire in the chimney."

"I cannot precisely agree with you," said Clifford, courte-ously bowing to the old gentleman, and at once taking up the clue of conversation which the latter had proffered.—"It had just occurred to me, on the contrary, that this admirable invention of the railroad—with the vast and inevitable im-provements to be looked for, both as to speed and convenience —is destined to do away with those stale ideas of home and fireside, and substitute something better."

"In the name of common sense," asked the old gentleman, rather testily, "what can be better for a man than his own parlor and chimney-corner?"

"These things have not the merit which many good people attribute to them," replied Clifford. "They may be said, in few and pithy words, to have ill-served a poor purpose! My impression is, that our wonderfully increased, and still in-creasing, facilities of locomotion are destined to bring us round again to the nomadic state. You are aware, my dear Sir—you must have observed it, in your own experience—that all hu-man progress is in a circle; or, to use a more accurate and beautiful figure, in an ascending spiral curve. While we fancy ourselves going straight forward, and attaining, at every step, an entirely new position of affairs, we do actually return to something long ago tried and abandoned, but which we now find etherealized, refined, and perfected to its ideal. The past is but a coarse and sensual prophecy of the present and the future. To apply this truth to the topic now under discussion! In the early epochs of our race, men dwelt in temporary huts, or bowers of branches, as easily constructed as a bird's nest, and which they built—if it should be called building, when such sweet homes of a summer-solstice rather grew, than were made with hands—which Nature, we will say, assisted them to rear, where fruit abounded, where fish and game were plentiful, or, most especially, where the sense of beauty was to be gratified by a lovelier shade than elsewhere, and a more exquisite arrangement of lake, wood, and hill. This life possessed a charm, which, ever since man quitted it, has vanished from existence. And it typified something better than itself. It had its drawbacks; such as hunger and thirst, inclement weather, hot sunshine, and weary and foot-blistering marches over barren and ugly tracts, that lay between the sites desirable for their fertility and beauty. But, in our ascending spiral, we escape all this. These railroads—could but the whistle be made musical, and the rumble and the jar got rid of—are positively the greatest blessing that the ages have wrought out for us. They give us wings; they annihilate the toil and dust of pilgrimage;[3] they spiritualize travel! Transition being so facile, what can be any man's inducement to tarry in one spot? Why, therefore, should he build a more cumbrous habitation than can readily be carried off with him? Why should he make himself a prisoner for life in brick, and stone, and old worm-eaten timber, when he may just as easily dwell, in one sense, nowhere—in a better sense, wherever the fit and beautiful shall offer him a home?"

Clifford's countenance glowed, as he divulged this theory; a youthful character shone out from within, converting the wrinkles and pallid duskiness of age into an almost transparent mask. The merry girls let their ball drop upon the floor, and gazed at him. They said to themselves, perhaps,

3. In "The Celestial Railroad" (1843), a parody-sequel to *The Pilgrim's Progress,* Hawthorne used the railroad to satirize his age's belief in science's ability to "annihilate the toil and dust" of spiritual and moral struggles.

that, before his hair was gray and the crow's feet tracked his temples, this now decaying man must have stamped the impress of his features on many a woman's heart. But, alas, no woman's eye had seen his face, while it was beautiful!

"I should scarcely call it an improved state of things," observed Clifford's new acquaintance, "to live everywhere, and nowhere!"

"Would you not?" exclaimed Clifford, with singular energy. "It is as clear to me as sunshine—were there any in the sky—that the greatest possible stumbling-blocks in the path of human happiness and improvement, are these heaps of bricks, and stones, consolidated with mortar, or hewn timber, fastened together with spike-nails, which men painfully contrive for their own torment, and call them house and home! The soul needs air; a wide sweep and frequent change of it. Morbid influences, in a thousand-fold variety, gather about hearths, and pollute the life of households. There is no such unwholesome atmosphere as that of an old home, rendered poisonous by one's defunct forefathers and relatives! I speak of what I know! There is a certain house within my familiar recollection—one of those peaked-gable, (there are seven of them,) projecting-storied edifices, such as you occasionally see, in our elder towns—a rusty, crazy, creaky, dry-rotted, damp-rotted, dingy, dark, and miserable old dungeon, with an arched window over the porch, and a little shop-door on one side, and a great, melancholy elm before it. Now, Sir, whenever my thoughts recur to this seven-gabled mansion—(the fact is so very curious that I must needs mention it)—immediately, I have a vision or image of an elderly man, of remarkably stern countenance, sitting in an oaken elbow-chair, dead, stone-dead, with an ugly flow of blood upon his shirt-bosom. Dead, but with open eyes! He taints the whole house, as I remember it. I could never flourish there, nor be happy, nor do nor enjoy what God meant me to do and enjoy!"

His face darkened, and seemed to contract, and shrivel itself up, and wither into age.

"Never, Sir!" he repeated. "I could never draw cheerful breath there!"

"I should think not," said the old gentleman, eyeing Clifford earnestly and rather apprehensively. "I should conceive not, Sir, with that notion in your head!"

"Surely not," continued Clifford; "and it were a relief to me, if that house could be torn down, or burnt up, and so the earth be rid of it, and grass be sown abundantly over its foundation. Not that I should ever visit its site again! For, Sir, the farther I get away from it, the more does the joy, the lightsome freshness, the heart-leap, the intellectual dance, the youth, in short—yes, my youth, my youth!—the more does it come back to me. No longer ago than this morning, I was old. I remember looking in the glass, and wondering at my own gray hair, and the wrinkles, many and deep, right across my brow, and the furrows down my cheeks, and the prodigious trampling of crow's feet about my temples! It was too soon! I could not bear it! Age had no right to come! I had not lived! But now do I look old? If so, my aspect belies me strangely; for—a great weight being off my mind—I feel in the very hey-day of my youth, with the world and my best days before me!"

"I trust you may find it so," said the old gentleman, who seemed rather embarrassed, and desirous of avoiding the observation which Clifford's wild talk drew on them both. "You have my best wishes for it!"

"For Heaven's sake, dear Clifford, be quiet!" whispered his sister. "They think you mad!"

"Be quiet yourself, Hepzibah!" returned her brother. "No matter what they think! I am not mad. For the first time in thirty years, my thoughts gush up and find words ready for them. I must talk, and I will!"

He turned again towards the old gentleman, and renewed the conversation.

"Yes, my dear Sir," said he, "it is my firm belief and hope, that these terms of roof and hearth-stone, which have so long been held to embody something sacred, are soon to pass out of men's daily use, and be forgotten. Just imagine, for a moment, how much of human evil will crumble away, with this one change! What we call real estate—the solid ground to build a house on—is the broad foundation on which nearly all the guilt of this world rests. A man will commit almost any wrong—he will heap up an immense pile of wickedness, as hard as granite, and which will weigh as heavily upon his soul, to eternal ages—only to build a great, gloomy, dark-chambered mansion, for himself to die in, and for his posterity to be miserable in. He lays his own dead corpse beneath the underpinning, as one may say, and hangs his frowning picture on the wall, and, after thus converting himself into an Evil Destiny, expects his remotest great-grandchildren to be happy there! I do not speak wildly. I have just such a house in my mind's eye!"

"Then, Sir," said the old gentleman, getting anxious to drop the subject, "you are not to blame for leaving it."

"Within the lifetime of the child already born," Clifford went on, "all this will be done away. The world is growing too ethereal and spiritual to bear these enormities a great while longer. To me—though, for a considerable period of time, I have lived chiefly in retirement, and know less of such things than most men—even to me, the harbingers of a better era are unmistakeable. Mesmerism, now! Will that effect nothing, think you, towards purging away the grossness out of human life?"

"All a humbug!" growled the old gentleman.

"These rapping spirits that little Phoebe told us of, the other day," said Clifford. "What are these but the messengers of the spiritual world, knocking at the door of substance? And it shall be flung wide open!"

"A humbug, again!" cried the old gentleman, growing more and more testy at these glimpses of Clifford's metaphysics.— "I should like to rap, with a good stick, on the empty pates of the dolts who circulate such nonsense!"

"Then there is electricity;—the demon, the angel, the mighty physical power, the all-pervading intelligence!" exclaimed Clifford. "Is that a humbug, too? Is it a fact—or have I dreamt it—that, by means of electricity, the world of matter has become a great nerve, vibrating thousands of miles in a breathless point of time? Rather, the round globe is a vast head, a brain, instinct with intelligence! Or, shall we say, it is itself a thought, nothing but thought, and no longer the substance which we deemed it?"

"If you mean the telegraph," said the old gentleman, glancing his eye towards its wire, alongside the rail-track, "it is an excellent thing;—that is, of course, if the speculators in cotton and politics don't get possession of it. A great thing indeed, Sir; particularly as regards the detection of bank-robbers and murderers!"

"I don't quite like it, in that point of view," replied Clifford. "A bank-robber—and what you call a murderer, likewise— has his rights, which men of enlightened humanity and conscience should regard in so much the more liberal spirit, because the bulk of society is prone to controvert their existence. An almost spiritual medium, like the electric telegraph, should be consecrated to high, deep, joyful, and holy missions. Lovers, day by day—hour by hour, if so often moved to do it— might send their heart-throbs from Maine to Florida, with some such words as these—'I love you forever!'—'My heart runs over with love!'—'I love you more than I can!'—and, again, at the next message—'I have lived an hour longer, and love you twice as much!' Or, when a good man has departed, his distant friend should be conscious of an electric thrill, as from the world of happy spirits, telling him—'Your dear friend is in bliss!' Or, to an absent husband, should come tidings thus—'An immortal being, of whom you are the father, has this moment come from God!'—and immediately its little voice would seem to have reached so far, and to be echoing in his heart. But for these poor rogues, the bank-robbers—who, after all, are about as honest as nine people in ten, except that they disregard certain formalities, and prefer to transact business at midnight, rather than 'Change-hours[4]—and for these murderers, as you phrase it, who are often excusable in the motives of their deed, and deserve to be ranked among public benefactors, if we consider only its result—for unfortunate individuals like these, I really cannot applaud the enlistment of an immaterial and miraculous power in the universal world-hunt at their heels!"

"You can't, hey?" cried the old gentleman, with a hard look.

"Positively, no!" answered Clifford. "It puts them too miserably at disadvantage. For example, Sir, in a dark, low, cross-beamed, panelled room of an old house, let us suppose a dead man, sitting in an arm-chair, with a blood-stain on his shirt-bosom—and let us add to our hypothesis another man, issuing from the house, which he feels to be over-filled with the dead man's presence—and let us lastly imagine him fleeing, Heaven knows whither, at the speed of a hurricane, by railroad! Now, Sir,—if the fugitive alight in some distant town, and find all the people babbling about that self-same dead man, whom he has fled so far to avoid the sight and thought of—will you not allow that his natural rights have been infringed? He has been deprived of his city of refuge, and, in my humble opinion, has suffered infinite wrong!"

"You are a strange man, Sir!" said the old gentleman, bringing his gimlet-eye to a point on Clifford, as if determined to bore right into him.—"I can't see through you!"

"No, I'll be bound you can't!" cried Clifford laughing. "And yet, my dear Sir, I am as transparent as the water of Maule's Well! But, come, Hepzibah! We have flown far

4. The hours during which business was transacted on the "Merchant's Exchange" in Boston.

enough for once. Let us alight, as the birds do, and perch ourselves on the nearest twig, and consult whither we shall fly next!"

Just then, as it happened, the train reached a solitary way-station. Taking advantage of the brief pause, Clifford left the car, and drew Hepzibah along with him. A moment afterwards, the train—with all the life of its interior, amid which Clifford had made himself so conspicuous an object—was gliding away in the distance, and rapidly lessening to a point, which, in another moment, vanished. The world had fled away from these two wanderers. They gazed drearily about them. At a little distance stood a wooden church, black with age, and in a dismal state of ruin and decay, with broken windows, a great rift through the main-body of the edifice, and a rafter dangling from the top of the square tower. Farther off was a farm-house in the old style, as venerably black as the church, with a roof sloping downward from the three-story peak to within a man's height of the ground. It seemed uninhabited. There were the relics of a wood-pile, indeed, near the door, but with grass sprouting up among the chips and scattered logs. The small rain-drops came down aslant; the wind was not turbulent, but sullen, and full of chilly moisture.[5]

Clifford shivered from head to foot. The wild effervescence of his mood—which had so readily supplied thoughts, fantasies, and a strange aptitude of words, and impelled him to talk from the mere necessity of giving vent to this bubbling up-gush of ideas—had entirely subsided. A powerful excitement had given him energy and vivacity. Its operation over, he forthwith began to sink.

"You must take the lead now, Hepzibah!" murmured he, with a torpid and reluctant utterance. "Do with me as you will!"

She knelt down upon the platform where they were standing, and lifted her clasped hands to the sky. The dull, gray

5. For the notebook entry (May 5, 1850) on which this passage is based, see "Passages from *The American Notebooks*," p. 327.

weight of clouds made it invisible; but it was no hour for disbelief;—no juncture this, to question that there was a sky above, and an Almighty Father looking down from it!

"Oh, God!" — ejaculated poor, gaunt Hepzibah — then paused a moment, to consider what her prayer should be— "Oh, God—our Father—are we not thy children? Have mercy on us!"

## XVIII

## GOVERNOR PYNCHEON

J UDGE PYNCHEON, while his two relatives have fled away with such ill-considered haste, still sits in the old parlor, keeping house, as the familiar phrase is, in the absence of its ordinary occupants. To him, and to the venerable House of the Seven Gables, does our story now betake itself, like an owl, bewildered in the daylight, and hastening back to his hollow tree.

The Judge has not shifted his position for a long while, now. He has not stirred hand or foot—nor withdrawn his eyes, so much as a hair's breadth, from their fixed gaze towards the corner of the room—since the footsteps of Hepzibah and Clifford creaked along the passage, and the outer door was closed cautiously behind their exit. He holds his watch in his left hand, but clutched in such a manner that you cannot see the dial-plate. How profound a fit of meditation! Or, supposing him asleep, how infantile a quietude of conscience, and what wholesome order in the gastric region, are betokened by slumber so entirely undisturbed with starts, cramp, twitches, muttered dream-talk, trumpet-blasts through the nasal organ, or any, the slightest, irregularity of breath! You must hold your own breath, to satisfy yourself whether he breathes at all. It is quite inaudible. You hear the ticking of his watch; his breath you do not hear. A most refreshing slumber, doubtless! And yet the Judge cannot be asleep. His eyes are open! A veteran politician, such as he, would never fall asleep with wide-open eyes; lest some enemy or mischief-maker, taking him thus at unawares, should peep through these windows into his consciousness, and make strange discoveries among the reminiscences, projects, hopes, apprehensions, weaknesses, and strong points, which he has heretofore shared with nobody. A cautious man is proverbially said to sleep with one eye open. That may be wisdom. But not with both; for this were heedlessness! No, no! Judge Pyncheon cannot be asleep.

It is odd, however, that a gentleman so burthened with engagements—and noted, too, for punctuality—should linger thus in an old, lonely mansion, which he has never seemed very fond of visiting. The oaken chair, to be sure, may tempt him with its roominess. It is, indeed, a spacious, and—allowing for the rude age that fashioned it—a moderately easy seat, with capacity enough, at all events, and offering no restraint to the Judge's breadth of beam. A bigger man might find ample accommodation in it. His ancestor, now pictured upon the wall, with all his English beef about him, used hardly to present a front extending from elbow to elbow of this chair, or a base that would cover its whole cushion. But there are better chairs than this—mahogany, black walnut, rosewood, spring-seated and damask-cushioned, with varied slopes, and innumerable artifices to make them easy, and obviate the irksomeness of too tame an ease;—a score of such might be at Judge Pyncheon's service. Yes; in a score of drawing-rooms, he would be more than welcome. Mamma would advance to meet him, with outstretched hand; the virgin daughter, elderly as he has now got to be—an old widower, as he smilingly describes himself—would shake up the cushion for the Judge, and do her pretty little utmost to make him comfortable. For the Judge is a prosperous man. He cherishes his schemes, moreover, like other people, and reasonably brighter than most others; or did so, at least, as he lay abed, this morning, in an agreeable half-drowse, planning the business of the day, and speculating on the probabilities of the next fifteen years. With his firm health, and the little inroad that age has made upon him, fifteen years, or twenty—yes, or perhaps five-and-twenty!—are no more than he may fairly call his own. Five-and-twenty years for the enjoyment of his real estate in town and country, his railroad, bank, and insurance shares, his United States stock, his wealth, in short, however invested, now in possession, or soon to be acquired; together with the public honors that have fallen upon him, and the weightier ones that are yet to fall! It is good! It is excellent! It is enough!

Still lingering in the old chair! If the Judge has a little time to throw away, why does not he visit the Insurance Office, as is his frequent custom, and sit awhile in one of their leathern-cushioned arm-chairs, listening to the gossip of the day, and dropping some deeply designed chance-word, which will be certain to become the gossip of tomorrow? And have not the Bank Directors a meeting, at which it was the Judge's purpose to be present, and his office to preside? Indeed they have; and the hour is noted on a card, which is, or ought to be, in Judge Pyncheon's right vest-pocket. Let him go thither, and loll at ease upon his money-bags! He has lounged long enough in the old chair.

This was to have been such a busy day! In the first place, the interview with Clifford. Half-an-hour, by the Judge's reckoning, was to suffice for that; it would probably be less, but—taking into consideration that Hepzibah was first to be dealt with, and that these women are apt to make many words where a few would do much better—it might be safest to allow half-an-hour. Half-an-hour? Why, Judge, it is already two hours, by your own undeviatingly accurate chronometer! Glance your eye down at it, and see. Ah; he will not give himself the trouble either to bend his head, or elevate his hand, so as to bring the faithful timekeeper within his range of vision. Time, all at once, appears to have become a matter of no moment with the Judge!

And has he forgotten all the other items of his memoranda? Clifford's affair arranged, he was to meet a State-street broker, who has undertaken to procure a heavy per-centage, and the best of paper, for a few loose thousands which the Judge happens to have by him, uninvested. The wrinkled note-shaver will have taken his railroad trip in vain. Half-an-hour later, in the street next to this, there was to be an auction of real estate, including a portion of the old Pyncheon property, originally belonging to Maule's garden-ground. It has been alienated from the Pyncheons, these fourscore years; but the Judge had kept it in his eye, and had set his heart on re-annexing it to the small demesne still left around the seven gables;— and now, during this odd fit of oblivion, the fatal hammer must have fallen, and transferred our ancient patrimony to some alien possessor! Possibly, indeed, the sale may have been postponed till fairer weather. If so, will the Judge make it convenient to be present, and favor the auctioneer with his bid, on the proximate occasion?

The next affair was to buy a horse for his own driving. The one, heretofore his favorite, stumbled, this very morning, on the road to town, and must be at once discarded. Judge Pyncheon's neck is too precious to be risked on such a contingency as a stumbling steed. Should all the above business be seasonably got through with, he might attend the meeting of a charitable society; the very name of which, however, in the multiplicity of his benevolence, is quite forgotten; so that this engagement may pass unfulfilled, and no great harm done. And if he have time, amid the press of more urgent matters, he must take measures for the renewal of Mrs. Pyncheon's tombstone, which, the sexton tells him, has fallen on its marble face, and is cracked quite in twain. She was a praiseworthy woman enough, thinks the Judge, in spite of her nervousness,

and the tears that she was so oozy with, and her foolish behavior about the coffee; and as she took her departure so seasonably, he will not grudge the second tombstone. It is better,
at least, than if she had never needed any! The next item on
his list was to give orders for some fruit-trees, of a rare variety,
to be deliverable at his country-seat, in the ensuing autumn.
Yes; buy them, by all means; and may the peaches be luscious
in your mouth, Judge Pyncheon! After this, comes something
more important. A committee of his political party has besought him for a hundred or two of dollars, in addition to his
previous disbursements, towards carrying on the fall-cam-
paign. The Judge is a patriot; the fate of the country is staked
on the November election; and besides, as will be shadowed
forth in another paragraph, he has no trifling stake of his own,
in the same great game. He will do what the committee asks;
nay, he will be liberal beyond their expectations; they shall
have a check for five hundred dollars, and more anon, if it be
needed. What next? A decayed widow, whose husband was
Judge Pyncheon's early friend, has laid her case of destitution
before him, in a very moving letter. She and her fair daughter
have scarcely bread to eat. He partly intends to call on her,
to-day—perhaps so—perhaps not—accordingly as he may happen to have leisure, and a small bank-note.

Another business, which, however, he puts no great weight
on—(it is well, you know, to be heedful, but not over anxious,
as respects one's personal health)—another business, then, was
to consult his family-physician. About what, for Heaven's
sake? Why, it is rather difficult to describe the symptoms. A
mere dimness of sight and dizziness of brain, was it?—or a
disagreeable choking, or stifling, or gurgling, or bubbling, in
the region of the thorax, as the anatomists say?—or was it a
pretty severe throbbing and kicking of the heart, rather cred-
itable to him than otherwise, as showing that the organ had
not been left out of the Judge's physical contrivance? No
matter what it was. The Doctor, probably, would smile at the

statement of such trifles to his professional ear; the Judge
would smile, in his turn; and meeting one another's eyes, they
would enjoy a hearty laugh, together! But, a fig for medical
advice! The Judge will never need it.

Pray, pray, Judge Pyncheon, look at your watch, now!
What, not a glance? It is within ten minutes of the dinner-
hour! It surely cannot have slipt your memory, that the
dinner of to-day is to be the most important, in its consequences, of all the dinners you ever ate. Yes; precisely the
most important; although, in the course of your somewhat
eminent career, you have been placed high towards the head
of the table, at splendid banquets, and have poured out your
festive eloquence to ears yet echoing with Webster's mighty
organ-tones. No public dinner this, however. It is merely a
gathering of some dozen or so of friends from several districts
of the State; men of distinguished character and influence,
assembling, almost casually, at the house of a common friend,
likewise distinguished, who will make them welcome to a
little better than his ordinary fare. Nothing in the way of
French cookery, but an excellent dinner, nevertheless! Real
turtle, we understand, and salmon, tautog, canvass-backs,
pig, English mutton, good roast-beef, or dainties of that serious kind, fit for substantial country-gentlemen, as these honorable persons mostly are. The delicacies of the season, in
short, and flavored by a brand of old Madeira which has been
the pride of many seasons. It is the Juno brand; a glorious
wine, fragrant, and full of gentle might; a bottled-up happiness, put by for use; a golden liquid, worth more than liquid
gold; so rare and admirable, that veteran wine-bibbers count
it among their epochs to have tasted it! It drives away the
heart-ache, and substitutes no head-ache! Could the Judge
but quaff a glass, it might enable him to shake off the unaccountable lethargy, which—(for the ten intervening minutes, and five to boot, are already past)—has made him such
a laggard at this momentous dinner. It would all but revive a

dead man! Would you like to sip it now, Judge Pyncheon?

Alas, this dinner! Have you really forgotten its true object? Then let us whisper it, that you may start at once out of the oaken chair, which really seems to be enchanted, like the one in Comus, or that in which Moll Pitcher imprisoned your own grandfather.[1] But ambition is a talisman more powerful than witchcraft. Start up, then, and hurrying through the streets, burst in upon the company, that they may begin before the fish is spoiled! They wait for you; and it is little for your interest that they should wait. These gentlemen—need you be told it?—have assembled, not without purpose, from every quarter of the State. They are practised politicians, every man of them, and skilled to adjust those preliminary measures, which steal from the people, without its knowledge, the power of choosing its own rulers. The popular voice, at the next gubernatorial election, though loud as thunder, will be really but an echo of what these gentlemen shall speak, under their breath, at your friend's festive board. They meet to decide upon their candidate. This little knot of subtle schemers will control the Convention, and, through it, dictate to the party. And what worthier candidate—more wise and learned, more noted for philanthropic liberality, truer to safe principles, tried oftener by public trusts, more spotless in private character, with a larger stake in the common welfare, and deeper grounded, by hereditary descent, in the faith and practice of the Puritans—what man can be presented for the suffrage of the people, so eminently combining all these claims to the chief rulership, as Judge Pyncheon here before us?

Make haste, then! Do your part! The meed for which you have toiled, and fought, and climbed, and crept, is ready for your grasp! Be present at this dinner!—drink a glass or two of that noble wine!—make your pledges in as low a whisper as you will!—and you rise up from table, virtually governor of the glorious old State! Governor Pyncheon of Massachusetts!

1. In John Milton's *Comus: A Masque* (1634), Comus imprisons the Lady "in an enchanted chair" and then tempts her virtue. Moll Pitcher, who died in 1813, was a famous clairvoyant in Lynn, Massachusetts, whose name became a generic term for "fortune-teller" in the nineteenth century.

And is there no potent and exhilarating cordial in a certainty like this? It has been the grand purpose of half your lifetime to attain it. Now, when there needs little more than to signify your acceptance, why do you sit so lumpishly in your great-great-grandfather's oaken chair, as if preferring it to the gubernatorial one? We have all heard of King Log;[2] but, in these jostling times, one of that royal kindred will hardly win the race for an elective chief-magistracy!

Well; it is absolutely too late for dinner. Turtle, salmon, tautog, woodcock, boiled turkey, Southdown mutton, pig, roast-beef, have vanished, or exist only in fragments, with lukewarm potatoes, and gravies crusted over with cold fat. The Judge, had he done nothing else, would have achieved wonders with his knife and fork. It was he, you know, of whom it used to be said, in reference to his ogre-like appetite, that his Creator made him a great animal, but that the dinner-hour made him a great beast. Persons of his large sensual endowments must claim indulgence, at their feeding-time. But, for once, the Judge is entirely too late for dinner. Too late, we fear, even to join the party at their wine! The guests are warm and merry; they have given up the Judge; and, concluding that the Free Soilers[3] have him, they will fix upon another candidate. Were our friend now to stalk in among them, with that wide-open stare, at once wild and stolid, his ungenial presence would be apt to change their cheer. Neither would it be seemly in Judge Pyncheon, generally so scrupulous in his attire, to show himself at a dinner-table with that crimson stain upon his shirt-bosom. By-the-by, how came it there? It is an ugly sight, at any rate; and the wisest way for the Judge is to button his coat closely over his breast, and, taking his horse and chaise from the livery-stable, to make all speed to his own house. There, after a glass of brandy and water, and a mutton-chop, a beef-steak, a broiled fowl, or some such hasty little dinner and supper, all in one, he had better spend the evening by the fireside. He must

2. A king who never makes his power felt; derived from the fable of the frogs who, upon complaining to Jupiter that the log he sent them as a king was spiritless, were sent a stork instead, which devoured them.
3. A political organization (1847–1854) opposed to the extension of slavery

toast his slippers a long while, in order to get rid of the chilliness, which the air of this vile old house has sent curdling through his veins.

Up, therefore, Judge Pyncheon, up! You have lost a day. But tomorrow will be here anon. Will you rise, betimes, and make the most of it? Tomorrow! Tomorrow! Tomorrow! We, that are alive, may rise betimes tomorrow. As for him that has died to-day, his morrow will be the resurrection-morn.

Meanwhile the twilight is glooming upward out of the corners of the room. The shadows of the tall furniture grow deeper, and at first become more definite; then, spreading wider, they lose their distinctness of outline in the dark, gray tide of oblivion, as it were, that creeps slowly over the various objects, and the one human figure sitting in the midst of them.[4] The gloom has not entered from without; it has brooded here all day, and now, taking its own inevitable time, will possess itself of everything. The Judge's face, indeed, rigid, and singularly white, refuses to melt into this universal solvent. Fainter and fainter grows the light. It is as if another double-handfull of darkness had been scattered through the air. Now it is no longer gray, but sable. There is still a faint appearance at the window; neither a glow, nor a gleam, nor a glimmer—any phrase of light would express something far brighter than this doubtful perception, or sense, rather, that there is a window there. Has it yet vanished? No!—yes!—not quite! And there is still the swarthy whiteness —we shall venture to marry these ill-agreeing words—the swarthy whiteness of Judge Pyncheon's face. The features are all gone; there is only the paleness of them left. And how looks it now? There is no window! There is no face! An infinite, inscrutable blackness has annihilated sight! Where is our universe? All crumbled away from us; and we, adrift in chaos, may hearken to the gusts of homeless wind, that go

---

in territories acquired by the Mexican War; hardly a party with which the conservative judge would align himself.

4. "The sunbeam that comes through a round-hole in the shutter of a darkened room, where a dead man sits in solitude." (*American Notebooks*,

sighing and murmuring about, in quest of what was once a world!

Is there no other sound? One other, and a fearful one. It is the ticking of the Judge's watch, which, ever since Hepzibah left the room in search of Clifford, he has been holding in his hand. Be the cause what it may, this little, quiet, never-ceasing throb of Time's pulse, repeating its small strokes with such busy regularity, in Judge Pyncheon's motionless hand, has an effect of terror, which we do not find in any other accompaniment of the scene.

But, listen! That puff of the breeze was louder; it had a tone unlike the dreary and sullen one, which has bemoaned itself, and afflicted all mankind with miserable sympathy, for five days past. The wind has veered about! It now comes boisterously from the north-west, and, taking hold of the aged frame-work of the seven gables, gives it a shake, like a wrestler that would try strength with his antagonist. Another, and another sturdy tustle with the blast! The old house creaks again, and makes a vociferous, but somewhat unintelligible bellowing in its sooty throat—(the big flue, we mean, of its wide chimney) partly in complaint at the rude wind, but rather, as befits their century-and-a-half of hostile intimacy, in tough defiance. A rumbling kind of a bluster roars behind the fire-board. A door has slammed above-stairs. A window, perhaps, has been left open, or else is driven in by an unruly gust. It is not to be conceived, beforehand, what wonderful wind-instruments are these old timber-mansions, and how haunted with the strangest noises, which immediately begin to sing, and sigh, and sob, and shriek—and to smite with sledge-hammers, airy, but ponderous, in some distant chamber—and to tread along the entries as with stately footsteps, and rustle up and down the staircase, as with silks miraculously stiff—whenever the gale catches the house with a window open, and gets fairly into it. Would that we were not an

entry made between February 16 and July 14, 1850.)

attendant spirit, here! It is too awful! This clamor of the wind through the lonely house; the Judge's quietude, as he sits invisible; and that pertinacious ticking of his watch!

As regards Judge Pyncheon's invisibility, however, that matter will soon be remedied. The north-west wind has swept the sky clear. The window is distinctly seen. Through its panes, moreover, we dimly catch the sweep of the dark, clustering foliage, outside, fluttering with a constant irregularity of movement, and letting in a peep of starlight, now here, now there. Oftener than any other object, these glimpses illuminate the Judge's face. But here comes more effectual light. Observe that silvery dance upon the upper branches of the pear-tree, and now a little lower, and now on the whole mass of boughs, while, through their shifting intricacies, the moonbeams fall aslant into the room. They play over the Judge's figure, and show that he has not stirred throughout the hours of darkness. They follow the shadows, in changeful sport, across his unchanging features. They gleam upon his watch. His grasp conceals the dial-plate; but we know that the faithful hands have met; for one of the city-clocks tells midnight.

A man of sturdy understanding, like Judge Pyncheon, cares no more for twelve o'clock at night, than for the corresponding hour of noon. However just the parallel, drawn in some of the preceding pages, between his Puritan ancestor and himself, it fails in this point. The Pyncheon of two centuries ago, in common with most of his contemporaries, professed his full belief in spiritual ministrations, although reckoning them chiefly of a malignant character. The Pyncheon of to-night, who sits in yonder chair, believes in no such nonsense. Such, at least, was his creed, some few hours since. His hair will not bristle, therefore, at the stories which—in times when chimney-corners had benches in them, where old people sat poking into the ashes of the past, and raking out traditions, like live coals—used to be told about this very room of his ancestral house. In fact, these tales are too absurd to bristle even childhood's hair. What sense, meaning, or moral, for example, such as even ghost-stories should be susceptible of, can be traced in the ridiculous legend, that, at midnight, all the dead Pyncheons are bound to assemble in this parlor! And, pray, for what? Why, to see whether the portrait of their ancestor still keeps its place upon the wall, in compliance with his testamentary directions! Is it worth while to come out of their graves for that?

We are tempted to make a little sport with the idea. Ghost-stories are hardly to be treated seriously, any longer. The family-party of the defunct Pyncheons, we presume, goes off in this wise.

First comes the ancestor himself, in his black cloak, steeple-hat, and trunk-breeches, girt about the waist with a leathern belt, in which hangs his steel-hilted sword; he has a long staff in his hand, such as gentlemen in advanced life used to carry, as much for the dignity of the thing, as for the support to be derived from it. He looks up at the portrait; a thing of no substance, gazing at its own painted image! All is safe. The picture is still there. The purpose of his brain has been kept sacred, thus long after the man himself has sprouted up in grave-yard grass. See; he lifts his ineffectual hand, and tries the frame. All safe! But, is that a smile?—is it not, rather, a frown of deadly import, that darkens over the shadow of his features? The stout Colonel is dissatisfied! So decided is his look of discontent as to impart additional distinctness to his features; through which, nevertheless, the moonlight passes, and flickers on the wall beyond. Something has strangely vexed the ancestor! With a grim shake of the head, he turns away. Here come other Pyncheons, the whole tribe, in their half-a-dozen generations, jostling and elbowing one another, to reach the picture. We behold aged men and grandames, a clergyman, with the Puritanic stiffness still in his garb and mien, and a red-coated officer of the Old French War;[5] and there comes the shopkeeping Pyncheon of a century ago, with the ruffles turned back from his wrists; and

5. The French and Indian War (1754–1760).

there the periwigged and brocaded gentleman of the artist's
legend, with the beautiful and pensive Alice, who brings no
pride, out of her virgin grave. All try the picture-frame.
What do these ghostly people seek? A mother lifts her child,
that his little hands may touch it! There is evidently a mystery about the picture, that perplexes these poor Pyncheons
when they ought to be at rest. In a corner, meanwhile, stands
the figure of an elderly man, in a leather jerkin and breeches,
with a carpenter's rule sticking out of his side-pocket; he
points his finger at the bearded Colonel and his descendants,
nodding, jeering, mocking, and finally bursting into obstreperous, though inaudible laughter.

Indulging our fancy in this freak, we have partly lost the
power of restraint and guidance. We distinguish an unlooked-
for figure in our visionary scene. Among those ancestral people, there is a young man, dressed in the very fashion of
to-day; he wears a dark frock-coat, almost destitute of skirts,
gray pantaloons, gaiter-boots of patent leather, and has a
finely wrought gold chain across his breast, and a little silver-
headed whalebone-stick in his hand. Were we to meet this
figure at noonday, we should greet him as young Jaffrey
Pyncheon, the Judge's only surviving child, who has been
spending the last two years in foreign travel. If still in life,
how comes his shadow hither? If dead, what a misfortune!
The old Pyncheon property, together with the great estate,
acquired by this young man's father, would devolve on
whom? On poor, foolish Clifford, gaunt Hepzibah, and rustic
little Phoebe! But another, and a greater marvel greets us!
Can we believe our eyes? A stout, elderly gentleman has
made his appearance; he has an aspect of eminent respectability, wears a black coat and pantaloons, of roomy width, and
might be pronounced scrupulously neat in his attire, but for
a broad crimson-stain, across his snowy neckcloth and down
his shirt-bosom. Is it the Judge, or no? How can it be Judge
Pyncheon? We discern his figure, as plainly as the flickering

moonbeams can show us anything, still seated in the oaken chair! Be the apparition whose it may, it advances to the picture, seems to seize the frame, tries to peep behind it, and turns away, with a frown as black as the ancestral one.

The fantastic scene, just hinted at, must by no means be considered as forming an actual portion of our story. We were betrayed into this brief extravagance by the quiver of the moonbeams; they dance hand-in-hand with shadows, and are reflected in the looking-glass, which, you are aware, is always a kind of window or door-way into the spiritual world. We needed relief, moreover, from our too long and exclusive contemplation of that figure in the chair. This wild wind, too, has tossed our thoughts into strange confusion, but without tearing them away from their one determined centre. Yonder leaden Judge sits immoveably upon our soul. Will he never stir again? We shall go mad, unless he stirs! You may the better estimate his quietude by the fearlessness of a little mouse, which sits on its hind-legs, in a streak of moonlight, close by Judge Pyncheon's foot, and seems to meditate a journey of exploration over this great, black bulk. Ha! What has startled the nimble little mouse? It is the visage of Grimalkin, outside of the window, where he appears to have posted himself for a deliberate watch. This Grimalkin has a very ugly look. Is it a cat watching for a mouse, or the Devil for a human soul? Would we could scare him from the window!

Thank Heaven, the night is well-nigh past! The moonbeams have no longer so silvery a gleam, nor contrast so strongly with the blackness of the shadows among which they fall. They are paler, now; the shadows look gray, not black. The boisterous wind is hushed. What is the hour? Ah! The watch has at last ceased to tick; for the Judge's forgetful fingers neglected to wind it up, as usual, at ten o'clock, being half-an-hour, or so, before his ordinary bed-time;—and it has run down, for the first time in five years. But the great world-clock of Time still keeps its beat. The dreary night—for, Oh, how dreary seems its haunted waste, behind us!—gives place to a fresh, transparent, cloudless morn. Blessed, blessed radiance! The day-beam—even what little of it finds its way into this always dusky parlor—seems part of the universal benediction, annulling evil, and rendering all goodness possible, and happiness attainable. Will Judge Pyncheon now rise up from his chair? Will he go forth, and receive the early sunbeams on his brow? Will he begin this new day—which God has smiled upon, and blessed, and given to mankind—will he begin it with better purposes than the many that have been spent amiss? Or are all the deep-laid schemes of yesterday as stubborn in his heart, and as busy in his brain, as ever?

In this latter case, there is much to do. Will the Judge still insist with Hepzibah on the interview with Clifford? Will he buy a safe, elderly gentleman's horse? Will he persuade the purchaser of the old Pyncheon property to relinquish the bargain, in his favor? Will he see his family-physician, and obtain a medicine that shall preserve him, to be an honor and blessing to his race, until the utmost term of patriarchal longevity? Will Judge Pyncheon, above all, make due apologies to that company of honorable friends, and satisfy them that his absence from the festive board was unavoidable, and so fully retrieve himself in their good opinion, that he shall yet be Governor of Massachusetts? And, all these great purposes accomplished, will he walk the streets again, with that dog-day smile of elaborate benevolence, sultry enough to tempt flies to come and buzz in it? Or will he—after the tomblike seclusion of the past day and night—go forth a humbled and repentant man, sorrowful, gentle, seeking no profit, shrinking from worldly honor, hardly daring to love God, but bold to love his fellow-man, and to do him what good he may? Will he bear about with him—no odious grin of feigned benignity, insolent in its pretence, and loathsome in its falsehood—but the tender sadness of a contrite heart, broken, at last, beneath its own weight of sin? For it is our belief, whatever show of honor he may have piled upon it, that there was heavy sin at the base of this man's being.

Rise up, Judge Pyncheon! The morning sunshine glimmers through the foliage, and, beautiful and holy as it is, shuns not to kindle up your face. Rise up, thou subtile, worldly, selfish, iron-hearted hypocrite, and make thy choice, whether still to be subtile, worldly, selfish, iron-hearted, and hypocritical, or to tear these sins out of thy nature, though they bring the life-blood with them! The Avenger is upon thee! Rise up, before it be too late!

What! Thou art not stirred by this last appeal? No; not a jot! And there we see a fly—one of your common house-flies, such as are always buzzing on the window-pane—which has smelt out Governor Pyncheon, and alights now on his forehead, now on his chin, and now, Heaven help us, is creeping over the bridge of his nose, towards the would-be chief-magistrate's wide-open eyes! Canst thou not brush the fly away? Art thou too sluggish? Thou man, that hadst so many busy projects, yesterday! Art thou too weak, that wast so powerful? Not brush away a fly! Nay, then, we give thee up!

And, hark! the shop-bell rings. After hours like these latter ones, through which we have borne our heavy tale, it is good to be made sensible that there is a living world, and that even this old, lonely mansion retains some manner of connection with it. We breathe more freely, emerging from Judge Pyncheon's presence into the street before the seven gables.

## XIX

## ALICE'S POSIES

U NCLE VENNER, trundling a wheelbarrow, was the earliest person stirring in the neighborhood, the day after the storm.

Pyncheon-street, in front of the House of the Seven Gables, was a far pleasanter scene than a by-lane, confined by shabby fences, and bordered with wooden dwellings of the meaner class, could reasonably be expected to present. Nature made sweet amends, that morning, for the five unkindly days which had preceded it. It would have been enough to live for, merely to look up at the wide benediction of the sky, or as much of it as was visible between the houses, genial once more with sunshine. Every object was agreeable, whether to be gazed at in the breadth, or examined more minutely. Such, for example, were the well-washed pebbles and gravel of the sidewalk; even the sky-reflecting pools in the centre of the street; and the grass, now freshly verdant, that crept along the base of the fences, on the other side of which, if one peeped over, was seen the multifarious growth of gardens. Vegetable productions, of whatever kind, seemed more than negatively happy, in the juicy warmth and abundance of their life. The Pyncheon-elm, throughout its great circumference, was all alive, and full of the morning sun and a sweetly tempered little breeze, which lingered within this verdant sphere, and set a thousand leafy tongues a-whispering all at once. This aged tree appeared to have suffered nothing from the gale. It had kept its boughs unshattered, and its full complement of leaves, and the whole in perfect verdure, except a single branch, that, by the earlier change with which the elm-tree sometimes prophesies the autumn, had been transmuted to bright gold. It was like the golden branch, that gained Æneas and the Sibyl admittance into Hades.[1]

This one mystic branch hung down before the main-entrance of the seven gables, so nigh the ground, that any passer-by might have stood on tiptoe and plucked it off. Presented at the door, it would have been a symbol of his right to enter, and be made acquainted with all the secrets of the house. So little faith is due to external appearance, that there was really an inviting aspect over the venerable edifice, conveying an idea that its history must be a decorous and happy one, and such as would be delightful for a fireside-tale. Its windows gleamed cheerfully in the slanting sunlight. The lines and tufts of green moss, here and there, seemed pledges of familiarity and sisterhood with Nature; as if this human dwelling-place, being of such old date, had established its prescriptive title among primeval oaks, and whatever other objects, by virtue of their long continuance, have acquired a gracious right to be. A person of imaginative temperament, while passing by the house, would turn, once and again, and peruse it well;—its many peaks, consenting together in the clustered chimney; the deep projection over its basement story; the arched window, imparting a look, if not of grandeur, yet of antique gentility, to the broken portal over which it opened; the luxuriance of gigantic burdocks, near the threshold;—he would note all these characteristics, and be conscious of something deeper than he saw. He would conceive the mansion to have been the residence of the stubborn old Puritan, Integrity, who, dying in some forgotten generation, had left a blessing in all its rooms and chambers,

1. In Book VI of Virgil's *Aeneid,* a golden bough admits Aeneas to the underworld of the dead, where his father shows him the splendid company of men who are to become their great Roman descendants. Havens (see Bibliography) argues that this implies the future brightness of the union

the efficacy of which was to be seen in the religion, honesty, moderate competence, or upright poverty, and solid happiness, of his descendants, to this day.

One object, above all others, would take root in the imaginative observer's memory. It was the great tuft of flowers—weeds, you would have called them, only a week ago—the tuft of crimson-spotted flowers, in the angle between the two front gables. The old people used to give them the name of Alice's Posies, in remembrance of fair Alice Pyncheon, who was believed to have brought their seeds from Italy. They were flaunting in rich beauty and full bloom, to-day, and seemed, as it were, a mystic expression that something within the house was consummated.

It was but little after sunrise, when Uncle Venner made his appearance, as aforesaid, impelling a wheelbarrow along the street. He was going his matutinal rounds to collect cabbage-leaves, turnip-tops, potato-skins, and the miscellaneous refuse of the dinner-pot, which the thrifty housewives of the neighborhood were accustomed to put aside, as fit only to feed a pig. Uncle Venner's pig was fed entirely and kept in prime order on these eleemosynary contributions; insomuch that the patched philosopher used to promise that, before retiring to his farm, he would make a feast of the portly grunter, and invite all his neighbors to partake of the joints and spare-ribs which they had helped to fatten. Miss Hepzibah Pyncheon's house-keeping had so greatly improved, since Clifford became a member of the family, that her share of the banquet would have been no lean one; and Uncle Venner, accordingly, was a good deal disappointed not to find the large earthen pan, full of fragmentary eatables, that ordinarily awaited his coming, at the back-doorstep of the seven gables.

"I never knew Miss Hepzibah so forgetful before," said the patriarch to himself. "She must have had a dinner, yesterday—no question of that! She always has one, now-a-days.

---

of Holgrave and Phoebe.

So where's the pot-liquor and potato-skins, I ask? Shall I knock, and see if she's stirring yet? No, no—'twon't do! If little Phoebe was about the house, I should not mind knocking; but Miss Hepzibah, likely as not, would scowl down at me, out of the window, and look cross, even if she felt pleasantly. So I'll come back at noon."

With these reflections, the old man was shutting the gate of the little back-yard. Creaking on its hinges, however, like every other gate and door about the premises, the sound reached the ears of the occupant of the northern gable; one of the windows of which had a side-view towards the gate.

"Good morning, Uncle Venner!" said the Daguerreotypist, leaning out of the window.—"Do you hear nobody stirring?"

"Not a soul!" said the man of patches. "But that's no wonder. 'Tis barely half-an-hour past sunrise, yet. But I'm really glad to see you, Mr. Holgrave! There's a strange, lonesome look about this side of the house; so that my heart misgave me, somehow or other, and I felt as if there was nobody alive in it. The front of the house looks a good deal cheerier; and Alice's Posies are blooming there beautifully; and if I were a young man, Mr. Holgrave, my sweetheart should have one of those flowers in her bosom, though I risked my neck climbing for it! Well!—and did the wind keep you awake, last night?"

"It did indeed!" answered the artist smiling. "If I were a believer in ghosts—and I don't quite know whether I am, or not—I should have concluded that all the old Pyncheons were running riot in the lower rooms; especially in Miss Hepzibah's part of the house. But it is very quiet, now."

"Yes; Miss Hepzibah will be apt to oversleep herself, after being disturbed, all night, with the racket," said Uncle Venner. "But it would be odd, now—wouldn't it?—if the Judge had taken both his cousins into the country along with him. I saw him go into the shop, yesterday."

"At what hour?" inquired Holgrave.

"Oh, along in the forenoon," said the old man. "Well, well; I must go my rounds, and so must my wheelbarrow. But I'll be back here at dinner-time; for my pig likes a dinner as well as a breakfast. No meal-time, and no sort of victuals, ever seems to come amiss to my pig. Good morning to you! And, Mr. Holgrave, if I were a young man, like you, I'd get one of Alice's Posies, and keep it in water till Phoebe comes back."

"I have heard," said the Daguerreotypist, as he drew in his head, "that the water of Maule's Well suits those flowers best."

Here the conversation ceased, and Uncle Venner went on his way. For half-an-hour longer, nothing disturbed the repose of the seven gables, nor was there any visitor, except a carrier-boy, who, as he passed the front-doorstep, threw down one of his newspapers; for Hepzibah, of late, had regularly taken it in. After awhile, there came a fat woman, making prodigious speed, and stumbling as she ran up the steps of the shop-door. Her face glowed with fire-heat; and, it being a pretty warm morning, she bubbled and hissed, as it were, as if all a-fry with chimney-warmth, and summer-warmth, and the warmth of her own corpulent velocity. She tried the shop-door; it was fast. She tried it again, with so angry a jar that the bell tinkled angrily back at her.

"The deuce take Old Maid Pyncheon!" muttered the irascible housewife. "Think of her pretending to set up a cent-shop, and then lying abed till noon! These are what she calls gentlefolk's airs, I suppose! But I'll either start her ladyship, or break the door down!"

She shook it accordingly; and the bell, having a spiteful little temper of its own, rang obstreperously, making its remonstrances heard—not, indeed, by the ears for which they were intended—but by a good lady on the opposite side of the street. She opened her window, and addressed the impatient applicant.

"You'll find nobody there, Mrs. Gubbins."

"But I must and will find somebody here!" cried Mrs. Gubbins, inflicting another outrage on the bell. "I want a half-pound of pork, to fry some first-rate flounders for Mr. Gubbins's breakfast; and, lady or not, Old Maid Pyncheon shall get up and serve me with it!"

"But do hear reason, Mrs. Gubbins!" responded the lady opposite.—"She, and her brother too, have both gone to their cousin, Judge Pyncheon's, at his country-seat. There's not a soul in the house but that young daguerreotype-man, that sleeps in the north-gable. I saw old Hepzibah and Clifford go away, yesterday; and a queer couple of ducks they were, paddling through the mud-puddles! They're gone, I'll assure you."

"And how do you know they're gone to the Judge's?" asked Mrs. Gubbins.—"He's a rich man; and there's been a quarrel between him and Hepzibah, this many a day, because he won't give her a living. That's the main reason of her setting up a cent-shop."

"I know that well enough," said the neighbor. "But they're gone—that's one thing certain. And who but a blood-relation, that couldn't help himself, I ask you, would take in that awful-tempered Old Maid, and that dreadful Clifford? That's it, you may be sure!"

Mrs. Gubbins took her departure, still brimming over with hot wrath against the absent Hepzibah. For another half-hour, or perhaps considerably more, there was almost as much quiet on the outside of the house, as within. The elm, however, made a pleasant, cheerful, sunny sigh, responsive to the breeze that was elsewhere imperceptible; a swarm of insects buzzed merrily under its drooping shadow, and became specks of light, whenever they darted into the sunshine; a locust sang, once or twice, in some inscrutable seclusion of the tree; and a solitary little bird, with plumage of pale gold, came and hovered about Alice's Posies.

At last, our small acquaintance Ned Higgins trudged up the street, on his way to school; and happening, for the first time in a fortnight, to be the possessor of a cent, he could by no means get past the shop-door of the seven gables. But it would not open. Again and again, however, and half-a-dozen other agains, with the inexorable pertinacity of a child, intent upon some object important to itself, did he renew his efforts for admittance. He had doubtless set his heart upon an elephant; or, possibly, with Hamlet, he meant to eat a crocodile.[2] In response to his more violent attacks, the bell gave now-and-then a moderate tinkle, but could not be stirred into clamor by any exertion of the little fellow's childish and tiptoe strength. Holding by the door-handle, he peeped through a crevice of the curtain, and saw that the inner door, communicating with the passage towards the parlor, was closed.

"Miss Pyncheon!" screamed the child, rapping on the window-pane. "I want an elephant!"

There being no answer to several repetitions of the summons, Ned began to grow impatient; and his little pot of passion quickly boiling over, he picked up a stone, with a naughty purpose to fling it through the window; at the same time blubbering and sputtering with wrath. A man, one of two who happened to be passing by, caught the urchin's arm.

"What's the trouble, old gentleman?" he asked.

"I want old Hepzibah, or Phoebe, or any of them!" answered Ned, sobbing. "They won't open the door; and I can't get my elephant!"

"Go to school, you little scamp!" said the man. "There's another cent-shop round the corner. 'Tis very strange, Dixey," added he to his companion, "what's become of all these Pyncheons! Smith, the livery-stable keeper, tells me Judge Pyncheon put his horse up, yesterday, to stand till after dinner, and has not taken him away, yet. And one of the Judge's hired men has been in, this morning, to make inquiry about him. He's a kind of person, they say, that seldom breaks his habits, or stays out o'nights."

"Oh, he'll turn up safe enough!" said Dixey. "And as for

2. At the grave of Ophelia, Hamlet, angered by Laertes' display of sorrow, and tormented with grief himself, says to Laertes: "Woo't weep? woo't fight? woo't fast? woo't tear thyself?/Woo't drink up esill? eat a crocodile?" (V, i, 262–3).

Old Maid Pyncheon, take my word for it, she has run in debt, and gone off from her creditors. I foretold, you remember, the first morning she set up shop, that her devilish scowl would frighten away customers. They couldn't stand it!"

"I never thought she'd make it go," remarked his friend. "This business of cent-shops is overdone among the women-folks. My wife tried it, and lost five dollars on her outlay!"

"Poor business!" said Dixey, shaking his head. "Poor business!"

In the course of the morning, there were various other attempts to open a communication with the supposed inhabitants of this silent and impenetrable mansion. The man of root-beer came, in his neatly painted wagon, with a couple of dozen full bottles, to be exchanged for empty ones; the baker, with a lot of crackers which Hepzibah had ordered for her retail-custom; the butcher, with a nice tidbit which he fancied she would be eager to secure for Clifford. Had any observer of these proceedings been aware of the fearful secret, hidden within the house, it would have affected him with a singular shape and modification of horror, to see the current of human life making this small eddy hereabouts; —whirling sticks, straws, and all such trifles, round and round, right over the black depth where a dead corpse lay unseen.

The butcher was so much in earnest with his sweetbread of lamb, or whatever the dainty might be, that he tried every accessible door of the seven gables, and at length came round again to the shop, where he ordinarily found admittance.

"It's a nice article, and I know the old lady would jump at it," said he to himself.—"She can't be gone away! In fifteen years that I have driven my cart through Pyncheon-street, I've never known her to be away from home; though, often enough, to be sure, a man might knock all day without bringing her to the door. But that was when she'd only herself to provide for."

Peeping through the same crevice of the curtain where,

only a little while before, the urchin of elephantine appetite had peeped, the butcher beheld the inner door, not closed, as the child had seen it, but ajar, and almost wide open. However it might have happened, it was the fact. Through the passage-way there was a dark vista into the lighter, but still obscure, interior of the parlor. It appeared to the butcher that he could pretty clearly discern what seemed to be the stalwart legs, clad in black pantaloons, of a man sitting in a large oaken chair, the back of which concealed all the remainder of his figure. This contemptuous tranquillity on the part of an occupant of the house, in response to the butcher's indefatigable efforts to attract notice, so piqued the man of flesh that he determined to withdraw.

"So," thought he, "there sits Old Maid Pyncheon's bloody brother, while I've been giving myself all this trouble! Why, if a hog hadn't more manners, I'd stick him! I call it demeaning a man's business to trade with such people; and from this time forth, if they want a sausage or an ounce of liver, they shall run after the cart for it!"

He tossed the tidbit angrily into his cart, and drove off in a pet.

Not a great while afterwards, there was a sound of music turning the corner, and approaching down the street, with several intervals of silence, and then a renewed and nearer outbreak of brisk melody. A mob of children was seen moving onward, or stopping, in unison with the sound, which appeared to proceed from the centre of the throng; so that they were loosely bound together by slender strains of harmony, and drawn along captive; with ever and anon an accession of some little fellow in an apron and straw hat, capering forth from door or gateway. Arriving under the shadow of the Pyncheon-elm, it proved to be the Italian boy, who, with his monkey and show of puppets, had once before played his hurdy-gurdy beneath the arched window. The pleasant face

of Phoebe—and doubtless, too, the liberal recompense which
she had flung him—still dwelt in his remembrance. His
expressive features kindled up, as he recognized the spot
where this trifling incident of his erratic life had chanced.
He entered the neglected yard, (now wilder than ever, with
its growth of hogweed and burdock,) stationed himself on
the door-step of the main-entrance, and opening his show-box,
began to play. Each individual of the automatic community
forthwith set to work, according to his or her proper vocation;
the monkey, taking off his highland bonnet, bowed and
scraped to the bystanders, most obsequiously, with ever an
observant eye to pick up a stray cent; and the young foreigner himself, as he turned the crank of his machine, glanced
upward to the arched window, expectant of a presence that
would make his music the livelier and sweeter. The throng
of children stood near; some on the sidewalk; some within the
yard; two or three establishing themselves on the very door-
step; and one squatting on the threshold. Meanwhile, the
locust kept singing, in the great, old Pyncheon-elm.

"I don't hear anybody in the house," said one of the children to another. "The monkey won't pick up anything here."

"There is somebody at home," affirmed the urchin on the
threshold. "I heard a step!"

Still the young Italian's eye turned sidelong upward; and
it really seemed as if the touch of genuine, though slight and
almost playful emotion, communicated a juicier sweetness to
the dry, mechanical process of his minstrelsy. These wanderers are readily responsive to any natural kindness—be it
no more than a smile, or a word, itself not understood, but
only a warmth in it—which befalls them on the roadside of
life. They remember these things, because they are the little
enchantments which, for the instant—for the space that reflects a landscape in a soap-bubble—build up a home about
them. Therefore, the Italian boy would not be discouraged

by the heavy silence, with which the old house seemed resolute to clog the vivacity of his instrument. He persisted in his
melodious appeals; he still looked upward, trusting that his
dark, alien countenance would soon be brightened by
Phoebe's sunny aspect. Neither could he be willing to depart
without again beholding Clifford, whose sensibility, like
Phoebe's smile, had talked a kind of heart's language to the
foreigner. He repeated all his music, over and over again,
until his auditors were getting weary. So were the little
wooden-people in his show-box, and the monkey most of all.
There was no response, save the singing of the locust.

"No children live in this house," said a schoolboy, at last.
"Nobody lives here but an old maid and an old man. You'll
get nothing here! Why don't you go along?"

"You fool, you, why do you tell him?" whispered a shrewd
little Yankee, caring nothing for the music, but a good deal
for the cheap rate at which it was had. "Let him play as long
as he likes. If there's nobody to pay him, that's his own
look-out!"

Once more, however, the Italian ran over his round of
melodies. To the common observer—who could understand
nothing of the case, except the music and the sunshine on
the hither side of the door—it might have been amusing to
watch the pertinacity of the street-performer. Will he succeed
at last? Will that stubborn door be suddenly flung open?
Will a group of joyous children, the young ones of the house,
come dancing, shouting, laughing, into the open air, and
cluster round the show-box, looking with eager merriment at
the puppets, and tossing each a copper for long-tailed Mammon, the monkey, to pick up?

But, to us, who know the inner heart of the seven gables,
as well as its exterior face, there is a ghastly effect in this repetition of light popular tunes at its door-step. It would be an
ugly business, indeed, if Judge Pyncheon (who would not
have cared a fig for Paganini's fiddle,[3] in his most harmonious

3. Niccolò Paganini (1782–1840), Italian composer and violinist, is considered
one of the great violin virtuosos of all time.

mood) should make his appearance at the door, with a bloody
shirt-bosom, and a grim frown on his swarthily white visage,
and motion the foreign vagabond away! Was ever before such
a grinding-out of jigs and waltzes, where nobody was in the
cue to dance? Yes; very often. This contrast, or intermingling
of tragedy with mirth, happens daily, hourly, momently. The
gloomy and desolate old house, deserted of life, and with awful Death sitting sternly in its solitude, was the emblem of
many a human heart, which, nevertheless, is compelled to
hear the trill and echo of the world's gaiety around it.

Before the conclusion of the Italian's performance, a couple
of men happened to be passing, on their way to dinner.

"I say, you young French fellow!" called out one of them,
—"come away from that door-step, and go somewhere else
with your nonsense! The Pyncheon family live there; and
they are in great trouble, just about this time. They don't
feel musical to-day. It is reported, all over town, that Judge
Pyncheon, who owns the house, has been murdered; and the
City Marshal is going to look into the matter. So be off with
you at once!"

As the Italian shouldered his hurdy-gurdy, he saw on the
door-step a card, which had been covered, all the morning,
by the newspaper that the carrier had flung upon it, but was
now shuffled into sight. He picked it up, and perceiving
something written in pencil, gave it to the man to read. In
fact, it was an engraved card of Judge Pyncheon's, with certain pencilled memoranda on the back, referring to various
businesses which it had been his purpose to transact during
the preceding day. It formed a prospective epitome of the
day's history; only that affairs had not turned out altogether
in accordance with the programme. The card must have been
lost from the Judge's vest-pocket, in his preliminary attempt
to gain access by the main-entrance of the house. Though
well-soaked with rain, it was still partially legible.

"Look here, Dixey!" cried the man. "This has something

to do with Judge Pyncheon. See;—here's his name printed on it; and here, I suppose, is some of his handwriting."

"Let's go to the City Marshal with it!" said Dixey. "It may give him just the clue he wants. After all," whispered he in his companion's ear, "it would be no wonder if the Judge has gone into that door, and never come out again! A certain cousin of his may have been at his old tricks. And Old Maid Pyncheon having got herself in debt by the cent-shop—and the Judge's pocket-book being well-filled—and bad blood amongst them already! Put all these things together, and see what they make!"

"Hush, hush!" whispered the other. "It seems like a sin to be the first to speak of such a thing. But I think, with you, that we had better go to the City Marshal."

"Yes, yes!" said Dixey. "Well!—I always said there was something devilish in that woman's scowl!"

The men wheeled about, accordingly, and retraced their steps up the street. The Italian, also, made the best of his way off, with a parting glance up at the arched window. As for the children, they took to their heels, with one accord, and scampered, as if some giant or ogre were in pursuit; until, at a good distance from the house, they stopt as suddenly and simultaneously as they had set out. Their susceptible nerves took an indefinite alarm from what they had overheard. Looking back at the grotesque peaks and shadowy angles of the old mansion, they fancied a gloom diffused about it, which no brightness of the sunshine could dispel. An imaginary Hepzibah scowled and shook her finger at them, from several windows at the same moment. An imaginary Clifford—for (and it would have deeply wounded him to know it) he had always been a horror to these small people —stood behind the unreal Hepzibah, making awful gestures, in a faded dressing-gown. Children are even more apt, if possible, than grown people, to catch the contagion of a panic terror. For the rest of the day, the more timid went whole streets about, for the sake of avoiding the seven gables; while the bolder signalized their hardihood by challenging their comrades to race past the mansion, at full speed.

It could not have been more than half-an-hour after the disappearance of the Italian boy, with his unseasonable melodies, when a cab drove down the street. It stopt beneath the Pyncheon-elm; the cabman took a trunk, a canvass-bag, and a bandbox, from the top of his vehicle, and deposited them on the door-step of the old house; a straw bonnet, and then the pretty figure of a young girl, came into view from the interior of the cab. It was Phoebe! Though not altogether so blooming as when she first tript into our story—for, in the few intervening weeks, her experiences had made her graver, more womanly, and deeper-eyed, in token of a heart that had begun to suspect its depths—still there was the quiet glow of natural sunshine over her. Neither had she forfeited her proper gift of making things look real, rather than fantastic, within her sphere. Yet we feel it to be a questionable venture, even for Phoebe, at this juncture, to cross the threshold of the seven gables. Is her healthful presence potent enough to chase away the crowd of pale, hideous, and sinful phantoms, that have gained admittance there, since her departure? Or will she, likewise, fade, sicken, sadden, and grow into deformity, and be only another pallid phantom, to glide noiselessly up and down the stairs, and affright children, as she pauses at the window?

At least, we would gladly forewarn the unsuspecting girl, that there is nothing in human shape or substance to receive her, unless it be the figure of Judge Pyncheon, who—wretched spectacle that he is, and frightful in our remembrance, since our night-long vigil with him!—still keeps his place in the oaken chair.

Phoebe first tried the shop-door. It did not yield to her

hand; and the white curtain, drawn across the window which formed the upper section of the door, struck her quick perceptive faculty as something unusual. Without making another effort to enter here, she betook herself to the great portal, under the arched window. Finding it fastened, she knocked. A reverberation came from the emptiness within. She knocked again, and a third time, and, listening intently, fancied that the floor creaked, as if Hepzibah were coming, with her ordinary tiptoe movement, to admit her. But so dead a silence ensued upon this imaginary sound, that she began to question whether she might not have mistaken the house, familiar as she thought herself with its exterior.

Her notice was now attracted by a child's voice, at some distance. It appeared to call her name. Looking in the direction whence it proceeded, Phoebe saw little Ned Higgins, a good way down the street, stamping, shaking his head violently, making deprecatory gestures with both hands, and shouting to her at mouth-wide screech.

"No, no, Phoebe!" he screamed. "Don't you go in! There's something wicked there! Don't—don't—don't go in!"

But, as the little personage could not be induced to approach near enough to explain himself, Phoebe concluded that he had been frightened, on some of his visits to the shop, by her Cousin Hepzibah; for the good lady's manifestations, in truth, ran about an equal chance of scaring children out of their wits, or compelling them to unseemly laughter. Still, she felt the more, for this incident, how unaccountably silent and impenetrable the house had become. As her next resort, Phoebe made her way into the garden, where, on so warm and bright a day as the present, she had little doubt of finding Clifford, and perhaps Hepzibah also, idling away the noontide in the shadow of the arbor. Immediately on her entering the garden-gate, the family of hens half ran, half flew, to meet her; while a strange Grimalkin, which was prowling under the parlor-window, took to his heels, clambered hastily over the fence, and vanished. The arbor was vacant, and its floor, table, and circular bench, were still damp, and bestrewn with twigs, and the disarray of the past storm. The growth of the garden seemed to have got quite out of bounds; the weeds had taken advantage of Phoebe's absence, and the long-continued rain, to run rampant over the flowers and kitchen-vegetables. Maule's Well had overflowed its stone-border, and made a pool of formidable breadth, in that corner of the garden.

The impression of the whole scene was that of a spot, where no human foot had left its print, for many preceding days—probably, not since Phoebe's departure—for she saw a side-comb of her own under the table of the arbor, where it must have fallen, on the last afternoon when she and Clifford sat there.

The girl knew that her two relatives were capable of far greater oddities, than that of shutting themselves up in their old house, as they appeared now to have done. Nevertheless, with indistinct misgivings of something amiss, and apprehensions to which she could not give shape, she approached the door that formed the customary communication between the house and garden. It was secured within, like the two which she had already tried. She knocked, however; and, immediately, as if the application had been expected, the door was drawn open, by a considerable exertion of some unseen person's strength, not widely, but far enough to afford her a sidelong entrance. As Hepzibah, in order not to expose herself to inspection from without, invariably opened a door in this manner, Phoebe necessarily concluded that it was her cousin who now admitted her.

Without hesitation, therefore, she stept across the threshold, and had no sooner entered, than the door closed behind her.

## XX

## THE FLOWER OF EDEN

PHOEBE, coming so suddenly from the sunny daylight, was altogether bedimmed in such density of shadow as lurked in most of the passages of the old house. She was not at first aware by whom she had been admitted. Before her eyes had adapted themselves to the obscurity, a hand grasped her own, with a firm, but gentle and warm pressure, thus imparting a welcome which caused her heart to leap and thrill with an indefinable shiver of enjoyment. She felt herself drawn along, not towards the parlor, but into a large and unoccupied apartment, which had formerly been the grand reception-room of the seven gables. The sunshine came freely into all the uncurtained windows of this room, and fell upon the dusty floor; so that Phoebe now clearly saw—what, indeed, had been no secret, after the encounter of a warm hand with hers—that it was not Hepzibah nor Clifford, but Holgrave, to whom she owed her reception. The subtle, intuitive communication, or, rather, the vague and formless impression of something to be told, had made her yield unresistingly to his impulse. Without taking away her hand, she looked eagerly in his face, not quick to forebode evil, but unavoidably conscious that the state of the family had changed, since her departure, and therefore anxious for an explanation.

The artist looked paler than ordinary; there was a thoughtful and severe contraction of his forehead, tracing a deep, vertical line between the eyebrows. His smile, however, was full of genuine warmth, and had in it a joy, by far the most vivid expression that Phoebe had ever witnessed, shining out of the New England reserve with which Holgrave habitually masked whatever lay near his heart. It was the look where-with a man, brooding alone over some fearful object, in a dreary forest or illimitable desert, would recognize the fa-miliar aspect of his dearest friend, bringing up all the peace-ful ideas that belong to home, and the gentle current of every-day affairs. And yet, as he felt the necessity of respond-ing to her look of inquiry, the smile disappeared.

"I ought not to rejoice that you have come, Phoebe!" said he. "We meet at a strange moment!"

"What has happened?" she exclaimed. "Why is the house so deserted? Where are Hepzibah and Clifford?"

"Gone! I cannot imagine where they are!" answered Hol-grave. "We are alone in the house!"

"Hepzibah and Clifford gone?" cried Phoebe. "It is not possible! And why have you brought me into this room, instead of the parlor? Ah, something terrible has happened! I must run and see!"

"No, no, Phoebe!" said Holgrave, holding her back. "It is as I have told you. They are gone, and I know not whither. A terrible event has indeed happened, but not to them, nor, as I undoubtingly believe, through any agency of theirs. If I read your character rightly, Phoebe," he continued, fixing his eyes on hers with stern anxiety, intermixed with tender-ness, "gentle as you are, and seeming to have your sphere among common things, you yet possess remarkable strength. You have wonderful poise, and a faculty which, when tested, will prove itself capable of dealing with matters that fall far out of the ordinary rule."

"Oh, no, I am very weak!" replied Phoebe trembling. "But tell me what has happened!"

"You are strong!" persisted Holgrave. "You must be both

strong and wise; for I am all astray, and need your counsel. It may be, you can suggest the one right thing to do!"

"Tell me!—tell me!" said Phoebe, all in a tremble. "It oppresses—it terrifies me—this mystery! Anything else, I can bear!"

The artist hesitated. Notwithstanding what he had just said, and most sincerely, in regard to the self-balancing power with which Phoebe impressed him, it still seemed almost wicked to bring the awful secret of yesterday to her knowledge. It was like dragging a hideous shape of death into the cleanly and cheerful space before a household fire, where it would present all the uglier aspect, amid the decorousness of everything about it. Yet it could not be concealed from her; she must needs know it.

"Phoebe," said he, "do you remember this?"

He put into her hand a daguerreotype; the same that he had shown her at their first interview, in the garden, and which so strikingly brought out the hard and relentless traits of the original.

"What has this to do with Hepzibah and Clifford?" asked Phoebe, with impatient surprise that Holgrave should so trifle with her, at such a moment. "It is Judge Pyncheon! You have shown it to me before!"

"But here is the same face, taken within this half-hour," said the artist, presenting her with another miniature. "I had just finished it, when I heard you at the door."

"This is death!" shuddered Phoebe, turning very pale. "Judge Pyncheon dead!"

"Such as there represented," said Holgrave, "he sits in the next room. The Judge is dead, and Clifford and Hepzibah have vanished! I know no more. All beyond is conjecture. On returning to my solitary chamber, last evening, I noticed no light, either in the parlor, or Hepzibah's room, or Clifford's;—no stir nor footstep about the house. This morning, there was the same deathlike quiet. From my window, I overheard the testimony of a neighbor, that your relatives were seen leaving the house, in the midst of yesterday's storm. A rumor reached me, too, of Judge Pyncheon being missed. A feeling which I cannot describe—an indefinite sense of some catastrophe, or consummation—impelled me to make my way into this part of the house, where I discovered what you see. As a point of evidence that may be useful to Clifford—and also as a memorial valuable to myself; for, Phoebe, there are hereditary reasons that connect me strangely with that man's fate—I used the means at my disposal to preserve this pictorial record of Judge Pyncheon's death."

Even in her agitation, Phoebe could not help remarking the calmness of Holgrave's demeanor. He appeared, it is true, to feel the whole awfulness of the Judge's death, yet had received the fact into his mind without any mixture of surprise, but as an event pre-ordained, happening inevitably, and so fitting itself into past occurrences, that it could almost have been prophesied.

"Why have not you thrown open the doors, and called in witnesses?" inquired she, with a painful shudder. "It is terrible to be here alone!"

"But Clifford!" suggested the artist. "Clifford and Hepzibah! We must consider what is best to be done in their behalf. It is a wretched fatality, that they should have disappeared. Their flight will throw the worst coloring over this event, of which it is susceptible. Yet how easy is the explanation, to those who know them! Bewildered and terror-stricken by the similarity of this death to a former one, which was attended with such disastrous consequences to Clifford, they have had no idea but of removing themselves from the scene. How miserably unfortunate! Had Hepzibah but shrieked aloud—had Clifford flung wide the door, and proclaimed Judge Pyncheon's death—it would have been, however awful in itself, an event fruitful of good consequences to them. As I view it, it would have gone far towards obliterating the black stain on Clifford's character."

"And how," asked Phoebe, "could any good come from what is so very dreadful?"

"Because," said the artist, "if the matter can be fairly considered, and candidly interpreted, it must be evident that Judge Pyncheon could not have come unfairly to his end. This mode of death has been an idiosyncrasy with his family, for generations past; not often occurring, indeed, but—when it does occur—usually attacking individuals of about the Judge's time of life, and generally in the tension of some mental crisis, or perhaps in an access of wrath. Old Maule's prophecy was probably founded on a knowledge of this physical predisposition in the Pyncheon race. Now, there is a minute and almost exact similarity in the appearances, connected with the death that occurred yesterday, and those recorded of the death of Clifford's uncle, thirty years ago. It is true, there was a certain arrangement of circumstances, unnecessary to be recounted, which made it possible—nay, as men look at these things, probable, or even certain—that old Jaffrey Pyncheon came to a violent death, and by Clifford's hands."

"Whence came those circumstances?" exclaimed Phoebe—"he being innocent, as we know him to be!"

"They were arranged," said Holgrave—"at least, such has long been my conviction—they were arranged, after the uncle's death, and before it was made public, by the man who sits in yonder parlor. His own death, so like that former one, yet attended with none of those suspicious circumstances, seems the stroke of God upon him, at once a punishment for his wickedness, and making plain the innocence of Clifford. But this flight—it distorts everything! He may be in concealment, near at hand. Could we but bring him back, before the discovery of the Judge's death, the evil might be rectified."

"We must not hide this thing, a moment longer!" said

Phoebe. "It is dreadful to keep it so closely in our hearts. Clifford is innocent. God will make it manifest! Let us throw open the doors, and call all the neighborhood to see the truth!"

"You are right, Phoebe," rejoined Holgrave. "Doubtless, you are right."

Yet the artist did not feel the horror, which was proper to Phoebe's sweet and order-loving character, at thus finding herself at issue with society, and brought in contact with an event that transcended ordinary rules. Neither was he in haste, like her, to betake himself within the precincts of common life. On the contrary, he gathered a wild enjoyment —as it were, a flower of strange beauty, growing in a desolate spot, and blossoming in the wind—such a flower of momentary happiness he gathered from his present position. It separated Phoebe and himself from the world, and bound them to each other, by their exclusive knowledge of Judge Pyncheon's mysterious death, and the counsel which they were forced to hold respecting it. The secret, so long as it should continue such, kept them within the circle of a spell, a solitude in the midst of men, a remoteness as entire as that of an island in mid-ocean;—once divulged, the ocean would flow betwixt them, standing on its widely sundered shores. Meanwhile, all the circumstances of their situation seemed to draw them together; they were like two children who go hand in hand, pressing closely to one another's side, through a shadow-haunted passage. The image of awful Death, which filled the house, held them united by his stiffened grasp.

These influences hastened the developement of emotions, that might not otherwise have flowered so soon. Possibly, indeed, it had been Holgrave's purpose to let them die in their undeveloped germs.

"Why do we delay so?" asked Phoebe. "This secret takes away my breath! Let us throw open the doors!"

"In all our lives, there can never come another moment like this!" said Holgrave. "Phoebe, is it all terror?—nothing but terror? Are you conscious of no joy, as I am, that has made this the only point of life, worth living for?"

"It seems a sin," replied Phoebe trembling, "to think of joy, at such a time!"

"Could you but know, Phoebe, how it was with me, the hour before you came!" exclaimed the artist. "A dark, cold, miserable hour! The presence of yonder dead man threw a great black shadow over everything; he made the universe, so far as my perception could reach, a scene of guilt, and of retribution more dreadful than the guilt. The sense of it took away my youth. I never hoped to feel young again! The world looked strange, wild, evil, hostile;—my past life, so lonesome and dreary; my future, a shapeless gloom, which I must mould into gloomy shapes! But, Phoebe, you crossed the threshold; and hope, warmth, and joy, came in with you! The black moment became at once a blissful one. It must not pass without the spoken word. I love you!"

"How can you love a simple girl, like me?" asked Phoebe, compelled by his earnestness to speak. "You have many, many thoughts, with which I should try in vain to sympathize. And I—I, too—I have tendencies with which you would sympathize as little. That is less matter. But I have not scope enough to make you happy."

"You are my only possibility of happiness!" answered Holgrave. "I have no faith in it, except as you bestow it on me!"

"And then—I am afraid!" continued Phoebe, shrinking towards Holgrave, even while she told him so frankly the doubts with which he affected her. "You will lead me out of my own quiet path. You will make me strive to follow you, where it is pathless. I cannot do so. It is not my nature. I shall sink down, and perish!"

"Ah, Phoebe!" exclaimed Holgrave, with almost a sigh, and a smile that was burthened with thought. "It will be far otherwise than as you forebode. The world owes all its on-ward impulse to men ill at ease. The happy man inevitably confines himself within ancient limits. I have a presentiment, that, hereafter, it will be my lot to set out trees, to make fences—perhaps, even, in due time, to build a house for another generation—in a word, to conform myself to laws, and the peaceful practice of society. Your poise will be more powerful than any oscillating tendency of mine."

"I would not have it so!" said Phoebe earnestly.

"Do you love me?" asked Holgrave. "If we love one another, the moment has room for nothing more. Let us pause upon it, and be satisfied. Do you love me, Phoebe?"

"You look into my heart," replied she, letting her eyes droop. "You know I love you!"

And it was in this hour, so full of doubt and awe, that the one miracle was wrought, without which every human existence is a blank. The bliss, which makes all things true, beautiful, and holy, shone around this youth and maiden. They were conscious of nothing sad nor old. They transfigured the earth, and made it Eden again, and themselves the two first dwellers in it. The dead man, so close beside them, was forgotten. At such a crisis, there is no Death; for Immortality is revealed anew, and embraces everything in its hallowed atmosphere.

But how soon the heavy earth-dream settled down again!

"Hark!" whispered Phoebe. "Somebody is at the street-door!"

"Now let us meet the world!" said Holgrave. "No doubt, the rumor of Judge Pyncheon's visit to this house, and the flight of Hepzibah and Clifford, is about to lead to the investigation of the premises. We have no way but to meet it. Let us open the door at once!"

But, to their surprise, before they could reach the street-door—even before they quitted the room in which the foregoing interview had passed—they heard footsteps in the farther passage. The door, therefore, which they supposed to be securely locked—which Holgrave, indeed, had seen to be so, and at which Phoebe had vainly tried to enter—must have been opened from without. The sound of footsteps was not harsh, bold, decided, and intrusive, as the gait of strangers would naturally be, making authoritative entrance into a dwelling where they knew themselves unwelcome. It was feeble, as of persons either weak or weary; there was the mingled murmur of two voices, familiar to both the listeners.

"Can it be!" whispered Holgrave.

"It is they!" answered Phoebe. "Thank God!—thank God!"

And then, as if in sympathy with Phoebe's whispered ejaculation, they heard Hepzibah's voice, more distinctly.

"Thank God, my brother, we are at home!"

"Well!—Yes!—thank God!" responded Clifford. "A dreary home, Hepzibah! But you have done well to bring me hither! Stay! That parlor-door is open. I cannot pass by it! Let me go and rest me in the arbor, where I used—Oh, very long ago, it seems to me, after what has befallen us—where I used to be so happy with little Phoebe!"

But the house was not altogether so dreary as Clifford imagined it. They had not made many steps—in truth, they were lingering in the entry, with the listlessness of an accomplished purpose, uncertain what to do next—when Phoebe ran to meet them. On beholding her, Hepzibah burst into tears. With all her might, she had staggered onward beneath the burden of grief and responsibility, until now that it was safe to fling it down. Indeed, she had not energy to fling it down, but only ceased to uphold it, and suffered it to press her to the earth. Clifford appeared the stronger of the two.

"It is our own little Phoebe!—Ah! and Holgrave with her," exclaimed he, with a glance of keen and delicate insight, and a smile, beautiful, kind, but melancholy. "I thought of you both, as we came down the street, and beheld Alice's Posies in full bloom. And so the flower of Eden has bloomed, likewise, in this old, darksome house, to-day!"

## XXI

# THE DEPARTURE

T HE SUDDEN DEATH of so prominent a member of the social world, as the Honorable Judge Jaffrey Pyncheon, created a sensation (at least, in the circles more immediately connected with the deceased) which had hardly quite subsided in a fortnight.

It may be remarked, however, that, of all the events which constitute a person's biography, there is scarcely one—none, certainly, of anything like a similar importance—to which the world so easily reconciles itself, as to his death. In most other cases and contingencies, the individual is present among us, mixed up with the daily revolution of affairs, and affording a definite point for observation. At his decease, there is only a vacancy, and a momentary eddy—very small, as compared with the apparent magnitude of the ingurgitated object—and a bubble or two, ascending out of the black depth, and bursting at the surface. As regarded Judge Pyncheon, it seemed probable, at first blush, that the mode of his final departure might give him a larger and longer posthumous vogue, than ordinarily attends the memory of a distinguished man. But when it came to be understood, on the highest professional authority, that the event was a natural, and—except for some unimportant particulars, denoting a slight idiosyncrasy—by no means an unusual form of death, the public, with its customary alacrity, proceeded to forget that he had ever lived. In short, the honorable Judge was beginning to be a stale subject, before half the county-newspapers had found time to put their columns in mourning, and publish his exceedingly eulogistic obituary.

Nevertheless, creeping darkly through the places which this excellent person had haunted in his lifetime, there was a hidden stream of private talk, such as it would have shocked all decency to speak loudly at the street-corners. It is very singular, how the fact of a man's death often seems to give people a truer idea of his character, whether for good or evil, than they have ever possessed while he was living and acting among them. Death is so genuine a fact that it excludes falsehood, or betrays its emptiness; it is a touch-stone that proves the gold, and dishonors the baser metal. Could the departed, whoever he may be, return in a week after his decease, he would almost invariably find himself at a higher or lower point than he had formerly occupied, on the scale of public appreciation. But the talk, or scandal, to which we now allude, had reference to matters of no less old a date than the supposed murder, thirty or forty years ago, of the late Judge Pyncheon's uncle. The medical opinion, with regard to his own recent and regretted decease, had almost entirely obviated the idea that a murder was committed, in the former case. Yet, as the record showed, there were circumstances irrefragably indicating that some person had gained access to old Jaffrey Pyncheon's private apartments, at or near the moment of his death. His desk and private drawers, in a room contiguous to his bed-chamber, had been ransacked; money and valuable articles were missing; there was a bloody handprint on the old man's linen; and, by a powerfully welded chain of deductive evidence, the guilt of the robbery and apparent murder had been fixed on Clifford, then residing with his uncle in the House of the Seven Gables.

Whencesoever originating, there now arose a theory that

undertook so to account for these circumstances as to exclude the idea of Clifford's agency. Many persons affirmed, that the history and elucidation of the facts, long so mysterious, had been obtained by the Daguerreotypist from one of those mesmerical seers, who, now-a-days, so strangely perplex the aspect of human affairs, and put everybody's natural vision to the blush, by the marvels which they see with their eyes shut.

According to this version of the story, Judge Pyncheon, exemplary as we have portrayed him in our narrative, was, in his youth, an apparently irreclaimable scapegrace. The brutish, the animal instincts, as is often the case, had been developed earlier than the intellectual qualities, and the force of character, for which he was afterwards remarkable. He had shown himself wild, dissipated, addicted to low pleasures, little short of ruffianly in his propensities, and recklessly expensive, with no other resources than the bounty of his uncle. This course of conduct had alienated the old bachelor's affection, once strongly fixed upon him. Now, it is averred—but whether on authority available in a court of justice, we do not pretend to have investigated—that the young man was tempted by the devil, one night, to search his uncle's private drawers, to which he had unsuspected means of access. While thus criminally occupied, he was startled by the opening of the chamber-door. There stood old Jaffrey Pyncheon, in his night-clothes! The surprise of such a discovery, his agitation, alarm, and horror, brought on the crisis of a disorder to which the old bachelor had an hereditary liability; he seemed to choke with blood, and fell upon the floor, striking his temple a heavy blow against the corner of a table. What was to be done? The old man was surely dead! Assistance would come too late! What a misfortune, indeed, should it come too soon; since his reviving consciousness would bring the recollection of the ignominious offence, which he had beheld his nephew in the very act of committing!

But he never did revive. With the cool hardihood, that always pertained to him, the young man continued his search of the drawers, and found a will of recent date, in favor of Clifford—which he destroyed—and an older one in his own favor, which he suffered to remain. But, before retiring, Jaffrey bethought himself of the evidence, in these ransacked drawers, that some one had visited the chamber with sinister purposes. Suspicion, unless averted, might fix upon the real offender. In the very presence of the dead man, therefore, he laid a scheme that should free himself at the expense of Clifford, his rival, for whose character he had at once a contempt and a repugnance. It is not probable, be it said, that he acted with any set purpose of involving Clifford in a charge of murder; knowing that his uncle did not die by violence, it may not have occurred to him, in the hurry of the crisis, that such an inference might be drawn. But, when the affair took this darker aspect, Jaffrey's previous steps had already pledged him to those which remained. So craftily had he arranged the circumstances, that, at Clifford's trial, his cousin hardly found it necessary to swear to anything false, but only to withhold the one decisive explanation, by refraining to state what he had himself done and witnessed.

Thus, Jaffrey Pyncheon's inward criminality, as regarded Clifford, was indeed black and damnable; while its mere outward show and positive commission was the smallest that could possibly consist with so great a sin. This is just the sort of guilt that a man of eminent respectability finds it easiest to dispose of. It was suffered to fade out of sight, or be reckoned a venial matter, in the Honorable Judge Pyncheon's long subsequent survey of his own life. He shuffled it aside, among the forgotten and forgiven frailties of his youth, and seldom thought of it again.

We leave the Judge to his repose. He could not be styled fortunate, at the hour of death. Unknowingly, he was a childless man, while striving to add more wealth to his only child's inheritance. Hardly a week after his decease, one of the Cunard steamers brought intelligence of the death, by cholera, of Judge Pyncheon's son, just at the point of embarkation for his native land. By this misfortune, Clifford became rich; so did Hepzibah; so did our little village-maiden, and through her, that sworn foe of wealth and all manner of conservatism —the wild reformer—Holgrave!

It was now far too late in Clifford's life for the good opinion of society to be worth the trouble and anguish of a formal vindication. What he needed was the love of a very few; not the admiration, or even the respect, of the unknown many. The latter might probably have been won for him, had those, on whom the guardianship of his welfare had fallen, deemed it advisable to expose Clifford to a miserable resuscitation of past ideas, when the condition of whatever comfort he might expect lay in the calm of forgetfulness. After such wrong as he had suffered, there is no reparation. The pitiable mockery of it, which the world might have been ready enough to offer, coming so long after the agony had done its utmost work, would have been fit only to provoke bitterer laughter than poor Clifford was ever capable of. It is a truth (and it would be a very sad one, but for the higher hopes which it suggests) that no great mistake, whether acted or endured, in our mortal sphere, is ever really set right. Time, the continual vicissitude of circumstances, and the invariable inopportunity of death, render it impossible. If, after long lapse of years, the right seems to be in our power, we find no niche to set it in. The better remedy is for the sufferer to pass on, and leave what he once thought his irreparable ruin far behind him.

The shock of Judge Pyncheon's death had a permanently invigorating and ultimately beneficial effect on Clifford. That strong and ponderous man had been Clifford's nightmare. There was no free breath to be drawn, within the sphere of so malevolent an influence. The first effect of freedom, as we have witnessed in Clifford's aimless flight, was a tremulous exhilaration. Subsiding from it, he did not sink into his former intellectual apathy. He never, it is true, attained to nearly the full measure of what might have been his faculties. But he recovered enough of them partially to light up his character, to display some outline of the marvellous grace that was abortive in it, and to make him the object of no less deep, although less melancholy interest than heretofore. He was evidently happy. Could we pause to give another picture of his daily life, with all the appliances now at command to gratify his instinct for the Beautiful, the garden-scenes, that seemed so sweet to him, would look mean and trivial in comparison.

Very soon after their change of fortune, Clifford, Hepzibah, and little Phoebe, with the approval of the artist, concluded to remove from the dismal old House of the Seven Gables, and take up their abode, for the present, at the elegant country-seat of the late Judge Pyncheon. Chanticleer and his family had already been transported thither; where the two hens had forthwith begun an indefatigable process of egg-laying, with an evident design, as a matter of duty and conscience, to continue their illustrious breed under better auspices than for a century past. On the day set for their departure, the principal personages of our story, including good Uncle Venner, were assembled in the parlor.

"The country-house is certainly a very fine one, so far as the plan goes," observed Holgrave, as the party were discussing their future arrangements.—"But I wonder that the late Judge—being so opulent, and with a reasonable prospect of transmitting his wealth to descendants of his own—should not have felt the propriety of embodying so excellent a piece of domestic architecture in stone, rather than in wood. Then, every generation of the family might have altered the interior, to suit its own taste and convenience; while the exterior, through the lapse of years, might have been adding venerableness to its original beauty, and thus giving that impression of permanence, which I consider essential to the happiness of any one moment."

"Why," cried Phoebe, gazing into the artist's face with infinite amazement, "how wonderfully your ideas are changed! A house of stone, indeed! It is but two or three weeks ago, that you seemed to wish people to live in something as fragile and temporary as a bird's nest!"

"Ah, Phoebe, I told you how it would be!" said the artist, with a half-melancholy laugh. "You find me a conservative already! Little did I think ever to become one. It is especially unpardonable in this dwelling of so much hereditary misfortune, and under the eye of yonder portrait of a model-conservative, who, in that very character, rendered himself so long the Evil Destiny of his race."

"That picture!" said Clifford, seeming to shrink from its stern glance. "Whenever I look at it, there is an old, dreamy recollection haunting me, but keeping just beyond the grasp of my mind. Wealth, it seems to say!—boundless wealth!—unimaginable wealth! I could fancy, that, when I was a child, or a youth, that portrait had spoken, and told me a rich secret, or had held forth its hand, with the written record of hidden opulence. But those old matters are so dim with me, now-a-days! What could this dream have been!"

"Perhaps I can recall it," answered Holgrave.—"See! There are a hundred chances to one, that no person, unacquainted with the secret, would ever touch this spring."

"A secret spring!" cried Clifford. "Ah, I remember now! I did discover it, one summer afternoon, when I was idling and dreaming about the house, long, long ago. But the mystery escapes me."

The artist put his finger on the contrivance to which he had referred. In former days, the effect would probably have been, to cause the picture to start forward. But, in so long a period of concealment, the machinery had been eaten through with rust; so that, at Holgrave's pressure, the portrait, frame and all, tumbled suddenly from its position, and lay face downward on the floor. A recess in the wall was thus brought to light, in which lay an object so covered with a century's dust, that it could not immediately be recognized as a folded sheet of parchment. Holgrave opened it, and displayed an ancient deed, signed with the hieroglyphics of several Indian sagamores, and conveying to Colonel Pyncheon and his heirs, forever, a vast extent of territory at the eastward.

"This is the very parchment, the attempt to recover which cost the beautiful Alice Pyncheon her happiness and life," said the artist, alluding to his legend. "It is what the Pyncheons sought in vain, while it was valuable; and now that they find the treasure, it has long been worthless."

"Poor Cousin Jaffrey! This is what deceived him," exclaimed Hepzibah. "When they were young together, Clifford probably made a kind of fairy-tale of this discovery. He was always dreaming hither and thither about the house, and lighting up its dark corners with beautiful stories. And poor Jaffrey, who took hold of everything as if it were real, thought my brother had found out his uncle's wealth. He died with this delusion in his mind!"

"But," said Phoebe, apart to Holgrave, "how came you to know the secret?"

"My dearest Phoebe," said Holgrave, "how will it please you to assume the name of Maule? As for the secret, it is the only inheritance that has come down to me from my ancestors. You should have known sooner, (only that I was afraid of frightening you away,) that, in this long drama of wrong and retribution, I represent the old wizard, and am probably as much of a wizard as ever he was. The son of the executed Matthew Maule, while building this house, took the opportunity to construct that recess, and hide away the Indian deed, on which depended the immense land-claim of the Pyncheons. Thus, they bartered their eastern-territory for Maule's garden-ground."

"And now," said Uncle Venner, "I suppose their whole claim is not worth one man's share in my farm yonder!"

"Uncle Venner," cried Phoebe, taking the patched philosopher's hand, "you must never talk any more about your farm! You shall never go there, as long as you live! There is a cottage in our new garden—the prettiest little, yellowish-brown cottage you ever saw; and the sweetest-looking place, for it looks just as if it were made of gingerbread—and we are going to fit it up and furnish it, on purpose for you. And you shall do nothing but what you choose, and shall be as happy as the day is long, and shall keep Cousin Clifford in spirits with the wisdom and pleasantness, which is always dropping from your lips!"

"Ah, my dear child," quoth good Uncle Venner, quite overcome, "if you were to speak to a young man as you do to an old one, his chance of keeping his heart, another minute, would not be worth one of the buttons on my waistcoat! And —soul alive!—that great sigh, which you made me heave, has burst off the very last of them! But never mind! It was the happiest sigh I ever did heave; and it seems as if I must have drawn in a gulp of heavenly breath, to make it with. Well, well, Miss Phoebe! They'll miss me in the gardens, hereabouts, and round by the back-doors; and Pyncheon-street, I'm afraid, will hardly look the same without old Uncle Venner, who remembers it with a mowing-field on one side, and the garden of the seven gables on the other. But either I must go to your country-seat, or you must come to my farm—that's one of two things certain; and I leave you to choose which!"

"Oh, come with us, by all means, Uncle Venner!" said Clifford, who had a remarkable enjoyment of the old man's mellow, quiet, and simple spirit. "I want you always to be within five minutes' saunter of my chair. You are the only philosopher I ever knew of, whose wisdom has not a drop of bitter essence at the bottom!"

"Dear me!" cried Uncle Venner, beginning partly to realize

what manner of man he was.—"And yet folks used to set me down among the simple ones, in my younger days! But I suppose I am like a Roxbury russet—a great deal the better, the longer I can be kept. Yes; and my words of wisdom, that you and Phoebe tell me of, are like the golden dandelions, which never grow in the hot months, but may be seen glistening among the withered grass, and under the dry leaves, sometimes as late as December. And you are welcome, friends, to my mess of dandelions, if there were twice as many!"

A plain, but handsome, dark-green barouche had now drawn up in front of the ruinous portal of the old mansion-house. The party came forth, and (with the exception of good Uncle Venner, who was to follow in a few days) proceeded to take their places. They were chatting and laughing very pleasantly together; and—as proves to be often the case, at moments when we ought to palpitate with sensibility—Clifford and Hepzibah bade a final farewell to the abode of their forefathers, with hardly more emotion than if they had made it their arrangement to return thither at tea-time. Several children were drawn to the spot, by so unusual a spectacle as the barouche and pair of gray horses. Recognizing little Ned Higgins among them, Hepzibah put her hand into her pocket, and presented the urchin, her earliest and staunchest customer, with silver enough to people the Domdaniel cavern[1] of his interior with as various a procession of quadrupeds, as passed into the ark.

Two men were passing, just as the barouche drove off.

"Well, Dixey," said one of them, "what do you think of this? My wife kept a cent-shop, three months, and lost five dollars on her outlay. Old Maid Pyncheon has been in trade just about as long, and rides off in her carriage with a couple of hundred thousand—reckoning her share, and Clifford's, and Phoebe's—and some say twice as much! If you choose to call it luck, it is all very well; but if we are to take it as the will of Providence, why, I can't exactly fathom it!"

1. A fabled vault under the ocean where magicians and enchanters meet with their disciples.

"Pretty good business!" quoth the sagacious Dixey. "Pretty good business!"

Maule's Well, all this time, though left in solitude, was throwing up a succession of kaleidoscopic pictures, in which a gifted eye might have seen fore-shadowed the coming fortunes of Hepzibah, and Clifford, and the descendant of the legendary wizard, and the village-maiden, over whom he had thrown love's web of sorcery. The Pyncheon-elm moreover, with what foliage the September gale had spared to it, whispered unintelligible prophecies. And wise Uncle Venner, passing slowly from the ruinous porch, seemed to hear a strain of music, and fancied that sweet Alice Pyncheon—after witnessing these deeds, this by-gone woe, and this present happiness, of her kindred mortals—had given one farewell touch of a spirit's joy upon her harpsichord, as she floated heavenward from the HOUSE OF THE SEVEN GABLES!

The End.

# Backgrounds and Sources

# Passages from
# The American Notebooks†

## [The Downward Path of Great Houses] [1]

### I.

The most curious object in [Gardiner, Maine] was the elegant new mansion of Robert Hallowell Gardiner.\*\*\* It is certainly a splendid structure; the material, granite from the vicinity. At the angles, it has small circular towers; the portal is lofty and imposing; relatively to the general style of domestic architecture in our country, it well deserves the name of a castle or palace.\*\*\* Nevertheless, this new palace, with all the fresh dust of the stone-cutting and the freshness of the quarry about it, conveys an impression quite as sad as could be produced by the most venerable ruin in Old England. The [projector] has undertaken a business beyond his proper means, and unsuited to the situation of our country.\*\*\* Should he ever finish it, it will be too splendid a residence for his impaired fortunes; and when his estate shall be divided among his children, this mansion, estimated at its cost, will be more than the share of any of them, leaving nothing to support the expenses of such a style of living. This subject offers hints of copious reflection, in reference to the indulgence of aristocratic pomp among democratic institutions. The doorway and lofty windows of the house were closed up with rough boards, except the windows of one or two chambers, which appeared to be furnished, probably for the residence of Mr. Cardiner's son, who must feel somewhat melancholy, amid the abortive effort of his father's vanity. The old gentleman—nor the young one for that matter—will never enjoy a single thrill of exultation within those spacious halls; on the contrary, it must already have become a humiliating and hateful idea to him; it has rendered him an object of pity to the public; and this edifice is likely to be known by the name of Gardiner's Folly, for centuries to come.

July 11, 1837

### II.

Sunday, walked with Cilley to see General Knox's old mansion —a large rusty-looking edifice of wood, with some grandeur in the architecture, standing on the banks of the river, close by the site of an old burial-ground, and near where an ancient fort had been erected for defence against the French and Indians. General Knox formerly owned a square of thirty miles in this part of the country;

---

† All selections from *The American Notebooks*, by Nathaniel Hawthorne, based upon the original manuscripts in the Pierpont Morgan Library and edited by Randall Stewart, are Copyright © 1932, 1960 by the Ohio State University Press. All Rights Reserved. Reprinted by permission of the Center for Textual Studies of the Ohio State University and the Ohio State University Press.

1. As the foregoing excerpts from his notebooks indicate, Hawthorne had long been impressed by the emblematic force of great houses gone to ruin. Both Holgrave (ch. XII) and Clifford (ch. XVII) give voice to the debilitating effects that

and he wished to settle it with a tenantry, after the fashion of English gentlemen. He would permit no edifices to be erected within a certain distance of his mansion. His patent covered, of course, the whole present town of Thomaston, together with Waldoboro', and divers other flourishing commercial and country villages; and would have been of incalculable value, could it have remained unbroken to the present time. But the General lived in grand style, and received throngs of visitors from foreign parts; and was obliged to part with large tracts of his possessions, till now there is little left but the ruinous mansion, and the ground immediately around it. His tomb stands near the house, a spacious receptacle, an iron door, at the end of a turf-covered mound, and surmounted by an obeslisk [sic] of the Thomaston marble. There are inscriptions to the memory of several of his family; for he had many children, male and female, all of whom are now dead but one daughter, a widow of fifty, recently married to Hon. John Holmes. There is a stone fence around the monument. On the outside of this are the grave-stones, and large flat tombstones of the ancient burial ground; the tomb-stones being of red freestone, with vacant spaces, formerly inlaid with slate, on which were the inscriptions and perhaps coats of arms. One of these spaces was in the shape of a heart. The people of Thomaston were very wrathful that the General should have laid out his grounds over this old burial-place; and he dared never throw down the grave-stones, though his wife, a haughty English lady, often teazed him to do so.*** The house and its vicinity, and the whole tract covered by Knox's patent, may be taken as an illustration of what must be the result of American schemes of aristocracy. It is not forty years, since this house was built, and Knox was in his glory; but now the house is all in decay, while, within a stone's throw of it, is a street of neat, smart, white edifices of one and two stories, occupied chiefly by thriving mechanics. But towns have grown up, where Knox probably meant to have forests and parks. On the banks of the river, where he meant to have only one wharf, for his own West-Indian vessels and yacht, there are our two wharves, with stores, and a lime-kiln. Little appertains to the mansion, except the tomb, and the old burial ground, and the old fort. The descendants are all poor; and the inheritance was merely sufficient to make a dissipated and drunken fellow of the one of the old General's sons, who survived to middle age.*** August 12, 1837

### III.

Sir William [Pepperell] had built an elegant house for his son and his intended wife; but after the death of the former, he never

---

pretentious mansions have upon those that inherit them. For the specific use made in the novel of General Knox's mansion, see Morton Griffiths' essays listed in the bibliography.

entered it.\*\*\* Very anxious to secure his property to his descendants, by the provisions of his will, which was drawn up by Judge Sewell, then a young lawyer. Yet the judge lived to see two of Sir William's grandchildren so reduced, that they were to have been numbered among the town's poor, and were only rescued from this fate by private charity. 1842

### IV.

A young girl inherits a family grave-yard—that being all that remains of rich hereditary possessions. 1842

### V.

The history of an Alms-House in a country village, from the eve of its foundation downward—a record of the remarkable occupants of it; and extracts from interesting portions of its annals. The rich of one generation might, in the next, seek for a home there, either in their own persons or those of their representatives. Perhaps the son and heir of the founder might have no better refuge.\*\*\* 1844

### VI.

Two or three miles from the Navy Yard, on Kittery Point, stands the former residence of Sir William Pepperell. It is a gamble [gambrel]-roofed house, very long and spacious, and looks venerable and imposing from its dimensions. A decent, respectable, intelligent woman admitted us, and showed us from bottom to top of her part of the house; she being a tenant of one half. The rooms were not remarkable for size, but were panelled on every side. The stair case is the best feature, ascending gradually, broad, and square, and with an elaborate balustrade; and over the front door there is a wide window, and a spacious breadth where the old baronet and his guests, after dinner, might sit and look out upon the water, and his ships at anchor.\*\*\* At no great distance, across the road, is a marble tomb, on the level slab of which is the Pepperell coat of arms, and an inscription in memory of Sir William's father, to whom the son seems to have erected it—although it is the family tomb. We saw no other trace of Sir William or his family. Precisely a hundred years since, he was in his glory. None of the name now exist here—or elsewhere, that I know of. A descendant of the Sparhawks, one of whom married Pepperell's daughter, is now keeper of a fort in the vicinity—a poor man. 1845

### [Marriage and the End of Family Hatreds] [2]

As we walked, he [Ebenezer Hathorne] kept telling stories of the family, who seem to have comprised many oddities, eccentric men and women, recluses &c. One of old Philip English (a Jersey

2. Except that Philip English came from Guernsey, not Jersey, all the facts in Ebenezer's account are essentially correct. It is quite possible that this anecdote of the descendants of persecutor and persecuted joining in marriage, espe-

man, the name originally l'Anglais) who had been persecuted by John Hathorne, of witch-time memory, and a violent quarrel ensued. When Philip lay on his death-bed, he consented to forgive his persecutor, "but if I get well," said he, "I'll be damned if I forgive him!" This Philip left some bastards; but only legitimate daughters, one of whom married, I believe, the son of the persecuting John.*** August 27, 1837

### [The Organ-Grinder's Monkey] [3]

In Boston, a man passing along Collonnade row grinding a barrel-organ, and attended by a monkey, dressed in frock and pantaloons, and with a tremendously thick tail appearing behind. While his master played on the organ, the monkey kept pulling off his hat, bowing and scraping to the spectators roundabout—sometimes, too, making a direct application to an individual—by all this dumb show, beseeching them to remunerate the organ-player. Whenever a coin was thrown on the ground, the monkey picked it up, clambered on his master's shoulder, and gave it into his keeping; then descended, and recommenced his pantomimic entreaties for more. His little, old, ugly, wrinkled face had an earnestness that looked just as if it came from the love of money deep within his soul; he peered round, looking for filthy lucre on all sides. With his tail and all, he might be taken for the Mammon of copper coin—a symbol of covetousness of small gains, the lowest form of the love of money. Doubtless, many a man passed by, whose moral being was not unfairly represented by this monkey.

Una was with me, holding by my forefinger, and walking decorously along the pavement. She stopped to contemplate the monkey, and after a while, shocked by his horrible ugliness, began to cry. October 11, 1845

### [The Tyranny of the Past] [4]

To represent the influence which Dead Men have among living affairs;—for instance, a Dead Man controls the disposition of wealth; a Dead Man sits on the judgment seat, and the living judges do but respect his decisions; Dead Men's opinions in all things control the living truth; we believe in Dead Men's religion; we laugh at Dead Men's jokes; we cry at Dead Men's pathos; everywhere and in all matters, Dead Men tyrannize inexorably over us. July 27-October 13, 1844

---

cially since it involved his own family, suggested to Hawthorne the union of Phoebe and Holgrave.
3. For the use Hawthorne made of this passage, see p. 164.
4. For the use Hawthorne made of this passage, see p. 183.

## [*The Locomotive*] ⁵

***On the Concord rail is the train of cars, with the locomotive puffing and blowing off its steam, and making a great bluster in that lonely place; while, along the other railroad, stretches the desolate track, with the withered weeds growing up betwixt the two lines of iron, all so desolate. And anon, you hear a low thunder running along these iron rails; it grows louder; an object is seen afar off, it approaches rapidly, and comes down upon you like fate, swift and inevitably. In a moment, it dashes along in front of the station-house and comes to a pause; the locomotive hissing and fuming, in its eagerness to go on. How much life has come at once into this lonely place! Four or five long cars, each, perhaps, with fifty people in it; reading newspapers, reading pamphlet novels, chattering, sleeping; all this vision of passing life! A moment passes, while the baggage men are putting on the trunks and packages; then the bell strikes a few times, and away goes the train again; quickly out of sight of those who remain behind, while a solitude of hours again broods over the Station House, which, for an instant, has thus been put in communication with far off cities, and then has only itself, with the old black, ruinous church, and the black old farm-house, both built years and years ago, before railroads were ever dreamed of. Meantime, the passenger, stepping from the solitary station-house into the train, finds himself in the midst of a new world, all in a moment; he rushes out of the solitude into a village; thence through woods and hills; into a large inland town; along beside the Merrimack, which has overflowed its banks, and eddies along, turbid as a vast mud-puddle, sometimes almost laving the doorstep of a house, and with trees standing in the flood, half-way up their trunks. Boys, with newspapers to sell, or apples, lozenges &c; many passengers departing and entering, at each new-station; the more permanent passenger, with his check or ticket stuck in his hatband, where the conductor may see it. A party of girls, playing at ball with a young man; altogether, it is a scene of stirring life, with which a person, who had been waiting long for the train to come by, might find it difficult at once to amalgamate himself.***

May 5, 1850

## [*The Station*] ⁶

I left Portsmouth last Wednesday, at three quarters past 12, by the Concord railroad, which, at Newcastle, unites with the Boston and Maine railroad, about ten miles from Portsmouth. The station

5.  For the use Hawthorne made of this passage, see p. 257.
6.  For the use Hawthorne made of this passage, see p. 266.

at Newcastle is a small wooden building with one railroad passing on one side, and another at another, and the two crossing each other at right angles. At a little distance, stands a black, large, old wooden church, with a square tower, and broken windows, and a great rift through the middle of the roof, all in a dismal stage of ruin and decay. A farmhouse of the old style, with a long sloping roof, and as black as the church, stands on the opposite side of the road, with its barns; and these are all the buildings in sight of the rail-road station.*** May 5, 1850

## Love Letters of Nathaniel Hawthorne (1907)

### [Mesmerism] [7]

*** [M]y spirit is moved to talk to thee to day about these magnetic miracles, and to beseech thee to take no part in them. I am unwilling that a power should be exercised on thee, of which we know neither the origin nor the consequence, and the phenomena of which seems rather calculated to bewilder us, than to teach us any truths about the present or future state of being. If I possessed such a power over thee, I should not dare to exercise it; nor can I consent to its being exercised by another. Supposing that this power arises from the transfusion of one spirit into another, it seems to me that the sacredness of an individual is violated by it; there would be an intrusion into thy holy of holies.***

# THOMAS HUTCHINSON

## The History of Massachusetts (1795)

### [Maule's Curse] [8]

One of these women [Sarah Good, an accused witch] being told at her execution by the minister Mr. Noyes, that he knew she was a

7. This letter (October 18, 1841) was written in response to Sophia's asking her fiancé's opinion of mesmerism as a possible cure for her chronic headaches. Sophia's sister, Elizabeth, had translated from the French an article about Mesmer, and Sophia's father shared his dental practice with a young dentist, Dr. Fiske, who used hypnotism for extractions. Sophia was soothed by Fiske's treatment, although he could never induce a hypnotic sleep in her. But when she found out what Hawthorne thought of mesmerism, she stopped the treatments.

In chapter XIII Hawthorne concedes to Holgrave "the rare and high quality of reverence for another's individuality. Let us allow him integrity, also, forever after to be confided in; since he forbade himself to twine that one link more, which might have rendered his spell over Phoebe indissoluble."

8. The story of Sarah Good's maledic-

witch, and therefore advised her to confess, she  replied, that *he lied, and that she was no more a witch than he was a wizard; and if he took her life away, God would give him blood to drink.*[9]


# JOSEPH B. FELT

## Annals of Salem (1849)

### [A Salem Murder] [1]

1830, Sept. 28. John Francis Knapp is hung at the north end of the Salem prison, in the yard.

Dec. 31. Joseph Jenkins Knapp, Jr., his brother, suffered the like punishment in the same place. More than 4,000 spectators witnessed each of their melancholy exits. As well known, their crime was conspiracy with Richard Crowninshield of Danvers, to murder Capt. Joseph White, one of our most noted and wealthy merchants, in his 82d year. The dreadful act, though previously intended at different times, was performed by Crowninshield in the night of April 6, for the price of $1,000. He entered the dwelling of his victim, proceeded to his chamber, where he was asleep, struck him on the head with a club and stabbed him several times near the heart. Having been imprisoned, and perceiving no pros-

tory farewell to Noyes, one of the judges at the Salem witchcraft trials in 1692, and of his subsequent death by hemorrhage, is Hawthorne's source for Maule's curse and the Pyncheons' form of death. When we recall that Hawthorne's great-great grandfather, John Hathorne, was also a judge at the trials, and that of this ancestor Hawthorne wrote (in "The Custom House") that the blood of the executed witches "may fairly be said to have left a stain upon him," then a pattern of psychological fusion—Noyes-Hathorne-Pyncheon—emerges.

Hutchinson's source for the story is Robert Calef's *More Wonders of the Invisible World* (1700), to which he refers in his footnote. Hawthorne probably came upon the anecdote in Hutchinson's book, which he knew well, having withdrawn it twice from the Salem library; he used Hutchinson on several occasions for source material and mentions him in his notebooks.

9. Calef—They have a tradition among the people of Salem that a peculiar circumstance attended the death of this gentleman, he having been choaked with blood, which makes them suppose her, if not a witch, a Pythonissa, at least, in

this instance [Hutchinson's note].

1. The murder of Captain White and the "murder" in the novel have in common the slaying of a rich old bachelor for the purposes of circumventing a will in favor of the murderer, and the unjust accusation of an innocent nephew through the strategems of the real villain. In the novel the nephew is imprisoned for thirty years, whereas in the White killing the nephew was exonerated in about four weeks.

Although Hawthorne probably knew the details of the White murder at first hand, since he was living in Salem at the time of the murder and Richard Crowninshield was Hawthorne's double third cousin, the account in Felt (which he withdrew from the Salem library in 1849) may have jogged his memory. Felt's book was one of Hawthorne's primary sources for Salem history; in "Alice Doane's Appeal" (1835), he pays the first edition of Felt's *Annals* (1827) this compliment: "Recently * * * an historian has treated the subject [of the witchcraft delusion] in a manner that will keep his name alive, * * * by converting * * * disgrace into an honorable monument of his antiquarian lore. * * * "

pect of escape from the demands of justice, he hung himself, June 15, in his cell. He left the subsequent warning. "May it (his own suicide) be the means of reforming many to virtue. Albeit they may meet with success at the commencement of vice, it is short lived, and, sooner or later, if they persist in it, they will meet with a fate similar to mine." Joseph J. Knapp, having married a relative of Capt. White, supposed, that by destroying his will and hastening him out of life, he should come to the possession of a large property. But he learned, too late, even before his apprehension, that his whole plan was futile; that he had "sowed to the wind and must reap the whirlwind." For weeks, strategems were so laid, that public suspicion fell on a nephew, a principal heir of Capt. White. He keenly felt the neglect of former friends, but conscious innocence sustained him, until truth developed the mystery. The untimely end of three young men, and the inexpressible anguish of their connections, with whom many a heart deeply sympathized, was the incalculable price of hastening to be rich in a most unwarrantable way. Right motive and virtuous action lead to possessions, which alone can be enjoyed in peaceful reflection, present fruition and anticipation of the future.

# ALFRED H. MARKS

## Hawthorne's Daguerreotypist: Scientist, Artist, Reformer †

Hawthorne's daguerreotypist in *The House of the Seven Gables* is a familiar figure, and his importance in the structure of that novel has long been recognized. Yet, although Holgrave's profession is seldom forgotten in discussions of the novel, too often daguerreotyping has been taken to be synonymous with photography as we know it today. A glance at the science of the daguerreotype as it existed in Hawthorne's time is instructive. Hawthorne's uses of the processes and terminology of that science are fairly direct and are only obscured by the fact that he does not seem to employ technical terms—there were few in existence. But not so clear are the interpretations Hawthorne places on the social and philosophical significance of the invention, the way in which he uses the daguerreotypist at the center of a satire on the super-

† From Alfred H. Marks, "Hawthorne's Daguerreotypist: Scientist, Artist, Reformer," *Ball State Teachers College Forum*, III (Spring, 1962), 61–74. Reprinted by permission of the editors of *Forum* and Professor Marks.

stitions excited by any new process and its practitioners, and finally the way in which his ironic method in the novel distorts the daguerreotypist into a figure at best peculiar in the eyes of the uninitiated. This paper hopes to clarify all of these points.

The birth-date of the daguerreotype vogue can be determined precisely. For it was on August 19, 1839, that the French government made public, by arrangement with Louis-Jacques-Mandé Daguerre, the details of this process, which up until then had been secret. Descriptions of the circumstances surrounding the announcement read like lines from a script of *You Are There*, so intense was the interest and so staid the bodies about which it centered. Both houses of the French legislature as well as the Academy of Science and the Academy of Fine Arts held extraordinary meetings to discuss the great discovery; and of the all-important August 19 joint meeting of the Academies, a would-be eyewitness writes that he was, "Banned from the hall like many others for having come only two hours beforehand. . . ."[1]

Shortly after the announcement Daguerre published a manual giving full particulars of the process, and "A few days later," writes Gaudin:

> . . . opticians' shops were crowded with amateurs panting for daguerreotype apparatus, and everywhere cameras were trained on buildings. Everyone wished to copy the view from his window, and he was lucky who at the first trial got a silhouette of roof tops against the sky. He went into ecstasies over chimney tops, he counted again and again roof tiles and chimney bricks,—in a word, the technique was so new and seemed so marvelous that even the poorest proof gave him an indescribable joy.[2]

In this manner, the daguerreotype art, which a writer in the American *Journal of the Franklin Institute* estimated, "Two centuries ago . . . would have been looked upon as the work of witchcraft. . . ."[3] and which the Leipzig *Anzeiger* in 1839 branded as sacrilegious,[4] turned almost overnight from a mystery to a piece of practically common knowledge.

Daguerre's manual, *Histoire et déscription des procédés du Daguerreotype* saw twenty-six editions in several countries and several languages before the end of 1839. A translation of significant passages was published in the *Journal of the Franklin Institute* for November, 1839;[5] and, using this translation, writes Newhall, "Joachim Bishop, a Philadelphia instrument maker . . .

1. M. A. Gaudin, *Traité Pratique de Photographie* (Paris, 1844), p. 6, quoted in Beaumont Newhall, *Photography, A Short Critical History* (New York, 1938), p. 22.
2. Newhall, *op. cit.*, pp. 22–3.
3. Antoine Claudet, "The Progress and Present State of the Daguerreotype Art," *Journal of the Franklin Institute*, XL (July, 1845), 49.
4. Newhall, *op. cit.*, p. 21.
5. *Journal of the Franklin Institute*, XXVIII, 303.

constructed three cameras in 1839 which follow Daguerre's description in every detail. . . ." [6]

But Daguerre's manual was too technical for the common taste; so the inventor was prevailed upon (he had been awarded a pension of 400 francs yearly by the French Government in return for his secret) to give weekly public demonstrations of the process. In these he showed his audience how he treated a silver-surfaced plate first with nitric acid and then with iodine, then with an exposure to the view from a window for "a period of five to forty minutes, according to the time of year and the state of the weather. . . ." After this Daguerre held the plate with silver downward, presumably to shield it from the light as much as possible, while several people peeped at it and said, "Nothing has been traced upon it." Then Daguerre developed the plate by fuming with mercury, fixed it in sodium hyposulphite or salt water, and passed the result around to the awed group.[7]

"It is interesting to observe," says Newhall, "that, of all countries, America adopted the daguerreotype with most enthusiasm, and that it lived longer here than elsewhere." He continues:

> New York, Boston and Philadelphia learned about the process almost simultaneously and from these centers traveling daguerreotypists, like the hero of Hawthorne's *The House of the Seven Gables*, circulated throughout the country.[8]

So, by 1851—the year Hawthorne published that novel—the daguerreotype had come a long way. In 1839 Samuel F. B. Morse had written to the New York paper of a daguerreotype:

> Objects moving are not impressed. The Boulevard, so constantly filled with a moving throng of pedestrians and carriages, was perfectly solitary, except an individual who was having his boots brushed. His feet were compelled, of course, to be stationary for some time, one being on the box of the boot black, and the other on the ground. Consequently his boots and legs were well defined, but he is without body or head, because these were in motion.[9]

But as early as October, 1840, J. W. Draper published in *American Repertory* a description of a process by which he had succeeded in taking daguerreotype pictures of those parts of the human image which were so commonly in motion. Draper used head clamps for rigidity and a four-inch lens to shorten the exposure. A New York technician named Walcott varied Draper's tech-

6. Newhall, *op. cit.*, p. 23.
7. *New York Star*, Oct. 14, 1839, cited in Newhall, *op. cit.*, pp. 23–5.
8. Newhall, *op. cit.*, p. 29.
9. Quoted in *Democratic Review*, V (May, 1839), 518. The daguerreotype described may be seen in Peter Pollack, *The Picture History of Photography* (New York, 1958), pp. 42–3.

nique at about the same time with a seven-inch elliptical mirror replacing the lens.[1] And by 1845, a writer on the subject was able to say, "The science of optics . . . is now in the hands of a thousand operators in photography. . . ." [2]

Hawthorne probably became informed on the details of the daguerreotype in many ways. He might well have read the 1839 article in the *Democratic Review*, a magazine which published at least two selections by him in 1838 and several more thereafter.[3] His relationships with artists, scientists, and literary men must have borne fruit in more knowledge of the art. Also likely is that he was able to glean what he knew from associations with daguerreotypists and their productions.

To read Hawthorne's statements on the photographic process as originated by Daguerre is to be transported into a world whose language gives evidence of keen, almost naive, observance of phenomena we now scarcely bother to analyze. When one hears Holgrave say to Phoebe, "In short, I make pictures out of sunshine. . . ." one is reminded of the appelation "sun picture" attached to the earliest productions of Daguerre.[4] One might compare Holgrave's words with the statement by the American reporter who attended one of Daguerre's 1839 lectures: "The plate prepared as above was placed in the camera . . . to remain until the action of the sun's rays on its surface was sufficient." [5] It becomes apparent that Hawthorne's time took this process much more literally than we do. It is not the scene of "the Tuileries, the Quay and the Seine" which is impressing itself on the plate here, as the twentieth century mind might characterize it. The picture is being made by the reflected light of the sun. As Holgrave says in another context, ". . . I misuse Heaven's blessed sunshine by tracing out human features through its agency." The language is both figurative and technical.

In the early years of the daguerreotype process, one may recall, light sources were so limited and photographic chemicals so rudimentary that human countenances, if reproduced at all, were seen on the plate with outlines blurred or features distorted from the ordeal of holding still while the long exposure was made. It was at this time that the advice was sagely rendered that ". . . the camera operation should be concluded before the features become wearied with one mode of expression." [6] And not long before the criticism had been voiced by Gaudin:

1. W. Goode, "The Daguerreotype and Its Applications," *American Journal of Science and Arts, XL* (Oct.-Dec., 1840), 142.
2. Antoine Claudet, *op. cit.*, p. 46.
3. Randall Stewart, ed., *The American Notebooks by Nathaniel Hawthorne* (New Haven, 1932), pp. 286, 290, 296–8, 310.
4. Cf. Oliver W. Larkin, *Life and Art in America* (New York, 1949), p. 194.
5. Newhall, *op. cit.*, p. 24.
6. W. Goode, *loc. cit.*, p. 142.

. . . the first proofs had several major faults which, in spite of the unparalleled perfection of certain details, troubled artists. The picture was reversed, the tone was harsh (criard), masses of greenery appeared only as silhouettes, and nowhere were any people to be seen; in a word color and life, the two parents of all poetry, were lacking.[7]

With an understanding of these facts about the early daguerreotype, Phoebe's answer to Holgrave's, "But would you like to see a specimen of my productions?" becomes clearer:

"A daguerreotype likeness, do you mean?
. . . I don't much like pictures of that sort, —they are so hard and stern; besides dodging away from the eye, and trying to escape altogether. They are conscious of looking very unamiable, I suppose, and therefore hate to be seen."

The daguerreotype is, however, more than a method of reproducing a more-or-less faithful image of reality in *The House of the Seven Gables*. Holgrave expresses its role clearly:

There is a wonderful insight in Heaven's broad and simple sunshine. While we give it credit only for depicting the merest surface, it actually brings out the secret character with a truth that no painter would venture upon, even could he detect it.

And the man whose "secret character" sunshine and the daguerreotype concentrate on bringing to light in the novel is Judge Pyncheon.

There are two sides to the Judge's character: one side he shows to the world in the form of a smile; the other side, the prevailing self, he tries to keep hidden, although it manifests itself fitfully on his face in the form of a frown which alternates with the smile. When the Judge is first introduced in the book the author takes two full pages, in the Riverside edition, to describe him. The sun is shining—in fact it is noon—but the Judge stands as if for his portrait in the shade of the Pyncheon elm. He is looking at the shop his cousin Hepzibah has just opened in the Pyncheon homestead. And as he watches, "both the frown and the smile passed successively over his countenance." "At first," it is related, the sight of Hepzibah's merchandise ". . . seemed not to please him,—nay, to cause him exceeding displeasure,—and yet, the very next moment, he smiled." But, "while the latter expression was yet on his lips, he caught a glimpse of Hepzibah . . . and then the smile changed from acrid and disagreeable to the sunniest complacency and benevolence."

Phoebe saw the smiles Judge Pyncheon flashed when she first

7. Newhall, *op. cit.*, p. 25.

met him. She also saw his frowns, but because she could not entertain the thought that "judges, clergymen, and other characters
of that eminent stamp and respectability, could really, in any
single instance, be otherwise than just and upright men . . . .
she chose for the time being to give the greater weight to the
smiles." The author explains her shortsightedness with the words:
". . . Phoebe, in order to keep the universe in its old place, was
fain to smother, in some degree, her own intuitions as to Judge
Pyncheon's character."

These "intuitions" had been planted in Phoebe's mind before
she met Judge Pyncheon. The daguerreotypist had shown her pictures of the Judge which she took  at first to be pictures of the
long-dead Colonel Pyncheon. But Holgrave corrected her on her
error, saying,

> "I can assure you that this is a modern face. . . . Now, the re-
> markable point is, that the original wears, to the world's eye . . .
> an exceedingly pleasant countenance, indicative of benevolence,
> openness of heart, sunny good-humor, and other praiseworthy
> qualities of that cast. The sun, as you see, tells quite another
> story, and will not be coaxed out of it, after half a dozen patient
> attempts on my part. Here we have the man, sly, subtle, hard,
> imperious, and, withal, cold as ice."

Although she dismissed the thought as improper a short time
later, Phoebe momentarily agreed with the daguerreotypist in her
first encounter with her wealthy cousin.

The Judge walked in the shop door expecting to meet Hepzibah
but upon meeting Phoebe was pleasantly surprised. And when he
discovered that she was his cousin he decided to avail himself of
a cousinly kiss. But, "just at the critical moment" she "drew
back." In response to the "cold, hard, immitigable" look the
thwarted Judge then gave her,

> it struck Phoebe that this very Judge Pyncheon was the original of
> the miniature which the daguerreotypist had shown her in the
> garden, and that the hard, stern, relentless look, now on his face,
> was the same that the sun had so inflexibly persisted in bringing
> out. Was it, therefore, no momentary mood, but, however skill-
> fully concealed, the settled temper of his life?

Hawthorne uses the daguerreotype as a kind of "truth de-
tector," recurring in the process, to at least four different interpretations of the powers of the invention. One interpretation provides
a simple mechanical and psychological explanation of the fidelity
of the daguerreotype in picturing Judge Pyncheon's character;
a second interpretation sees the daguerreotype as the favored ally
of a potent cosmic force; a third interpretation is based on a

transfer to photography of one of Hawthorne's desiderata of good portrait painting; and a fourth interpretation combines with a romantic view of illusion and reality and suffuses the entire book, closely implementing one of the principal themes.

Hawthorne takes the process in the first sense when he writes of Judge Pyncheon in the fourth chapter: "He would have made a good and massive portrait . . . although his look might grow positively harsh in the process of being fixed upon the canvas." The process of making a daguerreotype was not as tedious as that of painting a portrait, but in the short space of time that it did require the photograph made much greater demands on the subject's control of his facial muscles. As Phoebe said, the faces on daguerreotype plates were often "so hard and stern." Small wonder then that Judge Pyncheon's habitual frown should manifest itself on his face in spite of the daguerrotypist's repeated efforts to make a softer likeness of the Judge.

Throughout the book the daguerrotype is mentioned in connection with sunlight and often interchangeably with it. In this connection the daguerrotype has a second meaning, becoming an important agent of the light and dark imagery in the novel. It seems to derive some of the occult powers Hawthorne gives it from its ministries in the service of light. It may be pointed out that at the end of the book, after Judge Pyncheon has died and Clifford and Hepzibah have fled the scene, Holgrave leads Phoebe into an unoccupied portion of the Seven Gables: "The sunshine came freely into all the uncurtained windows of this room, and fell upon the dusty floor. . . ." Phoebe asks, "And why have you brought me into this room, instead of the parlor?" We know why she was not brought into the parlor, in which the corpse rests, and by another process we know why she was brought into this room, the only sunlit room in the house: for Holgrave is here leading not only Phoebe but the entire book—compared in chapter eighteen to "an owl, bewildered in the daylight"—out of the darkness and into the light. He is not primarily an active agent; as far as his profession is concerned his mission in the novel is truly in the service of light: to make matters clear. But more of that later.

There are four important pictures in *The House of the Seven Gables*. Two are paintings and two are photographs. One of the photographs—that of Judge Pyncheon in death—need not enter this discussion; but the other three pictures should, for the author, in a third way of looking at the daguerreotype, seems to rate them by the same criteria. The great portrait of Colonel Pyncheon has deteriorated greatly with age as the novel opens; yet, ". . . while the physical outline and substance were darkening away from the beholder's eye, the bold, hard, and, at the same time, indirect character of the man seemed to be brought out in a kind of spiritual relief." Hawthorne comments on this phenomenon as something "occasionally . . . observed in pictures of antique date."

> They acquire a look which an artist . . . would never dream of presenting to a patron as his own characteristic expression, but which, nevertheless, we at once recognize as reflecting the unlovely truth of a human soul. In such cases, the painter's deep conception of his subject's inward traits has wrought itself into the essence of the picture, and is seen after the superficial coloring has been rubbed off by time.

The second important painting is the miniature of Clifford that Hepzibah came to treasure so long, in making which the artist caught for his subject a look so "innately characteristic . . . that all the dusky years, and the burden of unfit calamity which had fallen upon him, did not suffice utterly to destroy it." It was not actually Holgrave, however, who saw and caught the no less "innately characteristic" frown which Judge Pyncheon wore in the daguerreotype under discussion. That frown was caught by sunlight and the natural properties inherent in the invention. And since it was made only incidentally by human agency, so much the more miraculous the Judge Pyncheon daguerreotype seems to have been.

Hawthorne is, thus, using the daguerreotype and the daguerreotypist here as the first signs of a new era in the history of art. Claudet saw them in a similar light in 1845, when he wrote:

> . . . henceforward young artists, of less genius, will be able, by studying the effects of the daguerreotype, to produce works of great merit.
>
> We may also assert that the great masters would have been still more perfect in their imitations of nature if the daguerreotype had been known to them. When Paul Delaroche, the celebrated painter, was asked his opinion of the invention of Daguerre, he unhesitatingly declared that ". . . this admirable discovery was an immense service rendered to the fine arts." [8]

But Hawthorne's daguerreotypist is doing more for the arts than providing photographs which painters might study. Holgrave is an artist in his own right, and it should not be forgotten that the author calls him "the artist" throughout the book. The point at which the genius of Holgrave stops and that of his medium begins is not finely drawn in the novel, but it is certain that Hawthorne looks at the invention as if in it science has perfected

8. *Op. cit.*, pp. 48–9.

something which can depict the "characteristic" and the essential with a perspicacity reminiscent of genius. This power might, as has been shown earlier, be ascribed to the way in which the long exposure-time of the plate caused the subject's features to grow tense and thereby to display a physiognomy not commonly associated with him. Also likely, however, is that Judge Pyncheon's smile was too evanescent to be photographed, so that the scowl, which reigned on his face most of the time—although few realized it—was the expression which finally impressed itself on the plate.

The latter effect is more than a mechanical—though perhaps not photographically accurate—phenomenon in *The House of the Seven Gables*. In fact, the ability of the daguerreotype to find the "secret character" or "settled temper" of Judge Pyncheon's life at times seems to represent for Hawthorne an illustration of the workings of a familiar romantic view of the world. The language used by one writer on the daguerreotype in 1839 is unwittingly suggestive—in the word "passing"—of the same idea:

> The absence of figures from the streets . . . is, at first sight, rather puzzling, though a little reflection satisfies one that passing objects do not remain long enough to make any perceptible impression. . . .[9]

What romantic writer interested in penetrating beneath the superfluities and superficialities of the world to the essential reality of life would not have been struck by this statement and the metaphoric possibilities of the invention it described?

Hawthorne applauded the feat of the painter of Colonel Pyncheon's portrait in finding the reality under the illusion: "the painter's deep conception of his subject's inward traits has wrought itself into the essence of the picture, and is seen after the superficial coloring has been rubbed off by time." He indirectly pointed out the same great quality in the miniature of Clifford in contexts suggesting one of the best-known exponents of the idea it was based on, Thomas Carlyle:

> . . . how worn and old were the soul's more immediate garments. . . . There he seemed to sit, with a dim veil of decay and ruin betwixt him and the world, but through which, at flitting intervals, might be caught the same expression . . . which Malbone . . . had imparted to the miniature!

And when the author described what anger did for Judge Pyncheon in his last living interview with Hepzibah—in the chapter entitled "The Scowl and the Smile"—he was describing an

9. Sir John Robison, writing on "Perfection of the Art," *American Journal of Science and Arts*, XXXVII (1839), 184–5.

effect the daguerreotype had wrought on the Judge many times before:

> The effect was as when the light, vapory clouds, with their soft coloring, suddenly vanish from the stony brow of a precipitous mountain, and leave there the frown which you at once feel to be eternal.

The lesson to be learned from the daguerreotype, then, was a profound one, and Hawthorne uses it in the following passage to develop the principal theme of the book:

> Was it, therefore . . . the settled temper of his life? And not merely so, but was it hereditary in him, and transmitted down, as a precious heirloom, from that bearded ancestor, in whose picture both the expression, and, to a singular degree, the features of the modern Judge were shown as by a kind of prophecy? . . .
> It implied that the weaknesses and defects, the bad passions, the mean tendencies, and the moral diseases which lead to crime are handed down from one generation to another, by a far surer process of transmission than human law has been able to establish in respect to the riches and honors which it seeks to entail upon posterity.

It is only another short step from this quotation to the moral of the novel stated in the first pages of the book, the "little-regarded truth, that the act of the passing generation is the germ which may and must produce good or evil fruit in a far-distant time; that, together with the seed of the merely temporary crop, which mortals term expediency, they inevitably sow the acorns of a more enduring growth, which may darkly overshadow their posterity." From what has been shown of the precise meaning Hawthorne gives to his imagery of light and dark in this novel, the meaning of the word "overshadow" may be seen as entering the context of the daguerreotype discussion. One task of the daguerreotypist is to bring sunlight into the shadows which have been thrown over the present "passing generation"; and with his camera, and perhaps even more his native intelligence, he is to bring out that which is eternal and exclude that which is, to the romantic, "passing." He is perhaps to the Seven Gables what the seer in the fifteenth chapter is to the stately mansion described there:

> Now and then, perchance, comes in a seer, before whose sadly gifted eye the whole structure melts into thin air, leaving only the hidden nook, the bolted closet, with the cobwebs festooned over its forgotten door, or the deadly hole under the pavement, and the decaying corpse within.

Hawthorne thus places many interpretations on the nature and possibilities of the daguerreotype process in *The House of the Seven Gables*. He refers to the process precisely, though in metaphor; he has his characters allude to certain defects of the process; he uses it as an instrument that can detect that which his villain has successfully hidden from society. From this point he expands it into an instrument of truth, a tool of Romantic epistemology, and a scientific art-form which does unfailingly what only genius has been able to do earlier; and finally he makes it an intermediary in the cause of light; it not only uses light; it brings light.

It is not easy for the reader to grant to Holgrave the admiration which his nature and role should call forth. The reason for this reluctance is that Hawthorne permits the reader to look at the young man from three points of view, all of which are unfair and two of which are downright misguided. Phoebe and Hepzibah provide two of these points of view; the author—in several direct interpolations in the novel—provides the third.

Holgrave enters the novel in the third chapter when he enters Hepzibah's cent shop as she is waiting for her first customer. His intention in dropping in he states is, "to offer my best wishes, and to ask if I can assist you any further in your preparations." The words "any further" make it clear that he has assisted somewhat in setting up the shop; in fact, what we see of Hepzibah's limited intercourse with the world and her comparative ineptitude at handling the merchandise seems to make it clear that Holgrave—whom Hepzibah terms in this chapter "her only friend"—was responsible for most of the physical preparation of the shop: ordering, getting the merchandise arranged, and readying the premises for business.

It also becomes clear in this chapter that Holgrave has had a great deal to do with Hepzibah's resolution to open up the shop in the first place. His errand here so early on her first day of business is obviously designed to cheer her and even to provide her with her first cash purchase. Hepzibah, who wants to "be a lady a moment longer," accepts no money from Holgrave; but she is cheered by his visit. In fact, his first words, asserted as taken by her as an "expression . . . of genuine sympathy" place Holgrave as not only an interested party but even a spiritual adviser in Hepzibah's project:

> "I am glad to see that you have not shrunk from your good purpose. I merely look in to offer my best wishes, and to ask if I can assist you any further in your preparations."

Holgrave's spiritual ministrations continue throughout the interview. Hepzibah fears that she cannot go through with it; Holgrave reminds her that her "long seclusion" has given her a distorted and unnecessarily frightening view of the world. She reminds the daguerreotypist that she is a "lady"; he informs her that the title is meaningless and even detrimental in their society. "These are new notions," Hepzibah counters, evincing one of her principal reasons for disagreement with, and even distrust of, the young man. "I shall never understand them; neither do I wish it. . . ." she concludes.

Although she does not agree with Holgrave on the principle, Hepzibah does carry out the actions counselled by him. And through the remainder of the book she slowly divests herself of her pride, and works, seemingly unconsciously, in pursuit of the answer to his rhetorical questions as to "whether it is not better to be a true woman than a lady." In this way "the shop-window" Holgrave seems to have assisted in opening becomes an entrance for more light than that shed by the sun. Yet, partly because Holgrave's ideas conflict with most of the preconceptions of her cherished upbringing, partly because he provides her with a scapegoat for all the embarrassment that this venture he counsels is causing her, and partly perhaps because of her unconscious hereditary ambivalence toward a Maule, whether known or disguised, Hepzibah fears and distrusts the daguerreotypist.

Hepzibah's distrust may also have been based on her fear of Holgrave's profession, which has already been shown as having been termed sacrilegious and even, hypothetically, "witchcraft" in the early years of its vogue. It is impossible to find all the roots of the indictment of Holgrave the spinster made to Phoebe when she first spoke to her young cousin about the man. Regardless, the following indirect quotation not only shows the twisted state of Hepzibah's critical faculties but also is a trenchant satire on the way in which ignorant and insulated people of any time or place treat men who have new ideas:

> . . . on seeing more of Mr. Holgrave, she hardly knew what to make of him. He had the strangest companions imaginable; men with long beards, and dressed in linen blouses, and other such new-fangled and ill-fitting garments; reformers, temperance lecturers, and all manner of cross-looking philanthropists; community-men, and come-outers, as Hepzibah believed, who acknowledged no law, and ate no solid food, but lived on the scent of other people's cookery, and turned up their noses at the fare. As for the daguerreotypist, she had read a paragraph in a penny paper, the other day, accusing him of making a speech full of wild and disorganizing matter, at a meeting of his banditti-like associates. For her own part, she had reason to believe that he practised animal magnetism, and, if such things were in fashion nowadays, should be apt to suspect him of studying the Black Art up there in his lonesome chamber.

Phoebe, little country girl that she is, hears her cousin out on the subject of the incendiary Mr. Holgrave and then shows that, far from being able to treat Hepzibah's statement critically, she is able to misinterpret it as being much more serious than it is:

> "But, dear cousin, if the young man is so dangerous, why do you let him stay? If he does nothing worse, he may set the house on fire!"

Phoebe is not only uneducated, she is also inherently conservative, one of those "whose essence it was to keep within the limits of law." So Hepzibah is permitted, paradoxically, by her seclusion and her brother's imprisonment to recognize more than her young cousin the worth of Holgrave's self-reliance—the Emersonian term is entirely *à propos* here. So when Phoebe protests about Holgrave's lawlessness, Hepzibah protects him: "Oh! I suppose he has a law of his own!"

Holgrave and Phoebe meet in the chapter entitled "Maule's Well." And in the Pyncheon garden their love takes root. It becomes clear early in the chapter that Holgrave is also the instrument by which organic nature, in the form of the rejuvenated garden, has been brought again into the lives of the inhabitants of the Seven Gables. Phoebe is disturbed by his meddlesome nature, but as they talk she loses some of her prejudice against him. He shows her the daguerreotype of Judge Pyncheon and contrasts it with the miniature of Clifford: the villain whom the world reveres against the gentle artist whom the world has imprisoned. Then they decide to share the work of caring for the garden and the chickens. They work for a time and part.

But Phoebe is not yet reassured about the young man's character. She is attracted toward him—still not immune to the old hereditary wizardry—but she resents the attraction. What bothers her most is the familiar confusion most of Hawthorne's women feel when they are in love. "The Maypole of Merry Mount" contains the best known example of this confusion. And Holgrave expresses the underlying idea for Phoebe later in the story:

> "This bemoaning of one's self . . . over the first, careless, shallow gayety of youth departed, and this profound happiness at youth regained,—so much deeper and richer than that we lost,—are essential to the soul's development."

Thus Phoebe and Hepzibah may be seen as mirrors which are unable by nature to reflect the true character of Holgrave. Their judgments of him are reflective more of their own qualities than of any qualities intrinsic to the young man. One complex of qualities may, however, be fairly accurately perceptible to them. These

are the traits which have accrued to Holgrave from his ancestors
and which are being worked into the symbolic structure of the
book because of their ambivalent affinity for the Pyncheon spirit.
Hawthorne isolates the basic trait in the Maule personality in
the first chapter of the novel:

> . . . they had been marked out from other men—not strikingly,
> nor as with a sharp line, but with an effect that was felt rather
> than spoken of—by an hereditary character of reserve. Their
> companions, or those who endeavored to become such, grew
> conscious of a circle round about the Maules, within the sanc-
> tity or the spell of which, in spite of an exterior of sufficient
> frankness and good-fellowship, it was impossible for any man to
> step. It was this indefinable peculiarity, perhaps, that, by in-
> sulating them from human aid, kept them always so unfortunate
> in life. It certainly operated to prolong in their case, and to con-
> firm to them as their only inheritance, those feelings of repug-
> nance and superstitious terror with which the people of the town,
> even after awakening from their frenzy, continued to regard the
> memory of the reputed witches.

Hepzibah perceives this trait directly, by inherited intuition, or
indirectly, by her suspicions of the strange profession which Holgrave's wizard blood causes him to adopt. Her discomfiture in his
presence may also be traced to the tone of dramatic irony—Hawthorne calls it at one point "half-hidden sarcasm"—Holgrave
seems to use when speaking with her on issues close to the
Pynchcon-Maule dispute. In these encounters his tone expresses
his knowledge of the secrets he dares not yet put in words.

The damage done the daguerreotypist by the attitudes of
Hepzibah and Phoebe is not difficult to explain away. But not so
easily dismissed are the criticisms leveled at him by the author.
These are contained, primarily, in the twelfth chapter of the book,
entitled "The Daguerreotypist." In this chapter four principal
charges are made against Holgrave. First, he moves from profession to profession "with the careless alacrity of an adventurer."
Second, he is too "cold." He is lacking in sympathy. "He was too
calm and cool an observer. Phoebe felt his eye, often; his heart,
seldom or never. . . . In his relations with them, he seemed to
be in quest of mental food, not heart-sustenance." Third, his lack
of sympathy is driving him  toward the greatest of all Hawthornian
sins: the violation of the sanctity of the human heart. Phoebe tells
him that she tries, to a limited extent, to understand Clifford's
moods: ". . . I venture to peep in, just as far as the light reaches,
but no further. It is holy ground where the shadow falls." But
Holgrave would go further. "Had I your opportunities," he informs Phoebe, "no scruples would prevent me from fathoming

Clifford to the full depth of my plummet-line." Fourth, in his youthful zeal he wants to effect too many sweeping changes in the world: "His error lay in supposing that this age, more than any past or future one, is destined to see the tattered garments of Antiquity exchanged for a new suit, instead of gradually renewing themselves by patchwork. . . ." Phoebe cannot contemplate his plan for the future without becoming "dizzy to think about such a shifting world!"

Each of these charges is mitigated or explained away, however, either in the same chapter or in the course of the remainder of the book. The complaint—if such it really was—about his lack of a settled profession is immediately qualified with a statement very much in the young man's favor:

> . . . amid all these personal vicissitudes, he had never lost his identity. Homeless as he had been,—continually changing his whereabouts, and, therefore, responsible neither to public opinion nor to individuals,—putting off one exterior, and snatching up another, to be soon shifted for a third,—he had never violated the innermost man, but had carried his conscience along with him.

This ability to change the outward man many times without contradicting one's inward nature—a Romantic and Transcendental virtue—is a positive good in this book. It stands in contrast to the falseness of Judge Pyncheon, the disparity between that man's real and apparent natures, his disdain for the sanctity of the "souls" of the people close to him—particularly Clifford—and, in the last analysis, his failure to recognize the importance and the sanctity of his own soul.

Holgrave's coldness takes on warmth as the book progresses, although the author does not show that Holgrave entirely conquers his propensity toward intellectual detachment and isolation. His love for Phoebe softens him a great deal—his smile when he greets her upon her return from the country is described as one of "genuine warmth." And his concern for Clifford and Hepzibah in the crisis of their flight from Judge Pyncheon's dead body shows that he comes to feel sympathy and responsibility for them. But in the last analysis Holgrave is still incomplete with respect to the possession of traits which would tie him closely to his fellow man. He realizes his lack, and on those terms pleads with Phoebe to marry him:

> "The world looked strange, wild, evil, hostile; my past life, so lonesome and dreary; my future, a shapeless gloom, which I must mould into gloomy shapes! But, Phoebe, you crossed the threshold; and hope, warmth, and joy came in with you!"

Phoebe also provides Holgrave with the test of his ability to respect the integrity of another human being, when she falls into a "mesmeric" trance after his reading of the story of Alice Pyncheon. Another Maule was not able to resist the temptation to place the will of another Pyncheon in bondage to him. But Holgrave does not make the same mistake, and the author—with unusual peremptoriness—interprets this decision as proof that he will always be able to resist the attractions of such a deed:

> To a disposition like Holgrave's, at once speculative and active, there is no temptation so great as the opportunity of acquiring empire over the human spirit; nor any idea more seductive to a young man than to become the arbiter of a young girl's destiny. Let us, therefore,—whatever his defects of nature and education, and in spite of his scorn for creeds and institutions,—concede to the daguerreotypist the rare and high quality of reverence for another's individuality. Let us allow him integrity, also, forever after to be confided in; since he forbade himself to twine that one link more which might have rendered his spell over Phoebe indissoluble.

The words "his scorn for creeds and institutions" provide the key to the last criticism voiced against Holgrave in the twelfth chapter. Much is said there about Holgrave's attitude toward institutions; yet, although Hawthorne points out that the daguerreotypist suffers from an excess of youthful interest in wholesale social reform, he does not entirely disparage that interest. In one sentence the author does clearly evince a fundamental disagreement with the idea of progress so sacred to the daguerreotypist:

> . . . he was a young man still, and therefore looked upon the world—that gray-bearded and wrinkled profligate, decrepit, without being venerable—as a tender stripling, capable of being improved into all that it ought to be, but scarcely yet had shown the remotest promise of becoming.

But in the next sentence the author shows that this belief, however erroneous, is not only excusable in a young man but is desirable, indeed necessary:

> He had that sense, or inward prophecy,—which a young man had better never have been born than not to have and a mature man had better die at once than utterly to relinquish,—that we are not doomed to creep on forever in the old bad way, but that, this very now, there are the harbingers abroad of a golden now to be accomplished in his own life-time.

Hawthorne then prophesies how time will temper Holgrave's radicalism, and shows—in words which are perhaps expressive of his own mature attitude toward man and his works—how the daguerreotypist will arrive at a faith possibly more in keeping with the nature of the world:

> And when, with the years settling more weightily upon him, his early faith should be modified by inevitable experience, it would be with no harsh and sudden revolution of his sentiments. He would still have faith in man's brightening destiny, and perhaps love him all the better, as he should recognize his helplessness in his own behalf; and the haughty faith with which he began life, would be well bartered for a humbler one at its close, in discerning that man's best directed effort accomplishes a kind of dream, while God is the sole worker of realities.

Perhaps the most ambiguous manifestation of Holgrave's character occurs at the end of the book, when he seems to have bartered all of his principles for Phoebe and her wealth. Throughout the book the author has directed irony against the young man by way of the inversion Hawthorne is working on all his characters in the novel. Thanks to this technique Judge Pyncheon is made to look attractive and magnanimous, and Hepzibah dementedly resentful of her cousin's part in her brother's imprisonment. Clifford is made to look insane, if not criminal, and Phoebe overly trustful and adolescent at best. Each of these ironies straightens itself at the end of the novel, and it is possible to see that Judge Pyncheon was thoroughly evil, that Hepzibah, correct in her appraisal of him, is now freed of her obsessive hate by his death, that Clifford's love of beauty can mitigate many of his faults now that the bane of his existence is gone, and that Phoebe will make the perfect mate—symbolically, at least—for Holgrave. The author spends the whole book making this inversion clear and trying to make his readers see the reality in these people's characters under their—save Phoebe's—delusive exteriors. But the act of making a new inversion, never to be resolved since it occurs in the last chapter, of the character of the man who throughout the book carries so much of the burden of making the other inversions clear, has the effect of upsetting the applecart of the whole moral.

The motivation of this last irony is complex and probably is based partly on another of these cosmic jokes Hawthorne is playing on the world of his readers, that forces him as Hyatt Waggoner implies,[1] to say things he doesn't mean and create Phoebes and Hildas in a world of Hepzibahs and Hesters and perhaps Hester's townswomen. Here he must end the novel in a way acceptable to fashion, in spite of the fact that, to refer to Wag-

---

1. *Hawthorne, A Critical Study* (Cambridge, Mass.: 1955), pp. 171–73 [pp. 404–413 of this Norton Critical Edition]. (Waggoner, however, considers the passage to be a "failure . . . the 'playful' side of Hawthorne at its weakest.")

goner again, his circle imagery [2] in the novel forces the inference that Judge Pyncheon's money is going to perpetuate the Pyncheon curse. For this reason, it seems, Hawthorne makes a joke of the entire problem, and places the burden of it on the shoulders of Holgrave, whose paradoxical role throughout the book has made him best fitted to carry it.

2.  *Ibid.*, pp. 154–6, 172–73.

# Reviews and Essays in Criticism

# EVERT AUGUSTUS DUYCKINCK

## [*The House of the Seven Gables*: Marble and Mud]†

In the preface to this work, the anxiously looked-for successor to the Scarlet Letter, Mr. Hawthorne establishes a separation between the demands of the novel and the romance, and under the privilege of the latter, sets up his claim to a certain degree of license in the treatment of the characters and incidents of his coming story. This license, those acquainted with the writer's previous works will readily understand to be in the direction of the spiritualitics of the piece, in favor of a process semi-allegorical, by which an acute analysis may be wrought out and the truth of feeling be minutely elaborated; an apology, in fact, for the preference of character to action, and of character for that which is allied to the darker elements of life—the dread blossoming of evil in the soul, and its fearful retributions. The House of the Seven Gables, one for each deadly sin, may be no unmeet adumbration of the corrupted soul of man. It is a ghostly, mouldy abode, built in some eclipse of the sun, and raftered with curses dark; founded on a grave, and sending its turrets heavenward, as the lightning rod transcends its summit, to invite the wrath supernal. Every darker shadow of human life lingers in and about its melancholy shelter. There all the passions allied to crime,—pride in its intensity, avarice with its steely gripe, and unrelenting conscience, are to be expiated in the house built on injustice. Wealth there withers, and the human heart grows cold: and thither are brought as accessories the chill glance of speculative philosophy, the descending hopes of the aged laborer, whose vision closes on the workhouse, the poor necessities of the humblest means of livelihood, the bodily and mental dilapidation of a wasted life.

> A residence for woman, child, and man,
> A dwelling place,—and yet no habitation;
> A Home,—but under some prodigious ban
> Of excommunication.
> O'er all these hung a shadow and a fear;
> A sense of mystery the spirit daunted,
> And said, as plain as whisper in the ear,
> The place is haunted!

Yet the sunshine casts its rays into the old building, as it must, were it only to show us the darkness.

† From a review of *The House of the Seven Gables, The Literary World*, VIII (April 26, 1851), 334–35.

In truth there is sunshine brought in among the inmates, and these wrinkled, cobwebbed spiritualities with gentle Phoebe,— but it is a playful, typical light of youth and goodness,—hardly crystallizing the vapory atmosphere of the romance into the palpable concretions of actual life.

Yet, withal, these scenes and vivid descriptions are dramatic and truthful: dramatic in the picturesque and in situation rather than in continuous and well developed action; true to the sentiment and inner reality, if not to the outer fact. The two death scenes of the founder of the family and of his descendant Judge Pyncheon, possess dramatic effect of a remarkable character; and various other groupings, at the fountain and elsewhere, separate themselves in our recollection. The chief perhaps, of the dramatis personae, is the house itself. From its turrets to its kitchen, in every nook and recess without and within, it is alive and vital, albeit of a dusty antiquity. We know it by sunlight and moonlight; by the elm which surmounts its roof, the mosses in its crevices, and its supernatural mist-swept blackness. Truly is it an actor in the scene. We move about tremblingly among its shadows,—the darkness of poverty and remorse dogging ruthlessly at our heels.

Verily this Hawthorne retains in him streaks of a Puritan ancestry. Some grave beater of pulpit cushions must lie among his ancestry; for of all laymen he will preach to you the closest sermons, probe deepest into the unescapable corruption, carry his lantern, like Belzoni among the mummies, into the most secret recesses of the heart; and he will do this with so vital a force in his propositions that they will transcend the individual example and find a precedent in every reader's heart. So true is it that when you once seize an actual thing you have in it a picture of universal life.

His Old Maid (Hepzibah) sacrificing pride to open her shop of small wares in one of the gables of the building, and her reluctant experiences of the first day, is not only a view of family pride in its shifts and reluctance, but covers all the doubts and irresolutions which beset a sensitive mind on the entrance upon any new sphere of duty in the great world.

These pictures are clear, distinct, full. The description is made out by repeated touches. There is no peculiar richness in the style: in some respects it is plain, but it flows on pellucid as a mountain rivulet, and you feel in its refreshing purity that it is fed by springs beneath.

You must be in the proper mood and time and place to read Hawthorne, if you would understand him. We think any one would·

be wrong to make the attempt on a rail-car, or on board a steamboat. It is not a shilling novel that you are purchasing when you buy the House of the Seven Gables, but a book—a book with lights and shades, parts and diversities, upon which you may feed and pasture, not exhausting the whole field at an effort, but returning now and then to uncropped fairy rings and bits of herbage. You may read the book into the small hours beyond midnight, when no sound breaks the silence but the parting of an expiring ember, or the groan of restless mahogany, and you find that the candle burns a longer flame, and that the ghostly visions of the author's page take shape about you. Conscience sits supreme in her seat, the fountains of pity and terror are opened; you look into the depths of the soul, provoked at so painful a sight—but you are strengthened as you gaze; for of that pain comes peace at last, and these shadows you must master by virtuous magic. Nathaniel Hawthorne may be the Cornelius Agrippa to invoke them, but you are the mirror in which they are reflected.

The story of the House of the Seven Gables is a tale of retribution, of expiation extending over a period of two hundred years, it taking all that while to lay the ghost of the earliest victim, in the time of the Salem witchcraft; for, by the way, it is to Salem that this blackened old dwelling, mildewed with easterly scud, belongs. The yeoman who originally struck his spade into the spot, by the side of a crystal spring, was hanged for a wizard, under the afflictive dispensation of Cotton Mather. His land passed by force of law under cover of an old sweeping grant from the State, though not without hard words and thoughts and litigations, to the possession of the Ahab of the Vineyard, Colonel Pyncheon, the founder of the house, whose statuesque death scene was the first incident of the strongly ribbed tenement built on the ground thus suspiciously acquired. It was a prophecy of the old wizard on his execution at Gallows Hill, looking steadfastly at his rival, the Colonel, who was there, watching the scene on horseback, that "God would give him blood to drink." The sudden death of apoplexy was thereafter ministered to the great magnates of the Pyncheon family. After an introductory chapter detailing this early history of the house, we are introduced to its broken fortunes of the present day, in its decline. An Old Maid is its one tenant, left there with a life interest in the premises by the late owner, whose vast wealth passed into the hands of a cousin, who, immediately, touched by this talisman of property, was transformed from a youth of dissipation into a high, cold, and worldly state of respectability. His portrait is drawn in this volume with the repeated limnings and labor of a Titian, who, it is known, would expend several years upon a human head. We see him in every light, walk leisurely round the vast circle of that magical outline, his respectability just mentioned, till we close in upon the man, narrowing slowly to his centre of falsity and selfishness. For a thorough witch laugh over fallen hollow-heartedness and pretence, there is a terrible sardonic greeting in the roll-call of that man's uncompleted day's performances as he sits in the fatal chamber, death-cold, having drunk the blood of the ancient curse. But this is to anticipate. Other inmates gather round Old Maid Hepzibah. A remote gable is rented to a young artist, a daguerreotypist, and then comes upon the scene the brother of the Old Maid, Clifford Pyncheon, one day let out from life incarceration for—what circumstantial evidence had brought home to him—the murder of the late family head. Thirty years had obliterated most of this man's moral and intellectual nature, save in a certain blending of the two with his physical instinct for the sensuous and beautiful. A rare character that for our spiritual limner to work upon! The agent he has provided, nature's ministrant to this feebleness and disease, to aid in the rebuilding of the man, is a sprig of unconscious, spontaneous girlhood—"a thing of beauty, and a joy for ever"—who enters the thick shades of the dwelling of disaster as a sunbeam, to purify and nourish its stagnant life. Very beautiful is this conception, and subtly wrought the chapters in which the relation is developed. Then we have the sacrifice of pride and solitary misanthropy in the petty retail shop Hepzibah opens for the increasing needs of the rusty mansion. This portion, as we have intimated, reaches the heart of the matter; and the moral here is as healthy as the emotion is keenly penetrated. What the tale-writer here says of his picture of the dilapidated figure of the Old Maid, applies to the poor and humble necessities of her position—"If we look through all the heroic fortunes of mankind, we find an entanglement of something mean and trivial with whatever is noblest in joy or sorrow. Life is made up of marble and mud. What is called poetic insight is the gift of discerning, in this sphere of strangely-mingled elements, the beauty and the majesty which are compelled to assume a garb so sordid." So, when gentility, and family decency, and the pride of life, seemed all to be sacrificed in the degradation and low vulgarities of the shop for boys and servant maids, a new ray of light breaks in upon the scene, quite unexpected and more noble than any form of magnificent selfishness. * * *

# HENRY FOTHERGILL CHORLEY

## [The Affluence of Fancy] †

The invention of 'The Scarlet Letter' involved so much crime and remorse, that—though never was tragedy on a similar theme more clear of morbid incitements,—we felt that in a journal like ours the tale could be characterized only, not illustrated by extracts. So powerful, however, was the effect of that novel—even on those who, like ourselves, were prepared to receive good things from Mr. Hawthorne's hands—as to justify no ordinary solicitude concerning his next effort in fiction. This is before us—in 'The House of the Seven Gables': a story widely differing from its predecessor,—exceeding it, perhaps, in artistic ingenuity—if less powerful, less painful also—rich in humours and characters —and from first to last individual. It is thus made evident that Mr. Hawthorne possesses the fertility as well as the ambition of Genius: and in right of these two tales few will dispute his claim to rank amongst the most original and complete novelists that have appeared in modern times.

Fantastic as the title of Mr. Hawthorne's new tale is, it is not misapplied. 'The House of the Seven Gables' is as perpetually present to the reader as was the Mother Church of Paris in M. Hugo's romance. This mansion was built long ago "in a by-street of one of our New England towns," as a family illustration and tenement; and the builder, a wealthy and prosperous man, one of the magnates of a new settlement, dug his foundations on land wrung (some said by chicanery licensed by law, though not by equity) from a poor mechanic having an evil reputation, who was burnt as a wizard. The race of neither the oppressor nor the oppressed became extinct. The Pyncheons and the Maules both transmitted strong and strange characteristics to their descendants, —those, family pride and insolence—these, a character for commanding sinister and malignant influences. The last is touched by Mr. Hawthorne with a master hand. We know nothing better than the manner in which he presses superstition into his service as a romancer: leaving the reader to guess and explain such marvels as at first seen down the dim vista of Time, are reproduced more faintly in the world of the real Present. * * *

† From a review of *The House of the Seven Gables*, *The Athenaeum* (May 24, 1851), 545–47.

Before, however, we leave this book, we have to note a fault in it not chargeable upon 'The Scarlet Letter,'—and one which, as having introduced Mr. Hawthorne to the English public, we mention in friendly jealousy, lest it grow into an affectation with him. That affluence of fancy, that delight in playing with an idea and placing it in every cameleon light of the prism, and that love of reverie, which are so fascinating in a humorous essayist—become importunate if employed in scenes of emotion and junctures of breathless suspense. The speculations, for instance, upon him who sat in the deserted house on the day of the catastrophe fret the reader with their prosy and tantalizing ingenuity. They would have been in their place in the study of a single figure; but as interrupting the current which is sweeping the fortunes of many persons to the brink of the cataract—they are frivolous and vexatious. We beg our vigorous inventor and finely finishing artist (Mr. Hawthorne is both) to mistrust himself whenever he comes to his second simile and his third suggestion. They weaken the reader's faith,—they exhaust, not encourage, in him that desire to consider "what might have happened" in such or such other cases which it is so essentially the privilege of first-class stories to generate.

# EDWIN PERCY WHIPPLE

## [*The House of the Seven Gables:* Humor and Pathos Combined] †

"The wrong-doing of one generation lives into the successive ones, and, divesting itself of every temporary advantage, becomes a pure and uncontrollable mischief"; this is the leading idea of Hawthorne's new romance, and it is developed with even more than his usual power. The error in "The Scarlet Letter," proceeded from the divorce of its humor from its pathos—the introduction being as genial as Goldsmith or Lamb, and the story which followed being tragic even to ghastliness. In "The House of the Seven Gables," the humor and the pathos are combined, and the whole work is stamped with the individuality of the author's genius, in all its variety of power. The first hundred pages of the volume are masterly in conception and execution, and can challenge comparison, in the singular depth and sweet-

† A review of *The House of the Seven Gables, Graham's Magazine*, XXXVIII (June, 1851), 467–68.

ness of their imaginative humor, with the best writing of the kind in literature. The other portions of the book have not the same force, precision, and certainty of handling, and the insight into character especially, seems at times to follow the processes of clairvoyance more than those of the waking imagination. The consequence is that the movement of the author's mind betrays a slight fitfulness toward the conclusion, and, splendid as is the supernaturally grotesque element which this ideal impatience introduces, it still somewhat departs from the integrity of the original conception, and interferes with the strict unity of the work. The mental nerve which characterizes the first part, slips occasionally into mental nervousness as the author proceeds.

We have been particular in indicating this fault, because the work is of so high a character that it demands, as a right, to be judged by the most exacting requirements of art. Taken as a whole, it is Hawthorne's greatest work, and is equally sure of immediate popularity and permanent fame. Considered as a romance, it does not so much interest as fasten and fascinate attention; and this attractiveness in the story is the result of the rare mental powers and moods out of which the story creatively proceeds. Every chapter proves the author to be, not only a master of narrative, a creator of character, an observer of life, and richly gifted with the powers of vital conception and combination, but it also exhibits him as a profound thinker and skillful metaphysician. We do not know but that his eye is more certain in detecting remote spiritual laws and their relations, than in the sure grasp of individual character; and if he ever loses his hold upon persons it is owing to that intensely meditative cast of his mind by which he views persons in their relations to the general laws whose action they illustrate. There is some discord in the present work in the development of character and sequence of events; the dramatic unity is therefore not perfectly preserved; but this cannot be affirmed of the unity of the law. That is always sustained, and if it had been thoroughly embodied, identified, and harmonized with the concrete events and characters, we have little hesitation in asserting that the present volume would be the deepest work of imagination ever produced on the American continent.

Before venturing upon any comments on the characters, we cannot resist the temptation to call the attention of our readers to the striking thoughts profusely scattered over the volume. These are generally quietly introduced, and spring so naturally out of the narrative of incidents, that their depth may not be at first appreciated. Expediency is the god whom most men really worship and obey, and few realize the pernicious consequences and poisonous vitality of bad deeds performed to meet an immediate difficulty. Hawthorne hits the law itself in this remark: "The net of the present generation is the germ which may and must produce good or evil fruit, in a far distant time; for, together with the seed of the merely temporary crop, which mortals term expediency, they inevitably sow the acorns of a more enduring growth, which may darkly overshadow their posterity." In speaking of the legal murder of old Matthew Maule for witchcraft, he says that Matthew "was one of the martyrs to that terrible delusion, which should teach us, among its other morals, that the influential classes, and those who take upon themselves to be leaders of the people, are fully liable to all the passionate error that has ever characterized the maddest mob." In reference to the hereditary transmission of individual qualities, it is said of Colonel Pyncheon's descendants, that "his character might be traced all the way down, as distinctly as if the colonel himself, a little diluted, had been gifted with a sort of intermittent immortality on earth." In a deeper vein is the account of the working of the popular imagination on the occasion of Col. Pyncheon's death. This afflicting event was ascribed by physicians to apoplexy; by the people to strangulation. The colonel had caused the death of a reputed wizard; and the fable ran that the lieutenant-governor, as he advanced into the room where the colonel sat dead in his chair, saw a skeleton hand at the colonel's throat, which vanished away as he came near him. Such touches as these are visible all over the volume, and few romances have more quotable felicities of thought and description.

The characters of the romance are among the best of Hawthorne's individualizations, and Miss Hepzibah and Phoebe are perhaps his masterpieces of characterization, in the felicity of their conception, their contrast, and their inter-action. Miss Hepzibah Pyncheon, the inhabitant of the gabled house, is compelled at the age of sixty to stoop from her aristocratic isolation from the world, and open a little cent shop, in order that she may provide for the subsistence of an unfortunate brother. The chapters entitled "The Little Shop-Window," "The First Customer," and a "Day Behind the Counter," in which her ludicrous humiliations are described, may be placed beside the best works of the most genial humorists, for their rapid alternations of smiles and tears, and the perfect April weather they make in the heart. The description of the little articles at the shop-window, the bars of soap, the leaden dragoons, the split peas, and the fantastic Jim Crow, "executing his world-renowned dance in gingerbread"; the attempts of the elderly maiden to arrange her articles aright, and the sad destruction she makes among them, crowned by upsetting that tumbler of marbles, "all of which roll different ways, and each individual marble, devil-directed, into the most difficult obscurity it can find"; the nervous irritation of her deportment as she puts her shop in order, the twitches of pride which agonize her breast, as stealing on tiptoe to the window, "as cautiously as if she conceived some bloody-minded villain to be watching behind the elm-tree, with intent to take her life," she stretches out her long, lank arm to put a paper of pearl-buttons, a Jew's harp, or what not, in its destined place, and then straitway vanishing back into the dusk, "as if the world need never hope for another glimpse of her"; the "ugly and spiteful little din" of the door-bell, announcing her first penny customer; all these, and many more minute details, are instinct with the life of humor, and cheerily illustrate that "entanglement of something mean and trivial with whatever is noblest in joy and sorrow," which it is the office of the humorist to represent and idealize.

The character of Phoebe makes the sunshine of the book, and by connecting her so intimately with Miss Hepzibah, a quaint sweetness is added to the native graces of her mind and disposition. The "homely witchcraft" with which she brings out the hidden capabilities of every thing, is exquisitely exhibited, and poor Uncle Venner's praise of her touches the real secret of her fascination. "I've seen," says that cheery mendicant, "a great deal of the world, not only in people's kitchens and back-yards, but at the street corners, and on the wharves, and in other places where my business calls me; but I'm free to say that I never knew a human creature do her work so much like one of God's angels as this child Phoebe does!" Holgrave, the young gentleman who carries off this pearl of womanhood, appears to us a failure. It is impossible for the reader to like him, and one finds it difficult to conceive how Phoebe herself can like him. The love scenes accordingly lack love, and a kind of magnetic influence is substituted for affection. The character of Clifford is elaborately drawn, and sustained with much subtle skill, but he occupies perhaps too much space, and lures the author too much into metaphysical analysis and didactic disquisition. Judge Pyncheon is powerfully delineated, and the account of his death is a masterpiece of fantastic description. It is needless, perhaps, to say that the characters of the book have, like those in "The Scarlet Letter," a vital relation to each other, and are developed not successively and separately, but mutually, each implying the other by a kind of artistic necessity.

The imagination in "The House of Seven Gables," is perhaps most strikingly exhibited in the power with which the house itself is pervaded with thought, so that every room and gable has a sort of human interest communicated to it, and seems to symbolize the whole life of the Pyncheon family, from the grim colonel, who built it, to that delicate Alice, "the fragrance of whose rich and delightful character lingered about the place where she lived, as a dried rose-bud scents the drawer where it has withered and perished."

In conclusion, we hope to have the pleasure of reviewing a new romance by Hawthorne twice a year at least. We could also hope that if Holgrave continues his contributions to the magazines, that he would send Graham some such a story as "Alice Pyncheon," which he tells so charmingly to Phoebe. "The Scarlet Letter," and "The House of Seven Gables," contain mental qualities which insensibly lead some readers to compare the author to other cherished literary names. Thus we have seen Hawthorne likened for this quality to Goldsmith, and for that to Irving, and for still another to Dickens; and some critics have given him the preference over all whom he seems to resemble. But the real cause for congratulation in the appearance of an original genius like Hawthorne, is not that he dethrones any established prince in literature, but that he founds a new principality of his own.

# HENRY JAMES

## [*The House of the Seven Gables*] †

\* \* \* *The House of the Seven Gables* comes nearer being a picture of contemporary American life than either of its companions; but on this ground it would be a mistake to make a large claim for it. It cannot be too often repeated that Hawthorne was not a realist. He had a high sense of reality—his Note-Books superabundantly testify to it; and fond as he was of jotting down the items that make it up, he never attempted to render exactly or closely the actual facts of the society that surrounded him. I have said—I began by saying—that his pages were full of its spirit, and of a certain reflected light that springs from it; but I was careful to add that the reader must look for his local and national qualities between the lines of his writing and in the *indirect* testimony of his tone, his accent, his temper, of his very omissions and suppressions. *The House of the Seven Gables* has, however, more literal actuality than the others, and if it were not too fanciful an account of it, I should say that it renders, to an initiated reader, the impression of a summer afternoon in an elm-shadowed New England town. It leaves upon the mind a

† From Henry James, *Hawthorne*, London, 1879. Pp. 124–130.

vague correspondence to some such reminiscence, and in stirring up the association it renders it delightful. The comparison is to the honour of the New England town, which gains in it more than it bestows. The shadows of the elms, in *The House of the Seven Gables*, are exceptionally dense and cool; the summer afternoon is peculiarly still and beautiful; the atmosphere has a delicious warmth, and the long daylight seems to pause and rest. But the mild provincial quality is there, the mixture of shabbiness and freshness, the paucity of ingredients. The end of an old race —this is the situation that Hawthorne has depicted, and he has been admirably inspired in the choice of the figures in whom he seeks to interest us. They are all figures rather than characters— they are all pictures rather than persons. But if their reality is light and vague, it is sufficient, and it is in harmony with the low relief and dimness of outline of the objects that surrounded them. They are all types, to the author's mind, of something general, of something that is bound up with the history, at large, of families and individuals, and each of them is the centre of a cluster of those ingenious and meditative musings, rather melancholy, as a general thing, than joyous, which melt into the current and texture of the story and give it a kind of moral richness. A grotesque old spinster, simple, childish, penniless, very humble at heart, but rigidly conscious of her pedigree; an amiable bachelor, of an epicurean temperament and an enfeebled intellect, who has passed twenty years of his life in penal confinement for a crime of which he was unjustly pronounced guilty; a sweet-natured and bright-faced young girl from the country, a poor relation of these two ancient decrepitudes, with whose moral mustiness her modern freshness and soundness are contrasted; a young man still more modern, holding the latest opinions, who has sought his fortune up and down the world, and, though he has not found it, takes a genial and enthusiastic view of the future: these, with two or three remarkable accessory figures, are the persons concerned in the little drama. The drama is a small one, but as Hawthorne does not put it before us for its own superficial sake, for the dry facts of the case, but for something in it which he holds to be symbolic and of large application, something that points a moral and that it behooves us to remember, the scenes in the rusty wooden house whose gables give its name to the story, have something of the dignity both of history and of tragedy. Miss Hepzibah Pyncheon, dragging out a disappointed life in her paternal dwelling, finds herself obliged in her old age to open a little shop for the sale of penny toys and gingerbread. This is the central incident of the tale, and, as Hawthorne relates it, it is an incident of the most impressive magnitude and most touching interest. Her dishonoured and vague-minded brother is released from prison at the same moment, and returns to the ancestral roof to deepen her perplexities. But, on the other hand, to alleviate them, and to introduce a breath of the air of the outer world into this long unventilated interior, the little country cousin also arrives, and proves the good angel of the feebly distracted household. All this episode is exquisite—admirably conceived and executed, with a kind of humorous tenderness, an equal sense of everything in it that is picturesque, touching, ridiculous, worthy of the highest praise. Hepzibah Pyncheon, with her near-sighted scowl, her rusty joints, her antique turban, her map of a great territory to the eastward which ought to have belonged to her family, her vain terrors, and scruples, and resentments, the inaptitude and repugnance of an ancient gentlewoman to the vulgar little commerce which a cruel fate has compelled her to engage in—Hepzibah Pyncheon is a masterly picture. I repeat that she is a picture, as her companions are pictures; she is a charming piece of descriptive writing, rather than a dramatic exhibition. But she is described, like her companions, too, so subtly and lovingly that we enter into her virginal old heart and stand with her behind her abominable little counter. Clifford Pyncheon is a still more remarkable conception, though he is, perhaps, not so vividly depicted. It was a figure needing a much more subtle touch, however, and it was of the essence of his character to be vague and unemphasised. Nothing can be more charming than the manner in which the soft, bright, active presence of Phoebe Pyncheon is indicated, or than the account of her relations with the poor, dimly sentient kinsman for whom her light-handed sisterly offices, in the evening of a melancholy life, are a revelation of lost possibilities of happiness. "In her aspect," Hawthorne says of the young girl, "there was a familiar gladness, and a holiness that you could play with, and yet reverence it as much as ever. She was like a prayer offered up in the homeliest beauty of one's mother-tongue. Fresh was Phoebe, moreover, and airy, and sweet in her apparel; as if nothing that she wore—neither her gown, nor her small straw bonnet, nor her little kerchief, any more than her snowy stockings—had ever been put on before; or, if worn, were all the fresher for it, and with a fragrance as if they had lain among the rose-buds." Of the influence of her maidenly salubrity upon poor Clifford, Hawthorne gives the prettiest description, and then, breaking off suddenly, renounces the attempt in language which, while pleading its inadequacy, conveys an exquisite satisfaction to the reader. I quote the passage for the sake of its extreme felicity, and of the charming image with which it concludes.

But we strive in vain to put the idea into words. No adequate expression of the beauty and profound pathos with which it impresses us is attainable. This being, made only for happiness, and heretofore so miserably failing to be happy—his tendencies so hideously thwarted that, some unknown time ago, the delicate springs of his character, never morally or intellectually strong, had given way, and he was now imbecile—this poor forlorn voyager from the Islands of the Blest, in a frail bark, on a tempestuous sea, had been flung by the last mountain-wave of his shipwreck into a quiet harbour. There, as he lay more than half lifeless on the strand, the fragrance of an earthly rose-bud had come to his nostrils, and, as odours will, had summoned up reminiscences or visions of all the living and breathing beauty amid which he should have had his home. With his native susceptibility of happy influences, he inhales the slight ethereal rapture into his soul, and expires!

I have not mentioned the personage in *The House of the Seven Gables* upon whom Hawthorne evidently bestowed most pains, and whose portrait is the most elaborate in the book; partly because he is, in spite of the space he occupies, an accessory figure, and partly because, even more than the others, he is what I have called a picture rather than a character. Judge Pyncheon is an ironical portrait, very richly and broadly executed, very sagaciously composed and rendered—the portrait of a superb, full-blown hypocrite, a large-based, full-nurtured Pharisee, bland, urbane, impressive, diffusing about him a "sultry" warmth of benevolence, as the author calls it again and again, and basking in the noontide of prosperity and the consideration of society; but in reality hard, gross, and ignoble. Judge Pyncheon is an elaborate piece of description, made up of a hundred admirable touches, in which satire is always winged with fancy, and fancy is linked with a deep sense of reality. It is difficult to say whether Hawthorne followed a model in describing Judge Pyncheon; but it is tolerably obvious that the picture is an impression—a copious impression—of an individual. It has evidently a definite starting-point in fact, and the author is able to draw, freely and confidently, after the image established in his mind. Holgrave, the modern young man, who has been a Jack-of-all-trades, and is at the period of the story a daguerreotypist, is an attempt to render a kind of national type—that of the young citizen of the United States whose fortune is simply in his lively intelligence, and who stands naked, as it were, unbiased and unencumbered alike, in the centre of the far-stretching level of American life. Holgrave is intended as a contrast; his lack of traditions, his democratic stamp, his condensed experience, are opposed to the desiccated prejudices and exhausted vitality of the race of which poor feebly-scowling, rusty-jointed Hepzibah is the most heroic representative. It is, perhaps, a pity that Hawthorne should not have proposed to himself to give the old Pyncheon qualities some embodiment which would help them to balance more fairly with the elastic properties of the young dagucrrcotypist—should not have painted a lusty conservative to match his strenuous radical. As it is, the mustiness and mouldiness of the tenants of the House of the Seven Gables crumble away rather too easily. Evidently, however, what Hawthorne designed to represent was not the struggle between an old society and a new, for in this case he would have given the old one a better chance; but simply, as I have said, the shrinkage and extinction of a family. This appealed to his imagination; and the idea of long perpetuation and survival always appears to have filled him with a kind of horror and disapproval. Conservative, in a certain degree, as he was himself, and fond of retrospect and quietude and the mellowing influences of time, it is singular how often one encounters in his writings some expression of mistrust of old houses, old institutions, long lines of descent. He was disposed, apparently, to allow a very moderate measure in these respects, and he condemns the dwelling of the Pyncheons to disappear from the face of the earth because it has been standing a couple of hundred years. In this he was an American of Americans; or, rather, he was more American than many of his countrymen, who, though they are accustomed to work for the short run rather than the long, have often a lurking esteem for things that show the marks of having lasted. I will add that Holgrave is one of the few figures, among those which Hawthorne created, with regard to which the absence of the realistic mode of treatment is felt as a loss. Holgrave is not sharply enough characterised; he lacks features; he is not an individual, but a type. But my last word about this admirable novel must not be a restrictive one. It is a large and generous production, pervaded with that vague hum, that indefinable echo, of the whole multitudinous life of man, which is the real sign of a great work of fiction.

# F. O. MATTHIESSEN

## [The House of the Seven Gables and American History] †

\* \* \* It is small wonder \* \* \* that turning away from what he considered the unrelieved gloom of *The Scarlet Letter*, [Hawthorne]

† From F. O. Matthiessen, *American Renaissance*, New York, 1941. Pp. 322–34. Copyright 1941 by Oxford University Press, Inc.; reprinted by permission.

thought *The Seven Gables* "more characteristic of my mind, and more proper and natural for me to write." The measure in which he intended the latter book as a criticism of his own age is somewhat obscured by his treatment of time. Even while he was examining his changing New England, he felt the past weighing heavily on the present's back. Unlike virtually all the other spokesmen for his day, he could never feel that America was a new world. Looking back over the whole history of his province, he was more struck by decay than by potentiality, by the broken ends to which the Puritan effort had finally come, by the rigidity that had been integral to its thought at its best, by modes of life in which nothing beautiful had developed. Furthermore, his contemporaries seemed still to be branded with lasting marks from the weight and strain of such effort. He was often reflecting on the loss in vitality, on such facts as that the "broad shoulders and well-developed busts" of the women of Hester Prynne's day had long since tended, along with their "boldness and rotundity of speech," to wither away like trees transplanted in too thin a soil. Even at Brook Farm, he had not been able to share in the declaration that the new age was the dawn of untried possibilities. Even there he had thought about how much old material enters into the freshest novelty, about the ages of experience that had passed over the world, about the fact that the very ground under their feet was "fathom-deep with the dust of deluded generations, on every one of which, as on ourselves, the world had imposed itself as a hitherto unwedded bride."

Consequently, as he meditated on time in this story of the old house with its "mysterious and terrible past," the present often seemed "this visionary and impalpable Now, which, if you once look closely at it, is nothing." He was not, however, in any doubt as to the focus of his plot; in fact, he held that the only basis for calling this book a romance rather than a novel was its attempt "to connect a bygone time with the very present that is flitting away from us. It is a legend prolonging itself . . . down into our own broad daylight." His treatment of this legend constituted his nearest approach to everyday contemporary life, since he did not cast it in the special circumstances of a Utopian community or of an art-colony, but chose materials more naturally at hand. His attitude towards them was in no sense different from that in his other books. He was always concerned with the enduring elements in human nature, but the structure he devised here enabled him to disclose better than elsewhere how "the Colonel Pyncheon of two centuries ago steps forward as the Judge of the passing moment." As a result Lowell wrote at once to tell him that this book was "the most valuable contribution to New

England history that has been made," since it typified the intimate connections between heredity and descent, which more mechanical historians had failed to establish. On the other hand, James, sending a letter half a century later to the celebration at Salem of its novelist's centenary, was impressed most by the "presentness," by Hawthorne's instinctive gift in finding his romance, "the quaintness or the weirdness, the interest *behind* the interest of things, as continuous with the very life we are leading . . . round about him and under his eyes." He saw it in *The Seven Gables* "as something deeply within us, not as something infinitely disconnected from us," and could consequently make this book a "singularly fruitful" example "of the real as distinguished from the artificial romantic note." Therefore, it will serve better than any of his others to answer the first of our two main questions about his equipment for writing tragedy; to what degree could he conceive of individuals who were representative of a whole interrelated condition of society?

The seventeenth-century house, grown black in the prevailing east wind, itself took on the status of a major theme. Hawthorne wrote to Fields that "many passages of this book ought to be finished with the minuteness of a Dutch picture, in order to give them their proper effect"; and that aim can be read in his careful drawing of the thick central chimney, the gigantic elm at the door, the long-since exhausted garden, the monotony of occurrences in the by-street in which the mansion now fronts, the faint stir of the outside world as heard in the church bells or the far whistle of a train. As he dwelt on this example of "the best and stateliest architecture" in a town whose houses, unaccountably to our eyes, generally struck him as having little pretense to varied beauty, he could feel that it had been "the scene of events more full of human interest, perhaps, than those of a gray feudal castle." This is worth noting since he seems to have forgotten it by the time he was writing the preface to *The Marble Faun*, where, developing the thought that romance needs ruin to make it grow, he took the conventional attitude about the thinness of material for the artist in America. Since this, in turn, gave the lead to James' famous enumeration of all "the items of high civilization," all the complexity of customs and manners that were left out of Hawthorne's scene, it is important that the Hawthorne of *The Seven Gables* believed that no matter how familiar and humble its incidents, "they had the earth-smell in them." He believed far more than that, for within the oak frame of the house, "so much of mankind's varied experience had passed . . . so much had been suffered, and something, too, enjoyed that . . . it was itself like a great human heart, with a life of its own, and full of rich and sombre reminiscences."

These furnished him with several other themes that were central to American history. The old spinster Hepzibah Pyncheon, at the opening of the book the sole possessor of the dark recesses of the mansion, is the embodiment of decayed gentility, sustained only by her delusion of family importance, lacking any revivifying touch with outward existence. Hawthorne knew how fully her predicament corresponded to the movement of the age, since "in this republican country, amid the fluctuating waves of our social life, somebody is always at the drowning-point." He made the young reformer Holgrave confront her with the unreality of her existence by declaring that the names of gentleman and lady, though they had once had a meaning and had conferred a value on their owners, "in the present—and still more in the future condition of society—they imply, not privilege, but restriction!" Indeed, by imprisoning herself so long in one place and in the unvarying round of a single chain of ideas, Hepzibah had grown to be a kind of lunatic, pathetic in her efforts to merge with human sympathies, since no longer capable of doing so. Hawthorne posed her genteel helplessness against the demurely charming self-reliance of her niece Phoebe. By pointing out that it was owing to her father's having married beneath his rank that Phoebe possessed such plebeian capabilities as being able to manage a kitchen or conduct a school, Hawthorne deliberately etched a contrast between the Pyncheon family and the rising democracy. This contrast is sustained even down to the inbred hens in the garden, who have a "rusty, withered aspect, and a gouty kind of movement," in consequence of too strict a watchfulness to maintain their purity of race. This accords again with Holgrave's statement to Phoebe that "once in every half-century, at longest, a family should be merged into the great, obscure mass of humanity, and forget all about its ancestors. Human blood, in order to keep its freshness, should run in hidden streams."

But there is more substance to Hawthorne's contrast than the tenuous if accurate notation of the gradual waning of the aristocracy, as against the solidly based energy of common life. He had observed in one of his early sketches of Salem that the influence of wealth and the sway of class "had held firmer dominion here than in any other New England town"; and he now traced those abuses to their source. The original power of the Pyncheons had been founded on a great wrong: the very land on which the house was built had first been occupied by the thatched hut of Matthew Maule, who had settled there because of the spring of fresh water, "a rare treasure on the sea-girt peninsula." But as the town expanded during its first generation, this treasure took on the aspect of a desired asset in real estate to the eyes of Colonel Pyncheon. A man of iron energy of purpose in obtaining whatever he had set his mind upon, he asserted a plausible claim to Maule's lot and a large adjacent tract of land, on the strength of a prior grant.

Hawthorne's treatment of this material is characteristic of his effort to suggest social complexity. He stated that since no written record of the dispute remained in existence, he could merely enter the doubt as to whether the Colonel's claim had not been unduly stretched. What strengthened that suspicion was the fact that notwithstanding the inequality of the two antagonists, in a period when well-to-do personal influence had great hereditary weight, the dispute remained unsettled for years and came to a close only with the death of Maule, who had clung stubbornly to what he considered his right. Moreover, the manner of his death affected the mind differently than it had at the time, since he was executed as one of the obscure "martyrs to that terrible delusion, which should teach us, among its other morals, that the influential classes, and those who take upon themselves to be leaders of the people, are fully liable to all the passionate error that has ever characterized the maddest mob." In the general frenzy it was hardly noted that Colonel Pyncheon had applied his whole bitter force to the persecution of Maule, though by stressing this origin of the condemned man's curse upon his enemy— "God will give him blood to drink"—Hawthorne recognized how economic motives could enter even into the charge of witchcraft.

By the time the justification for that curse began to be whispered around, the mansion was built, and "there is something so massive, stable, and almost irresistibly imposing in the exterior presentment of established rank and great possessions, that their very existence seems to give them a right to exist; at least, so excellent a counterfeit of right, that few poor and humble men have moral force enough to question it." The Maules, at any rate, kept their resentment to themselves; and as the generations went on, they were usually poverty-stricken, always plebeian. They worked with "unsuccessful diligence" at handicrafts, labored on the wharves, or went to sea before the mast. They lived here and there about the town in tenements, and went to the almshouse "as the natural home of their old age." Finally they had taken "the downright plunge" that awaits all families; and for the past thirty years no one of their name had appeared in the local directory.

The main theme that Hawthorne evolved from this history of the Pyncheons and the Maules was not the original curse on the house, but the curse that the Pyncheons have continued to bring upon themselves. Clifford may phrase it wildly in his sense of release at the Judge's death: "What we call real estate—the solid ground to build a house on—is the broad foundation on which nearly all the guilt of this world rests. A man will commit almost any wrong,—he will heap up an immense pile of wickedness, as hard as granite, and which will weigh as heavily upon his soul, to eternal ages,—only to build a great gloomy, dark-chambered mansion, for himself to die in, and for his posterity to be miserable in." But this also corresponds to Hawthorne's view in his preface, a view from which the dominating forces of his country had just begun to diverge most widely with the opening of California: "the folly of tumbling down an avalanche of ill-gotten gold, or real estate, on the heads of an unfortunate posterity, thereby to maim and crush them, until the accumulated mass shall be scattered abroad in its original atoms." Hawthorne's objections to the incumbrance of property often ran close to Thoreau's.

What Hawthorne set himself to analyze is this "energy of disease," this lust for wealth that has held the dominating Pyncheons in its inflexible grasp. After their original victory, their drive for power had long since shifted its ground, but had retained its form of oppressing the poor, for the present Judge steps forward to seize the property of his feeble cousins, Hepzibah and Clifford, with the same cold unscrupulousness that had actuated the original Colonel in his dealings with the Maules. The only variation is that, "as is customary with the rich, when they aim at the honors of a republic," he had learned the expediency, which had not been forced upon his freer ancestor, of masking his relentless will beneath a veneer of "paternal benevolence." Thus what Hawthorne saw handed down from one generation to another were not—and this paradoxical phrase was marked by Melville—"the big, heavy, solid unrealities" such as gold and hereditary position, but inescapable traits of character.

He did not, however, make the mistake of simplifying, by casting all his Pyncheons into one monotonous image. If the Judge typified the dominant strain in the family, Clifford, the most complex character in the book, could stand for the recessive. His gently sensuous, almost feminine face had received years ago its perfect recording in a Malbone miniature, since as a young man he had loved just such delicate charm. Hawthorne suggested the helplessness of his aesthetic temperament before the ruthless energy of the Judge, by saying that any conflict between them would be "like flinging a porcelain vase, with already a crack in it, against a granite column." By using that symbolic, almost Jamesian image, he gave further embodiment to the kind of contrast he had drawn between Owen Warland and his hostile environment. His implications also extended beyond the Pyncheon family, for the hard competitive drives that had crushed many potentialities of richer, less aggressive living, had been a distorting factor throughout the length of American experience.

But Hawthorne made no effort to idealize Clifford. Holgrave calls him an "abortive lover of the beautiful," and it is true that the fragile mainspring of his life has been shattered by his long imprisonment for the supposed murder of his uncle. This punishment had been especially cruel since the old man had actually died of an apoplectic seizure, the traditional Pyncheon disease, but under such suspicious circumstances that his other nephew Jaffrey, who coveted the whole inheritance, could cause it to appear an act of violence. As a result he had gained the fortune on which he was to build the career that led to the eminent respectability of a judgeship; and Hepzibah was left with only the life occupancy of the house. And to the house she clung tenaciously, though its proper maintenance was far beyond her impoverished means, in the hope that is finally realized, of welcoming home her brother after his belated release. But the man who returns no longer possesses any intellectual or moral fibre to control his sensibility. His tastes express themselves only in a selfish demand for luxuries and in an animal delight in food, an exaggeration of the defects that Hawthorne always felt to lie as a danger for the artistic temperament, whose too exclusive fondness for beauty might end by wearing away all human affections. Clifford has retrogressed until he is hardly more than an idiot, a spoiled child who takes a childish pleasure in any passing attraction that can divert him from the confused memories of his terrible years of gloom. But, occasionally, deeper forces stir within him, as one day when he is watching, from the arched window at the head of the stairs, a political procession of marching men with fifes and drums. With a sudden, irrepressible gesture, from which he is restrained just in time by Hepzibah and Phoebe, he starts forward as though to jump down into the street, in a kind of desperate effort at renewed contact with life outside himself, "but whether impelled by the species of terror that sometimes urges its victim over the very precipice which he shrinks from, or by a natural magnetism, tending towards the great centre of humanity," Hawthorne found it not easy to decide.

Melville considered this one of the two most impressive scenes in the book; and the currents that are stirring here rise to their climax in the chapter in which Hawthorne's imagination moves most freely, "The Flight of Two Owls," the poignant account of how Hepzibah is swept away by her brother's strange exhilaration at finding the Judge, who had come to threaten him, dead of a seizure. Clifford is now determined to leave the whole past behind, and impels Hepzibah to start off at once with him crazily in the rain. With no definite goal, his attention is suddenly attracted by a feature of the Salem scene unknown at the time of his imprisonment, a train at the depot. Before Hepzibah can protest, they are aboard and are started on a local towards Portsmouth. The fact that Hawthorne had made a record in his notebook, just the year before, of this very trip, seems to have helped him to catch the rhythm of kaleidoscopic impressions into which the two old people are caught up. With a giddy sense that he has finally merged with life, Clifford's excitement mounts in ever more reckless talk with a man across the aisle, in which Hawthorne ironically makes him develop the transcendental doctrine that evil is bound to disappear in the ascending spiral of human improvement. But just as the hard-eyed stranger's suspicions of his insanity are crystallizing into certitude, Clifford is seized by the impulse that he has now gone far enough. Taking advantage of the fact that the train has stopped for a moment, he again draws the bewildered Hepzibah after him and both get off. Another moment and they are alone on the open platform of a deserted way-station, under a sullen rain-swept sky. Clifford's unreal courage deserts him all at once, and he is once more helplessly dependent on his sister to get him home. The impression that Hawthorne has thus created of their solitude, of their decrepit inexperience in an uncomprehending and hostile world, may well have been part of the stimulus for the most effectively intense chapter in *Pierre*, where the adolescent couple arrive in New York at night, for the luridly brutal first impact of corruption upon innocence.

Still another theme is introduced through the role that is played by Holgrave. At the start of the book Hepzibah has taken him as her sole lodger, though she has become increasingly startled by his strange companions, "men with long beards, and dressed in linen blouses, and other such new-fangled and ill-fitting garments; reformers, temperance lecturers, and all manner of cross-looking philanthropists; community-men, and come-outers, as Hepzibah believed, who acknowledged no law, and ate no solid food." Moreover, she has read a paragraph in a paper accusing him of delivering a speech "full of wild and disorganizing matter." But though this has made her have misgivings whether she ought not send him away, she has to admit from her own contact with him that even by her formal standards he is a quiet and orderly young man. His first effect on Phoebe, after she has come to visit her aunt and really to take over the burden of running the house, is more disquieting, for his conversation seemed "to unsettle everything around her, by his lack of reverence for what was fixed."

In unrolling Holgrave's past history, which is made up in part from the histories of various characters whom Hawthorne had picked up in his country rambles, the novelist made clear that he believed he was tapping one of the richest sources of native material. He said at more explicit length than was customary to him: "A romance on the plan of Gil Blas, adapted to American society and manners, would cease to be a romance. The experience of many individuals among us, who think it hardly worth the telling, would equal the vicissitudes of the Spaniard's earlier life; while their ultimate success, or the point whither they tend, may be incomparably higher than any that a novelist would imagine for his hero." Holgrave himself told Phoebe somewhat proudly that he

. . . could not boast of his origin, unless as being exceedingly humble, nor of his education, except that it had been the scantiest possible, and obtained by a few winter-months' attendance at a district school. Left early to his own guidance, he had begun to be self-dependent while yet a boy; and it was a condition aptly suited to his natural force of will. Though now but twenty-two years old (lacking some months, which are years in such a life), he had already been, first, a country schoolmaster; next, a salesman in a country store; and either at the same time or afterwards, the political editor of a country newspaper. He had subsequently travelled New England and the Middle States, as a pedlar, in the employment of a Connecticut manufactory of cologne-water and other essences. In an episodical way he had studied and practiced dentistry, and with very flattering success, especially in many of the factory-towns along our inland streams. As a supernumerary official, of some kind or other, aboard a packet-ship, he had visited Europe, and found means, before his return, to see Italy, and part of France and Germany. At a later period he had spent some months in a community of Fourierists. Still more recently he had been a public lecturer on Mesmerism.

His present phase, as a daguerreotypist, was no more likely to be permanent than any of the preceding ones. He had taken it up "with the careless alacrity of an adventurer, who had his bread to earn."

Yet homeless as he had been, and continually changing his whereabouts, "and, therefore, responsible neither to public opinion nor to individuals," he had never violated his inner integrity of conscience, as Phoebe soon came to recognize. His hatred of the dead burden of the past was as thoroughgoing as possible; but he had read very little, and though he considered himself a thinker, with his own path to discover, he "had perhaps hardly yet reached the point where an educated man begins to think." "Altogether in his culture and want of culture"—as Hawthorne summed him up, somewhat laboriously, but with telling accuracy—"in his crude, wild, and misty philosophy, and the practical experience that counteracted some of its tendencies; in his magnanimous zeal for man's welfare, and his recklessness of whatever the ages had established in man's behalf; in his faith, and in his infidelity; in what he had and in what he lacked,—the artist might fitly enough stand forth as the representative of many compeers in his native land." His saving grace was the absence of arrogance in his ideas, which could otherwise have become those of a crank. He had learned enough of the world to be perplexed by it, and to begin to suspect "that a man's bewilderment is the measure of his wisdom." Melville checked that, as he did also the reflection that it would be hard to prefigure Holgrave's future, since in this country we are always meeting such jacks-of-all-trades, "for whom we anticipate wonderful things, but of whom, even after much and careful inquiry, we never happen to hear another word." In short, Hawthorne has presented a detailed portrait of one of Emerson's promising Young Americans.[1]

The course that is actually foreshadowed for him is devastating in its limitations. In consequence of the awakening of his love for Phoebe and her acceptance of him, society no longer looks hostile. When Phoebe is afraid that he will lead her out of her own quiet path, he already knows that the influence is likely to be all the other way. As he says, "the world owes all its onward impulses to men ill at ease," and he has a presentiment that it will hereafter be his lot to set out trees and to make fences, and to build a house for another generation. Thus he admits, with a half-melancholy laugh, that he feels the traditional values already asserting their power over him, even while he and Phoebe

1. Even Emerson, glutton for punishment though he was, finally reached the point where he refused to be excited by any more Charles Newcombs as potential Shakespeares. He wrote in his journal for 1842: "When I saw the sylvan youth, I said, 'Very good promise, but I cannot now watch any more buds': like the good Grandfather when they brought him the twentieth babe, he declined the dandling, he had said 'Kitty, Kitty,' long enough."

Hawthorne's analysis is also akin to the formulation which James made of the New England character in one of his early reviews (of Guérin's *Letters*, 1866): "A very good man or a very good woman in New England is an extremely complex being. They are as innocent as you please, but they are anything but ignorant. They travel; they hold political opinions; they are accomplished Abolitionists; they read magazines and newspapers, and write for them; they read novels and police reports; they subscribe to lyceum lectures and to great libraries; in a word, they are enlightened. The result of this freedom of enquiry is that they become profoundly self-conscious." This formulation led in turn to the kind of world James tried to project in *The Bostonians* (1886), where the mixture of reformers and blue-stockings is a late aftershine of Brook Farm and *Blithedale*. The general quality of mind common to both Holgrave and to James' New England type is the strain of exposed consciousness, which James could observe in his contemporaries just as Hawthorne had in his. This gives the most explicit reason for the continuity between them in the development of their inward subject-matter.

are still standing under the gaze of the portrait of Colonel Pyncheon, whom Holgrave recognizes as "a model conservative, who,
in that very character, rendered himself so long the evil destiny
of his race."

The conclusion of this book has satisfied very few. Although
Phoebe's marriage with Holgrave, who discloses himself at length
as a descendant of the Maules, is meant finally to transcend the
old brutal separation of classes that has hardened the poor family
against its oppressors, the reconciliation is somewhat too lightly
made. It is quite out of keeping with Hawthorne's seemingly deliberate answer in his preface to the new thought's doctrine of
Compensation, of the way good arises out of evil. For Hawthorne
said there that his book might illustrate the truth "that the wrong-
doing of one generation lives into the successive ones, and, divesting itself of every temporary advantage, becomes a pure and
uncontrollable mischief." That unrelenting strain was still at the
fore in his final reflections about Clifford. Although his feeble
spirits revived once the Judge's death had removed him from the
sphere of that malevolent influence, "after such wrong as he had
suffered, there is no reparation . . . No great mistake, whether
acted or endured, in our mortal sphere, is ever really set right.
Time, the continual vicissitude of circumstances, and the invariable
inopportunity of death, render it impossible. If, after long lapse
of years, the right seems to be in our power, we find no niche to
set it in."

In contrast to that tragic thought, Hawthorne's comparatively
flimsy interpretation of the young lovers derives from the fact that
he has not visualized their future with any precision. Trollope ob-
jected to this on the basic level of plot: "the hurrying up of the
marriage, and all the dollars which they inherit from the wicked
Judge, and the 'handsome dark-green barouche' prepared for their
departure, which is altogether unfitted to the ideas which the
reader has formed respecting them, are quite unlike Hawthorne,
and would seem almost to have been added by some every-day,
beef-and-ale, realistic novelist, into whose hands the unfinished
story had unfortunately fallen." As they leave for the new country
house that has tumbled into their hands, they seem to have made
the successful gesture of renouncing the worst of the past. The tone
of the last page could hardly be more different from that of the
end of *The Cherry Orchard*, where Chekhov dwells not on what
lies ahead, but on the mingled happiness and despair that have
been interwoven with the old house. But the Russian was aware of
the frustration and impending breakdown of a whole social class,
whereas Hawthorne assumed with confidence the continuance of
democratic opportunity. Yet in the poetic justice of bestowing

opulence on all those who had previously been deprived of it by the Judge, Hawthorne overlooked the fact that he was sowing all over again the same seeds of evil. \* \* \*

[T]he implications that lay ahead in the young couple's inheritance of several hundred thousand were equally beyond both Hawthorne's experience and imagination. He took for granted that in a democratic society the domineering influence of private wealth would not be able to hold the evil sway that it did in the narrowly autocratic era of Colonel Pyncheon. But the fact that he hardly cast a glance to examine what would prevail at the Holgraves' countryseat, prevented him from suggesting their participation in any definite state of existence, as, for instance, Tolstoy could suggest the Russia of which Pierre and Natasha had become part at the close of *War and Peace*.

Out of his savage revulsion from the America that had followed —the America of Sinclair Lewis' early satires, whose roots Veblen had probed with deeper thoroughness—Lawrence could make his free interpretation of Hawthorne's conclusion: "The new generation is having no ghosts or cobwebs. It is setting up in the photography line, and is just going to make a sound financial thing out of it." With all the old hates swept out of sight, "the vendetta-born young couple effect a perfect understanding under the black cloth of a camera and prosperity. *Vivat industria!* . . . How you'd have *hated* it if you'd had nothing but the prosperous, 'dear' young couple to write about! If you'd lived to the day when America was nothing but a Main Street." [2]

Hawthorne's inability, despite all his latent irony, to conceive

2. Lawrence, who could not bear any of Hawthorne's young girls, might have been better pleased with this picture, in *Our Old Home*, of the typical British female: "I have heard a good deal of the tenacity with which English ladies retain their personal beauty to a late period of life; but (not to suggest that an American eye needs use and cultivation before it can quite appreciate the charm of English beauty at any age) it strikes me that an English lady of fifty is apt to become a creature less refined and delicate, so far as her physique goes, than anything that we Western people class under the name of woman. She has an awful ponderosity of frame, not pulpy, like the looser development of our few fat women, but massive with solid beef and streaky tallow; so that (though struggling manfully against the idea) you inevitably think of her as made up of steaks and sirloins. When she walks, her advance is elephantine. When she sits down, it is on a great round space of her Maker's footstool, where she looks as if nothing could ever move her . . . Without anything positively salient, or actively offensive, or, indeed, unjustly formidable to her neighbors, she has the effect of a seventy-four gun-ship in time of peace; for, while you assure yourself that there is no real danger, you cannot help thinking how tremendous would be her onset if pugnaciously inclined, and how futile the effort to inflict any counter-injury . . . .

"You can meet this figure in the street, and live, and even smile at the recollection. But conceive of her in a ballroom, with the bare, brawny arms that she invariably displays there, and all the other corresponding development, such as is beautiful in the maiden blossom, but a spectacle to howl at in such an over-blown cabbage rose as this . . . . I wonder whether a middle-aged husband ought to be considered as legally married to all the accretions that have overgrown the slenderness of his bride, since he led her to the altar, and which make her so much more than he ever bargained for!"

any such world, made Eliot reflect, when he was about to start *The Waste Land*, that the thinness of the novelist's milieu was owing to no lack of intellectual life, but to the fact that "it was not corrupt enough." This circumstance involved also "the difficult fact that the soil which produced him with his essential flavor is the soil which produced, just as inevitably, the environment which stunted him." What that means in the evidence furnished by *The Seven Gables* is that Hawthorne could conceive evil in the world, but not an evil world. As a result his final pages drift away into unreal complacence. * * *

# LAWRENCE SARGENT HALL

## The Social Ethic †

*The House of the Seven Gables* constitutes Hawthorne's most forthright use of American democratic philosophy as a basis for a social ethic. The theme of this romance has to do with inherited sin, the sin of aristocratic pretensions against a moral order which, in the judgment of an equalitarian like Hawthorne, calls for a truer and higher evaluation of man. For the inheritance of the Pyncheon family proves to be no more than the antagonism of the old Colonel and his world toward things democratic.

Hawthorne was a shrewd enough student of history to be aware that the Puritan society of New England had been as aristocratic in its way as the feudal society of Europe, with which he was later to have a first-hand acquaintance. He saw clearly the sharp cleavage that existed then between the various members of the social group. The servants who stood inside the entrance to the House of the Seven Gables directing one class of people to the parlor and the other to the kitchen preside likewise over the social distinctions of the whole story, separating the Pyncheons from the Maules and gentility from democracy until the very end. It is Hawthorne's symbolism at its best.

In the days of the theocracy, Hawthorne is willing to admit, there may have been some "temporary advantage" to the division between high and low and the suppression of the one by the other. Though such suppression was wrong-doing regardless of extenuating circumstances, it was a type of evil that was less apparent in the days of the Colonel than it had since become.

† From Lawrence Sargent Hall, *Hawthorne: Critic of Society*, New Haven, 1944. Pp. 160–67. Reprinted by permission of Yale University Press.

There is something so massive, stable, and almost irresistibly imposing in the exterior presentment of established rank and great possessions, that their very existence seems to give them a right to exist; at least, so excellent a counterfeit of right, that few poor and humble men have moral force enough to question it, even in their secret minds. Such is the case now, after so many ancient prejudices have been overthrown; and it was far more so in ante-Revolutionary days, when the aristocracy could venture to be proud, and the low were content to be abased.

The Colonel who perpetrated the original wickedness belonged to a world whose social ethic was imperfectly developed. This fact makes his sin more normal than that of his heirs, yet no less culpable in the eyes of Holgrave or Hawthorne, both of whom measure it by an ethical absolute without reference to temporal variants. Meanwhile, each heir who accepts the Colonel's ill-gotten gain is an accessory after the fact. In times of growing social enlightenment when the heir cannot help knowing that his ancestor violated the rights of the commoner Maule, he is the wilful recipient of stolen goods. If he would share the spoils he must share the guilt.

> For various reasons, however, and from impressions often too vaguely founded to be put on paper, the writer cherishes the belief that many, if not most, of the successive proprietors of this estate were troubled with doubts as to their moral right to hold it. Of their legal tenure there could be no question; but old Matthew Maule, it is to be feared, trode downward from his own age to a far later one, planting a heavy footstep, all the way, on the conscience of a Pyncheon. If so, we are left to dispose of the awful query, whether each inheritor of the property—conscious of wrong, and failing to rectify it—did not commit anew the great guilt of his ancestor, and incur all its original responsibilities.

It was to a consciousness of similar sin against the democratic morality, which he felt was the only true social ethic, that Hawthorne later tried to arouse the British upper classes. Democracy, like Maule, should plant "a heavy footstep" on the conscience of any aristocracy.

The social sinfulness of aristocracy became specific, took on symbolic expression for the purposes of art in the crime which the arrogant old Colonel committed in usurping the home of the commoner Maule. It became more explicit still in the Colonel's effort to appropriate for himself and his heirs a tract of land somewhere in Maine. The fate of this abortive estate is especially significant. It reveals the natural destruction by democracy of the artificial, unethical arrangements of feudalism.

But, in course of time, the territory was partly regranted to more favored individuals, and partly cleared and occupied by actual settlers. These last, if they ever heard of the Pyncheon title, would have laughed at the idea of any man's asserting a right—on the strength of mouldy parchments, signed with the faded autographs of governors and legislators long dead and forgotten—to the lands which they or their fathers had wrested from the wild hand of nature by their own sturdy toil.

The family ambition to possess such an estate is so persistent that it even haunts the ascetic daydreams of poor Hepzibah, who clings wistfully to the hope that some sort of deed may yet appear to establish arbitrarily the claim of one family in default of the rights of all those common folk who have broken, cultivated, and inhabited the land for their livelihood. There is likelihood that Hawthorne was influenced here by Rousseau, whose works he had read extensively during June, July, and August of 1848. The following passage from *The Social Contract* can conceivably have had a strong conditioning effect on his thinking in connection with the land in Waldo County, Maine.

In general, to authorize the right of the first occupant upon any territory, the following conditions are necessary: first, that the land shall never have been occupied; second, that only such a quantity be occupied as will be necessary for subsistence; third, that it be taken possession of not by an empty ceremony but by labor and cultivation, for this is the only sign of ownership which, in default of legal title, should be respected by others.

By rendering the Pyncheon claim to such territory a snare and a delusion, Hawthorne signified the baselessness of the pretensions of gentility and its gradual absorption in the morally inevitable progress of society toward democracy.

But the Pyncheon family itself (like the illusion of property upon which still depended much of the pride that was the mainstay of their spirit) gradually became more and more attenuated as the falseness of their position was made clearer by the great movement of society toward the equalitarian ideal. In fact, by the time the story proper opens, the process by which their proudly accumulated mass of possessions (spiritual and material) "shall be scattered abroad in its original atoms" is nearly complete. Their coveted estate is occupied by common people who wrest a living from it with manual labor. One of their scions has married "a young woman of no family or property," died and left as only heir to the Pyncheon prejudices and delusions a daughter of democracy.

There are but two developments left before the final absorption of the family can be achieved; the working out of each of these is the schedule for the story. By marrying Holgrave, Phoebe must merge, under the healthy and joyous auspices of equalitarianism, the blood of the old Colonel with the blood of the commoner whom he wronged. Thus she will expiate the old social guilt by dissipating the false distinctions that underlay it. Simultaneously the grim pride of the Pyncheons, which has erected as its monument the House of the Seven Gables and maintained the house as a token of inviolateness and aloofness for generations, must be punctured and all its vital juices drawn off until there remains only a monstrous emptiness.

The undemocratic pride of the Pyncheons first manifested itself as a sin against society when the Colonel usurped the land of Matthew Maule, the commoner, on which to build a mansion to house his ill-founded pretensions. A self-destructive element in his behavior is implicit in the legend, which attributes his death to the fact that by his conduct he drew on his own head the curse of old Maule. Allegorically considered, Maule's curse is the moral sentence of society which a man inevitably brings on himself in sinning against his fellow. If we read from the legend, then, the sin of pride may be seen to contain the germ of its own annihilation.[1] And if we translate from the legend to the fact in terms of the action of the romance, we shall further see that it is the factor of isolation in the pride of the Pyncheons which automatically effects their ruin.

Like the chickens in the yard who pointedly resemble them, the Pyncheons had "existed too long in their distinct variety." In this parable is contained all the significance of an overweening self-interest operative within the carefully prescribed limits of one family for generation after generation. Deterioration is obvious in the blighted spinster who, with her hens and her brother, still clings to the last shreds of gentility.

Uncle Venner, the commoner, once remarked to Hepzibah that her family "never had the name of being an easy and agreeable set of folks. There was no getting close to them," he said. In the absence of a claim to anything more tangible except the house itself, this is the only inheritance of the last two inhabitants of Colonel Pyncheon's mansion. " 'Miss Hepzibah,' " observed Holgrave, " 'by secluding herself from society has lost all true relation with it, and is, in fact, dead. . . .' " "She had dwelt too much alone,—too long in the Pyncheon House—until her very brain was impregnated with the dry-rot of its timbers." "In her grief and wounded pride, Hepzibah had spent her life in divesting herself of friends; she had wilfully cast off the support which God

1. The fact that Judge Pyncheon is supposed to have ruined Clifford furthers the allegory of the family self-destruction.

has ordained his creatures to need from one another. . . ." Over against her gaunt and decadent individualism is set the contrasting figure of lively Phoebe, "a fair parallel between new Plebeianism and old Gentility." It is she who brings life into the dark house and hearts of Clifford and Hepzibah, and takes it away with her when she leaves.

But it is impossible in the present state of society even for the dark old sanctuary of Pyncheon gentility to preserve its insularity intact.

> Let us behold, in poor Hepzibah, the immemorial lady,—two hundred years old, on this side of the water, and thrice as many on the other,—with her antique portraits, pedigrees, coats of arms, records and traditions, in Pyncheon Street, under the Pyncheon Elm, and the Pyncheon House, where she has spent all her days,—reduced now, in that very house, to be the huckstress of a cent-shop.

The opening of the cent-shop to let the outside world into the stifling interior of the secluded house is a symbol of the salutary virtues of the Maule forces, or the forces of democracy, in contrast to the moribund condition of the Pyncheons. "In this republican country, amid the fluctuating waves of our social life," wrote Hawthorne, "somebody is always at the drowning point." The Pyncheons were drowning in their own separateness, unable to draw the breath of life because they had so entirely shut themselves away from it. The cent-shop is a kind of pulmonary connection from humanity to the almost strangled existence of the House of the Seven Gables.

> Hitherto, the life blood has been gradually chilling in your veins as you sat aloof, within your circle of gentility, while the rest of the world was fighting out its battle with one kind of necessity or another. Henceforth, you will at least have the sense of healthy and natural effort for a purpose, and of lending your strength— be it great or small—to the united struggle of mankind. This is success,—all the success that anybody meets with!

Holgrave was right; Hepzibah did undergo "the invigorating breath of a fresh outward atmosphere, after the long torpor and monotonous seclusion of her life." But the experience was transitory. She retained her aristocratic arrogance, and inwardly despised the people by whose pennies she hoped to be sustained. The democracy she still repudiated failed to provide for her because she tried to take it in on her own conditions, to pervert it to her own undemocratic ends. Hepzibah, "the recluse of half a lifetime," proved pathetically incapable of merging with humanity in the common struggle for existence. It is Phoebe who takes over the cent-shop.

The childish, ineffectual Clifford exemplifies if possible a worse maladjustment than his sister. He has what remains of the exquisite nature that Hawthorne describes as "always selfish in its essence." A person of his stamp "can always be pricked more acutely through his sense of the beautiful and harmonious than through his heart." Had his character been allowed an opportunity for full natural development his taste or aesthetic temper might have been so perfectly cultivated as to have "completely eaten out or filed away his affections," thus making even more complete his isolation from the human heart by which men live.

But Clifford too had moments in which he felt the regenerative urge to burst from the inner prison of himself into the stream of life. "With a shivering repugnance at the idea of personal contact with the world, a powerful impulse still seized on Clifford, whenever the rush and roar of the human tide grew strongly audible to him." On one such occasion he was watching from a window of the House of the Seven Gables when a political parade went by in the street below. It seemed "one broad mass of existence,— one great life,—one collected body of mankind, with a vast, homogeneous spirit animating it—a mighty river of life, massive in its tide, and black with mystery, and, out of its depths, calling to the kindred depth within him." So strong was the influence upon him to join in the march of his fellow men that it affected him as a sort of primal madness, and he could "hardly be restrained from plunging into the surging stream of human sympathies." He was impelled, Hawthorne suggests, by "a natural magnetism, tending towards the great centre of humanity." Breathlessly he remarked to the terrified Hepzibah that had he taken the plunge and survived it, it would have made him another man. Hawthorne interpolates again by saying that he "required to take a deep, deep plunge into the ocean of human life, and to sink down and be covered by its profoundness, and then to emerge, sobered, invigorated, restored to the world and to himself." In his desire shortly after this incident to join the villagers going to church on Sunday, he displayed a "similar yearning to renew the broken links of brotherhood with his kind." Yet he and Hepzibah were unable to go through with it once they stood on the front step in plain sight of the whole town and all its citizens. They retreated into the gloom of the house which was the historical and material symbol of the isolation of their hearts. "For, what other dungeon is so dark as one's own heart! What jailer so inexorable as one's self!"

Living arrangements like those of the later Pyncheons, as Hawthorne noted elsewhere, "assumed the form both of hypocrisy and exaggeration, by being inherited from the example and precept of other human beings, and not from an original and spiritual source." [2] The point Hawthorne is trying to make is the same one which Thoreau attempted to demonstrate by his life, and Emerson by his philosophy: namely, the moral necessity for all men to establish—as Emerson put it in *Nature*—"an original relation to the universe."

In one form or another this idea had dogged the subtler American democratic thinkers since Jefferson and Tom Paine insisted that each generation not only should be able but should be made to set up its own laws and contracts. Paine thought that to escape the infelicitous prejudices of the past it was necessary for men to think as though they were the first men who thought. We have already seen from the English romance that Hawthorne felt about his own generation as Holgrave feels about his. They must slough off the second-hand arrangements of the defunct past and work out their own relation to the world. This was their responsibility according to the best theories of democratic individualism. To fail in it as the Pyncheon progeny had was "sinister to the intellect, and sinister to the heart." It inevitably brought about "miserable distortions of the moral nature."

Thus the selfish individualism of a family so jealously guarding its interests through successive epochs, in defiance of newer trends and mores to which men at large are susceptible, is shown to be self-destructive. By preserving Colonel Pyncheon's proud egocentricity, the heirs cherished the very corrosive evil which eventually ate away their humanity. " 'The truth is,' " says Hawthorne's spokesman Holgrave, " 'that, once in every half-century, at longest, a family should be merged into the great, obscure mass of humanity, and forget all about its ancestors.' " Only in this way is it possible to avoid the arrogance which represents a sin against society, morally punishable by a fearful and hopeless ostracism.

This ostracism is the real legacy which Colonel Pyncheon left to his redoubtable progeny. "A man will commit almost any wrong," said Clifford, "—he will heap up an immense pile of wickedness, as hard as granite, and which will weigh as heavily upon his soul, to eternal ages,—only to build a great gloomy, dark chambered mansion, for himself to die in, and for his posterity to be miserable in." The dark chambered mansion is the human heart in isolation.

Maule's curse—the moral sentence passed by society—is that the Pyncheons shall be destroyed by their sin of selfishness

---

2. These comments occur in the sketch "Main Street," which was first published in Elizabeth Peabody's *Aesthetic Papers*, 1849, about a year before *The House of the Seven Gables* was begun.

against him and his class. But they shall meet destruction under the special and significant circumstances which are the consequences of their sin against the commoner. They shall ultimately be destroyed by the solitude which they built for themselves at Maule's expense in the shape of the House of the Seven Gables, where the Colonel died alone at the beginning of the story and where (reincarnated in the character of the Judge) he returns to die alone at the end.

A few hours earlier while impotent, friendless old Hepzibah cast futilely about, like someone in a nightmare, for succor from the wicked Judge, it seemed "as if the house stood in a desert, or, by some spell, was made invisible to those who dwelt around, or passed beside it." Here is the tragic crux of the story. This is the bitter atonement which the family has made for the guilt which it wilfully assumed for so many generations. And a few hours later—"The gloomy and desolate old house, deserted of life, and with awful Death sitting sternly in its solitude, was *the emblem of many a human heart*, which, nevertheless, is compelled to hear the thrill and echo of the world's gayety around it." The House is Hawthorne's master symbol of isolation. It stands for the spiritual condition of those who by their hostility to democracy sin against what he believed to be the true moral order, and as a result become evanescent through their utter separateness from mankind.

# CLARK GRIFFITH

## Substance and Shadow: Language and Meaning in *The House of the Seven Gables* †

In the opening pages of *The House of the Seven Gables* when Hawthorne first touches on the history of the Pyncheon family, he carefully notes how over the years the Pyncheon personality has assumed two widely varying shapes. Old Colonel Pyncheon himself typifies one distinct grouping within the family. Founder of the line and guilty of its original sin, he was a man of "iron energy," a schemer endowed with common sense "as massive and hard as blocks of granite," a practical man less interested in tradition than in providing his descendants with a "stable basis" and a "stately roof to shelter them." But while cer-

† From Clark Griffith, "Substance and Shadow: Language and Meaning in *The House of the Seven Gables*," *Modern Philology*, LI (Feb., 1954), 187–95. Copyright 1954 by the University of Chicago Press; reprinted by permission.

tain of his progeny have at intervals inherited something akin to the Colonel's "hard, keen sense," other Pyncheons seem bereft entirely of the foresight and tough forcefulness characterizing their ancestor. They tend to be ineffectual weaklings, "sluggish and dependent," given to vagaries of thought and action. Unfitted for a life of practical affairs, they brood endlessly over the past—in particular, over the "mouldy parchments, signed with faded autographs" which represent the "dead and forgotten" claims to an enormous land grant in Maine. And although, as Hawthorne says, these traditional titles are "impalpable," signify an "absurd delusion" and a "shadowy hope," still many a later Pyncheon has dwelt upon them because he finds "nothing more solid . . . to cherish."

Basically, these descriptive comments are intended to distinguish sharply between two sorts of characters; and both the purpose and the full consequences of the differentiation are matters to which we shall return. At this point, however, let us do no more than observe the linguistic, the actual word, differences contained in the passages. On the one hand, there are words like *iron, energy, massive, hard, granite, stable, stately.* Each connotes strength or vitality, the solidly real, the ponderous, the pre-eminently tangible. We might well refer to all of them as "substance words." Then, set over against these terms are such words as *sluggishness, mouldy, faded, dead, impalpable, delusion, shadowy.* Here the connotations suggest weakness or decay, dark unreality, the unsubstantial, the intangible. So plain, indeed, is the contrast that the second group may appropriately be designated "shadow words."

Substance words and shadow words. Throughout the remainder of the book, this verbal pattern, introduced at the outset, recurs and expands, proliferates into new terms, accumulates a greater symbolic richness. Ultimately the differences involved, extending beyond a mere contrast in human behavior, come to embrace other, more complex distinctions. By spelling out the several functions of this linguistic scheme, I hope to show that, far from being aesthetically slipshod or thematically unsatisfying, *The House of the Seven Gables* is, in the main, among Hawthorne's most effectively executed works of art, one in which exposition, symbolism, irony, drama, and meaning are alike subsumed under the far-reaching implications of substance and shadow.

## I

The most readily apparent example of Hawthorne's language pattern derives from his continuing technique of characterization. In the contemporary generation which occupies the foreground of the *House,* only three authentic Pyncheons remain. Each possesses in generous measure one or another of the traits prefigured in the family's summarized history. For example, we are insistently urged to regard Jaffrey Pyncheon as the substantial Colonel's substantial counterpart: as a "weighty citizen," a "solid specimen," a man driven by a "hard, relentless will," and one made offensively massive by the "animal substance" in his face. At the opposite extreme there is the recessive Clifford, with his "indistinct shadow of human utterance," his weak facial expressions that "waver and glimmer," his naturally torpid sluggishness which suffering has intensified rather than originated. Here, also, is Hepzibah, very nearly as tremulously weak as her brother, even more given than he to feeding upon the "shadowy food" and "airily magnificent" hopes of aristocratic pretensions.

In all, these terms or close cognates are repeated dozens of times in connection with each character. Yet their frequent reappearance is neither a tedious mannerism nor a flaw in Hawthorne's creative method. On the contrary, the two clusters of purely descriptive words prove to be indispensable to the total meaning of the *House*, and, as can immediately be seen, they serve as the basic distinction out of which subtler dissimilarities—especially those of a scenic and symbolic nature—quickly emerge.

Scenically, the book is somewhat unequally divided between the interior of the house, together with the dark and decaying garden, and its exterior, principally the street running along before it. Both scenes, we soon recognize, were designed to recapitulate the distinguishing features of the characters whom they contain. Overspread by a dreary, unrelieved gloom, the inner house is little more than a collection of shadows, vaguely, almost abstractly, described. And Hawthorne's various references to it—to the chill, the stagnation, the long lapse of mortal life within—are obviously intended to complement the moral and emotional disintegration of its inhabitants. As Hepzibah and Clifford acknowledge, this ghostly interior is not simply an encircling dungeon: like an organic extension of themselves, it has come to stand for—to be— their dismal and haunted hearts. Furthermore, the scenes outside the house, though far warmer and more real, nevertheless represent Jaffrey's physical background and are made to reflect something of his solid substantiality. If Hawthorne writes at great length of Judge Pyncheon's heavy, sultry, dog-day smile, he is hardly less voluble on the subject of the hot sunlight in the streets. Occasional references to the "'hard, keen'" business practices of the townspeople suggest Jaffrey's "vast ability in grasping . . . and appropriating"; indeed, the entire stress upon the palpable realities without reminds us that Jaffrey, more than most, eschews "all airy matter, and never mistakes a shadow for a substance."

Still it will scarcely do to establish too narrowly either of these scene-character identifications. Shortly after the book opens, both the inner and the outer house acquire a metaphorical as well as a literal significance; and when this happens, the verbal scheme broadens beyond descriptive matters and is reintroduced as symbolism. Consider the street. Although we are once or twice informed that it is only a quiet lane, Hawthorne's actual descriptions, abounding in masses of heavy surface detail, generally belie this picture. In fact, the sharply etched street scenes more often suggest a place of ceaseless turmoil—of processions and tradesmen, carts and omnibuses swarming constantly past. Hence the impression grows that, while on certain occasions the street may be a secluded byway, at other times it becomes a comprehensive symbol of the brisk nineteenth-century world. Here in the midst of robust housewives and fiercely energetic railroad trains, the present is a tangible, immediately felt reality. And when, by contrast, we turn back to the inner house, it is to come at once under the dark shadow of the past.

Nor is this so solely because Hepzibah dreams of faded gentility and Clifford of his wasted youth. Rather, an explicit past is symbolically embodied in several particular shadows which Hawthorne deftly singles out from the surrounding gloom: a chair (black with age), a mirror (shaded, shadowy), a map (dim and dusty), a portrait (faded, dusky), a harpsichord (black and coffin-like). One and all, these are the worthless heirlooms of the Pyncheon dynasty, relics rooted like the moldy parchments and illegible autographs in the very origins of the family.

They are not, however, meant merely to portray the past. Just as time and guilt are closely linked throughout the *House*, so these objects, converted into time images, look backward to earlier centuries and simultaneously point up the Pyncheons' sins. The portrait and ancestral chair were properties of the old Colonel. Really an elaborate drawing of the Maine estate, the map exemplifies the Pyncheons' greed, their hereditary yearning for wealth to which they have long since lost any title. The harpsichord belonged to Alice Pyncheon, whose overweening pride typified another family trait. Out of the dim mirror there flock the ghosts of all dead Pyncheons, each stamped with the mark of personal guilt. In short, the principal shadows inside the house are associated with moral degeneracy; and making this association, we come upon the most provocative of Hawthorne's symbolic distinctions. Shadow, the past, the inner house—all combine to symbolize the tragedy of human sin, while the substantial, contemporaneous world without provides a warmly optimistic atmosphere in which it seems possible to conceal this tragedy or to banish it or to live unaware that it even exists. Such, in turn, are the outlooks, the specious outlooks, imputed to Jaffrey, Holgrave, and Phoebe.

At first glance, to be sure, any conceptual frame flexible enough to include these characters, particularly Phoebe and Jaffrey, will seem highly improbable. Nevertheless, all belong to the world outside the house and are presented in terms of its key images. Each, for different reasons, resists the profounder implications of the inner house. As he deals with their respective states of "innocence," Hawthorne's language, turned now to symbolizing moral positions, remains remarkably self-consistent. Likening Jaffrey's entire life to a "tall and stately edifice," he writes that the Judge's sin lurks deep inside, a "corpse, half decayed, and still decaying . . . with the cobwebs festooned over its forgotten door." But citizen that he is of the outer world, Jaffrey never looks inward. To him, as he bluntly reminds Hepzibah, the past is sheerest nonsense. Around his own impurity he has arrayed the most imposing of exteriors—a sunny, benevolent smile and the "splendid halls" and "high cornices" betokening a guiltless life.

Now despite the signal differences between her and the Judge, it is noteworthy that Phoebe, too, is regularly associated with images of sunlight and substantiality; [1] and when closely examined, they turn out to be not simply the marks of her warm, generous affections. They symbolize as well the fact that her early responses to the seven-gabled house curiously parallel Jaffrey's attitude toward his life. Possessing none save the values of the outer world, Phoebe is honestly unprepared to recognize the presence of a "decaying corpse" within. Significantly, she knows little concerning the family's past, has forgotten most of what she once was told, remains profoundly incurious about Clifford's identity, Jaffrey's motives, the meaning of Maule's curse. What Phoebe's "real substance" lacks, as Hawthorne sometimes tries to show, is the modifying influence of tragic insight. While she fails as a character —fails because Hawthorne is only partially capable of demonstrating her maturation—Phoebe is, like Donatello or the bridal pair at Merrymount, an innocent whose defect is her very innocence.

To a considerable extent, therefore, Jaffrey the hypocrite and the guileless Phoebe are less representatives of any particular time than they are traditional character types in Hawthorne's writing; their relation to the outer house is a part of the general symbolic plan. Holgrave, on the other hand, does personify the distinctly modern world beyond the house and, it seems likely, the easy, fal-

---

1. To cite but a few of the many references, Phoebe is a "ray of sunshine"; she is "real! Holding her hand, you felt something; a tender something; a substance, and a warm one"; she is "a substance that could walk on earth." Considering the consistency of Haw- thorne's language scheme, we must, I think, suppose that these descriptive terms, applied equally to Jaffrey and Phoebe, were meant to suggest their common kinship with the real world beyond the house and with the values of that world.

lacious ethical perfectionism of the nineteenth century. Like this world of outward forms, he is a thoroughly externalized individual, a figure of many surfaces, forever "putting off one exterior and snatching up another to be soon shifted for a third." Moreover, his *social* radicalism, the subject of much critical comment, is only named, never fully analyzed; in terms of Hawthorne's imagery, it is actually the daguerreotypist's *moral* intransigency which is made to seem important. He rails not against economic injustices, that is, but against the past, that "dead corpse" which wastes the strength of the present. Loving " 'nothing mouldy,' " he deplores the old house with " 'its dark low-studded rooms . . . and sordidness.' " Were this possible, he would purify (and the verb is *purify*, not *transform*) the house with fire until only its ashes remained. The truth is that Holgrave, whose hypnotic powers imply his complete materialism,[2] would exorcise the same shadow wilfully concealed by Jaffrey and as yet unknown to Phoebe. Misguidedly intent upon abolishing evil, he is a forerunner of the materialistic purifiers at Blithedale.

Thus from simple, repetitious beginnings in the exposition of the novel, Hawthorne's language pattern passes over into symbolism, enriches the meaning of the time sequence, defines moral attitudes, and comes full circle to shed additional light on persons and places previously described. At the same time, the two groupings of words are further enlarged through their appearance in both the irony and the drama of the narrative.

## II

As much as *The Scarlet Letter*, the *House* is based upon irony. One difference, however, is that, where in the earlier book an irony of situation was emphasized (Dimmesdale's preaching to Hester, the community's celebration of Chillingworth's healing powers), Hawthorne has now turned to an irony of language, at its best more accurately termed "paradox." Again and again we encounter passages in which small linguistic byplays precisely restate Hawthorne's largest themes: Hepzibah ignores the "hard, little pellets" of Uncle Venner's advice while she builds castles in the air; Clifford's delicate soap bubbles burst against Jaffrey's massive face; the sunlight appropriated by Jaffrey for his smile also accentuates his dark depravity; his great wealth is composed of "solid unrealities." But the two richest and most effectively sustained ironies in the book work out at various places where those who take the greatest pride in their substantiality are reduced to

2. To the extent that he is a hypnotist, tempted to exert hypnotic powers over Phoebe, Holgrave is, of course, the counterpart of Westervelt in *The Blithedale Romance*. Westervelt is to be the complete materialist, the completely substantial man: "He was altogether earthy, worldly, made for time and its gross objects, and incapable—except by a sort of reflection from other minds—of so much as one spiritual idea."

shadows and where qualities heretofore seen as shadows are revealed as the prime realities.

In connection with the first, notice the old Colonel himself. If he thought to leave behind a stately roof, what in fact he did bequeath was a sin to "darkly overshadow [his] posterity." For all his "rough heartiness" and "great animal development," he has later come to represent merely a "dusky . . . frown . . '. lingering in the passage-way." Even in his portrait the "physical outline and substance" seem "darkening away," leaving only the sinful character of the man "to be brought out in a kind of spiritual relief." And toward the close of the narrative when Pyncheon ghosts flock through the magic mirror, there comes first the Colonel, "a thing of no substance," still re-enacting its old crime but doing so now with the wave of an ineffectual hand.

Quite in keeping with his resemblance to the Colonel, Jaffrey presently undergoes an identical metamorphosis. Although he never mistakes a shadow for a substance and does not " 'belong to the dreaming class of men,' " the Judge would violate Clifford's tranquillity for the sake of ancient papers which have no value and are so old and dusty that they all but crumble to the touch. Consequently, it is Jaffrey whom the moldy parchments, after all, mislead, for, as Hepzibah says, he " 'took hold of a dream as if it were real. He died with this delusion in his mind.' " Furthermore, once Jaffrey enters the house, proceeds beyond the shop door and into the inmost rooms, he does literally become a shadow, destroyed, so to speak, by the symbolic past— by Maule's legendary prophecy—and made to blend slowly, subtly, into the pervasive darkness. There is, unfortunately, rather little to be said for the tone of forced playfulness in the ensuing "wake." Yet Hawthorne's selection of details is reasonably successful when the images ironically contrast Jaffrey's love for solid forms (the ticking timepiece, the heavy cane, the references to food and wealth) with his present formlessness; when they are used to taunt the "great animal" for having fallen into an "unaccountable lethargy"; or when, at the end, they are maneuvered into showing both the sturdy, benevolent Judge and his shapeless apparition wearing a frown "as Black as the ancestral one."

What these ironic transformations suggest, of course, is that in the last analysis shadow may well outweigh substance. And since, as we have observed, shadow symbolizes sin, the case could hardly be otherwise. For evil, to repeat the oldest and truest of critical commonplaces, is the ultimate reality in Hawthorne's work, the inescapable part of every man's heritage which none can disguise or avoid or hope to argue away. Here where the initial criminal act lies buried in a dark past, so remote from the palpable present, guilt may appear to be an airy nothing. Yet it nonetheless continues and endures. If, as Holgrave protests, the past is dead, it likewise rests upon the present " 'like a giant's . . . body.' " Elsewhere Hawthorne comments on the greater ease of transmitting sin than of bequeathing tangible properties; and he dryly wonders that a "thumb's bigness" of Jaffrey's evil should overbalance in the scales a "mass of things not evil." Plainly, sin and the past and shadow symbolizing sin and the past are endowed with a power paradoxically at odds with their immateriality. In the *House* they function either to discipline the individual or, should he prove untractable, to destroy him. Out of the two processes, the superimposing of shadow over substantiality, evolves much of Hawthorne's drama.

Jaffrey, concerned to the last with external phenomena, simply becomes the decaying corpse he so long concealed. But the others symbolically identified with the exterior of the house pass inside to be instructed by its shadows. Halfway through the narrative the inner gloom touches Phoebe, disclosing to her truths deeper and more meaningful than those revealed " 'in broad day light or . . . in the ruddy light of a cheerful fire.' " Thereafter, her temperament is never again so unfailingly sunny. Her eyes look darker: their shadowiness is the token of her larger understanding. In Hawthorne's words, she is now "less girlish, but more a woman." Somewhat more plausible because better realized artistically, Holgrave's dramatic transformation is couched in a similar language. During the third long interview with Phoebe (chap. xiv), the daguerreotypist's hatred for the past and for the house is strangely subdued; his hard exterior seems mellowed. Although his pledge to lend Hepzibah and Clifford " 'whatever aid I can' " remains equivocal, he all but renounces his role as aloof spectator and moral purist. There is, he concedes, some "shallow gayety" in his own life which he has only commenced to comprehend.

Complete self-discovery is deferred until Holgrave, after coming upon Jaffrey's body, must spend a " 'dark, cold, miserable hour' " in the house alone. Then he first perceives the terrible substantiality of guilt. Then, too, he experiences a new gush of sympathy—expressed through his now unmistakable desire to protect Clifford —and a fresh insight into Phoebe's " 'hope, warmth, and joy.' " Notably, he declares his love for Phoebe inside the house where the shadows are darkest. His later wish—so patently absurd when taken literally—that the Judge had constructed his country house of stone rather than of wood is surely to be interpreted as Hawthorne's clumsy way of demonstrating how Holgrave has accepted the unassailable reality of the past. We note, in any case, that he utters the statement while standing directly beneath Colonel Pyncheon's faded portrait, then turns in the next breath to a comment on the immutability of the Colonel's old wrong.

Properly understood, then, the inner house and all it represents will chasten the individual, teach him charity and love, impress upon him the essential fact that sin is at once indestructible and the true basis for brotherhood. But there are dangers within as well as without. To dwell exclusively among the foul shadows of human depravity is to behold only their dark ugliness, never their power for ennobling. It is a life of isolation; and by living thus secludedly, Hepzibah and Clifford have aggravated and perpetuated the original sin, set it in motion anew. Accordingly, they must seek for their redemption in the outer world. Hepzibah, having spent her life proudly denying kinship with all others, "needs a walk along the noon day street to keep her sane," Clifford, his affections eaten away, requires restoration "to the world and to himself." The attempts of these two dim shadows to reestablish contact with the solid substantiality of the streets constitutes another aspect of the dramatic unfolding in the *House*.

Though both draw strength from Phoebe's warm and tender substance, there is no lasting salvation here. In the darkening garden Clifford still watches a dreary shadow break the light of Maule's well, still turns mournfully toward the sunlight and the street and cries out for his lost happiness. Once on a brilliantly warm Sabbath he and Hepzibah determine to leave the house for church, only to return immediately into an interior which now seems tenfold more dismal than before. Again, Clifford, shuddering and pale, is forcibly restrained from leaping through the arched window into the surging stream of life below. But following Jaffrey's death, the spell is temporarily broken. With a corpse behind them —and the image is important—the two recluses flee the house. Their flight becomes a striking instance of the language pattern translated into symbolic drama.

As if by instinct, Clifford leads Hepzibah to a train, one symbol, we noticed, of the vigorous external world and a symbol employed elsewhere in Hawthorne (particularly in "The Celestial Railroad") to express escape from sin and human responsibilities. Outside the cars, the rushing, varied landscape suggests again the panoramic street; inside, by the same token, Clifford suddenly espouses a confused jumble of theories which exactly duplicate the moral doctrines identified with that street. Like Jaffrey, he would ignore the shadow within (" 'Let such things slip aside. Here we are, in the world' "), and the wish is intensely ironic, since this particular shadow *is* Jaffrey. In another moment Clifford echoes Holgrave, calls for the destruction of roof and hearthstone and the evil they secrete, praises mesmerism as an instrument of human reform. His remarks gradually grow more frenzied until a fellow-passenger, "bringing his gimlet-eye to a point on Clifford," impatiently protests, " 'I can't see through you.' " At just this moment, however, the train reaches a way station, dreary, solitary, standing near a "venerably black" and apparently deserted farmhouse. Impulsively leaving the coach Clifford replies with a telling allusion: " 'No, I'll be bound you can't. . . . And yet, my dear sir, I am as transparent as the water of Maule's well!' "

Almost certainly this ambiguous exchange is fraught with symbolic undertones. Clifford's solid opacity, so oddly out of keeping with the ghostlike qualities formerly attributed to him, is, I should judge, the mark of his having entered the real world in the wrongest possible way. Plunging abruptly out of the house, he, too, readily acquired Jaffrey's ponderous indifference and Holgrave's heavy contempt for what lay behind. For a brief time he became wholly externalized, substance untempered by shadow. But only briefly, as the succeeding references make abundantly clear. Sin and the past are inexorable, and at the height of his liberation shadow—darkness, dreariness, the black house, the shadowy recesses of Maule's well—reclaims Clifford, just as it altered Jaffrey and Holgrave, whose language he began to speak. Instantly, the "wild effervescence of his mood . . . entirely subsided. A powerful excitement had given him energy and vivacity. Its operation over, he forthwith began to sink."

Nevertheless, the excursion has not failed. Even while the train rushes away from them, Hepzibah and Clifford are, like Phoebe and Holgrave, moving toward the achievement of a proper moral balance. Here on the rain-swept platform, Hepzibah, after failing twice when confined to the house, is finally able to pray.

### III

The human heart to be allegorized as a cavern; at the entrance there is sunshine, and flowers growing about it. You step within, but a short distance, and begin to find yourself surrounded with a terrible gloom, and monsters of divers kinds. . . . You are bewildered and wander long without hope. At last a light strikes upon you. You peep towards it, and find yourself in a region that seems, in some sort, to reproduce the flowers and sunny beauty of the entrance, but all perfect.[3]

The shortcoming of *The House of the Seven Gables* most frequently cited is, understandably enough, its plot of feud and reconciliation. Not only is this situation strained, hackneyed, and, as Austin Warren has remarked, a tiresome nuisance;[4] much more seriously, it seems forever threatening to rob the moral drama of

3.  *The American Notebooks by Nathaniel Hawthorne,* ed. Randal Stewart (New Haven, 1932), p. 98.

4.  *Rage for Order: Essays in Criticism* (Chicago, 1948), p. 99.

any slightest significance. If we are to presume that a kind of blanket amnesty is obtained through the marriage of Phoebe and Holgrave (Pyncheon and Maule), then our belief in the regenerative capacities of sin and, most especially, in a personal struggle for atonement is instantly negated. Freed by a trick, a purely mechanical plotting device, every character save the dead Jaffrey sallies forth from the dark, sin-ridden house. Guilt is painlessly transcended by the marriage vows. Hawthorne has sacrificed the moral depths of the better tales and of *The Scarlet Letter* for a trivial coincidence, a case of concealed identity, and a happy ending which would do no great credit to the sentimental novelists whom he despised.

But is this an accurate presumption, a just estimate of the book? Actually, a close consideration of the text indicates how remarkably little attention is paid to the continuing antipathies of Maules toward Pyncheons. Whether or not Hawthorne originally intended this, the specific quarrel serves as point of departure for a study of generalized guilt and then is itself thrust swiftly and decisively into the background. Always keenly aware of the Pyncheons' sins, we nonetheless tend to lose sight of their injured victims; they so far slipped Hawthorne's own mind, apparently, that he was obliged to resort to an awkward, obviously contrived flashback (chap. xiii) in order to reintroduce them. Hence it seems permissible to shift away from the plot and to look for the meaning of the *House* in its pervasive symbolism rather than in its slight, superficial story. My feeling is that, far more than a suitable redress for the Maules, the crucial moral test in the book is posed by the dreary inner house.

Symbolically, this dark interior resembles the forest of temptation through which Dimmesdale wandered on his way to eventual confession. Or it is like the catacombs in *The Marble Faun*, where, as Hawthorne was afterward to write, "all men must descend if they would know anything beyond the surface and illusive pleasures of existence." Or, in what is perhaps the happiest analogy, it is akin to the figure of a heart cavern sketched out by Hawthorne in one of his journal entries.[5] Before its door, as before the cavern, there are flowers and sunlight, seemingly substantial, but actually artificial—as artificial as Jaffrey's feigned innocence, Phoebe's untutored naïveté, Holgrave's unrealistic reforms, Clifford's wild mood in the train. Inside the house, as within the cavern, are hideous shadows of "divers kinds," terribly

5. It is interesting to note that Hawthorne once or twice uses a heart figure to describe the inner house: "So much of mankind's varied experience had passed there . . . that the very timbers were oozy, as with the moisture of a heart. It was itself like a great human heart." He also comments on how the darkness of the interior falls over Clifford's face "as if the shadow of a cavern or dungeon had come over it."

real, but also dreadfully distorted, even as Hepzibah and Clifford are twisted beyond all resemblance to their fellow-beings and as the roses in the Pyncheon garden are blighted by a rotting mold. But at the far end of the cavern, Hawthorne added, there lay "a region that seems in some sort to reproduce the flowers and sunny beauty of the entrance, but all perfect." And, however weakly uninspired the concluding pages of *The House of the Seven Gables* prove to be, the great bulk of the narrative would suggest that Hawthorne meant to present this region at its close.

For as we have seen, to pass into the house is necessary; yet the human heart decays when it lingers there. To pass out of the house is necessary; yet the heart is hardened when it abandons those inmost meanings which the house contains. But to pass *into* and *through* and then *out* of the house, as Phoebe and Holgrave and Hepzibah and Clifford ultimately do—herein lies the correct moral balance and, therefore, the way toward redemption. It is to see the Pyncheons' blackest weeds blossom into the flowers of Eden. It is to hear a strong note of joy struck on Alice Pyncheon's dusky harpsichord. Above all, as Hawthorne's language shows, it is to seize upon the wisdom that true reality and the truly compassionate heart are neither entirely substance nor entirely shadow but an inextricable compound of them both.

# RUDOLPH VON ABELE

## Holgrave's Curious Conversion †

*The House of the Seven Gables* is the only one of Hawthorne's major writings of which it *might* be said that it is "comic," in that the conflict it encloses between the Pyncheon family and the world *appears* susceptible of resolution. Whether this is actually so or not makes a neat problem in interpretation. On the surface the last scene is nothing but comedy: the ogre Jeffrey Pyncheon is dead, the houses of Maule and Pyncheon — unlike those of Montague and Capulet—are finally cemented by the power of love, a great and ancient wrong is "righted," and everybody rolls off in a green barouche to the late Judge's country acres, while the chorus, to an accompaniment given out *andante affetuoso* by the wraith of Alice Pyncheon upon her harpsi-

† From Rudolph Von Abele, "Holgrave's Curious Conversion," *The Death of the Artist: A Study of Hawthorne's Disintegration*, The Hague, 1955. Pp. 58–69. Copyright by Martinus Nijhoff, Publishers of The Hague; reprinted by permission of Martinus Nijhoff.

chord, makes the comment, "Pretty good business, pretty good business!" The tableau is in spirit if in nothing else not unlike that of the close of Artemus Ward's version of the "Osawatomie Brown" shows:

> Tabloo—Old Brown on a platform, pintin upards, the staige lited up with red fire. Goddiss of Liberty also on, platform, pintin upards. A dutchman in the orkestry warbles on a base drum. Curtin falls. Moosic by the band.

And Sophia Hawthorne, to whom he read the manuscript of the romance, wrote of it: "There is unspeakable grace and beauty in the conclusion, throwing back upon the sterner tragedy of the commencement an ethereal light, and a dear home-loveliness and satisfaction." Whether she interpreted the conclusion—or the book, for that matter, as a whole—properly, is certainly open to question; but there is no doubt that superficially taken the last pages do sound like this.

The pivot of this final scene is the abrupt "conversion" of Holgrave, the last surviving Maule, from a bearded, peripatetic and enthusiastic reformer to a settled and weary conservative—in part through the yeasty work of his love for Phoebe Pyncheon, but also, one imagines, in part through the influence of the fortune into most of which he is destined to come if he marries her. But one finds it impossible to accept this "conversion" at face value: it comes much too neatly, and is scarcely prepared for in the body of the book. And as a matter of fact, this is no trivial affair, inasmuch as the significance of the entire book hangs on how this "transformation" is regarded.

This is hinted at, though not very plainly, by a trivial detail in Hawthorne's description of the Pyncheon elm on the morning succeeding the equinoctial storms. A branch of this elm has been by the weather turned to "bright gold," and resembles, Hawthorne says, "the golden branch that gained Aeneas and the Sibyl admittance into Hades." Aeneas, wanderer and planter of cities, is not Clifford Pyncheon but Holgrave, and the Sibyl would appear then to be Phoebe, through whom he is led into membership in the Pynchron family, that is, the "house" of which the House itself is but the symbol. Reformism, for Holgrave, is like wandering for Aeneas, an expression of youthful energy preceding his discovery of his "true self." Now as for the golden branch: the figure associated with gold throughout the book is of course Jaffrey Pyncheon, who carries a gold-headed cane, wears gold-bowed spectacles, and is respectably well off. Early in the romance he has been seen in all his glory standing at the threshold of the house, "as if you had seen him touching the twigs of the Pyncheon-elm, and Midas-like, transmuting them to gold." As it happens, the Judge's death *does* transmute the elm, and everything else about the dingy old house, to gold; but it is that kind of gold, commercially amassed material wealth, to possess which is indeed to enter hell, the very hell in which the Judge has himself been living all his days. But in accepting this wealth, Holgrave and Phoebe commit the identical fault: and they too enter hell. Holgrave may have recovered what his forebears lost; he may have achieved justice; but wealth in the nineteenth century of industrial capitalism is not wealth in the seventeenth century sense of primitive accumulation. If it were not an impropriety to pursue one's hero out of the book in which he appears, one would have to nourish the fear that Holgrave will use Jaffrey's money to underwrite a Lowell cotton mill that sweats its operatives and runs on the fourteen-hour day.

If it were not an impropriety—but a line of thought resembling this does inhabit the book, in the image of "wise Uncle Venner" (venerable), that "miscellaneous old gentleman," who battens on other people's garbage: he is intended to figure a contrast in pastoral terms to the lures of wealth. Hawthorne, it is true, chaffs him a good deal, but he chaffs everybody in this book, for some odd reason—perhaps merely the one that since people complained of the gloominess of *The Scarlet Letter*, he is going to make this work funny come hell or high water. At the end the "venerable uncle" is gathered up and taken off to the country estate also, where he will be court jester and still the happiest person in the book.

There is, moreover, the "germ" phrase in the notebooks from whence the romance is supposed to derive: "To inherit a great fortune. To inherit a great misfortune." This is true not only of all the original Pyncheons, but of Jaffrey as well, and through him of Holgrave and Phoebe. And the departure from the House of the Seven Gables, which might be taken as a symbolic shift of scene, a break with the past of which the house has been the chiefest emblem, is in fact no such thing. The break is only nominal; as Emerson remarked of the mania for travel, "I carry my giant with me wherever I go." For the old House is exchanged a new House, but the difference between them is only the difference between the rough individualism of old Colonel Pyncheon and the suave foxiness of Jaffrey, in whom, as Hawthorne remarks, can be seen a distinct physical decline over his ancestor as well.

So the conclusion can be read ironically, and, as the chorus says, it *is* all "good business." *Revanche* is attained with the sacrifice of neither love nor money—not only for old Colonel Pyncheon's dispossession and persecution of Matthew Maule, but for young Matthew Maule's failure to win Alice Pyncheon honestly too. Holgrave (a point I wish to return to later) refrains from practicing mesmerism to win Phoebe, and gains her love in a natural way; but Matthew Maule, scorned by Alice Pyncheon, "violated" her by practicing black arts upon her. Hence the ghostly harpsichord on the very last page: for that instrument has not been played on since Alice's death, and now that a later Pyncheon is to lose her virginity in a proper way, it becomes possible for it to "sound" again.[1]

How much credence are we to put in Hawthorne's dismissal of an economic interpretation of the romance in his preface to it on the ground that "When romances do really teach anything . . . it is usually through a far more subtle process than the ostensible one"? Which might also mean that what they teach is far more "subtile" than what they seem to teach. Yet had he not intended to stress the economic interpretation he would hardly have mentioned it. One wonders what other notion Hawthorne might have had of the book, not only beyond this but beyond the burden of satire, in the figure of Jaffrey, of Charles Upham, the Salem clergyman who helped to get him fired from his customs post, and of the satire on the Hawthorne family saga of lands in Maine. A possible reading, not necessarily Hawthorne's own, can be made to focus on Holgrave as an aesthetic rather than an economic symbol. One merit of such a view is that it brings, without doing it violence, the *Seven Gables* into line with the other three finished romances, in each of which is the same concern with the problem of the artist.

Let us make the preliminary hypothesis, as we did also in studying *The Scarlet Letter*, that not merely one, but all the protagonists of this book are to be regarded as projections of different sides of Hawthorne's nature; in this case a definition of the contrasts between Maules and Pyncheons is obviously required. Holgrave is the last surviving representative of a family whose line has long been supposed extinct; a family whose characteristics, while it was known, consisted mainly in much personal reserve and a reputation for occult power over others. The surviving Pyncheons are representatives of the family responsible for the low ebb of the Maules—a family whose dominant characteristics are a certain venality and hardness of temper, coupled with a fitful practical energy. Whenever, as occasionally happens, a Pyncheon appears who is less Pyncheon than something else, perhaps

1. Hepzibah, by the way, whose name ironically means "My delight is in her," once took harpsichord lessons, but, one infers, because she was neither musically clever nor sexually attractive, her father forbade her the use of Alice's instrument. Like it, she is never "played on" during her life, and as a result is always "out of tune."

Maule, he is suppressed, as Clifford Pyncheon was by Jaffrey.

Now as for Holgrave: He is an artist of sorts when we first see him (though, given his polymorphous history, there is no guarantee that he will remain one), a daguerreotypist whose art, presumably because it operates with the assistance of the sun, that is, of Nature—of which Phoebe, bringing her "sunshine" and her country butter and her ways with chickens and vegetables, is the symbol—whose art represents reality as the best portraiture cannot. His two pictures of Jaffrey, one made while the subject was alive, the other after he was dead, are revelations of the "man beneath the mask," as the sensitive Phoebe notices at once. Moreover, he is also a writer, whose name has figured "on the covers of Graham and Godey," and who reads to Phoebe one afternoon from manuscript a story about his and her common ancestors, cast in the mold of many of Hawthorne's own Twice-Told Tales. It is well-known that his angry outburst against the past—"Shall we never, never get rid of this Past! . . . It lies upon the Present like a giant's dead body!" etc.—is an almost exact transcription of a passage from the Hawthorne notebooks, a passage which, whether or not he believed it when he put it into Holgrave's mouth, Hawthorne assuredly *once* believed. Like Hawthorne himself, and others of his surrogates, Holgrave figures largely as a "spectator" of the "drama" being "enacted" around him: Phoebe accuses him on this ground of being "coldhearted," of treating the house as merely a "theatre," and Clifford and Hepzibah as actors in a "tragedy . . . played exclusively for [his] amusement." Elsewhere she thinks him "too calm and cool an observer," as he goes about his business of watching, like the lens of one of his own cameras, a drama into which he steps at the end as chief protagonist upon the Judge's death. It is also worth noting that, like Hawthorne himself, and like several other of Hawthorne's fictive surrogates, Holgrave is a handsome young man with a swarthy complexion.

Now the arts of this young man, daguerreotypy and literature, are connected by Hawthorne with his gift of mesmeric power, a naturalist version of the occult powers said to have been owned by his forebears, and for the possession of which Matthew Maule the elder was hanged, and Matthew Maule the younger obliged to fall into an obscure poverty. And as in the case of the younger Matthew, whose career is the theme of Holgrave's short story, delivered one afternoon in the Pyncheon garden to Phoebe as audience, the exercise of occult powers is related to the sexual impulse,—quite as if, by the by, a "gift" for some sort of "magic" were either adjunct to, or symbolic of, virility. Holgrave's recitation of his legend almost mesmerises Phoebe, almost puts her into an extremely suggestible state, where she may become amenable to Holgrave's amorous overtures. It is true that Hawthorne obliquely satirizes this "gift" of the young reformer's by showing him in the act, somewhat earlier, of hypnotizing one of the Pyncheon chickens; but this may be because Holgrave is never really going to use his powers, which therefore do not represent a real peril; the seriousness of Hawthorne's use of mesmerism as a symbol of unlawful influence (like art?) is generally evident. Holgrave has, we must assume, the power to do to Phoebe what the younger Matthew Maule did to Alice Pyncheon—which is what Westervelt, in *The Blithedale Romance*, does to Priscilla. His abstention from doing it is therefore crucial to the book.

So, two centuries before, was hanged for witchcraft, at Colonel Pyncheon's instigation, old Matthew Maule: and for "Colonel Pyncheon" we are, by autobiographical authority, to read "John Hathorne." This Maule's son built the House of the Seven Gables, and his son in turn, the younger Matthew, was also a carpenter, which is to say, an artisan, in a day in which to be a carpenter was to be an architect as well. Is it too much to hazard that Hawthorne is promulgating, in the Maule and Pyncheon family lines, images of the artist and the anti-artist in himself? in which case, first, Holgrave would represent something of a decadence from the social usefulness of his ancestors' calling, much as Owen Warland's interest in artificial insects, and Dimmesdale's adulterous passion, represent fallings-off from their respective proper occupations and, second, Jaffrey Pyncheon (and hence Judge John Hathorne) would become the "type" of all influences in Hawthorne's personality that strove so hard to overthrow the Maule in him. Now it is true that Hawthorne's attitude toward the Salem witchcraft trials, in which Judge Hathorne played a prominent role, was critical; that he even imputed to old Colonel Pyncheon in this romance a motive more economic than sectarian. Yet it is also true that the power witches represented, the power to control the souls of others, impressed him as dangerous, and dangerous because it was undemocratic. This is made very plain in the extraordinary early fragment, "Alice Doane's Appeal," written as far back as 1825. Mesmerism is simply a nineteenth-century version of witchcraft; and Hawthorne's attitude, toward the Maules as well as the Pyncheons, is really, I think, one of even-handed condemnation. This is so at least on the plane of this discussion.

Holgrave as artist, possessing quasi-magical powers which he may use to further his own ends, and artistic power that enable him to "see through" appearances and, like the painter in "The Prophetic Portraits," reveal the essence of a personality, abjures these endowments to become a wealthy bourgeois. He does so even though he has been Hawthorne's ideal artist: one who has had much experience of life, one who despite all fortune's tumblings has never lost his identity, and one who can work the highest miracle of which art is capable. And Jaffrey Pyncheon, who actually, and ironically, succeeds by dying in corrupting the Maule power for good, is the typical Victorian *paterfamilias*, like old Mr Osborne in *Vanity Fair:* a localized image of the terrifying father, Zeus, with his "rough beard," his "cold, hard, immitigable" face that resembles the "brow of a precipitous mountain," and his emblem of power, the gold-headed cane. And if he is Zeus, he is an old, lascivious Zeus, become a "great beast" at table, emitting an odor of venery when he leans over the counter to kiss Phoebe: "the man . . . the sex, was entirely too prominent in [his] demonstration." * * * And if Jaffrey is Zeus (therefore also Jehovah), Clifford, the epicene childman, is what Hawthorne calls him: "a thunder-smitten Adam," who for his innocence and his epicureanism was tricked by his cousin Jaffrey to prison, in which place both his artistic gifts and his sexual potency were totally destroyed. Had he been allowed to "live," he might have become an artist; but imprisonment has kept him a child who indulges tantrums, notices women's clothes, likes to blow soapbubbles, eats with refined voracity, is terrified of steam-engines, and is completely virgin. Having never "quaffed the cup of passionate love," he knows "that it [is] now too late." Holgrave the swarthy worldling is not the only surrogate for Hawthorne's artistry: in the pitiful figure of Clifford it seems to me that we can read a symbolic accusation by his creator against the world that, at least in his own opinion, forced him into isolation in order to write. After all, the clergyman Charles Upham, in seeing to it that Hawthorne was replaced in his job with the customs after the change in administrations from Democratic to Whig in 1848, was in a sense condemning him to go back to the prison of the artist's study from which he had, since 1846, been seeking to liberate himself.

The upshot of the book's organization, then, is that the Pyncheon, or bourgeois, power, epitomized in Jaffrey, indelibly corrupts, even though extinguishing itself, in the process, the Maule power, as represented by the artist Holgrave. The catastrophe, as in *The Scarlet Letter*, is general, is suicidal. Holgrave's capitulation to Jaffrey's money is, however, nonetheless abrupt, surprising, dishonorable, for all that; and the way it is huddled up into the last pages, with a sweetening of pastoralism and sentimentalism leads me to suspect Hawthorne of being both confused and uncomfortable while he wrote it. The confusion and embarrassment follow, too, I think, not only from his abstract recognition of a bad situation, that in a democratic society not only the aristocratic but the artistic tempers must become corrupted by the power of economics, but also from his recognition of something else, more deeply personal.

Phoebe plays an interesting role in this romance: among these weary towndwellers, living in the dry-rot of civilization, she is the apostle of Nature, a "country cousin" who brings life and light to a "decaying" and "weather-beaten" house. She is as "pleasant about the house as a gleam of sunshine falling on the floor." When she arrives she is wearing a yellow straw hat; she comes bringing country butter in gift; the windows of her room open on the east; she presides over the weekly gathering in the garden, which occurs on Sundays; the Indian cakes she prepares for Clifford are yellower than those made by Hepzibah. She dissipates "the shadows of gloomy events," and to Holgrave she confides that she dislikes moonlight, mystery, riddles. As in *The Blithedale Romance* Zenobia's departure brings on equinoctial weather, so when Phoebe goes September gales begin, nor does the sun return till the morning she returns. In fine, she is continually linked with that life-giving thing, the sun, which is also responsible for the "truthfulness" of Holgrave's daguerreotypes. Her name itself is the feminine form of *Phoebus*. And as such she is being offered through the body of the book as an implicit alternative to Jaffrey, whose power, not of the sun, not "natural," is derived from the opposite of it, usury. He is a speculator; his life is sterile; after his death comes that of his only son, by cholera; as Phoebe comes and goes with the sun, so he is a sun unto himself—a light of a "sultry," "dog-day" quality is said to "dry up," or sterilize, the streets. As it is her role to bring and foster life, it is his to unman others, as he does his cousin.

It is in a sense neat that Holgrave, who has been "living by the sun," should at the end of the book turn to its sun-goddess for succor. The only trouble is the irony which, like presented bayonets of palace guards, confronts us no matter where we try to enter this romance: when he turns to her it is within a week of her falling heiress to Jaffrey's estate, or a large portion of it; and "Love's web," so busily being spun in the anteroom to where the Judge sits stiffly dead, is a deception at last, that only betrays Holgrave into the green barouche. The "comic" resolution of the book is, in this as in other perspectives, most unsatisfying. We may take it, of course, to read as though Holgrave's turning conservative may be only the impulse of a moment (but the consequences of impulses cannot be so easily shrugged off as the impulses can be felt), or, with F. O. Matthiessen, as if Hawthorne were being in deadly earnest in writing the conclusion, which is then expressive of his inability to see the evil potentialities of American capitalism. Neither view accounts, however, for the machinery by which Hawthorne pushes this legacy into the laps of his two protagonists: the death of Jaffrey's only son, which is quite baldly an auctorial device for forcing a certain kind of conclusion, but one so at variance with the rest of his book that it must be intended as an irony.

Of course, as has been said,[2] there is a question of "poetic justice" involved here, inasmuch as the Pyncheon name, to atone for its aristocratic exclusiveness and unapproachability, must disappear: which makes it imperative that Jaffrey's son should die and leave behind only the epicene Clifford, the virgin Hepzibah, and the female Phoebe. But first, the manner of this son's death smells loudly of the *deus ex machina* (it is a clumsy device that fails to be convincing), and second, Phoebe does not have to marry Holgrave since her name will go in the act of marriage with no matter whom. The retort to this is that she must marry Holgrave because history must come full circle. But must Holgrave be damned in order to achieve the justice that is, on this view, his right?

*The House of the Seven Gables* appears to be Hawthorne's major recording of his social egalitarianism; the warped conclusion of the book may, I think, stem out of his complicating of the theme of egalitarianism with that of art, and so producing the kind of muddle in the book that Hawthorne's mind was always in about his respective loyalties to art and to his politics. That isolation and misunderstanding was an almost necessary role for the serious artist in his America can hardly be doubted. It is not for nothing that his great sinners were men and women isolated from their fellows, and in many instances guilty of detached, instead of attached, analysis. Having made Holgrave, not only a defrauded heir, but also an artist, and having endowed him with certain of his own features, he could not make and keep him a radical democrat, without being unfaithful to his inner ambivalences, for the simple reason that books must have resolutions, whereas lives have none save the resolution of death, which is by definition uncognizable. So long as he was in public service Hawthorne found it impossible to work creatively; he fell back on sketches and notebook-keeping; and the latter of these may be regarded as the making of promises to the self to come back to creative effort *mañana*, later. At the Old Manse, or later at Lenox, where he consorted with almost the only intelligentsia America

2. See L. S. Hall, *Hawthorne, Critic of Society* (New Haven, 1944), pp. 160–67    [p. 376 of this Norton Critical Edition].

could show, it was another story: but whereas Hawthorne could, in an awkward way, live two lives in one body, one or the other of Holgraves's roles must go. Hawthorne solved this problem by trundling out his machine and eliminating both roles together.

It might be pointed out that when Holgrave comes to the House of the Seven Gables he has no intention of staying there, or of mingling his fortunes with those of the Pyncheons: though he may know the whole situation as they do not, his aim, so long as he is a radical, must be to avoid it. This is much as if Hawthorne were looking back to his own early years in Salem and saying, "My intentions also were to use this only as a way-station." But the House is contagious; and having once entered it, Holgrave cannot get out without surrendering utterly—just as once incarcerated in his "prison,". Clifford can never escape it either, especially not once he has been released. In his "dismal chamber" Hawthorne also fell a victim to the power of the past —the New England past which was his heritage; nor was he able afterward to get out of it, and if he could, it would be only at the cost of . surrendering his artistic soul. This amounts almost to saying that for Hawthorne it was worse to be Holgrave than it was to be Jaffrey Pyncheon; which may be pursuing the thread somewhat too rigorously, but despite its Humpty-Dumpty aspects strikes me as more faithful to the book than the customary interpretations. In one respect Hawthorne may be said to be trying to "save" Holgrave, but even this goes sour: if we look at his marriage with Phoebe as that of an intellectual to a non-intellectual, we may think we are witnessing Hawthorne bestowing on his hero a pastoral benediction. For Phoebe is not only a sun-goddess, she is also a child, in the penumbra of maturity, but still a child, innocent, simple, happy. But there is still the irony of her being drowned in stocks and bonds, and being forced to abandon her naive rural scene for a grand country estate, where the garden, instead of running wild, is ordered on the best principles of Andrew Jackson Downing. Always there is the irony, which, really not confined to the end of the book merely, suffices to turn its whole face from one of pretended comedy to one of bitterness.

A word in conclusion about the romance's structure: by comparison with that of *The Scarlet Letter* it is loose and atomistic. In neither book is there any strong narrative line, but whereas in the earlier romance Hawthorne imposed control by constructing the book in terms of a series of antitheses and balances all revolving round the pivotal twelfth chapter, in which Dimmesdale stands on the scaffold at midnight, there is here no such symmetry. Things simply "happen": Phoebe comes, Clifford comes, Jaffrey grows importunate, Jaffrey dies, Clifford and Hepzibah flee, Holgrave and Phoebe fall in love; aside from the entries these characters make, there is nothing in their relations that would forbid the dénouement from occurring all at once. No temporal, no motivational reason exists for the lapse of several months that separates Jaffrey's initial foray on Clifford from the final one which brings about his death. The only justification that can be made is that of the desirability of a certain "suspense"; but this for its own sake merely produces only padding. What the book then shows in the way of structure is an initial gathering-together and a resolution, lacking a middle, and having in its stead a number of lyric flights about Clifford's, Hepzibah's and Holgrave's personalities, which take up fully a third of the book (between the seventh and fifteenth chapters) without contributing anything but a kind of irrelevant whimsicality for the most part. Hawthorne's attack upon the sustained piece of prose fiction, that is, begins to go wrong at the outset; which is not due entirely to his wish to produce something that will please many people by its "sunniness" and "optimism," but also to his inherent inability to conceive in terms of anything larger than the *nouvelle*.

# HYATT H. WAGGONER

## [The Ascending Spiral Curve] †

\* \* \* It is paradoxically true of *The House of the Seven Gables* that it is at once more realistic and more consistently allegorical than *The Scarlet Letter*. It has a richer evocation of atmosphere, a more palpable recreation of a definite time and place and way of life than Hawthorne's masterpiece. But it is also more directly and completely controlled by a conscious conceptual framework, a framework involving the most abstract levels of thought. If the work is to be recovered for mature readers in our time, it can only I think be through an appreciation of its symbolic structure. This may not be possible, but we shall not know whether it is possible or not until we see how far Hawthorne succeeded in conveying "more of various modes of truth" than he could grasp "by a direct effort."

The first of the themes to demand comment is the one that Hawthorne emphasizes in the preface and continues to under-

† From Hyatt H. Waggoner, *"The House of the Seven Gables," Hawthorne: A Critical Study*, Cambridge, 1963, revised edition. Pp. 176-87. Copyright 1955, 1963, by the President and Fellows of Harvard College; reprinted by permission of the publishers, The Belknap Press of Harvard University Press.

score throughout, the relation of past and present. Superficially, the relation seems to be one of contrast. Past evil makes present suffering, past wealth leads to present poverty, the house once magnificent is now decayed. When the inadequacy of this insight becomes clear, we find another, which turns out to be its very antithesis, emerging from the pattern: there is nothing new under the sun, past and present are essentially identical, as seen in the deaths of colonel and judge. But this too turns out to be only a partial insight, needing correction. The correction, we discover, has been foreshadowed from the very beginning by the symbolism of the elm, which experiences yearly death and rebirth, and by the symbolism of Maule's well, which combines permanence and change.

But when we relate these conceptions to the image patterns we discover what seems to be an essential ambiguity. The angles of the house are associated only with death and the *illusion* of permanence and linear progress, but the circles of the elm are associated both with sterile repetition and redemptive renewal, with the death of the judge and with Phoebe's coming. We must somehow distinguish between the movement of the hands around the face of the dead judge's watch and the circles of light shed by Phoebe.

The "light" shed by the judge's sultry smile is deceptive. Despite his appearance he is really a creature of darkness. If he had his way he would continue and compound the original injustice. He is therefore unable to escape the compulsive cycles of nature. The circles in which he is involved are his only reality; his dreams of achievement, his plans for his day and for the continued building of his fortune, are as illusory as the dreams of permanent magnificence his ancestor embodied in the house. The circles associated with Phoebe, on the other hand, are not compulsive but liberating. Her light is as real as the sunshine and as healing as love. Hers are the circles of nature, but nature completed and illumined by grace. She is natural, but as the flowers are natural: like the lilies of the field, she is not worried about achieving security or ambitious to achieve distinction. She is emblematic, Hawthorne might have said of her, as he said often of his wife in his love letters, of the redemptive power of love, by which alone man may break out of the cycles of futile repetition and participate by choice in a cycle of a different kind.

But if Phoebe illumines and transforms nature by the power of love, we are still left with a difficulty. How can the circles of nature and grace be so different and yet look so much the same? If we conceive of the circles of history in terms of the ancient figure of the wheel of fate, then the death of the judge and much else in the history of the family would make it appear that the wheel is merely going around. But the union of Pyncheon and Maule suggests that the wheel is moving somewhere as it revolves.

Is progress real or merely apparent? A closer look at Clifford's speech on the train will yield a partial clue. Hawthorne's irony in this scene is constant and much more subtle than we have yet noted. Its final effect is to reinforce the meanings he had expressed earlier in "The Celestial Railroad." Thus in reading Clifford's words about how the past is only a "coarse and sensual prophecy" of the present and future, we may emphasize, as Clifford does, the inferiority of the past because it was coarse and sensual. But if the past provides a *prophecy*, it must be because the repetitions of history suggest that man's nature and condition are essentially unchanged. If so, hope for real progress now must rest where it has always rested.

Again, in Clifford's phrase about the present repeating the past, but the past "etherealized, refined, and perfected to its ideal," we may, with Clifford, take "ideal" to mean simply "better," more desirable. But there are implications here that Clifford does not see. "Perfected to its ideal" may also mean "made more truly itself." Evil as well as good may be purged, refined, rendered purer, in short "spiritualized," as Hawthorne very well knew. His really evil characters are guilty not of the gross and sensual sins, not of obvious expressions of self-centeredness like murder, but of intellectual and spiritual pride. "Spiritual" is not necessarily a plus-valued word, though it tended to be for Hawthorne's age. It may be quite neutral: there are spiritual enormities as well as physical ones. That Hawthorne thought so is implied everywhere in his work. But if it is possible to read Clifford's phrase as meaning that evil as well as good continues, both being gradually "refined" or rendered more "spiritual," then "progress" becomes a very equivocal term and the irony of history has not really been dissolved. History itself then would offer no adequate basis for hope.

One of Hawthorne's own comments as narrator in his last chapter corroborates our impression that "perfected to its ideal" is a more ambiguous phrase than Clifford knew. Commenting on the fact that it was too late in his life for Clifford to benefit from any formal vindication of his good name, Hawthorne broadens the observation to include all wrongs done and suffered: "It is a truth (and it would be a very sad one but for the higher hopes which it suggests) that no great mistake, whether acted or endured, in our mortal sphere, is ever really set right." If this is true, whatever meaning the idea of progress has in the novel, it cannot be that of utopianism or secular liberalism.

Yet both internal and external evidence suggests that the ideas

Clifford voiced on the train—ideas central in the liberalism of the time—had a strong appeal for Hawthorne. The structure of the novel as a whole, with the departure from the house and the marriage combining to make a happy ending, would seem to suggest that Hawthorne approves of Clifford's understanding of history as figured in an ascending spiral curve, even if he does not approve of the reasons Clifford gives for his hopeful view. But how can he do so if he also believes that no great wrong is ever set right? Does the leaving of the old house for a new one at the end mean real progress or does it not? Is the novel confused because Hawthorne simply cannot make up his mind?

There is certainly a conflict of attitudes involved here but there is also, I think, a sufficient resolution of the conflict to keep the paradox from becoming a complete antinomy. Hawthorne demonstrates a Keatsian sort of "negative capability" in entertaining sympathetically two opposed views, but there is finally as much clarity in the implications of his work as we have any right to demand. He provides a partial resolution of the conflict both on the level of belief and on the level of feeling and imagination. On the level of belief, the resolution is dependent on our taking more seriously than we have yet the parenthetical part of the statement I have quoted about the great wrong Clifford suffered. The truth the narrator asserts would be a very sad one—and one thoroughly in conflict with the hopeful cast of Clifford's view of history—if it did not inspire "higher hopes." In short, the irremediable injustices of this life are a reason for believing in the life eternal, in which there will be perfect justice. Hawthorne's belief in immortality comes to the support of his desire to believe in progress.

But Hawthorne was no philosopher, and his ideas about progress tend to fit his mood and the occasion rather than add up to a consistent theory. Truth for him was to be found in the image, as well as conveyed by the image. When we turn from the statements we have been considering, we find that most of what seemed like inconsistency disappears. Here as elsewhere, Hawthorne was able to convey through his art "more of various modes of truth" than he could grasp by direct effort—or state philosophically.

The common impression that the work simply wavers between belief in progress and despair of any escape from the past may be corrected by a closer look at the implications of the emphatic Eden imagery and at what Hawthorne has said, chiefly through imagery, in the chapter on the flight in which Clifford's words occur. By his references to Eden, Hawthorne locates the house of the seven gables in the spiritual geography of his imagination. When Phoebe returns after her visit to the country and goes into the garden, she finds it ruined and deserted. The idyllic summer afternoons she spent there reading to Clifford will never come again. Hawthorne devotes a paragraph to describing the garden's emptiness and disarray, making this the most emphatic reminder in the book of the mythic overtones of his tale.

The implications of this passage and of the explicit references to Eden elsewhere in the book are clear enough. Man is a fallen creature in a fallen world. Any redemption possible for him is offered only on condition that he recognize this fact. Clifford's brief dream of an easy escape made possible by the newest thing in locomotion is a delusion. There is and will be no celestial railroad so long as man's essential condition remains unchanged. Like R. P. Warren's characters who find that flight westward changes nothing, does not permit escape from the guilt of the past, Clifford and Hepzibah must return to the house.

What has already been implied by his Eden allusions Hawthorne amply reinforces by the way he manages the abortive flight. In the first place, the "two owls" have to leave the house in the middle of a great storm, and Hawthorne makes it clear that his image is a metaphor for a stormy world. As Hepzibah and Clifford face the east wind, its pitiless blast makes them "death-a-cold." Hepzibah, more sensitive than Clifford on this occasion, experiences "a moral sensation, mingling itself with the physical chill, and causing her to shake more in spirit than in body. The world's broad, bleak atmosphere was all so comfortless!" And Hawthorne makes sure that we do not dismiss Hepzibah's impression as one appropriate only to the Hepzibahs of the world. Exercising his right as intrusive author, he comments in the next sentence, "Such, indeed, is the impression which it makes on every new adventurer, even if he plunge into it while the warmest tide of life is bubbling through his veins."

Fallen man in a stormy world: the combination makes what Hawthorne calls "a very sombre picture." In such a world it would be a delusion to suppose that progress would be easy. And Hawthorne suggests the extent of Clifford's delusion by having him support his argument for progress by espousing two opinions that were precisely the opposite of Hawthorne's and one which he found at least questionable. Clifford thinks that mesmerism represents a great advance, since it will do much "towards purging away the grossness out of human life." Hawthorne himself lumped mesmerism with spiritualism and considered them both to be, if not fraud, then both religiously irrelevant and morally dangerous. Clifford also thinks it an unmitigated advantage to "do away with those stale ideas of home and fireside, and substitute something better." The extent of his delusion may be tested by noting the symbolic implications of the hearth or family fireside image throughout Hawthorne's work, from beginning to end. The opening of this chapter parallels the situation in "Night Sketches," as the two old people who have been sheltered from life plunge into a stormy world and discover what it is really like, but Clifford's several references to the advantages of giving up the outmoded hearth reverse the meaning of the end of the sketch, in which the light of faith is known to be trustworthy just because its flame was kindled at the hearth.

But if Clifford's words are ironic, containing meanings the opposite of those he intends to express, they should not be taken as completely destroying the tension Hawthorne has set up between the conservative and the liberal views of history. Clifford may speak wildly and without recognizing all the implications of what he is saying, but that Hawthorne does not mean to undercut Clifford's hope entirely is implied in many ways in the book, perhaps most clearly in the implications, on the political and social level, of the marriage of Phoebe and Holgrave. This is a marriage of conservative and radical, of heart and head. Woman is the conserver and the conservative, man the speculator whose thought may undermine even that which is most sacred, even the hearth and the altar. The marriage of Phoebe and Holgrave, then, though we see more of its effect on Holgrave than we do on Phoebe, still at least theoretically preserves some sort of balance between the two attitudes. Hawthorne makes explicit what, in his view, Holgrave's "error" was. It was excessive confidence in man and lack of respect for the past. "As to the better centuries that are coming, the artist was surely right." Marriage to Phoebe should not lessen his "faith in man's brightening destiny" but increase his feeling for the values of the hearth, so that he might come to realize that "God is the sole worker of realities." Only on the religious level, in the higher hope motivated by the spectacle of history, did Hawthorne dissolve his ambiguity.

The best evidence of what the hearth meant to Hawthorne is to be found in "Fire Worship." There, in a tone that at least partly takes back what he is saying, he declares he will never be reconciled to the "enormity" of the iron stove that has replaced the open hearth.

> Truly may it be said that the world looks darker for it. In one way or another, here and there and all around us, the inventions of mankind are fast blotting the picturesque, the poetic, and the beautiful out of human life. . . . While a man was true to the fireside, so long would he be true to country and law, to the God whom his fathers worshipped, to the wife of his youth, and to

all things else which instinct or religion has taught us to consider sacred.

Fire, in short, at least fire in the open fireplace, is "the great conservative of Nature." But if the tone of the sketch did not make it sufficiently clear that Hawthorne's views are not confined within the limits of such conservatism, evidence elsewhere would do so. Only in a playful tone could Hawthorne write of "these evil days" in which "physical science has nearly succeeded in extinguishing" the "sacred trust" of the household fire. He is exaggerating as much as Clifford when he asks, "What reform is left for our children to achieve, unless they overthrow the altar too?" The conflicting claims of liberal and conservative are being balanced here as they are in the comment on reformers in "The Hall of Fantasy," where Hawthorne writes, "Be the individual theory as wild as fancy could make it, still the wiser spirit would recognize the struggle of the race after a better and purer life than had yet been realized on earth. My faith revived even while I rejected all their schemes."

Still, the irony in Clifford's words about the hearth prepares us to find his discussion of the significance of the new theories of electricity similarly mistaken. Yet once again, the ideas he voices are not *entirely* mistaken. Electricity, he thinks, supports idealism in its view that the world is essentially mind, not matter. Its implication is that "the world of matter has become a great nerve." Indeed, it is even more thoroughly spiritual, more nonmaterial, than would be suggested by "nerve": it is "instinct with intelligence," not material at all, really, but "a thought, nothing but thought, and no longer the substance which we deemed it." Metaphysical idealism seems to Clifford so thoroughly to support his hope of escape that he is not disturbed by the old gentleman's warning that the practical application of electrical theory in the newly invented telegraph may merely make the work of bank robbers and murderers easier.

The reader, if not Clifford, is prepared then for what faced "the two wanderers" when they got off the train:

> They gazed drearily about them. At a little distance stood a wooden church, black with age, and in a dismal state of ruin and decay, with broken windows, a great rift through the main body of the edifice, and a rafter dangling from the top of the square tower. Farther off was a farm-house, in the old style, as venerably black as the church . . . uninhabited.

No wonder "Clifford shivered from head to foot" now, as Hepzibah had at the beginning of their flight. The realities of a stormy world have supplied an answer to the question of whether his momentary idealism was justified or not. The deserted church and the deserted house measure the extent of his and Holgrave's delusions and prepare us for the way Hawthorne ends the chapter. Hepzibah kneels and prays, lifting her hands to the sky.

> The dull, gray weight of clouds made it invisible; but it was no hour for disbelief,—no juncture this to question that there was a sky above, and an Almighty Father looking from it!
> "O God!"—ejaculated poor, gaunt Hepzibah,—then paused a moment, to consider what her prayer should be,—"O God,—our Father,—are we not thy children? Have mercy on us!"

If Clifford in his disdain of the hearth has reversed the meaning and imagery of "Night Sketches" Hepzibah in her final prayer has repeated both. She has not, like the narrator in the early sketch, been granted a glimpse of a true light. The storm still hides the sky toward which she directs her prayer. But she takes the lead now in guiding Clifford back to the hearth. The hearth even of such a house as the one she thinks she must return to for good is better than what she has discovered in her first real experience of the world. In as stormy a world as this, one learns the true value of the hearth.

Hawthorne ends his novel by refusing to declare himself on the reality of secular Progress, falling back instead on the "higher hopes" he had said were inspired by the vision of time as unredeemable. "The Pyncheon Elm . . . with what foliage the September gale had spared to it, whispered unintelligible prophecies." "Wise Uncle Venner," meanwhile, imagines Alice Pyncheon, the most pathetic victim of the evil of the past, floating "heavenward from the HOUSE OF THE SEVEN GABLES!" She at least has escaped what Hepzibah and Clifford could not escape by physical flight. As for the living characters, Hawthorne seems to want to encourage us to hope.

But why should not the fine new house in the suburbs generate the same evils the old house did? There is, after all, even a new fortune to go with it—or rather, an old, tainted one, newly acquired. Must we then read the ending as ironic? Or should we simply say that it is unconvincing?

If the book itself were thought not to make it sufficiently clear that the ending is meant to be taken seriously, without irony, all that we can find out about Hawthorne and his beliefs and attitudes from the total record he left us would show that he intended no irony here. Before he wrote it, he decided he wanted his next book to be more hopeful than *The Scarlet Letter*, and when he had finished it he thought he had succeeded. A more careful reading than it has generally been given will show that in it he made no unqualified declarations that he *needed* to undercut with an ironic ending. Thematically, the ending follows from what precedes it and in no way changes the meaning. Hawthorne has both shown us and told us that it is a stormy world that Holgrave and Phoebe will have to live in. Whether they will be destroyed by it or not is left as undecided here as was the fate of the young lovers in "The Canterbury Pilgrims." In both cases we are invited simply to hope that their love will last and prove redemptive. Hawthorne has implied that the new house will be an improvement over the old, but he has even more strongly implied that, as man's condition remains essentially unchanged, those who inhabit it will have to face problems as old as Eden itself.

He has said, in effect, that both change and permanence are real, and that we are not to think of them as being one good and the other bad. Instead, we must think about them in terms of the necessary distinctions between superficial and profound, external and internal, physical and moral. He has said that what his century chiefly meant by progress, that is, technology, solve some problems but not others; and that the ones it does not solve are more important than the ones it does. The way he handles Clifford's reference to the telegraph epitomizes all he has to say on technology: "it is an excellent thing,—that is, of course, if the speculators in cotton and politics don't get possession of it."

As for what he has said about redemption through love, it would never have occurred to him to be ironical about that. If the prophecies of the elm at the end are "unintelligible," that is because in a dark world where much must remain obscure, the only meanings worthy of the heart's trust are those that emerge when Scripture corroborates and completes Nature: the "higher hopes," again, and the flowers growing from the rotting roof, life coming out of death. Here nature and Scripture agree. The voice of Nature alone is either undecipherable or insufficient. It is September, and the great storm has torn off most of the elm's leaves. Nature is under going its seasonal death even as Uncle Venner fancies Alice Pyncheon ascending in corroboration of our higher hopes. Hawthorne meant his ending to be taken seriously.

But the modern reader inevitably finds it difficult to do so, for two reasons. First, he is likely to bring to his reading a stubborn skepticism directed toward both Hawthorne's idea of the redemptive power of married love and his faith in immortality, his higher hopes. That of course is not Hawthorne's fault, but suspension of disbelief may be even more difficult than suspension of belief.

And Hawthorne makes it unnecessarily difficult by the way he handles Phoebe, Holgrave, and their courtship and marriage. Hawthorne felt he had been "saved" by his own marriage, and he idealized Sophia much as Mark Twain idealized Libby. Writing the novel, he felt little need to convince the reader that Phoebe ought to be taken as a visible sign of Grace, that marriage to her would transform Holgrave's views, or that marriage itself was a blessed state. Did he not know it to be true, from his own experience? So he lavished his care on Hepzibah, principally, though also on Clifford and the Judge, as more difficult problems for the artist, and gave the less challenging portraits less attention.

But with a Phoebe who is both too good to be believed and too quickly symbolic in her goodness, a Holgrave who is much more interesting on a thematic level than he is convincing as a created character, and a marriage that comes too suddenly and may seem a mere contrivance, so that we have as much trouble believing in the love as we do in the lovers, it is not very surprising that many readers have failed to be convinced of the validity of the hope Hawthorne proffers in his ending. It is hard to believe that love will save us if we cannot believe in *the* love that is supposed to have saved the Pyncheons and the Maules.

But it is too easy to emphasize the failure. It is, anyway, I suspect, as much ours as Hawthorne's. And insofar as it is Hawthorne's, the reasons that have been given for it have not always been good ones. Hawthorne said in his Preface that he was writing a romance, but we tend to demand of him the very "minute fidelity . . . to the probable and ordinary course of man's experience" he said it was not his aim to produce. Whether it is possible to grant him his aim without feeling that it is inferior even while we grant it, is an open question. But at any rate it should be clear that it is only on this "novelistic" level that the work fails, if it does. As a mythopoetic fiction, it is one of the greatest works in American literature.

## ALFRED H. MARKS

### Who Killed Judge Pyncheon?
### The Role of the Imagination in
### *The House of the Seven Gables* †

Judge Jaffrey Pyncheon has been dead for over one hundred years, and according to F. O. Matthiessen the chapter on his death was one of the "favorite showpieces" of the age of Nathaniel

† From Alfred H. Marks, "Who Killed Judge Pyncheon? The Role of the Imagination in *The House of the Seven Gables*," *PMLA*, LXXI (June, 1956), 355–69. Reprinted by permission of the Modern Language Association and Professor Marks.

Hawthorne.[1] Yet there is doubt—if one may be pardoned for borrowing for a moment the pose of the hack who rewrites accounts of old murders—that the facts surrounding his death have been properly explored. Did he simply die of some kind of pulmonary hemorrhage, to which his ancestors were prone? Was no one present when he died? If he did die a natural death, is it possible that his "hereditary liability" was helped somehow, by circumstances taking place in the room with him, in precipitating his final seizure?

*The House of the Seven Gables* is Hawthorne's most humorous novel, but it is also the work in which he is most serious in his devotion to the powers of beauty and the imagination and in his hatred of economic materialism and Philistinism. And Judge Pyncheon is both materialist and Philistine in this book. He is also the most unambiguous figure in this strange romance. There is doubt as to who its hero and its heroine are, but there is no doubt that Judge Pyncheon is the villain. To establish what killed the evil judge is therefore to establish what the romance holds up as good. The search for the man who killed him is even more important; for that man, if he exists, should logically be the hero of this book.

To start, let it be said that Hawthorne is more than an accessory to this act. No murder was ever planned so calculatedly as was Judge Pyncheon's demise in this novel. He died as full of gore and as close to the scene of many of his crimes as were Penelope's suitors when Odysseus slew them. There might have been tragic irony in his death when he was about to be proposed for the governorship, but the irony is used against the Judge instead of in his favor. The long chapter mentioned by Matthiessen, in which Hawthorne sheds almost entirely the disguise usually worn by the author, practically to dance with enthusiasm around the Judge's body, should be all the proof one needs to believe that Hawthorne wanted the Judge dead and enjoyed having him die.

When Hawthorne was anticipating being removed from his post at the Salem Custom House, he wrote a letter to Longfellow in which he said: "If they will pay no reverence to the imaginative power when it causes herbs of grace and sweet-scented flowers to spring up along their pathway, then they should be taught what it can do in the way of producing nettles, skunk-cabbage, deadly night-shade, wolf's bane, dog-wood." [2] He was given the opportunity of producing "nettles, skunk-cabbage," and all the rest for the education of his former colleagues in "The Custom House";

---

1. *The American Renaissance* (New York, 1941), p. 214 [p. 364 of this Norton Critical Edition].

2. Cited by Randall Stewart, *The American Notebooks by Nathaniel Hawthorne* (New Haven, 1932), p. 298.

and teach them he did. But *The House of the Seven Gables* is an even greater victory of the imagination over those who hate it and do not know enough also to fear it, for in this work the defeat of the Philistine is brought about under carefully planned conditions. The author could not show the imagination winning in objective reality without being guilty of a confusion in terms—as in making a scientific analysis of a miracle. So in *The House of the Seven Gables* the imagination is both subject matter and process: Hawthorne calls upon the reader to recognize the validity of imaginative truth by means of the imagination itself. Roy R. Male, Jr., in a recent article writes of "Rappaccini's Daughter": "the real question of the story is whether Giovanni has the ability to attain and hold against the challenge of materialistic scepticism a religious faith or heavenly love." [3] In *The House of the Seven Gables*, "the real question" is similar, but here it involves the reader, who must continue to pay, in spite of "the challenge of materialistic scepticism," the "reverence to the imaginative power" Hawthorne prized.

The room in which Judge Pyncheon was to spend his last minutes is described in the second chapter of *The House of the Seven Gables*: "It was a low-studded room, with a beam across the ceiling, panelled with dark wood, and having a large chimney-piece." Its furniture includes two tables and six or seven chairs. "Half a dozen" of the chairs, we are told, are "straight and stiff, and so ingeniously contrived for the discomfort of the human person that they were irksome even to sight." There is one chair, however, that is an "exception . . . a very antique elbow-chair, with a high back, carved elaborately in oak, and a roomy depth within its arms." The rest of the furnishings of the room include principally the "map of the Pyncheon territory" and the portrait of the long-dead Colonel Pyncheon.

The one comfortable chair will be particularly important later in the work, not only because Judge Pyncheon will die in it, but also because it is the favorite diurnal resting place of Clifford throughout the story. We know that it is this, the only comfortable chair in the room, that Clifford occupies because at the end of chapter seven we are told that his chair is "deep and softly cushioned . . ." and in chapter nine that it is "his great chair." Hawthorne gives enough evidence to establish this coincidence and little more; yet it lies at the center of a cluster of facts—all bearing on the death of Judge Pyncheon—which the reader can only determine by inference from it. We are not explicitly asked to use the occult methods Holgrave was rumored to have used in find-

3. "The Dual Aspects of Evil in 'Rappaccini's Daughter'," *PMLA*, LXIX (March, 1954), 102.

ing out the circumstances surrounding the death of Judge Pyncheon's uncle: "Many persons affirmed that the history and educidation of the facts, long so mysterious, had been obtained by the daguerreotypist from one of those mesmerical seers, who, nowadays, so strangely perplex the aspect of human affairs, and put everybody's natural vision to the blush, by the marvels which they see with their eyes shut." But it seems to be clear that Hawthorne wanted his reader to draw many inferences from the facts which, baldly stated, are as follows:

Judge Pyncheon died on the fifth day of an easterly storm which had descended on his town and the Seven Gables. Clifford had not risen at his usual time on the morning Judge Pyncheon died, although, we are told, "during four days of this miserable storm, Clifford wrapt himself in an old cloak, and occupied his customary chair." His occupancy of this chair at this time was one of long habit; six chapters earlier we were told, "In the morning, very shortly after breakfast, it was Clifford's custom to fall asleep in this chair; nor, unless accidentally disturbed, would he emerge from a dense cloud of slumber or the thinner mists that flitted to and fro, until well toward noonday."

Before Clifford made his appearance before his sister on that fateful morning, Judge Pyncheon came to visit, unannounced and uninvited. The Judge had made several half-hearted and at least one determined effort to see Clifford earlier, but had been turned away either by unfavorable circumstances or outright rebuff each time. There was doubt that he had yet seen Clifford—who stood in mortal terror of him—since that poor man had returned from what Judge Pyncheon seems to have acknowledged as having been "a living tomb," although he might have got a glimpse of Clifford one day when Clifford stood behind a shower of soap bubbles in the gloom beside one of the windows in the upper story of the Seven Gables. The Judge, on this—his last—visit, managed to coerce Hepzibah to summon Clifford, then wearily sat down to wait his arrival in Clifford's chair, the "ancestral chair," the same oaken chair that their ancestor had died in when the house was new.

Hepzibah did not go to Clifford's room directly, but first entered another wing of the house to enlist the aid of the daguerreotypist Holgrave in this crisis. Holgrave was not in his room, and, as Hepzibah soon discovered, Clifford was not in his. She was shocked by Clifford's seeming disappearance. She perhaps had forgotten that she had heard someone play Alice Pyncheon's prophetic harpsichord earlier that day. It did not seem to occur to her that Clifford might have descended to the first floor while she was in search of Holgrave. Her principal fear was that he had fled, and "in the old-fashioned garments which he wore about the house. . . . This figure of her wretched brother would go wandering through the city, attracting all eyes, and everybody's wonder and repugnance, like a ghost, the more to be shuddered at because visible at noontide."

Hepzibah distractedly descended the stairs, peered into the shadows of the room in which she had left Judge Pyncheon, and announced that Clifford was gone. Whereupon her brother appeared, coming from inside the room, "preternaturally pale"—even for Clifford—and unnaturally exhilarated. He then took her into the room and showed her that Judge Pyncheon was dead. She noticed that her brother was "all in a tremor and a quake, from head to foot, while, amid these commoted elements of passion or alarm, still flickered his gusty mirth." She noticed also—although the author seems to have made Clifford's habit sufficiently clear earlier—"that Clifford had on a cloak,—a garment of long ago,—in which he had constantly muffled himself during these days of easterly storm." Then, at Clifford's instigation, Hepzibah and her brother almost guiltily flee the premises of the Seven Gables, leaving the corpse behind them.

Many inferences can be drawn from these facts, and the validity of a few of those inferences may be additionally supported by a discussion of Hawthorne's theme and method in the novel.

Seldom in Hawthorne's works, and perhaps in the works of any author, can one affirm that a given interpretation of one of the themes of a work must be so because the author believed in the theme and carried it into his own life. But the theme of the superiority of the way of the imagination over the way of the senses is one important theme of *The House of the Seven Gables* that one can affirm on such authority. One could say that merely as a matter of vested interest and personal prejudice Hawthorne felt that the artist, the man of the imagination, is superior to those who create only sublunary reality; but to say only that would not be enough. His own statements in justification of that viewpoint are cogent enough to be considered as more than rationalizations.

In "The New Adam and Eve" Hawthorne makes the strong claim: "It is only through the medium of the imagination that we can lessen those iron fetters, which we call truth and reality, and, make ourselves even partially sensible what prisoners we are." And in "A Select Party" he reviles the men who lack "the imaginative faith" and fail to recognize "the truth, that the dominions which the spirit conquers for itself, among unrealities become a thousand times more real than the earth whereon they stamp their feet, saying, 'This is solid and substantial; this may be called a fact'." Finally, in "The Artist of the Beautiful," he states categorically that imaginative reality—here, the beautiful—is more real than the reality perceived by the senses: "When the artist rose high enough to achieve the beautiful, the symbol by which he made it perceptible to mortal senses became of little value in his eyes while his spirit possessed itself in the enjoyment of the reality."

*The House of the Seven Gables* is in many ways a companion piece with "The Artist of the Beautiful" and also "The Snow Image." In "The Snow Image" the traits of Mrs. Lindsey "that survived out of her imaginative youth" and the sensibilities of the "imaginative little beings" that are her daughters are opposed to the "common sense view" of Mr. Lindsey. The melting of the snow child in this tale represents the way in which the matter-of-fact world destroys the creations of the imagination. In "The Artist of the Beautiful," similarly, Owen Warland's "intellect . . . imagination . . . sensibility . . . soul" are opposed to the "main strength and reality" of Robert Danforth, the sympathy tempered by secret scorn of Annie, and the malevolent "hard scepticism" of Peter Hovenden. The destruction of the butterfly represents the material victory of the Danforth-Hovenden forces. But in this tale, unlike "The Snow Image," the spiritual forces of Warland are shown as being unconquerable.

In the novel the opposition is more subtle than in the tales. The key adjective is still "imaginative," referring to thoughts, usually connected with art, which have no plausible physical referents. Also important, as in "The Artist of the Beautiful," is the word "ethereal," referring to the physical appearance of the "imaginative," and the word "spiritual," roughly synonymous with "imaginative." In *The House of the Seven Gables*, however, the reader is not only deprived of the statements on the superiority of the "beautiful," the "spiritual," or the "imaginative" over the "practical," so frequent in "The Artist of the Beautiful," he is at the same time required to accept a principal character who is even more puny than Owen Warland—the emaciated Clifford. In other words, in the novel Hawthorne takes the idea of the super-physical strength of the ethereal embodiment of the imagination as far as it can go. He gives the reader a lover of beauty who is senile and who has seen his physique practically destroyed by thirty years of imprisonment. Even Owen Warland's victory would seem to be scant consolation for Clifford.

When Clifford is first introduced in the novel, it may be recalled, "the spirit of the man . . . could not walk." But when he catches sight of Phoebe, "he made a salutation" that seems to spring from a certain valuable innate quality in the man: "Imperfect as it was, however, it conveyed an idea, or, at least, gave a hint of indescribable grace, such as no practised art of external manners could have attained." As he eats his first meal since returning home, his "spiritual part" fitfully returns, as if "doing its best to kindle the heart's household fire, and light up intellectual lamps in the dark and ruinous mansion, where it was doomed to be a forlorn inhabitant." This look which returns "at flitting intervals," we are soon informed, is "the same expression, so refined, so softly imaginative, which Malbone . . . had imparted to the miniature" Hepzibah had treasured for so long. And when he has his first drink of coffee the meaning of this "innately characteristic" look is finally made clear. It is the evidence of "a certain fine temper of being . . . changeably and imperfectly betrayed, of which it was the function to deal with all beautiful and enjoyable things."

Somehow, through thirty years of imprisonment, this love of beauty has remained alive. And it is probable that Hawthorne intended in epithets like a "substantial emptiness, a material ghost," combined with descriptions of the fitfully flashing "characteristic" look, to show Clifford's imaginative love of beauty as the only means by which he can be led back to spiritual and therefore physical health. One engrossing problem of the novel after Clifford enters it is to bring about that rehabilitation. It is brought about with the aid of Phoebe, who can reach Clifford with her beauty and sustain him with her practicality, "She was real!" Holgrave, imaginative, radical, disturbing, helps. So does Uncle Venner, with statements like "I'm one of those people who think that infinity is big enough for us all—and eternity long enough." And, of course, Hepzibah's love, however little Clifford acknowledges it, is ethereal enough fare for him. All minister to him in the organic,[4] though dilapidated, garden behind the Seven Gables. And finally, when Judge Pyncheon, the living symbol of the curse Clifford's artistic spirit inherited at the moment of his birth into the Pyncheon family, dies, Clifford is set free of this slightly less confining prison—if organic, at best an "outworn shell"—that is the Seven Gables. He is ready to take his place in the dynamic world outside. His and Hepzibah's spiritual rebirth is symbolized by their ride in the dynamic railway train, in which, at first, "Everything was unfixed from its age-long rest, and moving at whirlwind speed in a direction opposite to their own."

The materialism of Judge Pyncheon is, of course, diametrically opposed to the way of Clifford. In his clothing of "wide and rich gravity . . . that must have been a characteristic of the wearer" and in his smile, "unctuous, rather than spiritual," with the "dignity of his character and his broad personal basis" he is the epitome of physical existence. Hawthorne accomplishes an inversion of the Judge and Clifford on a theme and metaphor identical with

4. I am employing designedly here the key terms of Morse Peckham's "Toward a Theory of Romanticism," *PMLA*, LXVI (March, 1951), 5–23.

the principal theme and metaphor of Carlyle's *Sartor Resartus.* "No better model need be sought," he writes of the Judge Pyncheon later to be seen as evil, ". . . of a very high order of respectability, which, by some indescribable magic, not merely expressed itself in his looks and gestures, but even governed the fashion of his garments, and rendered them all proper and essential to the man." And of the ethereal, imaginative Clifford he writes, "how worn and old were the soul's more immediate garments." To Hawthorne Clifford must have been the superior. And the author could have demonstrated this fact theoretically without trouble. But to show in the living, moving, earthly contexts of a novel that the artistic, half-cracked, senile Clifford was superior to the practical, sane, well-fed Judge must have seemed like an impossible task. And to attempt this when the nature of the problem demanded that Clifford be made no less ethereal, and the nature of his character and years precludes his being made much less senile, might seem to make more difficult what was already impossible. Yet, in spite of the difficulties, Clifford's superiority under these conditions was something that Hawthorne attempted to posit; and in doing so he engaged himself in perhaps his most intricate artistic problem.

It was easy to deprive the Judge of his plethora of substance. Hawthorne was able simply to bring in all-conquering death to accomplish that task. Before he kills the Judge off, however, the author, besides throwing ironic stilettos by the dozen at the massive figure of the man, his smile, and his kindly manner, plays at least one prank on the Judge in order to bring his way of looking at the world into question. This occurs when Hawthorne has the Judge try unsuccessfully to kiss Phoebe. At the "critical moment" the girl "drew back; so that her highly respectable kinsman, with his body bent over the counter, and his lips protruded, was betrayed into the rather absurd predicament of kissing the empty air." Hawthorne removes the incident from the realm of low comedy and establishes it as ironic with the comment, "It was a modern parallel to the case of Ixion embracing a cloud, and was so much the more ridiculous, as the Judge prided himself on eschewing all airy matter, and never mistaking a shadow for a substance."

But it was impossible to deprive Clifford of his plethora of spirituality, by giving him physical strength, without surrendering the whole issue. So Hawthorne has the two men come into overt conflict only once. The contact is overt, yet most indirect: Clifford accidentally hits the Judge with a soap bubble. The Judge calls to him in "the obscurity behind the arched window"—we do not know whether he saw Clifford, or simply inferred his presence— "Aha, Cousin Clifford! What! still blowing soap-bubbles!" Clifford did not miss the sarcasm in his tone, and "an absolute palsy of fear came over him." This is the only time in the book the men are brought close enough to each other to react mutually for the reader's benefit. Clifford comes off the worse for the contact; that is clear. But the reader can find a great deal of evidence for Clifford's superiority in other ways than by seeing the men in direct contact with each other.

Important is the effect on the two men of the ancestral chair, which—it was established earlier in this paper—they occupied at different times. Clifford falls asleep in this chair on his first morning home, and thereafter he naps away every morning in it, awakening refreshed, presumably. The Judge, however, will not sit long in this chair and remain living. We do not know whether the revival of Clifford's energies has somehow charged the chair to the extent of making it lethal to the Judge—as if Clifford were a Beatrice Rappaccini who was able to kill by indirect as well as direct contact. (In many ways, also, the chair has the avenging qualities of the mantle of Lady Eleanore.) But most important, and most simply, the chair is the symbol of the Pyncheon line, which has grown to a state of being incompatible with that of the Judge. It should be noted that of all the exhortations and exorcisms—literally—Hawthorne directs at the Judge's corpse in his efforts to wake it up in the "Governor Pyncheon" chapter, all save the last are directed to the practical sensibilities of the Judge—"Make haste, then! Do your part! The meed for which you have toiled, and climbed, and crept, is ready for your grasp!" They, of course, do not waken the Judge. And when on his final attempt the author does not succeed in waking the Judge with a moral and spiritual plea—which would have been beyond his ken alive or dead—the author gives up in disgust.

Chapter sixteen of the novel deals with Hepzibah's trip, at Judge Pyncheon's behest, to bring her brother down for an audience with his stern cousin. Hepzibah fears for her brother's safety, "Of so slight a nature, and so shattered by his previous calamities, it could not well be short of utter ruin to bring him face to face with the hard, relentless man, who has been his evil destiny through life." She feels that Clifford is powerless to resist the Judge, "For what, in the grasp of a man like this, was to become of Clifford's soft poetic nature." Incredulously she ridicules the idea that Clifford has anything to give the Judge: "Clifford had none but shadowy gold at his command; and it was not the stuff to satisfy Judge Pyncheon!"

Only when she finds "no other pretext for deferring the torture that she was to inflict on Clifford" does Hepzibah knock at her brother's door. Then she imagines what her brother would do if he were able to divine her reason for summoning him: "Clifford would turn his face to the pillow, and cover his head beneath the bedclothes, like a startled child at midnight." When she does not find him in his room, Hepzibah fancies, among other things, that he is hiding under some squash vines in the garden. She conjectures that he might have fled into the street. She then reasons that he might fall off one of the wharves girdling the town, and with that Hepzibah runs down to enlist Judge Pyncheon's aid in the search.

The reader who knows what is to happen to Judge Pyncheon can feel the dramatic irony in these lines. This is a technique so common in Hawthorne's works that many of them—"My Kinsman, Major Molineux," "Mr. Higginbotham's Catastrophe," the early chapters of *The Scarlet Letter*, to name a few—can be understood only in small part when read for the first time. But he who reads these lines informed not only by a knowledge of Judge Pyncheon's fate but also by the knowledge that Hawthorne sympathizes with Clifford and thinks him in possession of something much stronger than his cousin's "big, heavy, solid unrealities" must also see something close to low comedy in the sister's fear that her brother might hide under his blankets or even a squash-patch to avoid an audience with the Judge.

An example of the combination of humor with this dramatic-irony-of-the-knowing-reader is to be found in the preceding chapter, in which the Judge forces Hepzibah to do his bidding:

> "Of my uncle's unquestionably great estate, as I have said, not the half—no, not one third, as I am fully convinced—was apparent after his death. Now, I have the best possible reasons for believing that your brother Clifford can give me a clew to the recovery of the remainder."
>
> "Clifford!—Clifford know of any hidden wealth?—Clifford have it in his power to make you rich?" cried the old gentlewoman, affected with a sense of something like ridicule, at the idea. "Impossible! You deceive yourself! It is really a thing to laugh at!"
>
> "It is as certain as that I stand here!" said Judge Pyncheon, striking his gold-headed cane on the floor, and at the same time stamping his foot, as if to express his conviction the more forcibly by the whole emphasis of his substantial person. "Clifford told me so himself!"
>
> "No, no!" exclaimed Hepzibah, incredulously. "You are dreaming, Cousin Jaffrey!"
>
> "I do not belong to the dreaming class of men," said the Judge quietly.

The last statement is laughable because it is so unnecessary, and the entire conversation takes on a different hue when one understands that Clifford, "idling and dreaming about the house, long long ago" actually made a discovery which would have led his cousin to the long missing deed to the Pyncheon's eastern territories. The way in which Hepzibah ridicules the Judge at one of the few times in his life when he is believing in something produced by the imagination, and the way in which he vouches for the truth with the fact of his existence—in his last hour on earth —combine to make an ironic mélange exhibiting great workmanship.

In interpreting the circumstances surrounding the death of Judge Pyncheon, however, more than a knowledge of Hawthorne's theme and a degree of prescience as to what he is going to do in the remainder of the book is demanded of the reader. It was well that Hepzibah, after seeing Judge Pyncheon's corpse, was "full of horror at what she had seen, and afraid to inquire, or almost to imagine, how it had come to pass"; she, poor woman, can be excused for her timidity. Yet we read that even she was not too frightened to imagine what had happened. The reader, seemingly, must conquer his lethargy, if not his squeamishness, and do as much as Hepzibah, although he has more facts than she had to go on.

Clifford, from all we know, was the first person to see Judge Pyncheon dead. We don't know whether the Judge was still alive when Clifford came into the room, but we can be fairly certain that Clifford would not have gone into the room of his own volition if he had known his arch-tormentor was there, alive or dead. Clifford's entrance there, to sit down in his accustomed spot for his morning nap, has however been motivated throughout the earlier chapters sufficiently to enable us to understand fairly clearly why he does enter the room. And the description of the darkness of the room given somewhat later helps us to understand why he would not have seen the Judge until he had gotten fairly close to him: ". . . what with the shade of the branches across the windows, and the smoke-blackened ceiling, and the dark oak-panelling of the walls, there was hardly so much daylight that Hepzibah's imperfect sight could accurately distinguish the Judge's figure." The hypothesis is fairly strong, then, that Clifford entered the room to carry out a habitual act and inadvertently came upon Judge Pyncheon in the chair he was about to sit down in. If Judge Pyncheon is to be taken as already dead then, we need conjecture no more. But Hawthorne gives us a great deal of assistance in imagining what might have happened were Judge Pyncheon alive.

Let it be mentioned again here that the story of the death of the Judge's uncle comes to us later through the medium of the imagination of the daguerreotypist. Let it also be pointed out that many of the details of the death of Colonel Pyncheon—some of which are confirmed late in the book—come to us by way of fireside tradition, old-wives' tales, and even Holgrave's short story of Alice Pyncheon. The stories about the Colonel centered around the fact that his death had been brought about at least by witchcraft if not by physical foul play. The earlier Jaffrey, we were told, did not die without outside influence: "his agitation, alarm, and horror" at seeing his nephew ransacking his office "brought on the crisis of a disorder to which the old bachelor had an hereditary liability; he seemed to choke with blood, and fell upon the floor, striking his temple a heavy blow against the corner of a table." The author reports few rumors on the death of Judge Pyncheon, although it is at least as mysterious as the other two deaths. Clearly, therefore, the reader must assemble his own explanation.

We do not know how Clifford acted when he saw Judge Pyncheon in his chair, but we can infer how he must have acted. "An absolute palsy of fear," at least, must have come over him. And what he must have looked like at this time perhaps even Hawthorne was not able to express. The author had called him a "ghost" throughout the book. All we know about his appearance at this moment is that when Hepzibah saw him several minutes later, "His face was preternaturally pale; so deadly white, indeed, that, through all the glimmering indistinctness of the passage-way, Hepzibah could discern his features, as if a light fell on them alone." Clifford's appearance at the moment when he came upon the Judge in his chair is important, however; for, if the Judge was still alive at this moment, Clifford's shocked expression must have been a revelation to him! The Judge had waited so long to see his cousin. And as he sat in the ancestral chair, we are told, "it may be no wearier man had ever sunk into the chair than this same Judge Pyncheon." Hawthorne's final comment on the living Judge Pyncheon is: "Surely, it must have been at no slight cost that he had thus fortified his soul with iron. Such calmness is a mightier effort than the violence of weaker men. And there was yet a heavier task for him to do. Was it a little matter,—a trifle to be prepared for in a single moment, and to be rested from in another moment,—that he must now, after thirty years, encounter a kinsman risen from a living tomb again?" After all this, would it have been any wonder if Clifford looked like a ghost to Judge Pyncheon? Hawthorne labors the point so much that Clifford's similarity to a ghost might appear to be a mere figure of speech to the reader. But would it have been that to the Judge, viewing him at close range for the first time in thirty years, in this haunted environment?

Once having made the initial assumption that Judge Pyncheon was alive when Clifford first encountered him in the chair, one can find a great deal of evidence for the inference as to what would have followed: the Judge's fatigue, the witchery of the room, the old wrapper worn by Clifford and redundantly alluded to a second time by the author when Hepzibah first saw her brother after the Judge's death.[5] (One might even conjecture that the garment belonged to the last prosperous occupant of the house—the man of whose death Judge Pyncheon was, in a way, the agent.) Even the interpolation, "a trifle to be prepared for in a moment, and to be rested from in another moment," could be interpreted as covertly referring to the confrontation with Clifford that came without warning and yet required so much rest. To this last interpretation, however, the reader might well react with the words Hawthorne used in interpreting the moral of the barrel-organ: "But rather than swallow this last too acrid ingredient, we reject the whole moral of the show."

It would not be going too far, however, to assert that the triumphant irony lurking here—in which a man who "prided himself on . . . never mistaking a shadow for a substance" would seem to have died because he had mistaken a substance for a shadow, an irony which Clifford, in his "gusty mirth," perhaps appreciated —does not conflict in any way with techniques Hawthorne exhibits in less ambiguous passages. The underlying irony is the same as that Hawthorne uses in the blinding of the Cynic in "The Great Carbuncle," but what a world of artistry has been added in the intervening years!

Lest we of the twentieth century, with our gadgets and our growing mastery over the physical universe, feel allied with Judge Pyncheon and threatened by Hawthorne's irony, however, it should be pointed out that the Judge's materialism was not simply a love of reality. The reality he believed in was devoid not only of the ghost, but also of the spirit in the broadest sense. He seemed to care nothing about morality. He seemed to have little sense of family, save for the son who would continue his own corporeal materialization. His treatment of his wife while she lived and her memory after she died shows him insensitive to love. And his personal resemblance to the long defunct Colonel Pyncheon emphasizes Hepzibah's accusation near the end of the book: "Alas, Cousin Jaffrey, this hard and grasping spirit has run in our blood these two hundred years. You are but doing over again, in another

5. In the Salem House reputed to be the historical original of the house in the novel, a secret staircase runs from what is assumed as being Clifford's room to the room in which the Judge was sitting. The motivation of the novel would support the interpretation that Clifford had somehow stumbled on the secret of the staircase on this morning when he had even had the temerity to play Alice Pyncheon's harpsichord. Hawthorne's dislike, however, of "bringing his fancy-pictures almost into positive contact with the realities of the moment" would seem to rule out the inference that Clifford emerged from this passage before the Judge's incredulous eyes.

shape, what your ancestor before you did, and sending down to your posterity the curse inherited from him!"

The entire book is, of course, concerned with relating the effects of this curse and the way that it is finally lifted. The curse operates most of the time through the house itself and the lost map of the Pyncheon territories, representing in the Preface "an avalanche of ill-gotten gold, or real estate . . . tumbling down . . . on the heads of an unfortunate posterity, thereby to maim and crush them, until the accumulated mass shall be scattered abroad in its original atoms." On account of the map, the Pyncheon line, personified by Alice Pyncheon, was allegorically sold into bondage of the Maules by Gervayse Pyncheon, the Colonel's grandson. And after her tragic death her harpsichord remained to allegorize the denial of music and probably art to the Pyncheons following her. Holgrave comes into this book to marry Phoebe and lead the posterity out from under the curse—the author shows him, in fact, successfully resisting the temptation seized upon by an earlier Maule when Holgrave refuses to exploit the mesmeric trance in which his story of Alice Pyncheon has placed Phoebe. But Holgrave and Phoebe are subordinate to Clifford and Hepzibah in this story, not only as their roles direct, but also from the standpoint of space and emphasis.

Against Clifford the Pyncheon curse, as stated in the Preface, "divesting itself of every temporary advantage [now that the map and the claim have long lost their validity] becomes a pure and uncontrollable mischief." His imprisonment for thirty years is allegorically dependent on the curse of Alice Pyncheon, for Clifford's artistic spirit is something the grasping spirit of the Pyncheons has placed in bondage. And his liberation from prison is carried out by the Judge for the purpose of placing that imaginative spirit further in bondage by trying to wring from it the secret of the lost claim. The fact that Judge Pyncheon dies while in the process of attempting this feat is one important and particularly ironic instance of the "pure and uncontrollable mischief" of the curse. Why the Judge wanted to acquire the useless map is difficult to determine, but that he died in the pursuit of it is undeniable.

By the Judge's death the curse is removed. In the marriage of Holgrave to Phoebe the heiress, the author, with some levity, has Holgrave—"I have become a conservative already!"—indicate that thanks to wealth and real estate a new curse may be acquired or the old one, in a way, be perpetuated. But the effect on Clifford of the removal of the curse is clear. In the central chapters of the book he is somewhat reborn to enjoyment of the world, and so-

ciety, and even progress—symbolized by the railroad. He sees his
sister finally able to worship and to pray, and even says, "Well—
Yes!—thank God!" himself when he returns to the Seven Gables
after his railroad trip. He came to know love through Phoebe and
sees its fruition, in another way, in her marriage to Holgrave. But
until the death of the Judge a cloud would periodically come
over his emotions. So, in the last chapter the author writes,

> The shock of Judge Pyncheon's death had a permanently in-
> vigorating and ultimately beneficial effect on Clifford. That strong
> and ponderous man had been Clifford's nightmare. There was
> no free breath to be drawn, within the sphere of so malevolent
> an influence. The first effect of freedom, as we have witnessed
> in Clifford's aimless flight, was a tremulous exhilaration. Sub-
> siding from it, he did not sink into his former intellectual
> apathy. He never, it is true, attained to nearly the full measure
> of what might have been his faculties. But he recovered enough
> of them partially to light up his character, to display some out-
> line of the marvellous grace that was abortive in it, and to make
> him the object of no less deep, although less melancholy interest
> than heretofore. He was evidently happy. Could we pause to give
> another picture of his daily life, with all the appliances now at
> his command to gratify his instinct for the Beautiful, the garden
> scenes, that seemed so sweet to him, would look mean and trivial
> in comparison.

It is not necessary that Clifford become completely rehabili-
tated physically in the novel. Hawthorne's plan throughout
the book seems to have dictated that Clifford could be fully
developed only to the degree that he was shadowy and under-
nourished, and there is no need of changing that plan at the end.
The author seems to have understood, however, the implications
for his reader of this incongruity between his intent and his execution, if it was Clifford he was talking about when he wrote of
*The House of the Seven Gables:* "I should not wonder if I had refined upon the principal character a little too much for popular
appreciation." [6] But Herman Melville, at least, appreciated Clifford, although it is difficult to determine whether he was thinking
of Clifford as deriving his strength from his immateriality
when he wrote, "Clifford is full of an awful truth throughout. He
is conceived in the finest, truest spirit. He is no caricature. He is
Clifford." [7]
In "P's Correspondence" Hawthorne drew John Keats to dimensions similar to those he uses with Clifford, and dressed him

6. Letter to Bridge, Lenox, 15 March,
1851 (*Recollections*, p. 125).
7. Letter to Hawthorne, Pittsfield,
Wednesday morning (*Hawthorne and His Wife*, I, 387).

428 · *Alfred H. Marks*

in similar ironies: "The truth is, Keats has all his life felt the effects of that terrible bleeding at the lungs caused by the article on his Endymion in the Quarterly Review, and which so nearly brought him to the grave. Ever since he has glided about the world like a ghost, sighing a melancholy tone in the ear of here and there a friend, but never sending forth his voice to greet the multitude. I can hardly think him a great poet. The burden of a mighty genius would never have been imposed upon shoulders so physically frail and a spirit so infirmly sensitive. Great poets should have iron sinews." And in the same sketch he appended to an imaginative description of an overweight, though long dead Byron, an explicit statement of the irony he used implicitly on Judge Pyncheon: "But, to say the truth, a prodigiously fat man impresses me as a kind of hobgoblin; in the very extravagance of his mortal system I find something akin to the immateriality of a ghost."

Melville wrote of Hawthorne's attitude toward the certainties of life: "There is the grand truth about Nathaniel Hawthorne. He says NO! in thunder; but the Devil himself cannot make him say yes." [8] But important in *The House of the Seven Gables* is the fact that Hawthorne is here working out the impossible problem of saying yes in a negative way. For in this work the way of Judge Pyncheon—anti-spiritual, unscrupulous, opportunistic, narrowly this-worldly, static—is clearly defeated. And the way of Clifford, Hepzibah, Phoebe, and Holgrave—spiritual, imaginative, religious, affectionate, intellectually active, dynamic—even though the banner it holds aloft has been tattered by the author's irony, is clearly victorious. The death of Judge Pyncheon stands, of course, as the key to the material well-being of the principal characters of the book. But material well-being is not what Hawthorne has principally in mind for these people. Their imaginative and spiritual qualities are what he prizes. And as to the death of Judge Pyncheon, the material facts are not what concern him. Clifford might have killed the Judge by frightening him to death; there is evidence in favor of this interpretation, though not enough to hold up in court. But the best evidence in its favor, paradoxically, is the fact that the definition of the imagination, the central concept in this novel, would require Hawthorne to stop short of giving unequivocal proof. Thus an important part of Hawthorne's task in *The House of the Seven Gables* is to oppose narrow materialism with the imagination, and in the death of Judge Pyncheon he seems to bring about the victory of the imagination on its own terms.

8. *Ibid.*, p. 388.

## ROY R. MALE

### Evolution and Regeneration: *The House of the Seven Gables* †

In *The House of the Seven Gables* the basic elements of the moral situation are once again placed before us. But the characters, tone, and guiding metaphor have radically changed from those of *The Scarlet Letter*. The ambiguous qualities of womanhood are subsumed in the dark house; the masculine traits are symbolized in the various inhabitants of the street; and the central metaphor is drawn from the process of evolution. Before we proceed to the book itself we ought to consider briefly Hawthorne's attitude toward evolution.

Nothing could be further from Darwinian descendentalism than the brief report on "Species of Men" that Hawthorne cranked out for *The American Magazine of Useful and Entertaining Knowledge* in August, 1836. Using the classifications of Linnaeus for his guide, he compared men with orangutans and concluded in favor of Homo sapiens.[1] In later years, when he visited the British Museum, the Ethnographical Rooms left him cold. "I care little for the varieties of the human race," he said, "all that is really important and interesting being found in our own variety." Indeed, one interested in the relation of science to American literature might draw up a list of items showing Hawthorne's apathy toward the contemporary furor about evolution: no references to Lamarck or Lyell; no reaction to Chambers' *Vestiges of the Natural History of Creation* (1844); no evidence that he knew of Charles Darwin's existence; a lifelong indifference to fossils; little or no curiosity about geology and astronomy. Here surely is exemplified what Austin Warren meant when he said that Hawthorne was "nearly impervious to the intellectual movements of his day." [2] All we have to do is contrast his notebooks with Emerson's journals, studded with allusions to Lyell, Oken, Goethe, Stallo, and Darwin.

† From Roy R. Male, "Evolution and Regeneration: *The House of the Seven Gables*," *Hawthorne's Tragic Vision*, Austin, 1957. Pp. 119–38. Copyright 1957 by the University of Texas Press. First published in The Norton Library 1964. Reprinted by permission of W. W. Norton & Company and Professor Male.

1. *Hawthorne as Editor*, ed. Arlin Turner (Louisiana State University Press, Baton Rouge, La., 1941), pp. 209–10.
2. Austin Warren, ed., *Hawthorne: Representative Selections* (American Book Company, New York, 1934), p. xi.

Yet this is superficial and negative evidence. Though Emerson was more interested in contemporary science, nothing he ever wrote compares with Hawthorne's artistic representation of growth, continuity, and change. Unimpressed by collections of scientific data, Hawthorne was fascinated by the interaction of past and present, heredity and environment. He was always a sympathetic and attentive observer of plant life. What stimulated him was the process of growth: the development of the "crook-necked winter squashes, from the first little bulb with the withered blossom adhering to it, until they lay strewn upon the soil, big round fellows, hiding their heads beneath the leaves, but turning up their great yellow rotundities to the noontide sun." Gazing at his garden at "The Old Manse," he felt that "something worth living for had been done. A new substance was born into the world."

As he observed the cycle of the seasons and the maturing of his plants in the garden near the Concord River, Hawthorne naturally followed the practice of his time in drawing parallels between man and nature. But he never fell into the excesses of the German *Naturphilosophie*, blurring the distinctions between man and other forms of life. "However close upon our heels the inferior tribes of creation may seem to tread," he wrote, "there is one great and invariable mark of distinction." Man has increasing knowledge and responsibility; the orangutan does not. The essential soundness of this position need not be labored today, since the spokesmen for a gladiatorial theory of existence have fallen into disrepute. But it is heartening to see the morality of knowledge and responsibility expounded by a modern authority on evolution. In *The Meaning of Evolution*, probably the best general explanation that has yet appeared, George Gaylord Simpson approaches his subject from a broad knowledge of paleontology, and thus his method is a far cry from Hawthorne's. In the second part of his book, however, Simpson searches for an evolutionary ethic. Distinguishing between the "old evolution" universal to all organisms and the "new evolution" peculiar to man, Simpson decries the fallacious tooth-and-claw morality of the early Darwinians. "The old evolution was and is essentially amoral. The new evolution involves knowledge, including the knowledge of good and evil." [3] Here he and Hawthorne are on common ground. This is the province of *The House of the Seven Gables*.

When it was first erected, the House of the Seven Gables typified the mechanical Colonel Pyncheon. But it has developed through the years until by Hepzibah's time it has become

3. George G. Simpson, *The Meaning of Evolution* (Yale University Press, New Haven, Conn., 1949), p. 311.

humanized. Hawthorne typically portrays this mellowing by making the house become almost organic. The Pyncheon elm "sweeps the whole black roof with its pendent foliage," so that the house seems "part of nature." In the yard and "especially in the angles of the building" can be seen "an enormous fertility of burdocks" with leaves two or three feet long. Green moss has gathered over the window and on the roof; flower shrubs (Alice's posies) appear in the nook between two of the gables. The history of the house is thus a record of continuity and change and suggests the book's main problem, which, using the term in the mid-nineteenth-century sense, we may define as one of evolution. The explicitly stated theme is that "the weaknesses and defects, the bad passions, the mean tendencies, and the moral diseases which lead to crime are handed down from one generation to another, by a far surer process of transmission than human law." In short, Hawthorne is here concerned with the moral aspects of what in modern terms would be called the "ontogenetic problem," with the quite apparent but nonetheless mysterious similarities and differences that exist between progenitor and offspring. Like all his contemporaries, including Charles Darwin, he shared the assumption, stated most emphatically by Lamarck, that some acquired characteristics are inherited. Writing in the pre-Mendelian era, he also assumed that heredity factors are somehow transmitted "in the blood."

The fact that *The House of the Seven Gables* would now hardly bear scrutiny as a scientific treatise in genetics should not blind us to its essentially genetic point of view, in which an understanding of the house and its occupants depends upon knowledge of their history. The most obvious clues to the subject of the book are the terms used to describe the Pyncheons and the Maules. The old Colonel is called "the progenitor"; his offspring are "specimens of the breed"; the "elder stock" in this country have had "little or no intercourse" with the "English branch" of the family; Phoebe is "one little offshoot" who has acquired variety and hence new vitality. Her practical sense comes from her mother's side, while something about her mouth reminds Jaffrey of her father. Decrepit Hepzibah and recessive Clifford are paralleled by "a few species of antique and hereditary flowers, in no very flourishing condition" and more notably, of course, by the chickens—"pure specimens of a breed which had been transmitted down as an heirloom in the Pyncheon family." Like Hepzibah, the chickens have degenerated because they have been kept too pure a species. "These feathered people had existed too long in their distinct variety; a fact of which the present representatives, judging by their lugubrious deportment, seemed to be aware."

Then there is the Pyncheon elm, the family tree, one branch of which represents Jaffrey Pyncheon and is transmuted to gold after his death. The Maules, on their side, have transmitted a "hereditary character of reserve" that has contributed to their poverty and isolation.

Evolution, as we know, favors those who have the most offspring, and Hawthorne did not ignore the sexual element in the genetic history of the Pyncheons. One of the ironies of this history has been the way in which the sexual aggressiveness of the dominant strain has limited its children. Colonel Pyncheon "had worn out three wives" by the "remorseless weight and hardness of his character in the conjugal relation." The equally animalistic Jaffrey exhausts his wife in three or four years, and his only son dies of cholera. Hawthorne deftly hints at the Judge's sexual behavior by describing his contribution to agriculture "through the agency of the famous Pyncheon bull." The sterility of the recessive strain, on the other hand, can be seen in Clifford, who has "never quaffed the cup of passionate love," and Hepzibah, the "time-stricken virgin" who has never known "what love technically means." Thus, as Hawthorne rather laboriously puts it, "in respect to natural increase, the breed had not thriven."

The plot of the book and the moral growth of its characters depend upon a subtle interaction between heredity and environment, the house and the street. These two elements, introduced in the first paragraph and gradually developed into a "mighty contrast," need to be carefully examined, for they provide our clearest insight into the way in which Hawthorne fused biological, social, and moral materials into a work of art. The house is a complex symbol of various hereditary forces. On the whole it is, as Simpson has described heredity, "a conservative factor tending to keep succeeding generations within a common pattern." [4] Resembling a great human heart, which Hawthorne elsewhere described as "the great conservative," the house also objectifies the inner life of the psyche. Through its dusky mirror flow shades of the past that blend into the present. Its realm is that of "real time," or duration, as Bergson described it;[5] within its shadowy depths the spatial elements of extension and solidity tend to melt away. This process is exemplified in the portrait of Colonel Pyncheon: its "physical outline and substance" seem to be "darkening away" as "the superficial coloring has been rubbed off by time."

As a veritable "womb of time," the house is also the repository of the word. Hidden within its depths are the "letters and parch-

4. *Ibid.*, p. 212.
5. Henri Bergson, *Creative Evolution*, trans. Arthur Mitchell (Henry Holt and Company, Inc., New York, 1911), pp. 37–40.

ments" that old Colonel Pyncheon had bequeathed to his posterity
—documents that will turn out to be worthless for the present
generation. Equally lifeless for Clifford and Hepzibah are volumes
of what had once been brilliant comedies during the Restoration
and in the eighteenth century. Hawthorne mentions Dryden's
*Miscellany Poems, The Tatler,* and especially Pope's *The Rape of
the Lock,* which was singled out, perhaps, because its title fits
into the sexual imagery and the eventual penetration by Judge
Pyncheon into the house. As Hepzibah reads aloud from these
volumes, her croaking voice transforms their once witty pages into
lugubrious monotony.

The orientation of the house signifies its place midway between
two civilizations. It faces the commerce of the street on the west,
while to the rear on the east is an old garden. Its exterior
darkened by the "prevalent east wind," the house contains within
its gloomy halls a map of what is consistently referred to as the
"Eastern claim." Though the land itself is only as far east as
Waldo County in Maine, it is associated with the "princely territory" of Europe and symbolizes the aristocratic tradition of the
Pyncheon clan, with its "antique portraits, pedigrees, coats of
arms." This trait was personified in "foreign-bred" Gervayse Pyncheon, grandson of the old Colonel, whose efforts to obtain the
Eastern claim were motivated by his desire to return to England,
"that more congenial home." His daughter Alice was also in-
ordinately proud, but her beauty, her flowers, and her music indicate the beneficial contribution of the exotic strain. During her
stay, the house seemed jolly-looking and alive, heated by the
hearty warmth of the great chimney.

The darkness of the house, however, is more impressive than
its vitality. Within its depths are shadowy emblems of the past,
each representing evil geniuses (we would call them "genes") of
the Pyncheon family. The ancestral chair is a reminder not only
of the old Colonel but also of the family's susceptibility to apoplexy (Maule's curse); the portrait and the map are dimly visible
tokens of his inflexible sternness and greed. The harpsichord is
now like a coffin and recalls Alice Pyncheon's fatal pride. None of
these objects can be distinguished very clearly in the darkness,
but it is one of the book's purposes to show that they have an
inescapable reality.

Certainly their burden weighs heavily upon the present incum-
bents of the house. Hepzibah's unbending and decadent gentility
is matched by the stiff chairs, her beetle-browed frown by the
front of the house as it lowers on the street. The essential nobility
of her character is masked by her grotesque exterior. The exotic
strain recurs in Clifford, whose undisciplined sensibility and faded

beauty remind us of Gervayse Pyncheon and his daughter. The long intervening years and Clifford's unjust imprisonment have weakened and coarsened the traits of his ancestors. Where Gervayse had savored fine imported wines, Clifford voraciously gulps coffee and breakfast cakes (Hepzibah is unable to produce a meal from the cookbook full of English recipes); where Alice played hauntingly beautiful melodies on the harpsichord, Clifford must be content with their modern counterpart, the creaky music of the Italian's hurdy-gurdy.

To move from the sepulchral darkness of the house to the dusty sunlight of the street is to discover the hubbub of the contemporary environment. Though Hawthorne occasionally describes the street as a quiet byway, he obviously intended to capture in it the whole throbbing turmoil of nineteenth-century life in this country. It is a struggle for existence, a "battle with one kind of necessity or another," in which the poorhouse awaits those who lose. The street becomes "a mighty river of life, massive in its tide," brimming with loquacious housewives and raucous vendors; the world is like a train or "an omnibus, with its populous interior, dropping here and there a passenger, and picking up another." In these two dominant images, Hawthorne clearly perceived that aspect of American society which Theodore Dreiser and H. L. Mencken were later to seize upon as characteristic: its bewildering and ceaseless fluidity. In its aimless flux some people rise above the surface while others submerge, and, as in Dreiser's *Sister Carrie*, there seems little real connection between individuals as they meet on the way up or down. The current of life on the train that carries Clifford and Hepzibah away from the old house is typical. "New people continually entered. Old acquaintances —for such they soon grew to be, in this rapid current of affairs— continually departed."

In a fluctuating society where the shadowy barriers of caste seem to have disappeared, external appearances and mechanical precision are of the utmost importance. It is a world of shimmering shop windows, a glittering bazaar dominated by "a multitude of perfumed and glossy salesmen, smirking, smiling, bowing, and measuring out the goods." Typified by the pantomime of the hurdy-gurdy operator, it is "an automatic community" in which the cobbler, the blacksmith, and the scholar dance to one identical tune, work with feverish activity, and "bring nothing finally to pass." For in this epitome of life in the street, the movement of time, like the melody, is frozen in space. "At the cessation of the music, everybody was petrified, at once, from the most extravagant life into a dead torpor." The meanest aspect of this life can be seen in the organ-grinder's monkey, whose outstretched paw and "strangely man-like expression" form an image of covetousness. "Doubtless, more than one New-Englander passed by, and threw a look at the monkey, and went on, without imagining how nearly his own moral condition was here exemplified."

Where the house is organic, temporal, feminine, and integrated, the street is essentially mechanical, spatial, masculine, and atomistic—a congeries of inert particles related only in so far as they are governed by the solar system. Judge Pyncheon, Uncle Venner, and Holgrave are the street's chief representatives. Its worst features, its incessant emphasis upon the "big, heavy, solid unrealities" of gold, real estate, and clothes, are embodied in the Judge. Distinguished by the "studied propriety of his dress and equipment," he and his benign smile are as superficial as the shine on his boots. In ironic contrast to Hepzibah, the "snowy whiteness" of his linen hides the dark, corpselike soul within. Like Mammon, he is a creature of the pavement, keeping in constant touch with it by means of his gold-headed cane. He is a superpatriot: "The fate of the country is staked on the November election" in which he hopes to become governor. A devotee of the "scale and balance system," he wishes to retain of time only what can be spread out all at once in space.[6]

The philosopher of the street is harmless Uncle Venner, who has "studied the world at street corners." " 'Give no credit!'— these were some of his golden maxims,—'never take paper-money! Look well to your change.' " While Hepzibah is trying to digest these "hard little pellets" of wisdom, he advises her above all to put on the signet of the street, a "warm, sunny smile." The years of plodding up and down the gravel and pavement have left their mark on Uncle Venner's attire: he is patched together of different epochs, a veritable "epitome of times and fashions." Never having possessed the corrupting power of Judge Pyncheon, he is tough and vigorous without being hard. Sheer antiquity has mellowed him so that he is as familiar within several family circles as he is outside on the street. He looks forward with pathetic cheer to ending his days at his "farm"— the poorhouse. He is one of Hawthorne's few unforgettable minor characters.

Early in the first chapter Hawthorne cites the prediction that old Matthew Maule's ghost would haunt the "new apartments" of the Pyncheon house. This prophecy comes true in the person of Holgrave, who lives in "a remote gable" of the house, barred from the main portion. He dwells in the house only to learn how to hate it, for, as his chameleonic past indicates, his real home

6. Compare Bergson's description in *ibid.*, p. 37: "The essence of mechanical explanation, in fact, is to regard the future and the past as calculable functions of the present, and thus to claim that *all is given*."

has been the street. His education has been the result of "passing through the thoroughfare of life"; among other trades, he has been a salesman and a traveling peddler. In his present occupation as daguerreotypist he makes pictures out of the street's element, the sunlight. But he is neither a man of patches like Uncle Venner nor an empty monument of fashion like Judge Pyncheon. His clothes—a simple inexpensive suit and clean linen—are an indication that he has retained his integrity despite past vicissitudes. He resembles the seeker for truth in "The Intelligence Office": "somewhat too rough-hewn and brawny for a scholar" and yet motivated by an intellectual curiosity of which his daguerreotypes are emblems. As Fogle has pointed out, his pictures lack depth and chiaroscuro. They penetrate Jaffrey's exterior but, like Holgrave's limited vision, offer no insight into the complex shadows of the house and its occupants; they abstract the particular individual from his context. Typical of many of his compeers, Holgrave has cut himself off from tradition, even to the extent of changing his name. Though he does not realize it at first, he is a man in search of roots. Beneath his shifting political beliefs and his varied occupations lies a yearning for stability.

Mediating between the dark house and the sunlit street is the little shop, "where the projection of the second story and the thick foliage of the elm-tree, as well as the commodities at the window, created a sort of *gray medium*." Catering chiefly to the juvenile trade, the shop forms a sequestered, childlike imitation of the grinding commerce in the street. A second spot where elements from the house and street converge is the garden. It provides a refuge from their stark realities and is a "green play-place of flickering light," where aristocratic flowers and plebeian vegetables, rank weeds and white rosebushes may intermingle. Here Holgrave and Uncle Venner, Clifford and Hepzibah may converse and watch undisturbed the "paltry rivulet of life." But the real mistress of both shop and garden is Phoebe. In the early part of the book she moves freely through house and street without being fully aware of their implications. Her room fronts on the garden while Holgrave's faces the street, but both the young people lack depth of vision. In her girlish innocence Phoebe sees nothing in Maule's well but the colored pebbles at the bottom.

The two massive symbols of house and street thus pervade the book, and the conflict between them sets the stage for its most memorable scenes. Hepzibah is introduced to us at the moment "when the patrician lady is to be transformed into the plebeian woman. . . . She must earn her own food, or starve." The urgent necessity for her to adapt herself to the brisk ways of the street is underscored by Hawthorne's grim reminder that "in this republican country, amid the fluctuating waves of our social life, somebody is

always at the drowning-point." Her situation reminds us of the
modern evolutionary doctrine that extinction is caused by a change
in the organism-environment integration that requires the orga-
nism to make an adaptive change it is unable to make. As G. G.
Simpson puts it, "When a group is already waning and approaching the danger of extinction, its local interbreeding populations
eventually fall below the size where random, inadaptive mutations
are regularly eliminated without becoming fixed in an undue proportion of the population. This, with accompanying excessive in-
breeding also likely in such a situation, may tend to produce
bizarre, sickly, or generally inadaptive forms." [7] Hepzibah, like
her chickens, is such a bizarre and inadaptive form. But she is
also and above all an indomitable human being, one who knows
when to join, when to compromise, and when to fight. Her
pathetic failure as an "aristocratic huckstress" is overshadowed
by her love for Clifford, her kindness to Phoebe, and her staunch
resistance to the Judge.

If Hepzibah needs "a walk along the noonday street to keep
her sane," Clifford requires an even greater shock. An inveterate
conservative, he has more difficulty than she does in adjusting to
the street. Alternately attracted and repelled by its incessant activity, he is baffled by such novelties as the omnibus, the water
cart, and the train, all of which oppress him with "the idea of
terrible energy." In his retrogressive condition, he finds himself
most at home with the girlish Phoebe in the garden. To be reborn,
he needs to immerse himself in the destructive element, "to take
a deep, deep plunge into the ocean of human life, and to sink
down and be covered by its profoundness, and then to emerge,
sobered, invigorated, restored to the world and to himself." Enveloped in his damask dreams of the past, he makes two abortive
gestures toward reunion with the life of the present: once when
he nearly jumps from the window into the midst of a political
procession and again when he and Hepzibah desperately strive to
attend church.

The chapter describing Clifford's temporary but invigorating escape from the house is probably the high point of the book. Jaffrey's death seems to lift the whole burden of the past; Clifford
excitedly throws off his damask dressing gown, dons a cloak,
and triumphantly guides Hepzibah out of the house into the street.
Almost instinctively, he guides her to a train, which * * * is one
of Hawthorne's symbolic representations of the contemporary
scene. As the train gathers speed and the landscape with its emblems of the past melts away in the gloom of the stormy afternoon, Clifford immediately adopts a marvelous hodgepodge of
contemporary ideas. In an ironic parallel with Holgrave, he hys-

7. Simpson, *The Meaning of Evolution*, p. 204.

terically denounces the evils that accumulate around roof and hearthstone and urges their destruction by fire. With Emersonian optimism he describes evolution as an ever ascending spiral of progress in which material crudities are gradually spiritualized. "These railroads—could but the whistle be made musical, and the rumble and the jar got rid of—are positively the greatest blessing that the ages have wrought out for us," he says to a gimlet-eyed stranger. "They give us rings; they annihilate the toil and dust of pilgrimage; they spiritualize travel!" As further evidence that the world is growing ethereal, he cites the phenomena of mesmerism and spiritualism. His excitement grows to a feverish pitch when he exalts the vitalizing power of electricity. "Then there is electricity,—the demon, the angel, the mighty physical power, the all-pervading intelligence!" he exclaims. "Is it a fact— or have I dreamt it—that, by means of electricity, the world of matter has become a great nerve, vibrating thousands of miles in a breathless point of time? Rather, the round globe is a vast head, a brain, instinct with intelligence." These speculations, faintly reminiscent of *Naturphilosophie*, are climaxed by Clifford's praise of the telegraph, which, like Thoreau, he considers to be "an almost spiritual medium."

Clifford's new acquaintance is understandably bewildered by all this. But his parting comment, as the two wanderers prepare to alight from the train, unwittingly reveals one of the ironies attendant upon Clifford's paean to spiritualization. "I can't see through you!" the stranger says, pointing up the fact that Clifford's excursion into the world has given him an opacity inconsonant with his former shadowy status in the house.[8] This mood is temporary, however, for at the lonely train station Clifford and Hepzibah are confronted by two relics of the past—a wooden church "black with age" and a farmhouse "in the old style." Clifford's tremulous exhilaration bubbles away, and he turns once again to Hepzibah for guidance. Yet their trip has not been a total failure, for here on the isolated platform, lifting her hands to the dull, gray sky, Hepzibah is able to pray—something she has been unable to do in the house.

While the two fugitives are embarked on their wild flight through the street and Clifford is temporarily assuming its substantial veneer, the corpse of Judge Pyncheon gradually fades into the shadows of the house. Throughout his life he has clutched at the solid "realities" of the past—the real estate—while shrugging off the intangible hereditary factors that contain his ultimate doom. On the surface (and this, of course, is as far as his self-

8. Here I am indebted to Clark Griffith, "Substance and Shadow: Language and Meaning in *The House of the Seven Gables,*" *Modern Philology,* LI (February, 1954), 187–95 [p. 383 in this Norton Critical Edition].

analysis would go), his motives are clear. Clifford has been released from prison through the Judge's political influence; he will either divulge the whereabouts of the map or Jaffrey will have him declared insane. Yet from the start, when Hepzibah opens her shop and the Judge scrutinizes the house from "the opposite side" of the street, one feels that his efforts to get inside the house subconsciously stem from something deeper than greed. He must exorcize that black dram of evil which, a few hours of the year, keeps overbalancing all his good works; he must wrench out and analyze the secret of the interior. Though this obsession is never made explicit, Hepzibah hints at it when she tells him, "mournfully, not passionately," that "it is you that are diseased in mind, not Clifford!" The macabre chapter in which Hawthorne gloats over the Judge's death has repelled some modern tastes. But it climaxes the subtle interaction between space and time that permeates the book. One of the massive ironies in the Judge's demise lies in the distinction between abstract and real time. As we have noted he has been a devotee of the mechanical system in which time is measured spatially. It is a knife-edge point of view that assumes that our experience takes place at discrete instants. The essence of this attitude, as Bergson observed, is "to regard the future and the past as calculable functions of the present, and thus to claim that all is given." The little card that falls out of Jaffrey's pocket on the doorstep forms "a prospective epitome of the day's history"; his unerringly accurate watch has measured the distance between his various engagements. One might say, indeed, that the Judge's watch has replaced his pulse. But now, in the darkening inner parlor of the house, both watch and pulse run down; the Judge is overwhelmed by real time; "the great world-clock of Time still keeps its beat." Hawthorne compresses the outcome in one sarcastic pun: "Time, all at once, appears to have become a matter of no moment with the Judge!"

The rhetoric of this chapter is not just a showpiece; it functions as part of the irony. The house, as we have noted, is the custodian of the word: it holds the documents, books, and poetry from the past. Now, in his gross material fashion, the Judge has tried to effect the kind of synthesis of the Light and the Word in the Act that we examined in *The Scarlet Letter*. He has always possessed plenty of light and considerable oily eloquence, but he feels the need of the old word—the document—and the act, that is, the "deed." The attempt kills him.[9] Hawthorne buries this creature of modern sunshine and festive eloquence

9. Alfred H. Marks has convincingly argued that Judge Pyncheon was frightened to death by the ghostlike Clifford, who embodied the values of the imagination. See "Who Killed Judge Pyncheon? The Role of the Imagination in *The House of the Seven Gables*," *Publications of the Modern Language Association*, LXXI (June, 1956), 355–69 [p. 413 in this Norton Critical Edition].

under seventeenth-century rhetoric. The devices of Petrus Ramus and the slogans of the Puritans come back to haunt Jaffrey Pyncheon:

> Rise up, Judge Pyncheon! The morning sunshine glimmers through the foliage, and beautiful and holy as it is, shuns not to kindle up your face. Rise up, thou subtle, worldly, selfish, iron-hearted hypocrite, and make thy choice whether still to be subtle, worldly, selfish, iron-hearted, and hypocritical, or to tear these sins out of thy nature, though they bring the life-blood with them! The Avenger is upon thee! Rise up, before it be too late!

The metamorphosis of Phoebe and Holgrave is less effective than that of Clifford, Hepzibah, and Jaffrey. One reason for this is that they initially possess so many good traits that not much change is necessary for them to attain moral balance. As Holgrave's story of Alice Pyncheon shows, the development of the Pyncheons and the Maules may in some instances be morally progressive. Phoebe has Alice's beauty and her love of music without her arrogance; Holgrave possesses Matthew Maule's hypnotic powers but, unlike his ancestor, reveres the individuality of others. Hawthorne's problem is to portray the gradual maturation of his young couple. With Phoebe he is not very successful; we are told that her association with the house has made her less girlish, more a woman, but we do not feel it.

Holgrave's growth, though it is perhaps too rapid to be credible, is more interesting because it is partly unfolded through the action. The worst aspect of his "oscillating tendency" appears when Hepzibah, confronted by the inexorable Judge, seeks aid in defending Clifford. Her thoughts naturally turn to Holgrave, who might well become "the champion of a crisis." But when she unlocks the door to his room, she discovers that he is not there. At the time when he is needed most, the daguerreotypist is "at his public rooms." Later, however, after he has spent a miserable, lonely hour with Jaffrey's body, Holgrave discovers the reality of duration, of guilt and retribution, and in doing so discovers himself.

Hawthorne wrote to Evert Duyckinck that he had intended to bring *The House of the Seven Gables* to a "prosperous close." [1] By this he probably meant that he had attempted to reconcile the values of past and present in a "sunny" ending. But when he reached this point, he was apparently unable or unwilling to take the proposed reconciliation seriously, and the final pages degenerate into flimsy farce. Good old Uncle Venner, it turns out, is not going to end his days in the poorhouse but will dwell

---

1. The letter is quoted in Eleanor Melville Metcalf, *Herman Melville: Cycle and Epicycle* (Harvard University Press, Cambridge, Mass., 1953), pp. 102–104.

in a little gingerbread cottage at the country estate. (Chanticleer and his hens have already moved there and have begun an indefatigable orgy of egg-laying.) Holgrave, having completely surrendered to Phoebe, is contemplating do-it-yourself projects, including a cut-stone house in suburbia. Hepzibah, now worth a couple of hundred thousand dollars, is prodigal in her gifts. Maule's well, formerly notable for its profound depths, is now vomiting up a succession of kaleidoscopic pictures. The whole conclusion is summed up in a vision of Alice Pyncheon floating to heaven on her harp.

The feeble ending is, perhaps, as E. M. Forster has suggested, a defect inherent in the novel form, and Hawthorne's failure here does not seriously lessen his solid achievement in the book. Unlike *The Scarlet Letter*, which is pure tragedy, *The House of the Seven Gables* is tragicomedy. Less intense than the earlier book, it is more massive in its carefully selected realistic detail and its structure. The lapse of two centuries between Colonel Pyncheon and the present generation provides Hawthorne with a deep well of concealed activity from which he can draw at will. He pulls the reader into this past by constant allusion and by the deliberate distortion of straightforward narrative in Chapter XXII. The main structural element is the contrast between the house and the street, which forms an arched window, as it were, through which we view the moral evolution of the Pyncheons. At the apex of the arch are the two chapters in which Clifford and Jaffrey simultaneously invade alien domains: for as Clifford hails the annihilation of time, Jaffrey is engulfed by it; while Clifford emerges into the Light, Jaffrey is buried under the Word. By juxtaposing these two chapters Hawthorne temporarily halts the time flow of the narrative and concentrates our attention upon the ironic correlation of the events of one stormy afternoon. The result is a structural emphasis upon the book's theme— the interpenetration of the past and the present.

# MARIUS BEWLEY

## [Aristocracy Versus Democracy and the Chain of Humanity] †

If *The Scarlet Letter* is a study of the breaking of the magnetic chain of humanity on a spatial plane, *The House of the Seven*

† From Marius Bewley, "Hawthorne's Novels," *The Eccentric Design*, New York, 1959. Pp. 175–83. Reprinted by permission of Columbia University Press.

*Gables* may be described as a variation on the theme from a temporal point of view. It is a study of guilt transmitted through time, from generation to generation, rather than of guilt seen in a widening circle which gradually encompasses surrounding society. The focus is less psychological than historical, and the political note is more dominant than in *The Scarlet Letter*. The original transgression from which the whole action of the story begins is not, as with Hester and Dimmesdale, a private moral action, but a public one—an action involving laws of inheritance and the transference of property from one generation to the next. We encounter here another of those basic tensions in American life of which I spoke earlier—the tension between past and present. In *The American Renaissance*, F. O. Matthiessen writes: "A peculiar kind of social understanding made Hawthorne hold to both the contradicting terms of this paradox of being at once a democrat and a conservative." Matthiessen is not very enlightening on the nature of this "social understanding," but it would seem to go back to that fundamental ambivalence in American experience which created the apparent contradiction between Cooper's European political novels and the Littlepage trilogy. I think we might simply define this ambivalence as the recognition on the part of the best Americans that either the excessive democracy or the excessive conservatism of the extremists on either side of the equation was impracticable. In *The House of the Seven Gables* Hawthorne carries on the same kind of debate between the respective claims, on one hand, of the past, inherited wealth, and aristocratic status; on the other, of the present, and of democratic equality, both financial and social. But the debate does not come off successfully. The resolution is as slippery for Hawthorne as for Cooper. This conflict can be illustrated by juxtaposing two quotations from *The House of the Seven Gables*. The first is from Chapter XII:

> "Shall we never, never get rid of this past?" cried he [Holgrave], keeping up the earnest tone of his preceding conversation. "It lies upon the Present like a giant's dead body! In fact, the case is just as if a young giant were compelled to waste all his strength in carrying about the corpse of the old giant, his grandfather, who died a long while ago, and only needs to be decently buried. Just think a moment, and it will startle you to see what slaves we are to bygone times,—to Death, if we give the matter the right word!"
> "But I do not see it," observed Phoebe.
> "For example, then," continued Holgrave: "a dead man if he happen to have made a will, disposes of wealth no longer his own; or, if he die intestate, it is distributed in accordance with the notions of men much longer dead than he. A dead man sits on all our judgment seats; and living judges do but search out and

repeat his decisions. We read in dead men's books! We laugh at
dead men's jokes, and cry at dead men's pathos! We are sick of
dead men's diseases, physical and moral, and die of the same
remedies with which dead doctors killed their patients! We worship the living Deity according to dead men's forms and creeds.
Whatever we seek to do, of our own free motion, a dead man's
icy hand obstructs us! Turn our eyes to what point we may, a
dead man's white immitigable face encounters them, and freezes
our very heart! And we must be dead ourselves before we can
begin to have our proper influence on our own world, which
will then be no longer our world, but the world of another generation, with which we shall have no shadow of a right to interfere.
I ought to have said, too, that we live in dead men's houses; as,
for instance, in this of the Seven Gables!"

"And why not," said Phoebe, "so long as we can be comfortable
in them?"

"But we shall live to see the day, I trust," went on the artist,
"when no man shall build his house for posterity. Why should he?
. . . If each generation were allowed and expected to build its
own houses, that single change, comparatively unimportant in
itself, would imply almost every reform which society is now
suffering for. I doubt whether even our public edifices—our
capitols, state-houses, courthouses, city-halls, and churches—
ought to be built of such permanent materials as stone or brick.
It were better that they should crumble to ruin once in twenty
years, or thereabouts, as a hint to the people to examine into and
reform the institutions which they symbolize."

Basically, this is the purest and extremest Jeffersonianism. Jefferson's philosophy of constitutions was based on the principle
that the earth belongs to the living. Each generation was, or
should be, independent of those who had lived and legislated before it, and consequently every constitution required revision
every nineteen years. Albert Jay Nock points out in his *Jefferson*
that for Jefferson the length of a generation was counted as a majority of men "born on the same day, reaching maturity at twenty-
one years of age, dying on the same day, thirty-four years later," [1]
hardly a very logical point of view. The laws and constitutions
made by one generation could be preserved in existence only by
the will of the majority of men of that generation which devised
them. If they were "enforced longer it is an act of force and not of
right":

. . . no society can make a perfect constitution, or even a perpetual law. The earth belongs always to the living generation.
They may manage it then, and what proceeds from it, as they
please during their usufruct. They are masters of their own
persons, and consequently may govern them as they please. But

1. Albert Jay Nock, *Jefferson* (New York, 1926), pp. 68–70.

persons and property make the sum of the objects of government. The constitution and the laws of their predecessors, extinguished them, in their natural course, with those whose will gave them being. This could preserve that being till it ceased to be itself, and no longer. . . .[2]

We may assume that the words Hawthorne puts into Holgraves's mouth are to be taken with some seriousness, for the same sentiments can be duplicated easily in *The English Notebooks*. The sudden transition which occurs in Holgrave's character in the final chapter is, then, not only disconcerting—it fails to the point of appearing grotesque:

Very soon after their change of fortune, Clifford, Hepzibah, and little Phoebe, with the approval of the artist, concluded to remove from the dismal old House of Seven Gables, and take up their abode for the present, at the elegant country seat of the late Judge Pyncheon. . . .

"The country house is certainly a very fine one, so far as the plan goes," observed Holgrave, as the party were discussing their future arrangements. "But I wonder that the late Judge—being so opulent, and with a reasonable prospect of transmitting his wealth to descendants of his own—should not have felt the propriety of embodying so excellent a piece of domestic architecture in stone, rather than wood. Then, every generation of the family might have altered the interior, to suit its own taste, and convenience; while the exterior through the lapse of years, might have been adding venerableness to its original beauty, and thus giving that impression of permanence which I consider essential to the happiness of any one moment."

"Why," cried Phoebe, gazing into the artist's face with infinite amazement, "how wonderfully your ideas are changed! A house of stone, indeed! It is but two or three weeks ago that you seemed to wish people to live in something as fragile and temporary as a bird's nest!"

"Ah, Phoebe, I told you how it would be!" said the artist, with a half-melancholy laugh. "You find me a conservative already! Little did I think ever to become one."

The juxtaposition of these two passages illustrates the tension in Hawthorne, but at its dullest level. The quotations confront each other with the nerveless, lumpish opposition of two lifelessly held ideas that can generate no creative activity between them. Matthiessen's kindly attempt at justification, which I have cited above, is as good as any that can be made about the ending, but it remains unconvincing. When he was dealing with ideas, Hawthorne was inferior. His mind lacked the intellectual rigour,

2. Paul L. Ford, ed., *The Writings of Thomas Jefferson* (New York, 1892–9), V, p. 121.

consistency, and logical courage of Cooper's. If he was greater as an artist, as a dealer in ideas he was a conventional bore, and in these passages the fatigue that would later overwhelm him is anticipated. The form of the whole novel seems to split up at the end on Holgrave's schizophrenia. The conflict in attitudes is nowhere absorbed into a more comprehensive viewpoint. At best, it is a matter of petty weighing, measuring and counting to see which has the larger balance on the credit side.

In a novel like *The Spoils of Poynton*, Henry James was able to build up an attitude around the same theme, but with a subtle complexity we do not find in *The House of the Seven Gables*. Mrs. Gereth's house, with its wonderful antiques, becomes a symbol of what can happen when the values of the past—represented by her purchased treasures—are substituted for human values. And yet so delicate is James's touch that the whole thing is capable of being stated from several conflicting points of view, in contrast to which Holgrave's sudden reversal is heavy and embarrassing. It is not that, carefully analysed, James's attitudes would have been greatly different. But he retained a wonderful control of tone that was to disappear from Hawthorne's novels after *The Scarlet Letter*. For example, we can see this tone operating at an elementary but marvellously effective level in Arthur Townsend's speech in *Washington Square* in which he speaks of the virtues of the perennial New York habit of tearing down the city every few years for the sake of putting up something equally unsure of itself:

"At the end of three or four years we'll move. That's the way to live in New York—to move every three or four years. Then you always get the last thing. It's because the city's growing so quick—you've got to keep up with it. It's going straight up town—that's where New York's going. If I wasn't afraid Marian would be lonely, I'd go up there—right up to the top—and wait for it. But Marian says she wants some neighbours—she doesn't want to be a pioneer. She says that if she's got to be the first settler she had better go out to Minnesota. I guess we'll move up little by little; when we get tired of one street we'll go higher. So you see we'll always have a new house; it's a great advantage to have a new house; you get all the latest improvements. They invent everything all over again about every five years, and it's a great thing to keep up with the new things. I always try to keep up with the new things of every kind. Don't you think that's a good motto for a young couple—to keep 'going higher'? That's the name of that piece of poetry—what do they call it?—*Excelsior!*"

The playful Jamesian irony that permeates Arthur Townsend's speech is itself a delightful commentary on this exhibition of the tension between past and present in the American mind. And one may well pause to consider if Arthur Townsend, for all his rather attractive giddiness, was any more of a featherbrain than the solemn young Holgrave whom Hawthorne takes so seriously. My point simply is that the tension we have been considering here can be resolved in art only in terms of finely controlled tone. It is not amenable to the sort of intellectual solemnity into which Hawthorne falls so disastrously.

But if *The House of the Seven Gables* at one level treats of the American tension between past and present, it also makes another statement on Hawthorne's old theme of human isolation, of the individual cut off from society and reality. This aspect of the story is centred in Clifford, and the parts of the story in which he appears are the most significant. The House of the Seven Gables is a richly evocative symbol. While Hawthorne's control is not as sure as in *The Scarlet Letter*, the decayed old house carries with it almost as many meanings as Hester's ambiguous A. It symbolizes all those human motives—greed, selfishness, pride—that explain Clifford's unjust imprisonment thirty years before the novel opens, and at the same time it renders visible his isolation from human society, his exclusion from the inner sphere of reality. Out of prison after thirty years of unjust confinement, Clifford at Seven Gables continues to be imprisoned in himself, shut off from the world as much as he had been before. * * *

There is one important difference between Clifford and all the other characters in Hawthorne's work who are excluded from the inner sphere of reality. Clifford is the only one who is perfectly innocent, and entirely the victim. He has not, like Hester, co-operated with the guilt of society by developing a bold speculativeness of mind. Possibly he resembles Owen Warland in "The Artist of the Beautiful" more than anyone else: "the hard coarse world" has proved too much for him. There is an episode at the close of Chapter XI which tells us something of the meaning Hawthorne meant to embody in him. He shows us the aged Clifford blowing soap bubbles into the street from the window in Seven Gables: "Little impalpable worlds were those soap-bubbles, with the big world depicted, in hues bright as imagination, on the nothing of their surface."

Hawthorne more than most artists husbanded his technical resources, and this passage reminds one of the similar symbolism employed in "Endicott and the Red Cross" and *The Scarlet Letter* in passages in which the surrounding features of the Puritan world are reflected in the armour of Endicott and Governor Bellingham respectively. In those passages, as Mr. Yvor Winters has pointed out, we have the disparate and scattered elements of Puritan society reduced to a symbolic microcosm in the rounded, burnished steel of the breastplate and helmet—images providing us a commentary on the hard martial quality, and intolerant spirituality of Puritanism. But here the world of Clifford's vision is reflected, not in martial steel, but on the surface of bubbles. Clifford is a type of the artist for Hawthorne, and the one "creative" character in his work to whom he shows any generosity. But Clifford provides an even sadder commentary on Hawthorne's conception of the artist than the others. Those soap bubbles are significant, and one's spontaneous embarrassment is wholly justified. They come out of the same part of Hawthorne's mind in which Owen Warland's ghastly little mechanical butterfly flutters limply about. Art is not for "the hard coarse world," but, presumably, for the illustrated souvenir gift books.

But the passage is not intended to be at Clifford's expense. Perhaps it exemplifies Hawthorne's meaning as much as anything in the novel. Unlike houses of stone and timber, or landed estates, or gold, soap bubbles are too perishable to be inherited or willed to posterity, and yet (Hawthorne thinks) their momentary beauty embodies a life that is denied to more durable things. But once in touch with more durable things, they break and vanish, just as Clifford's own life had broken on the crude and harsh unscrupulousness of Judge Pyncheon.

The sign of Clifford's saving grace is that he endeavours to break down the barriers that keep him isolated from men. He does not welcome his solitude as Wakefield seemed to do, nor accept his exclusion from inner reality with Gervayse Hastings's sense of inevitability. There are two occasions in the novel in which he makes a great effort to break out from his solitude and become a living part of the democratic community. Sitting at an upstairs window, he observes a tawdry political procession going down the street with banners and a band and he is irresistibly impelled to join it:

> He shuddered; he grew pale; he threw an appealing look at Hepzibah and Phoebe, who were with him at the window. They comprehended nothing of his emotions, and supposed him merely disturbed by the unaccustomed tumult. At last, with tremulous limb, he started up, set his foot on the window-sill, and in an instant more would have been in the unguarded balcony. As it was, the whole procession might have seen him, a wild, haggard, figure, his grey locks floating in the wind that waved their banners; a lonely being, estranged from his race, but now feeling himself man again, by virtue of the irrepressible instinct that possessed him. Had Clifford attained the balcony, he would probably have leaped into the street; but whether impelled by the species of terror that sometimes urges its victim over the very precipice which he shrinks from, or by a natural magnetism, tending towards the centre of humanity, it were not easy to decide. Both

impulses might have wrought on him at once.

"Clifford, Clifford! are you crazy?" cried his sister.

"I hardly know, Hepzibah," said Clifford, drawing a long breath. "Fear nothing,—it is over now,—but had I taken that plunge, and survived it, methinks it would have made me another man!"

One is reminded here (at least as far as meaning goes; there is no artistic equality between them) of how Robin in Hawthorne's most masterly story, "My Kinsman, Major Molineux," by momentarily participating in the terrible merriment of the torchlight procession which is persecuting his noble old kinsman, proves his worthiness to become a part of the new American humanity which, it must be added, looks even less attractive than Clifford's political procession. Hawthorne frequently suggests that some violent act of the will, possibly involving a high degree of sacrifice, is sometimes necessary either to sustain the magnetic chain of humanity in unbroken integrity, or make it whole again. And Clifford shows himself ready for such a sacrifice: "Had I taken that plunge and survived it, methinks it would have made me another man!"

The second occasion on which Clifford endeavours to establish communication with society is in the chapter called "The Flight of the Two Owls," in which he and Hepzibah flee through a storm to the railway station, and take their aimless excursion on the train. The chapter is beautifully done, and as it closes with Hepzibah and Clifford standing in the cold rain on the deserted platform, Hawthorne's artistry reaches a higher point, perhaps, than elsewhere in the book. He has managed in his description here to externalize very skilfully the hopelessness and emptiness that have followed this aged couple in their flight to the world, and in the course of the chapter he has managed to present visible everyday reality in such a way that it seems more of a dream than the visions that haunt Clifford in the shadowy corners of Seven Gables itself.

I have already commented on the happy story-book ending of *The House of the Seven Gables.* It has been praised recently for its positive affirmation of life-values which, supposedly, stand out in dominant contrast to the elements of the past represented by the old house itself. The dialectic is certainly there: tradition and the past disputing with the American future. But the most casual reader can hardly escape recognizing that the successful portions of the novels are those in which Hawthorne, forgetting his democratic American axe, describes the shadows of the ancient house, and not the plumbing improvements of the suburban villa into which everybody moves at last.

# WILLIAM B. DILLINGHAM

## Structure and Theme in *The House of the Seven Gables* †

Most critics of *The House of the Seven Gables* fail to discover any structural pattern. The usual conclusion is that the book consists of a series of episodes tied loosely together by the theme of an inherited curse. Rudolph Von Abele has written that *The House*, in regard to structure, is "loose and atomistic." He objects to the "lyric flights about Clifford's, Hepzibah's and Holgrave's personalities," which "take up fully a third of the book . . . without contributing anything but a kind of irrelevant whimsicality. . . ."[1] For Herbert Gorman, the work "is no more than a series of tales relating to one family. . . . As a novel the book falls to pieces and the reader is confronted with varying ingredients that do not, by any manner of reasoning, form a unified ensemble."[2] Newton Arvin states that "the principle of coherence" among the "scenes" is "less dramatic than pictorial."[3] George Woodberry sees *The House* as "a succession of stories bound together" with a "lax unity."[4]

Admittedly, the plot of *The House*, as Austin Warren has said, can be viewed as an "unavoidable nuisance."[5] It is frequently in-

† From William B. Dillingham, "Structure and Theme in *The House of the Seven Gables*," *Nineteenth-Century Fiction*, XIV (June, 1959), 59–70. Copyright 1959 by the Regents of the University of California; reprinted by permission of the Regents and Professor Dillingham.
1. Rudolph Von Abele, *The Death of the Artist: A Study of Hawthorne's Disintegration* (The Hague, 1955), pp. 68–69 [p. 394 of this Norton Critical Edition].
2. Herbert Gorman, *Hawthorne: A Study in Solitude* (New York, 1927), pp. 95–96.
3. Newton Arvin, *Hawthorne* (Boston, 1929), p. 213.
4. George E. Woodberry, *Nathaniel Hawthorne* (Boston, 1902), pp. 209–210. Those critics who do consider *The House* more than merely a collection of episodes often remove it from its temporal form and compare it with another medium. Maurice Beebe, for example, pictures the structure as "a circle spinning out from a central core, its conclusion contained in its starting point. Or, better, the geometric figure which more accurately describes *The House of the Seven Gables* is, as Clifford Pyncheon says of life in general, an 'ascending spiral curve.'" To illustrate, Beebe asks the reader to "visualize a bed spring observed from above rather than from the side" ("The Fall of the House of Pyncheon," *Nineteenth-Century Fiction*, XI [June, 1956], 3, 15). Hyatt H. Waggoner also analyzes the novel's structure largely in spatial terms, comparing it to various geometric figures. "When in the last chapter," he writes, "Pyncheon and Maule are united and depart from the house, the theme which has been rendered visible by straight lines and angles is overcome by that embodied in curves, circles, and cycles" (*Hawthorne: A Critical Study* [Cambridge, Mass., 1955], p. 154) [for Waggoner, see p. 404 of this volume].
5. Austin Warren, *Rage for Order* (Chicago, 1948), p. 99.

terrupted by long character delineations, flights into the past, musings over matters that are irrelevant to the action of the story. When the various episodes and apparent digressions are considered thematically, however, the work takes on a unity not recognizable when it is viewed solely as a narrative. Despite the superficial motif of an inherited curse, the real theme concerns the necessity of man's participation in what Holgrave terms "the united struggle of mankind." Hawthorne projects his theme in a series of antitheses. Poverty is contrasted with riches, the present with the past, aristocracy with democracy, youth with age, greed with unselfishness, the complex with the simple, appearance with reality, pride with humbleness, the isolated with the unisolated. And each contrast subtly throws light on the theme. For example, the character delineations of Clifford and Phoebe, ridiculed by the critics, show an isolated character contrasted with an unisolated character and deftly point up the pathos and hopelessness of a state of psychological isolation. Again, the scene in chapter xviii that pictures the dead Judge alone in the House of the Seven Gables offers a contrast between the real and the apparent, between the real Judge Pyncheon and the Judge as the deceived people of his town see him. It is a dramatic representation of the hypocrisy that results from Judge Pyncheon's psychological isolation from the "united struggle of mankind."

Thus the "varying ingredients," although not all contributing to the plot, do contribute to the theme, the most important unifying element. Of the various contrasts that pervade the entire novel, three are especially dominant in three different parts, and to these principal contrasts the novel owes its major theme. The first six chapters stress the desirability of a democratic way of life over an aristocratic one. With the introduction of Clifford in chapter vii the theme of psychological isolation comes into the foreground and is emphasized through chapter xiv, mainly in contrasts of Clifford, Hepzibah, and the Judge with unisolated characters. The last seven chapters constantly reflect the main theme by pointing up the dichotomy between appearance and reality. To illustrate the structural pattern and theme a rather detailed consideration of each of the three parts is necessary.

I

In chapter i the conflict between the aristocrat Colonel Pyncheon and the plebeian Matthew Maule sets the stage for the strong antithesis of aristocracy and democracy that remains in the foreground for six chapters. When the ancient House of the Seven Gables is first erected by Colonel Pyncheon, he has an open-house celebration to which he invites both the aristocratic and the plebeian classes. But each class receives different treatment. Two servants observe the guests as they arrive, "pointing some of the guests to the neighborhood of the kitchen, and ushering others into the statelier rooms,—hospitable alike to all, but still with a scrutinizing regard to the high or low degree of each." Thus early in the history of the house a pride in high social degree becomes a part of the Pyncheon tradition, which, like all aristocratic traditions, is based on a flimsy foundation. The symbol of the Pyncheons' absurd claim to superiority is the missing deed to the territory in Maine.

This impalpable claim, therefore, resulted in nothing more solid than to cherish, from generation to generation, an absurd delusion of family importance, which all along characterized the Pyncheons. It caused the poorest member of the race to feel as if he inherited a kind of nobility, and might yet come into possession of princely wealth to support it.

The decline of the Pyncheon aristocracy is indicated in terms of Hepzibah's having to open a cent-shop in order to earn a livelihood. Hawthorne pictures the old maid sympathetically, but, by placing her in opposition to the life around her, also reveals her emptiness and the necessity for her coming out of her proud shell of tradition and becoming a part of the populace. She is

the final throe of what called itself old gentility. A lady—who had fed herself from childhood with the shadowy food of aristocratic reminiscences, and whose religion it was that a lady's hand soils itself irremediably by doing aught for bread. . . .

She must at last step down from her proud and isolated pedestal of aristocracy. And it is her "great life-trial," for this "poorest member of the race" feels as if she "inherited a kind of nobility." Democracy's triumph over aristocracy is again emphasized in chapter iii with the introduction of a strong representative of democracy, Holgrave, the descendant of Matthew Maule. Speaking to Holgrave of her "gentility," Hepzibah says: "But I was born a lady, and have always lived one; no matter in what narrowness of means, always a lady!" But Holgrave sees through the superficiality of these faded and meaningless titles of "lady" and "gentleman." Rather than conferring any special privileges, they restrict the holder of the titles to an artificial code of behavior that renders him useless to himself and to society. To Hepzibah's statement, Holgrave answers:

"But I was not born a gentleman; neither have I lived like one . . . so . . . you will hardly expect me to sympathize with sensibilities of this kind; though . . . I have some imperfect comprehension of them. These names of gentleman and lady had a meaning, in the past history of the world, and conferred privileges, desirable or otherwise, on those entitled to bear them. In the present—and still more in the future condition of society—they imply, not privilege, but restriction!"

Holgrave speaks further for social equality in answering Hepzibah's complaint that, since she is a "lady," she cannot become involved in the operation of a common cent-shop:

> "Hitherto, the life-blood has been gradually chilling in your veins as you sat aloof, within your circle of gentility, while the rest of the world was fighting out its battle with one kind of necessity or another. Henceforth, you will at least have the sense of healthy and natural effort for a purpose, and of lending your strength—be it great or small—to the united struggle of mankind."

In chapter iv Phoebe comes to live in Hepzibah's ancient house and to work in the cent-shop. A Pyncheon in name only, she serves as a foil to her traditional surroundings: "The young girl, so fresh, so unconventional, and yet so orderly and obedient to common rules . . . was widely in contrast . . . with everything about her." In chapter v, "May and November," the antithesis of aristocracy and democracy is most explicit in Hepzibah's lament that Phoebe is an excellent shopkeeper, but not a "lady." But "it would be preferable," writes Hawthorne, "to regard Phoebe as the example of feminine grace and availability combined, in a state of society, if there were any such, where ladies did not exist." In direct contrast with Phoebe, Hawthorne pictures Hepzibah, who is a lady but less desirable in every way:

> To find the born and educated lady, on the other hand, we need look no farther than Hepzibah, our forlorn old maid, in her rustling and rusty silks, with her deeply cherished and ridiculous consciousness of long descent. . . . It was a fair parallel between new Plebeianism and old Gentility.

Chapter vi brings together two members of the new democracy. Phoebe and Holgrave, in the traditionally aristocratic Pyncheon garden with its "grass, and foliage, and aristocratic flowers." The deteriorating effect of the social snobbery implicit in an aristocratic way of life is symbolized by the diminutive Pyncheon hens. Like the Pyncheons, the isolated chickens "had degenerated . . . in consequence of too strict a watchfulness" to keep them aloof and pure.

An aristocracy emphasizes the excellence and privileges of a few and leads to a dangerous and unwise withdrawal from the world's "united struggle." Thus the express superiority of a state of social equality represents the main theme of the first six chapters. The center of Part I is Hepzibah, the major symbol of a fallen aristocracy. Within this part, Hawthorne arranges each scene so that there are never more than two characters together—usually one plebeian and one aristocrat.

## II

Man's need to participate in the world's "united struggle" becomes more apparent in Part II (chapters vii–xiv) as the isolated characters, Clifford, Hepzibah, and the Judge, are studied in contrast to those who are a part of the human brotherhood. Hepzibah, Clifford, and Judge Pyncheon represent three distinct ways in which man is isolated from his fellows. Hepzibah is isolated through pride in tradition and an aristocratic way of life; Clifford through his extreme love of only the beautiful; and Judge Pyncheon through greed. All three have only a partial view of reality. They cannot see life as it is because they are blinded by their characteristic weakness of pride, extreme aesthetic sensibility, and greed.

As Hepzibah is the chief figure of a degraded aristocracy in Part I, Clifford, beginning with his introduction in chapter vii, is the main figure of isolation in Part II. Like Hepzibah (but for a different reason), Clifford has always been outside the realm of reality. He had "nothing to do with sorrow; nothing with strife; nothing with the martyrdom which . . . awaits those who have the heart, and will, and conscience, to fight a battle with the world." Clifford's nature isolates him, for "it seemed Clifford's nature to be a Sybarite." He can have no part in the "united struggle of mankind" for he can accept only the beautiful. He cannot feel even the closeness of kinship and love for Hepzibah that she feels for him, for she does not possess the beauty his nature requires for adoration. "How could he—so yellow as she was, so wrinkled, so sad of mien, with that odd uncouthness of a turban on her head, and the most perverse of scowls contorting her brow,—how could he love to gaze at her?" But "did he owe her no affection for so much as she had silently given? He owed her nothing. A nature like Clifford's can contract no debts of that kind." Rather than a detriment to his well-being, therefore, the long imprisonment may have been the instrument that saved what little affection Clifford is capable of feeling. For, if

> Clifford . . . had enjoyed the means of cultivating his taste to its utmost perfectibility, that subtle attribute might, before his period, have completely eaten out or filed away his affections. Shall we venture to pronounce, therefore, that his long and black calamity may not have had a redeeming drop of mercy at the bottom?

The third major character, Judge Pyncheon, enters the novel in chapter viii. He represents in his generation a long line of avaricious Pyncheons. Like his ancestors, he is afflicted by "the moral diseases which lead to crime" and "are handed down from one generation to another, by a far surer process of transmission than human law has been able to establish in respect to the riches and honors which it seeks to entail upon posterity." To the world Judge Pyncheon seems kindly and philanthropic. Actually, however, he is separated from mankind. In chapter viii he attempts to bestow his affection upon Phoebe in the cent-shop. He offers to kiss her as a symbol of "acknowledged kindred," but Phoebe, "without design, or only with such instinctive design as gives no account of itself to the intellect," draws away and refuses the kiss. Despite the ties of blood between them, she realizes that he is a stranger to her world.

In the first part of chapter viii, the comparison of Judge Pyncheon with his ancestor, the Colonel, indicates the reason for the isolation of both these characters: greed. For, "tradition affirmed that the Puritan had been greedy of wealth; the Judge, too, with all the show of liberal expenditure, was said to be as closefisted as if his grip were of iron." Not only is he selfish with what he already has, but he is ruthless in obtaining more, as is indicated in his first attempted interview with Clifford. This incident establishes the Judge as the villain and reveals the growing conflict between him and his poorer relations, which is the central action of the plot. His "hot fellness of purpose, which annihilated everything but itself," isolates him from mankind. He has upset the necessary equilibrium in life by allowing the head to overcome the dictates of the heart. Like Roger Chillingworth, Ethan Brand, and Rappaccini, Judge Pyncheon follows one major ambition to his doom.

In chapter ix the complex and melancholy Clifford again assumes the central position in the theme of isolation as he is contrasted with the bright little Phoebe. As a consequence of Clifford's partial acceptance of reality, "the world never wanted him." Phoebe's nature, on the other hand,

> was not one of those . . . which are most attracted by what is strange and exceptional in human character. The path which would best have suited her was the well-worn track of ordinary life; the companions in whom she would most have delighted were such as one encounters at every turn.

Possessing a freshness derived from her kinship with humanity, she is the "only representative of womanhood" who is at least partly able to bring Clifford "back into the breathing world." For, Hawthorne explains, "Persons who have wandered, or been expelled, out of the common track of things . . . desire nothing so much as to be led back. They shiver in their loneliness, be it on a mountain-top or in a dungeon."

The pathos involved in Clifford's isolation is evident as he gazes from behind the arched window upon as much of "the great world's movement" as possible. Hawthorne describes the

> pale, gray, childish, aged, melancholy, yet often simply cheerful, and sometimes delicately intelligent aspect of Clifford, peering from behind the faded crimson of the curtain,—watching the monotony of every-day occurrences with a kind of inconsequential interest and earnestness, and, at every petty throb of his sensibility, turning for sympathy to the eyes of the bright young girl!

In the middle chapter of *The House* (chapter xi) the theme of isolation reaches its peak of intensity in Clifford's actions. As he and Phoebe watch the parade march with all its pomp past the House of the Seven Gables, he realizes his state of isolation from the "one broad mass of existence,—one great life,—one collected body of mankind," and he cannot resist an actual physical attempt to plunge down into the "surging stream of human sympathy."

> He shuddered; he grew pale. . . . At last, with tremulous limbs, he started up, set his foot on the window-sill, and in an instant more would have been in the unguarded balcony. . . . [He was] a wild, haggard figure, his gray locks floating in the wind that waved their banners; a lonely being, estranged from his race. . . .

Then Hawthorne clearly describes Clifford's great need to become reunited with the world and hints that this reunion can be accomplished only by death.

> He needed a shock; or perhaps he required to take a deep, deep plunge into the ocean of human life, and to sink down and be covered by its profoundness, and then to emerge, sobered, invigorated, restored to the world and to himself. Perhaps, again, he required nothing less than the great final remedy—death.

In the latter part of chapter xi a second attempt "to renew the broken links of brotherhood" involves Hepzibah, who, like Clifford, is cognizant of her aloofness from mankind. Indeed, she

> yearned to take him by the hand, and go and kneel down, they two together,—both so long separate from the world, and, as she now recognized, scarcely friends with Him above,—to kneel down among the people, and be reconciled to God and man at once.

But as the two pathetic figures attempt to follow Phoebe to church, they realize that they have lived too long in solitude and that there is no returning. "We have no right among human beings," Clifford says, "no right anywhere but in this old house. . . ." As they retreat to the dismal mansion, there is a contrast between the free air of the outside world and the heavy atmosphere of their "jail," the house.

The last three chapters of Part II are concerned mainly with Holgrave, with the story he reads to Phoebe, and with Phoebe's departure. In spite of the immaturity of Holgrave's notions about reform, he does possess some wisdom in matters relating to the isolating effect of the past on the present. "It [the past] lies upon the Present like a giant's dead body!" he tells Phoebe.

> "In fact, the case is just as if a young giant were compelled to waste all his strength in carrying about the corpse of the old giant, his grandfather, who died a long while ago, and only needs to be decently buried. Just think a moment, and it will startle you to see what slaves we are to bygone times. . . ."

The story which Holgrave reads to Phoebe emphasizes the two traits which have brought about Maule's Curse and isolated the Pyncheons: greed and pride. Gervayse Pyncheon upset the balance of head and heart and sacrificed his daughter for the promise of wealth. Gervayse's fate is similar to that of Colonel Pyncheon and, much later, to that of Judge Pyncheon.

Except for the Judge, all of the main characters are brought together in chapter xiv as Phoebe leaves the old mansion. The contrast between the hopelessly isolated Clifford and Phoebe as she says good-by to him is striking. Her departure takes him even further into the world of solitude. His parting remark to her is: "Go, now!—I feel lonelier than I did." Phoebe's departure terminates the second structural part of the novel. Holgrave sets the scene for the climax, which comes at the beginning of Part III, when he says to Phoebe before she leaves: "I cannot help fancying that Destiny is arranging its fifth act for a catastrophe." From Judge Pyncheon's attempted interview with Clifford in chapter viii to Holgrave's portentous remarks at the end of Part II, there is a general movement of the plot, a building up of the major conflict between Hepzibah, Clifford, and the Judge, toward the climactic scene, which occurs in chapter xv and ends in the Judge's death. The theme of isolation is thus predominant in Part II, and is stressed by the study of the isolated in contrast to the unisolated. As the narrative progresses, it becomes increasingly evident that the isolated figures cannot become reconciled with the world.

### III

From the time when Hepzibah's scowl is contrasted with the Judge's smile in chapter xv to the end of the novel, where the events of the story ostensibly terminate in complete felicity, things are clearly not as they seem. Judge Pyncheon, who casts his shadow over this last part of the novel, is portrayed on two levels: as he appears and as he really is. The very title of chapter xv

("The Scowl and the Smile") hints at Hawthorne's concern with the deceptiveness of outward appearance as typified in Hepzibah and the Judge. The townspeople think Hepzibah's scowl reflects her inward nature. Although she is, in reality, warm and kind, her myopic frown stamps her as sour and bitter. In contrast, the Judge seems benevolent but is really a villain of the first order. To the world, he is

> a man of eminent respectability. The church acknowledged it; the state acknowledged it. It was denied by nobody. In all the very extensive sphere of those who knew him . . . there was not an individual—except Hepzibah, and . . . the daguerreotypist . . . who would have dreamed of seriously disputing his claim to a high and honorable place in the world's regard.

He is like a marvelously well-built palace with a "deadly hole under the pavement" that contains, unseen from the outside, some secret decay. For, "beneath the show of a marble palace . . . is this man's miserable soul!"

The growing conflict between the avaricious Judge and his relatives in the House of the Seven Gables reaches a climax in chapter xvi, when the Judge demands to see Clifford. In his twisted mind he is sure that Clifford knows the location of a long-lost Pyncheon treasure. The climax of the novel is thus brought about by the Judge's reliance on false judgment made from appearance. For, the only gold Clifford has "at his command" is "but shadowy gold," and is "not the stuff to satisfy Judge Pyncheon!" Appearance then leads to another misunderstanding. Hepzibah finds the Judge dead, and Clifford urges her to flee with him from the house. Everything points to the conclusion that Clifford has murdered the Judge and thus ended the constant threat to his well-being.

In chapter xviii, Hawthorne offers a clue to the chief theme in the section by the title of the chapter, "Governor Pyncheon." The labels "Governor," "Colonel," and "Judge" represent titles which to the world signify integrity and honor, but which, in the case of the Judge and his ancestors, denote, in truth, a marked dishonesty. Hawthorne pictures the dead Judge sitting alone in the House of the Seven Gables while a storm rages outside; and by describing all his scheduled activities for the day in which he dies, reveals the dichotomy between appearance and reality in the Judge's life.

The last three chapters compose the dénouement of the novel, and there is much explication of plot details in these chapters. The Judge's death is a natural one of the same type that overcame the Colonel, not murder as it has seemed to be. The daguerreotypist is shown in his true identity as a descendant of Matthew Maule. Many other details, such as the location of the missing document, are explained and the story comes to a close with no questions unanswered.

In these final chapters a constant undertone reminds us of the contrast between appearance and reality, both in plot details and in Judge Pyncheon's life. The morning after the Judge's death, when the summer storm has subsided, even the ancient House of the Seven Gables appears to be a place with a pleasant history (chapter xix). "So little faith is due to external appearance, that there was really an inviting aspect over the venerable edifice, conveying an idea that its history must be a decorous and happy one. . . ." This undertone is exemplified down through the last chapter of the book in remarks concerning Judge Pyncheon. In chapter xxi, Hawthorne writes: "Thus Jaffrey Pyncheon's inward criminality . . . was, indeed, black and damnable; while its mere outward show and positive commission was the smallest that could possibly consist with so great a sin."

Thematically the most important, and indeed the most striking, example of this ironic undertone comes in the ending. Hepzibah, Clifford, Holgrave, and Phoebe leave the ancient house to live in the Judge's country home with the intention of having the "patched philosopher," Uncle Venner, join them later. These actions seem to indicate that happiness has at last been achieved by Hepzibah and Clifford, who have inherited the Judge's fortune and are rid of his threat. But the level of the apparent here, as in other places in Part III, is not to be mistaken for the real. A recent criticism maintains that

> the Maule-Pyncheons ride happily away from the House of the Seven Gables to possess the future in a merger of bright fortunes —almost a fairy story ending for Clifford and Hepzibah. . . . It's about as pessimistic as Cinderella. . . . Old Maid Pyncheon closes up her cent shop and rides off in her carriage with a couple of hundred thousand. . . .[6]

And this is precisely what happens. But to assume that the fortune which Hepzibah and Clifford inherit will mean perfect bliss for them is a failure to understand the fundamental traits of these characters and the main theme of the novel. Hepzibah had been fortunate indeed when she was forced to open a cent-shop, step down from her isolated pedestal of "imaginary rank," and become a part of the "surging stream of human sympathy." The epoch of Hepzibah's contact with the human struggle is short-lived, however. With her inheritance of the Judge's fortune she can step back upon her pedestal of gentility, there to remain isolated and lost.

6. Henry G. Fairbanks, "Sin, Free Will, and 'Pessimism' in Hawthorne," *PMLA*, LXXI (1956), 988. For another expression of *The House* as a novel with a happy ending see Ernest Erwin Leisy, *American Literature* (New York, 1929), p. 98.

Clifford, we should remember, is a Sybarite. With the loss of Phoebe, "his only representative of womanhood," to Holgrave, Clifford has passed his greatest happiness. He now has "the means of cultivating his taste to its utmost perfectibility." In the closing pages Hawthorne writes that Clifford has "all the appliances now at command to gratify his instinct for the Beautiful. . . ." And the result can only be isolation and an "eating out of his affections." For the three chief characters of the novel, the ending is anything but happy, in spite of appearances. The Judge dies isolated from man and God because of his greed. Hepzibah will again be a "lady," isolated from the "united struggle," and Clifford will no longer be forced to see life as it is; he can now view only the Beautiful. Ironically, therefore, Holgrave's remark in chapter xiv that "Destiny is arranging its fifth act for a catastrophe" applies not to the death of Judge Pyncheon, which certainly is no catastrophe, but to the tragedy that is to befall Hepzibah and Clifford upon their inheritance of the Judge's fortune. It is an echo of the statement Hawthorne recorded in his notebooks: "To inherit a great fortune. To inherit a great misfortune." [7]

Structurally, then, *The House* is composed of a series of antitheses with three particular contrasts dominating the book. To these dominant contrasts the work owes its major theme: the necessity of man's close communion with his fellow beings. Primarily because of its basic weakness in plot, *The House* is not Hawthorne's best work. It is, nevertheless, much more than a series of unrelated tales that contribute nothing to the total effect but a kind of "irrelevant whimsicality." Organized under a pervading theme, the seemingly diverse elements of the novel can be said to form a "unified ensemble."

## ALFRED J. LEVY

### *The House of the Seven Gables:* The Religion of Love [†]

In an acute analysis, Maurice Beebe contends that Hawthorne's *The House of the Seven Gables* is "unified not only as static picture, but also as dramatic narrative." In his largely successful at-

7. *The American Notebook*, ed. Randall Stewart (New Haven, 1932), p. 130.
† From Alfred J. Levy, *"The House of the Seven Gables:* The Religion of Love," *Nineteenth-Century Fiction*, XVI (December, 1961), 189–203. Copyright 1961 by the Regents of the University of California; reprinted by permission of the Regents and Professor Levy.

tempt to dispute those critics who emphasize the romance's static rather than dynamic qualities, Beebe sees the geometric figure of the ascending spiral curve as an equivalent of the book's total structure. In his concentration, however, on the "house-human relationship" and in his relegation of both Holgrave and Phoebe to minor roles as unifying agents in the total structure, Beebe has underemphasized elements which contribute much to the organic unity of the romance—elements which would, in fact, complement his thesis about the spiral curve.

It is my contention that the characters themselves, especially Phoebe, provide the vital structural backbone and account as well for thematic unity. The house-human relationship, although it reveals the thematic background against which the action is played, could not account for complete organic unity. Consequently, I would like to look more closely at the characters, at their motives and tensions, to discover what Hawthorne means by his remark in the preface, "A high truth, indeed, fairly, finally, and skilfully wrought out, brightening at every step, and crowning the final development of a work of fiction may add an artistic glory, but is never any truer, and seldom any more evident at the first page than at the last."

It is only by considering the final grouping of the characters, after they have lived out their total dramatic lives, that the full impact strikes. The Pyncheon house is important but subordinate to the characters who move within its physical and spiritual confines.

The house is in a state of decay because its inhabitants have withdrawn from worldly business. This deliberate isolation is an unnatural choice that leads to inversion and imbalance; Hawthorne's attitude toward this distortion of man's social function is reflected in his symbolic treatment of the house. There is no light, either in house or inhabitants. All normal intercourse with the world is avoided, and even the chickens are a scrawny replica of the once healthy Pyncheon breed.

Hepzibah Pyncheon is thoroughly dominated by the past, by what she believes is a familial curse of bloody, violent deaths for all male Pyncheons. She is powerless, before she opens her cent shop, to cope with the present. She is an old and feeble lady, who has missed her chance for a vigorous life. Her enforced isolation has enervated her; she has become somewhat unbalanced, "a kind of lunatic." Even in her most strenuous attempt to repudiate the past—her train ride with Clifford—she is overwhelmed by what she is doing and fundamentally adheres to her fixed idea of the past by imagining that the train was "passing up and down Pyncheon Street."

Hawthorne, however, with characteristic sympathy, does not reject the old woman. Although she has been too weak and has made bad choices, Hawthorne implies that what saved her from atheism was her ability to discern the essential goodness and divine design behind the bewildering complexities of life's surface. Hawthorne sounds a key theme when he admits that "life is made up of marble and mud" and that "without all the deeper trust in a comprehensive sympathy above us, we might hence be led to suspect the insult of a sneer, as well as an immitigable frown, on the iron countenance of fate."

Hepzibah attempts two solutions to her artificial isolation. If eventually neither succeeded, they were, nevertheless, the right kinds of effort. Both gestures fail, however, because Hepzibah is too old to carry them through with vigor; the final affirmation, implicit in the spiral curve, remains for the young people, who, nevertheless, learn from the old lady. If this romance looks back at the past, it also looks to the future. A fundamental theme reveals that the past bequeaths a heritage that cannot be denied; nevertheless, the past need not dominate the present. Poor Hepzibah has lived too long in the past; this has resulted in her special lunacy. Hawthorne does not repudiate her efforts to regain a normal tempo, but he implies in her failures that she is no longer equipped to succeed. That he accepts her solution, however, can be seen in the final actions of Holgrave and Phoebe.

At any rate, her efforts are of a kind. They both involve a kind of love, an earnest desire to help her neighbors. Her first coin from the cent shop seems to her "a talisman, fragrant with good, and deserving to be set in gold and worn next her heart." Her second effort costs her more: she has lived a loveless life and attempts to solve her personal isolation by lavishing affection on her brother, himself a relic of the past. To a very limited extent she succeeds, but it is significant that Phoebe eventually takes over both the cent shop and the care of Clifford. Hawthorne calls the old lady's efforts "pitiful, yet magnanimous."

If Hepzibah's attempts to restore a healthy equilibrium to her mutilated life fail, Clifford's efforts are more pathetic, if none the less significant. Thrown into jail by the false accusations of Judge Pyncheon, Clifford makes continuous attempts after his release to move back into the life from which he had been so artificially separated. Even more significantly, he tries to return to the innocence of his childhood ("He had not merely grown young;—he was a child again"), by which device he "kept his heart the fresher." Clifford is not, of course, the ideal Hawthorne hero; he is far too weak. But his efforts to reassociate himself with the world about him inadvertently teach Phoebe and Holgrave certain things which are of great use to them in their final decision.

Clifford, like his sister, makes strenuous efforts to renew a normal association with the world. Like her he perceives the futility of his isolation and tries to overcome it; like her he is doomed to failure because he had already made his fundamental choice to live in the past. Essentially, he accepts the tyranny of the past, and this disqualifies him as hero. The Hawthorne hero never loses his sense of the past and the debt he owes to past experience; conspicuously a man in history, he can never allow the past to dominate him so that he loses moral responsibility for his actions. Accepting the past as irrevocable is a way of predestining a man to a given course of action, a way of robbing him of his free will and, ultimately, of his dignity as a human being. Hawthorne thus rejects Clifford.

Clifford's forays take many forms. First, he and Hepzibah decide to go to church, to worship with their neighbors; the moment they step into the sun, however, they see it is no use. They are relics of an outworn culture, and the house sucks them back into the vortex of the past. "For, what other dungeon is so dark as one's own heart! What jailer so inexorable as one's self." In his second attempt, Clifford is watching a parade. As he watches from the window, he sways toward the pulsing life as a child will instinctively search for salt or sugar, some lack in his diet, without knowing precisely what the lack is. The most explicit attempt is the train trip. A remarkable change comes over Clifford once he is beyond the stultifying atmosphere of Salem. In a fit of divine madness, he recaptures youthful powers of perception, sees incisively what will happen to him, to his sister, and to Phoebe and Holgrave. As Beebe perceives, Clifford uses the figure of the ascending spiral curve to signify human progress. The figure can be further related to a main theme: Clifford, one of the guardians of the past, becomes an apostle of progress, but a progress, as the spiral suggests, based on the best achievements of the past.

In a lyrical outburst, Clifford shows what he has learned from experience. He makes it more than apparent that man is predestined to nothing that wise choices cannot abrogate. Ultimately, man's passive acceptance of the onus of the past prevents progress; man can, by wise and intelligent choice, perfect himself in this life.

"It is as clear to me as sunshine,—were there any in the sky,—that the greatest possible stumbling-blocks in the path of human happiness and improvement are these heaps of brick and stones, consolidated with mortar, or hewn timber, fastened together with spike nails, which men painfully contrive for their one torment, and call house and home! The soul needs air; a wide sweep and frequent change of it. Morbid influences, in a thousand-fold variety, gather about hearths, and pollute the life of households. There is no such unwholesome atmosphere as that of an old home, rendered poisonous by one's defunct forefathers and relatives. I speak of what I know."

Much as Clifford perceives, he is incapable of translating these insights into action. Much as he abhors the old mansion, he and Hepzibah crawl back to it to await deliverance by stronger characters who live in the present.

Many critics have remarked that Holgrave acts inconsistently, that his repudiation of his early position is unmotivated and, in fact, sentimental. I quite agree with Beebe that there is a consistent line of development in Holgrave, and that his final adjustment is foreshadowed in a major crisis. I hope to show also that this change was decisively influenced by an ingenuous girl, who did not realize her powers. Holgrave, it is true enough, is at first a brash young man. He has radical tendencies, entertains strange looking men, and displays an affinity for various reform movements of his day. Even early in the romance, however, Hawthorne does not intend to be wholly satirical. He is more in sympathy with Holgrave than critics have admitted. Nor is he assailing the idea of reform as a whole; he is depicting a vigorous man who wanted sincerely to change for the better the world in which he lived. As Hawthorne remarks, "Man's own youth is the world's youth; at least he feels as if it were, and imagines that the earth's granite substance is something not yet hardened, and which he can mold into whatever shape he likes."

Phoebe accurately perceives that Holgrave has not found the means with which to gain the ends he desires. Reflected in her instinctive recoil from him is Hawthorne's characteristic preoccupation with the head and heart dichotomy; Holgrave is wrong only in his methods. "In his relation with them [the Pyncheons], he seemed to be in quest of mental food, not heart-sustenance. Phoebe could not conceive what interested him so much in her friends and herself, intellectually, since he cared nothing for them, or, comparatively, so little, as objects of human affection."

Hawthorne clearly praises this trait of wanting to do good (although he censures Holgrave for other things); as a matter of fact, he maintains that this innate idealism in man's best hope.

> He had that sense, or inward prophecy,—which a young man had better never have been born than not to have, and a mature man had better die at once than utterly to relinquish,—that we are not doomed to creep on forever in the old bad way, but that, this very now, there are the harbingers abroad of a golden era, to be accomplished in his own lifetime. . . . And when, with the years settling down more weightily upon him, his early faith

should be modified by inevitable experience, it would be with no harsh and sudden revolution of his sentiments.

Holgrave is a radical and Hawthorne is not; Holgrave wants to recast everything in the image of his age and consequently of himself. Hawthorne, however, thought this pride, and realized that change, in and for itself, is not necessarily good, that progress must be built carefully on the pyramid of the past. Nowhere does Hawthorne suggest that man cease his efforts on behalf of humanity. Youthful ardor seeks too abrupt changes, is too vigorous and at times misdirected, but this enthusiasm is desirable nonetheless; when it is modified by wisdom and judgment, it produces men of real worth. The young engraver needs desperately a permanent ethical and moral base from which to move, some direction for his enormous energy—and he finds it in Phoebe. If, early in his career, Holgrave is a relativist in some matters, he always preserves undefiled his personal integrity—and this matters most to Hawthorne. Holgrave had never sought to impose his will arbitarily upon another, "had never violated the innermost man, but had carried his conscience along with him." It is in this spirit of altruism that Holgrave protests to Phoebe of the debilitating effect of the past (in the well known speech equating the past with a dead giant's body). We must keep constantly in mind that Holgrave is a Maule, one of the family who had sought to impose the curse of the past on the present. Presumably his identity is preying upon his mind as he utters his words. The irony heightens the tension.

The Maules had always had a talent for mesmerism, and Holgrave is a Maule. While he is telling Phoebe the story of Alice Pyncheon, she becomes so enthralled that she nearly falls under his spell. It will require but a final act of will to bring her completely into a hypnotic state and presumably to her death—another Pyncheon victim to another Maule. If Holgrave were to make this act of will (no single situation in Hawthorne so implies his belief that man can make his own destiny), he would be acceding to the past and approving the evil the past has bequeathed. His refusal to hypnotize Phoebe repudiates the past and prepares for the eradication of the curse. Actually, as Beebe has noted, this is the first step in the reconstruction process. From here to the close, there is a definite lightening of tone, imagery, and theme, with the single parenthesis on the death of Judge Pyncheon, who wants to drape the corpse of the past on the present. An instance of this lighter tone and imagery occurs after Holgrave refuses to hypnotize Phoebe; the tone reveals that the young man has won through to a more profound understanding of and harmony with the world about him. All nature acquiesces in his decision.

So sweetly cool was the atmosphere, after all the feverish day, that the summer eve might be fancied as sprinkling dews and liquid moonlight, with a dash of icy temper in them, out of a silver vase. Here and there, a few drops of freshness were scattered on a human heart, and gave it youth again, and sympathy with the eternal youth of nature. The artist chanced to be one on whom the reviving influence fell.

Holgrave's long speech on the possibilities of reform which begins within man's heart reflects Hawthorne's profound yet paradoxically simple attitude toward man's efforts to achieve happiness. This is a mirror image of Hawthorne's many portraits of evil and depravity and quite as relevant in reflecting the author's views about mankind. In spite of his intellectual tag as a reactionary, Hawthorne is merely cautious and realistic with respect to man's efforts to improve. He believed that man could improve, but he resented attempts at improvement based on shaky foundations. He also disliked any reform that was imposed artificially from without, that did not take into account the primacy of the inner man. One thing Hawthorne did preserve from his Puritan ancestors was a sharp sense of the duality of man's nature, coupled with a definite emphasis on the inner man. Any reform which did not begin with his inner self was futile. That he did not, however, repudiate the possibility of reform can be seen, as L. S. Hall has conclusively shown, in his lifelong adherence to the Jacksonian Democrats.

Despite all the introspection and tangled debate over sin and its effects on mind and soul, Hawthorne's personal belief about the fact of evil is deceptively uncomplicated. Sin and evil are stumbling blocks for the man in search of happiness, but these obstacles are wholly products of the empirical world; they are not a priori bequests with which man comes fully equipped. All of Hawthorne's ethical ideals are firmly centered on the concept of a beneficent, not a malignant creator, and he never swerves from this belief even in what appear on the surface his gloomiest pieces. When Holgrave refuses to hypnotize Phoebe, he reflects this ethical position, and from this point on Hawthorne is quite in sympathy with the young man. As a direct result of his refusal to take possession of Phoebe's will, Holgrave has discovered the balance or equipoise between energy and restraint.

When Holgrave comes, therefore, to modify his earlier radical position, it is the result of a well-pointed, consistent development. He moves toward a mature awareness of individual prerogative balanced by social and moral responsibility. Phoebe is the agent of this maturation, and he acknowledges her stabilizing influence. He uses his new views on building houses to measure for us precisely how far he has modified his earlier position that each generation should build its own homes.

> "It will be far otherwise than as you forebode. The world owes all its onward impulses to men ill at ease. The happy man inevitably confines himself within ancient limits. I have a presentiment that, hereafter, it will be my lot to set out trees, to make fences,—perhaps, even, in due time, to build a house for another generation,—in a word, to conform myself to laws, and the peaceful practice of society. Your poise will be more powerful than any oscillating tendency of mine."

Holgrave-Maule does not promise to abandon his efforts to improve man's lot; his efforts will, however, be guided by a new sense of responsibility born of his life with Phoebe. Commensurate with Hawthorne's oft-stated position, Holgrave abandons only his efforts to impose artificially conceived schemes upon mankind, before he has set his own house in order. He has simply begun his reform with himself.

The main reason for the critical complaint about the melodramatic ending as well as the apparent inconsistency in Holgrave's character results from a tendency to underrate Phoebe's effect on the engraver in particular and on the action of the book in general. Quite probably, this tendency to demote Phoebe is a natural result of the reading tastes of the twentieth century. There is not much doubt that Hawthorne did lapse into occasional sentimentality in his treatment of Phoebe, but in itself that is not sufficient reason for invalidating her role, a role which Hawthorne is at some pains to emphasize. He treats her with no irony whatever, and this has caused her frequently to be regarded with a condescension born of disbelief. Our century puts a premium on irony and, correlatively, tends to deny that a wholly ideal character can exist substantially beside other characters less ideal and more human. The twentieth century takes what it wants from Hawthorne and neglects what it thinks it does not need. This type of criticism neglects the fundamental question of what Phoebe meant to Hawthorne. If Phoebe is a sentimental character, therefore, might not this sentimental strain be essential to a thorough understanding of Hawthorne's mind?

Phoebe was real to Hawthorne, as real as the dark and mysterious Miriam or the proud Lady Eleonore or as real as the curse of the Maules. Perhaps Hawthorne has created the curse and the blackness with more artistic success, but he means us to accept Phoebe's credibility as well; he treats her in a painfully sincere way, never sarcastically or satirically. To be sure, she represents for him an ideal as well as a real character, and she exists on both levels at once. Undoubtedly, it was for Hawthorne infinitely more difficult to give Phoebe realistic dimension. She represents an ideal which he had never known (with the possible exception of Sophia), an ideal which he believed, however, could be attained. The blackness he had known and could depict from experience; the ideal he had to imagine. Both extremes coexist in his creative mind.

Soon after her introduction, Hawthorne goes to some lengths to establish her on both the realistic and symbolic levels. He does this by associating a realistic detail (the white roses of her bedchamber) with her, to indicate her symbolic repudiation of the complex web of evil spun round the musty old house. She brings to the dying mansion pleasant qualities—light laughter and bubbling life. It is, however, of tremendous significance that she is partly a Pyncheon. She is, as are so many of Hawthorne's protagonists, a person in history, but she refuses to allow the past to dominate her. She has in her ". . . the stern old stuff of Puritanism with a gold thread in the web."

The chapter titled "May and November" is devoted to establishing the symbolic basis for her future actions in contrast to the November which Hepzibah represents. Phoebe stands for all that is young and growing, all that is hopeful and has no reason to be disillusioned. There is not an ounce of hypocrisy or pride in her; all that she does rises out of an intuitive love for her fellow man, and what she does is never repudiated by Hawthorne either explicitly or implicitly. Her good works do accomplish her announced goal; they do not lead to chaos or confusion, because she is incapable by nature of an evil act. For Hawthorne to have created Phoebe was daring, but the fact that he did create her has been slighted too often. There is no germ of depravity in her, and her good works lead only to a graceful repudiation of the familial curse. It is a subtle irony that this unspotted and innocent girl should be a daughter of the Puritans.

Characteristically, she is unable to believe evil even of Jaffrey Pyncheon, the villainous descendant of the old Colonel. When he offers aid to Clifford and Hepzibah, Phoebe merely asks, "Is he so very wicked? . . . Yet his offers were surely kind!" and the more experienced Hepzibah had to add, "Do not speak of them [the offers]—he has a heart of iron."

Holgrave immediately perceives this divine innocence about Phoebe and compares her implicitly to his portraits. He has a gift of bringing out the inner truth of character in his prints, a gift Hawthorne bestows deliberately, so that when the engraver speaks of Phoebe he will be believed. Phoebe, however, dislikes this Paul Pry tendency of standing apart and coldly exposing people without desiring to help them. With all his varied activities on behalf of mankind, apparently Holgrave never really had an affection for people. For Phoebe, on the other hand, living is synonymous with loving; essentially this is what she teaches Holgrave and what leads to his capitulation. Her words paraphrase her instinctive realization of the basic ethical rule, "Love thy neighbor."

"How is it possible to see people in distress, without desiring, more than anything else, to help and comfort them? You talk as if this old house were a theatre; and you seem to look at Hepzibah's and Clifford's misfortunes, and those of generations before them, as a tragedy, such as I have seen acted in the hall of a country hotel, only the present one appears to be played exclusively for your amusement. I do not like this. The play costs the performers too much, and the audience is too cold-hearted."

Phoebe, by her consistent actions, gives substance to these words. Where Holgrave stood apart coldly exercising a restraining influence on his will and choosing a proud isolation worse, in a sense, than the passive isolation of Clifford and Hepzibah, Phoebe plunges into the darkest corners with a serene conviction that she is helping her neighbors to overcome their woes. She enters the tomb of the seven gables where all seems divorced from normal relationships, and she restores an equilibrium to all three of the isolated inhabitants. That she does this too easily has brought a charge of sentimentality, but Hawthorne is at great pains, in an authorial aside, to establish her on a realistic level. She is authentic evidence for a beneficent creator and an ordered world.

She was real! Holding her hand you felt something; a tender something; a substance, and a warm one: and so long as you should feel its grasp . . . you might be certain that your place was good in the whole sympathetic chain of human nature. The world was no longer a delusion.

Apparently, Phoebe was real enough to bring three people out of their isolations. She does it only by ministering love which can overcome any evil. Hepzibah dimly perceives the panacea of love but is not strong enough to break the bonds of the past. Clifford comes to depend on Phoebe while the old lady glides gratefully into the background, realizing instinctively that she cannot supply the reservoir of spirit and intellect that her brother requires to draw himself out of his shell. In a long aside, Hawthorne speaks of Phoebe's "activity of body, intellect, and heart" accomplishing her goals. Hepzibah is invalidated, and Phoebe becomes the primary force from this point. Although she is a Pyncheon with stern Puritan ancestors, Phoebe is innocent, not naturally depraved. She is the very antithesis of evil. She recoils by instinct from objectified evil in the form of Jaffrey Pyncheon once she recognizes him for what he is—even though her first impulse (like Huckleberry Finn's) is to believe that no one is unworthy of human and divine sympathy.

Against Phoebe are arrayed imposing forces. Jaffrey, who represents "the weaknesses and defects, the bad passions, the mean tendencies, and the moral diseases which lead to crime," tries consciously to transmit the evil of the past to the inexperience of the present. Clifford and Hepzibah are, in a sense, even more deceptive opponents, since they draw upon themselves a sympathy which obscures their weakness of passivity. Finally, Holgrave-Maule, embittered by the earlier Pyncheon's crime against his ancestor, sees the basic problem of past dominating present, but he intellectualizes and seeks to impose erratically conceived solutions. Phoebe confronts them, bests the first in direct combat, brings the next two to a modest awareness of their own powers, and utilizes the tremendous potential of the last by giving him an equipoise he never possessed alone. This is what Hawthorne means when he speaks of her "activity of body, intellect, and heart."

It is of paramount importance to realize that Phoebe is a special type of reformer. She accomplishes her goal "with no sense of a mission to perform." Her method is always to draw the potential from the individual, never to impose her will on another—the cardinal sin for Hawthorne. The entire problem of imposition of will is dealt with on two levels. On the personal level there is the Matthew Maule-Alice Pyncheon affair and the Holgrave-Phoebe counterpoint. Abstractly, there is the attempt of past generations to impose their wills upon the present, exemplified in the familial curse. On both levels this is a horrible crime, and on both levels Phoebe is victorious. It is one of Hawthorne's better ironies that she uses methods quite antithetical to those of her opponents. She steadfastly refuses to accept the fact that she is liable for the burdens of the past, and by consistent choices governed by her ethic of love, she proves a belief in a beneficent deity. By her refusal to believe the worst of her fellow man, she reveals that man has the privilege and power of working out his destiny.

Hawthorne does not ignore the real presence of evil, and Jaffrey Pyncheon is his objective realization of it in this particular frame. If, however, Jaffrey represents total evil, Phoebe represents total good. Hawthorne saw Phoebe victorious on both the realistic and symbolic levels. He surrounds her with imagery of light and beauty that indicates her victory at his deepest level of consciousness. The simple ethic that refutes the stern evil of Jaffrey Pyncheon defies Hawthorne's descriptive powers, so he tells us what Phoebe ultimately means to him as well as to those she has helped. The following passage consitutes for me the strongest kind of evidence for Hawthorne's belief in the essential goodness of mankind—provided man himself believes in his own goodness. Everything in Phoebe is totally opposed to evil and depravity, and still Hawthorne insists that she is a real person, not merely an ideal impossible of attainment. She is not an intellectual, she is not afflicted with missionary zeal, but her simple ethic of love transforms her into an angel come to vivid life and transforms what she stands for to a religion. "The girl [Phoebe] waved her hand to Hepzibah and Clifford, and went up the street; a religion in herself, warm, simple, true, with a substance that could walk on earth, and a spirit that was capable of heaven."

This equation of Phoebe with angelic qualities of innocence and purity is not uncalculated, for Hawthorne consistently underscores the young girl's unspoiled nature as well as her restorative powers, which revived chickens, houses, and people with an equal degree of success. If old Jaffrey is aligned with the forces of darkness, Phoebe has restored the lost innocence of Eden to the rotting old house.

*The House of the Seven Gables* produces no tragic struggle and therefore no catharsis, but since the curse is man-made, it can be successfully purged by enlightened man's efforts. When man stumbles and deliberately chooses evil (as in the original imposition of the curse), the reality of evil overwhelms him. However, the curse is not predestined; it has been invoked by fallible man who can revoke it at his will. This revocation must begin internally, that is with someone who has a personal stake in the curse—in this case Holgrave-Maule. As Beebe has remarked, if Holgrave were not a Maule and Phoebe not a Pyncheon, their actions would be unaccountable. However, they complement each other's actions leading to the abrogation of the curse, Holgrave in his deliberate refusal to hypnotize Phoebe, and Phoebe in her leavening effect upon the violent and misdirected energies of Holgrave. It is both structurally and dramatically proper, therefore, that they meet on the middle ground of compromise.

There are, however, victims of the curse. Clifford and Hepzibah have lost the vitality of their lives. Their suffering is due not to a malignant power but to their own inability to cope with the crucial problem of their lives. Jaffrey Pyncheon chooses evil and dies a victim of his own malicious agency. He is evil incarnate, hiding his intentions beneath a cloak of hypocrisy, and Hawthorne brilliantly reflects the hypocrisy of his life in the sustained irony of Jaffrey's mock eulogy.

It is remarkable how each character's fate is almost wholly the product of his own actions and choices. For instance, Holgrave has the tradition of two generations of familial hate behind him and only the love for Phoebe to compensate; yet he chooses not to violate her soul by placing his grip upon it. Phoebe is a daughter of the Puritans but repudiates their sternness by her actions. Clifford and Hepzibah succumb to a nearly fatal passivity, and although they find a token happiness, the best they can do is to provide some insights for younger and more vigorous minds. Jaffrey, of course, chooses evil consistently and gets precisely what he deserves. Despite the insistence of early biographers, Hawthorne did not believe that man was an island unto himself. He went through a period of youthful introspection, but his mature fiction advocated the open union of all men in love and in sincerity. What is deceptive about Hawthorne is that he dwells at length upon the isolated individual in an effort to show the imbalance and unhappiness that result from social maladjustment. This romance, however, belongs to people who reject isolation for a normal life in society. Ultimately, the charge of sentimentality fails, because Hawthorne has carefully accounted and prepared for all of the final actions.

Hawthorne has inserted one of his customarily illuminating sidelights charged with allegorical significance. In this particular scene, Phoebe and Clifford are watching a sideshow being performed beneath their window by an organ grinder with puppets. Hawthorne cannot resist these observations:

> Possibly some cynic, at once merry and bitter, had desired to signify in this pantomimic scene, that we mortals, whatever our business or amusement,—however serious, however trifling,—all dance to one identical tune, and, in spite of our ridiculous activity, bring nothing finally to pass. For the most remarkable aspect of the affair was, that, at the cessation of the music, everybody was petrified, at once, from the most extravagant life into a dead torpor. Neither was the cobbler's shoe finished, nor the blacksmith's iron shaped out; nor was there a drop less of brandy in the toper's bottle, nor a drop more of milk in the milkmaid's pail, nor one additional coin in the miser's strongbox, nor was the scholar a page deeper in his book. All were precisely in the same condition as before they made themselves so ridiculous by their haste to toil, to enjoy, to accumulate gold, and to become wise. Saddest of all, moreover, the lover was none the happier for the maiden's granted kiss! But, rather than swallow this last too acrid ingredient, we reject the whole moral of the show.

Hawthorne's reflections on the sideshow reject automatism in favor of free-will and underscore as well the basic theme of the romance. Everything is here sketched in miniature, and Hawthorne's attitude is clear. There is first the cynical position that all man's efforts mean nothing toward the accomplishment of a planned goal. Extended, this denies that man has any freedom of will—and this Hawthorne rejects. The analogy between the world of puppets and the world of men allows none of the actors happiness, suggesting a malignant and unmerciful deity—and this Hawthorne rejects. Finally, the gesture of love is rendered useless and cold—and this Hawthorne utterly rejects. Although evil exists, man has a real choice between alternatives. Ultimately, the responsibility for the individual's actions rests with him, therefore, and earns him a self-imposed stature.

The romance denies both that man was by nature totally depraved and that he was necessarily predisposed to evil. Hawthorne saw no easy solution in man's propensity for choosing evil. Likewise, his realistic understanding of human nature let him see that evil might be passively permitted by those incapable of stopping it. Finally, the positive forces win out—in the persons of a young girl who gravitates naturally toward goodness and love, and a young man whose idealistic fervor needs to be channeled into areas where it can do some constructive good. This is a book with faith in young people; it is, fundamentally, optimistic.

# DANIEL G. HOFFMAN

## Paradise Regained at Maule's Well †

In *The House of the Seven Gables* Hawthorne would seem to have gone to some lengths not to emulate the taut economy of *The Scarlet Letter*. His tale is spread over six generations in time, his plot divagates into the destinies of ten characters instead of three, and there is no single controlling symbol like the letter to unify these dispersed materials. The manner, too, lacks the unification of tone of the earlier romance. There is the novelistic realism involved in presenting a social background more extensive than Hawthorne attempts elsewhere; there is also the machinery of Gothic romance, including an interpolated fable which recapitulates many of the themes of the work in which it is embedded.

Although its unity is flawed by the unassimilated presence of these several modes, and by the introduction of more materials than the fiction effectively uses, *The House of the Seven Gables* has nonetheless an almost-successful ethical consistency. Such a consistency was among the chief of Hawthorne's aims; in his preface he calls it "the truth of the human heart." In its evocation, he insists, the author "has fairly a right" to choose or create his

† From Daniel G. Hoffman, "Paradise Regained at Maule's Well," *Form and Fable in American Fiction*, New York, 1961. Pp. 187–201. Copyright 1961 by Daniel G. Hoffman; reprinted by permission of Oxford University Press.

circumstances, including the prerogative "to mingle the Marvellous" with the realistic elements of his scene. These are the responsibilities of the author of a romance, which, "as a work of art, must rigidly subject itself to laws." This is about as much as we get from Hawthorne of a direct aesthetic statement; since the structure of each of his romances is unique, it would appear that the laws to which he made himself subject were revealed in the process of composition. Each of his works is an experiment, an attempt to discover these laws.

Hawthorne presents his work as a romance, and his reason for distinguishing this form from the novel appears to have been defensive. He would prepare the reader to grant him license to escape the necessity of aiming "at a very minute fidelity, not merely to the possible, but to the probable and ordinary course of man's experience." Aiming instead at the revelation of universal truths, he must free himself from too-close subjection to circumstances, expecially contemporary circumstances. For these he finds inimical to the imaginative idealization of experience. What he needed, then, were patterns of possible conflict whose working-out would demonstrate the truths of the heart. Hence his dependence upon both the mythical and the marvellous—the mythical for a substructure of thematic action, the marvellous for the concretization of detail. But *The House of the Seven Gables* is also a determinedly historical novel whose issues can be presented only in terms of the culture of a particular place. On this account the mythical and the marvellous elements of the romance have to be subsumed into the novelistic values of a probable reality. The fusion of techniques is incomplete, because the materials are by nature incompatible. On the ethical level, however, as I have said, Hawthorne achieved a near-success. Thematically, this near-success unwittingly expounds the failure of hopefulness.

*The House of the Seven Gables* is built on an implicit substructure of Puritan myth. On this is erected an historical reconstruction of folk belief in witchcraft as it varied over two centuries. This witchcraft—and the sins it represents—is superseded by the ebullient optimism of the contemporary Yankee character. Doubtless this is among the reasons for the book's great popularity among his contemporaries. Yet while *The House of the Seven Gables* reflects the spirit of popular culture, its avoidance of tragic fate goes against the grain of Hawthorne's own convictions. Not even the grace and shadowed charm of its style can mend this flaw in the conception of the book.

## I

Maule's Well is the fountain that fouls Eden in the New World. In *The Scarlet Letter* Hawthorne had explored the themes of original sin, retribution, and redemption. In *The House of the Seven Gables* his version of the myth of the Fortunate Fall dramatizes expulsion from Eden and the visiting upon the sons of the sins of their fathers. There is a curse upon the house of Pyncheon, a curse well earned, which cannot be expiated or escaped until the inherited pattern of complicity and reduplication of the original sin is broken. Each generation has the chance to exercise free will in breaking the fateful pattern, but this happy ending to mankind's heritage of woe takes place only in contemporary New England. After two centuries of guilt and sorrow, the bloodlines of the wronged Maules and the blighted Pyncheons at last produce a generation of the new unfallen Americans whose advent Crèvecœur had so confidently announced.

Hawthorne draws with good effect upon the two chief traditions of early New England folklore in the working-out of his ambitiously conceived panorama. Providences and witch lore give him a sombre, chiaroscuro palette with which to depict the fate of his fallen, ambitious, worldly Pyncheons, who would presume to found a great house on the grave of a wronged man. To rescue both Pyncheons and Maules from an eternity of suffering he creates his most optimistic character. Holgrave is a representative man of the nineteenth century. Although actually a descendant of old Matthew Maule, the lineage of Hawthorne's daguerreotypist leads straight back to the Yankee—to Dominicus Pike, to Robin come to a confident and happy end.

Holgrave's first forebear, Matthew Maule, had cleared "an acre or two of earth . . . out of the primeval forest, to be his garden ground and homestead." Almost at once he is despoiled of his incipient Eden by Colonel Pyncheon, the type of the aggressive man of iron:

> The Puritan—so, at least, says chimney-corner tradition, which often preserves traits of character with marvellous fidelity—was bold, imperious, relentless, crafty; laying his purposes deep, and following them out with an inveteracy of pursuit that knew neither rest nor conscience; trampling on the weak, and, when essential to his ends, doing his utmost to beat down the strong.

Chimney-corner tradition, in this romance, speaks the ultimate truths of the heart. "Ancient superstitions," Hawthorne writes, "after being steeped in human hearts and embodied in human breath . . . through a series of generations, become imbued with an effect of homely truth . . . By long transmission among household facts, they grow to look like them." Thus folk belief is invoked as the voice of the heart's truth, whose revelations must be heeded in the conflict with the crafty and relentless Puritan. Hawthorne's men of iron have no hearts. Colonel Pyncheon is akin to Ethan Brand and Roger Chillingworth.

The Colonel not only dispossessed Maule from his plot, but took a zealous part in declaring Maule a wizard. The plebeian was hanged for witchcraft, while Colonel Pyncheon—like Cotton Mather at the execution of George Burroughs—"sat on horseback, grimly gazing at the scene." Maule, who "declared himself hunted to death for his spoil," curses Pyncheon with his dying words: "God will give him blood to drink!"

Colonel Pyncheon is in no way deterred by this curse from his plan of founding a dynasty. His holdings are enlarged by the grant of a vast tract of territory in Maine, "more extensive than many a dukedom, or even a reigning prince's territory, on European soil." But the title remained in some doubt, and in succeeding generations the land was "partly cleared and occupied by actual settlers." Their situation repeats that of Maule with regard to the Pyncheons' dubious claim to the original property. The first element in the Pyncheon birthright is an aggravation of the clan's inherent materialism, "an absurd delusion of family importance" based on their expectation of claiming the dubious tract and "ultimately forming a princedom for themselves." The Pyncheons, then, are fated to play the painful role of the disinherited aristocrat. But they have other roles too, none happier.

Their second birthright is their inherited guilt. What shall they make of "the awful query, whether each inheritor of the property —conscious of wrong, and failing to rectify it—did not commit anew the great guilt of his ancestor, and incur all its original responsibilities"?

The curse completes their inheritance. The first Pyncheon, building his mansion over the unquiet grave of Matthew Maule, gives the wizard's ghost "a kind of privilege to haunt its new apartments." At the opening of his house, Colonel Pyncheon has an apoplectic seizure, and dies with his own blood gurgling in his throat. In recent times the Pyncheons have endured "the heaviest calamity that ever befell the race; no less than the violent death—for so it was adjudged—of one member of the family by the criminal act of another." The victim was a repentant Pyncheon who, concluding that his ancestor had swindled and then murdered Maule, raised the question "whether it were not imperative upon him, even at this late hour, to work restitution to Maule's posterity." This Christian gentleman, naturally enough, was murdered by one of his kin. The crime was attributed to Clifford Pyncheon, whose sister Hepzibah now lives alone in the house while his cousin Judge Pyncheon flourishes downtown. Clifford languishes in jail until, midway in the book, he is returned, ruined in spirit, to the House of the Seven Gables. Now that the blood the Pyncheons drink is one another's, the Maules have disappeared from view. The curse combines the repetition of a Remarkable Judgment with the legend of Cain and Abel.

This chronicle of inherited guilt, reduplicated sin, and repeated retribution comprises the history of the House. Yet the setting, the actual land, continues to be paradisal in its attractiveness, as though the Pyncheon garden, with its bees "plying their golden labor," would become an Eden in truth, were its inhabitants worthy of such grace. It seems most paradisal to the characters most innocent—to Phoebe, the country cousin of the Pyncheons, and to Holgrave, who says to Phoebe, "What a good world we live in! How good and beautiful! How young it is, too . . . the garden would every day be virgin soil, with the earth's first freshness in the flavor of its beans and squashes; and the house!—it would be like a bower in Eden, blossoming with the earliest roses that God ever made." The penultimate chapter, in which Judge Pyncheon's death finally releases the remaining innocents from the curse, is called "The Flower of Eden." Phoebe, of course, is the flower, and is promptly grafted onto Holgrave's family tree. Not only does *The House of the Seven Gables* tell of man's long exile from Paradise, but it strongly hints that its American lovers will return there.

What credence we give to this conclusion depends in large part on our confidence in Holgrave as "the representative of many compeers in his native land." Holgrave's character, as I have said, is significantly rooted in the folk traditions of Yankee metamorphosis and optimism. But if the folklore of Yankee character contributes to the book's optimistic conclusion, the folklore of witchcraft and necromancy determines the difficulties which must first be overcome.

## II

Witchcraft in *The House of the Seven Gables* begins in the season of Salem's horror. But as the Pyncheon story is an historical chronicle stretched over two centuries, the treatment of witchcraft changes with the changing times. Hawthorne shows scrupulous fidelity to both historical fact and oral tradition in recording the transformation from the Puritan to the contemporary version of folk belief. Just as the Puritan faith was relaxed and liberalized in the Unitarian and Transcendental periods, so too folk faith in witchcraft transformed itself to accord with the new spirit of the age. Yet Hawthorne manages to keep his modern version of witchcraft alive as a manifestation of active spiritual evil, even though he must turn his latter-day necromancer into a hypnotist. At the end, the last of the Maules, who by birthright should have inherited his ancestors' evil powers, renounces his opportunity to avenge again the wrongs done his line by the Pyncheons. Holgrave, as we have seen, marries Phoebe instead of bewitching her.

Is it often noticed that the original Maule was not a witch at all? He was completely innocent, falsely accused by Colonel Pyncheon. Yet a curse from the lips of a dying man is ever an especially terrifying portent. Hawthorne describes Old Maule as "one of the martyrs to that terrible delusion, which should teach us, among its other morals, that . . . those who take upon themselves to be leaders of the people, are fully liable to all the passionate error that has ever characterized the wildest mob." At the same time, though, "The mode of his death . . . blasted with strange horror the humble name . . . and made it seem almost a religious act to drive the plough over the little area of habitation, and obliterate his place and memory from among men." This is another alternative choice in which both the literal, rational statement and the superstitious one are true.

That is to say, although Matthew Maule was innocent when alive, both his ghost and his posterity become witches. They have been wronged, they have been invested by "ancient superstitions . . . steeped in human hearts and embodied in human breath . . ." with the malignity of witchcraft. They seek revenge upon the Pyncheons, thus implicating themselves in that contagion of original sin which Colonel Pyncheon's pride and avarice began. Old Maule's curse is fulfilled as the Pyncheons of one generation after another are struck dead with a gurgle of blood in their throats. His son, Thomas Maule, a master carpenter, actually served Colonel Pyncheon as architect of the House of the Seven Gables. Not until much later, from Holgrave's interpolated fable of "Alice Pyncheon," do we learn of Thomas's revenge upon his father's persecutor. He secreted the title to the Maine estate behind the Colonel's portrait, denying the Pyncheons' posterity their hope of aristocratic preferment.

There are two later generations of Maules in the romance. One is Thomas Maule's son, named Matthew like his grandfather; the other is the contemporary Holgrave. We learn of Matthew's vengeful witchcraft from Holgrave's story. Among his many other accomplishments the latest Maule is a fiction-writer, and he reads his manuscript to Phoebe in the paradisal garden of the House of the Seven Gables. Thus the witchcraft in "Alice Pyncheon" is presented as the literary exercise of a young man of the most advanced rationalistic ideas. Yet the fable presents Matthew's necromancy with the same seriousness that Hawthorne shows toward sortilege in Puritan times.

Even the witchcraft alleged of Old Maule showed the tradition in a state of decay, compared to its full rendering in "Young Goodman Brown." We hear nothing of covens or sexual orgies, nor, as in *The Scarlet Letter*, is there mention of the Black Man and the Devil's compact. Instead there is generalized dread, a sense of active malignity worked by supernatural means. Old Maule's spirit and his descendants earn their repute as witches through the exercise of personal vengeance, not through their search for the Unpardonable Sin. Now the common witch of New England folk tradition, as we have seen, is the malicious night-rider—a lone operator, not the Sweet Devil's covenanters whom we find in the Lancashire trials. Hawthorne, describing popular beliefs about the Maules, presents their evil prowess in this early passage:

> They were half believed to inherit mysterious attributes; the family eye was said to possess strange power. Among other good-for-nothing properties and privileges, one was especially assigned them,—of exercising an influence over other people's dreams. The Pyncheons, if all stories were true, haughtily as they bore themselves in the noon-day streets of their native town, were no better than bond-servants to these plebeian Maules, on entering the topsy-turvy commonwealth of sleep. Modern psychology, it may be, will endeavour to reduce these alleged necromancies within a system, instead of rejecting them as altogether fabulous.

The reduction of these necromancies to a system of modern psychology occurs in *The Blithedale Romance*. Here Hawthorne is content to identify the power of witchcraft with the malign possession of another's soul in "the topsy-turvy commonwealth of sleep." We remember his raising the possibility that Young Goodman Brown had merely fallen asleep and dreamed in the forest. This might have been true, but if so it would in no way have negated the truth of the story. The possession of a soul is both real and evil, whether in dreams or waking.

Some of the lore in Holgrave's tale parallels oral traditions reported in Whittier's *Supernaturalism of New England:* the unquiet ghost who protests the division of his estate, and the use of hypnotism to enter the world of spirits. Matthew Maule has the Evil Eye, with its powers of "blighting corn, and drying children into mummies with the heartburn." In 1837 Hawthorne had read Sir Walter Scott's *Letters on Demonology and Witchcraft;* he may there have found the suggestion for his statement that what most influenced popular belief in Matthew Maule's wizardry was not even his Evil Eye but "the suspicion of his holding heretical tenets in matters of religion and polity."

In the story of "Alice Pyncheon" the double drama of reduplicated guilt is played again in the third generation since the proud

Colonel and the wizard Maule. Gervayse Pyncheon has lived abroad with his daughter; returning to the House of the Seven Gables, he finds that provincial manse too narrow to contain his ambitions of great estate. He is determined to prosecute the claim to the lands in Maine, and summons Matthew Maule the carpenter for an interview. There are persistent popular traditions of "some mysterious connection and dependence, existing between the family of the Maules and these vast unrealized possessions of the Pyncheons." Here Hawthorne cites folklore and providences: an old crone, dead now, had been used to say "in her fireside talk, that miles and miles of the Pyncheon lands had been shoveled into Maule's grave." Again, "it was a by-word" that the missing deed "would never be found, unless in the wizard's skeleton hand." Gervayse Pyncheon's lawyers had even searched Old Maule's grave. "Nothing was discovered, however, except that, unaccountably, the right hand of the skeleton was gone."

All these, of course, are the traditions of time past. What now ensues is that Matthew Maule agrees to furnish the document, in return for two conditions: surrender of the grounds and the House; and "the favor of a little talk with your fair daughter Alice." So strong is Gervayse's desire to become Lord Pyncheon, the Earl of Waldo, that he consents to both.

Alice is so beautiful that "her presence imparted an indescribable grace and faint witchery to the whole edifice." Though haughty toward the menial, she finds Maule sexually attractive at first glance—a glance which "the carpenter never forgave." Her father begins to have misgivings:

> Had not [the wizard] bequeathed a legacy of hatred against the Pyncheons to this only grandson, who, as it appeared, was now about to exercise a subtle influence over the daughter of his enemy's house? Might not this influence be the same that was called witchcraft?

Alice, however, is confident "that a lady, while true to herself," can fear no one. Her father muses on the dowry which Matthew Maule will make possible—and on her marrying an English duke or German prince instead of a New England lawyer. "The ambitious father almost consented, in his heart, that, if the devil's power were needed to the accomplishment of this great object, Maule might evoke him. Alice's own purity would be her safeguard."

But there are evils against which purity is powerless. Maule puts Alice into a trance. "She is mine!" he gloats, "Mine, by the right of the strongest spirit!" He now uses the hypnotized girl to establish communication with the ghosts of old Matthew and Thomas

Maule and Colonel Pyncheon. But this interview with the departed is frustrated by the revenant Maules, who prevent the Colonel's ghost from revealing the secret. "It will never be allowed," young Matthew tells Gervayse. "The custody of this secret, that would so enrich his heirs, makes part of your grandfather's retribution. He must choke with it. . . ." Gervayse Pyncheon tries to speak, "but—what with fear and passion—could make only a gurgling murmur in his throat."

Alice is now roused from her trance, but Matthew has not yet had his revenge upon her for her haughtiness. Henceforth she is "Maule's slave." "A power that she little dreamed of had laid its grasp upon her maiden soul. A will . . . constrained her to do its grotesque and fantastic bidding." Seated at his fireside, the carpenter commands her "Alice, laugh!" or "Alice, be sad!" or "Alice, dance." "It seemed to be Maule's impulse, not to ruin Alice, nor to visit her with any black or gigantic mischief, which would have crowned her sorrows with the grace of tragedy, but to wreak a low, ungenerous scorn upon her. Thus all dignity of life was lost." Her ultimate ignominy is to wait attendance on Maule's bride, a laborer's daughter. Returning homeward in the snow, she takes sick and dies. At her funeral Maule gnashes his teeth in frustration, for death has cheated him of his revenge.

As he finishes his tale Holgrave discovers that he has put Phoebe to sleep. Here is his chance—to repeat Matthew's invasion of Alice's soul. That he is competent to do so we already know, for in the preceding chapter

> he had been a public lecturer on Mesmerism, for which science (as he assured Phoebe, and, indeed, satisfactorily proved, by putting Chanticleer, who happened to be scratching near by, to sleep) he had very remarkable endowments.

But somehow, suffering has purified the bloodline of the Maules. Perhaps it is through his immersion in contemporary America, with its unlimited opportunities for personal development and advancement, that Holgrave has freed himself from the obsessive revenge which cursed his ancestors. At any rate he has that matchless probity and innocence which "never violated the innermost man." Holgrave repudiates his opportunity to repeat his ancestors' sin of vengeance. He is no longer a Puritan, nor a Puritan witch, but a New England Yankee.

### III

Hawthorne rarely committed himself to the comic mode, yet surely, despite its dark details, *The House of the Seven Gables* has claims to be considered a comedic romance. This warrant lies in Holgrave's character, which redeems the history from what had hitherto been its seemingly predestined pattern of woe. Holgrave is the only hero in Hawthorne's major romances who has the positive power of self-transformation. Like the folk heroes of popular culture, young Holgrave is a master of metamorphosis. Though not yet twenty-two, he has already been a country schoolmaster, a salesman, a political editor, a travelling peddler and dentist, a shipboard official and European tourist, and member of a Fourierist colony, as well as a lecturer on mesmerism. When we meet him "his present phase" is a daguerreotypist, and Hawthorne underscores the point that "amid all these personal vicissitudes, he had never lost his identity. . . . but had carried his conscience along with him." This observation emphasizes what Hawthorne felt to be the inherent moral threat of the power of transformation. The buoyant optimism with which he tries to resolve the dilemma of this romance is supported by his conception of the bridegroom's character.

Sympathetic though Hawthorne's portrait is of this young evangel of the latest doctrines, the picture is yet tinged with ironical qualifications. "He considered himself a thinker, and was certainly of a thoughtful turn, but, with his own path to discover, had perhaps hardly yet reached the point where an educated man begins to think." This incipient philosopher demands, "Shall we never, never get rid of this Past? It lies upon the Present like a giant's dead body. . . . We read in dead men's books! We laugh at dead men's jokes, and cry at dead men's pathos! We are sick of dead men's diseases, physical and moral, and . . . We worship the living Deity according to dead men's forms and creeds." Here is popular exemplar of Emersonian self-reliance. His strictures against the past are all perfectly justified by the facts of his own situation, yet he is quite unwilling to acknowledge the ineluctability of its influence upon *his* life. His image of himself is again the popular conception of the unfallen, self-created man whose own will determines his destiny.

In his rejection of the past and in his immature philosophy of self-determined metamorphosis Holgrave is of course a foil to the aristocratic illusions of the declining Pyncheons. The contrast between their fortunes and their views of fate was for Hawthorne an inevitable one. Indeed, the opportunities afforded in an egalitarian society for changes in rank and status seemed to Hawthorne much more likely to lead to a fallen aristocracy than to the upward climb of the sober, industrious, and honest yeoman celebrated by Crèvecœur, Franklin, and the popular mythology of the day.[1] Holgrave and Dominicus Pike are the signal instances of

1. In this work Hawthorne views such a career as Franklin's—one wholly concerned with the outward display of good works and of apparent service to society

Hawthorne's accepting the popular myth, the peddler in a rural, agrarian context, the daguerreotypist in a more complex society of commerce. Elsewhere Hawthorne characteristically turns the popular myth upside down. For him metamorphosis in a viable society has the obsessive implication of descent, degradation, decrepitude. His notebooks record many instances of social mobility downward,[2] and this is the common pattern of social change in his fiction.

Since Hawthorne makes the reader aware of other influences on Holgrave's fortune than those the youth himself acknowledges, there is a special interest in his occupation as daguerreotypist. On the one hand his camera links him with all the magic portraits and mirrors in Hawthorne's Gothic repertoire. But on the other the daguerreotype signifies that Holgrave *deals* in representations of personal identity—the portraits of persons. And this links him with his author's prepossessive concern with identity and its vicissitudes in an egalitarian culture. The case histories of Hepzibah and Clifford Pyncheon show that sudden changes of wealth and status do not leave untouched the souls that suffer them. Holgrave's ebullient denials of any but the smiling possibilities of change make it seem unlikely that the ancestral curse in *The House of the Seven Gables* can be as readily exorcised as the contrivance of its plot maintains. Here is the basic flaw of Hawthorne's only full-length attempt at a happy ending. It contradicts his own fundamental conception of "the truth of the human heart."

—with much the same attitude that Melville showed in *Israel Potter*. Hawthorne presents Judge Pyncheon (in chapter 15) as almost a parody of Franklin, a confidence-man taken in by his own hypocrisies:

"We might say . . . that there was enough of splendid rubbish in his life to cover up and paralyze a more active and subtile conscience than the Judge was ever troubled with. The purity of his judicial character, while on the bench; the faithfulness of his public service in subsequent capacities; . . . his remarkable zeal as president of a Bible society; his unimpeachable integrity as treasurer of a widow's and orphan's fund; his benefits to horticulture, by producing two much-esteemed varieties of the pear, and to agriculture, through the agency of the famous Pyncheon bull; the cleanness of his moral deportment, for a great many years past; . . . his efforts in furtherance of the temperance cause; . . . the studied propriety of his dress and equipment; . . . the smile of a broad benevolence wherewith he made it a point to gladden the whole world, —what room could possibly be found

for darker traits in a portrait made up of lineaments like these?"

The other side of Franklin's character appears in the genial folk-wisdom of simple Uncle Venner, whose maxims could be taken for Poor Richard's: "Give no credit! Never take paper money! Look well to your change! . . . At your leisure hours, knit children's woollen socks and mittens! Brew your own yeast, and make your own ginger-beer!"

2. The annals of Sir William Pepperill's and Governor Knox's families lead from the mansion to the poorhouse. Lawyer Haynes's fortunes decline from professional eminence to maimed penury. Hawthorne meets an unemployed naval officer, "a man of splendid epaulets, and very aristocratical equipment and demeanor," now "without position, and changed into a brandy-burnt and rowdyish sort of personage." At Parker's grog-shop he sees an "elderly ragamuffin . . . who had been in decent circumstances . . . there is a sort of shadow or delusion of respectability about him; and sobriety too, and a kind of decency, in his groggy and red-nosed destitution." (*American Notebooks*, ed. Stewart, pp. 94, 116, 22–3, 36–7, 255–6, 248.)

# Selected Bibliography

Abel, Darrel. "Hawthorne's House of Tradition," *South Atlantic Quarterly,* LII (October, 1953), 561–78.

Beebe, Maurice. "The Fall of the House of Pyncheon," *Nineteenth-Century Fiction,* XI (June, 1956), 1–17.

Bell, Millicent. *Hawthorne's View of the Artist,* New York, 1962. Pp. 159–65, 185–90.

Bewley, Marius. *The Eccentric Design,* New York, 1959. Pp. 175–83.

Birdsall, Virginia Ogden. "Hawthorne's Fair-Haired Maidens: The Fading Light," *PMLA,* LXXV (June, 1960), 250–56.

Cunliffe, Marcus. "*The House of Seven Gables,*" in *Hawthorne Centenary Essays,* ed. Roy Harvey Pearce, Columbus, Ohio, 1964. Pp. 79–101.

Dameron, J. Lasley. "Hawthorne's *The House of the Seven Gables:* A Serpent Image," *Notes & Queries,* VI (July-August, 1959), 289–90.

Dillingham, William B. "Structure and Theme in *The House of the Seven Gables,*" *Nineteenth-Century Fiction,* XIV (June, 1959), 59–70.

Emry, Hazel T. "Two Houses of Pride: Spenser's and Hawthorne's," *Philological Quarterly,* XXXIII (January, 1954), 91–94.

Farmer, Norman, Jr. "Maule's Curse and the Rev. Nicholas Noyes: A Note on Hawthorne's Source," *Notes & Queries,* XI (June, 1964), 224–25.

Faust, Bertha. *Hawthorne's Contemporaneous Reputation,* Philadelphia, 1939. Pp. 87–97.

Fogle, Richard H. *Hawthorne's Fiction: The Light and the Dark,* Norman, Okla., 1952. Pp. 122–39.

Griffith, Ben W., Jr. "Hawthorne's *The House of the Seven Gables,*" *Georgia Review,* VIII (1954), 235–37.

Griffith, Clark. "Substance and Shadow: Language and Meaning in *The House of Seven Gables,*" *Modern Philology,* LI (February, 1954), 187–95.

Griffiths, Thomas. " 'Montpelier' and 'Seven Gables': Knox's Estate and Hawthorne's Novel," *New England Quarterly,* XVI (September, 1943), 432–43.

———. *Maine Sources in "The House of the Seven Gables,"* Waterville, Me., 1945. Pp. 3–49.

Hall, Lawrence Sargent. *Hawthorne: Critic of Society,* New Haven, 1944. Pp. 160–67.

Havens, Elmer A. "The 'Gold Branch' as Symbol in *The House of the Seven Gables,*" *Modern Language Notes,* LXXIV (January, 1954), 20–22.

Hoffman, Daniel G. "Paradise Regained at Maule's Well," *Form and Fable in American Fiction,* New York, 1961. Pp. 187–201.

James, Henry. *Hawthorne,* London, 1879. Pp. 122–30. Reissued by Cornell University Press, 1956, in its Great Seal Books.

Levin, Harry. *The Power of Blackness: Hawthorne, Poe, Melville,* New York, 1960. Pp. 79–86.

Levy, Alfred J. "*The House of the Seven Gables:* The Religion of Love," *Nineteenth-Century Fiction,* XVI (December, 1961), 189–203.

Male, Roy R. *Hawthorne's Tragic Vision,* Austin, Texas, 1957. Pp. 119–38. Reissued by W. W. Norton & Co., 1964, in The Norton Library.

Marks, Alfred H. "Hawthorne's Daguerreotypist: Scientist, Artist, Reformer," *Ball State Teachers College Forum,* III (Spring, 1962), 61–74.

———. "Who Killed Judge Pyncheon? The Role of the Imagination in *The House of the Seven Gables,*" *PMLA,* LXXI (June, 1956), 355–69.

Martin, Terrence. *Nathaniel Hawthorne,* New York, 1965. Pp. 128–44.

Matthiessen, F. O. *American Renaissance,* New York, 1941. Pp. 322–37.

Orel, Harold. "The Double Symbol," *American Literature,* XXIII (March, 1951), 1–6.

Pearson, Norman Holmes. "The Pynchons and Judge Pyncheon," *Essex Institute Historical Collections,* C (October, 1964), 235–55.

Ragan, James F. "Social Criticism in *The House of the Seven Gables,*" in *Literature and Society,* ed. Bernice Slote, Lincoln, Neb. 1964. Pp. 112–20.

Sherbo, Arthur. "Albert Brisbane and Hawthorne's Holgrave and Hollingsworth," *New England Quarterly,* XXVII (December, 1954), 531–34.

Stanton, Robert. "Hawthorne, Bunyan, and the American Romances," *PMLA*, LXXI (March, 1956), 155–65.
Stein, William B. *Hawthorne's Faust*, Gainesville, Fla., 1953. Pp. 123–26.
Van Doren, Mark. *Hawthorne*, New York, 1949. Pp. 171–78.
Von Abele, Rudolph. *The Death of the Artist: A Study in Hawthorne's Disintegration*, The Hague, 1955. Pp. 58–69.
Waggoner, Hyatt H. *Hawthorne: A Critical Study*, Cambridge, Mass. revised edition, 1963. Pp. 160–87.
Warren, Austin. "Nathaniel Hawthorne," *Rage for Order*, Chicago, 1948. Pp. 97–103. Reissued by University of Michigan Press, 1959, in Ann Arbor Paperbacks.